TONO-BUNGAY

&

A MODERN UTOPIA

TONO-BUNGAY

and

A MODERN UTOPIA

by

H. G. WELLS

ODHAMS PRESS LIMITED
LONDON, W.C.2

Printed in Great Britain

TONO-BUNGAY

CONTENTS

Book One

The Days before Tono-Bungay was Invented

Chapter   Page

I.   OF BLADESOVER HOUSE, AND MY MOTHER ; AND THE CONSTITUTION OF SOCIETY   11

II. OF MY LAUNCH INTO THE WORLD AND THE LAST I SAW OF BLADESOVER   37

III. THE WIMBLEHURST APPRENTICESHIP   55

Book Two

The Rise of Tono-Bungay

I.   HOW I BECAME A LONDON STUDENT, AND WENT ASTRAY   79

II. THE DAWN COMES, AND MY UNCLE APPEARS IN A NEW SILK HAT   100

III. HOW WE MADE TONO-BUNGAY HUM   115

IV. MARION   128

Book Three

The Great Days of Tono-Bungay

I.   THE HARDINGHAM HOTEL, AND HOW WE BECAME BIG PEOPLE   165

CONTENTS

Chapter   Page

II.   OUR PROGRESS FROM CAMDEN TOWN TO CREST
         HILL   183

III. SOARING   216

IV.   HOW I STOLE THE HEAPS OF QUAP FROM MORDET
         ISLAND   242

Book Four

The Aftermath of Tono-Bungay

I.   THE STICK OF THE ROCKET   269

II.   LOVE AMONG THE WRECKAGE   290

III. NIGHT AND THE OPEN SEA   300

Book One

The Days before
Tono-Bungay was Invented

CHAPTER ONE

OF BLADESOVER HOUSE, AND MY MOTHER ; AND THE CONSTITUTION OF SOCIETY

§ I

Most people in this world seem to live " in character " ; they have a beginning, a middle and an end, and the three are congruous one with another and true to the rules of their type. You can speak of them as being of this sort of people or that. They are, as theatrical people say, no more (and no less) than " character actors." They have a class, they have a place, they know what is becoming in them and what is due to them, and their proper size of tombstone tells at last how properly they have played the part. But there is also another kind of life that is not so much living as a miscellaneous tasting of life. One gets hit by some unusual transverse force, one is jerked out of one's stratum and lives crosswise for the rest of the time, and, as it were, in a succession of samples. That has been my lot, and that is what has set me at last writing something in the nature of a novel. I have got an unusual series of impressions that I want very urgently to tell. I have seen life at very different levels, and at all these levels I have seen it with a sort of intimacy and in good faith. I have been a native in many social countries. I have been the unwelcome guest of a working baker, my cousin, who has since died in the Chatham infirmary ; I have eaten illegal snacks—the unjustifiable gifts of footmen—in pantries, and been despised for my want of style (and subsequently married and divorced) by the daughter of a gasworks clerk ; and—to go to my other extreme —I was once—oh, glittering days !—an item in the house-party of a countess. She was, I admit, a countess with a financial aspect, but still, you know, a countess. I've seen these people at various angles. At the dinner-table I've met not simply the titled but the great. On one occasion— it is my brightest memory—I upset my champagne over the trousers of the greatest statesman in the empire—Heaven forbid I should be so invidious as to name him !—in the warmth of our mutual admiration.

And once (though it is the most incidental thing in my life) I murdered a man. . . .

Yes, I've seen a curious variety of people and ways of living altogether. Odd people they all are, great and small, very much alike at bottom and curiously different on their surfaces. I wish I had ranged just a little further both up and down, seeing I have ranged so far. Royalty must be worth knowing and very great fun. But my contacts with princes have been limited to quite public occasions, nor at the other end of the scale have I had what I should call an inside acquaintance with that dusty but attractive class of people who go about on the high roads drunk but *en famille* (so redeeming the minor lapse), in the summer-time, with a perambulator, lavender to sell, sun-brown children, a smell, and ambiguous bundles that fire the imagination. Navvies, farm-labourers, sailormen, and stokers, all such as sit in 1834 beer-houses, are beyond me also, and I suppose must remain so now for ever. My intercourse with the ducal rank, too, has been negligible ; I once went shooting with a duke, and in an outburst of what was no doubt snobbishness, did my best to get him in the legs. But that failed.

I'm sorry I haven't done the whole lot, though. . . .

You will ask by what merit I achieved this remarkable social range, this extensive cross-section of the British social organism. It was the Accident of Birth. It always is in England. Indeed, if I may make the remark so cosmic, everything is. But that is by the way. I was my uncle's nephew, and my uncle was no less a person than Edward Ponderevo, whose comet-like transit of the financial heavens happened—it is now ten years ago ! Do you remember the days of Ponderevo, the *great* days, I mean, of Ponderevo ? Perhaps you had a trifle in some world-shaking enterprise ! Then you know him only too well. Astraddle on Tono-Bungay, he flashed athwart the empty heavens—like a comet —rather, like a stupendous rocket !—and overawed investors spoke of his star. At his zenith he burst into a cloud of the most magnificent promotions. What a time that was ! The Napoleon of domestic conveniences ! . . .

I was his nephew, his peculiar and intimate nephew. I was hanging on to his coat-tails all the way through. I made pills with him in the chemist's shop at Wimblehurst before he began. I was, you might say, the stick of his rocket ; and after our tremendous soar, after he had played with millions, a golden rain in the sky, after my bird's-eye view of the modern world, I fell again, a little scarred and blistered perhaps, two-and-twenty years older, with my youth gone, my manhood eaten in upon, but greatly edified, into this Thames-side yard, into these white heats and hammerings, amidst the fine realities of steel—to think it all over in my leisure and jot down the notes and inconsecutive observations that make this book. It was more, you know, than a figurative soar. The zenith of that career was surely our flight across the channel in the Lord Roberts β . . . .

I warn you this book is going to be something of an agglomeration. I want to trace my social trajectory (and my uncle's) as the main line of my story ; but as this is my first novel and almost certainly my last, I want to get in, too all sorts of things that struck me, things that amused me and impressions I got—even although they don't minister directly

to my narrative at all. I want to set out my own queer love
experiences, too, such as they are, for they troubled and distressed and swayed me hugely ; and they still seem to me
to contain all sorts of irrational and debatable elements
that I shall be the clearer-headed for getting on paper. And
possibly I may even flow into descriptions of people who are
really no more than people seen in transit, just because it
amuses me to recall what they said and did to us, and more
particularly how they behaved in the brief but splendid
glare of Tono-Bungay and its still more glaring offspring.
It lit some of them up, I can assure you ! Indeed, I want
to get in all sorts of things. My ideas of a novel all through
are comprehensive rather than austere. . . .

Tono-Bungay still figures on the hoardings, it stands in
rows in every chemist's store-room, it still assuages the coughs
of age and brightens the elderly eye and loosens the elderly
tongue ; but its social glory, its financial illumination, have
faded from the world for ever. And I, sole scorched survivor
from the blaze, sit writing of it here in an air that is never
still for the clang and thunder of machines, on a table littered
with working drawings, and amid fragments of models and notes
about velocities and air and water pressures and trajectories—
of an altogether different sort from that of Tono-Bungay.

§ 2

I write that much and look at it, and wonder whether,
after all, this is any fair statement of what I am attempting
in this book. I've given, I see, an impression that I want
to make simply a hotch-potch of anecdotes and experiences
with my uncle swimming in the middle as the largest lump
of victual. I'll own that here, with the pen already started,
I realise what a fermenting mass of things learnt and emotions
experienced and theories formed I've got to deal with, and
how, in a sense, hopeless my book must be from the very
outset. I suppose what I'm really trying to render is nothing
more nor less than Life—as one man has found it. I want
to tell—*myself*, and my impressions of the thing as a whole,
to say things I have come to feel intensely of the laws, traditions, usages, and ideas we call society, and how we poor
individuals get driven and lured and stranded among these
windy, perplexing shoals and channels. I've got, I suppose,
to a time of life when things begin to take on shapes that
have an air of reality, and become no longer material for
dreaming but interesting in themselves. I've reached the
criticising, novel-writing age, and here I am writing mine—
my one novel—without having any of the discipline to refrain
and omit that I suppose the regular novel-writer acquires.

I've read an average share of novels and made some starts
before this beginning, and I've found the restraints and rules
of the art (as I made them out) impossible for me. I like

to write, I am keenly interested in writing, but it is not my
technique. I'm an engineer with a patent or two and a set
of ideas ; most of whatever artist there is in me has been
given to turbine machines and boat-building and the problem
of flying, and do what I will I fail to see how I can be other
than a lax, undisciplined story-teller. I must sprawl and
flounder, comment and theorise, if I am to get the thing out
I have in mind. And it isn't a constructed tale I have to
tell but unmanageable realities. My love-story—and if only
I can keep up the spirit of truth-telling all through as strongly
as I have now, you shall have it all—falls into no sort of neat
scheme of telling. It involves three separate feminine persons.
It's all mixed up with the other things. . . .

But I've said enough, I hope, to excuse myself for the
method or want of method in what follows, and I think I
had better tell without further delay of my boyhood and
my early impressions in the shadow of Bladesover House.

§ 3

There came a time when I realised that Bladesover House
was not all it seemed, but when I was a little boy I took the
place with the entirest faith as a complete authentic micro-
cosm. I believed that the Bladesover system was a little working model—and not so very little either—of the whole world.

Let me try and give you the effect of it.

Bladesover lies up on the Kentish Downs, eight miles
perhaps from Ashborough ; and its old pavilion, a minute
wooden parody of the temple of Vesta at Tibur, upon the
hill-crest behind the house, commands in theory at least a
view of either sea, of the Channel southward and the Thames
to the north-east. The park is the second largest in Kent,
finely wooded with well-placed beeches, many elms and some
sweet chestnuts, abounding in little valleys and hollows
of bracken, with springs and a stream and three fine ponds
and multitudes of fallow deer. The house was built in the
eighteenth century, it is of pale red brick in the style of a
French château, and save for one pass among the crests
which opens to blue distances, to minute, remote, oast-set
farm-houses and copses and wheatfields and the occasional
gleam of water, its hundred and seventeen windows look
on nothing but its own wide and handsome territories. A
semicircular screen of great beeches masks the church and
village, which cluster picturesquely about the high roads
along the skirts of the great park. Northward, at the
remotest corner of that enclosure, is a second dependent
village, Ropedean, less fortunate in its greater distance and
also on account of a rector. This divine was indeed rich,
but he was vindictively economical because of some shrink-
age of his tithes ; and by reason of his use of the word
Eucharist for the Lord's Supper he had become altogether

estranged from the great ladies of Bladesover. So that
Ropedean was in the shadows through all that youthful time.

Now the unavoidable suggestion of that wide park and
that fair large house, dominating church, village and the
country-side, was that they represented the thing that mattered
supremely in the world, and that all other things had significance only in relation to them. They represented the Gentry,
the Quality, by and through and for whom the rest of the
world, the farming folk and the labouring folk, the trades-
people of Ashborough, and the upper servants and the lower
servants and the servants of the estate, breathed and lived
and were permitted. And the Quality did it so quietly and
thoroughly, the great house mingled so solidly and effectually
with earth and sky, the contrast of its spacious hall and saloon
and galleries, its airy housekeeper's room and warren of offices
with the meagre dignities of the vicar, and the pinched and
stuffy rooms of even the post-office people and the grocer,
so enforced these suggestions, that it was only when I was a
boy of thirteen or fourteen and some queer inherited strain
of scepticism had set me doubting whether Mr. Bartlett, the
vicar, did really know with certainty all about God, that as
a further and deeper step in doubting I began to question
the final rightness of the gentlefolk, their primary necessity
in the scheme of things. But once that scepticism had
awakened it took me fast and far. By fourteen I had achieved
terrible blasphemies and sacrilege ; I had resolved to marry a
viscount's daughter, and I had blacked the left eye—I think it
was the left—of her half-brother, in open and declared rebellion.

But of that in its place.

The great house, the church, the village, and the labourers
and the servants in their stations and degrees, seemed to
me, I say, to be a closed and complete social system. About
us were other villages and great estates, and from house to
house, interlacing, correlated, the Gentry, the fine Olympians,
came and went. The country towns seemed mere collections
of shops, marketing places for the tenantry, centres for such
education as they needed, as entirely dependent on the gentry
as the village and scarcely less directly so. I thought this
was the order of the whole world. I thought London was
only a greater country town where the gentlefolk kept town-
houses and did their greater shopping under the magnificent
shadow of the greatest of gentlewomen, the Queen. It
seemed to be in the divine order. That all this fine appearance was already sapped, that there were forces at work that
might presently carry this elaborate social system in which my
mother instructed me so carefully that I might understand my
" place," to Limbo, had scarcely dawned upon me even by
the time that Tono-Bungay was fairly launched upon the world.

There are many people in England to-day upon whom
it has not yet dawned. There are times when I doubt

whether any but a very inconsiderable minority of English people realise how extensively this ostensible order has even now passed away. The great houses stand in the parks still, the cottages cluster respectfully on their borders, touching their eaves with their creepers, the English countryside—you can range through Kent from Bladesover northward and see—persists obstinately in looking what it was. It is like an early day in a fine October. The hand of change rests on it all, unfelt, unseen; resting for a while, as it were half reluctantly, before it grips and ends the thing for ever. One frost and the whole face of things will be bare, links snap, patience end, our fine foliage of pretences lie glowing in the mire.

For that we have still to wait a little while. The new order may have gone far towards shaping itself, but just as in that sort of lantern show that used to be known in the village as the "Dissolving Views," the scene that is going remains upon the mind, traceable and evident, and the newer picture is yet enigmatical long after the lines that are to replace those former ones have grown bright and strong, so that the new England of our children's children is still a riddle to me. The ideas of democracy, of equality, and above all of promiscuous fraternity have certainly never really entered into the English mind. But what *is* coming into it? All this book, I hope, will bear a little on that. Our people never formulates; it keeps words for jests and ironies. In the meanwhile the old shapes, the old attitudes remain, subtly changed and changing still, sheltering strange tenants. Bladesover House is now let furnished to Sir Reuben Lichtenstein, and has been since old Lady Drew died; it was my odd experience to visit there, in the house of which my mother had been housekeeper, when my uncle was at the climax of Tono-Bungay. It was curious to notice then the little differences that had come to things with this substitution. To borrow an image from my mineralogical days, these Jews were not so much a new British gentry as "pseudomorphous" after the gentry. They are a very clever people, the Jews, but not clever enough to suppress their cleverness. I wished I could have gone downstairs to savour the tone of the pantry. It would have been very different I know. Hawksnest, over beyond, I noted, had its pseudomorph too; a newspaper proprietor of the type that hustles along with stolen ideas from one loud sink-or-swim enterprise to another, had bought the place outright; Redgrave was in the hands of brewers.

But the people in the villages, so far as I could detect, saw no difference in their world. Two little girls bobbed and an old labourer touched his hat convulsively as I walked through the village. He still thought he knew his place—and mine. I did not know him, but I would have liked dearly to have asked him if he remembered my mother, if either my uncle or old Lichtenstein had been man enough to stand being given away like that.

In that English country-side of my boyhood every human being had a " place." It belonged to you from your birth like the colour of your eyes, it was inextricably your destiny. Above you were your betters, below you were your inferiors, and there were even an unstable questionable few, cases so disputable that you might, for the rough purposes of every day at least, regard them as your equals. Head and centre of our system was Lady Drew, her " leddyship," shrivelled, garrulous, with a wonderful memory for genealogies and very, very old, and beside her and nearly as old, Miss Sommerville, her cousin and companion. These two old souls lived like dried-up kernels in the great shell of Bladesover House, the shell that had once been gaily full of fops, of fine ladies in powder and patches and courtly gentlemen with swords ; and when there was no company they spent whole days in the corner parlour just over the housekeeper's room, between reading and slumber and caressing their two pet dogs. When I was a boy I used always to think of these two poor old creatures as superior beings living, like God, somewhere through the ceiling. Occasionally they bumped about a bit and one even heard them overhead, which gave them a greater effect of reality without mitigating their vertical pre-dominance. Sometimes too I saw them. Of course if I came upon them in the park or in the shrubbery (where I was a trespasser) I hid or fled in pious horror, but I was upon due occasion taken into the Presence by request. I remember her " leddyship " then as a thing of black silks and a golden chain, a quavering injunction to me to be a good boy, a very shrunken loose-skinned face and neck, and a ropy hand that trembled a half-crown into mine. Miss Somerville hovered behind, a paler thing of broken lavender and white and black, with screwed-up, sandy-lashed eyes. Her hair was yellow and her colour bright, and when we sat in the housekeeper's room of a winter's night warming our toes and sipping elder wine, her maid would tell us the simple secrets of that belated flush. . . . After my fight with young Garvell I was of course banished, and I never saw those poor old painted goddesses again.

Then there came and went on these floors over our respectful heads, the Company ; people I rarely saw, but whose tricks and manners were imitated and discussed by their maids and valets in the housekeeper's room and the steward's room— so that I had them through a medium at second hand. I gathered that none of the company was really Lady Drew's equal, they were greater and lesser—after the manner of all things in our world. Once I remember there was a Prince, with a real live gentleman in attendance, and that was a little above our customary levels and excited us all, and perhaps raised our expectations unduly. Afterwards Rabbits, the butler, came into my mother's room downstairs, red with

indignation and with tears in his eyes. " Look at *that* ! "
gasped Rabbits. My mother was speechless with horror.
That was a sovereign, a mere sovereign, such as you might get
from any commoner !

After Company, I remember, came anxious days, for the
poor old women upstairs were left tired and cross and
vindictive, and in a state of physical and emotional indigestion
after their social efforts. . . .

On the lowest fringe of these real Olympians hung the
vicarage people, and next to them came those ambiguous
beings who are neither quality nor subjects. The vicarage
people certainly hold a place by themselves in the typical
English scheme ; nothing is more remarkable than the progress the Church has made—socially—in the last two hundred
years. In the early eighteenth century the vicar was rather
under than over the house-steward, and was deemed a fitting
match for the housekeeper or any not too morally discredited
discard. The eighteenth-century literature is full of his
complaints that he might not remain at table to share the pie.
He rose above these indignities because of the abundance
of younger sons. When I meet the large assumptions of the
contemporary cleric, I am apt to think of these things. It is
curious to note that to-day that down-trodden, organ-playing
creature, the Church of England village schoolmaster, holds
much the same position as the seventeenth-century parson.
The doctor in Bladesover ranked below the vicar but above
the " vet " ; artists and summer visitors squeezed in above
or below this point according to their appearance and expenditure ; and then in a carefully arranged scale came the
tenantry, the butler and housekeeper, the village shopkeeper,
the head keeper, the cook, the publican, the second keeper,
the blacksmith (whose status was complicated by his daughter
keeping the post office—and a fine hash she used to make of
telegrams, too !), the village shopkeeper's eldest son, the first
footman, younger sons of the village shopkeeper, his first
assistant, and so forth. . . .

All these conceptions and applications of a universal
precedence and much else I drank in at Bladesover, as I
listened to the talk of valets, ladies'-maids, Rabbits the butler
and my mother in the much cupboarded, white-painted,
chintz-brightened housekeeper's room where the upper
servants assembled, or of footmen and Rabbits and estate
men of all sorts among the green baize and Windsor chairs of
the pantry—where Rabbits, being above the law, sold beer
without a licence or any compunction—or of housemaids and
still-room maids in the bleak, matting-carpeted still-room,
or of the cook and her kitchen maids and casual friends among
the bright copper and hot glow of the kitchens.

Of course their own ranks and places came by implication
to these people, and it was with the ranks and places of the

Olympians that the talk mainly concerned itself. There was an old peerage and a Crockford together with the books of recipes, the *Whitaker's Almanack*, the *Old Moore's Almanack*, and the eighteenth-century dictionary, on the little dresser that broke the cupboards on one side of my mother's room ; there was another peerage, with the covers off, in the pantry ; there was a new peerage in the billiard-room, and I seem to remember another in the anomalous apartment that held the upper servants' bagatelle board, and in which, after the Hall dinner, they partook of the luxury of sweets. And if you had asked any of those upper servants how such and such a Prince of Battenberg was related to, let us say, Mr. Cunninghame Grahame or the Duke of Argyle, you would have been told upon the nail. As a boy, I heard a great deal of that sort of thing, and if to this day I am still a little vague about courtesy titles and the exact application of honorifics, it is, I can assure you, because I hardened my heart, and not from any lack of adequate opportunity of mastering these succulent particulars.

Dominating all these memories is the figure of my mother —my mother who did not love me because I grew liker my father every day—and who knew with inflexible decision her place and the place of every one in the world except the place that concealed my father—and in some details mine. Subtle points were put to her. I can see and hear her saying now, "No, Miss Fison, peers of England go in before peers of the United Kingdom, and he is merely a peer of the United King-dom." She had much exercise in placing people's servants about her tea-table, where the etiquette was very strict. I wonder sometimes if the etiquette of housekeepers' rooms is as strict to-day, and what my mother would have made of a chauffeur. . . .

On the whole I am glad that I saw so much as I did of Bladesover—if for no other reason than because seeing it when I did, quite naïvely, believing in it thoroughly, and then coming to analyse it, has enabled me to understand much that would be absolutely incomprehensible in the structure of English society. Bladesover is, I am convinced, the clue to almost all that is distinctively British and per-plexing to the foreign inquirer in England and the English-speaking peoples. Grasp firmly that England was all Blades-over two hundred years ago ; that it has had Reform Acts indeed, and such-like changes of formula, but no essential revolution since then ; that all that is modern and different has come in as a thing intruded or as a gloss upon this pre-dominant formula, either impertinently or apologetically ; and you will perceive at once the reasonableness, the necessity, of that snobbishness which is the distinctive quality of English thought. Everybody who is not actually in the shadow of a Bladesover is as it were perpetually seeking after lost orientations. We have never broken with our tradition, never even symbolically hewed it to pieces, as the French did in quivering fact in the Terror. But all the organising ideas have slackened, the old habitual bonds have relaxed or altogether come undone. And America too, is, as it were, a detached, outlying part of that estate which has expanded in queer ways. George Washington, Esquire, was of the gentlefolk, and he came near being a King. It was Plutarch, you know, and nothing intrinsically American, that prevented George Washington being a King. . . .

§ 4

I hated tea-time in the housekeeper's room more than anything else at Bladesover. And more particularly I hated it when Mrs. Mackridge and Mrs. Booch and Mrs. Latude-Fernay were staying in the house. They were, all three of them, pensioned-off servants. Old friends of Lady Drew's had rewarded them posthumously for a prolonged devotion to their minor comforts, and Mrs. Booch was also trustee for a favourite Skye terrier. Every year Lady Drew gave them an invitation—a reward and encouragement of virtue with especial reference to my mother and Miss Fison, the maid. They sat about in black and shiny and flouncey clothing adorned with gimp and beads, eating great quantities of cake, drinking much tea in a stately manner and reverberating remarks.

I remember these women as immense. No doubt they were of negotiable size, but I was only a very little chap and they have assumed nightmare proportions in my mind. They loomed, they bulged, they impended. Mrs. Mackridge was large and dark ; there was a marvel about her head, inasmuch as she was bald. She wore a dignified cap, and in front of that upon her brow hair was *painted*. I have never seen the like since. She had been maid to the widow of Sir Roderick Blenderhasset Impey, some sort of governor or such-like potent in the East Indies, and from her remains— in Mrs. Mackridge—I judge Lady Impey was a very stupendous and crushing creature indeed. Lady Impey had been of the Juno type, haughty, unapproachable, given to irony and a caustic wit. Mrs. Mackridge had no wit, but she had acquired the caustic voice and gestures along with the old satins and trimmings of the great lady. When she told you it was a fine morning, she seemed also to be telling you you were a fool and a low fool to boot ; when she was spoken to, she had a way of acknowledging your poor tinkle of utterance with a voluminous, scornful "Haw!" that made you want to burn her alive. She also had a way of saying "Indade!" with a droop of the eyelids.

Mrs. Booch was a smaller woman, brown haired, with queer little curls on either side of her face, large blue eyes, and a small set of stereotyped remarks that constituted her entire mental range. Mrs. Latude-Fernay has left, oddly enough, no memory at all except her name and the effect of a green-grey silk dress, all set with gold and blue buttons. I fancy she was a large blonde. Then there was Miss Fison, the maid who served both Lady Drew and Miss Somerville, and at the end of the table opposite my mother, sat Rabbits the butler. Rabbits, for a butler, was an un-assuming man, and at tea he was not as you know butlers, but in a morning coat and a black tie with blue spots. Still, he was large, with side whiskers, even if his clean-shaven mouth was weak and little. I sat among these people on a high, hard, early Georgian chair, trying to exist, like a feeble seedling amidst great rocks, and my mother sat with an eye upon me, resolute to suppress the slightest manifestation of vitality. It was hard on me, but perhaps it was also hard upon these rather over-fed, ageing, pretending people, that my youthful restlessness and rebellious, unbelieving eyes should be thrust in among their dignities.

Tea lasted for nearly three-quarters of an hour, and I sat it out perforce ; and day after day the talk was exactly the same.

" Sugar, Mrs. Mackridge ? " my mother used to ask. " Sugar, Mrs. Latude-Fernay ? "

The word " sugar " would stir the mind of Mrs. Mackridge. " They say," she would begin, issuing her proclamation—at least half her sentences began " they say "—" sugar is fatt-an-ing, nowadays. Many of the best people do not take it now at all."

" Not with their tea, ma'am," said Rabbits, intelligently.

" Not with anaything," said Mrs. Mackridge, with an air of crushing repartee, and drank.

" What won't they say next ? " said Miss Fison.

" They do say such things ! " said Mrs. Booch.

" They say," said Mrs. Mackridge, inflexibly, " the doctors are not recomm-an-ding it now."

MY MOTHER : " No, ma'am ? "

MRS. MACKRIDGE : " No, ma'am."

Then, to the table at large : " Poor Sir Roderick before he died, consumed great quan-ta-ties of sugar. I have sometimes fancied it may have hastened his end."

This ended the first skirmish. A certain gloom of manner and a pause was considered due to the sacred memory of Sir Roderick.

" George," said my mother, " don't kick the chair ! "

Then, perhaps, Mrs. Booch would produce a favourite piece from her repertoire. " The evenings are drawing out nicely," she would say, or if the season was decadent, " How the evenings draw in ! " It was an invaluable remark to her ; I do not know how she would have got along without it.

My mother, who sat with her back to the window, would always consider it due to Mrs. Booch to turn about and regard the evening in the act of elongation or contraction, whatever phase it might be.

A brisk discussion of how long we were to the longest or shortest day would ensue, and die away at last exhausted.

Mrs. Mackridge, perhaps, would reopen. She had many intelligent habits ; among others she read the paper—*The Morning Post*. The other ladies would at times tackle that sheet, but only to read the births, marriages, and deaths on the front page. It was, of course, the old *Morning Post* that cost threepence, not the brisk, coruscating young thing of to-day. "They say," she would open, "that Lord Tweedums is to go to Canada."

"Ah !" said Mr. Rabbits ; "dew they ? "

"Isn't he," said my mother, "the Earl of Slumgold's cousin ? " She knew he was ; it was an entirely irrelevant and unnecessary remark, but still, something to say.

"The same, ma'am," said Mrs. Mackridge. "They say he was extremelay popular in New South Wales. They looked up to him greatlay. I knew him, ma'am, as a young man. A very nice pleasant young fella."

Interlude of respect.

"'Is predecessor," said Rabbits, who had acquired from some clerical model a precise emphatic articulation without acquiring at the same time the aspirates that would have graced it, "got into trouble at Sydney."

"Haw ! " said Mrs. Mackridge, scornfully, "so I am tawled."

"'E came to Templemorton after 'e came back, and I remember them talking 'im over after 'e'd gone again."

"Haw ? " said Mrs. Mackridge, interrogatively.

"'*Is* fuss was quotin' poetry, ma'am. 'E said—what was it 'e said ?—' They lef' their country for their country's good,' which in some way was took to remind them of their being originally convic's, though now reformed. Every one I 'eard speak, agreed it was takless of 'im."

"Sir Roderick used to say," said Mrs. Mackridge, "that the First Thing "—here Mrs. Mackridge paused and looked dreadfully at me—"and the Second Thing "—here she fixed me again—"and the Third Thing "—now I was released— "needed in a colonial governor is Tact." She became aware of my doubts again, and added predominantly, "It has always struck me that that was a Singularly True Remark."

I resolved that if ever I found this polypus of Tact growing up in my soul, I would tear it out by the roots, throw it forth and stamp on it.

"They're queer people—colonials," said Rabbits, "very queer. When I was at Templemorton I see something ov 'em. Queer fellows, some of 'em. Very respectful of course, free with their money in a spasammy sort of way, but—— Some of 'em, I must confess, make me nervous. They have an eye on you. They watch you—as you wait. They let themselves appear to be lookin' at you. . . ."

My mother said nothing in that discussion. The word

" colonies " always upset her. She was afraid, I think, that if she turned her mind in that direction my errant father might suddenly and shockingly be discovered, no doubt conspicuously bigamic and altogether offensive and revolutionary. She did not want to rediscover my father at all.

It is curious that when I was a little listening boy I had such an idea of our colonies that I jeered in my heart at Mrs. Mackridge's colonial ascendancy. These brave, emancipated sunburnt English of the open, I thought, suffer these aristocratic invaders as a quaint anachronism, but as for being gratified——!

I don't jeer now. I'm not so sure.

§ 5

It is a little difficult to explain why I did not come to do what was the natural thing for any one in my circumstances to do, and take my world for granted. A certain innate scepticism, I think, explains it—and a certain inaptitude for sympathetic assimilation. My father, I believe, was a sceptic ; my mother was certainly a hard woman.

I was an only child, and to this day I do not know whether my father is living or dead. He fled my mother's virtues before my distincter memories began. He left no traces in his flight, and she, in her indignation, destroyed every vestige that she could of him. Never a photograph nor a scrap of his handwriting have I seen ; and it was, I know, only the accepted code of virtue and discretion that prevented her destroying her marriage certificate and me, and so making a clean sweep of her matrimonial humiliation. I suppose I must inherit something of the moral stupidity that could enable her to make a holocaust of every little personal thing she had of him. There must have been presents made by him as a lover, for example—books with kindly inscriptions, letters perhaps, a flattened flower, a ring, or such-like gage. She kept her wedding-ring, of course, but all the others she destroyed. She never told me his Christian name or indeed spoke a word to me of him, though at times I came near daring to ask her ; and what I have of him—it isn't much—I got from his brother, my hero, my Uncle Ponderevo. She wore her ring ; her marriage certificate she kept in a sealed envelope in the very bottom of her largest trunk, and me she sustained at a private school among the Kentish hills. You must not think I was always at Bladesover—even in my holidays. If at the time these came round, Lady Drew was vexed by recent Company, or for any other reason wished to take it out of my mother, then she used to ignore the customary reminder my mother gave her, and I " stayed on " at the school.

But such occasions were rare, and I suppose that between ten and fourteen I averaged fifty days a year at Bladesover.

Don't imagine I deny that was a fine thing for me. Bladesover, in absorbing the whole country-side, had not altogether
missed greatness. The Bladesover system has at least done
one good thing for England, it has abolished the peasant habit
of mind. If many of us still live and breathe pantry and
housekeeper's room, we are quit of the dream of living by
economising parasitically on hens and pigs. . . . About that
park there were some elements of a liberal education ; there
was a great space of greensward not given over to manure
and food grubbing ; there was mystery, there was matter
for the imagination. It was still a park of deer. I saw something of the life of these dappled creatures, heard the belling
of stags, came upon young fawns among the bracken, found
bones, skulls, and antlers in lonely places. There were
corners that gave a gleam of meaning to the word forest,
glimpses of unstudied natural splendour. There was a slope
of bluebells in the broken sunlight under the newly green
beeches in the west wood that is now precious sapphire in
my memory ; it was the first time that I knowingly met Beauty.

And in the house there were books. The rubbish old
Lady Drew read I never saw ; stuff of the Maria Monk type,
I have since gathered, had a fascination for her ; but back
in the past there had been a Drew of intellectual enterprise,
Sir Cuthbert, the son of Sir Matthew who built the house ;
and thrust away, neglected and despised, in an old room
upstairs were books and treasures of his that my mother
let me rout among during a spell of wintry wet. Sitting
under a dormer window on a shelf above great stores of tea
and spices, I became familiar with much of Hogarth in a big
portfolio, with Raphael—there was a great book of engravings from the stanzas of Raphael in the Vatican—and with
most of the capitals of Europe as they had looked about 1780,
by means of several big iron-moulded books of views. There
was also a broad eighteenth-century atlas with huge wandering maps that instructed me mightily. It had splendid adornments about each map title ; Holland showed a fisherman and
his boat ; Russia a Cossack ; Japan, remarkable people
attired in pagodas—I say it deliberately, " pagodas." There
were Terræ Incognitæ in every continent then, Poland,
Sarmatia, lands since lost ; and many a voyage I made with
a blunted pin about that large, incorrect, and dignified world.
The books in that little old closet had been banished, I suppose,
from the saloon during the Victorian revival of good taste
and emasculated orthodoxy, but my mother had no suspicion
of their character. So I read and understood the good sound
rhetoric of Tom Paine's *Rights of Man*, and his *Common
Sense*—excellent books, once praised by bishops and since
sedulously lied about. Gulliver was there unexpurgated,
strong meat for a boy, perhaps, but not too strong, I hold—
I have never regretted that I escaped niceness in these affairs.

The satire of Traldragdubh made my blood boil as it was meant to do, but I hated Swift for the Houyhnhnms and never quite liked a horse afterwards. Then I remember also a translation of Voltaire's *Candide*, and *Rasselas*; and, vast book though it was, I really believe I read, in a muzzy sort of way, of course, from end to end, and even with some reference now and then to the Atlas, Gibbon—in twelve volumes.

These readings whetted my taste for more, and surreptitiously I raided the bookcases in the big saloon. I got through quite a number of books before my sacrilegious temerity was discovered by Ann, the old head-housemaid. I remember that among others I tried a translation of Plato's *Republic* then, and found extraordinarily little interest in it ; I was much too young for that ; but *Vathek*—*Vathek* was glorious stuff. That kicking affair ! When everybody *had* to kick !

The thought of *Vathek* always brings back with it my boyish memory of the big saloon at Bladesover.

It was a huge, long room with many windows opening upon the park, and each window—there were a dozen or more reaching from the floor up—had its elaborate silk or satin curtains, heavily fringed, a canopy (is it ?) above, its complex white shutters folding into the deep thickness of the wall. At either end of that great still place was an immense marble chimney-piece ; the end by the bookcase showed the wolf and Romulus and Remus, with Homer and Virgil for supporters ; the design of the other end I have forgotten. Frederick, Prince of Wales, swaggered flatly over the one, twice life-size, but mellowed by the surface gleam of oil ; and over the other was an equally colossal group of departed Drews as sylvan deities, scantily clad, against a storm-rent sky. Down the centre of the elaborate ceiling were three chandeliers, each bearing some hundreds of dangling glass lustres, and over the interminable carpet—it impressed me as about as big as Sarmatia in the store-room Atlas—were islands and archipelagos of chintz-covered chairs and couches, tables, great Sèvres vases on pedestals, a bronze man and horse. Somewhere in this wilderness one came, I remember, upon a big harp beside a lyre-shaped music-stand, and a grand piano. . . .

The book-borrowing raid was one of extraordinary dash and danger. One came down the main service stairs—that was legal. Illegality began on a little landing when, very cautiously, one went through a red baize door. A short passage led to the hall, and here one reconnoitred for Ann, the old head-housemaid—the younger housemaids were friendly and did not count. Ann located, came a dash across the open space at the foot of that great staircase that has never been properly descended since powder went out of fashion, and so to the saloon door. A beast of an oscillating Chinaman in china, as large as life, grimaced and quivered to

one's lightest steps. That door was the perilous place ; it
was double, with the thickness of the wall between, so that one
could not listen beforehand for the whisk of the feather-brush
on the other side. Oddly rat-like, is it not, this darting into
enormous places in pursuit of the abandoned crumbs of thought?

And I found Langhorne's *Plutarch* too, I remember, on
those shelves. It seems queer to me now to think that I
acquired pride and self-respect, the idea of a state and the
germ of public spirit, in such a furtive fashion ; queer, too,
that it should rest with an old Greek, dead these eighteen
hundred years, to teach me that.

§ 6

The school I went to was the sort of school the Bladesover
system permitted. The public schools that had come into
existence in the brief glow of the Renascence had been taken
possession of by the ruling class ; the lower classes were not
supposed to stand in need of schools, and our middle stratum
got the schools it deserved, private schools, schools any unqualified pretender was free to establish. Mine was kept
by a man who had had the energy to get himself a college
of Preceptors diploma, and considering how cheap his charges
were, I will readily admit the place might have been worse.
The building was a dingy, yellow-brick residence outside the
village, with the schoolroom as an outbuilding of lath and plaster.

I do not remember that my schooldays were unhappy—
indeed, I recall a good lot of fine mixed fun in them—but I
cannot without grave risk of misinterpretation declare that
we were at all nice and refined. We fought much, not sound
formal fighting but " scrapping " of a sincere and murderous
kind, into which one might bring one's boots—it made us
tough at any rate—and several of us were the sons of London
publicans, who distinguished " scraps " where one meant to
hurt from ordered pugilism, practising both arts, and having,
moreover, precocious linguistic gifts. Our cricket-field was
bald about the wickets, and we played without style and
disputed with the umpire ; and the teaching was chiefly in
the hands of a lout of nineteen, who wore ready-made clothes
and taught despicably. The head master and proprietor
taught us arithmetic, algebra, and Euclid, and to the older
boys even trigonometry, himself ; he had a strong mathematical bias, and I think now that by the standard of a British
public school he did rather well by us.

We had one inestimable privilege at that school, and that
was spiritual neglect. We dealt with one another with the
forcible simplicity of natural boys, we " cheeked " and
" punched " and " clouted " ; we thought ourselves Red
Indians and cowboys and such-like honourable things, and
not young English gentlemen ; we never felt the strain of
" Onward, Christian soldiers," nor were swayed by any

premature piety in the cold oak pew of our Sunday devotions. All that was good. We spent our rare pennies in the un-censored reading matter of the village dame's shop, on the *Boys of England* and honest penny dreadfuls—ripping stuff, stuff that anticipated Haggard and Stevenson, badly printed and queerly illustrated, and very, very good for us. On our half-holidays we were allowed the unusual freedom of rambling in twos and threes wide and far about the land, talking ex-perimentally, dreaming wildly. There was much in those walks! To this day the landscape of the Kentish weald, with its low, broad distances, its hop gardens and golden stretches of wheat, its oasts and square church towers, its background of downland and hangers, has for me a faint sense of adventure added to the pleasure of its beauty. We smoked on occasion, but nobody put us up to the proper " boyish " things to do ; we never " robbed an orchard," for example, though there were orchards all about us : we thought stealing was sinful ; we stole incidental apples and turnips and strawberries from the fields, indeed, but in a criminal in-glorious fashion, and afterwards we were ashamed. We had our days of adventure, but they were natural accidents, our own adventures. There was one hot day when several of us, walking out towards Maidstone, were incited by the devil to despise ginger beer, and we fuddled ourselves dreadfully with ale ; and a time when our young minds were infected to the pitch of buying pistols, by the legend of the Wild West. Young Roots from Highbury, came back with a revolver and cartridges, and we went off six strong to live a free, wild life one holiday afternoon. We fired our first shot deep in the old flint mine at Chiselstead, and nearly burst our ear-drums ; then we fired in a primrose-studded wood by Pick-thorn Green, and I gave a false alarm of " keeper," and we fled in disorder for a mile. After which Roots suddenly shot at a pheasant in the high road by Chiselstead, and then young Barker told lies about the severity of the game laws and made Roots sore afraid, and we hid the pistol in a dry ditch outside the school field. A day or so after we got it again, and ignoring a certain fouling and rusting of the barrel, tried for a rabbit at three hundred yards. Young Roots blew a molehill at twenty paces into a dust cloud, burnt his fingers, and scorched his face ; and the weapon having once displayed this strange disposition to flame upon the shooter, was not subsequently fired.

One main source of excitement for us was " cheeking " people in vans and carts upon the Goudhurst road ; and getting myself into a monstrous white mess in the chalk pits beyond the village, and catching yellow jaundice as a sequel to bathing stark naked with three other Adamites, Old Ewart leading that function, in the rivulet across Hick-son's meadows, are among my *memorabilia*. Those free, imaginative afternoons ! how much they were for us ! how much they did for us ! All streams came from the then un-discovered " sources of the Nile " in those days, all thickets were Indian jungles, and our best game, I say it with pride, I invented. I got it out of the Bladesover saloon. We found a wood where " Trespassing " was forbidden, and did the " Retreat of the Ten Thousand " through it from end to end, cutting our way bravely through a host of nettle beds that barred our path, and not forgetting to weep and kneel when at last we emerged within sight of the High Road Sea. So we have burst at times, weeping and rejoicing, upon startled wayfarers. Usually I took the part of that distinguished general Xenōphon—and please note the quantity of the ō. I have all my classical names like that—Socrates rhymes with Bates for me, and except when the bleak eye of some scholar warns me of his standards of judgment, I use those dear old mispronunciations still. The little splash into Latin made during my days as a chemist washed off nothing of the habit. Well,—if I met those great gentlemen of the past with their accents carelessly adjusted I did at least meet them alive, as an equal, and in a living tongue. Altogether my school might easily have been worse for me, and among other good things it gave me a friend who has lasted my life out.

This was Ewart, who is now a monumental artist at Woking, after many vicissitudes. Dear chap, how he did stick out of his clothes to be sure ! He was a long-limbed lout, ridiculously tall beside my more youthful compactness, and except that there was no black moustache under his nose blob, he had the same round knobby face he has to-day, the same bright and active hazel-brown eyes, the stare, the medita-tive moment, the insinuating reply. Surely no boy ever played the fool as Bob Ewart used to play it, no boy had a readier knack of mantling the world with wonder. Common-ness vanished before Ewart, at his expository touch all things became memorable and rare. From him I first heard tell of love, but only after its barbs were already sticking in my heart. He was, I know now, the bastard of that great improvident artist, Rickmann Ewart ; he brought the light of a lax world that at least had not turned its back upon beauty, into the growing fermentation of my mind.

I won his heart by a version of Vathek, and after that we were inseparable yarning friends. We merged our intellectual stock so completely that I wonder sometimes how much I did not become Ewart, how much Ewart is not vicariously and derivatively me. . . .

§ 7

And then when I had newly passed my fourteenth birth-day, came my tragic disgrace.

It was in my midsummer holidays that the thing happened,

and it was through the Honourable Beatrice Normandy. She had " come into my life," as they say, before I was twelve.

She descended unexpectedly into a peaceful interlude that followed the annual going of those Three Great Women. She came into the old nursery upstairs, and every day she had tea with us in the housekeeper's room. She was eight, and she came with a nurse called Nannie; and to begin with, I did not like her at all.

Nobody liked this irruption into the downstairs rooms; the two " gave trouble "—a dire offence; Nannie's sense of duty to her charge led to requests and demands that took my mother's breath away. Eggs at unusual times, the reboiling of milk, the rejection of an excellent milk pudding —not negotiated respectfully, but dictated as of right. Nannie was a dark, long-featured, taciturn woman in a grey dress; she had a furtive inflexibility of manner that finally dismayed and crushed and overcame. She conveyed she was " under orders "—like a Greek tragedy. She was that strange product of the old time, a devoted, trusted servant; she had, as it were, banked all her pride and will with the greater, more powerful people who employed her, in return for a life-long security of servitude—the bargain was none the less binding for being implicit. Finally they were to pension her, and she would die the hated treasure of a boarding-house. She had built up in herself an enormous habit of reference to these up-stairs people, she had curbed down all discordant murmurings of her soul, her very instincts were perverted or surrendered. She was sexless, her personal pride was all transferred, she mothered another woman's child with a hard, joyless devotion that was at last entirely compatible with a stoical separation. She treated us all as things that counted for nothing save to fetch and carry for her charge. But the Honourable Beatrice could condescend.

The queer chances of later years come between me and a distinctly separated memory of that childish face. When I think of Beatrice, I think of her as I came to know her at a later time, when at last I came to know her so well that indeed now I could draw her, and show a hundred little delicate things you would miss in looking at her. But even then I remember how I noted the infinite delicacy of her childish skin and the fine eyebrow, finer than the finest feather that ever one felt on the breast of a bird. She was one of those elfin, rather precocious little girls, quick coloured, with dark hair, naturally curling dusky hair that was sometimes astray over her eyes, and eyes that were sometimes impishly dark and sometimes a clear brown-yellow. And from the very out-set, after a most cursory attention to Rabbits, she decided that the only really interesting thing at the tea-table was myself.

The elders talked in their formal, dull way—telling Nannie the trite old things about the park and the village that they told every one, and Beatrice watched me across the table with a pitiless little curiosity that made me uncomfortable.

"Nannie," she said, pointing, and Nannie left a question of my mother's disregarded to attend to her; " is he a servant boy ? "

" S-s-sh," said Nannie.   " He's Master Ponderevo."

" Is he a servant boy ? " repeated Beatrice.

" He's a schoolboy," said my mother.

" Then may I talk to him, Nannie ? "

Nannie surveyed me with brutal inhumanity.   " You mustn't talk too much," she said to her charge, and cut cake into fingers for her.   " No," she added decisively, as Beatrice made to speak.

Beatrice became malignant.   Her eyes explored me with unjustifiable hostility.   " He's got dirty hands," she said, stabbing at the forbidden fruit.   " And there's a fray to his collar."

Then she gave herself up to cake with an appearance of entire forgetfulness of me that filled me with hate and a passionate desire to compel her to admire me. . . . And the next day before tea, I did for the first time in my life, freely, without command or any compulsion, wash my hands.

So our acquaintance began, and presently was deepened by a whim of hers.   She had a cold and was kept indoors, and confronted Nannie suddenly with the alternative of being hopelessly naughty, which in her case involved a generous amount of screaming unsuitable for the ears of an elderly, shaky, rich aunt, or having me up to the nursery to play with her all the afternoon.   Nannie came downstairs and borrowed me in a careworn manner, and I was handed over to the little creature as if I was some large variety of kitten.   I had never had anything to do with a little girl before, I thought she was more beautiful and wonderful and bright than anything else could possibly be in life, and she found me the gentlest of slaves—though at the same time, as I made evident, fairly strong.   And Nannie was amazed to find the afternoon slip cheerfully and rapidly away.   She praised my manners to Lady Drew and to my mother, who said she was glad to hear well of me, and after that I played with Beatrice several times.   The toys she had remain in my memory still as huge, splendid things, gigantic to all my previous experience of toys, and we even went to the great doll's house on the nursery landing to play discreetly with that, the great doll's house that the Prince Regent had given Sir Harry Drew's first-born (who died at five), that was a not ineffectual model of Bladesover itself, and contained eighty-five dolls and had cost hundreds of pounds. I played under imperious direction with that toy of glory.

I went back to school when that holiday was over, dreaming of beautiful things, and got Ewart to talk to me of love ; and I made a great story out of the doll's house, a story that, taken over into Ewart's hands, speedily grew to an island doll's city all our own.

One of the dolls, I privately decided, was like Beatrice.

One other holiday there was when I saw something of her—oddly enough my memory of that second holiday in which she played a part is vague—and then came a gap of a year, and then my disgrace.

§ 8

Now I sit down to write my story and tell over again things in their order, I find for the first time how inconsecutive and irrational a thing the memory can be. One recalls acts and cannot recall motives ; one recalls quite vividly moments that stand out inexplicably—things adrift, joining on to nothing, leading nowhere. I think I must have seen Beatrice and her half-brother quite a number of times in my last holiday at Bladesover, but I really cannot recall more than a little of the quality of the circumstances. That great crisis of my boyhood stands out very vividly as an effect, as a sort of cardinal thing for me, but when I look for details—particularly details that led up to the crisis—I cannot find them in any developing order at all. This half-brother, Archie Garvell, was a new factor in the affair. I remember him clearly as a fair-haired, supercilious-looking, weedily-lank boy, much taller than I, but I should imagine very little heavier, and that we hated each other by a sort of instinct from the beginning ; and yet I cannot remember my first meeting with him at all.

Looking back into these past things—it is like rummaging in a neglected attic that has experienced the attentions of some whimsical robber — I cannot even account for the presence of these children at Bladesover. They were, I know, among the innumerable cousins of Lady Drew, and according to the theories of downstairs, candidates for the ultimate possession of Bladesover. If they were, their candidature was unsuccessful. But that great place, with all its faded splendour, its fine furniture, its large traditions, was entirely at the old lady's disposition ; and I am inclined to think it is true that she used this fact to torment and dominate a number of eligible people. Lord Osprey was among the number of these, and she showed these hospitalities to his motherless child and stepchild, partly, no doubt, because he was poor, but quite as much, I nowadays imagine, in the dim hope of finding some affectionate or imaginative outcome of contact with them. Nannie had dropped out of the world this second time, and Beatrice was in the charge of an extremely amiable and ineffectual poor army-class young woman whose name I never knew. They were, I think, two remarkably ill-managed and enterprising children. I seem to remember, too, that it was understood that I was not a fit companion for them, and that our meetings had to be as unostentatious as possible. It was Beatrice who insisted upon our meeting.

I am certain I knew quite a lot about love at fourteen, and that I was quite as much in love with Beatrice then as any impassioned adult could be, and that Beatrice was, in her way, in love with me. It is part of the decent and useful pretences of our world that children of the age at which we were, think nothing, feel nothing, know nothing of love. It is wonderful what people the English are for keeping up pretences. But indeed I cannot avoid telling that Beatrice and I talked of love and kissed and embraced one another.

I recall something of one talk under the overhanging bushes of the shrubbery—I on the park side of the stone wall, and the lady of my worship a little inelegantly astride thereon. Inelegantly do I say ? You should have seen the sweet imp as I remember her. Just her poise on the wall comes suddenly clear before me, and behind her the light various branches of the bushes of the shrubbery that my feet might not profane, and far away and high behind her, dim and stately, the cornice of the great façade of Bladesover rose against the dappled sky. Our talk must have been serious and businesslike, for we were discussing my social position.

"I don't love Archie," she had said, apropos of nothing ; and then in a whisper, leaning forward with the hair about her face, "I love *you* !"

But she had been a little pressing to have it clear that I was not and could not be a servant.

"You'll never be a servant—ever ! "

I swore that very readily, and it is a vow I have kept by nature.

"What will you be ? " said she.

I ran my mind hastily over the professions.

"Will you be a soldier ? " she asked.

"And be bawled at by duffers ? No fear ! " said I. "Leave that to the plough-boys."

"But an officer ? "

"I don't know," I said, evading a shameful difficulty. "I'd rather go into the navy."

"Wouldn't you like to fight ? "

"I'd like to fight," I said. "But a common soldier—it's no honour to have to be told to fight and to be looked down upon while you do it, and how could I be an officer ? "

"Couldn't you be ? " she said, and looked at me doubtfully ; and the spaces of the social system opened between us.

Then, as became a male of spirit, I took upon myself to brag and lie my way through this trouble. I said I was a poor man, and poor men went into the navy ; that I "knew" mathematics, which no army officer did ; and I claimed Nelson for an exemplar, and spoke very highly of my outlook upon blue water. "He loved Lady Hamilton," I said, "although she *was* a lady—and I will love you."

We were somewhere near that when the egregious governess became audible, calling " Beeee-âtrice ! Beeee-e-e-âtrice ! "

" Snifty beast ! " said my lady, and tried to get on with the conversation ; but that governess made things impossible.

" Come here ! " said my lady suddenly, holding out a grubby hand ; and I went very close to her, and she put her little head down upon the wall until her black fog of hair tickled my cheek.

" You are my humble, faithful lover ? " she demanded in a whisper, her warm flushed face near touching mine, and her eyes very dark and lustrous.

" I am your humble, faithful lover," I whispered back.

And she put her arm about my head and put out her lips, and we kissed, and boy though I was, I was all a-tremble. So we two kissed for the first time.

" *Beeee-e-e*-â-trice ! "—fearfully close.

My lady had vanished, with one wild kick of her black-stockinged legs. A moment after, I heard her sustaining the reproaches of her governess, and explaining her failure to answer with an admirable lucidity and disingenuousness.

I felt it was unnecessary for me to be seen just then, and I vanished guiltily round the corner into the West Wood, and so to love-dreams and single-handed play, wandering along one of those meandering bracken valleys that varied Bladesover park. And that day and for many days that kiss upon my lips was a seal, and by night the seed of dreams.

Then I remember an expedition we made—she, I, and her half-brother—into those West Woods—they two were supposed to be playing in the shrubbery—and how we were Indians there, and made a wigwam out of a pile of beech logs, and how we stalked deer, crept near and watched rabbits feeding in a glade, and almost got a squirrel. It was play seasoned with plentiful disputing between me and young Garvell, for each firmly insisted upon the leading rôles, and only my wider reading—I had read ten stories to his one— gave me the ascendancy over him. Also I scored over him by knowing how to find the eagle in a bracken stem. And somehow—I don't remember what led to it at all—I and Beatrice, two hot and ruffled creatures, crept in among the tall bracken and hid from him. The great fronds rose above us, five feet or more, and as I had learnt how to wriggle through that undergrowth with the minimum of betrayal by tossing greenery above, I led the way. The ground under bracken is beautifully clear and faintly scented in warm weather ; the stems come up black and then green ; if you crawl flat, it is a tropical forest in miniature. I led the way and Beatrice crawled behind, and then as the green of the farther glade opened before us, stopped. She crawled up to me, her hot little face came close to mine ; once more she looked and breathed close to me, and suddenly she flung her arm about my neck and dragged me to earth beside her, and kissed me and kissed me again. We kissed, we embraced and kissed again, all without a word ; we desisted, we stared and hesitated—then in a suddenly damped mood and a little perplexed at ourselves, crawled out, to be presently run down and caught in the tamest way by Archie.

That comes back very clearly to me, and other vague memories—I know old Hall and his gun, out shooting at jackdaws, came into our common experiences, but I don't remember how ; and then at last, abruptly, our fight in the Warren stands out. The Warren, like most places in England that have that name, was not particularly a warren, it was a long slope of thorns and beeches through which a path ran, and made an alternative route to the downhill carriage road between Bladesover and Ropedean. I don't know how we three got there, but I have an uncertain fancy it was connected with a visit paid by the governess to the Ropedean vicarage people. But suddenly Archie and I, in discussing a game, fell into a dispute for Beatrice. I had made him the fairest offer : I was to be a Spanish nobleman, she was to be my wife, and he was to be a tribe of Indians trying to carry her off. It seems to me a fairly attractive offer to a boy to be a whole tribe of Indians with a chance of such a booty. But Archie suddenly took offence.

" No," he said ; " we can't have that ! "

" Can't have what ? "

" You can't be a gentleman, because you aren't. And you can't play Beatrice is your wife. It's—it's impertinent."

" But——" I said, and looked at her.

Some earlier grudge in the day's affair must have been in Archie's mind. " We let you play with us," said Archie ; " but we can't have things like that."

" What rot ! " said Beatrice. " He can if he likes."

But he carried his point. I let him carry it, and only began to grow angry three or four minutes later. Then we were still discussing play and disputing about another game. Nothing seemed right for all of us.

" We don't want you to play with us at all," said Archie.

" Yes, we do," said Beatrice.

" He drops his aitches like anything."

" No, E doesn't," said I, in the heat of the moment.

" There you go ! " he cried. " E, he says. E ! E ! E ! "

He pointed a finger at me. He had struck to the heart of my shame. I made the only possible reply by a rush at him. " Hallo ! " he cried, at my blackavised attack. He dropped back into an attitude that had some style in it, parried my blow, got back at my cheek, and laughed with surprise and relief at his own success. Whereupon I became a thing of murderous rage. He could box as well or better than I—he had yet to realise I knew anything of that at all— but I had fought once or twice to a finish with bare fists,

I was used to inflicting and enduring savage hurting, and I doubt if he had ever fought. I hadn't fought ten seconds before I felt this softness in him, realised all that quality of modern upper-class England that never goes to the quick, that hedges about rules and those petty points of honour that are the ultimate comminution of honour, that claims credit for things demonstrably half done. He seemed to think that first hit of his and one or two others were going to matter, that I ought to give in when presently my lip bled and dripped blood upon my clothes. So before we had been at it a minute he had ceased to be aggressive except in momentary spurts, and I was knocking him about almost as I wanted to do, and demanding breathlessly and fiercely, after our school manner, whether he had had enough, not knowing that by his high code and his soft training it was equally impossible for him to either buck-up and beat me, or give in.

I have a very distinct impression of Beatrice dancing about us during the affair in a state of unladylike appreciation, but I was too preoccupied to hear much of what she was saying. But she certainly backed us both, and I am inclined to think now—it may be the disillusionment of my ripened years—whichever she thought was winning.

Then young Garvell, giving way before my slogging, stumbled and fell over a big flint, and I, still following the tradition of my class and school, promptly flung myself on him to finish him. We were busy with each other on the ground when we became aware of a dreadful interruption.

" Shut up, you *fool* ! " said Archie.

" Oh, Lady Drew ! " I heard Beatrice cry. " They're fighting ! They're fighting something awful ! "

I looked over my shoulder. Archie's wish to get up became irresistible, and my resolve to go on with him vanished altogether.

I became aware of the two old ladies, presences of black and purple silk and fur and shining dark things ; they had walked up through the Warren while the horses took the hill easily, and so had come upon us. Beatrice had gone to them at once with an air of taking refuge, and stood beside and a little behind them. We both rose dejectedly. The two old ladies were evidently quite dreadfully shocked, and peering at us with their poor old eyes ; and never had I seen such a tremblement in Lady Drew's lorgnettes.

" You've never been fighting ? " said Lady Drew. " You have been fighting."

" It wasn't proper fighting," snapped Archie, with accusing eyes on me.

" It's Mrs. Ponderevo's George ! " said Miss Somerville, so adding a conviction for ingratitude to my evident sacrilege.

" How could he *dare* ? " cried Lady Drew, becoming very awful.

" He broke the rules," said Archie, sobbing for breath. " I
slipped, and—he hit me while I was down. He knelt on me."

" How could you *dare* ? " said Lady Drew.

I produced an experienced handkerchief rolled up into
a tight ball, and wiped the blood from my chin, but I offered
no explanation of my daring. Among other things that
prevented that, I was too short of breath.

" He didn't fight fair," sobbed Archie. . . .

Beatrice, from behind the old ladies, regarded me intently
and without hostility. I am inclined to think the modification of my face through the damage to my lip interested
her. It became dimly apparent to my confused intelligence
that I must not say these two had been playing with me.
That would not be after the rules of their game. I resolved
in this difficult situation upon a sulky silence, and to take
whatever consequences might follow.

§ 9

The powers of justice in Bladesover made an extraordinary
mess of my case.

I have regretfully to admit that the Honourable Beatrice
Normandy did, at the age of ten, betray me, abandon me,
and lie most abominably about me. She was, as a matter
of fact, panic-stricken about me, conscience-stricken, too ;
she bolted from the very thought of my being her affianced
lover and so forth, from the faintest memory of kissing ; she
was indeed altogether disgraceful and human in her betrayal.
She and her half-brother lied in perfect concord, and I was
presented as a wanton assailant of my social betters. They
were waiting about in the Warren, when I came up and spoke
to them, etc.

On the whole, I now perceive Lady Drew's decisions were,
in the light of the evidence, reasonable and merciful.

They were conveyed to me by my mother, who was, I
really believe, even more shocked by the grossness of my
social insubordination than Lady Drew. She dilated on her
ladyship's kindnesses to me, on the effrontery and wickedness
of my procedure, and so came at last to the terms of my
penance. " You must go up to young Mr. Garvell, and beg
his pardon."

" I won't beg his pardon," I said, speaking for the first time.

My mother paused, incredulous.

I folded my arms on her tablecloth, and delivered my
wicked little ultimatum. " I won't beg his pardon nohow,"
I said. " See ? "

" Then you will have to go off to your Uncle Frapp at
Chatham."

" I don't care where I have to go or what I have to do, I
won't beg his pardon," I said.

And I didn't.

After that I was one against the world. Perhaps in my mother's heart there lurked some pity for me, but she did not show it. She took the side of the young gentleman ; she tried hard, she tried very hard, to make me say I was sorry I had struck him. Sorry !

I couldn't explain.

So I went into exile in the dog-cart to Redwood station, with Jukes the coachman, coldly silent, driving me, and all my personal belongings in a small American-cloth portmanteau behind.

I felt I had much to embitter me ; the game had not the beginnings of fairness by any standards I knew. . . . But the thing that embittered me most was that the Honourable Beatrice Normandy should have repudiated and fled from me as though I was some sort of leper, and not even have taken a chance or so, to give me a good-bye. She might have done that anyhow ! Supposing I had told on her ! But the son of a servant counts as a servant. She had forgotten and now remembered. . . .

I solaced myself with some extraordinary dream of coming back to Bladesover, stern, powerful, after the fashion of Coriolanus. I do not recall the details, but I have no doubt I displayed great magnanimity. . . .

Well, anyhow, I never said I was sorry for pounding young Garvell, and I am not sorry to this day.

CHAPTER TWO

OF MY LAUNCH INTO THE WORLD AND THE LAST I SAW
OF BLADESOVER

§ I

WHEN I was thus banished from Bladesover House, as it was then thought for good and all, I was sent by my mother in a vindictive spirit, first to her cousin Nicodemus Frapp, and then, as a fully indentured apprentice, to my uncle Ponderevo.

I ran away from the care of my cousin Nicodemus back to Bladesover House.

My cousin Nicodemus Frapp was a baker in a back street— a slum rather—just off that miserable, narrow, mean, high road that threads those exquisite beads, Rochester and Chatham. He was, I must admit, a shock to me, much dominated by a young, plump, prolific, malingering wife ; a bent, slow-moving, unwilling, dark man, with flour in his hair and eyelashes, in the lines of his face and the seams of his coat. I've never had a chance to correct my early impression of him, and he still remains an almost dreadful memory, a sort of caricature of incompetent simplicity. As I remember him, indeed, he presented the servile tradition perfected. He had no pride in his person, fine clothes and dressing up wasn't " for the likes of " him, so that he got his wife, who was no artist at it, to cut his black hair at irregular intervals, and let his nails become disagreeable to the fastidious eye ; he had no pride in his business nor any initiative, his only virtues were not doing certain things and hard work. " Your uncle," said my mother—all grown-up cousins were uncles by courtesy among the Victorian middle class—" isn't much to look at or talk to, but he's a Good Hard-Working Man." There was a sort of base honourableness about toil, however needless, in that system of inversion. Another point of honour was to rise at or before dawn, and then laboriously muddle about. It was very distinctly impressed on my mind that the Good Hard-Working Man would have thought it " fal-lallish " to own a pocket-handkerchief. Poor old Frapp—dirty and crushed by-product of Bladesover's magnificence ! He made no fight against the world at all, he was floundering in small debts that were not so small but that finally they over-whelmed him, whenever there was occasion for any exertion his wife fell back upon pains and her "condition," and God sent them many children, most of whom died, and so, by their coming and going, gave a double exercise in the virtues of submission.

Resignation to God's will was the common device of these people in the face of every duty and every emergency. There were no books in the house, I doubt if either of them had retained the capacity for reading consecutively for more than a minute or so, and it was with amazement that day after day, over and above stale bread, one beheld food and again more food amidst the litter that held permanent session on the living-room table.

One might have doubted if either of them felt discomfort in this dusty darkness of existence, if it was not that they did visibly seek consolation. They sought this and found it of a Sunday, not in strong drink and raving, but in imaginary draughts of blood. They met with twenty or thirty other darkened and unclean people, all dressed in dingy colours that would not show the dirt, in a little brick-built chapel equipped with a spavined roarer of a harmonium, and there solaced their minds on the thought that all that was fair and free in life, all that struggled, all that planned and made, all pride and beauty and honour, all fine and enjoyable things, were irrevocably damned to everlasting torments. They were the self-appointed confidants of God's mockery of His own creation. So at any rate they stick in my mind. Vaguer, and yet hardly less agreeable than this cosmic jest, this coming " Yah, clever ! " and general serving out and " showing up " of the lucky, the bold, and the cheerful, was their own pre-destination to Glory.

" There is a Fountain filled with Blood
    Drawn from Emmanuel's Veins,"

so they sang. I hear the drone and wheeze of that hymn
now. I hated them with the bitter, uncharitable condemnation of boyhood, and a twinge of that hate comes back to me.
As I write the words, the sounds and then the scene return,
these obscure, undignified people, a fat woman with asthma,
an old Welsh milk-seller with a tumour on his bald head,
who was the intellectual leader of the sect, a huge-voiced
haberdasher with a big black beard, a white-faced, extraordinarily pregnant woman, his wife, a spectacled rate-
collector with a bent back. . . . I hear the talk about souls,
the strange, battered old phrases that were coined ages ago
in the seaports of the sun-dry Levant, of balm of Gilead and
manna in the desert, of gourds that give shade and water in
a thirsty land ; I recall again the way in which at the conclusion of the service the talk remained pious in form but
became medical in substance, and how the women got together
for obstetric whisperings. I, as a boy, did not matter, and
might overhear. . . .

If Bladesover is my key for the explanation of England,
I think my invincible persuasion that I understand Russia
was engendered by the circle of Uncle Frapp.

I slept in a dingy-sheeted bed with the two elder survivors
of Frapp fecundity, and spent my week-days in helping in
the laborious disorder of the shop and bake-house, in incidental
deliveries of bread and so forth, and in parrying the probings
of my uncle into my relations with the Blood, and his confidential explanations that ten shillings a week—which was
what my mother paid him—was not enough to cover my
accommodation. He was very anxious to keep that, but
also he wanted more. There were neither books nor any seat
nor corner in that house where reading was possible, no
newspaper ever brought the clash of worldly things into its
heavenward seclusion, horror of it all grew in me daily, and
whenever I could I escaped into the streets and tramped about
Chatham. The news shops appealed to me particularly.
One saw there smudgy illustrated sheets, the *Police News*
in particular, in which vilely-drawn pictures brought home
to the dullest intelligence an interminable succession of squalid
crimes, women murdered and put into boxes, buried under
floors, old men bludgeoned at midnight by robbers, people
thrust suddenly out of trains, happy lovers shot, vitrioled,
and so forth by rivals. I got my first glimpse of the life of
pleasure in foully-drawn pictures of " police raids " on this
and that. Interspersed with these sheets were others in
which Sloper, the urban John Bull, had his fling with gin
bottle and obese umbrella, or the kindly, empty faces of the
Royal Family appeared and reappeared, visiting this, opening

that, getting married, getting offspring, lying in state, doing everything but anything, a wonderful, good-meaning, impenetrable race apart. . . .

I have never revisited Chatham ; the impression it has left on my mind is one of squalid compression, unlit by any gleam of a maturer charity. All its effects arranged themselves as antithetical to the Bladesover effects. They confirmed and intensified all that Bladesover suggested. Bladesover declared itself to be the land, to be essentially England ; I have already told how its airy spaciousness, its wide dignity, seemed to thrust village, church, and vicarage into corners, into a secondary and conditional significance. Here one gathered the corollary of that. Since the whole wide country of Kent was made up of contiguous Bladesovers and for the gentlefolk, the surplus of population, all who were not good tenants nor good labourers, Church of England, submissive and respectful, were necessarily thrust together, jostled out of sight, to fester as they might in this place that had the colours and even the smells of a well-packed dust-bin. They should be grateful even for that ; that, one felt, was the theory of it all.

And I loafed about this wilderness of crowded dinginess with young, receptive, wide-open eyes, and through the blessing (or curse) of some fairy godmother of mine, asking and asking again : " But after all, *why*—— ? "

I wandered up through Rochester once, and had a glimpse of the Stour valley above the town, all horrible with cement works and foully smoking chimneys and rows of workmen's cottages, minute, ugly, uncomfortable, and grimy. So I had my first intimation of how industrialism must live in a landlord's land. I spent some hours, too, in the streets that give upon the river, drawn by the spell of the sea. But I saw barges and ships stripped of magic and mostly devoted to cement, ice, timber, and coal. The sailors looked to me gross and slovenly men, and the shipping struck me as clumsy, ugly, old, and dirty. I discovered that most sails don't fit the ships that hoist them, and that there may be as pitiful and squalid a display of poverty with a vessel as with a man. When I saw colliers unloading, watched the workers in the hold filling up silly little sacks and the succession of blackened, half-naked men that ran to and fro with these along a plank over a thirty-foot drop into filth and mud, I was first seized with admiration of their courage and toughness and then, " But after all, *why*—— ? " and the stupid ugliness of all this waste of muscle and endurance came home to me. Among other things it obviously wasted and deteriorated the coal. . . . And I had imagined great things of the sea ! . . .

Well, anyhow, for a time that vocation was stilled.

But such impressions came into my leisure, and of that I had no excess. Most of my time was spent doing things for Uncle Frapp, and my evenings and nights perforce in the company of the two eldest of my cousins. One was errand boy at an oil shop and fervently pious, and of him I saw nothing until the evening except at meals; the other was enjoying the midsummer holidays without any great elation, a singularly thin and abject, stunted creature he was, whose chief liveliness was to pretend to be a monkey, and who I am now convinced had some secret disease that drained his vitality away. If I met him now I should think him a pitiful little creature and be extremely sorry for him. Then I felt only a wondering aversion. He sniffed horribly, he was tired out by a couple of miles of loafing, he never started any conversation, and he seemed to prefer his own company to mine. His mother, poor woman, said he was the " thoughtful one."

Serious trouble came suddenly out of a conversation we held in bed one night. Some particularly pious phrase of my elder cousin's irritated me extremely, and I avowed outright my entire disbelief in the whole scheme of revealed religion. I had never said a word about my doubts to any one before, except to Ewart, who had first evolved them. I had never settled my doubts until at this moment when I spoke. But it came to me then that the whole scheme of salvation of the Frapps was not simply doubtful but impossible. I fired this discovery out into the darkness with the greatest promptitude.

My abrupt denials certainly scared my cousins amazingly.

At first they could not understand what I was saying, and when they did I fully believe they expected an instant answer in thunderbolts and flames. They gave me more room in the bed forthwith, and then the elder sat up and expressed his sense of my awfulness. I was already a little frightened at my temerity, but when he asked me categorically to unsay what I had said, what could I do but confirm my repudiation ?

" There's no hell," I said, " and no eternal punishment. No God would be such a fool as that."

My elder cousin cried aloud in horror, and the younger lay scared, but listening.

" Then you mean," said my eldest cousin, when at last he could bring himself to argue, " you might do just as you liked ? "

" If you were cad enough," said I.

Our little voices went on interminably, and at one stage my cousin got out of bed and made his brother do likewise, and knelt in the night dimness and prayed at me. That I found trying, but I held out valiantly. " Forgive him," said my cousin, " he knows not what he sayeth."

" You can pray if you like," I said, " but if you're going to cheek me in your prayers I draw the line."

The last I remember of that great discussion was my cousin deploring the fact that he " should ever sleep in the same bed with an Infidel ! "

The next day he astonished me by telling the whole business

to his father. This was quite outside all my codes. Uncle Nicodemus sprang it upon me at the midday meal.

" You been sayin' queer things, George," he said abruptly. " You better mind what you're saying."

" What did he say, father ? " said Mrs. Frapp.

" Things I couldn' repeat," said he.

" What things ? " I asked hotly.

" Ask *'im*," said my uncle, pointing with his knife to his informant, and making me realise the nature of my offence. My aunt looked at the witness. " Not—— ? " she framed a question.

" Wuss," said my uncle. " Blarsphemy."

My aunt couldn't touch another mouthful. I was already a little troubled in my conscience by my daring, and now I began to feel the black enormity of the course upon which I had embarked.

" I was only talking sense," I said.

I had a still more dreadful moment when presently I met my cousin in the brick alley behind the yard, that led back to his grocer's shop.

" You sneak ! " I said, and smacked his face hard forthwith. " Now then," said I.

He started back, astonished and alarmed. His eyes met mine, and I saw a sudden gleam of resolution. He turned his other cheek to me.

" 'It it," he said ; " 'it it. *I'll* forgive you."

I felt I had never encountered a more detestable way of evading a licking. I shoved him against the wall and left him there, forgiving me, and went back into the house.

" You'd better not speak to your cousins, George," said my aunt, " till you're in a better state of mind."

I became an outcast forthwith. At supper that night a gloomy silence was broken by my cousin saying, " 'E 'it me for telling you, and I turned the other cheek, muvver."

" 'E's got the evil one be'ind 'im now, a ridin' on 'is back," said my aunt, to the grave discomfort of the eldest girl, who sat beside me.

After supper my uncle, in a few ill-chosen words, prayed me to repent before I slept.

" Suppose you was took in your sleep, George," he said ; " where'd you be then ? You jest think of that, me boy." By this time I was thoroughly miserable and frightened, and this suggestion unnerved me dreadfully, but I kept up an impenitent front. " To wake in 'ell," said Uncle Nicodemus, in gentle tones. " You don't want to wake in 'ell, George, burnin' and screamin' for ever, do you ? You wouldn't like that ? "

He tried very hard to get me to " jest 'ave a look at the bake'ouse fire " before I retired. " It might move you," he said.

I was awake longest that night. My cousins slept the

sleep of faith on either side of me. I decided I would whisper my prayers, and stopped midway because I was ashamed, and perhaps also because I had an idea one didn't square God like that.

"No," I said, with a sudden confidence, "damn me if you're coward enough. . . . But you're not. . . . No ! You couldn't be ! "

I woke my cousins up with emphatic digs, and told them as much triumphantly, and went very peacefully to sleep with my act of faith accomplished.

I slept not only through that night, but for all my nights since then. So far as any fear of Divine injustice goes, I sleep soundly, and shall, I know, to the end of things. That declaration was an epoch in my spiritual life.

§ 2

But I didn't expect to have the whole meeting on Sunday turned on to me.

It was. It all comes back to me, that convergence of attention, even the faint leathery smell of its atmosphere returns, and the coarse feel of my aunt's black dress beside me in contact with my hand. I see again the old Welsh milkman " wrestling " with me—they all wrestled with me, by prayer or exhortation. And I was holding out stoutly, though convinced now by the contagion of their universal conviction that by doing so I was certainly and hopelessly damned. I felt that they were right, that God was probably like them, and that on the whole it didn't matter. And to simplify the business thoroughly, I had declared I didn't believe anything at all. They confuted me by texts from Scripture, which I now perceive was an illegitimate method of reply. When I got home, still impenitent and eternally lost and secretly very lonely and miserable and alarmed, Uncle Nicodemus docked my Sunday pudding.

One person only spoke to me like a human being on that day of wrath, and that was the younger Frapp. He came up to me in the afternoon while I was confined upstairs with a Bible and my own thoughts.

" 'Ello," he said, and fretted about.

" D'you mean to say there isn't—no one ? " he said, funking the word.

" No one ? "

" No one watching yer—always."

" Why should there be ? " I asked.

" You can't 'elp thoughts," said my cousin, " any'ow. . . . You mean——" He stopped hovering. " I s'pose I oughtn't to be talking to you."

He hesitated and flitted away with a guilty back glance over his shoulder. . . .

The following week made life quite intolerable for me ;

these people forced me at last into an Atheism that terrified me. When I learnt that next Sunday the wrestling was to be resumed, my courage failed me altogether.

I happened upon a map of Kent in a stationer's window on Saturday, and that set me thinking of one form of release. I studied it intently for half an hour, perhaps, on Saturday night, got a route list of villages well fixed in my memory, and got up and started for Bladesover about five on Sunday morning while my two bedmates were still fast asleep.

§ 3

I remember something, but not so much of it as I should like to recall, of my long tramp to Bladesover House. The distance from Chatham is almost exactly seventeen miles, and it took me until nearly one. It was very interesting and I do not think I was over-fatigued, though I got rather pinched by one boot.

The morning must have been very clear, because I remember that near Itchinstow Hall I looked back and saw the estuary of the Thames, that river that has since played so large a part in my life. But at the time I did not know it was the Thames, I thought this great expense of mud flats and water was the sea, which I had never yet seen nearly. And out upon it stood ships, sailing ships and a steamer or so, going up to London or down out into the great seas of the world. I stood for a long time watching these and thinking whether after all I should not have done better to have run away to sea.

The nearer I drew to Bladesover, the more doubtful I grew of the quality of my reception, and the more I regretted that alternative. I suppose it was the dirty clumsiness of the shipping I had seen nearly, that put me out of mind of that. I took a short cut through the Warren across the corner of the main park to intercept the people from the church. I wanted to avoid meeting any one before I met my mother, and so I went to a place where the path passed between banks, and without exactly hiding, stood up among the bushes. This place, among other advantages, eliminated any chance of seeing Lady Drew, who would drive round by the carriage road.

Standing up to waylay in this fashion, I had a queer feeling of brigandage, as though I was some intrusive sort of bandit among these orderly things. It is the first time I remember having that outlaw feeling distinctly, a feeling that has played a large part in my subsequent life. I felt there existed no place for me—that I had to drive myself in.

Presently, down the hill, the servants appeared, straggling by twos and threes, first some of the garden people and the butler's wife with them, then the two laundry maids, odd, inseparable old creatures, then the first footman talking to the butler's little girl, and at last, walking grave and breathless beside old Ann and Miss Fison, the black figure of my mother.

My boyish mind suggested the adoption of a playful form of appearance. " Coo-ee, mother ! " said I, coming out against the sky, " Coo-ee ! "

My mother looked up, went very white, and put her hand to her bosom. . . .

I suppose there was a fearful fuss about me. And of course I was quite unable to explain my reappearance. But I held out stoutly, " I won't go back to Chatham ; I'll drown myself first." The next day my mother carried me off to Wimble-hurst, took me fiercely and aggressively to an uncle I had never heard of before, near though the place was to us. She gave me no word as to what was to happen, and I was too subdued by her manifest wrath and humiliation at my last mis-demeanour to demand information. I don't for one moment think Lady Drew was " nice " about me. The finality of my banishment was endorsed and underlined and stamped home. I wished very much now that I had run away to sea, in spite of the coaly dust and squalor Rochester had revealed to me. Perhaps overseas one came to different lands.

§ 4

I do not remember much of my journey to Wimblehurst with my mother except the image of her as sitting bolt upright, as rather disdaining the third-class carriage in which we travelled, and how she looked away from me out of the window when she spoke of my uncle. " I have not seen your uncle," she said, " since he was a boy. . . ." She added grudgingly, " Then he was supposed to be clever."

She took little interest in such qualities as cleverness.

" He married about three years ago, and set up for himself in Wimblehurst. . . . So I suppose she had some money."

She mused on scenes she had long dismissed from her mind. " Teddy," she said at last in the tone of one who has been feeling in the dark and finds. " He was called Teddy . . . about your age . . . Now he must be twenty-six or seven."

I thought of my uncle as Teddy directly I saw him ; there was something in his personal appearance that in the light of that memory phrased itself at once as Teddiness—a certain Teddidity. To describe it in any other terms is more difficult. It is nimbleness without grace, and alertness without intelli-gence. He whisked out of his shop upon the pavement, a short figure in grey and wearing grey carpet slippers ; one had a sense of a young fattish face behind gilt glasses, wiry hair that stuck up and forward over the forehead, an irregular nose that had its aquiline moments, and that the body betrayed an equatorial laxity, an incipient " bow window " as the image goes. He jerked out of the shop, came to a stand on the pavement outside, regarded something in the window with infinite appreciation, stroked his chin, and, as abruptly, shot

sideways into the door again, charging through it as it were
behind an extended hand.

"That must be him," said my mother, catching at her breath.

We came past the window whose contents I was presently
to know by heart, a very ordinary chemist's window except
that there was a frictional electrical machine, an air-pump
and two or three tripods and retorts replacing the customary
blue, yellow, and red bottles above. There was a plaster of
Paris horse to indicate veterinary medicines among these
breakables, and below were scent packets and diffusers and
sponges and soda-water syphons and such-like things. Only
in the middle there was a rubricated card, very neatly painted
by hand, with these words :—

Buy Ponderevo's Cough Linctus *Now*.

NOW !

WHY ?

Twopence Cheaper than in Winter.

You Store Apples !. why not the Medicine

You are Bound to Need ?

---

in which appeal I was to recognise presently my uncle's
distinctive note.

My uncle's face appeared above a card of infants' com-
forters in the glass pane of the door. I perceived his eyes
were brown, and that his glasses creased his nose. It was
manifest he did not know us from Adam. A stare of scrutiny
allowed an expression of commercial deference to appear in
front of it, and my uncle flung open the door.

"You don't know me ? " panted my mother.

My uncle would not own he did not, but his curiosity was
manifest. My mother sat down on one of the little chairs
before the soap and patent-medicine-piled counter, and her
lips opened and closed.

"A glass of water, madam," said my uncle ; waved his
hand in a sort of curve, and shot away.

My mother drank the water and spoke. "That boy,"
she said, "takes after his father. He grows more like him
every day, . . . and so I have brought him to you."

"His father, madam ? "

"George."

For a moment the chemist was still at a loss. He stood
behind the counter with the glass my mother had returned
to him in his hand. Then comprehension grew.

"By Gosh ! " he said. "Lord ! " he cried. His glasses fell

off. He disappeared, replacing them, behind a pile of boxed-up bottles of blood mixture. " Eleven thousand virgins ! " I heard him cry. The glass was banged down. " O-ri-ental Gums ! "

He shot away out of the shop through some masked door. One heard his voice. " Susan ! Susan ! "

Then he reappeared with an extended hand. " Well, how *are* you ? " he said. " I was never so surprised in my life. Fancy ! . . . *You !* "

He shook my mother's impassive hand and then mine very warmly, holding his glasses on with his left forefinger.

" Come right in ! " he cried, " come right in ! Better late than never ! " and led the way into the parlour behind the shop.

After Bladesover that apartment struck me as stuffy and petty, but it was very comfortable in comparison with the Frapp living-room. It had a faint, disintegrating smell of meals about it, and my most immediate impression was of the remarkable fact that something was hung about or wrapped round or draped over everything. There was bright-patterned muslin round the gas-bracket in the middle of the room, round the mirror over the mantel, stuff with ball-fringe along the mantel and casing in the fireplace—I first saw ball-fringe here—and even the lamp on the little bureau wore a shade like a large muslin hat. The tablecloth had ball-fringe, and so had the window curtains, and the carpet was a bed of roses. There were little cupboards on either side of the fire-place, and in the recesses, ill-made shelves packed with books and enriched with pinked American cloth. There was a dictionary lying face downward on the table, and the open bureau was littered with foolscap paper and the evidences of recently abandoned toil. My eye caught, " The Ponderevo Patent Flat, a Machine you can Live in," written in large firm letters. My uncle opened a little door like a cupboard door in the corner of this room, and revealed the narrowest twist of staircase I had ever set eyes upon. " Susan ! " he bawled again. " Wantje. Some one to see you. Surprisin'."

There came an inaudible reply, and a sudden loud bump over our heads as of some article of domestic utility pettishly flung aside, then the cautious steps of some one descending the twist, and then my aunt appeared in the doorway with her hand upon the jamb.

" It's Aunt Ponderevo," cried my uncle. " George's wife —and she's brought over her son ! " His eye roved about the room. He darted to the bureau with a sudden impulse and turned the sheet about the patent flat face down. Then he waved his glasses at us, " *You* know, Susan, my elder brother George. I told you about 'im lots of times."

He fretted across to the hearthrug and took up a position there, replaced his glasses and coughed.

My Aunt Susan seemed to be taking it in. She was then

rather a pretty slender woman of twenty-three or four, I
suppose, and I remember being struck by the blueness of her
eyes and the clear freshness of her complexion. She had little
features, a button nose, a pretty chin, and a long, graceful
neck that stuck out of her pale blue cotton morning dress.
There was a look of half-assumed perplexity on her face,
a quizzical wrinkle of the brow that suggested a faintly
amused attempt to follow my uncle's mental operations, a
vain attempt and a certain hopelessness that had in succession
become habitual. She seemed to be saying, "Oh, Lord!
What's he giving me *this* time?" And as I came to know
her better I detected, as a complication of her effort of apprehension, a subsidiary riddle to "What's he giving me?" and
that was—to borrow a phrase from my schoolboy language—
"Is it keeps?" She looked at my mother and me, and back
to her husband again.

"You know," he said. "George!"

"Well," she said to my mother, descending the last three
steps of the staircase and holding out her hand, "you're
welcome. Though it's a surprise. . . . I can't ask you to
have anything, I'm afraid, for there isn't anything in the
house." She smiled, and looked at her husband banteringly.
"Unless he makes up something with his old chemicals,
which he's quite equal to doing."

My mother shook hands stiffly, and told me to kiss my
aunt. . . .

"Well, let's all sit down," said my uncle, suddenly whistling
through his clenched teeth, and briskly rubbing his hands
together. He put up a chair for my mother, raised the blind
of the window, lowered it again, and returned to his hearthrug. "I'm sure," he said, as one who decides, "I'm very
glad to see you."

§ 5

As they talked I gave my attention pretty exclusively
to my uncle.

I noted him in great detail. I remember now his partially
unbuttoned waistcoat, as though something had occurred
to distract him as he did it up, and a little cut upon his chin.
I liked a certain humour in his eyes. I watched, too, with
the fascination these things have for an observant boy, the
play of his lips—they were slightly oblique, and there was
something "slipshod," if one may strain a word so far, about
his mouth so that he lisped and sibilated ever and again—
and the coming and going of a curious expression, triumphant
in quality it was, upon his face as he talked. He fingered his
glasses, which did not seem to fit his nose, fretted with things
in his waistcoat-pockets or put his hands behind him, looked
over our heads, and ever and again rose to his toes and dropped
back on his heels. He had a way of drawing air in at times

through his teeth that gave a whispering zest to his speech. It's a sound I can only represent as a soft Zzzz.

He did most of the talking. My mother repeated what she had already said in the shop, " I have brought George over to you," and then desisted for a time from the real business in hand. " You find this a comfortable house ? " she asked ; and this being affirmed : " It looks—very convenient. . . . Not too big to be a trouble—no. You like Wimblehurst, I suppose ? "

My uncle retorted with some inquiries about the great people of Bladesover, and my mother answered in the character of a personal friend of Lady Drew's. The talk hung for a time, and then my uncle embarked upon a dissertation upon Wimblehurst.

" This place," he began, " isn't, of course, quite the place I ought to be in."

My mother nodded as though she had expected that.

" It gives me no Scope," he went on. " It's dead-and-alive. Nothing happens."

" He's always wanting something to happen," said my Aunt Susan. " Some say he'll get a shower of things and they'll be too much for him."

" Not they," said my uncle, buoyantly.

" Do you find business—slack ? " asked my mother.

" Oh ! one rubs along. But there's no Development— no Growth. They just come along here and buy pills when they want 'em—and a horseball or such. They've got to be ill before there's a prescription. That sort they are. You can't get 'em to launch out, you can't get 'em to take up anything new. F'rinstance, I've been trying lately—induce them to buy their medicines in advance, and in larger quantities. But they won't look at it ! Then I tried to float a little notion of mine, sort of an insurance scheme for colds ; you pay so much a week, and when you've got a cold you get a bottle of Cough Linctus so long as you can produce a substantial sniff. See ? But Lord ! they've no capacity for ideas, they don't catch on ; no Jump about the place, no Life ! Live !—they trickle, and what one has to do here is to trickle too—Zzzz."

" Ah ! " said my mother.

" It doesn't suit me," said my uncle. " I'm the cascading sort."

" George was that," said my mother after a pondering moment.

My Aunt Susan took up the parable with an affectionate glance at her husband.

" He's always trying to make his old business jump," she said. " Always putting fresh cards in the window, or getting up to something. You'd hardly believe. It makes *me* jump sometimes."

" But it does no good," said my uncle.

" It does no good," said his wife.   " It's not his *miloo*. . . ."

Presently they came upon a wide pause.

From the beginning of their conversation there had been the promise of this pause, and I pricked my ears.   I knew perfectly what was bound to come ; they were going to talk of my father.   I was enormously strengthened in my persuasion when I found my mother's eye resting thoughtfully upon me in the silence, and then my uncle looked at me and then my aunt.   I struggled unavailingly to produce an expression of meek stupidity.

" I think," said my uncle, " that George will find it more amusing to have a turn in the market-place than to sit here talking with us.   There's a pair of stocks there, George—very interesting.   Old-fashioned stocks."

" I don't mind sitting here," I said.

My uncle rose and in the most friendly way led me through the shop.   He stood on his doorstep and jerked amiable directions to me.

" Ain't it sleepy, George, eh ?   There's the butcher's dog over there, asleep in the road—half an hour from midday ! If the last Trump sounded I don't believe it would wake. Nobody would wake !   The chaps up there in the churchyard —they'd just turn over and say : " Naar—you don't catch us, you don't !   See ? " . . . Well, you'll find the stocks just round that corner."

He watched me out of sight.

So I never heard what they said about my father after all.

§ 6

When I returned, my uncle had in some remarkable way become larger and central.   " Tha'chu, George ? " he cried, when the shop-door bell sounded.   " Come right through " ; and I found him, as it were, in the chairman's place before the draped grate.

The three of them regarded me.

" We have been talking of making you a chemist, George," said my uncle.

My mother looked at me.   " I had hoped," she said, " that Lady Drew would have done something for him——"   She stopped.

" In what way ? " said my uncle.

" She might have spoken to some one, got him into something, perhaps. . . ."   She had the servant's invincible persuasion that all good things are done by patronage.

" He is not the sort of boy for whom things are done," she added, dismissing these dreams.   " He doesn't accommodate himself.   When he thinks Lady Drew wishes a thing, he seems not to wish it.   Towards Mr. Redgrave, too, he has been—disrespectful—he is like his father."

" Who's Mr. Redgrave ? "

" The Vicar."

" A bit independent ? " said my uncle briskly.

" Disobedient," said my mother. " He has no idea of his place. He seems to think he can get on by slighting people and flouting them. He'll learn, perhaps, before it is too late."

My uncle stroked his cut chin and regarded me. " Have you learnt any Latin ? " he asked abruptly.

I said I had not.

" He'll have to learn a little Latin," he explained to my mother, " to qualify. H'm. He could go down to the chap at the grammar school here—it's just been routed into existence again by the Charity Commissioners—and have lessons."

" What, me learn Latin ! " I cried, with emotion.

" A little," he said.

" I've always wanted——" I said, and " *Latin !* "

I had long been obsessed by the idea that having no Latin was a disadvantage in the world, and Archie Garvell had driven the point of this pretty earnestly home. The literature I had read at Bladesover had all tended that way. Latin had had a quality of emancipation for me that I find it difficult to convey. And suddenly, when I had supposed all learning was at an end for me, I heard this !

" It's no good to you, of course," said my uncle, " except to pass exams with, but there you are ! "

" You'll have to learn Latin because you have to learn Latin," said my mother, " not because you *want* to. And afterwards you will have to learn all sorts of other things. . . ."

The idea that I was to go on learning, that to read and master the contents of books was still to be justifiable as a duty, overwhelmed all other facts. I had had it rather clear in my mind for some weeks that all that kind of opportunity might close to me for ever. I began to take a lively interest in this new project.

" Then shall I live here ? " I asked, " with you, and study . . . as well as work in the shop ? . . ."

" That's the way of it," said my uncle.

I parted from my mother that day in a dream, so sudden and important was this new aspect of things to me. I was to learn Latin ! Now that the humiliation of my failure at Bladesover was past for her, now that she had a little got over her first intense repugnance at this resort to my uncle and contrived something that seemed like a possible provision for my future, the tenderness natural to a parting far more significant than any of our previous partings crept into her manner.

She sat in the train to return, I remember, and I stood at the open door of her compartment, and neither of us knew how soon we should cease for ever to be a trouble to one another.

" You must be a good boy, George," she said. " You must learn. . . . And you mustn't set yourself up against those who are above you and better than you. . . . Or envy them."

" No, mother," I said.

I promised carelessly. Her eyes were fixed upon me. I was wondering whether I could by any means begin Latin that night.

Something touched her heart then, some thought, some memory; perhaps some premonition. . . . The solitary porter began slamming carriage doors.

" George," she said hastily, almost shamefully, " kiss me ! "

I stepped up into her compartment as she bent forward. She caught me in her arms quite eagerly, she pressed me to her—a strange thing for her to do. I perceived her eyes were extraordinarily bright, and then this brightness burst along the lower lids and rolled down her cheeks.

For the first and last time in my life I saw my mother's tears. Then she had gone, leaving me discomforted and perplexed, forgetting for a time even that I was to learn Latin, thinking of my mother as of something new and strange.

The thing recurred though I sought to dismiss it ; it stuck itself into my memory against the day of fuller understanding. Poor, proud, habitual, sternly narrow soul ! poor, difficult, and misunderstanding son ! it was the first time that ever it dawned upon me that my mother also might perhaps feel.

§ 7

My mother died suddenly and, it was thought by Lady Drew, inconsiderately, the following spring. Her ladyship instantly fled to Folkestone with Miss Somerville and Fison, until the funeral should be over and my mother's successor installed.

My uncle took me over to the funeral. I remember there was a sort of prolonged crisis in the days preceding this, because, directly he heard of my loss, he had sent a pair of check trousers to the Judkins people in London to be dyed black, and they did not come back in time. He became very excited on the third day, and sent a number of increasingly fiery telegrams without any result whatever, and succumbed next morning with a very ill grace to my Aunt Susan's insistence upon the resources of his dress-suit. In my memory those black legs of his, in a particularly thin and shiny black cloth—for evidently his dress-suit dated from adolescent and slenderer days—straddle like the Colossus of Rhodes over my approach to my mother's funeral. Moreover, I was inconvenienced and distracted by a silk hat he had bought me, my first silk hat, much ennobled, as his was also, by a deep mourning band.

I remember, but rather indistinctly, my mother's white-panelled housekeeper's room and the touch of oddness about it that she was not there, and the various familiar faces made strange by black, and I seem to recall the exaggerated self-consciousness that arose out of their focused attention. No doubt the sense of the new silk hat came and went and came again in my emotional chaos. Then something comes out clear and sorrowful, rises out clear and sheer from among all these rather base and inconsequent things, and once again I walk before all the other mourners close behind her coffin as it is carried along the churchyard path to her grave, with the old vicar's slow voice saying regretfully and unconvincingly above me, triumphant solemn things.

"I am the resurrection and the life, saith the Lord; he that believeth in Me, though he were dead, yet shall he live: and whosoever liveth and believeth in Me shall never die."

Never die! The day was a high and glorious morning in spring, and all the trees were budding and bursting into green. Everywhere there were blossoms and flowers; the pear-trees and cherry-trees in the sexton's garden were sunlit snow, there were nodding daffodils and early tulips in the graveyard beds, great multitudes of daisies, and everywhere the birds seemed singing. And in the middle was the brown coffin end, tilting on men's shoulders, and half occluded by the vicar's Oxford hood.

And so we came to my mother's waiting grave. . . .

For a time I was very observant, watching the coffin lowered, hearing the words of the ritual. It seemed a very curious business altogether.

Suddenly as the service drew to its end, I felt something had still to be said which had not been said, realised that she had withdrawn in silence, neither forgiving me nor hearing from me—those now lost assurances. Suddenly I knew I had not understood. Suddenly I saw her tenderly; remembered not so much tender or kindly things of her as her crossed wishes and the ways in which I had thwarted her. Surprisingly I realised that behind all her hardness and severity she had loved me, that I was the only thing she had ever loved, and that until this moment I had never loved her. And now she was there and deaf and blind to me, pitifully defeated in her designs for me, covered from me so that she could not know.

I dug my nails into the palms of my hands, I set my teeth, but tears blinded me, sobs would have choked me had speech been required of me. The old vicar read on, there came a mumbled response—and so on to the end. I wept as it were internally, and only when we had come out of the churchyard could I think and speak calmly again.

Stamped across this memory are the little black figures of my uncle and Rabbits, telling Avebury, the sexton and undertaker, that "it had all passed off very well—very well indeed."

§ 8

That is the last I shall tell of Bladesover. The drop-scene falls on that, and it comes no more as an actual presence into this novel. I did, indeed, go back there once again, but under circumstances quite immaterial to my story. But in a sense Bladesover has never left me ; it is, as I said at the outset, one of those dominant explanatory impressions that makes the framework of my mind. Bladesover illuminates England ; it has become all that is spacious, dignified, pretentious, and truly conservative in English life. It is my social datum. That is why I have drawn it here on so large a scale.

When I came back at last to the real Bladesover on an inconsequent visit, everything was far smaller than I could have supposed possible. It was as though everything had shivered and shrivelled a little at the Lichtenstein touch. The harp was still in the saloon, but there was a different grand piano with a painted lid and a metrostyle pianola, and an extraordinary quantity of artistic litter and bric-à-brac scattered about. There was the trail of the Bond Street showroom over it all. The furniture was still under chintz, but it wasn't the same sort of chintz although it pretended to be, and the lustre-dangling chandeliers had passed away. Lady Lichtenstein's books replaced the brown volumes I had browsed among—they were mostly presentation copies of contemporary novels, and the *National Review* and the *Empire Review* and the *Nineteenth Century and After* jostled current books on the tables—English new books in gaudy catchpenny " artistic " covers, French and Italian novels in yellow, German art handbooks of almost incredible ugliness. They were abundant evidences that her ladyship was playing with the Keltic renascence, and a great number of ugly cats made of china—she " collected " china and stoneware cats—stood about everywhere—in all colours, in all kinds of deliberately comic, highly glazed distortion. . . .

It is nonsense to pretend that finance makes any better aristocrats than rent. Nothing can make an aristocrat but pride, knowledge, training, and the sword. These people were no improvement on the Drews, none whatever. There was no effect of a beneficial replacement of passive unintelligent people by active intelligent ones. One felt that a smaller but more enterprising and intensely undignified variety of stupidity had replaced the large dullness of the old gentry, and that was all. Bladesover, I thought, had undergone just the same change between the 'seventies and the new century that had overtaken the dear old *Times*, and heaven knows how much more of the decorous British fabric. These Lichtensteins and their like seem to have no promise in them at all of any fresh vitality for the kingdom. I do not believe in their intelligence or their power—they have nothing new about them at all, nothing creative nor rejuvenescent, no more than a disorderly instinct of acquisition ; and the prevalence of them and their kind is but a phase in the broad, slow decay of the great social organism of England. They could not have made Bladesover, they cannot replace it ; they just happen to break out over it—saprophytically.

Well—that was my last impression of Bladesover.

CHAPTER THREE

THE WIMBLEHURST APPRENTICESHIP

§ I

So far as I can remember now, except for that one emotional phase by the graveside, I passed through all these experiences rather callously. I had already, with the facility of youth, changed my world, ceased to think at all of the old school routine, and put Bladesover aside for digestion at a later stage. I took up my new world in Wimblehurst with the chemist's shop as its hub, set to work at Latin and materia medica, and concentrated upon the present with all my heart. Wimblehurst is an exceptionally quiet and grey Sussex town, rare among south of England towns in being largely built of stone. I found something very agreeable and picturesque in its clean, cobbled streets, its odd turnings and abrupt corners, and in the pleasant park that crowds up one side of the town. The whole place is under the Eastry dominion, and it was the Eastry influence and dignity that kept its railway station a mile and three-quarters away. Eastry House is so close that it dominates the whole ; one goes across the market-place (with its old lock-up and stocks), past the great pre-Reformation church, a fine, grey shell, like some empty skull from which the life has fled, and there at once are the huge wrought-iron gates, and one peeps through them to see the façade of this place, very white and large and fine, down a long avenue of yews. Eastry was far greater than Bladesover, and an altogether completer example of the eighteenth-century system. It ruled not two villages but a borough, that had sent its sons and cousins to Parliament almost as a matter of right so long as its franchise endured. Every one was in the system, every one—except my uncle. He stood out and complained.

My uncle was the first real breach I found in the great front of Bladesover the world had presented me, for Chatham was not so much a breach as a confirmation. But my uncle had no respect for Bladesover and Eastry—none whatever. He did not believe in them. He was blind even to what they were. He propounded strange phrases about them, he exfoliated and wagged about novel and incredible ideas.

"This place," said my uncle surveying it from his open doorway in the dignified stillness of a summer afternoon, "wants Waking Up ! "

I was sorting up patent medicines in the corner.

"I'd like to let a dozen young Americans loose into it," said my uncle "Then we'd see."

I made a tick against Mother Shipton's Sleeping Syrup. We had cleared our forward stock.

"Things must be happening *somewhere*, George," he broke out in a querulously rising note as he came back into the little shop. He fiddled with the piled dummy boxes of fancy soap and scent and so forth that adorned the end of the counter, then turned about petulantly, stuck his hands deeply into his pockets and withdrew one to scratch his head. "I must do *something*," he said. "I can't stand it.

"I must invent something. And shove it. . . . I could.

"Or a play. There's a deal of money in a play, George. What would you think of me writing a play—eh? . . . There's all sorts of things to be done.

"Or the stog-igschange."

He fell into that meditative whistling of his.

"Sac-ramental wine!" he swore, "this isn't the world— it's Cold Mutton Fat! That's what Wimblehurst is! Cold Mutton Fat!—dead and stiff! And I'm buried in it up to the arm-pits. Nothing ever happens, nobody wants things to happen 'scept me! Up in London, George, things happen. America! I wish to Heaven, George, I'd been born American —where things hum.

"What can one *do* here? How can one grow? While we're sleepin' here with our Capital oozing away—into Lord Eastry's pockets for rent—men are up there. . . ." He indicated London as remotely over the top of the dispensing counter, and then as a scene of great activity by a whirl of the hand and a wink and a meaning smile at me.

"What sort of things do they do?" I asked.

"Rush about," he said. "Do things! Somethin' glorious. There's cover gambling. Ever heard of that, George?" He drew the air in through his teeth. "You put down a hundred, say, and buy ten thousand pounds' worth. See? That's a cover of one per cent. Things go up one, you sell, realise cent. per cent.; down, whiff, it's gone! Try again! Cent. per cent., George, every day. Men are made or done for in an hour. And the shoutin'! Zzzz. . . . Well, that's one way, George. Then another way—there's Corners!"

"They're rather big things, aren't they?" I ventured.

"Oh, if you go in for wheat or steel—yes. But suppose you tackled a little thing, George. Just some leetle thing that only needed a few thousands. Drugs, for example. Shoved all you had into it—staked your liver on it, so to speak. Take a drug—take ipecac, for example. Take a lot of ipecac. Take all there is! See? There you are! There aren't unlimited supplies of ipecacuanha—can't be!—and it's a thing people *must* have. Then quinine again! You

watch your chance, wait for a tropical war breaking out,
let's say, and collar all the quinine. Where *are* they ? Must
have quinine, you know. Eh ? Zzzz.

"Lord ! there's no end of things—no end of *little* things.
Dill-water—all the suff'ring babes yowling for it. Eucalyptus
again—cascara—witch hazel—menthol—all the toothache
things. Then there's antiseptics, and curare, cocaine. . . ."

" Rather a nuisance to the doctors," I reflected.

" They got to look out for themselves. By Jove, yes.
They'll do you if they can, and you do them. Like brigands.
That makes it romantic. That's the Romance of Commerce,
George. You're in the mountains there ! Think of having
all the quinine in the world, and some millionaire's pampud
wife gone ill with malaria, eh ? That's a squeeze, George, eh ?
Eh ? Millionaire in his carriage outside, offering you any
price you liked. That 'ud wake up Wimblehurst. . . . Lord !
You haven't an Idea down here. Not an idea. Zzzz."

He passed into a rapt dream, from which escaped such
fragments as : " Fifty per cent. advance, sir ; security—
to-morrow. Zzzz."

The idea of cornering a drug struck upon my mind then
as a sort of irresponsible monkey-trick that no one would
ever be permitted to do in reality. It was the sort of nonsense
one would talk to make Ewart laugh and set him going on
to still odder possibilities. I thought it was part of my uncle's
way of talking. But I have learnt differently since. The
whole trend of modern money-making is to foresee something
that will presently be needed and put it out of reach, and then
to haggle yourself wealthy. You buy up land upon which
people will presently want to build houses, you secure rights
that will bar vitally important developments, and so on, and
so on. Of course, the naïve intelligence of a boy does not
grasp the subtler developments of human inadequacy. He
begins life with a disposition to believe in the wisdom of
grown-up people, he does not realise how casual and disingenuous has been the development of law and custom, and
he thinks that somewhere in the state there is a power as
irresistible as a head master's to check mischievous and
foolish enterprises of every sort. I will confess that when
my uncle talked of cornering quinine, I had a clear impression
that any one who contrived to do that would pretty certainly
go to jail. Now I know that any one who could really bring
it off would be much more likely to go to the House of Lords !

My uncle ranged over the gilt labels of his bottles and
drawers for a while, dreaming of corners in this and that. But
at last he reverted to Wimblehurst again.

" You got to be in London when these things are in hand.
Down here—— !

" Jee-rusalem ! " he cried. " Why did I plant myself here ?
Everything's done. The game's over. Here's Lord Eastry,

and he's got everything, except what his lawyers get, and
before you get any more change this way you'll have to
dynamite him—and them. *He* doesn't want anything more
to happen. Why should he? Any change 'ud be a loss to
him. He wants everything to burble along and burble along
and go on as it's going for the next ten thousand years. Eastry
after Eastry, one parson down, another come, one grocer dead,
get another! Any one with any ideas better go away. They
have gone away! Look at all these blessed people in this
place! Look at 'em! All fast asleep, doing their business
out of habit—in a sort of dream. Stuffed men would do just
as well—just. They've all shook down into their places.
They don't want anything to happen either. They're all
broken in. There you are! Only what are they all alive
for? . . .

  " Why can't they get a clockwork chemist? "

He concluded as he often concluded these talks. " I must
invent something—that's about what I must do. Zzzz.
Some convenience. Something people want. . . . Strike
out. . . . You can't think, George, of anything everybody
wants and hasn't got? I mean something you could turn
out retail under a shilling, say? Well, *you* think, whenever
you haven't got anything better to do. See? "

§ 2

So I remember my uncle in that first phase, young, but
already a little fat, restless, fretful, garrulous, putting in
my fermenting head all sorts of discrepant ideas. Certainly
he was educational. . . .

For me the years at Wimblehurst were years of pretty
active growth. Most of my leisure and much of my time
in the shop I spent in study. I speedily mastered the modicum
of Latin necessary for my qualifying examinations, and—a
little assisted by the Government Science and Art Department
classes that were held in the Grammar School—went on with
my mathematics. There were classes in physics, in chemistry,
in mathematics, and machine drawing, and I took up all these
subjects with considerable avidity. Exercise I got chiefly
in the form of walks. There was some cricket in the summer
and football in the winter sustained by young men's clubs
that levied a parasitic blackmail on the big people and the
sitting member, but I was never very keen at these games. I
didn't find any very close companions among the youths of
Wimblehurst. They struck me, after my Cockney school-
mates, as loutish and slow, servile and furtive, spiteful and
mean. *We* used to swagger, but these countrymen dragged
their feet and hated an equal who didn't; we talked loud,
but you only got the real thoughts of Wimblehurst in a knowing undertone behind its hand. And even then they weren't
much in the way of thoughts.

No, I didn't like those young countrymen, and I'm no believer in the English country-side under the Bladesover system as a breeding-ground for honourable men. One hears a frightful lot of nonsense about the Rural Exodus and the degeneration wrought by town life upon our population. To my mind, the English townsman even in the slums is infinitely better spiritually, more courageous, more imaginative and cleaner, than his agricultural cousin. I've seen them both when they didn't think they were being observed, and I know. There was something about my Wimblehurst companions that disgusted me. It's hard to define. Heaven knows that at that Cockney boarding-school at Goudhurst we were coarse enough, the Wimblehurst youngsters had neither words nor courage for the sort of thing we used to do—for our bad language, for example ; but, on the other hand, they displayed a sort of sluggish, real lewdness—lewdness is the word—a baseness of attitude. Whatever we exiled urbans did at Goudhurst was touched with something, however coarse, of romantic imagination. We had read the *Boys of England,* and told each other stories. In the English country-side there are no books at all, no songs, no drama, no valiant sin even ; all these things have never come or they were taken away and hidden generations ago, and the imagination aborts and bestialises. That, I think, is where the real difference against the English rural man lies. It is because I know this that I do not share in the common repinings because our country-side is being depopulated, because our population is passing through the furnace of the towns. They starve, they suffer, no doubt, but they come out of it hardened, they come out of it with souls. . . .

Of an evening the Wimblehurst blade, shiny-faced from a wash and with some loud finery, a coloured waistcoat or a vivid tie, would betake himself to the Eastry Arms billiard-room, or to the bar parlour of some minor pub where nap could be played. One soon sickened of his slow knowingness, the cunning observation of his deadened eyes, his idea of a " good story," always, always told in undertones, poor dirty worm ! his shrewd, elaborate manœuvres for some petty advantage, a drink to the good or such-like deal. There rises before my eyes as I write, young Hopley Dodd, the son of the Wimblehurst auctioneer, the pride of Wimblehurst, its finest flower, with his fur waistcoat and his bulldog pipe, his riding-breeches—he had no horse—and his gaiters, as he used to sit, leaning forward and watching the billiard-table from under the brim of his artfully tilted hat. A half-dozen phrases constituted his conversation : " Hard lines ! " he used to say, and " Good baazness," in a bass bleat. Moreover, he had a long, slow whistle that was esteemed the very cream of humorous comment. Night after night he was there. . . .

Also, you know, he would not understand that *I* could

play billiards, and regarded every stroke I made as a fluke. For a beginner I didn't play so badly, I thought. I'm not so sure now ; that was my opinion at the time. But young Dodd's scepticism and the " good baazness " finally cured me of my disposition to frequent the Eastry Arms, and so these noises had their value in my world.

I made no friends among the young men of the place at all, and though I was entering upon adolescence I have no love-affair to tell of here. Not that I was not waking up to that aspect of life in my middle teens. I did, indeed, in various slightly informal ways, scrape acquaintance with casual Wimblehurst girls ; with a little dressmaker's apprentice I got upon shyly speaking terms, and a pupil teacher in the National School went further and was " talked about " in connection with me ; but I was not by any means touched by any reality of passion for either of these young people ; love—love as yet came to me only in my dreams. I only kissed these girls once or twice. They rather disconcerted than developed those dreams. They were so clearly not " it." I shall have much to say of love in this story, but I may break it to the reader now that it is my rôle to be a rather ineffectual lover. Desire I know well enough—indeed, too well ; but love I have been shy of. In all my early enterprises in the war of the sexes, I was torn between the urgency of the body and a habit of romantic fantasy that wanted every phase of the adventure to be generous and beautiful. And I had a curiously haunting memory of Beatrice, of her kisses in the bracken and her kiss upon the wall, that somehow pitched the standard too high for Wimblehurst's opportunities. I will not deny I did in a boyish way attempt a shy, rude adventure or so in love-making at Wimblehurst ; but through these various influences, I didn't bring things off to any extent at all. I left behind me no devastating memories, no splendid reputation. I came away at last, still inexperienced and a little thwarted, with only a natural growth of interest and desire in sexual things.

If I fell in love with any one in Wimblehurst it was with my aunt. She treated me with a kindliness that was only half maternal—she petted my books, she knew about my certificates, she made fun of me in a way that stirred my heart to her. Quite unconsciously I grew fond of her. . . .

My adolescent years at Wimblehurst were on the whole laborious, uneventful years that began in short jackets and left me in many ways nearly a man, years so uneventful that the Calculus of Variations is associated with one winter, and an examination in Physics for Science and Art Department Honours marks an epoch. Many divergent impulses stirred within me, but the master impulse was a grave young dis- position to work and learn, and thereby in some not very clearly defined way get out of the Wimblehurst world into which I had fallen. I wrote with some frequency to Ewart

self-conscious, but, as I remember them, not unintelligent
letters, dated in Latin and with lapses into Latin quotation
that roused Ewart to parody. There was something about
me in those days more than a little priggish. But it was, to
do myself justice, something more than the petty pride of
learning. I had a very grave sense of discipline and preparation that I am not ashamed at all to remember. I was
serious. More serious than I am at the present time. More
serious, indeed, than any adult seems to be. I was capable
then of efforts—of nobilities. . . . They are beyond me now.
I don't see why, at forty, I shouldn't confess I respect my
own youth. I had dropped being a boy quite abruptly. I
thought I was presently to go out into a larger and quite
important world and do significant things there. I thought
I was destined to do something definite to a world that had
a definite purpose. I did not understand then, as I do now,
that life was to consist largely in the world's doing things to
me. Young people never do seem to understand that aspect
of things. And as I say, among my educational influences
my uncle, all unsuspected, played a leading part, and perhaps
among other things gave my discontent with Wimblehurst,
my desire to get away from that clean and picturesque emptiness, a form and expression that helped to emphasise it. In
a way that definition made me patient. " Presently I shall
get to London," I said, echoing him.

I remember him now as talking, always talking, in those
days. He talked to me of theology, he talked of politics, of
the wonders of science and the marvels of art, of the passions
and the affections, of the immortality of the soul and the
peculiar actions of drugs ; but predominantly and constantly
he talked of getting on, of enterprises, of inventions and great
fortunes, of Rothschilds, silver kings, Vanderbilts, Goulds,
flotations, realisations and the marvellous ways of Chance
with men—in all localities, that is to say, that are not
absolutely sunken to the level of Cold Mutton Fat.

When I think of those early talks, I figure him always in
one of three positions. Either we were in the dispensing lair
behind a high barrier, he pounding up stuff in a mortar,
perhaps, and I rolling pill-stuff into long rolls and cutting it
up with a sort of broad, fluted knife, or he stood looking out
of the shop door against the case of sponges and spray-diffusers,
while I surveyed him from behind the counter, or he leant
against the little drawers behind the counter, and I hovered
dusting in front. The thought of those early days brings back
to my nostrils the faint smell of scent that was always in the air,
marbled now with streaks of this drug and now of that, and
to my eyes the rows of jejune glass bottles with gold labels,
mirror-reflected, that stood behind him. My aunt, I remember, used sometimes to come into the shop in a state of aggressive sprightliness, a sort of connubial ragging expedition, and

get much fun over the abbreviated Latinity of those gilt inscriptions. " Ol Amjig, George," she would read derisively, "and he pretends it's almond oil ! Snap !—and that's mustard. Did you *Ever*, George ?

" Look at him, George, looking dignified. I'd like to put an old label on to *him* round the middle like his bottles are, with Ol Pondo on it. That's Latin for Impostor, George—*must* be. He'd look lovely with a stopper."

" *You* want a stopper," said my uncle, projecting his face. . . .

My aunt, dear soul, was in those days quite thin and slender, with a delicate rosebud complexion and a disposition to connubial badinage, to a sort of gentle skylarking. There was a silvery ghost of lisping in her speech. She was a great humorist, and as the constraint of my presence at meals wore off, I became more and more aware of a filmy but extensive net of nonsense she had woven about her domestic relations until it had become the reality of her life. She affected a derisive attitude to the world at large, and applied the epithet " old " to more things than I have ever heard linked to it before or since. " Here's the old newspaper," she used to say to my uncle. " Now don't go and get it in the butter, you silly old Sardine ! "

" What's the day of the week, Susan ? " my uncle would ask.

" Old Monday, Sossidge," she would say, and add, " I got all my Old Washing to do. Don't I *know* it ! " . . .

She had evidently been the wit and joy of a large circle of schoolfellows, and this style had become a second nature with her. It made her very delightful to me in that quiet place. Her customary walk even had a sort of hallo ! in it. Her chief preoccupation in life was, I believe, to make my uncle laugh, and when by some new nickname, some new quaintness or absurdity, she achieved that end, she was, behind a mask of sober amazement, the happiest woman on earth. My uncle's laugh when it did come, I must admit, was, as Baedeker says, " rewarding." It began with gusty blowings and snortings, and opened into a clear " Ha ha ! " but in its fullest development it included, in those youthful days, falling about anyhow and doubling up tightly, and whackings of the stomach, and tears and cries of anguish. I never in my life heard my uncle laugh to his maximum except at her, he was commonly too much in earnest for that, and he didn't laugh much at all, to my knowledge, after those early years. Also she threw things at him to an enormous extent in her resolve to keep things lively in spite of Wimble- hurst ; sponges out of stock she threw, cushions, balls of paper, clean washing, bread ; and once up the yard when they thought that I and the errand boy and the diminutive maid of all work were safely out of the way, she smashed a boxful of eight-ounce bottles I had left to drain, assaulting my uncle with a new soft broom. Sometimes she would shy things at me—but not often. There seemed always laughter round and about her—all three of us would share hysterics at times—and on one occasion the two of them came home from church shockingly ashamed of themselves, because of a storm of mirth during the sermon. The vicar, it seems, had tried to blow his nose with a black glove as well as the customary pocket-handkerchief. And afterwards she had picked up her own glove by the finger, and looking innocently but intently sideways, had suddenly by this simple expedient exploded my uncle altogether. We had it all over again at dinner.

"But it shows you," cried my uncle, suddenly becoming grave, "what Wimblehurst is, to have us all laughing at a little thing like that ! We weren't the only ones that giggled. Not by any means ! And, Lord ! it *was* funny ! "

Socially, my uncle and aunt were almost completely isolated. In places like Wimblehurst the tradesmen's wives always are isolated socially, all of them, unless they have a sister or a bosom friend among the other wives, but the husbands met in various bar-parlours or in the billiard-room of the Eastry Arms. But my uncle, for the most part, spent his evenings at home. When first he arrived in Wimblehurst I think he had spread his effect of abounding ideas and enterprise rather too aggressively ; and Wimblehurst, after a temporary subjugation, had rebelled and done its best to make a butt of him. His appearance in a public-house led to a pause in any conversation that was going on.

"Come to tell us about everything, Mr. Pond'revo ? " some one would say politely.

"You wait," my uncle used to answer, disconcerted, and sulk for the rest of his visit.

Or some one with an immense air of innocence would remark to the world generally, " They're talkin' of rebuildin' Wimblehurst all over again, I'm told. Anybody heard anything of it ? Going to make it a reg'lar smart-goin', enterprisin' place—kind of Crystal Pallas."

"Earthquake and a pestilence before you get *that*," my uncle would mutter, to the infinite delight of every one, and add something inaudible about " Cold Mutton Fat." . . .

§ 3

We were torn apart by a financial accident to my uncle of which I did not at first grasp the full bearings. He had developed what I regarded as an innocent intellectual recreation which he called stock-market meteorology. I think he got the idea from the use of curves in the graphic presentation of associated variations that he saw me plotting. He secured some of my squared paper and, having cast about for a time, decided to trace the rise and fall of certain mines and railways. "There's something in this, George," he said, and I little

dreamt that among other things that were in it, was the whole
of his spare money and most of what my mother had left to
him in trust for me.

"It's as plain as can be," he said. " See, here's one system
of waves and here's another ! These are prices for Union
Pacifics—extending over a month. Now next week, mark
my words, they'll be down one whole point. We're getting
near the steep part of the curve again. See ? It's absolutely
scientific. It's verifiable. Well, and apply it ! You buy in
the hollow and sell on the crest, and—there you are ! "

I was so convinced of the triviality of this amusement that
to find at last that he had taken it in the most disastrous
earnest overwhelmed me.

He took me for a long walk to break it to me, over the
hills towards Yare and across the great gorse commons by
Hazelbrow.

" There are ups and downs in life, George," he said—half-
way across that great open space, and paused against the
sky. . . . " I left out one factor in the Union Pacific analysis."

" *Did* you ? " I said, struck by the sudden change in his
voice. " But you don't mean—— ? "

I stopped and turned on him in the narrow sandy rut of
pathway, and he stopped likewise.

" I do, George. I *do* mean. It's bust me ! I'm a bank-
rupt here and now."

" Then—— ? "

" The shop's bust too. I shall have to get out of that."

" And me ? "

" Oh, you !—*you're* all right. You can transfer your
apprenticeship, and—er—well, I'm not the sort of man to
be careless with trust-funds, you can be sure. I kept that
aspect in mind. There's some of it left, George—trust me !—
quite a decent little sum."

" But you and aunt ? "

" It isn't *quite* the way we meant to leave Wimblehurst,
George ; but we shall have to go. Sale ; all the things shoved
about and ticketed—lot a hundred and one. Ugh ! . . .
It's been a larky little house in some ways. The first we had.
Furnishing—a spree in its way. . . . Very happy. . . ."
His face winced at some memory. " Let's go on, George,"
he said shortly, near choking, I could see.

I turned my back on him, and did not look round again
for a little while.

" That's how it is, you see, George," I heard him after a time.

When we were back in the high road again he came along-
side, and for a time we walked in silence.

" Don't say anything home yet," he said presently.
" Fortunes of War. I got to pick the proper time with Susan
—else she'll get depressed. Not that she isn't a first-rate
brick whatever comes along."

" All right," I said, " I'll be careful," and it seemed to me for the time altogether too selfish to bother him with any further inquiries about his responsibility as my trustee. He gave a little sigh of relief at my note of assent, and was presently talking quite cheerfully of his plans. . . . But he had, I remember, one lapse into moodiness that came and went suddenly. " Those others ! " he said, as though the thought had stung him for the first time.

" What others ? " I asked.

" Damn them ! " said he.

" But what others ? "

" All those damned stick-in-the-mud-and-die-slowly trades-people : Ruck, the butcher, Marbel, the grocer. Snape ! Gord ! George, *how* they'll grin ! " . . .

I thought him over in the next few weeks, and I remember now in great detail the last walk we had together before he handed over the shop and me to his successor. For he had the good luck to sell his business, " lock, stock, and barrel " —in which expression I found myself and my indentures included. The horrors of a sale by auction of the furniture even were avoided.

I remember that either coming or going on that occasion, Ruck, the butcher, stood in his doorway and regarded us with a grin that showed his long teeth.

" You half-witted hog ! " said my uncle. " You grinning hyena " ; and then, " Pleasant day, Mr. Ruck."

" Goin' to make your fortun' in London, than ? " said Mr. Ruck with slow enjoyment.

That last excursion took us along the causeway to Beeching, and so up the downs and round almost as far as Steadhurst, home. My moods, as we went, made a mingled web. By this time I had really grasped the fact that my uncle had, in plain English, robbed me ; the little accumulations of my mother, six hundred pounds and more, that would have educated me and started me in business, had been eaten into and was mostly gone into the unexpected hollow that ought to have been a crest of the Union Pacific curve, and of the remainder he still gave no account. I was too young and inexperienced to insist on this or know how to get it, but the thought of it all made streaks of decidedly black anger in that scheme of interwoven feelings. And you know, I was also acutely sorry for him—almost as sorry as I was for my Aunt Susan. Even then I had quite found him out. I knew him to be weaker than myself ; his incurable, irresponsible childish-ness was as clear to me then as it was on his death-bed, his redeeming and excusing imaginative silliness. Through some odd mental twist, perhaps, I was disposed to exonerate him even at the cost of blaming my poor old mother who had left things in his untrustworthy hands.

I should have forgiven him altogether, I believe, if he had

been in any manner apologetic to me ; but he wasn't that.
He kept reassuring me in a way I found irritating. Mostly,
however, his solicitude was for Aunt Susan and himself.

" It's these Crises, George," he said, " try Character.
Your aunt's come out well, my boy."

He made meditative noises for a space.

" Had her cry, of course "—the thing had been only too
painfully evident to me in her eyes and swollen face—" who
wouldn't ? But now—buoyant again ! . . . She's a Corker.

" We'll be sorry to leave the little house, of course. It's
a bit like Adam and Eve, you know. Lord ! what a chap
old Milton was !

> " The world was all before them, where to choose
> Their place of rest, and Providence their guide."

It sounds, George. . . . Providence their guide ! . . . Well
—thank goodness there's no imeedgit prospect of either Cain
or Abel !

" After all, it won't be so bad up there. Not the scenery,
perhaps, or the air we get here, but—*Life* ! We've got very
comfortable little rooms, very comfortable considering, and
I shall rise. We're not done yet, we're not beaten ; don't
think that, George. I shall pay twenty shillings in the pound
before I've done—you mark my words, George—twenty-five
to you. . . . I got this situation within twenty-four hours—
others offered. It's an important firm—one of the best in
London. I looked to that. I might have got four or five
shillings a week more—elsewhere. Quarters I could name.
But I said to them plainly, wages to go on with, but opportunity's my game—development. We understood each other."

He threw out his chest, and the little round eyes behind
his glasses rested valiantly on imaginary employers.

We would go on in silence for a space while he revised and
restated that encounter. Then he would break out abruptly
with some banal phrase.

" The Battle of Life, George, my boy," he would cry, or
" Ups and Downs ! "

He ignored or waived the poor little attempts I made to
ascertain my own position. " That's all right," he would say ;
or, " Leave all that to me. *I'll* look after them." And he
would drift away towards the philosophy and moral of the
situation. What was I to do ?

" Never put all your resources into one chance, George ;
that's the lesson I draw from this. Have forces in reserve.
It was a hundred to one, George, that I was right—a hundred
to one. I worked it out afterwards. And here we are spiked
on the off-chance. If I'd have only kept back a little, I'd
have had it on U.P. next day, like a shot, and come out on
the rise. There you are ! "

His thoughts took a graver turn.

" It's when you bump up against Chance like this, George, that you feel the need of religion. Your hard and fast scientific men—your Spencers and Huxleys—they don't understand that. I do. I've thought of it a lot lately—in bed and about. I was thinking of it this morning while I shaved. It's not irreverent for me to say it, I hope—but God comes in on the off-chance, George. See ? Don't you be too cocksure of anything, good or bad. That's what I make out of it. I could have sworn. Well, do you think I—particular as I am —would have touched those Union Pacifics with trust-money at all, if I hadn't thought it a thoroughly good thing—good without spot or blemish ? . . . And it was bad !

" It's a lesson to me. You start in to get a hundred per cent. and you come out with that. It means, in a way, a reproof for Pride. I've thought of that, George—in the Night Watches. I was thinking this morning when I was shaving, that that's where the good of it all comes in. At bottom I'm a mystic in these affairs. You calculate you're going to do this or that, but at bottom who knows at all *what* he's doing ? When you most think you're doing things, they're being done right over your head. *You're* being done —in a sense. Take a hundred-to-one chance, or one to a hundred—what does it matter ? You're being Led."

It's odd that I heard this at the time with unutterable contempt, and now that I recall it—well, I ask myself, what have I got better ?

" I wish," said I, becoming for a moment outrageous, " *you* were being Led to give me some account of my money, Uncle."

" Not without a bit of paper to figure on, George, I can't. But you trust me about that, never fear. You trust me."

And in the end I had to.

I think the bankruptcy hit my aunt pretty hard. There was, so far as I can remember now, a complete cessation of all those cheerful outbreaks of elasticity—no more skylarking in the shop or scampering about the house. But there was no fuss that I saw, and only little signs in her complexion of the fits of weeping that must have taken her. She didn't cry at the end, though to me her face with its strain of self-possession was more pathetic than any weeping. " Well," she said to me as she came through the shop to the cab, " Here's old orf, George ! Orf to Mome number two ! Good-bye !" And she took me in her arms and kissed me and pressed me to her. Then she dived straight for the cab before I could answer her.

My uncle followed, and he seemed to me a trifle too valiant and confident in his bearing for reality. He was unusually white in the face. He spoke to his successor at the counter. " Here we go ! " he said. " One down, the other up. You'll find it a quiet little business so long as you run it on quiet lines—a nice, quiet little business. There's nothing more ? No ? Well, if you want to know anything write to me. I'll

always explain fully. Anything—business, place, or people.
You'll find Pil. Antibil. a little overstocked, by the bye. I
found it soothed my mind the day before yesterday making
'em, and I made 'em all day. Thousands! And where's
George? Ah! there you are! I'll write to you, George,
fully, about all that affair. Fully!"

It became clear to me, as if for the first time, that I was
really parting from my Aunt Susan. I went out on to the
pavement and saw her head craned forward, her wide-open
blue eyes and her face intent on the shop that had combined for her all the charms of a big doll's house and a little
home of her very own. "Good-bye!" she said to it and to
me. Our eyes met for a moment—perplexed. My uncle
bustled out and gave a few totally unnecessary directions to
the cabman and got in beside her. "All right?" asked the
driver. "Right," said I; and he woke up the horse with a
flick of his whip. My aunt's eyes surveyed me again. "Stick
to your old science and things, George, and write and tell me
when they make you a Professor," she said cheerfully.

She stared at me for a second longer with eyes growing
wider and brighter and a smile that had become fixed, glanced
again at the bright little shop still saying " Ponderevo " with
all the emphasis of its fascia, and then flopped back hastily out
of sight of me into the recesses of the cab. Then it had gone
from before me, and I beheld Mr. Snape, the hairdresser, inside
his shop regarding its departure with a quiet satisfaction and
exchanging smiles and significant headshakes with Mr. Marbel.

§ 4

I was left, I say, as part of the lock, stock, and barrel at
Wimblehurst with my new master, a Mr. Mantell; who plays
no part in the progress of this story except in so far as he
effaced my uncle's traces. So soon as the freshness of this
new personality faded, I began to find Wimblehurst not only
a dull but a lonely place, and to miss my Aunt Susan immensely. The advertisements of the summer terms for
Cough Linctus were removed; the bottles of coloured water
—red, green, and yellow—restored to their places; the horse
announcing veterinary medicine, which my uncle, sizzling
all the while, had coloured in careful portraiture of a Good-
wood favourite, rewhitened; and I turned myself even more
resolutely than before to Latin (until the passing of my preliminary examination enabled me to drop that), and then
to mathematics and science.

There were classes in Electricity and Magnetism at the
Grammar School. I took a little " elementary " prize in that
in my first year and a medal in my third; and in Chemistry
and Human Physiology and Sound, Light, and Heat, I did
well. There was also a lighter, more discursive subject called
Physiography, in which one ranged among the sciences and

encountered Geology as a process of evolution from Eozoon
to Eastry House, and Astronomy as a record of celestial
movements of the most austere and invariable integrity. I
learnt out of cheap, badly-written condensed text-books, and
with the minimum of experiment, but still I learnt. Only
thirty years ago it was, and I remember I learnt of the electric
light as an expensive, impracticable toy, the telephone as a
curiosity, electric traction as a practical absurdity. There
was no argon, no radium, no phagocytes—at least to my
knowledge, and aluminium was a dear infrequent metal.
The fastest ships in the world went then at nineteen knots,
and no one but a lunatic here and there ever thought it
possible that men might fly.

Many things have happened since then, but the last glance
I had of Wimblehurst two years ago remarked no change
whatever in its pleasant tranquillity. They had not even
built any fresh houses—at least not actually in the town,
though about the station there had been some building. But
it was a good place to do work in, for all its quiescence. I
was soon beyond the small requirements of the Pharmaceutical
Society's examination, and as they do not permit candidates
to sit for that until one-and-twenty, I was presently filling
up my time and preventing my studies becoming too desultory
by making an attack upon the London University degree of
Bachelor of Science, which impressed me then as a very
splendid but almost impossible achievement. The degree in
mathematics and chemistry appealed to me as particularly
congenial—albeit giddily inaccessible. I set to work. I had
presently to arrange a holiday and go to London to matricu-
late, and so it was I came upon my aunt and uncle again.
In many ways that visit marked an epoch. It was my first
impression of London at all. I was then nineteen, and by
a conspiracy of chances my nearest approach to that human
wilderness had been my brief visit to Chatham. Chatham,
too, had been my largest town. So that I got London at
last with an exceptional freshness of effect, as the sudden
revelation of a whole unsuspected other side to life.

I came to it on a dull and smoky day by the South-Eastern
Railway, and our train was half an hour late, stopping and
going on and stopping again. I marked beyond Chislehurst
the growing multitude of villas, and so came stage by stage
through multiplying houses and diminishing interspaces of
market garden and dingy grass to regions of interlacing
railway lines, big factories, gasometers and wide reeking swamps
of dingy little homes, more of them and more and more.
The number of these and their dinginess and poverty increased,
and here rose a great public-house and here a Board School
and here a gaunt factory ; and away to the east there loomed
for a time a queer, incongruous forest of masts and spars.
The congestion of houses intensified and piled up presently

into tenements; I marvelled more and more at this boundless
world of dingy people; whiffs of industrial smell, of leather,
of brewing, drifted into the carriage, the sky darkened, I
rumbled thunderously over bridges, van-crowded streets,
peered down on and crossed the Thames with an abrupt
éclat of sound. I got an effect of tall warehouses, of grey
water, barge crowded, of broad banks of indescribable mud,
and then I was in Cannon Street Station—a monstrous, dirty
cavern with trains packed across its vast floor, and more
porters standing along the platform than I had ever seen in
my life before. I alighted with my portmanteau and struggled
along, realising for the first time just how small and weak I
could still upon occasion feel. In this world, I felt, an Honours
medal in Electricity and Magnetism counted for nothing
at all.

Afterwards I drove in a cab down a cañon of rushing street
between high warehouses, and peeped up astonished at the
blackened greys of Saint Paul's. The traffic of Cheapside—
it was mostly in horse omnibuses in those days—seemed
stupendous, its roar was stupendous; I wondered where the
money came from to employ so many cabs, what industry
could support the endless jostling stream of silk-hatted, frock-
coated, hurrying men. Down a turning I found the Temperance Hotel Mr. Mantell had recommended to me. The porter
in a green uniform who took over my portmanteau, seemed,
I thought, to despise me a good deal.

§ 5

Matriculation kept me for four full days, and then came
an afternoon to spare, and I sought out Tottenham Court
Road through a perplexing network of various and crowded
streets. But this London was vast! it was endless! it
seemed the whole world had changed into packed frontages
and hoardings and street spaces. I got there at last and made
inquiries, and I found my uncle behind the counter of the
pharmacy he managed, an establishment that did not impress
me as doing a particularly high-class trade. "Lord!" he said
at the sight of me, "I was wanting something to happen!"

He greeted me warmly. I had grown taller, and he, I
thought, had grown shorter and smaller and rounder, but
otherwise he was unchanged. He struck me as being rather
shabby, and the silk hat he produced and put on when, after
mysterious negotiations in the back premises he achieved his
freedom to accompany me, was past its first youth; but he
was as buoyant and confident as ever.

"Come to ask me about all *that*?" he cried. "I've never
written yet."

"Oh! among other things," said I with a sudden regrettable politeness, and waived the topic of his trusteeship to ask
after my Aunt Susan.

"We'll have her out of it," he said suddenly; "we'll go somewhere. We don't get you in London every day."

"It's my first visit," I said; "I've never seen London before"; and that made him ask me what I thought of it, and the rest of the talk was London, London, to the exclusion of all smaller topics. He took me up the Hampstead Road almost to the Cobden statue, plunged into some back streets to the left, and came at last to a blistered front door that responded to his latch-key, one of a long series of blistered front doors with fanlights and apartment cards above. We found ourselves in a drab-coloured passage that was not only narrow and dirty but desolatingly empty, and then he opened a door and revealed my aunt sitting at the window, with a little sewing-machine on a bamboo occasional table before her, and "work"—a plum-coloured walking dress, I judged, at its most analytical stage—scattered over the rest of the apartment.

At the first glance I judged my aunt was plumper than she had been, but her complexion was just as fresh and her China blue eyes as bright as in the old days.

"London," she said, didn't "get blacks" on her.

She still "cheeked" my uncle, I was pleased to find. "What are you old Poking in for at *this* time—*Gubbitt*?" she said when he appeared, and she still looked with a practised eye for the facetious side of things. When she saw me behind him, she gave a little cry and stood up radiant. Then she became grave.

I was surprised at my own emotion in seeing her. She held me at arm's length for a moment, a hand on each shoulder, and looked at me with a sort of glad scrutiny. She seemed to hesitate, and then pecked a little kiss off my cheek

"You're a man, George," she said, as she released me, and continued to look at me for a while.

Their *ménage* was one of a very common type in London. They occupied what is called the dining-room floor of a small house, and they had the use of a little inconvenient kitchen in the basement that had once been a scullery. The two rooms, bedroom behind and living-room in front, were separated by folding doors that were never now thrown back, and indeed, in the presence of a visitor, not used at all. There was, of course, no bathroom or anything of that sort available, and there was no water supply except to the kitchen below. My aunt did all the domestic work, though she could have afforded to pay for help if the build of the place had not rendered that inconvenient to the pitch of impossibility. There was no sort of help available except that of indoor servants, for whom she had no accommodation. The furniture was their own; it was partly second-hand, but on the whole it seemed cheerful to my eye, and my aunt's bias for cheap, gay-figured muslin had found ample scope. In many ways

I should think it must have been an extremely inconvenient and cramped sort of home, but at the time I took it, as I was taking everything, as being there and in the nature of things. I did not see the oddness of solvent, decent people living in a habitation so clearly neither designed nor adapted for their needs, so wasteful of labour and so devoid of beauty as this was, and it is only now as I describe this that I find myself thinking of the essential absurdity of an intelligent community living in such makeshift homes. It strikes me now as the next thing to wearing second-hand clothes.

You see, it was a natural growth, part of that system to which Bladesover, I hold, is the key. There are wide regions of London, miles of streets of houses, that appear to have been originally designed for prosperous middle-class homes of the early Victorian type. There must have been a perfect fury of such building in the 'thirties, 'forties, and 'fifties. Street after street must have been rushed into being, Camden Town way, Pentonville way, Brompton way, West Kensington way, in the Victoria region and all over the minor suburbs of the south side. I am doubtful if many of these houses had any long use as the residences of single families, if from the very first almost their tenants did not makeshift and take lodgers and sub-let. They were built with basements, in which their servants worked and lived—servants of a more submissive and troglodytic generation who did not mind stairs—the dining-room (with folding doors) was a little above the ground-level, and in that the wholesome boiled and roast with damp boiled potatoes and then pie to follow, was consumed, and the numerous family read and worked in the evening, and above was the drawing-room (also with folding doors), where the infrequent callers were received. That was the vision at which those industrious builders aimed. Even while these houses were being run up, the threads upon the loom of fate were shaping to abolish altogether the type of household that would have fitted them. Means of transit were developing to carry the moderately prosperous middle-class families out of London, education and factory employment were whittling away at the supply of rough, hardworking, obedient girls who would stand the subterranean drudgery of these places, new classes of hard-up middle-class people such as my uncle, employees of various types, were coming into existence, for whom no homes were provided. None of these classes have ideas of what they ought to be, or fit in any legitimate way into the Bladesover theory that dominates our minds. It was nobody's concern to see them housed under civilised conditions, and the beautiful laws of supply and demand had free play. They had to squeeze in. The landlords came out financially intact from their blundering enterprise. More and more these houses fell into the hands of married artisans or struggling widows or old servants with savings, who

became responsible for the quarterly rent and tried to sweat
a living by sub-letting furnished or unfurnished apartments.

I remember now that a poor, grey-haired old woman, who
had an air of having been roused from a nap in the dust-
bin, came out into the area and looked up at us as we three
went out from the front door to " see London " under my
uncle's direction. She was the sub-letting occupier, she
squeezed out a precarious living by taking the house whole
and sub-letting it in detail, and she made her food and got
the shelter of an attic above and a basement below by the
transaction. And if she didn't chance to " let " steadily,
out she went to pauperdom and some other poor sordid old
adventurer tried in her place. . . .

It is a foolish community that can house whole classes,
useful and helpful, honest and loyal classes, in such squalidly
unsuitable dwellings. It is by no means the social economy
it seems, to use up old women's savings and inexperience
in order to meet the landlord's demands. But any one who
doubts this thing is going on right up to to-day need only
spend an afternoon in hunting for lodgings in any of the
regions of London I have named.

But where has my story got to ? My uncle, I say, decided
I must be shown London, and out we three went as soon as
my aunt had got her hat on, to catch all that was left of
the day.

§ 6

It pleased my uncle extremely to find I had never seen
London before. He took possession of the metropolis forthwith. " London, George," he said, " takes a lot of understanding. It's a great place. Immense. The richest town
in the world, the biggest port, the greatest manufacturing
town, the Imperial city—the centre of civilisation, the heart
of the world ! See those sandwich men down there ! That
third one's hat ! Fair treat ! You don't see poverty like
that in Wimblehurst, George ! And many of them high
Oxford honours men, too. Brought down by drink ! It's a
wonderful place, George—a whirlpool, a maelstrom ! whirls
you up and whirls you down."

I have a very confused memory of that afternoon's inspection of London. My uncle took us to and fro showing
us over his London, talking erratically, following a route of
his own. Sometimes we were walking, sometimes we were
on the tops of great staggering horse omnibuses in a heaving
jumble of traffic, and at one point we had tea in an Aerated
Bread Shop. But I remember very distinctly how we passed
down Park Lane under an overcast sky, and how my uncle
pointed out the house of this child of good fortune and that
with succulent appreciation.

I remember, too, that as he talked I would find my aunt

watching my face as if to check the soundness of his talk by my expression.

"Been in love yet, George?" she asked suddenly, over a bun in the tea-shop.

"Too busy, aunt," I told her.

She bit her bun extensively, and gesticulated with the remnant to indicate that she had more to say.

"How are *you* going to make your fortune?" she said so soon as she could speak again. "You haven't told us that."

"'Lectricity," said my uncle, taking breath after a deep draught of tea.

"If I make it at all," I said. "For my part I think I shall be satisfied with something less than a fortune."

"We're going to make ours—suddenly," she said. "So *he* old says." She jerked her head at my uncle. "He won't tell me when—so I can't get anything ready. But it's coming. Going to ride in our carriage and have a garden. Garden—like a bishop's."

She finished her bun and twiddled crumbs from her fingers. "I shall be glad of the garden," she said. "It's going to be a real big one with rosaries and things. Fountains in it. Pampas grass. Hothouses."

"You'll get it all right," said my uncle, who had reddened a little.

"Grey horses in the carriage, George," she said. "It's nice to think about when one's dull. And dinners in restaurants often and often. And theatres—in the stalls. And money and money and money."

"You may joke," said my uncle, and hummed for a moment.

"Just as though an old Porpoise like him would ever make money," she said, turning her eyes upon his profile with a sudden lapse to affection. "He'll just porpoise about."

"I'll do something," said my uncle, "you bet! Zzzz!" and rapped with a shilling on the marble table.

"When you do you'll have to buy me a new pair of gloves," she said, "anyhow. That finger's past mending. Look! you Cabbage—you." And she held the split under his nose, and pulled a face of comical fierceness.

My uncle smiled at these sallies at the time, but afterwards, when I went back with him to the Pharmacy—the low-class business grew brisker in the evening and they kept open late— he reverted to it in a low, expository tone. "Your aunt's a bit impatient, George. She gets at me. It's only natural. . . . A woman doesn't understand how long it takes to build up a position. No. . . . In certain directions now—I am— quietly—building up a position. Now here. . . . I get this room. I have my three assistants. Zzzz. It's a position that, judged by the criterion of immeedjit income, isn't perhaps so good as I deserve, but strategically—yes. It's what I want. I make my plans. I rally my attack."

" What plans," I said, " are you making ? "

" Well, George, there's one thing you can rely upon. I'm doing nothing in a hurry. I turn over this idea and that, and I don't talk—indiscreetly. There's— No ! I don't think I can tell you that. And yet, why *not* ? "

He got up and closed the door into the shop. " I've told no one," he remarked, as he sat down again. " I owe you something."

His face flushed slightly, he leant forward over the little table towards me.

" Listen ! " he said.

I listened.

" Tono-Bungay," said my uncle very slowly and distinctly.

I thought he was asking me to hear some remote, strange noise. " I don't hear anything," I said reluctantly to his expectant face.

He smiled undefeated. " Try again," he said, and repeated, " Tono-Bungay."

" Oh, *that* ! " I said.

" Eh ? " said he.

" But what is it ? "

" Ah ! " said my uncle, rejoicing and expanding. " What *is* it ? That's what you got to ask ? What *won't* it be ? " He dug me violently in what he supposed to be my ribs. " George," he cried—" George, watch this place ! There's more to follow."

And that was all I could get from him.

That, I believe, was the very first time that the words Tono-Bungay were heard on earth—unless my uncle indulged in monologues in his chamber—a highly probable thing. Its utterance certainly did not seem to me at the time to mark any sort of epoch, and had I been told this word was the Open Sesame to whatever pride and pleasure the grimy front of London hid from us that evening, I should have laughed aloud.

" Coming now to business," I said after a pause, and with a chill sense of effort ; and I opened the question of his trust.

My uncle sighed, and leant back in his chair. " I wish I could make all this business as clear to you as it is to me," he said. " However—— Go on ! Say what you have to say."

§ 7

After I left my uncle that evening I gave way to a feeling of profound depression. My uncle and aunt seemed to me to be leading—I have already used the word too often but I must use it again—*dingy* lives. They seemed to be adrift in a limitless crowd of dingy people, wearing shabby clothes, living uncomfortably in shabby second-hand houses, going to and fro on pavements that had always a thin veneer of greasy, slippery mud, under grey skies that showed no gleam of hope of anything for them but dinginess until they died. It seemed absolutely clear to me that my mother's little savings had been swallowed up and that my own prospect was all too certainly to drop into and be swallowed up sooner or later by this dingy London ocean. The London that was to be an adventurous escape from the slumber of Wimblehurst, had vanished from my dreams. I saw my uncle pointing to the houses in Park Lane and showing a frayed shirt-cuff as he did so. I heard my aunt : " I'm to ride in my carriage then. So he old says.''

My feelings towards my uncle were extraordinarily mixed. I was intensely sorry not only for my Aunt Susan but for him —for it seemed indisputable that as they were living then so they must go on—and at the same time I was angry with the garrulous vanity and silliness that had clipped all my chance of independent study, and imprisoned her in those grey apartments. When I got back to Wimblehurst I allowed myself to write him a boyishly sarcastic and sincerely bitter letter. He never replied. Then, believing it to be the only way of escape for me, I set myself far more grimly and resolutely to my studies than I had ever done before. After a time I wrote to him in more moderate terms, and he answered me evasively. And then I tried to dismiss him from my mind and went on working.

Yes, that first raid upon London under the moist and chilly depression of January had an immense effect upon me. It was for me an epoch-making disappointment. I had thought of London as a large, free, welcoming, adventurous place, and I saw it slovenly and harsh and irresponsive.

I did not realise at all what human things might be found behind those grey frontages, what weakness that whole forbidding façade might presently confess. It is the constant error of youth to overestimate the Will in things. I did not see that the dirt, the discouragement, the discomfort of London could be due simply to the fact that London was a witless old giantess of a town. too slack and stupid to keep herself clean and maintain a brave face to the world. No ! I suffered from the sort of illusion that burnt witches in the seventeenth century. I endured her grubby disorder with a sinister and magnificent quality of intention.

And my uncle's gestures and promises filled me with doubt and a sort of fear for him. He seemed to me a lost little creature, too silly to be silent, in a vast implacable condemnation. I was full of pity and a sort of tenderness for my Aunt Susan, who was doomed to follow his erratic fortunes mocked by his grandiloquent promises. . . .

I was to learn better. But I worked with the terror of the grim underside of London in my soul during all my last year at Wimblehurst.

END OF BOOK I

Book Two

The Rise of
Tono-Bungay

CHAPTER ONE

§ 1

I CAME to live in London, as I shall tell you, when I was nearly twenty-two. Wimblehurst dwindles in perspective, is now in this book a little place far off, Bladesover no more than a small pinkish speck of frontage among the distant Kentish hills; the scene broadens out, becomes multitudinous and limitless, full of the sense of vast irrelevant movement. I do not remember my second coming to London as I do my first, nor my early impressions, save that an October memory of softened amber sunshine stands out, amber sunshine falling on grey house fronts, I know not where. That, and a sense of a large tranquillity. . . .

I could fill a book, I think, with a more or less imaginary account of how I came to apprehend London, how first in one aspect and then another it grew in my mind. Each day my accumulating impressions were added to and qualified and brought into relationship with new ones, they fused inseparably with others that were purely personal and accidental. I find myself with a certain comprehensive perception of London, complex indeed, incurably indistinct in places and yet in some way a whole that began with my first visit and is still being mellowed and enriched.

London !

At first, no doubt, it was a chaos of streets and people and buildings and reasonless going to and fro. I do not remember that I ever struggled very steadily to understand it, or explored it with any but a personal and adventurous intention. Yet in time there has grown up in me a kind of theory of London ; I do think I see lines of an ordered structure out of which it has grown, detected a process that is something more than a confusion of casual accidents, though indeed it may be no more than a process of disease.

I said at the outset of my first book that I find in Bladesover the clue to all England. Well, I certainly imagine it is the clue to the structure of London. There have been no revolutions, no deliberate restatements or abandonments of opinion in England since the days of the fine gentry, since 1688 or thereabouts, the days when Bladesover was built ; there have been changes, dissolving forces, replacing forces, if you will ; but then it was that the broad lines of the English system set firmly. And as I have gone to and fro in London, in certain regions constantly the thought has recurred, this is Bladesover House, this answers to Bladesover House. The fine gentry may have gone ; they have indeed largely gone, I think ; rich merchants may have replaced them, financial

adventurers or what not. That does not matter ; the shape
is still Bladesover.

I am most reminded of Bladesover and Eastry by all those
regions round about the West End parks, for example, estate
parks, each more or less in relation to a palace or group of
great houses. The roads and back ways of Mayfair and all
about St. James's again, albeit perhaps of a later growth in
point of time, were of the very spirit and architectural texture
of the Bladesover passages and yards ; they had the same
smells, the space, the large cleanness, and always going to and
fro there one met unmistakable Olympians, and even more
unmistakable valets, butlers, footmen in mufti. There were
moments when I seemed to glimpse down areas the white
panelling, the very chintz of my mother's room again.

I could trace out now on a map what I would call the Great-
House region ; passing south-westward into Belgravia, becoming diffused and sporadic westward, finding its last
systematic outbreak round and about Regent's Park. The
Duke of Devonshire's place in Piccadilly, in all its insolent
ugliness, pleases me particularly, it is the quintessence of the
thing, Apsley House is all in the manner of my theory, Park
Lane has its quite typical mansions, and they run along the
border of the Green Park and St. James's. And I struck out
a truth one day in Cromwell Road quite suddenly, as I looked
over the Natural History Museum : " By Jove ! " said I,
" but this is the little assemblage of cases of stuffed birds and
animals upon the Bladesover staircase grown enormous, and
yonder as the corresponding thing to the Bladesover curios
and porcelain is the Art Museum, and there in the observa-
tories in Exhibition Road is old Sir Cuthbert's Gregorian telescope that I hunted out in the storeroom and put together."
And diving into the Art Museum under this inspiration I came
to a reading-room and found, as I had inferred, old brown books !

It was really a good piece of social comparative anatomy
I did that day ; all these museums and libraries that are
dotted over London between Piccadilly and West Kensington,
and indeed the museum and library movement throughout
the world, sprang from the elegant leisure of the gentlemen
of taste. Theirs were the first libraries, the first houses of
culture ; by my rat-like raids into the Bladesover saloon I
became, as it were, the last dwindled representative of such a
man of letters as Swift. But now these things have escaped out
of the Great House altogether, and taken on a strange independent life of their own.

It is this idea of escaping parts from the seventeenth-century
system of Bladesover, of proliferating and overgrowing
elements from the Estates, that to this day seems to me the
best explanation, not simply of London, but of all England.
England is a country of great Renascence landed gentlefolk
who have been unconsciously outgrown and overgrown. The

proper shops for Bladesover custom were still to be found in
Regent Street and Bond Street in my early London days—
in those days they had been but lightly touched by the American's profaning hand—and in Piccadilly. I found the doctor's
house of the country village or country town up and down
Harley Street, multiplied but not otherwise different, and the
family solicitor (by the hundred) further eastward in the
abandoned houses of a previous generation of gentlepeople,
and down in Westminster, behind Palladian fronts, the public
offices sheltered in large Bladesoverish rooms and looked out on
St. James's Park. The Parliament Houses of lords and gentlemen, the parliament house that was horrified when merchants
and brewers came thrusting into it a hundred years ago, stood out
upon its terrace gathering the whole system together into a head.

And the more I have paralleled these things with my
Bladesover-Eastry model, the more evident it has become to
me that the balance is not the same, and the more evident is
the presence of great new forces, blind forces of invasion, of
growth. The railway termini on the north side of London have
been kept as remote as Eastry had kept the railway-station
from Wimblehurst, they stop on the very outskirts of the
estates, but from the south, the South-Eastern railway had
butted its great stupid, rusty iron head of Charing Cross station
—that great head that came smashing down in 1905—clean
across the river, between Somerset House and Whitehall. The
south side had no protecting estates. Factory chimneys smoke
right over against Westminster with an air of carelessly not
having permission, and the whole effect of industrial London
and of all London east of Temple Bar and of the huge, dingy
immensity of London port, is to me of something dispropor-
tionately large, something morbidly expanded, without plan or
intention, dark and sinister toward the clean, clear, social
assurance of the West End. And south of this central London,
south-east, south-west, far west, north-west, all round the
northern hills, are similar disproportionate growths, endless
streets of undistinguished houses, undistinguished industries,
shabby families, second-rate shops, inexplicable people who in
a once fashionable phrase do not "exist." All these aspects
have suggested to my mind at times, do suggest to this day,
the unorganised, abundant substance of some tumorous
growth-process, a process which indeed bursts all the outlines
of the affected carcass and protrudes such masses as ignoble,
comfortable Croydon, as tragic, impoverished West Ham. To
this day I ask myself will those masses ever become structural,
will they indeed shape into anything new whatever, or is
that cancerous image their true and ultimate diagnosis ? . . .

Moreover, together with this hypertrophy there is an
immigration of elements that have never understood and
never will understand the great tradition, wedges of foreign
settlement embedded in the heart of this yeasty English

Expansion. One day I remember wandering eastward out
of pure curiosity—it must have been in my early student days
—and discovering a shabbily bright foreign quarter, shops
displaying Hebrew placards and weird, unfamiliar commodities, and a concourse of bright-eyed, eagle-nosed people talking
some incomprehensible gibberish between the shops and the
barrows. And soon I became quite familiar with the devious,
vicious, dirtily-pleasant exoticism of Soho. I found those
crowded streets a vast relief from the dull grey exterior of
Brompton where I lodged and lived my daily life. In Soho,
indeed, I got my first inkling of the factor of replacement that
is so important in both the English and the American process.

Even in the West End, in Mayfair and the squares about
Pall Mall, Ewart was presently to remind me the face of the
old aristocratic dignity was fairer than its substance, here were
actors and actresses, here moneylenders and Jews, here bold
financial adventurers, and I thought of my uncle's frayed cuff
as he pointed out this house in Park Lane and that. That was
so-and-so's who made a corner in borax, and that palace belonged to that hero among modern adventurers, Barmentrude,
who used to be an I.D.B.—an illicit diamond buyer, that is to
say. A city of Bladesovers, the capital of a kingdom of Bladesovers, all much shaken and many altogether in decay, parasitically occupied, insidiously replaced by alien, unsympathetic
and irresponsible elements ;—and withal ruling an adventitious
and miscellaneous empire of a quarter of this daedal earth.
Complex laws, intricate social necessities, disturbing, insatiable
suggestions, followed from this. Such was the world into
which I had come, into which I had in some way to thrust
myself and fit my problem, my temptations, my efforts, my
patriotic instinct, all my moral instincts, my physical appetites,
my dreams and my vanity.

London ! I came up to it, young and without advisers,
rather priggish, rather dangerously open-minded and very open-
eyed, and with something—it is I think the common gift of
imaginative youth, and I claim it unblushingly—fine in me,
finer than the world and seeking fine responses. I did not
want simply to live or simply to live happily or well, I wanted
to serve and do and make—with some nobility. It was in me.
It is in half the youth of the world.

§ 2

I had come to London as a scholar. I had taken the Vincent-
Bradley scholarship of the Pharmaceutical Society, but I threw
this up when I found that my work of the Science and Art
Department in mathematics, physics, and chemistry had
given me one of the minor Technical Board Scholarships at the
Consolidated Technical Schools at South Kensington. This
latter was in mechanics and metallurgy ; and I hesitated
between the two. The Vincent-Bradley gave me £70 a year

and quite the best start-off a pharmaceutical chemist could
have ; the South Kensington thing was worth about twenty-
two shillings a week, and the prospects it opened were vague.
But it meant far more scientific work than the former, and I
was still under the impulse of that great intellectual appetite
that is part of the adolescence of men of my type.   Moreover,
it seemed to lead towards engineering, in which I imagined—
I imagine to this day—my particular use is to be found.   I
took its greater uncertainty as a fair risk.   I came up very
keen, not doubting that the really hard and steady industry
that had carried me through Wimblehurst would go on still
in the new surroundings.

Only from the very first it didn't. . . .

When I look back now at my Wimblehurst days, I still find
myself surprised at the amount of steady grinding study, of
strenuous self-discipline that I maintained throughout my
apprenticeship.   In many ways I think that time was the most
honourable period in my life.   I wish I could say with a
certain mind that my motives in working so well were large
and honourable too.   To a certain extent they were so ; there
was a fine sincere curiosity, a desire for the strength and power
of scientific knowledge and a passion for intellectual exercise ;
but I do not think those forces alone would have kept me at
it so grimly and closely if Wimblehurst had not been so dull,
so limited, and so observant.   Directly I came into the London
atmosphere, tasting freedom, tasting irresponsibility and the
pull of new forces altogether, my discipline fell from me like a
garment.   Wimblehurst to a youngster in my position offered
no temptations worth counting, no interests to conflict with
study, no vices—such vices as it offered were coarsely stripped
of any imaginative glamour—dull drunkenness, clumsy, leer-
ing, shameful lust, no social intercourse even to waste one's
time, and on the other hand it would minister greatly to the
self-esteem of a conspicuously industrious student.   One was
marked as " clever," one played up to the part, and one's little
accomplishment stood out finely in one's private reckoning
against the sunlit small ignorance of that agreeable place.
One went with an intent rush across the market square, one
took one's exercises with as dramatic a sense of an ordered day
as an Oxford don, one burnt the midnight oil quite consciously
at the rare, respectful, benighted passer-by.   And one was
magnificent and memorable in the local paper with one's unapproachable yearly harvest of certificates.   Thus I was not
only a genuinely keen student but also a prig and poseur in
those days—and the latter kept the former at it, as London
made clear.   Moreover, Wimblehurst had given me no outlet
in any other direction.

But I did not realise all this when I came to London, did not
perceive how the change of atmosphere began at once to warp
and distribute my energies.   In the first place I became in-

visible. If I idled for a day, no one except my fellow-students
(who evidently had no awe of me) remarked it. No one saw
my midnight taper ; no one pointed me out as I crossed the
street as an astonishing intellectual phenomenon. In the next
place I became inconsiderable. In Wimblehurst I felt I stood
for Science ; nobody there seemed to have so much as I and
to have it so fully and completely. In London I walked
ignorant in an immensity, and it was clear that among my
fellow-students from the midlands and the north I was ill-
equipped and under-trained. With the utmost exertion I
should only take a secondary position among them. And
finally, in the third place, I was distracted by voluminous new
interests ; London took hold of me, and Science, which had
been the universe, shrank back to the dimensions of tiresome
little formulæ compacted in a book. I came to London in late
September, and it was a very different London from that great
greyly-overcast, smoke-stained house-wilderness of my first
impressions. I reached it by Victoria and not by Cannon
Street, and its centre was now in Exhibition Road. It shone
pale amber, blue-grey, and tenderly spacious and fine under
clear autumnal skies, a London of hugely handsome buildings
and vistas and distances, a London of gardens and labyrinthine
tall museums, of old trees and remote palaces and artificial
waters. I lodged near by in West Brompton at a house in
a little square.

So London faced me the second time, making me forget
altogether for a while the grey, drizzling city visage that had
first looked upon me. I settled down and went to and fro to
my lectures and laboratory ; in the beginning I worked hard,
and only slowly did the curiosity that presently possessed me
to know more of this huge urban province arise, the desire to
find something beyond mechanism that I could serve, some use
other than learning. With this was a growing sense of loneliness, a desire for adventure and intercourse. I found myself
in the evenings poring over a map of London I had bought,
instead of copying out lecture notes—and on Sundays I made
explorations, taking omnibus rides east and west and north and
south, and so enlarging and broadening the sense of great
swarming hinterlands of humanity with whom I had no dealings, of whom I knew nothing. . . .

The whole illimitable place teemed with suggestions of
indefinite and sometimes outrageous possibility, of hidden but
magnificent meanings.

It wasn't simply that I received a vast impression of space
and multitude and opportunity ; intimate things also were
suddenly dragged from neglected, veiled, and darkened corners
into an acute vividness of perception. Close at hand in the
big art museum I came for the first time upon the beauty of
nudity, which I had hitherto held to be a shameful secret,
flaunted and gloried in ; I was made aware of beauty as not

only permissible but desirable and frequent, and of a thousand hitherto unsuspected rich aspects of life. One night in a real rapture, I walked round the upper gallery of the Albert Hall and listened for the first time to great music, I believe now that it was a rendering of Beethoven's Ninth Symphony. . . .

My apprehension of spaces and places was reinforced by a quickened apprehension of persons. A constant stream of people passed by me, eyes met and challenged mine and passed —more and more I wanted them to stay—if I went eastward towards Piccadilly, women who seemed then to my boyish inexperience softly splendid and alluring, murmured to me as they passed. Extraordinarily life unveiled. The very hoardings clamoured strangely at one's senses and curiosities. One bought pamphlets and papers full of strange and daring ideas transcending one's boldest ; in the parks one heard men discussing the very existence of God, denying the rights of property, debating a hundred things that one dared not think about in Wimblehurst. And after the ordinary overcast day, after dull mornings, came twilight, and London lit up and became a thing of white and yellow and red jewels of light and wonderful floods of golden illumination and stupendous and unfathomable shadows—and there were no longer any mean or shabby people—but a great mysterious movement of unaccountable beings. . . .

Always I was coming on the queerest new aspects. Late one Saturday night I found myself one of a great slow-moving crowd between the blazing shops and the flaring barrows in the Harrow Road ; I got into conversation with two bold-eyed girls, bought them boxes of chocolate, made the acquaintance of father and mother and various younger brothers and sisters, sat in a public-house hilariously with them all, standing and being stood drinks, and left them in the small hours at the door of " home," never to see them again. And once I was accosted on the outskirts of a Salvation Army meeting in one of the parks by a silk-hatted young man of eager and serious discourse, who argued against scepticism with me, invited me home to tea into a clean and cheerful family of brothers and sisters and friends, and there I spent the evening singing hymns to the harmonium (which reminded me of half-forgotten Chatham) and wishing all the sisters were not so obviously engaged. . . .

Then on the remote hill of this boundless city-world I found Ewart.

§ 3

How well I remember the first morning, a bright Sunday morning in early October, when I raided in upon Ewart ! I found my old schoolfellow in bed in a room over an oil-shop in a back street at the foot of Highgate Hill. His landlady, a pleasant, dirty young woman with soft brown eyes, brought

down his message for me to come up ; and up I went. The
room presented itself as ample and interesting in detail and
shabby with a quite commendable shabbiness. I had an impression of brown walls—they were papered with brown paper
—of a long shelf along one side of the room with dusty plaster
casts and a small, cheap lay figure of a horse, of a table and
something of grey wax partially covered with a cloth, and of
scattered drawings. There was a gas stove in one corner and
some enamelled ware that had been used overnight for cooking.
The oilcloth on the floor was streaked with a peculiar white
dust. Ewart himself was not in the first instance visible, but
only a fourfold canvas screen at the end of the room from which
shouts proceeded of " Come on ! " then his wiry black hair,
very much rumpled, and a staring red-brown eye and his stump
of a nose came round the edge of this at a height of about three
feet from the ground. " It's old Ponderevo ! " he said, " the
Early Bird ! And he's caught the worm ! By Jove, but it's
cold this morning ! Come round here and sit on the bed ! "
    I walked round, wrung his hand, and we surveyed one another.
    He was lying on a small wooden fold-up bed, the scanty
covering of which was supplemented by an overcoat and an
elderly but still cheerful pair of check trousers, and he was
wearing pyjamas of a virulent pink and green. His neck
seemed longer and more stringy than it had been even in our
schooldays, and his upper lip had a wiry black moustache.
The rest of his ruddy, knobby countenance, his erratic hair and
his general hairy leanness, had not even—to my perceptions—
grown.
    " By Jove ! " he said, " you've got quite decent-looking,
Ponderevo ! What do you think of me ? "
    " You're all right. What are you doing here ? "
    " Art, my son—sculpture ! And incidentally——" He
hesitated. " I ply a trade. Will you hand me that pipe and
those smoking things ? So ! You can't make coffee, eh ?
Well, try your hand. Cast down this screen—no—fold it up and
so we'll go into the other room. I'll keep in bed all the same.
The fire's a gas stove. Yes. Don't make it bang too loud as
you light it—I can't stand it this morning. You won't smoke?
. . . Well, it does me good to see you again, Ponderevo.
Tell me what you're doing, and how you're getting on."
    He directed me in the service of his s mple hospitality, and
presently I came back to his bed and sat down and smiled at
him there, smoking comfortably with his hands under his
head, surveying me.
    " How's Life's Morning, Ponderevo ? By Jove, it must be
nearly six years since we met ! We've got moustaches.
We've fleshed ourselves a bit, eh ? And you—— ? "
    I felt a pipe was becoming after all, and that lit, I gave him a
favourable sketch of my career.
    " Science ! And you've worked like that ! While I've been

pottering round doing odd jobs for stone-masons and people, and trying to get to sculpture. I've a sort of feeling that the chisel—— I began with painting, Ponderevo, and found I was colour-blind, colour-blind enough to stop it. I've drawn about and thought about—thought more particularly. I give myself three days a week as an art student, and the rest of the time—I've a sort of trade that keeps me. And we're still in the beginning of things, young men starting. Do you remember the old times at Goudhurst, our doll's-house island, the Retreat of the Ten Thousand, Young Holmes and the rabbits, eh ? It's surprising, if you think of it, to find we are still young. And we used to talk of what we would be, and we used to talk of love ! I suppose you know all about that now, Ponderevo."

I flushed and hesitated on some vague, foolish lie. " No," I said, a little ashamed of the truth. " Do you ? I've been too busy."

" I'm just beginning—just as we were then. Things happen——"

He sucked at his pipe for a space and stared at the plaster cast of a flayed hand that hung on the wall.

" The fact is, Ponderevo, I'm beginning to find life a most extraordinary queer set-out ; the things that pull one, the things that don't. The wants—— This business of sex. It's a net. No end to it, no way out of it, no sense in it. There are times when women take possession of me, when my mind is like a painted ceiling at Hampton Court with the pride of the flesh sprawling all over it. *Why ?* . . . And then again sometimes when I have to encounter a woman, I am overwhelmed by a terror of tantalising boredom—I fly, I hide, I do anything. You've got your scientific explanations, perhaps ; what's Nature and the universe up to in that matter ? "

" It's her way, I gather, of securing the continuity of the species."

" But it doesn't," said Ewart. " That's just it ! No. I have succumbed to—dissipation—down the hill there. Euston Road way. And it was damned ugly and mean, and I hate having done it. And the continuity of the species—lord ! . . . And why does Nature make a man so infernally ready for drinks ? There's no sense in that anyhow." He had sat up in bed, to put this question with the greater earnestness. " And why has she given me a most violent desire towards sculpture and an equally violent desire to leave off work directly I begin it, eh ? . . . Let's have some more coffee. I put it to you, these things puzzle me, Ponderevo. They dishearten me. They keep me in bed."

He had an air of having saved up these difficulties for me for some time. He sat with his chin almost touching his knees, sucking at his pipe.

" That's what I mean," he went on, " when I say life is

getting on to me as extraordinary queer. I don't see my
game, nor why I was invited. And I don't make anything
of the world outside either. What do *you* make of it ? "

" London," I began. " It's—so enormous ! "

" Isn't it ! And it's all up to nothing. You find chaps
keeping grocers' shops—why the *devil*, Ponderevo, do they
keep grocers' shops ? They all do it very carefully, very
steadily, very meanly. You find people running about and
doing the most remarkable things—being policemen, for
example, and burglars. They go about these businesses quite
gravely and earnestly. I—somehow—can't go about mine.
Is there any sense in it at all—anywhere ? "

" There must be sense in it," I said. " We're young."

" We're young—yes. But one must inquire. The grocer's
a grocer because, I suppose, he sees he comes in there. Feels
that on the whole it amounts to a call. . . . But the bother
is I don't see where I come in at all. Do you ? "

" Where *you* come in ? "

" No, where *you* come in."

" Not exactly, yet," I said. " I want to do some good in
the world—something—something effectual before I die. I
have a sort of idea my scientific work—— I don't know."

" Yes," he mused. " And I've got a sort of idea my
sculpture,—but *how* it is to come in and *why*,—I've no idea
at all." He hugged his knees for a space. " That's what
puzzles me, Ponderevo, no end."

He became animated. " If you will look in that cupboard,"
he said, " you will find an old respectable-looking roll on a
plate and a knife somewhere and a gallipot containing butter.
You give them me and I'll make my breakfast, and then if
you don't mind watching me paddle about at my simple
toilet I'll get up. Then we'll go for a walk and talk about
this affair of life further. And about Art and Literature
and anything else that crops up on the way. . . . Yes, that's
the gallipot. Cockroach got in it ? Chuck him out—damned
interloper. . . ."

So in the first five minutes of our talk, as I seem to remember it now, old Ewart struck the note that ran through
all that morning's intercourse. . . .

To me it was a most memorable talk because it opened
out quite new horizons of thought. I'd been working rather
close and out of touch with Ewart's free, gesticulating way.
He was pessimistic that day and sceptical to the very roots
of things. He made me feel clearly, what I had not felt at
all before, the general adventurousness of life, particularly
of life at the stage we had reached, and also the absence of
definite objects, of any concerted purpose in the lives that
were going on all round us. He made me feel, too, how ready
I was to take up commonplace assumptions. Just as I had
almost imagined that somewhere in social arrangements

there was certainly a Head Master who would intervene if one went too far, so I had always had a sort of implicit belief that in our England there were somewhere people who understood what we were all, as a nation, about. That crumpled into his pit of doubt and vanished. He brought out, sharply cut and certain, the immense effect of purposelessness in London that I was already indistinctly feeling. We found ourselves at last returning through Highgate Cemetery and Waterlow Park—and Ewart was talking.

" Look at it there," he said, stopping and pointing to the great vale of London spreading wide and far. " It's like a sea—and we swim in it. And at last down we go, and then up we come—washed up here." He swung his arm to the long slopes about us, tombs and headstones in long perspectives, in limitless rows. " We're young, Ponderevo, but sooner or later our whitened memories will wash up on one of these beaches, on some such beach as this. George Ponderevo, F.R.S., Sidney Ewart, R.I.P. Look at the rows of 'em ! "

He paused. " Do you see that hand ? The hand, I mean, pointing upward, on the top of a blunted obelisk. Yes. Well, that's what I do for a living—when I'm not thinking, or drinking, or prowling, or making love, or pretending I'm trying to be a sculptor without either the money or the morals for a model. See ? And I do those hearts afire and those pensive angel guardians with the palm of peace. Damned well I do 'em and damned cheap ! I'm a sweated victim, Ponderevo. . . ."

That was the way of it, anyhow. I drank deep of talk that day, we went into theology, into philosophy ; I had my first glimpse of socialism. I felt as though I had been silent in a silence since I and he had parted. At the thought of socialism Ewart's moods changed for a time to a sort of energy. " After all, all this confounded vagueness *might* be altered. If you could get men to work together. . . .

It was a good talk that rambled through all the universe. I thought I was giving my mind refreshment, but indeed it was dissipation. All sorts of ideas, even now, carry me back, as it were, to a fountain-head, to Waterlow Park and my resuscitated Ewart. There stretches away south of us long garden slopes and white gravestones and the wide expanse of London and somewhere in the picture is an old red wall, sun-warmed, and a great blaze of Michaelmas daisies set off with late golden sunflowers and a drift of mottled, blood-red, fallen leaves. It was with me that day as though I had lifted my head suddenly out of dull and immediate things and looked at life altogether. . . . But it played the very devil with the copying up of my arrears of notes to which I had vowed the latter half of that day.

After that reunion Ewart and I met much and talked much, and in our subsequent encounters his monologue was

interrupted and I took my share. He had exercised me so
greatly that I lay awake at nights thinking him over, and
discoursed and answered him in my head as I went in the
morning to the College. I am by nature a doer and only by
the way a critic ; his philosophical assertion of the incalculable
vagueness of life which fitted his natural indolence roused
my more irritable and energetic nature to active protests.
" It's all so pointless," I said, " because people are slack and
because it's in the ebb of an age. But you're a socialist.
Well, let's bring that about ! And there's a purpose. There
you are ! "

Ewart gave me all my first conceptions of socialism ; in a
little while I was an enthusiastic socialist and he was a passive
resister to the practical exposition of the theories he had
taught me   " We must join some organisation," I said.
" We ought to do things. . . . We ought to go and speak at
street corners. People don't know." You must figure me a
rather ill-dressed young man in a state of great earnestness,
standing up in that shabby studio of his and saying these
things, perhaps with some gesticulations, and Ewart with a
clay-smudged face, dressed perhaps in a flannel shirt and
trousers, with a pipe in his mouth, squatting philosophically
at a table, working at some chunk of clay that never got
beyond suggestion.

" I wonder why one doesn't want to," he said. . . .

It was only very slowly I came to gauge Ewart's real
position in the scheme of things, to understand how deliberate
and complete was this detachment of his from the moral
condemnation and responsibilities that played so fine a part
in his talk. His was essentially the nature of an artistic
appreciator ; he could find interest and beauty in endless
aspects of things that I marked as evil, or at least as not
negotiable ; and the impulse I had towards self-deception,
to sustained and consistent self-devotion, disturbed and
detached and pointless as it was at that time, he had indeed
a sort of admiration for, but no sympathy. Like many
fantastic and ample talkers he was at bottom secretive, and
he gave me a series of little shocks of discovery throughout
our intercourse. The first of these came in the realisation
that he quite seriously meant to do nothing in the world at
all towards reforming the evils he laid bare in so easy and
dexterous a manner. The next came in the sudden appearance of a person called " Milly "—I've forgotten her surname
—whom I found in his room one evening, simply attired in
a blue wrap—the rest of her costume behind the screen—
smoking cigarettes and sharing a flagon of an amazingly cheap
and self-assertive grocer's wine Ewart affected, called " Canary
Sack." " Hallo ! " said Ewart, as I came in. " This is
Milly, you know. She's been being a model—she *is* a model
really. . . . (Keep calm, Ponderevo !) Have some sack ? "

Milly was a woman of thirty, perhaps, with a broad, rather pretty face, a placid disposition, a bad accent, and delightful blonde hair that waved off her head with an irrepressible variety of charm ; and whenever Ewart spoke she beamed at him. Ewart was always sketching this hair of hers and embarking upon clay statuettes of her that were never finished. She was, I know now, a woman of the streets, whom Ewart had picked up in the most casual manner, and who had fallen in love with him, but my inexperience in those days was too great for me to place her then, and Ewart offered no elucidations. She came to him, he went to her, they took holidays together in the country when certainly she sustained her fair share of their expenditure. I suspect him now even of taking money from her. Odd old Ewart ! It was a relationship so alien to my orderly conceptions of honour, to what I could imagine any friend of mine doing, that I really hardly saw it with it there under my nose. But I see it and I think I understand it now. . . .

Before I fully grasped the discursive manner in which Ewart was committed to his particular way in life, I did, I say, as the broad, constructive ideas of socialism took hold of me, try to get him to work with me in some definite fashion as a socialist.

" We ought to join on to other socialists," I said. " They've got something."

" Let's go and look at 'em first."

After some pains we discovered the office of the Fabian Society, lurking in a cellar in Clement's Inn ; and we went and interviewed a rather discouraging secretary who stood astraddle in front of a fire and questioned us severely and seemed to doubt the integrity of our intentions profoundly. He advised us to attend the next open meeting in Clifford's Inn and gave us the necessary data. We both contrived to get to the affair, and heard a discursive gritty paper on Trusts and one of the most inconclusive discussions you can imagine. Three-quarters of the speakers seemed under some jocular obsession which took the form of pretending to be conceited. It was a sort of family joke, and as strangers to the family we did not like it. . . .

As we came out through the narrow passage from Clifford's Inn to the Strand, Ewart suddenly pitched upon a wizened, spectacled little man in a vast felt hat and a large orange tie.

" How many members are there in this Fabian Society of yours ? " he asked.

The little man became at once defensive in his manner.

" About seven hundred," he said ; " perhaps eight."

" Like—like the ones here ? "

The little man gave a nervous, self-satisfied laugh. " I suppose they're up to sample," he said.

The little man dropped out of existence and we emerged

upon the Strand. Ewart twisted his arm into a queerly
eloquent gesture that gathered up all the tall façades of the
banks, the business places, the projecting clock and towers
of the Law Courts, the advertisements, the luminous signs,
into one social immensity, into a capitalistic system gigantic
and invincible.

"These socialists have no sense of proportion," he said.
"What can you expect of them?"

§ 4

Ewart, as the embodiment of talk, was certainly a leading
factor in my conspicuous failure to go on studying. Social
theory in its first crude form of Democratic Socialism gripped
my intelligence more and more powerfully. I argued in the
laboratory with the man who shared my bench until we
quarrelled and did not speak. And also I fell in love.

The ferment of sex had been creeping into my being like
a slowly advancing tide through all my Wimblehurst days,
the stimulus of London was like the rising of a wind out of
the sea that brings the waves in fast and high. Ewart had
his share in that. More and more acutely and unmistakably
did my perception of beauty in form and sound, my desire
for adventure, my desire for intercourse, converge on this
central and commanding business of the individual life. I
had to get me a mate.

I began to fall in love faintly with girls I passed in the
street, with women who sat before me in trains, with girl
fellow-students, with ladies in passing carriages, with loiterers
at the corners, with neat-handed waitresses in shops and tea-
rooms, with pictures even of girls and women. On my rare
visits to the theatre I always became exalted, and found the
actresses and even the spectators about me mysterious,
attractive creatures of deep interest and desire. I had a
stronger and stronger sense that among these glancing, passing
multitudes there was somewhere one who was for me. And
in spite of every antagonistic force in the world, there was
something in my very marrow that insisted: "Stop! Look at
this one! Think of her! Won't she do? This signifies—this
before all things signifies! Stop! Why are you hurrying by?
This may be the predestined person—before all others."

It is odd that I can't remember when first I saw Marion,
who became my wife—whom I was to make wretched, who
was to make me wretched, who was to pluck that fine generalised possibility of love out my early manhood and make it
a personal conflict. I became aware of her as one of a number
of interesting attractive figures that moved about in my
world, that glanced back at my eyes, that flitted by with a
kind of averted watchfulness. I would meet her coming
through the Art Museum, which was my short cut to the

Brompton Road, or see her sitting, reading, as I thought, in one of the bays of the Education Library. But really, as I found out afterwards, she never read. She used to come there to eat a bun in quiet. She was a very gracefully-moving figure of a girl then, very plainly dressed, with dark brown hair, I remember, in a knot low on her neck behind that confessed the pretty roundness of her head and harmonised with the admirable lines of ears and cheek, the grave serenity of mouth and brow.

She stood out among the other girls very distinctly because they dressed more than she did, struck emphatic notes of colour, startled one by novelties in hats and bows and things. I've always hated the rustle, the disconcerting colour boundaries, the smart, unnatural angles of women's clothes. Her plain black dress gave her a starkness. . . .

I do remember though, how one afternoon I discovered the peculiar appeal of her form for me. I had been restless with my work and had finally slipped out of the Laboratory and come over to the Art Museum to lounge among the pictures. I came upon her in an odd corner of the Sheepshanks gallery intently copying something from a picture that hung high. I had just been in the gallery of casts from the antique, my mind was all alive with my newly awakened sense of line, and there she stood with face upturned, her body drooping forward from the hips just a little—memorably graceful—feminine.

After that I know I sought to see her, felt a distinctive emotion at her presence, began to imagine things about her. I no longer thought of generalised womanhood or of this casual person or that. I thought of her.

An accident brought us together. I found myself one Monday morning in an omnibus staggering westward from Victoria—I was returning from a Sunday I'd spent at Wimblehurst in response to a unique freak of hospitality on the part of Mr. Mantell. She was the sole other inside passenger. And when the time came to pay her fare, she became an extremely scared, disconcerted, and fumbling young woman she had left her purse at home.

Luckily I had some money.

She looked at me with startled, troubled brown eyes ; she permitted my proffered payment to the conductor with a certain ungraciousness that seemed a part of her shyness; and then as she rose to go, she thanked me with an obvious affectation of ease.

"Thank you so much," she said in a pleasant, soft voice ; and then less gracefully, "Awfully kind of you, you know."

I fancy I made polite noises. But just then I wasn't disposed to be critical. I was full of the sense of her presence, her arm was stretched out over me as she moved past me, the gracious slenderness of her body was near me. The words

T.-B.—M.U.   D

we used didn't seem very greatly to matter. I had vague
ideas of getting out with her—and I didn't.

That encounter, I have no doubt, exercised me enormously,
I lay awake at night rehearsing it, and wondering about the
next phase of our relationship. That took the form of the
return of my twopence. I was in the Science Library, digging
something out of the *Encyclopædia Britannica*, when she
appeared beside me and placed on the open page an evidently premeditated thin envelope, bulgingly confessing the coins within.

" It was so very kind of you," she said, " the other day.
I don't know what I should have done, Mr.——"

I supplied my name. " I knew," I said, " you were a
student here."

" Not exactly a student. I——"

" Well, anyhow, I knew you were here frequently. And
I'm a student myself at the Consolidated Technical Schools."

I plunged into autobiography and questionings, and so
entangled her in a conversation that got a quality of intimacy
through the fact that, out of deference to our fellow-readers,
we were obliged to speak in undertones. And I have no
doubt that in substance it was singularly banal. Indeed, I
have an impression that all our early conversations were
incredibly banal. We met several times in a manner half-
accidental, half-furtive, and wholly awkward. Mentally I
didn't take hold of her. I never did take hold of her mentally.
Her talk, I now know all too clearly, was shallow, pretentious,
evasive. Only—even to this day—I don't remember it as
in any way vulgar. She was, I could see quite clearly, anxious
to overstate or conceal her real social status, a little desirous
to be taken for a student in the art school and a little ashamed
that she wasn't. She came to the museum to " copy things,"
and this, I gathered, had something to do with some way of
partially earning her living that I wasn't to inquire into. I
told her things about myself, vain things that I felt might
appeal to her, but that I learnt long afterwards made her
think me " conceited." We talked of books, but there she
was very much on her guard and secretive, and rather more
freely of pictures. She " liked " pictures. I think from the
outset I appreciated and did not for a moment resent that
hers was a commonplace mind, that she was the unconscious
custodian of something that had gripped my most intimate
instinct, that she embodied the hope of a possibility, was the
careless proprietor of a physical quality that had turned my
head like strong wine. I felt I had to stick to our acquaintance, flat as it was. Presently we should get through these
irrelevant exterior things, and come to the reality of love
beneath.

I saw her in dreams released, as it were, from herself,
beautiful, worshipful, glowing. And sometimes when we
were together, we would come on silences through sheer lack

of matter, and then my eyes would feast on her and the silence seemed like the drawing back of a curtain—her superficial self. Odd, I confess. Odd, particularly, the enormous hold of certain things about her upon me, a certain slight rounded duskiness of skin, a certain perfection of modelling in her lips, her brow, a certain fine flow about the shoulders. She wasn't, indeed, beautiful to many people—these things are beyond explaining. She had manifest defects of form and feature, and they didn't matter at all. Her complexion was bad, but I don't think it would have mattered if it had been positively unwholesome. I had extraordinarily limited, extraordinarily painful, desires. I longed intolerably to kiss her lips.

§ 5

The affair was immensely serious and commanding to me. I don't remember that in these earlier phases I had any thought of turning back at all. It was clear to me that she regarded me with an eye entirely more critical than I had for her, that she didn't like my scholarly untidiness, my want of even the most commonplace style. " Why do you wear collars like that ? " she said, and sent me in pursuit of gentlemanly neckwear. I remember when she invited me a little abruptly one day to come to tea at her home on the following Sunday and meet her father and mother and aunt, that I immediately doubted whether my hitherto unsuspected best clothes would create the impression she desired me to make on her belongings. I put off the encounter until the Sunday after, to get myself in order. I had a morning coat made and I bought a silk hat, and had my reward in the first glance of admiration she ever gave me. I wonder how many of my sex are as preposterous. I was, you see, abandoning all my beliefs—all my conventions unasked. I was forgetting myself—immensely. And there was a conscious shame in it all. Never a word did I breathe to Ewart—to any living soul—of what was going on.

Her father and mother and aunt struck me as the dismalest of people, and her home in Walham Green was chiefly notable for its black and amber tapestry carpets and curtains and tablecloths, and the age and irrelevance of its books, mostly books with faded gilt on the covers. The windows were fortified against the intrusive eye by cheap lace curtains and an " art pot " upon an unstable octagonal table. Several framed Art School drawings of Marion's, bearing official South Kensington marks of approval, adorned the room, and there was a black and gilt piano with a hymn-book on the top of it. There were draped mirrors over all the mantels, and above the sideboard in the dining-room in which we sat at tea was a portrait of her father villainously truthful after the manner of such works. I couldn't see a trace of the beauty I found in her in either parent, yet she somehow contrived to be like them both.

These people pretended in a way that reminded me of the Three Great Women in my mother's room, but they had not nearly so much social knowledge and did not do it nearly so well. Also, I remarked, they did it with an eye on Marion. They had wanted to thank me, they said, for the kindness to their daughter in the matter of the bus fare, and so accounted for anything unusual in their invitation. They posed as simple gentle-folk, a little hostile to the rush and gadding-about of London, preferring a secluded and unpretentious quiet.

When Marion got out the white tablecloth from the side-board-drawer for tea, a card bearing the word " APARTMENTS " fell to the floor. I picked it up and gave it to her before I realised from her quickened colour that I should not have seen it ; that probably it had been removed from the window in honour of my coming.

Her father spoke once in a large, remote way of the claims of business engagements, and it was only long afterwards I realised that he was a supernumerary clerk in the Walham Green Gas Works and otherwise a useful man at home. He was a large, loose, fattish man with unintelligent brown eyes magnified by spectacles ; he wore an ill-fitting frock-coat and a paper collar, and he showed me, as his great treasure and interest, a large Bible which he had grangerised with photographs of pictures. Also he cultivated the little garden-yard behind the house, and he had a small greenhouse with tomatoes. " I wish I 'ad 'eat," he said. " One can do such a lot with 'eat. But I suppose you can't 'ave every-thing you want in this world."

Both he and Marion's mother treated her with a deference that struck me as the most natural thing in the world. Her own manner changed, became more authoritative and watchful, her shyness disappeared. She had taken a line of her own, I gathered, draped the mirror, got the second-hand piano, and broken her parents in. Her mother must once have been a pretty woman ; she had regular features and Marion's hair without its lustre, but she was thin and careworn. The aunt, Miss Ramboat, was a large, abnormally shy person, very like her brother, and I don't recall anything she said on this occasion.

To begin with there was a good deal of tension—Marion was frightfully nervous, and every one was under the necessity of behaving in a mysteriously unreal fashion until I plunged, became talkative and made a certain ease and interest. I told them of the schools, of my lodgings, of Wimblehurst and my apprenticeship days. " There's a lot of this Science about nowadays," Mr. Ramboat reflected ; " but I sometimes wonder a bit what good it is ? "

I was young enough to be led into what he called " a bit

of a discussion," which Marion truncated before our voices became unduly raised. "I dare say," she said, "there's much to be said on both sides."

I remember Marion's mother asked me what church I attended, and that I replied evasively. After tea there was music and we sang hymns. I doubted if I had a voice when this was proposed, but that was held to be a trivial objection, and I found sitting close beside the sweep of hair from Marion's brow had many compensations. I discovered her mother sitting in the horsehair arm-chair and regarding us sentimentally. I went for a walk with Marion towards Putney Bridge, and then there was more singing and a supper of cold bacon and pie, after which Mr. Ramboat and I smoked. During that walk, I remember, she told me the import of her sketchings and copyings in the museum. A cousin of a friend of hers whom she spoke of as Smithie, had developed an original business in a sort of tea-gown garment which she called a Persian Robe, a plain wrap with a gaily embroidered yoke, and Marion went there and worked in the busy times. In the times that weren't busy she designed novelties in yokes by an assiduous use of eyes and notebook in the museum, and went home and traced out the captured forms on the foundation material. "I don't get much," said Marion, "but it's interesting, and in the busy times we work all day. Of course, the workgirls are dreadfully common, but we don't say much to them. And Smithie talks enough for ten."

I quite understood the workgirls were dreadfully common.

I don't remember that Walham Green *ménage* and the quality of these people, nor the light they threw on Marion, detracted in the slightest degree at that time from the intent resolve that held me to make her mine. I didn't like them. But I took them as part of the affair. Indeed, on the whole, I think they threw her up by an effect of contrast ; she was so obviously controlling them, so consciously superior to them.

More and more of my time did I give to this passion that possessed me. I began to think chiefly of ways of pleasing Marion, of acts of devotion, of treats, of sumptuous presents for her, of appeals she would understand. If at times she was manifestly unintelligent, if her ignorance became indisputable, I told myself her simple instincts were worth all the education and intelligence in the world. And to this day I think I wasn't altogether wrong about her. There was, I still recognise, something fine about her, something simple and high, that flickered in and out of her ignorance and commonness and limitations like the tongue from the mouth of a snake. . . .

One night I was privileged to meet her and bring her home from an entertainment at the Birkbeck Institute. We came back on the underground railway and we travelled first-class —that being the highest class available. We were alone in the carriage, and for the first time I ventured to put my arm about her.

" You mustn't," she said feebly.

" I love you," I whispered suddenly with my heart beating wildly, drew her to me, drew all her beauty to me and kissed her cool and unresisting lips.

" Love me ? " she said, struggling away from me. "Don't!" and then, as the train ran into a station, " You must tell no one. . . . I don't know. . . . You shouldn't have done that. . . ."

Then two other people got in with us and terminated my wooing for a time.

When we found ourselves alone together, walking towards Battersea, she had decided to be offended. I parted from her unforgiven and terribly distressed.

When we met again, she told me I must never do "that" again.

I had dreamt that to kiss her lips was ultimate satisfaction. But it was indeed only the beginning of desires. I told her my one ambition was to marry her.

" But," she said, " you're not in a position—— What's the good of talking like that ? "

I stared at her. " I mean to," I said.

" You can't," she answered. " It will be years——"

" But I love you," I insisted.

I stood not a yard from the sweet lips I had kissed ; I stood within arm's length of the inanimate beauty I desired to quicken, and I saw opening between us a gulf of years, toil, waiting, disappointments, and an immense uncertainty.

" I love you," I said. " Don't you love me ? "

She looked me in the face with grave, irresponsive eyes.

" I don't know," she said. " I *like* you, of course. . One has to be sensible. . . ."

I can remember now my sense of frustration by her un-resilient reply. I should have perceived then that for her my ardour had no quickening fire. But how was I to know ? I had let myself come to want her, my imagination endowed her with infinite possibilities. I wanted her and wanted her, stupidly and instinctively. . . .

" But," I said ; " Love—— ! "

" One has to be sensible," she replied. " I like going about with you. Can't we keep as we are ? "

§ 6

Well, you begin to understand my breakdown now. I have been copious enough with these apologia. My work got more and more spiritless, my behaviour degenerated, my punctuality declined ; I was more and more out-classed in the steady grind by my fellow-students. Such supplies of moral energy as I still had at command shaped now in the direction of serving Marion rather than science.

I fell away dreadfully, more and more I shirked and skulked ;
the humped men from the north, the pale men with thin,
clenched minds, the intent, hard-breathing students I found
against me, fell at last from keen rivalry to moral contempt.
Even a girl got above me upon one of the lists. Then indeed
I made it a point of honour to show by my public disregard of
every rule that I really did not even pretend to try. . . .

So one day I found myself sitting in a mood of considerable
astonishment in Kensington Gardens, reflecting on a recent
heated interview with the school Registrar in which I had
displayed more spirit than sense. I was astonished chiefly
at my stupendous falling away from all the militant ideas of
unflinching study I had brought up from Wimblehurst. I
had displayed myself, as the Registrar put it, " an unmitigated
rotter." My failure to get marks in the written examination
had only been equalled by the insufficiency of my practical work.

" I ask you," the Registrar had said, " what will become
of you when your scholarship runs out ? "

It certainly was an interesting question. What *was* going
to become of me ?

It was clear there would be nothing for me in the schools
as I had once dared to hope ; there seemed, indeed, scarcely
anything in the world except an ill-paid assistantship in some
provincial organised Science School or grammar school. I
knew that for that sort of work, without a degree or any
qualification, one earned hardly a bare living and had little
leisure to struggle up to anything better. If only I had even
as little as fifty pounds I might hold out in London and take
my B.Sc. degree, and quadruple my chances ! My bitterness
against my uncle returned at the thought. After all, he had
some of my money still, or ought to have. Why shouldn't
I act within my rights, threaten to "take proceedings " ?
I meditated for a space on the idea, and then returned to the
Science Library and wrote him a very considerable and
occasionally pungent letter.

That letter to my uncle was the nadir of my failure. Its
remarkable consequences, which ended my student days
altogether, I will tell in the next chapter.

I say "my failure." Yet there are times when I can even
doubt whether that period was a failure at all, when I become
defensively critical of those exacting courses I did not follow,
the encyclopædic process of scientific exhaustion from which
I was distracted. My mind was not inactive even if it fed on
forbidden food. I did not learn what my professors and demon-
strators had resolved I should learn, but I learnt many things.
My mind learnt to swing wide and to swing by itself.

After all, those other fellows who took high places in the
college examinations and were the professor's model boys,
haven't done so amazingly. Some are professors themselves,
some technical experts ; not one can show things done such

as I, following my own interest, have achieved. For I have
built boats that smack across the water like whip-lashes, no
one ever dreamt of such boats until I built them ; and I
have surprised three secrets that are more than technical
discoveries, in the unexpected hiding-places of Nature. I
have come nearer flying than any man has done. Could I
have done as much if I had had a turn for obeying those
rather mediocre professors at the college who proposed to
train my mind ? If I had been *trained* in research—that
ridiculous contradiction in terms—should I have done more
than produce additions to the existing store of little papers
with blunted conclusions, of which there are already too
many ? I see no sense in mock modesty upon this matter.
Even by the standards of worldly success I am, by the side
of my fellow-students, no failure. I had my F.R.S. by the
time I was thirty-seven, and if I am not very wealthy, poverty
is as far from me as the Spanish Inquisition. Suppose I had
stamped down on the head of my wandering curiosity, locked
my imagination in a box just when it wanted to grow out to
things, worked by so-and-so's excellent method and so-and-
so's indications, where should I be now ? . . .

I may be all wrong in this. It may be I should be a far more
efficient man than I am if I had cut off all those divergent
expenditures of energy, plugged up my curiosity about society
with some currently acceptable rubbish or other, abandoned
Ewart, evaded Marion instead of pursuing her, concentrated.
But I don't believe it !

However, I certainly believed it completely and was filled
with remorse on that afternoon when I sat dejectedly in
Kensington Gardens and reviewed, in the light of the
Registrar's pertinent questions, my first two years in London.

CHAPTER TWO

THE DAWN COMES, AND MY UNCLE APPEARS IN A NEW SILK HAT

§ I

THROUGHOUT my student days I had not seen my uncle.
I refrained from going to him in spite of an occasional
regret that in this way I estranged myself from my
Aunt Susan, and I maintained a sulky attitude of mind
towards him. And I don't think that once in all that time
I gave a thought to that mystic word of his that was to alter
all the world for us. Yet I had not altogether forgotten it.
It was with a touch of memory, dim transient perplexity if

no more—why did this thing seem in some way personal ?—
that I read a new inscription upon the hoardings :—

THE SECRET OF VIGOUR,

TONO-BUNGAY.

That was all.   It was simple and yet in some way arresting.
I found myself repeating the word after I had passed, it
roused one's attention like the sound of distant guns.   " Tono "
—what's that ? and deep, rich, unhurrying ;—" *Bun*—gay ! "
Then came my uncle's amazing telegram, his answer to
my hostile note, which must have followed him from place to
place :   " *Come to me at once you are wanted three hundred a
year certain tono-bungay.*"
" By Jove ! " I cried, " of course !
" It's something——.   A patent-medicine ! I wonder
what he wants with me ? "
In his Napoleonic way my uncle had omitted to give an
address.   His telegram had been handed in at Farringdon
Road, and after complex meditations I replied to Ponderevo,
Farringdon Road, trusting to the rarity of our surname to
reach him.
" Where are you ? " I asked.
His reply came promptly :
" 192A Raggett Street, E.C."
The next day I took an unsanctioned holiday after the
morning's lecture.   I discovered my uncle in a wonderfully
new silk hat—oh, a splendid hat ! with a rolling brim that
went beyond the common fashion.   It was decidedly too big
for him—that was its only fault.   It was stuck on the back
of his head, and he was in a white waistcoat and shirt sleeves.
He welcomed me with a forgetfulness of my bitter satire
and my hostile abstinence that was almost divine.   His
glasses fell off at the sight of me.   His round, inexpressive
eyes shone brightly.   He held out his plump, short hand.
" Here we are, George ! What did I tell you ? Needn't
whisper it now, my boy.   Shout it—*loud* ! Spread it about !
Tell every one ! Tono—TONO—TONO-BUNGAY ! "
Raggett Street, you must understand, was a thoroughfare
over which some one had distributed large quantities of
cabbage stumps and leaves.   It opened out of the upper end
of Farringdon Street, and 192A was a shop with the plate-
glass front coloured chocolate, on which several of the same
bills I had read upon the hoardings had been stuck.   The
floor was covered by street mud that had been brought in on
dirty boots, and three energetic young men of the hooligan
type, in neck-wraps and caps, were packing wooden cases
with papered-up bottles, amidst much straw and confusion.

The counter was littered with these same swathed bottles, of a pattern then novel but now amazingly familiar in the world, the blue paper with the coruscating figure of a genially nude giant, and the printed directions of how under practically all circumstances to take Tono-Bungay. Beyond the counter on one side opened a staircase down which I seemed to remember a girl descending with a further consignment of bottles, and the rest of the background was a high partition, also chocolate, with " Temporary Laboratory " inscribed upon it in white letters, and over a door that pierced it, " Office." Here I rapped, inaudible amid much hammering, and then entered unanswered to find my uncle, dressed as I have described, one hand gripping a sheaf of letters, and the other scratching his head as he dictated to one of three toiling typewriter girls. Behind him was a further partition and a door inscribed " ABSOLUTELY PRIVATE—NO ADMISSION " thereon. This partition was of wood painted the universal chocolate up to about eight feet from the ground and then of glass. Through the glass I saw dimly a crowded suggestion of crucibles and glass retorts, and—by Jove—yes !—the dear old Wimblehurst air-pump still ! It gave me quite a little thrill—that air-pump ! And beside it was the electrical machine—but something—some serious trouble—had happened to that. All these were evidently placed on a shelf just at the level to show.

" Come right into the sanctum," said my uncle, after he had finished something about " esteemed consideration," and whisked me through the door into a room that quite amazingly failed to verify the promise of that apparatus. It was papered with dingy wall-paper that had peeled in places ; it contained a fireplace, an easy-chair with a cushion, a table on which stood two or three big bottles, a number of cigar-boxes on the mantel, a whisky Tantalus and a row of soda syphons. He shut the door after me carefully.

" Well, here we are ! " he said. " Going strong ! Have a whisky, George ? No !—Wise man ! Neither will I ! You see me at it ! At it—hard ! "

" Hard at what ? "

" Read it," and he thrust into my hand a label—that label that has now become one of the most familiar objects of the chemist's shop, the greenish-blue rather old-fashioned bordering, the legend, the name in good black type, very clear, and the strong man all set about with lightning flashes above the double column of skilful lies in red—the label of Tono-Bungay. " It's afloat," he said, as I stood puzzling at this. " It's afloat. I'm afloat ! " And suddenly he burst out singing in that throaty tenor of his—

" I'm afloat, I'm afloat on the fierce flowing tide,
    The ocean's my home and my bark is my bride ! "

"Ripping song that is, George. Not so much a bark as a solution, but still—it does! Here we are at it! By the bye! Half a mo'! I've thought of a thing." He whisked out, leaving me to examine this nuclear spot at leisure, while his voice became dictatorial without. The den struck me as in its large, grey, dirty way quite unprecedented and extraordinary. The bottles were all labelled simply A, B, C, and so forth, and that dear old apparatus above, seen from this side, was even more patently "on the shelf" than when it had been used to impress Wimblehurst. I saw nothing for it but to sit down in the chair and await my uncle's explanations. I remarked a frock-coat with satin lapels behind the door; there was a dignified umbrella in the corner and a clothes-brush and a hat-brush stood on a side-table. My uncle returned in five minutes looking at his watch—a gold watch—"Gettin' lunch-time, George," he said. "You'd better come and have lunch with me!"

"How's Aunt Susan?" I asked.

"Exuberant. Never saw her so larky. This has bucked her up something wonderful—all this."

"All what?"

"Tono-Bungay."

"What *is* Tono-Bungay?" I asked.

My uncle hesitated. "Tell you after lunch, George," he said. "Come along!" and having locked up the sanctum after himself, led the way along a narrow, dirty pavement, lined with barrows and swept at times by avalanche-like porters bearing burthens to vans, to Farringdon Street. He hailed a passing cab superbly, and the cabman was infinitely respectful. "Schäfers's," he said, and off we went side by side —and with me more and more amazed at all these things—to Schäfers's Hotel, the second of the two big places with huge, lace curtain-covered windows near the corner of Blackfriars Bridge.

I will confess I felt a magic change in our relative proportions as the two colossal, pale-blue-and-red liveried porters of Schäfers's held open the inner doors for us with a salutation that in some manner they seemed to confine wholly to my uncle. Instead of being about four inches taller, I felt at least the same size as he, and very much slenderer. Still more obsequious waiters relieved him of the new hat and the dignified umbrella, and took his orders for our lunch. He gave them with a fine assurance.

He nodded to several of the waiters.

"They know me, George, already," he said. "Point me out. Live place! Eye for coming men!"

The detailed business of the lunch engaged our attention for a while, and then I leant across my plate. "And *now*?" said I.

"It's the secret of vigour. Didn't you read that label?"

"Yes, but——"

"It's selling like hot cakes."

" And what is it ? " I pressed.

" Well," said my uncle, and then leant forward and spoke softly under cover of his hand, " It's nothing more or less than . . ."

(But here an unfortunate scruple intervenes. After all, Tono-Bungay is still a marketable commodity and in the hands of purchasers, who bought it from—among other vendors—me. No ! I am afraid I cannot give it away.)

" You see," said my uncle in a slow, confidential whisper, with eyes very wide and a creased forehead, " it's nice because of the " (here he mentioned a flavouring matter and an aromatic spirit), " it's stimulating because of " (here he mentioned two very vivid tonics, one with a marked action on the kidney). "And the " (here he mentioned two other ingredients) " makes it pretty intoxicating. Cocks their tails. Then there's " (but I touch on the essential secret). " And there you are. I got it out of an old book of recipes—all except the " (here he mentioned the more virulent substance, the one that assails the kidneys), " which is my idea. Modern touch ! There you are ! "

He reverted to the direction of our lunch.

Presently he was leading the way to the lounge—a sumptuous place in red morocco and yellow glazed crockery, with incredible vistas of settees and sofas and things, and there I found myself grouped with him in two excessively upholstered chairs with an earthenware Moorish table between us bearing coffee and Benedictine, and I was tasting the delights of a tenpenny cigar. My uncle smoked a similar cigar in an habituated manner, and he looked energetic and knowing and luxurious and most unexpectedly a little bounder, round the end of it. It was just a trivial flaw upon our swagger, perhaps, that we both were clear our cigars had to be " mild." He got obliquely across the spaces of his great arm-chair so as to incline confidentially to my ear, he curled up his little legs, and I, in my longer way, adopted a corresponding receptive obliquity. I felt that we should strike an unbiased observer as a couple of very deep and wily and developing and repulsive persons.

" I want to let you into this "—puff—" George," said my uncle round the end of his cigar. " For many reasons."

His voice grew lower and more cunning. He made explanations that to my inexperience did not completely explain. I retain an impression of a long credit and a share with a firm of wholesale chemists, of a credit and a prospective share with some pirate printers, of a third share for a leading magazine and newspaper proprietor.

" I played 'em off one against the other," said my uncle. I took his point in an instant. He had gone to each of them in turn and said the others had come in.

" I put up four hundred pounds," said my uncle, " myself and my all. And you know——"

He assumed a brisk confidence. " I hadn't five hundred pence. " At least——"

For a moment he really was just a little embarrassed. " I *did*," he said, " produce capital. You see, there was that trust affair of yours—I ought, I suppose—in strict legality —to have put that straight first. Zzzz. . . .

" It was a bold thing to do," said my uncle, shifting the venue from the region of honour to the region of courage. And then with a characteristic outburst of piety, " Thank God it's all come right !

" And now, I suppose, you ask where do *you* come in ? Well, fact is, I've always believed in you, George. You've got—it's a sort of dismal grit. Bark your shins, rouse you, and you'll go ! You'd rush any position you had a mind to rush. I know a bit about character, George—trust me. You've got——" He clenched his hands and thrust them out suddenly, and at the same time said, with explosive violence, " Wooosh ! Yes. You have ! The way you put away that Latin at Wimblehurst ; I've never forgotten it. Wo-oo-oo-osh ! Your science and all that ! Wo-oo-oo-osh ! I know my limitations. There's things I can do, and " (he spoke in a whisper, as though this was the first hint of his life's secret) " there's things I can't. Well, I can create this business, but I can't make it go. I'm too voluminous—I'm a boiler-over, not a simmering stick-at-it. *You* keep on *hotting up and hotting up*. Papin's digester. That's you, steady and long and piling up—then, wo-oo-oo-oo-osh. Come in and stiffen these niggers. Teach them that wo-oo-oo-osh. There you are ! That's what I'm after. You ! Nobody else believes you're more than a boy. Come right in with me and be a man. Eh, George ? Think of the fun of it—a thing on the go—a Real Live Thing ! Wooshing it up ! Making it buzz and spin ! Whoo-oo-oo."—He made alluring expanding circles in the air with his hand. " Eh ? "

His proposal, sinking to confidential undertones again, took more definite shape. I was to give all my time and energy to developing and organising. " You shan't write a single advertisement, or give a single assurance," he declared. " I can do all that." And the telegram was no flourish ; I was to have three hundred a year. Three hundred a year. ("That's nothing," said my uncle, " the thing to freeze on to, when the time comes, is your tenth of the vendor's share.")

Three hundred a year certain, anyhow ! It was an enormous income to me. For a moment I was altogether staggered. Could there be that much money in the whole concern ? I looked about me at the sumptuous furniture of Schäfers's Hotel. No doubt there were many such incomes.

My head was spinning with unwonted Benedictine and Burgundy.

"Let me go back and look at the game again," I said. "Let me see upstairs and round about."

I did.

"What do you think of it all ? " my uncle asked at last.

"Well, for one thing," I said, "why don't you have those girls working in a decently ventilated room ? Apart from any other consideration, they'd work twice as briskly. And they ought to cover the corks before labelling round the bottle——"

"Why ? " said my uncle.

"Because—they sometimes make a mucker of the cork job, and then the label's wasted."

"Come and change it, George," said my uncle, with sudden fervour. "Come here and make a machine of it. You can. Make it all slick, and then make it woosh. I know you can. Oh ! I know you can."

<h2 style="text-align:center">§ 2</h2>

I seem to remember very quick changes of mind after that lunch. The muzzy exultation of the unaccustomed stimulants gave way very rapidly to a mood of pellucid and impartial clairvoyance which is one of my habitual mental states. It is intermittent ; it leaves me for weeks together, I know, but back it comes at last like justice on circuit, and calls up all my impressions, all my illusions, all my wilful and passionate proceedings. We came downstairs again into that inner room which pretended to be a scientific laboratory through its high glass lights, and indeed was a lurking place. My uncle pressed a cigarette on me, and I took it and stood before the empty fireplace while he propped his umbrella in the corner, deposited the new silk hat that was a little too big for him on the table, blew copiously and produced a second cigar.

It came into my head that he had shrunken very much in size since the Wimblehurst days, that the cannon ball he ahd swallowed was rather more evident and shameless than it had been, his skin less fresh and the nose between his glasses, which still didn't quite fit, much redder. And just then he seemed much laxer in his muscles and not quite as alertly quick in his movements. But he evidently wasn't aware of the degenerative nature of his changes as he sat there, looking suddenly quite little under my eyes.

"Well, George ! " he said, quite happily unconscious of my silent criticism, "what do you think of it all ? "

"Well," I said, "in the first place—it's a damned swindle !"

"Tut ! tut ! " said my uncle. "It's as straight as—— It's fair trading ! "

"So much the worse for trading," I said.

"It's the sort of thing everybody does. After all, there's no harm in the stuff—and it may do good. It might do a lot of good—giving people confidence, f'rinstance, against an epidemic. See ? Why not ? I don't see where your swindle comes in."

" H'm," I said.   " It's a thing you either see or don't see."

" I'd like to know what sort of trading isn't a swindle in its way.   Everybody who does a large advertised trade is selling something common on the strength of saying it's uncommon. Look at Chickson—they made him a baronet.   Look at Lord Radmore, who did it on lying about the alkali in soap !   Rippin' ads those were of his, too ! "

" You don't mean to say you think doing this stuff up in bottles and swearing it's the quintessence of strength and making poor devils buy it at that, is straight ? "

" Why not, George ?   How do we know it mayn't be the quintessence to them so far as they're concerned ? "

" Oh ! " I said, and shrugged my shoulders.

" There's Faith.   You put Faith in 'em. . . . I grant our labels are a bit emphatic.   Christian Science, really.   No good setting people against the medicine.   Tell me a solitary trade nowadays that hasn't to be—emphatic.   It's the modern way !   Everybody understands it—everybody allows for it."

" But the world would be no worse, and rather better, if all this stuff of yours was run down a conduit into the Thames."

" Don't see that, George, at all.   'Mong other things, all our people would be out of work.   Unemployed !   I grant you Tono-Bungay *may* be—not *quite* so good a find for the world as Peruvian bark, but the point is, George—*it makes trade !* And the world lives on trade.   Commerce !   A romantic exchange of commodities and property.   Romance.   'Magination.   See ?   You must look at these things in a broad light. Look at the wood—and forget the trees !   And hang it, George !   we got to do these things !   There's no way unless you do.   What do *you* mean to do—anyhow ? "

" There's ways of living," I said, " without either fraud or lying."

" You're a bit stiff, George.   There's no fraud in this affair, I'll bet my hat !   But what do you propose to do ?   Go as chemist to some one who *is* running a business, and draw a salary without a share like I offer you.   Much sense in that ! It comes out of the swindle—as you call it—just the same."

" Some businesses are straight and quiet, anyhow ; supply a sound article that is really needed, don't shout advertisements."

" No, George.   There you're behind the times.   The last of that sort was sold up 'bout five years ago."

" Well, there's scientific research."

" And who pays for that ?   Who put up that big City and Guilds place at South Kensington ?   Enterprising business men !   They fancy they'll have a bit of science going on, they want a handy Expert ever and again, and there you are ! And what do you get for research when you've done it ?   Just

a bare living and no outlook. They just keep you to make
discoveries, and if they fancy they'll use 'em they do."

" One can teach."

" How much a year, George ? How much a year ? I
suppose you must respect Carlyle ! Well—you take Carlyle's
test—solvency. (Lord ! what a book that French Revolution
of his is !) See what the world pays teachers and discoverers
and what it pays business men ! That shows the ones it really
wants. There's a justice in these big things, George, over and
above the apparent injustice. I tell you it wants trade. It's
Trade that makes the world go round. Argosies ! Venice !
Empire ! "

My uncle suddenly rose to his feet.

" You think it over, George. You think it over ! And
come up on Sunday to the new place—we got rooms in Gower
Street now—and see your aunt. She's often asked for you,
George—often and often, and thrown it up at me about that
bit of property—though I've always said and always will, that
twenty-five shillings in the pound is what I'll pay you and
interest up to the nail. And think it over. It isn't me I ask
you to help. It's yourself. It's your Aunt Susan. It's the
whole concern. It's the commerce of your country. And we
want you badly. I tell you straight, I know my limitations.
You could take this place, you could make it go ! I can see
you at it—looking rather sour. Woosh is the word, George."

And he smiled endearingly.

" I got to dictate a letter," he said, ending the smile, and
vanished into the outer room.

§ 3

I didn't succumb without a struggle to my uncle's allure-
ments. Indeed, I held out for a week while I contemplated
life and my prospects. It was a crowded and muddled contemplation. It invaded even my sleep.

My interview with the Registrar, my talk with my uncle,
my abrupt discovery of the hopeless futility of my passion for
Marion, had combined to bring me to a sense of crisis. What
was I going to do with life ?

I remember certain phases of my indecisions very well.

I remember going home from our talk. I went down
Farringdon Street to the Embankment because I thought to go
home by Holborn and Oxford Street would be too crowded for
thinking. . . . That piece of Embankment from Blackfriars
to Westminster still reminds me of that momentous hesitation.

You know, from first to last, I saw the business with my
eyes open, I saw its ethical and moral values quite clearly.
Never for a moment do I remember myself faltering from my
persuasion that the sale of Tono-Bungay was a thoroughly
dishonest proceeding. The stuff was, I perceived, a mis-

chievous trash, slightly stimulating, aromatic, and attractive,
likely to become a bad habit and train people in the habitual
use of stronger tonics, and insidiously dangerous to people with
defective kidneys. It would cost about sevenpence the large
bottle to make, including bottling, and we were to sell it at half
a crown plus the cost of the patent medicine stamp. A thing
that I will confess deterred me from the outset far more than
the sense of dishonesty in this affair, was the supreme silliness
of the whole concern. I still clung to the idea that the world
of men was or should be a sane and just organisation, and the
idea that I should set myself gravely, just at the fine spring-
time of my life, to developing a monstrous bottling and packing
warehouse, bottling rubbish for the consumption of foolish,
credulous, and depressed people, had in it a touch of insanity.
My early beliefs still clung to me. I felt assured that somewhere there must be a hitch in the fine prospect of ease and
wealth under such conditions ; that somewhere, a little overgrown, perhaps, but still traceable, lay a neglected, wasted
path of use and honour for me.

My inclination to refuse the whole thing increased rather
than diminished at first as I went along the Embankment.
In my uncle's presence there had been a sort of glamour that
had prevented an outright refusal. It was a revival of affection
for him I felt in his presence I think, in part, and in part an
instinctive feeling that I must consider him as my host. But
much more was it a curious persuasion he had the knack of
inspiring—a persuasion not so much of his integrity and
capacity as of the reciprocal and yielding foolishness of the
world. One felt that he was silly and wild, but in some way
silly and wild after the fashion of the universe. After all,
one must live somehow. I astonished him and myself by
temporising.

" No," said I, " I'll think it over ! "

And as I went along the Embankment, the first effect was
all against my uncle. He shrank—for a little while he continued to shrink—in perspective until he was only a very small
shabby little man in a dirty back street, sending off a few
hundred bottles of rubbish to foolish buyers. The great
buildings on the right of us, the Inns and the School Board
place—as it was then—Somerset House, the big hotels, the
great bridges, Westminster's outlines ahead, had an effect of
grey largeness that reduced him to the proportions of a busy
blackbeetle in a crack in the floor.

And then my eye caught the advertisements on the south
side of " Sorber's Food," of " Cracknell's Ferric Wine," very
bright and prosperous signs, illuminated at night, and I
realised how astonishingly they looked at home there, how
evidently part they were in the whole thing.

I saw a man come charging out of Palace Yard—the policeman touched his helmet to him—with a hat and a bearing

astonishingly like my uncle's. After all—didn't Cracknell himself sit in the House ? . . .

Tono-Bungay shouted at me from a hoarding near Adelphi Terrace, I saw it afar off near Carfax Street, it cried out again upon me in Kensington High Street and burst into a perfect clamour, six or seven times I saw it, as I drew near my diggings. It certainly had an air of being something more than a dream. . . .

Yes, I thought it over—thoroughly enough. . . . Trade rules the world. Wealth rather than trade ! The thing was true, and true too was my uncle's proposition that the quickest way to get wealth is to sell the cheapest thing possible in the dearest bottle. He was frightfully right after all. *Pecunia non olet*—a Roman emperor said that. Perhaps my great heroes in Plutarch were no more than such men, fine now only because they are distant ; perhaps after all this Socialism to which I had been drawn was only a foolish dream, only the more foolish because all its promises were conditionally true. Morris and these others played with it wittingly ; it gave a zest, a touch of substance to their æsthetic pleasures. Never would there be good faith enough to bring such things about. They knew it ; every one, except a few fools, knew it. As I crossed the corner of St. James's Park wrapped in thought, I dodged back just in time to escape a prancing pair of greys. A stout, common-looking woman, very magnificently dressed, regarded me from the carriage with a scornful eye. " No doubt," thought I, " a pill-vendor's wife. . . ."

Running through all my thoughts, surging out like a refrain, was my uncle's master-stroke, his admirable touch of praise : " Make it all slick—and then make it Woosh. I know you can ! Oh ! I *know* you can ! "

§ 4

Ewart as a moral influence was unsatisfactory. I had made up my mind to put the whole thing before him, partly to see how he took it, and partly to hear how it sounded when it was said. I asked him to come and eat with me in an Italian place near Panton Street where one could get a curious, interesting, glutting sort of dinner for eighteen-pence. He came with a disconcerting black-eye that he wouldn't explain. " Not so much a black-eye," he said, " as the aftermath of a purple patch. . . . What's your difficulty ? "

" I'll tell you with the salad," I said.

But as a matter of fact I didn't tell him. I threw out that I was doubtful whether I ought to go into trade, or stick to teaching in view of my deepening socialist proclivities ; and he, warming with the unaccustomed generosity of a sixteen-penny Chianti, ran on from that without any further inquiry as to my trouble.

His utterances roved wide and loose.

" The reality of life, my dear Ponderevo," I remember him saying very impressively and punctuating with the nut-crackers as he spoke, " is Chromatic Conflict . . . and Form. Get hold of that and let all these other questions go. The Socialist will tell you one sort of colour and shape is right, the Individualist another. What does it all amount to ? What *does* it all amount to ? *Nothing !* I have no advice to give any one, none—except to avoid regrets. Be yourself—seek after such beautiful things as your own sense determines to be beautiful. And don't mind the headache in the morning. . . . For what, after all, *is* a morning, Ponderevo ? It isn't like the upper part of a day ! "

He paused impressively.

" What Rot ! " I cried, after a confused attempt to apprehend him.

" Isn't it ! And it's my bedrock wisdom in the matter ! Take it or leave it, my dear George ; take it or leave it." . . . He put down the nut-crackers out of my reach and lugged a greasy-looking notebook from his pocket. " I'm going to steal this mustard pot," he said.

I made noises of remonstrance.

" Only as a matter of design. I've got to do an old beast's tomb. Wholesale grocer. I'll put it on his corners,—four mustard pots. I dare say he'd be glad of a mustard plaster now to cool him, poor devil, where he is. But anyhow—here goes ! "

§ 5

It came to me in the small hours that the real moral touch-stone for this great doubting was Marion. I lay composing statements of my problem and imagined myself delivering them to her—and she, goddess-like and beautiful, giving her fine, simply-worded judgment.

" You see, it's just to give one's self over to the Capitalistic System," I imagined myself saying in good socialist jargon ; " it's surrendering all one's beliefs. We *may* succeed, we *may* grow rich, but where would the satisfaction be ? "

Then she would say, " No ! That wouldn't be right."

" But the alternative is to wait ! "

Then suddenly she would become a goddess. She would turn upon me frankly and nobly, with shining eyes, with arms held out. " No," she would say, " we love one another. Nothing ignoble shall ever touch us. We love one another. Why wait to tell each other that, dear ? What does it matter that we are poor and may keep poor ? " . . .

But indeed the conversation didn't go at all in that direction. At the sight of her my nocturnal eloquence became preposterous and the moral values altered completely. I had waited for her outside the door of the Persian-robe establishment in Kensington High Street, and walked home with her thence. I remember how she emerged into the warm evening light, and that she wore a brown straw hat that made her for once not only beautiful but pretty.

" I like that hat," I said by way of opening ; and she smiled her rare, delightful smile at me.

" I love you," I said in an undertone, as we jostled closer on the pavement.

She shook her head forbiddingly, but she still smiled. Then—

" Be sensible ! "

The High Street pavement is too narrow and crowded for conversation and we were some way westward before we spoke again.

" Look here," I said ; " I want you, Marion. Don't you understand ? I want you."

" Now ! " she cried warningly.

I do not know if the reader will understand how a passionate love, an immense admiration and desire, can be shot with a gleam of positive hatred. Such a gleam there was in me at the serene self-complacency of that " *Now !* " It vanished almost before I felt it. I found no warning in it of the antagonisms latent between us.

" Marion," I said, " this isn't a trifling matter to me. I love you. I would die to get you. . . . Don't you care ? "

" But what is the good ? "

" You don't care ! " I cried. " You don't care a rap ! "

" You know I care," she answered. " If I didn't—— If I didn't like you very much should I let you come and meet me— go about with you ? "

" Well, then," I said, " promise to marry me ! "

" If I do, what difference will it make ? "

We were separated by two men carrying a ladder, who drove between us unawares.

" Marion," I asked when we got together again, " I tell you I want you to marry me."

" We can't."

" Why not ? "

" We can't marry—in the street."

" We could take our chance ! "

" I wish you wouldn't go on talking like this. What *is* the good ? "

She suddenly gave way to gloom. " It's no good marry- ing," she said. " One's only miserable. I've seen other girls. When one's alone one has a little pocket-money anyhow, one can go about a little. But think of being married and no money, and perhaps children—you can't be sure. . . ."

She poured out this concentrated philosophy of her class and type in jerky, uncompleted sentences, with knitted brows, with discontented eyes towards the westward glow—forgetful, it seemed, for a moment even of me.

" Look here, Marion," I said abruptly, " what would you marry on ? "

" What *is* the good ? " she began.

" Would you marry on three hundred a year ? "

She looked at me for a moment. " That's six pounds a week," she said. " One could manage on that—easily. Smithie's brother—— No, he only gets two hundred and fifty. He married a typewriting girl."

" Will you marry me if I get three hundred a year ? "

She looked at me again, with a curious gleam of hope.

" *If !* " she said.

I held out my hand and looked her in the eyes. " It's a bargain," I said.

She hesitated and touched my hand for an instant. " It's silly," she remarked as she did so.   " It means really we're—— She paused.

" Yes ? " said I.

" Engaged. You'll have to wait years. What good can it do you ? "

" Not so many years," I answered.

For a moment she brooded.

Then she glanced at me with a smile, half-sweet, half-wistful, that has stuck in my memory for ever.

" I like you," she said.   " I shall like to be engaged to you."

And, faint on the threshold of hearing, I caught her ventured " dear ! " It's odd that in writing this down my memory passes over all that intervened and I feel it all again, and once again I am Marion's boyish lover taking great joy in such rare and little things.

§ 6

At last I went to the address my uncle had given me in Gower Street, and found my Aunt Susan waiting tea for him.

Directly I came into the room I appreciated the change in outlook that the achievement of Tono-Bungay had made almost as vividly as when I saw my uncle's new hat. The furniture of the room struck upon my eye as almost stately. The chairs and sofa were covered with chintz, which gave it a dim, remote flavour of Bladesover ; the mantel, the cornice, the gas pendant were larger and finer than the sort of thing I had grown accustomed to in London. And I was shown in by a real housemaid with real tails to her cap, and great quantities of reddish hair. There was my aunt, too, looking bright and pretty, in a blue-patterned tea-wrap with bows that seemed to me the quintessence of fashion. She was sitting in a chair by the open window with quite a pile of yellow-labelled books on the occasional table beside her. Before the large, paper-decorated fireplace stood a three-tiered cake-stand displaying assorted cakes, and a tray with all the tea equipage except the teapot was on the large central table.

The carpet was thick, and a spice of adventure was given it by a number of dyed sheepskin mats.

"Hel-*lo* !" said my aunt as I appeared. "It's George !"

"Shall I serve the tea now, Mem ?" said the real housemaid, surveying our greetings coldly.

"Not till Mr. Ponderevo comes, Meggie," said my aunt, and grimaced with extraordinary swiftness and virulence as the housemaid turned her back.

"Meggie, she calls herself," said my aunt as the door closed, and left me to infer a certain want of sympathy.

"You're looking very jolly, aunt," said I.

"What do you think of all this old Business he's got ?" asked my aunt.

"Seems a promising thing," I said.

"I suppose there is a business somewhere ?"

"Haven't you seen it ?"

"'Fraid I'd say something *at* it, George, if I did. So he won't let me. It came on quite suddenly. Brooding he was and writing letters and sizzling something awful—like a chestnut going to pop. Then he come home one day saying Tono-Bungay till I thought he was clean off his onion, and singing—what was it ?"

"' I'm afloat, I'm afloat,' " I guessed.

"The very thing. You've heard him. And saying our fortunes were made. Took me out to the Ho'born Restaurant, George—dinner, and we had champagne, stuff that blows up the back of your nose and makes you go *So*, and he said at last he'd got things worthy of me—and we moved here next day It's a swell house, George. Three pounds a week for the rooms. And he says the Business'll stand it."

She looked at me doubtfully.

"Either do that or smash," I said profoundly.

We discusssed the question for a moment mutely with our eyes. My aunt slapped the pile of books from Mudie's.

"I've been having such a Go of reading, George. You never did !"

"What do you think of the business ?" I asked.

"Well, they've let him have money," she said, and thought and raised her eyebrows.

"It's been a time, she went on. "The flapping about ! Me sidding doing nothing and him on the go like a rocket. He's done wonders. But he wants you, George—he wants you. Sometimes he's full of hope—talks of when we're going to have a carriage and be in society—makes it seem so natural and topsy-turvy, I hardly know whether my old heels aren't up here listening to him, and my old head on the floor. . . . Then he gets depressed. Says he wants restraint. Says he can make a splash but can't keep on. Says if you don't come in everything will smash—— But you *are* coming in ?"

She paused and looked at me.

" Well——"

" You don't say you won't come in."

" But look here, aunt," I said, "do you understand quite ? It's a quack medicine.   It's trash."

" There's no law against selling quack medicine that I know of," said my aunt.   She thought for a minute and became unusually grave.   " It's our only chance, George," she said. " If it doesn't go . . ."

There came the slamming of a door, and a loud bellowing from the next apartment through the folding doors.   " Here —er Shee *Rulk* lies *Poo* Tom Bo—oling."

" Silly old Concertina !   Hark at him, George ! "   She raised her voice.   " Don't sing that, you old Walrus you ! Sing 'I'm afloat !' "

One leaf of the folding doors opened and my uncle appeared.

" Hallo, George !   Come along at last ?   Gossome tea-cake, Susan ?

" Thought it over, George ? " he said abruptly.

" Yes," said I

" Coming in ? "

I paused for a last moment and nodded yes.

" Ah ! " he cried.   " Why couldn't you say that a week ago ? "

" I've had false ideas about the world," I said. . . .   " Oh ! they don't matter now !   Yes, I'll come, I'll take my chance with you, I won't hesitate again."

And I didn't.   I stuck to that resolution for seven long years.

CHAPTER THREE

HOW WE MADE TONO-BUNGAY HUM

§ 1

SO I made my peace with my uncle and we set out upon this bright enterprise of selling slightly injurious rubbish at one-and-three-halfpence and two-and-nine a bottle, including the Government stamp.   We made Tono-Bungay hum !   It brought us wealth, influence, respect, the con- fidence of endless people.   All that my uncle promised me proved truth and understatement ; Tono-Bungay carried me to freedoms and powers that no life of scientific research, no pas- sionate service of humanity could ever have given me. . . .

It was my uncle's genius that did it.   No doubt he needed me—I was, I will admit, his indispensable right hand ; but his was the brain to conceive.   He wrote every advertisement ; some of them even he sketched.   You must remember that those were the days before the *Times* took to enterprise and the vociferous hawking of that antiquated *Encyclopædia*.   That alluring, button-holing, let-me-just-tell-you-quite-soberly-something-you-ought-to-know style of newspaper advertisement, with every now and then a convulsive jump of some attractive phrase into capitals, was then almost a novelty. " Many people who are MODERATELY well think they are QUITE well," was one of his early efforts. The jerks in capitals were, " DO NOT NEED DRUGS OR MEDICINE," and " SIMPLY A PROPER REGIMEN TO GET YOU IN TONE." One was warned against the chemist or druggist who pushed " much advertised nostrums " on one's attention. That trash did more harm than good. The thing needed was regimen—and Tono-Bungay!

Very early, too, was that bright little quarter column, at least it was usually a quarter column, in the evening papers : " HILARITY—TONO-BUNGAY. Like Mountain Air in the Veins." The penetrating trio of questions : " Are you bored with your Business ? Are you bored with your Dinner ? Are you bored with your Wife ? "—that, too, was in our Gower Street days. Both these we had in our first campaign when we worked London south, central, and west ; and then, too, we had our first poster—the HEALTH, BEAUTY, AND STRENGTH one. That was his design ; I happen still to have got by me the first sketch he made for it. I have reproduced it here with one or two others to enable the reader to understand the mental quality that initiated these familiar ornaments of London. (The second one is about eighteen months later, the germ of the well-known " Fog " poster ; the third was designed for an influenza epidemic, but never issued.)

These things were only incidentally in my department. I had to polish them up for the artist and arrange the business of printing and distribution, and after my uncle had had a violent and needless quarrel with the advertisement manager of the *Daily Regulator* about the amount of display given to one of his happy thoughts, I also took up the negotiation of advertisements for the press.

We discussed and worked out distribution together— first in the drawing-room floor in Gower Street, with my aunt sometimes helping very shrewdly, and then, with a steadily improving type of cigar and older and older whisky, in his snuggery at their first house, the one in Beckenham. Often we worked far into the night—sometimes until dawn.

We really worked infernally hard, and, I recall, we worked with a very decided enthusiasm, not simply on my uncle's part, but mine. It was a game, an absurd but absurdly interesting game, and the points were scored in cases of bottles. People think a happy notion is enough to make a man rich, that fortunes can be made without toil. It's a dream, as every millionaire (except one or two lucky gamblers) can testify ; I doubt if J. D. Rockefeller in the early days of Standard Oil worked harder than we did. We worked far into the night—and we also worked all day. We

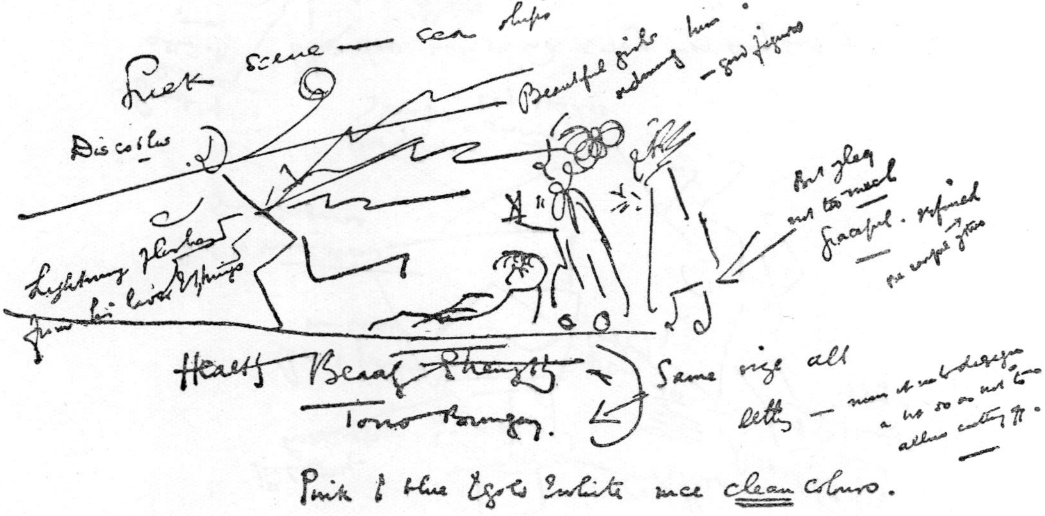

Same size all
Tono Bungay.
Pink & blue
nice clean colours.

Picture of David 15

Cap hair

Miserable figure scene

I think Fag.

Arms folded in chest.

Cap no. Casting 13

Yet so much Want Sunshine

Sunk eyes, sharp, 3mg = big strides

Stage of life Dont seem alike it

He does not mind a Fag. — in any sort of weather

Tone Amagay by day. Sitters hold his tight

Please asking for more.

The Happy Phagocyte

Do you know what a Phagocyte is?

(Large — Stomach in set about. Phagocytes needn't up mix). So that what two Bungay scalf is is a sort of Worster Sauce for the Phagocyte. It gives it an appetite. It makes it a perfect hog for the Influenza Bacillus.

made a rule to be always dropping in at the factory unannounced to keep things right—for at first we could afford no properly responsible underlings—and we travelled London, pretending to be our own representatives and making all sorts of special arrangements.

But none of this was my proper work, and as soon as we could get other men in, I dropped the travelling, though my uncle found it particularly interesting and kept it up for years. " Does me good, George, to see the chaps behind their counters like I was once," he explained. My special and distinctive duty was to give Tono-Bungay substance and an outward and visible bottle, to translate my uncle's great imaginings into the creation of case after case of labelled bottles of nonsense, and the punctual discharge of them by railway, road, and steamer towards their ultimate goal in the Great Stomach of the People. By all modern standards the business was, as my uncle would say, " absolutely *bona fide*." We sold our stuff and got the money, and spent the money honestly in lies and clamour to sell more stuff. Section by section we spread it over the whole of the British Isles ; first working the middle-class London suburbs, then the outer suburbs, then the home counties, then going (with new bills and a more pious style of " ad ") into Wales, a great field always for a new patent-medicine, and then into Lancashire. My uncle had in his inner office a big map of England, and as we took up fresh sections of the local press and our consignments invaded new areas, flags for advertisements and pink underlines for orders showed our progress.

" The romance of modern commerce, George ! " my uncle would say, rubbing his hands together and drawing in air through his teeth. " The romance of modern commerce, eh ? Conquest. Province by province. Like sogers."

We subjugated England and Wales ; we rolled over the Cheviots with a special adaptation containing eleven per cent. of absolute alcohol : " Tono-Bungay. Thistle Brand." We also had the Fog poster adapted to a kilted Briton in a misty Highland scene.

Under the shadow of our great leading line we were presently taking subsidiary specialities into action ; " Tono-Bungay Hair Stimulant " was our first supplement. Then came " Concentrated Tono-Bungay " for the eyes. That didn't go, but we had a considerable success with the Hair Stimulant. We broached the subject, I remember, in a little catechism beginning : " Why does the hair fall out ? Because the follicles are fagged. What are the follicles ? . . ." So it went on to the climax that the Hair Stimulant contained all " The essential principles of that most reviving tonic, Tono-Bungay, together with an emollient and nutritious oil derived from crude Neat's Foot Oil by a process of refinement, separation, and deodorisation. . . . It will be manifest to any one of scientific attainments that in Neat's Foot Oil derived from the hoofs and horns of beasts, we must necessarily have a *natural* skin and hair lubricant."

And we also did admirable things with our next subsidiaries, "Tono-Bungay Lozenges," and "Tono-Bungay Chocolate." These we urged upon the public for their extraordinary nutritive and recuperative value in cases of fatigue and strain. We gave them posters and illustrated advertisements showing climbers hanging from marvellously vertical cliffs, cyclist champions upon the track, mounted messengers engaged in Aix-to-Ghent rides, soldiers lying out in action under a hot sun. "You can GO for twenty-four hours," we declared, "on Tono-Bungay Chocolate." We didn't say whether you could return on the same commodity. We also showed a dreadfully barristerish barrister, wig, side-whiskers, teeth, a horribly life-like portrait of all existing barristers, talking at a table, and beneath, this legend : "A Four Hours' Speech on Tono-Bungay Lozenges, and as fresh as when he began." That brought in regiments of school-teachers, revivalist ministers, politicians and the like. I really do believe there was an element of "kick" in the strychnine in these lozenges, especially in those made according to our earlier formula. For we altered all our formulæ — invariably weakening them enormously as sales got ahead.

In a little while—so it seems to me now—we were employing travellers and opening up Great Britain at the rate of a hundred square miles a day. All the organisation throughout was sketched in a crude, entangled, half-inspired fashion by my uncle, and all of it had to be worked out into a practicable scheme of quantities and expenditure by me. We had a lot of trouble finding our travellers ; in the end at least half of them were Irish-Americans, a wonderful breed for selling medicine. We had still more trouble over our factory manager, because of the secrets of the inner room, and in the end we got a very capable woman, Mrs. Hampton Diggs, who had formerly managed a large millinery workroom, whom we could trust to keep everything in good working order without finding out anything that wasn't put exactly under her loyal and energetic nose. She conceived a high opinion of Tono-Bungay and took it in all forms and large quantities so long as I knew her. It didn't seem to do her any harm. And she kept the girls going quite wonderfully.

My uncle's last addition to the Tono-Bungay group was the Tono-Bungay Mouthwash. The reader has probably read a hundred times that inspiring inquiry of his, "You are Young Yet, but are you Sure Nothing has Aged your Gums ? "

And after that we took over the agency for three or four good American lines that worked in with our own, and could be handled with it : Texan Embrocation, and "23—to clear the system " were the chief. . . .

I set down these bare facts. To me they are all linked
with the figure of my uncle. In come of the old seventeenth
and early eighteenth-century prayer-books at Bladesover
there used to be illustrations with long scrolls coming out
of the mouths of the wood-cut figures. I wish I could write
all this last chapter on a scroll coming out of the head of my
uncle, show it all the time as unfolding and pouring out from
a short, fattening, small-legged man with stiff, cropped hair,
disobedient glasses on a perky little nose, and a round stare
behind them. I wish I could show you him breathing hard
and a little through his nose as his pen scrabbled out some
absurd inspiration for a poster or a picture page, and make
you hear his voice, charged with solemn import like the voice
of a squeaky prophet, saying " George ! list'n ! I got an
ideer. I got a notion, George ! "

I should put myself into the same picture. Best setting
for us, I think, would be the Beckenham snuggery, because
there we worked hardest. It would be the lamplit room
of the early 'nineties, and the clock upon the mantel would
indicate midnight or later. We would be sitting on either
side of the fire, I with a pipe, my uncle with cigar or cigarette.
There would be glasses standing inside the brass fender.
Our expressions would be very grave. My uncle used to sit
right back in his arm-chair ; his toes always turned in when
he was sitting down and his legs had a way of looking curved,
as though they hadn't bones or joints but were stuffed with
sawdust.

" George, whad'yer think of T.-B. for seasickness ? " he
would say.

" No good that I can imagine."

" Oom ! No harm *trying*, George. We can but try."

I would suck my pipe. " Hard to get at. Unless we sold
our stuff specially at the docks. Might do a special at Cook's
office, or in the Continental Bradshaw."

" It 'ud give 'em confidence, George."

He would Zzzz, with his glasses reflecting the red of the
glowing coals.

" No good hiding our light under a Bushel," he would
remark. . . .

I never really determined whether my uncle regarded
Tono-Bungay as a fraud, or whether he didn't come to believe
in it in a kind of way by the mere reiteration of his own
assertions. I think that his average attitude was one of
kindly, almost parental toleration. I remember saying on one
occasion, " But you don't suppose this stuff ever did a human
being the slightest good at all ? " and how his face assumed a
look of protest, as one of reproving harshness and dogmatism.

" You've a hard nature, George," he said. " You're too
ready to run things down. How can one *tell* ? How can one
venture to *tell* ? . . ."

I suppose any creative and developing game would have interested me in those years. At any rate, I know I put as much zeal into this Tono-Bungay as any young lieutenant could have done who suddenly found himself in command of a ship. It was extraordinarily interesting to me to figure out the advantage accruing from this shortening of the process or that, and to weigh it against the capital cost of the alteration. I made a sort of machine for sticking on the labels, that I patented ; to this day there is a little trickle of royalties to me from that. I also contrived to have our mixture made concentrated, got the bottles, which all came sliding down a guarded slant-way, nearly filled with distilled water at one tap, and dripped our magic ingredients in at the next. This was an immense economy of space for the inner sanctum. For the bottling we needed special taps, and these, too, I invented and patented.

We had a sort of endless band of bottles sliding along an inclined glass trough made slippery with running water. At one end a girl held them up to the light, put aside any that were imperfect and placed the others in the trough, the filling was automatic ; at the other end a girl slipped in the cork and drove it home with a little mallet. Each tank, the little one for the vivifying ingredients and the big one for distilled water, had a level indicator, and inside I had a float arrangement that stopped the slide whenever either had sunk too low. Another girl stood ready with my machine to label the corked bottles and hand them to the three packers, who slipped them into their outer papers and put them, with a pad of corrugated paper between each pair, into a little groove from which they could be made to slide neatly into position in our standard packing-case. It sounds wild, I know, but I believe I was the first man in the city of London to pack patent medicines through the side of the packing-case, to discover there was a better way in than by the lid. Our cases packed themselves, practically ; had only to be put into position on a little wheeled tray and when full pulled to the lift that dropped them to the men downstairs, who padded up the free space and nailed on top and side. Our girls, more-over, packed with corrugated paper and matchbox-wood box partitions when everybody else was using expensive young men to pack through the top of the box with straw, many breakages and much waste and confusion.

§ 2

As I look back at them now, these energetic years seem all compacted to a year or so ; from the days of our first hazardous beginning in Farringdon Street with barely a thousand pounds' worth of stuff or credit all told—and that got by something perilously like snatching—to the days when my uncle went to the public on behalf of himself and

me (one-tenth share) and our silent partners, the drug whole-
salers and the printing people and the owner of that group
of magazines and newspapers, to ask with honest confidence
for £150,000. Those silent partners were remarkably sorry,
I know, that they had not taken larger shares and given
us longer credit when the subscriptions came pouring in.
My uncle had a clear half to play with (including the one-tenth
understood to be mine).

£150,000—think of it !—for the goodwill in a string of
lies and a trade in bottles of mitigated water ! Do you realise
the madness of the world that sanctions such a thing ? Perhaps
you don't. At times use and wont certainly blinded me. If
it had not been for Ewart, I don't think I should have had
an inkling of the wonderfulness of this development of my
fortunes ; I should have grown accustomed to it, fallen in
with all its delusions as completely as my uncle presently
did. He was immensely proud of the flotation. " They've
never been given such value," he said, " for a dozen years."
But Ewart, with his gesticulating hairy hands and bony
wrists, is single-handed chorus to all this as it plays itself
over again in my memory, and he kept my fundamental
absurdity illuminated for me during all this astonishing time.

" It's just on all-fours with the rest of things," he remarked ;
" only more so. You needn't think you're anything out of
the way."

I remember one disquisition very distinctly. It was just
after Ewart had been to Paris on a mysterious expedition to
" rough in " some work for a rising American sculptor. This
young man had a commission for an allegorical figure of
Truth (draped, of course) for his State Capitol, and he needed
help. Ewart had returned with his hair cut *en brosse* and
with his costume completely translated into French. He
wore, I remember, a bicycling suit of purplish-brown, baggy
beyond imagining—the only creditable thing about it was
that it had evidently not been made for him—a voluminous
black tie, a decadent soft felt hat and several French expletives
of a sinister description. " Silly clothes, aren't they ? " he
said at the sight of my startled eye. " I don't know why I
got 'm. They seemed all right over there." He had come
down to our Raggett Street place to discuss a benevolent
project of mine for a poster by him, and he scattered remarkable discourse over the heads (I hope it was over the heads) of
our bottlers.

" What I like about it all, Ponderevo, is its poetry. . . .
That's where we get the pull of the animals. No animal
would ever run a factory like this. Think ! . . . One remembers the Beaver, of course. He might very possibly
bottle things, but would he stick a label round 'em and sell
'em ? The Beaver is a dreamy fool I'll admit, him and his
dams, but, after all, there's a sort of protection about 'em, a

kind of muddy practicality ! They prevent things getting at
him. And it's not your poetry only. It's the poetry of the
customer, too. Poet answering to poet—soul to soul. Health,
Strength, and Beauty—in a bottle—the magic philtre ! Like
a fairy tale. . . .

"Think of the people to whom your bottles of footle go !
(I'm calling it footle, Ponderevo, out of praise," he said in
parenthesis.)

"Think of the little clerks and jaded women and overworked people. People overstrained with wanting to do,
people overstrained with wanting to be. . . . People, in fact,
overstrained. . . . The real trouble of life, Ponderevo, isn't
that we exist—that's a vulgar error ; the real trouble is
that we *don't* really exist and we want to. That's what this
—in the highest sense—muck stands for ! The hunger to be
—for once—really alive—to the finger-tips ! . . .

"Nobody wants to do and be the things people are—
nobody. *You* don't want to preside over this—this bottling,
I don't want to wear these beastly clothes and be led about
by you, nobody wants to keep on sticking labels on silly
bottles at so many farthings a gross. That isn't existing !
That's—sus—*substratum.* None of us want to be what we
are, or to do what we do. Except as a sort of basis. What
do we want ? *You* know. *I* know. Nobody confesses.
What we all want to be is something perpetually young and
beautiful—young Joves—young Joves, Ponderevo "—his
voice became loud, harsh, and declamatory—" pursuing coy
half-willing nymphs through everlasting forests . . ."

There was a just-perceptible listening hang in the work
about us.

"Come downstairs," I interrupted, " we can talk better
there."

" I can talk better here," he answered.

He was just going on, but fortunately the implacable face
of Mrs. Hampton Diggs appeared down the aisle of bottling
machines.

" All right," he said, " I'll come. . ."

In the little sanctum below, my uncle was taking a digestive
pause after his lunch and by no means alert. His presence
sent Ewart back to the theme of modern commerce, over
the excellent cigar my uncle gave him. He behaved with the
elaborate deference due to a business magnate from an
unknown man.

" What I was pointing out to your nephew, sir," said
Ewart, putting both elbows on the table, " was the poetry
of commerce. He doesn't, you know, seem to see it at all."

My uncle nodded brightly. " Whad I tell 'im," he said
round his cigar.

" You are artists. You and I, sir, can talk, if you will
permit me, as one artist to another. It's advertisement has

—done it. Advertisement has revolutionised trade and industry ; it is going to revolutionise the world. The old merchant used to tote about commodities ; the new one creates values. Doesn't need to tote. He takes something that isn't worth anything—or something that isn't particularly worth anything, and he makes it worth something. He takes mustard that is just like anybody else's mustard, and he goes about saying, shouting, singing, chalking on walls, writing inside people's books, putting it everywhere, " Smith's Mustard is the Best." And behold it *is* the Best ! "

" True," said my uncle, chubbily and with a dreamy sense of mysticism ; " true ! "

" It's just like an artist ; he takes a lump of white marble on the verge of a limekiln, he chips it about, he makes—he makes a monument to himself—and others—a monument the world will not willingly let die. Talking of mustard, sir, I was at Clapham Junction the other day, and all the banks are overgrown with horseradish that's got loose from a garden somewhere. You know what horseradish is—grows like wildfire—spreads—spreads. I stood at the end of the platform looking at the stuff and thinking about it. ' Like fame,' I thought, ' Rank and wild where it isn't wanted. Why don't the really good things in life grow like horseradish ? ' I thought. My mind went off in a peculiar way it does from that to the idea that mustard costs a penny a tin—I bought some the other day for a ham I had. It came into my head that it would be ripping good business to use horseradish to adulterate mustard. I had a sort of idea that I could plunge into business on that, get rich and come back to my own proper monumental art again. And then I said. ' But *why* adulterate ? I don't like the idea of adulteration.' "

" Shabby," said my uncle, nodding his head. " Bound to get found out ! "

" And totally unnecessary too ! Why not do up a mixture —three-quarters pounded horseradish and a quarter mustard —give it a fancy name—and sell it at twice the mustard price. See ? I very nearly started the business straight away, only something happened. My train came along."

" Jolly good ideer," said my uncle. He looked at me. " That really *is* an ideer, George," he said.

" Take shavin's, again ! You know that poem of Longfellow's, sir, that sounds exactly like the first declension. What is it ?—' man's a maker men say ! ' "

My uncle nodded and gurgled some quotation that died away.

" Jolly good poem, George," he said in an aside to me.

" Well, it's about a carpenter and a poetic Victorian child, you know, and some shavin's. The child made no end out of the shavin's. So might you. Powder 'em. They might be anything. Soak 'em in jipper—Xylo-tobacco ! Powder 'em and get a little tar and turpentinous smell in—wood-

packing for hot baths—a Certain Cure for the scourge of
Influenza! There's all these patent grain foods—what
Americans call cereals. I believe I'm right, sir, in saying
they're sawdust."

"No!" said my uncle, removing his cigar; "as far as I can find
out it's really grain—spoilt grain. . . . I've been going into that."

"Well, there you are!" said Ewart. "Say it's spoilt
grain. It carries out my case just as well. Your modern
commerce is no more buying and selling than—sculpture.
It's mercy—it's salvation. It's rescue work! It takes all
sorts of fallen commodities by the hand and raises them.
Cana isn't in it. You turn water—into Tono-Bungay."

"Tono-Bungay's all right," said my uncle, suddenly grave.
"We aren't talking of Tono-Bungay."

"Your nephew, sir, is hard; he wants everything to go to
a sort of predestinated end; he's a Calvinist of Commerce.
Offer him a dust-bin full of stuff; he calls it refuse—passes
by on the other side. Now, *you*, sir—you'd make cinders
respect themselves."

My uncle regarded him dubiously for a moment. But there
was a touch of appreciation in his eye.

"Might make 'em into a sort of sanitary brick," he reflected
over his cigar end.

"Or a friable biscuit. Why *not*? You might advertise:
'Why are Birds so Bright? Because they digest their food
perfectly! Why do they digest their food so perfectly?
Because they have a gizzard! Why hasn't man a gizzard?
Because he can buy Ponderevo's Ashpit Triturating Friable
Biscuit—Which is Better.' "

He delivered the last words in a shout, with his hairy hand
flourished in the air. . . .

"Damn clever fellow," said my uncle, after he'd gone.
"I know a man when I see one. He'll do. Bit drunk, I
should say. But that only makes some chaps brighter. If
he *wants* to do that poster, he can. Zzzz. That ideer of his
about the horseradish. There's something in that, George.
I'm going to think over that. . . ."

I may say at once that my poster project came to nothing
in the end, though Ewart devoted an interesting week to the
matter. He let his unfortunate disposition to irony run
away with him. He produced a picture of two Beavers with
a subtle likeness, he said, to myself and my uncle—the likeness
to my uncle certainly wasn't half bad—and they were bottling
rows and rows of Tono-Bungay, with the legend "Modern
Commerce." It certainly wouldn't have sold a case, though
he urged it on me one cheerful evening on the ground that
it would "arouse curiosity." In addition, he produced a
quite shocking study of my uncle, excessively and needlessly
nude but, so far as I was able to judge, an admirable likeness,
engaged in feats of strength of a Gargantuan type before

an audience of deboshed and shattered ladies. The legend,
" Health, Beauty, Strength " below, gave a needed point to
his parody. This he hung up in the studio over the oil shop,
with a flap of brown paper by way of a curtain over it to
accentuate its libellous offence.

CHAPTER FOUR

MARION

§ I

AS I look back on those days in which we built up the
great Tono-Bungay property out of human hope and
a credit for bottles and rent and printing, I see my
life, as it were, arranged in two parallel columns of unequal
width, a wider, more diffused, eventful, and various one which
continually broadens out, the business side of my life, and a
narrow, darker and darkling one shot ever and again with a
gleam of happiness, my home life with Marion. For of course
I married Marion.

I didn't, as a matter of fact, marry her until a year after
Tono-Bungay was thoroughly afloat, and then only after
conflicts and discussions of a quite strenuous sort. By that
time I was twenty-four. It seems the next thing to childhood
now. We were both in certain directions unusually ignorant
and simple ; we were temperamentally antagonistic, and
we hadn't—I don't think we were capable of—an idea in
common. She was young and extraordinarily conventional
—she seemed never to have an idea of her own but always
the idea of her class—and I was young and sceptical, enterprising and passionate ; the two links that held us together
were the intense appeal her physical beauty had for me, and
her appreciation of her importance in my thoughts. There can
be no doubt of my passion for her. In her I had discovered
woman desired. The nights I have lain awake on account of
her, writhing, biting my wrists in a fever of longing ! . . .

I have told how I got myself a silk hat and black coat to
please her on Sunday—to the derision of some of my fellow-
students who chanced to meet me—and how we became
engaged. But that was only the beginning of our differences.
To her that meant the beginning of a not unpleasant little
secrecy, an occasional use of verbal endearments, perhaps
even kisses. It was something to go on indefinitely, inter-
fering in no way with her gossiping spells of work at Smithie's.
To me it was a pledge to come together into the utmost
intimacy of soul and body so soon as we could contrive it. . . .

I don't know if it will strike the reader that I am setting
out to discuss the queer unwise love relationship and my

bungle of a marriage with excessive solemnity. But to me it seems to reach out to vastly wider issues than our little personal affair. I've thought over my life. In these last few years I've tried to get at least a little wisdom out of it. And in particular I've thought over this part of my life. I'm enormously impressed by the ignorant, unguided way in which we two entangled ourselves with each other. It seems to me the queerest thing in all this network of misunderstandings and misstatements and faulty and ramshackle conventions which make up our social order as the individual meets it, that we should have come together so accidentally and so blindly. Because we were no more than samples of the common fate. Love is not only the cardinal fact in the individual life, but the most important concern of the community ; after all, the way in which the young people of this generation pair off determines the fate of the nation ; all the other affairs of the State are subsidiary to that. And we leave it to flushed and blundering youth to stumble on its own significance, with nothing to guide it but shocked looks and sentimental twaddle and base whisperings and cant-smeared examples.

I have tried to indicate something of my own sexual development in the preceding chapter. Nobody was ever frank and decent with me in this relation, nobody, no book, ever came and said to me thus and thus is the world made and so-and-so is necessary. Everything came obscurely, indefinitely, perplexingly ; and all I knew of law or convention in the matter had the form of threatenings and prohibitions. Except through the furtive, shameful talk of my coevals at Goudhurst and Wimblehurst, I was not even warned against quite horrible dangers. My ideas were made partly of instinct, partly of a romantic imagination, partly woven out of a medley of scraps of suggestion that came to me haphazard. I had read widely and confusedly : *Vathek*, Shelley, Tom Paine, Plutarch, Carlyle, Hæckel, William Morris, the Bible, the *Free-thinker*, the *Clarion*, *The Woman Who Did*—I mention the ingredients that come first to mind. All sorts of ideas were jumbled up in me and never a lucid explanation. But it was evident to me that the world regarded Shelley, for example, as a very heroic as well as beautiful person ; and that to defy convention and succumb magnificently to passion was the proper thing to do to gain the respect and affection of all decent people.

And the make-up of Marion's mind in the matter was an equally irrational affair. Her training had been one not simply of silences, but suppressions. An enormous force of suggestion had so shaped her that the intense natural fastidiousness of girlhood had developed into an absolute perversion of instinct. For all that is cardinal in this essential business of life she had one inseparable epithet—" horrid."

Without any such training she would have been a shy lover,
but now she was an impossible one. For the rest she had
derived, I suppose, partly from the sort of fiction she got
from the Public Library, and partly from the workroom talk
at Smithie's. So far as the former origin went, she had an
idea of love as a state of worship and service on the part of
the man and of condescension on the part of the woman.
There was nothing " horrid " about it in any fiction she had
read. The man gave presents, did services, sought to be in
every way delightful. The woman "went out" with him,
smiled at him, was kissed by him in decorous secrecy, and if
he chanced to offend, denied her countenance and presence.
Usually she did something "for his good" to him, made him
go to church, made him give up smoking or gambling,
smartened him up. Quite at the end of the story came a
marriage, and after that the interest ceased.

That was the tenor of Marion's fiction ; but I think the
work-table conversation at Smithie's did something to modify
that. At Smithie's it was recognised, I think, that a " fellow "
was a possession to be desired ; that it was better to be
engaged to a fellow than not ; that fellows had to be kept—
they might be mislaid, they might even be stolen. There was
a case of stealing at Smithie's, and many tears.

Smithie I met before we were married, and afterwards she
became a frequent visitor to our house at Ealing. She was
a thin, bright-eyed, hawk-nosed girl of thirty-odd, with
prominent teeth, a high-pitched, eager voice, and a disposition
to be urgently smart in her dress. Her hats were startling
and various but invariably disconcerting, and she talked
in a rapid, nervous flow that was hilarious rather than witty,
and broken by little screams of " Oh, my *dear* ! " and " You
never did ! " She was the first woman I ever met who used
scent. Poor old Smithie ! What a harmless, kindly soul
she really was, and how heartily I detested her ! Out of the
profits on the Persian robes she supported a sister's family of
three children, she " helped " a worthless brother and overflowed in help even to her work-girls, but that didn't weigh with
me in those youthfully-narrow times. It was one of the intense
minor irritations of my married life that Smithie's whirlwind
chatter seemed to me to have far more influence with Marion
than anything I had to say. Before all things I coveted her
grip upon Marion's inaccessible mind.

In the workroom at Smithie's, I gathered, they always spoke
of me demurely as "A Certain Person." I was rumoured to be
dreadfully " clever," and there were doubts—not altogether
without justification—of the sweetness of my temper.

§ 2

Well, these general explanations will enable the reader to
understand the distressful times we two had together when

presently I began to feel on a footing with Marion and to
fumble conversationally for the mind and the wonderful
passion I felt, obstinately and stupidly, must be in her.   I think
she thought me the maddest of sane men ; " clever," in fact,
which at Smithie's was, I suppose, the next thing to insanity, a
word intimating incomprehensible and incalculable motives. . . .

She could be shocked at anything, she misunderstood
everything, and her weapon was a sulky silence that knitted
her brows, spoiled her mouth and robbed her face of beauty.
" Well, if we can't agree, I don't see why we should go on
talking," she used to say.   That would always enrage me
beyond measure.   Or, " I'm afraid I'm not clever enough to
understand that."

Silly little people !   I see it all now, but then I was no
older than she and I couldn't see anything but that Marion,
for some inexplicable reason, wouldn't come alive.

We would contrive semi-surreptitious walks on Sunday,
and part speechless with the anger of indefinable offences.
Poor Marion !   The things I tried to put before her, my
fermenting ideas about theology, about Socialism, about
æsthetics—the very words appalled her, gave her the faint
chill of approaching impropriety, the terror of a very present
intellectual impossibility.   Then by an enormous effort
I would suppress myself for a time and continue a talk that
made her happy, about Smithie's brother, about the new
girl who had come to the workroom, about the house we
would presently live in.   But there we differed a little.   I
wanted to be accessible to St. Paul's or Cannon Street Station,
and she had set her mind quite resolutely upon Ealing. . . .
It wasn't by any means quarrelling all the time, you understand.   She liked me to play the lover " nicely " ; she liked
the effect of going about—we had lunches, we went to Earl's
Court, to Kew, to theatres and concerts, but not often to
concerts because, though Marion " liked " music, she didn't
like " too much of it," to picture shows—and there was a
nonsensical sort of baby-talk I picked up—I forget where
now—that became a mighty peacemaker.

Her worst offence for me was an occasional excursion into
the Smithie style of dressing, debased West Kensington.   For
she had no sense at all of her own beauty.   She had no comprehension whatever of beauty of the body, and she could
slash her beautiful lines to rags with hat-brims and trimmings.
Thank Heaven a natural refinement, a natural timidity and
her extremely slender purse kept her from the real Smithie
efflorescence !   Poor, simple, beautiful, kindly, limited
Marion !   Now that I am forty-five, I can look back at her
with all my old admiration and none of my old bitterness,
with a new affection and not a scrap of passion, and take her
part against the equally stupid, drivingly-energetic, sensuous,
intellectual sprawl I used to be.   I was a young beast for her

to have married—a young beast. With her it was my business to understand and control—and I exacted fellowship,
passion. . . .

We became engaged, as I have told ; we broke it off and
joined again. We went through a succession of such phases.
We had no sort of idea what was wrong with us. Presently
we were formally engaged. I had a wonderful interview
with her father in which he was stupendously grave and
h-less, wanted to know about my origins and was tolerant
(exasperatingly tolerant) because my mother was a servant,
and afterwards her mother took to kissing me and I bought
a ring. But the speechless aunt, I gathered, didn't approve
—having doubts of my religiosity. Whenever we were
estranged we could keep apart for days ; and to begin with,
every such separation was a relief. And then I would want
her ; a restless longing would come upon me. I would think
of the flow of her arms, of the soft, gracious bend of her body.
I would lie awake or dream of a transfigured Marion of light
and fire. It was indeed Dame Nature driving me on to
womankind in her stupid, inexorable way ; but I thought it
was the need of Marion that troubled me. So I always went
back to Marion at last and made it up and more or less conceded or ignored whatever thing had parted us, and more and
more I urged her to marry me. . . .

In the long run that became a fixed idea. It entangled my
will and my pride, I told myself I was not going to be beaten.
I hardened to the business. I think, as a matter of fact, my
real passion for Marion had waned enormously long before we
were married, that she had lived it down by sheer irresponsive-
ness. When I felt sure of my three hundred a year she stipulated for delay, twelve months' delay, "to see how things
would turn out." There were times when she seemed simply
an antagonist holding out irritatingly against something I had
to settle. Moreover, I began to be greatly distracted by the
interest and excitement of Tono-Bungay's success, by the
change and movement in things, the going to and fro. I would
forget her for days together, and then desire her with an irritating intensity. At last, one Saturday afternoon, after a brooding morning, I determined almost savagely that these delays
must end.

I went off to the little home at Walham Green, and made
Marion come with me to Putney Common. Marion wasn't at
home when I got there, and I had to fret for a time and talk to
her father, who was just back from his office, he explained, and
enjoying himself in his own way in the greenhouse.

"I'm going to ask your daughter to marry me," I said.
"I think we've been waiting long enough."

"I don't approve of long engagements either," said her
father. "But Marion will have her own way about it anyhow.
Seen this new powdered fertiliser ? "

I went in to talk to Mrs. Ramboat. " She'll want time to get her things," said Mrs. Ramboat. . . .

I and Marion sat down together on a little seat under some trees at the top of Putney Hill, and I came to my point abruptly.

" Look here, Marion," I said, " are you going to marry me or are you not ? "

She smiled at me. " Well," she said, " we're engaged—aren't we ? "

" That can't go on for ever. Will you marry me next week ? "

She looked me in the face. " We can't," she said.

" You promised to marry me when I had three hundred a year."

She was silent for a space. " Can't we go on for a time as we are ? We *could* marry on three hundred a year. But it means a very little house. There's Smithie's brother. They manage on two hundred and fifty, but that's very little. She says they have a semi-detached house almost on the road, and hardly a bit of garden. And the wall to next-door is so thin, they hear everything. When her baby cries—they rap. And people stand against the railings and talk. . . . Can't we wait ? You're doing so well."

An extraordinary bitterness possessed me at this invasion of the stupendous, beautiful business of love by sordid necessity. I answered her with immense restraint.

" If," I said, " we could have a double-fronted, detached house—at Ealing, say—with a square patch of lawn in front and a garden behind—and—and a tiled bathroom."

" That would be sixty pounds a year at least."

" Which means five hundred a year. . . . Yes, well, you see, I told my uncle I wanted that, and I've got it."

" Got what ? "

" Five hundred pounds a year."

" Five hundred pounds ! "

I burst into laughter that had more than a taste of bitterness.

" Yes," I said, " really ! and *now* what do you think ? "

" Yes," she said, a little flushed ; " but be sensible ! Do you really mean you've got a Rise, all at once, of two hundred a year ? "

" To marry on—yes."

She scrutinised me a moment. " You've done this as a surprise ! " she said, and laughed at my laughter. She had become radiant, and that made me radiant too.

" Yes," I said, " yes," and laughed no longer bitterly. She clasped her hands and looked me in the eyes.

She was so pleased that I forgot absolutely my disgust of a moment before. I forgot that she had raised her price two hundred pounds a year and that I had bought her at that.

" Come ! " I said, standing up ; " let's go towards the sun-

set, dear, and talk about it all.   Do you know—this is a most
beautiful world, an amazingly beautiful world, and when the
sunset falls upon you it makes you into shining gold.   No,
not gold—into golden glass. . . .   Into something better than
either glass or gold." . . .

And for all that evening I wooed her and kept her glad.
She made me repeat my assurances over again and still
doubted a little.

We furnished that double-fronted house from attic—it ran
to an attic—to cellar, and created a garden.

"Do you know Pampas Grass?" said Marion.   "I love
Pampas Grass . . . if there is room."

"You shall have Pampas Grass," I declared.

And there were moments as we went in imagination about
that house together, when my whole being cried out to take her
in my arms—now.   But I refrained.   On that aspect of life
I touched very lightly in that talk, very lightly, because I had
had my lesson.

She promised to marry me within two months' time.
Shyly, reluctantly, she named a day, and next afternoon, in
heat and wrath, we "broke it off" again for the last time.
We split upon procedure.   I refused flatly to have a normal
wedding with wedding cake, white favours, carriages and the
rest of it.   It dawned upon me suddenly in conversation with
her and her mother, that this was implied.   I blurted out my
objection forthwith, and this time it wasn't any ordinary
difference of opinion ; it was a "row."   I don't remember a
quarter of the things we flung out in that dispute.   I remember
her mother reiterating in tones of gentle remonstrance : "But,
George dear, you *must* have a cake—to send round."   I think
we all reiterated things.   I seem to remember a refrain of my
own : "A marriage is too sacred a thing, too private a thing,
for this display."   Her father came in and stood behind me
against the wall, and her aunt appeared beside the sideboard
and stood with folded arms, looking from speaker to speaker,
a sternly gratified prophetess.   It didn't occur to me then how
painful it was to Marion for these people to witness my rebellion.

"But, George," said her father, "what sort of marriage do
you want ?   You don't want to go to one of those there
registary offices ? "

"That's exactly what I'd like to do.   Marriage is too private
a thing——"

"I shouldn't feel married," said Mrs. Ramboat.

"Look here, Marion," I said ; "we are going to be married
at a registry office.   I don't believe in all these—fripperies and
superstitions, and I won't submit to them.   I've agreed to all
sorts of things to please you."

"What's he agreed to ? " said her father—unheeded.

"I can't marry at a registry office," said Marion, sallow-white.

"Very well," I said.   "I'll marry nowhere else."

"I can't marry at a registry office."

"Very well," I said, standing up, white and tense ; and it amazed me, but I was also exultant ; "then we won't marry at all."

She leant forward over the table, staring blankly at nothing.

"I don't think we'd better," she said in a low tone ; "if it's to be like this."

"It's for you to choose," I said. I stood for a moment watching the cloud of sulky offence that veiled her beauty.

"It's for you to choose," I repeated ; and regardless of the others, walked to the door, slammed it behind me, and so went out of the house.

"That's over," I said to myself in the road, and was full of a desolating sense of relief. . . .

But presently her half-averted face began to haunt me as she had sat at the table, and her arm and the long droop of her shoulder.

§ 3

The next day I did an unexampled thing. I sent a telegram to my uncle, "*Bad temper not coming to business*," and set off for Highgate and Ewart. He was actually at work—on a bust of Millie, and seemed very glad for any interruption.

"Ewart, you old Fool," I said, "knock off and come for a day's gossip. I'm rotten. There's a sympathetic sort of lunacy about you. Let's go to Staines and paddle up to Windsor."

"Girl ? " said Ewart, putting down a chisel.

"Yes."

That was all I told him of my affair.

"I've got no money," he remarked, to clear up any ambiguity in my invitation.

We got a jar of shandy-gaff, some food, and, on Ewart's suggestion, two Japanese sunshades in Staines ; we demanded extra cushions at the boathouse and we spent an enormously soothing day in discourse and meditation, our boat moored in a shady place this side of Windsor. I seem to remember Ewart with a cushion forward, only his heels and sunshade and some black ends of hair showing, a voice and no more, against the shining, smoothly-streaming mirror of the trees and bushes.

"It's not worth it," was the burthen of the voice.

"You'd better get yourself a Millie, Ponderevo, and then you wouldn't feel so upset."

"No," I said decidedly, "that's not my way." . . .

A thread of smoke ascended from Ewart for a while, like smoke from an altar. . . .

"Everything's a muddle, and you think it isn't. Nobody knows where we are—because, as a matter of fact, we aren't anywhere. Are women property—or are they fellow-creatures ? Or a sort of proprietary goddesses ? They're so obviously fellow-creatures. You believe in the goddess ? "

" No," I said, " that's not my idea."

" What is your idea ? "

" Well——"

" H'm," said Ewart, in my pause.

" My idea," I said, " is to meet one person who will belong to me—to whom I shall belong—body and soul. No half-gods ! Wait till she comes. If she comes at all. . . . We must come to each other young and pure."

" There's no such thing as a pure person or an impure person. . . . Mixed to begin with."

This was so manifestly true that it silenced me altogether.

" And if you belong to her and she to you, Ponderevo—which end's the head ? "

I made no answer except an impatient " Oh ! "

For a time we smoked in silence. . . .

" Did I tell you, Ponderevo, of a wonderful discovery I've made ? " Ewart began presently.

" No," I said, " what is it ? "

" There's no Mrs. Grundy."

" No ? "

" No ! Practically not. I've just thought all that business out. She's merely an instrument, Ponderevo. She's borne the blame. Grundy's a man. Grundy unmasked. Rather lean and out of sorts. Early middle age. With bunchy black whiskers and a worried eye. Been good so far, and it's fretting him ! Moods ! . . . There's Grundy in a state of sexual panic, for example—' For God's sake cover it up ! They get together—they get together ! It's too exciting ! The most dreadful things are happening ! ' Rushing about—long arms going like a windmill. ' They must be kept apart ! ' Starts out for an absolute obliteration of everything—absolute separations. One side of the road for men, and the other for women, and a hoarding—without posters—between them. Every boy and girl to be sewn up in a sack and sealed, just the head and hands and feet out until twenty-one. Music abolished, calico garments for the lower animals ! Sparrows to be suppressed—ab-so-lutely."

I laughed abruptly.

" Well, that's Mr. Grundy in one mood—and it puts Mrs. Grundy—— She's a much maligned person, Ponderevo—a rake at heart—and it puts her in a most painful state of fluster—most painful ! She's an amenable creature. When Grundy tells her things are shocking, she's shocked—pink and breathless. She goes about trying to conceal her profound sense of guilt behind a haughty expression. . . .

" Grundy meanwhile is in a state of complete whirlabout. Long, lean, knuckly hands pointing and gesticulating ! ' They're still thinking of things—thinking of things ! It's dreadful ! They get it out of books. I can't imagine where they get it ! I must watch ! There're people over there

whispering ! Nobody ought to whisper ! There's something
suggestive in the mere act ! Then, pictures ! In the museums
—things too dreadful for words. Why can't we have pure
art—with the anatomy all wrong and pure and nice—and pure
fiction, pure poetry, instead of all this stuff with allusions—
allusions ? . . . Excuse me ! There's something up behind
that locked door ! The keyhole ! In the interests of public
morality—yes, Sir, as a pure good man—I insist—*I'll* look—
it won't hurt me—I insist on looking—my duty—M,m,m—
the keyhole ! ' "

He kicked his legs about extravagantly, and I laughed again.
"That's Grundy in one mood, Ponderevo. It isn't Mrs.
Grundy. That's one of the lies we tell about women. They're
too simple. Simple ! Women *are* simple ! They take on
just what men tell 'em. . ."

Ewart meditated for a space. "Just exactly as it's put to
them," he said, and resumed the moods of Mr. Grundy.

"Then you get old Grundy in another mood. Ever caught
him nosing, Ponderevo ? Mad with the idea of mysterious,
unknown, wicked, delicious things. Things that aren't
respectable. Wow ! Things he mustn't do ! . . . Any one
who knows about these things, knows there's just as much
mystery and deliciousness about Grundy's forbidden things
as there is about eating ham. Jolly nice if it's a bright
morning and you're well and hungry and having breakfast in
the open air. Jolly unattractive if you're off colour. But
Grundy's covered it all up and hidden it and put mucky
shades and covers over it until he's forgotten it. Begins to
fester round it in his mind. Has dreadful struggles with
himself about impure thoughts. . . . Then you get Grundy
with hot ears—curious in undertones. Grundy on the loose,
Grundy in a hoarse whisper and with furtive eyes and convulsive movements—making things indecent. Evolving—in
dense vapours—indecency !

"Grundy sins. Oh yes, he's a hypocrite. Sneaks round
a corner and sins ugly. It's Grundy and his dark corners
that make vice, vice ! We artists—we have no vices. And
then he's frantic with repentance. And wants to be cruel to
fallen women and decent harmless sculptors of the simple
nude—like me—and so back to his panic again."

"Mrs. Grundy, I suppose, doesn't know he sins," I remarked.

"No ? I'm not so sure. . . . But, bless her heart ! she's
a woman. . . . She's a woman.

"Then again you get Grundy with a large greasy smile—
like an accident to a butter tub—all over his face, being Liberal
Minded—Grundy in his Anti-Puritan moments, ' trying not to
see Harm in it '—Grundy the friend of innocent pleasure. He
makes you sick with the Harm he's trying not to see in it. . . .

"And that's why everything's wrong, Ponderevo. Grundy,
damn him ! stands in the light, and we young people can't see.

His moods affect us. We catch his gusts of panic, his disease
of nosing, his greasiness. We don't know what we may think,
what we may say. He does his silly utmost to prevent our
reading and seeing the one thing, the one sort of discussion
we find—quite naturally and properly—supremely interesting. So we don't adolesce ; we blunder up to sex. Dare—
dare to look—and he may dirt you for ever ! The girls are
terror-stricken to silence by his significant whiskers, by the
bleary something in his eyes."

Suddenly Ewart, with an almost Jack-in-the-box effect,
sat up.

"He's about us everywhere, Ponderevo," he said very
solemnly. "Sometimes—sometimes I think he is—in our
blood. In *mine*."

He regarded me for my opinion very earnestly, with his
pipe in the corner of his mouth.

"You're the remotest cousin he ever had," I said. . . .

I reflected. "Look here, Ewart," I asked, "how would
you have things different ? "

He wrinkled up his queer face, regarded the water, and
made his pipe gurgle for a space, thinking deeply.

"There are complications, I admit. We've grown up under
the terror of Grundy and that innocent—but docile and—yes—
formidable lady, his wife. I don't know how far the complications aren't a disease, a sort of bleaching under the Grundy
shadow. . . . It is possible there are things I have still to
learn about women. . . . Man has eaten of the Tree of Knowledge. His innocence is gone. You can't have your cake and
eat it. We're in for knowledge ; let's have it plain and
straight. I should begin, I think, by abolishing the ideas of
decency and indecency. . . ."

"Grundy would have fits ! " I injected.

"Grundy, Ponderevo, would have cold douches—publicly
—if the sight was not too painful—three times a day. . .
But I don't think, mind you, that I should let the sexes run
about together. No. The fact behind the sexes—is sex.
It's no good humbugging. It trails about—even in the best
mixed company. Tugs at your ankle. The men get showing
off and quarrelling—and the women. Or they're bored. I
suppose the ancestral males have competed for the ancestral
females ever since they were both some sort of grubby little
reptile. You aren't going to alter that in a thousand years or
so. . . . Never should you have a mixed company, never—
except with only one man or only one woman. How would
that be ? . . .

"Or duets only ? . . ."

"How to manage it ? Some rule of etiquette, perhaps."
. . . He became portentously grave.

Then his long hand went out in weird gestures.

"I seem to see—I seem to see—a sort of City of Women,

Ponderevo. Yes. . . . A walled enclosure—good stone-mason's work—a city wall, high as the walls of Rome, going about a garden. Dozens of square miles of garden—trees—fountains—arbours—lakes. Lawns on which the women play, avenues in which they gossip, boats. . . . Women like that sort of thing. Any woman who's been to a good eventful girls' school lives on the memory of it for the rest of her life. It's one of the pathetic things about women—the superiority of school and college to anything they get afterwards. And this city-garden of women will have beautiful places for music, places for beautiful dresses, places for beautiful work. Everything a woman can want. Nurseries. Kindergartens. Schools. And no man—except to do rough work, perhaps—ever comes in. The men live in a world where they can hunt and engineer, invent and mine and manufacture, sail ships, drink deep, and practise the arts, and fight——"

"Yes," I said ; "but——"

He stilled me with a gesture.

"I'm coming to that. The homes of the women, Ponderevo, will be set in the wall of their city ; each woman will have her own particular house and home, furnished after her own heart in her own manner—with a little balcony on the outside wall. Built into the wall—and a little balcony. And there she will go and look out, when the mood takes her, and all round the city there will be a broad road and seats and great shady trees. And men will stroll up and down there when they feel the need of feminine company ; when, for instance, they want to talk about their souls or their characters or any of the things that only women will stand. . . . The women will lean over and look at the men and smile and talk to them as they fancy. And each woman will have this ; she will have a little silken ladder she can let down if she chooses—if she wants to talk closer. . . ."

"The men would still be competing."

"There perhaps—yes. But they'd have to abide by the women's decisions."

I raised one or two difficulties, and for a while we played with this idea.

"Ewart," I said, "this is like Dolls' Island. . . ." "Suppose," I reflected, "an unsuccessful man laid siege to a balcony and wouldn't let his rival come near it ? "

"Move him on," said Ewart, "by a special regulation. As one does organ-grinders. No difficulty about that. And you could forbid it—make it against the etiquette. No life is decent without etiquette. . . . And people obey etiquette sooner than laws. . . ."

"Hm," I said, and was struck by an idea that is remote in the world of a young man. "How about children ? " I asked ; "in the City ? Girls are all very well. But boys for example—grow up."

" Ah ! " said Ewart.   " Yes.   I forgot.   They mustn't grow
up inside. . . . They'd turn out the boys when they were
seven.   The father must come with a little pony and a little
gun and manly wear, and take the boy away.   Then one could
come afterwards to one's mother's balcony. . . . It must
be fine to have a mother.   The father and the son. . . ."

" This is all very pretty in its way," I said at last, " but it's
a dream.   Let's come back to reality.   What I want to know
is, what are you going to do in Brompton, let us say, or Walham
Green *now* ? "

" Oh ! damn it ! " he remarked, " Walham Green !   What
a chap you are, Ponderevo ! " and he made an abrupt end to
his discourse.   He wouldn't even reply to my tentatives for a
time. . . .

" While I was talking just now," he remarked presently,
" I had a quite different idea."

" What ? "

" For a masterpiece.   A series.   Like the busts of the
Cæsars.   Only not heads, you know.   We don't see the people
who do things to us nowadays. . . ."

" How will you do it, then ? "

" Hands—a series of hands !   The hands of the Twentieth
Century.   I'll do it.   Some day some one will discover it
—go there—see what I have done, and what is meant by it."

" See it where ? "

" On the tombs.   Why not ?   The Unknown Master of the
Highgate Slope !   All the little, soft feminine hands, the
nervous ugly males, the hands of the flops, and the hands of
the snatchers !   And Grundy's loose, lean, knuckly affair—
Grundy the terror !—the little wrinkles and the thumb !
Only it ought to hold all the others together—in a slightly
disturbing squeeze. . . . Like Rodin's great Hand—you
know the thing ! "

§ 4

I forget how many days intervened between that last
breaking off of our engagement and Marion's surrender.   But
I recall now the sharpness of my emotion, the concentrated
spirit of tears and laughter in my throat as I read the words
of her unexpected letter—" I have thought over everything,
and I was selfish. . . ."

I rushed off to Walham Green that evening to give back all
she had given me, to beat her altogether at giving.   She was
extraordinarily gentle and generous that time, I remember,
and when at last I left her, she kissed me very sweetly.

So we were married.

We were married with all the customary incongruities.
I gave—perhaps after a while not altogether ungrudgingly
—and what I gave, Marion took, with a manifest satisfaction.
After all, I was being sensible.   So that we had three livery

carriages to the church (one of the pairs of horses matched) and coachmen—with an improvised flavour and very shabby silk hats—bearing white favours on their whips, and my uncle intervened with splendour and insisted upon having a wedding-breakfast sent in from a caterer's in Hammersmith. The table had a great display of chrysanthemums, and there was orange blossom in the significant place and a wonderful cake. We also circulated upwards of a score of wedges of that accompanied by silver-printed cards in which Marion's name of Ramboat was stricken out by an arrow in favour of Ponderevo. We had a little rally of Marion's relations, and several friends and friends' friends from Smithie's appeared in the church and drifted vestry-ward. I produced my aunt and uncle—a select group of two. The effect in that shabby little house was one of exhilarating congestion. The sideboard, in which lived the tablecloth and the " Apartments " card, was used for a display of the presents, eked out by the unused balance of the silver-printed cards.

Marion wore the white raiment of a bride, white silk and satin, that did not suit her, that made her seem large and strange to me ; she obtruded bows and unfamiliar contours. She went through all this strange ritual of an English wedding with a sacramental gravity that I was altogether too young and egotistical to comprehend. It was all extraordinarily central and important to her ; it was no more than an offensive, complicated, and disconcerting intrusion of a world I was already beginning to criticise very bitterly, to me. What was all this fuss for ? The mere indecent advertisement that I had been passionately in love with Marion ! I think, however, that Marion was only very remotely aware of my smouldering exasperation at having in the end behaved " nicely." I had played-up to the extent of dressing my part ; I had an admirably cut frock-coat, a new silk hat, trousers as light as I could endure them—lighter, in fact—a white waistcoat, light tie, light gloves. Marion, seeing me despondent, had the unusual enterprise to whisper to me that I looked lovely ; I knew too well I didn't look myself. I looked like a special coloured supplement to *Men's Wear*, or *The Tailor and Cutter*, Full Dress For Ceremonial Occasions. I had even the disconcerting sensations of an unfamiliar collar. I felt lost—in a strange body, and when I glanced down myself for reassurance, the straight, white abdomen, the alien legs confirmed that impression.

My uncle was my best man, and looked like a banker—a little banker—in flower. He wore a white rose in his button-hole. He wasn't, I think, particularly talkative. At least I recall very little from him.

" George," he said once or twice, " this is a great occasion for you—a very great occasion."

He spoke a little doubtfully.

You see I had told him nothing about Marion until about

a week before the wedding ; both he and my aunt had been taken altogether by surprise. They couldn't, as people say, "make it out." My aunt was intensely interested, much more than my uncle ; it was then, I think, for the first time that I really saw that she cared for me. She got me alone, I remember, after I had made my announcement. "Now, George," she said, "tell me everything about her. Why didn't you tell me—*me* at least—before ? "

I was surprised to find how difficult it was to tell her about Marion. I perplexed her.

" Then is she beautiful ? " she asked at last.

" I don't know what you'll think of her," I parried. " I think——"

" Yes ? "

" I think she might be the most beautiful person in the world."

" And isn't she ? To you ? "

" Of course," I said, nodding my head. " Yes. She *is*. . . ."

And while I don't remember anything my uncle said or did at the wedding, I do remember very distinctly certain little things, scrutiny, solicitude, a curious rare flash of intimacy in my aunt's eyes. It dawned on me that I wasn't hiding anything from her at all. She was dressed very smartly, wearing a big-plumed hat that made her neck seem longer and slendered than ever, and when she walked up the aisle with that rolling stride of hers and her eye all on Marion, perplexed into self-forgetfulness, it wasn't somehow funny. She was, I do believe, giving my marriage more thought than I had done, she was concerned beyond measure at my black rage and Marion's blindness, she was looking with eyes that knew what loving is—for love.

In the vestry she turned away as we signed, and I verily believe she was crying, though to this day I can't say why she should have cried, and she was near crying too when she squeezed my hand at parting—and she never said a word or looked at me, but just squeezed my hand. . . .

If I had not been so grim in spirit, I think I should have found much of my wedding amusing. I remember a lot of ridiculous detail that still declines to be funny, in my memory. The officiating clergyman had a cold, and turned his " n's " to " d's," and he made the most mechanical compliment conceivable about the bride's age when the register was signed. Every bride he had ever married had had it, one knew. And two middle-aged spinsters, cousins of Marion's and dressmakers at Barking, stand out. They wore marvellously bright and gay blouses and dim old skirts, and had an immense respect for Mr. Ramboat. They threw rice ; they brought a whole bag with them and gave handfuls away to unknown little boys at the church door and so created a Lilliputian riot, and one had meant to throw a slipper. It was a very worn old silk slipper, I know, because she dropped it out of a pocket in the aisle—there was a sort of jumble in the aisle—and I picked it up for her. I don't think she actually threw it, for as we drove away from the church I saw her in a dreadful, and it seemed to me hopeless, struggle with her pocket ; and afterwards my eye caught the missile of good fortune lying, it or its fellow, most obviously mislaid, behind the umbrella-stand in the hall. . . .

The whole business was much more absurd, more incoherent, more human than I had anticipated, and I was far too young and serious to let the latter quality atone for its shortcomings. I am so remote from this phase of my youth that I can look back at it all as dispassionately as one looks at a picture—at some wonderful, perfect sort of picture that is unexhaustible ; but at the time these things filled me with unspeakable resentment. Now I go round it all, look into its details, generalise about its aspects. I'm interested, for example, to square it with my Bladesover theory of the British social scheme. Under stress of tradition we were all of us trying in the fermenting chaos of London to carry out the marriage ceremonies of a Bladesover tenant or one of the chubby middling sort of people in some dependent country town. There a marriage is a public function with a public significance. There the church is to a large extent the gathering-place of the community, and your going to be married a thing of importance to every one you pass on the road. It is a change of status that quite legitimately interests the whole neighbourhood. But in London there are no neighbours, nobody knows, nobody cares. An absolute stranger in an office took my notice, and our banns were proclaimed to ears that had never previously heard our names. The clergyman, even, who married us had never seen us before, and didn't in any degree intimate that he wanted to see us again.

Neighbours in London ! The Ramboats did not know the names of the people on either side of them. As I waited for Marion before we started off upon our honeymoon flight, Mr. Ramboat, I remember, came and stood beside me and stared out of the window.

" There was a funeral over there yestiday," he said by way of making conversation, and moved his head at the house opposite. " Quite a smart affair it was—with a glass 'earse. . . ."

And our little procession of three carriages with white-favour-adorned horses and drivers, went through all the huge, noisy, indifferent traffic like a lost china image in the coal-chute of an ironclad. Nobody made way for us, nobody cared for us ; the driver of an omnibus jeered ; for a long time we crawled behind an unamiable dust-cart. The irrelevant clatter and tumult gave a queer flavour of indecency to this public coming-together of lovers. We seemed to have

obtruded ourselves shamelessly. The crowd that gathered
outside the church would have gathered in the same spirit
and with greater alacrity for a street accident. . . .

At Charing Cross—we were going to Hastings—the experienced eye of the guard detected the significance of our unusual
costume, and he secured us a compartment.

" Well," said I as the train moved out of the station,
" *That's* all over ! " And I turned to Marion—a little unfamiliar still, in her unfamiliar clothes—and smiled.

She regarded me gravely, timidly.

" You're not cross ? " she asked.

" Cross ! Why ? "

" At having it all proper."

" My dear Marion ! " said I, and by way of answer took and
kissed her white-gloved, leather-scented hand. . . .

I don't remember much else about the journey, an hour
or so it was of undistinguished time—for we were both confused and a little fatigued and Marion had a slight headache
and did not want caresses. I fell into a reverie about my
aunt, and realised as if it were a new discovery, that I cared
for her very greatly. I was acutely sorry I had not told her
earlier of my marriage. . . .

But you will not want to hear the history of my honeymoon.
I have told all that was needed to serve my present purpose.
Thus and thus it was the Will in things had its way with me.
Driven by forces I did not understand, diverted altogether
from the science, the curiosities and work to which I had once
given myself, I fought my way through a tangle of traditions,
customs, obstacles and absurdities, enraged myself, limited
myself, gave myself to occupations I saw with the clearest
vision were dishonourable and vain, and at last achieved the
end of purblind Nature, the relentless immediacy of her desire,
and held, far short of happiness, Marion weeping and reluctant
in my arms.

§ 5

Who can tell the story of the slow estrangement of two
married people, the weakening of first this bond and then
that of that complex contact ? Least of all can one of the
two participants. Even now, with an interval of fifteen
years to clear it up for me, I still find a mass of impressions
of Marion as confused, as discordant, as unsystematic and
self-contradictory as life. I think of this thing and love her,
of that and hate her—of a hundred aspects in which I can
now see her with an unimpassioned sympathy. As I sit
here trying to render some vision of this infinitely confused
process, I recall moments of hard and fierce estrangement,
moments of unclouded intimacy, the passages of transition all
forgotten. We talked a little language together when we

were " friends," and I was " Mutney " and she was " Ming," and we kept up such an outward show that till the very end Smithie thought our household the most amiable in the world.

I cannot tell to the full how Marion thwarted me and failed in that life of intimate emotions which is the kernel of love. That life of intimate emotions is made up of little things. A beautiful face differs from an ugly one by a difference of surfaces and proportions that are sometimes almost infinitesimally small. I find myself setting down little things and little things ; none of them do more than demonstrate those essential temperamental discords I have already sought to make clear. Some readers will understand—to others I shall seem no more than an unfeeling brute who couldn't make allowances. . . . It's easy to make allowances now ; but to be young and ardent and to make allowances, to see one's married life open before one, the life that seemed in its dawn a glory, a garden of roses, a place of deep sweet mysteries and heart throbs and wonderful silences, and to see it a vista of tolerations and baby-talk ! A compromise. The least effectual thing in all one's life.

Every love romance I read seemed to mock our dull inter-course, every poem, every beautiful picture reflected upon the uneventful succession of grey hours we had together. I think our real difference was one of æsthetic sensibility.

I do still recall as the worst and most disastrous aspect of all that time, her absolute disregard of her own beauty. It's the pettiest thing to record, I know, but she could wear curl-papers in my presence. It was her idea too, to " wear out " her old clothes and her failures at home when " no one was likely to see her "—" no one " being myself. She allowed me to accumulate a store of ungracious and slovenly memories. . . .

All our conceptions of life differed. I remember how we differed about furniture. We spent three or four days in Tottenham Court Road, and she chose the things she fancied with an inexorable resolution—sweeping aside my suggestions with—" Oh, *you* want such queer things." She pursued some limited, clearly seen and experienced ideal—that excluded all other possibilities. Over every mantel was a mirror that was draped, our sideboard was wonderfully good and splendid with bevelled glass, we had lamps on long metal stalks and cosy corners and plants in grog-tubs. Smithie approved it all. There wasn't a place where one could sit and read in the whole house. My books went upon shelves in the dining-room recess. And we had a piano, though Marion's playing was at an elementary level. . . .

You know, it was the cruellest luck for Marion that I, with my restlessness, my scepticism, my constantly developing ideas, had insisted upon marriage with her. She had no faculty of growth or change ; she had taken her mould, she

had set in the limited ideas of her peculiar class.   She preserved
her conception of what was right in drawing-room chairs and
in marriage ceremonial and in every relation of life with a
simple and luminous honesty and conviction, with an immense
unimaginative inflexibility—as a tailor-bird builds its nest
or a beaver makes its dam.

Let me hasten over this history of disappointments and
separation. I might tell of waxings and wanings of love
between us, but the whole was waning.   Sometimes she would
do things for me, make me a tie or a pair of slippers, and fill
me with none the less gratitude because the things were
absurd.   She ran our home and our one servant with a hard,
bright efficiency.   She was inordinately proud of house and
garden.   Always, by her lights, she did her duty by me. . . .

Presently the rapid development of Tono-Bungay began
to take me into the provinces, and I would be away sometimes
for a week together.   This she did not like ; it left her " dull,"
she said, but after a time she began to go to Smithie's again
and to develop an independence of me.   At Smithie's she
was now a woman with a position ; she had money to spend.
She would take Smithie to theatres and out to lunch and talk
interminably of the business, and Smithie became a sort of
permanent week-ender with us.   Also Marion got a spaniel
and began to dabble with the minor arts, with poker-work
and a Kodak and hyacinths in glasses.   She called once on
a neighbour.   Her parents left Walham Green—her father
severed his connection with the gas-works—and came to live in a
small house I took for them near us, and they were much with us.

Odd the littleness of the things that exasperate when the
fountains of life are embittered !   My father-in-law was
perpetually catching me in moody moments and urging me to
take to gardening.   He irritated me beyond measure.

" You think too much," he would say.   " If you was to let
in a bit with a spade, you might soon 'ave that garden of yours
a Vision of Flowers.   That's better than thinking, George."

Or in a tone of exasperation, " I *carn't* think, George, why
you don't get a bit of glass 'ere.   This sunny corner you c'd
do wonders with a bit of glass."

And in the summer time he never came in without per-
forming a sort of conjuring trick in the hall, and taking
cucumbers and tomatoes from unexpected points of his
person.   " All out o' *my* little bit," he'd say in exemplary
tones.   He left a trail of vegetable produce in the most unusual
places, on mantelboards, sideboards, the tops of pictures.
Heavens ! how the sudden unexpected tomato could annoy
me ! . . .

It did much to widen our estrangement that Marion and my
aunt failed to make friends, became, by a sort of instinct,
antagonistic.

My aunt, to begin with, called rather frequently, for she

was really anxious to know Marion. At first she would
arrive like a whirlwind and pervade the house with an atmosphere of hello ! She dressed already with that cheerfully
extravagant abandon that signalised her accession to fortune,
and dressed her best for these visits. She wanted to play
the mother to me, I fancy, to tell Marion occult secrets about
the way I wore out my boots and how I never could think to
put on thicker things in cold weather. But Marion received
her with that defensive suspiciousness of the shy person,
thinking only of the possible criticism of herself ; and my
aunt, perceiving this, became nervous and slangy. . . .

"She says such queer things," said Marion once, discussing
her. " But I suppose it's witty."

" Yes," I said ; " it *is* witty."

" If I said things like she does——"

The queer things my aunt said were nothing to the queer
things she didn't say. I remember her in our drawing-room
one day, and how she cocked her eye—it's the only expression
—at the india-rubber plant in a Doulton-ware pot which
Marion had placed on the corner of the piano.

She was on the very verge of speech. Then suddenly she
caught my expression, and shrank up like a cat that has been
discovered looking at the milk.

Then a wicked impulse took her.

" Didn't say an old word, George," she insisted, looking
me full in the eye.

I smiled. " You're a dear," I said, " not to," as Marion
came lowering into the room to welcome her. But I felt
extraordinarily like a traitor—to the india-rubber plant,
I suppose—for all that nothing had been said. . . .

" Your aunt makes Game of people," was Marion's verdict,
and, open-mindedly : " I suppose it's all right . . . for her."

Several times we went to the house in Beckenham for lunch,
and once or twice to dinner. My aunt did her peculiar best
to be friends, but Marion was implacable. She was also, I
know, intensely uncomfortable, and she adopted as her social
method an exhausting silence, replying compactly and without
giving openings to anything that was said to her.

The gaps between my aunt's visits grew wider and wider.

My married existence became at last like a narrow deep
groove in the broad expanse of interests in which I was living.
I went about the world ; I met a great number of varied
personalities ; I read endless books in trains as I went to and
fro. I developed social relationships at my uncle's house that
Marion did not share. The seeds of new ideas poured in upon
me and grew in me. Those early and middle years of one's
third decade are, I suppose, for a man the years of greatest
mental growth. They are restless years and full of vague
enterprise.

Each time I returned to Ealing, life there seemed more

alien, narrow and unattractive—and Marion less beautiful and more limited and difficult—until at last she was robbed of every particle of her magic. She gave me always a cooler welcome, I think, until she seemed entirely apathetic. I never asked myself then what heartaches she might hide or what her discontents might be. I would come home hoping nothing, expecting nothing. This was my faded life and I had chosen it. I became more sensitive to the defects I had once disregarded altogether ; I began to associate her sallow complexion with her temperamental insufficiency, and the heavier lines of her mouth and nostril with her moods of discontent. We drifted apart ; wider and wider the gap opened. I tired of baby-talk and stereotyped little fondlings ; I tired of the latest intelligence from those wonderful work-rooms, and showed it all too plainly ; we hardly spoke when we were alone together. The mere unreciprocated physical residue of my passion remained—an exasperation between us.

No children came to save us. Marion had acquired at Smithie's a disgust and dread of maternity. All that was the fruition and quintessence of the " horrid " elements in life, a disgusting thing, a last indignity that overtook unwary women. I doubt indeed a little if children would have saved us ; we should have differed so fatally about their up-bringing.

Altogether, I remember my life with Marion as a long distress, now hard, now tender. It was in those days that I first became critical of my life and burthened with a sense of error and maladjustment. I would lie awake in the night, asking myself the purpose of things, reviewing my unsatisfying, ungainly home-life, my days spent in rascal enterprise and rubbish-selling, contrasting all I was being and doing with my adolescent ambitions, my Wimblehurst dreams. My circum-stances had an air of finality, and I asked myself in vain why I had forced myself into them.

§ 6

The end of our intolerable situation came suddenly and unexpectedly, but in a way that I suppose was almost inevit-able. My alienated affections wandered, and I was unfaithful to Marion.

I won't pretend to extenuate the quality of my conduct. I was a young and fairly vigorous man ; all my appetite for love had been roused and whetted and none of it had been satisfied by my love affair and my marriage. I had pursued an elusive gleam of beauty to the disregard of all else, and it had failed me. It had faded when I had hoped it would grow brighter. I despaired of life, and was embittered. And things happened as I am telling. I don't draw any moral at all in the matter, and as for social remedies, I leave them to the social reformer. I've got to a time of life when the only theories that interest me are generalisations about realities.

To go to our inner office in Raggett Street I had to walk through a room in which the typists worked. They were the correspondence typists ; our books and invoicing had long since overflowed into the premises we had had the luck to secure on either side of us. I was, I must confess, always in a faintly cloudily-emotional way aware of that collection of for the most part round-shouldered femininity, but presently one of the girls detached herself from the others and got a real hold upon my attention. I appreciated her at first as a straight little back, a neater back then any of the others ; as a softly rounded neck with a smiling necklace of sham pearls ; as chestnut hair very neatly done—and as a side-long glance. Presently as a quickly turned face that looked for me.

My eye would seek her as I went through on business things—I dictated some letters to her and so discovered she had pretty, soft-looking hands with pink nails. Once or twice, meeting casually, we looked one another for the flash of a second in the eyes.

That was all. But it was enough in the mysterious free-masonry of sex to say essential things. We had a secret between us.

One day I came into Raggett Street at lunch time and she was alone, sitting at her desk. She glanced up as I entered, and then became very still, with a downcast face and her hands clenched on the table. I walked right by her to the door of the inner office, stopped, came back and stood over her.

We neither of us spoke for quite a perceptible time. I was trembling violently.

" Is that one of the new typewriters ? " I asked at last for the sake of speaking.

She looked up at me without a word, with her face flushed and her eyes alight, and I bent down and kissed her lips. She leaned back to put an arm about me, drew my face to her and kissed me again and again. I lifted her and held her in my arms. She gave a little smothered cry to feel herself so held.

Never before had I known the quality of passionate kisses. . . .

Somebody became audible in the shop outside.

We started back from one another with flushed faces and bright and burning eyes.

" We can't talk here," I whispered with a confident intimacy. " Where do you go at five ? "

" Along the Embankment to Charing Cross," she answered as intimately. " None of the others go that way. . . ."

" About half-past five ? "

" Yes, half-past five. . . ."

The door from the shop opened, and she sat down very quickly.

"I'm glad," I said in a commonplace voice, "that these new typewriters are all right."

I went into the inner office and routed out the pay-sheet in order to find her name—Effie Rink. And I did no work at all that afternoon. I fretted about that dingy little den like a beast in a cage.

When presently I went out, Effie was working with an extraordinary appearance of calm—and there was no look for me at all. . .

We met and had our talk that evening, a talk in whispers when there was none to overhear; we came to an understanding. It was strangely unlike any dream of romance I had ever entertained.

§ 7

I came back after a week's absence to my home again—a changed man. I had lived out my first rush of passion for Effie, had come to a contemplation of my position. I had gauged Effie's place in the scheme of things, and parted from her for a time. She was back in her place at Raggett Street after a temporary indisposition. I did not feel in any way penitent or ashamed, I know, as I opened the little cast-iron gate that kept Marion's front garden and Pampas Grass from the wandering dog. Indeed, if anything, I felt as if I had vindicated some right that had been in question. I came back to Marion with no sense of wrong-doing at all—with, indeed, a new friendliness towards her. I don't know how it may be proper to feel on such occasions ; that is how I felt.

I found her in our drawing-room, standing beside the tall lamp-stand that half filled the bay as though she had just turned from watching for me at the window. There was something in her pale face that arrested me. She looked as if she had not been sleeping. She did not come forward to greet me.

"You've come home," she said.

"As I wrote to you."

She stood very still, a dusky figure against the bright window.

"Where have you been ? " she asked.

"East Coast," I said easily.

She paused for a moment. " I *know*," she said.

I stared at her. It was the most amazing moment in my life. . . .

"By Jove ! " I said at last, " I believe you do ! "

"And then you come home to me ! "

I walked to the hearthrug and stood quite still there, regarding this new situation.

"I didn't dream," she began. "How could you do such a thing ? "

It seemed a long interval before either of us spoke another word.

" Who knows about it ? " I asked at last.

" Smithie's brother.   They were at Cromer."

" Confound Cromer !   Yes ! "

" How could you bring yourself——"

I felt a spasm of petulant annoyance at this unexpected catastrophe.

" I should like to wring Smithie's brother's neck," I said. . . .

Marion spoke in dry, broken fragments of sentences.   " You . . . I'd always thought that anyhow *you* couldn't deceive me. . . . I suppose all men are horrid—about this."

" It doesn't strike me as horrid.   It seems to me the most necessary consequence—and natural thing in the world."

I became aware of some one moving about in the passage, and went and shut the door of the room.   Then I walked back to the hearthrug and turned.

" It's rough on you," I said.   " But I didn't mean you to know.   You've never cared for me.   I've had the devil of a time.   Why should you mind ? "

She sat down in a draped arm-chair.   " I *have* cared for you," she said.

I shrugged my shoulders.

" I suppose," she said, " *she* cares for you ? "

I had no answer.

" Where is she now ? "

" Oh ! does it matter to you ? . . . Look here, Marion ! This—this I didn't anticipate.   I didn't mean this thing to smash down on you like this.   But, you know, something had to happen.   I'm sorry—sorry to the bottom of my heart that things have come to this between us.   But indeed, I'm taken by surprise.   I don't know where I am—I don't know how we got here.   Things took me by surprise.   I found myself alone with her one day.   I kissed her.   I went on. It seemed stupid to go back.   And besides—why should I have gone back ?   Why should I ?   From first to last, I've hardly thought of it as touching you. . . . Damn ! "

She scrutinised my face, and pulled at the ball-fringe of the little table beside her.

" To think of it," she said.   " I don't believe . . . I can ever touch you again."

We kept a long silence.   I was only beginning to realise in the most superficial way the immense catastrophe that had happened between us.   Enormous issues had rushed upon us.   I felt unprepared and altogether inadequate.   I was unreasonably angry.   There came a rush of stupid expressions to my mind that my rising sense of the supreme importance of the moment saved me from saying.   The gap of silence widened until it threatened to become the vast memorable margin of some one among a thousand trivial possibilities of speech that would fix our relations for ever.

Our little general servant tapped at the door—Marion always liked the servant to tap—and appeared.

"Tea, M'm," she said—and vanished, leaving the door open.

"I will go upstairs," said I, and stopped. "I will go upstairs," I repeated, "and put my bag in the spare room."

We remained motionless and silent for a few seconds.

"Mother is having tea with us to-day," Marion remarked at last, and dropped the worried end of ball-fringe and stood up slowly. . . .

And so, with this immense discussion of our changed relations hanging over us, we presently had tea with the unsuspecting Mrs. Ramboat and the spaniel. Mrs. Ramboat was too well trained in her position to remark upon our sombre preoccupation. She kept a thin trickle of talk going, and told us, I remember, that Mr. Ramboat was "troubled" about his cannas.

"They don't come up and they won't come up. He's been round and had an explanation with the man who sold him the bulbs—and he's very heated and upset."

The spaniel was a great bore, begging and doing small tricks first at one and then at the other of us. Neither of us used his name. You see we had called him Miggles, and made a sort of trio in the baby-talk of Mutney and Miggles and Ming.

§ 8

Then presently we resumed our monstrous, momentous duologue. I can't now make out how long that duologue went on. It spread itself, I know, in heavy fragments over either three days or four. I remember myself grouped with Marion, talking sitting on our bed in her room, talking standing in our dining-room, saying this thing or that. Twice we went for long walks. And we had a long evening alone together, with jaded nerves and hearts that fluctuated between a hard and dreary recognition of facts and, on my part at least, a strange unwonted tenderness. Because in some extraordinary way this crisis had destroyed our mutual apathy and made us feel one another again.

It was a duologue that had discrepant parts, that fell into lumps of talk that failed to join on to their predecessors, that began again at a different level, higher or lower, that assumed new aspects in the intervals and assimilated new considerations. We discussed the fact that we two were no longer lovers ; never before had we faced that. It seems a strange thing to write, but as I look back, I see clearly that those several days were the time when Marion and I were closest together, looked for the first and last time faithfully and steadfastly into each other's soul. For those days only, there were no pretences, I made no concessions to her nor she to me ; we concealed nothing, exaggerated nothing. We had done with pretending. We had it out plainly and soberly with each other. Mood followed mood and got its stark expression.

Of course there was quarrelling between us, bitter quarrelling, and we said things to one another—long pent-up things that bruised and crushed and cut. But over it all in my memory now is an effect of deliberate confrontation, and the figure of Marion stands up, pale, melancholy, tear-stained, injured, implacable and dignified.

"You love her?" she asked once, and jerked that doubt into my mind.

I struggled with tangled ideas and emotions. "I don't know what love is. It's all sorts of things—it's made of a dozen strands twisted in a thousand ways."

"But you want her? You want her now—when you think of her?"

"Yes," I reflected. "I want her—right enough."

"And me? Where do I come in?"

"I suppose you come in here."

"Well, but what are you going to do?"

"Do!" I said, with the exasperation of the situation growing upon me. "What do you want me to do?"

As I look back on all that time—across a gulf of fifteen active years—I find I see it with an understanding judgment. I see it as if it were the business of some one else—indeed of two other people—intimately known yet judged without passion. I see now that this shock, this sudden immense disillusionment, did in real fact bring out a mind and soul in Marion; that for the first time she emerged from habits, timidities, imitations, phrases and a certain narrow will-impulse, and became a personality.

Her ruling motive at first was, I think, an indignant and outraged pride. This situation must end. She asked me categorically to give up Effie, and I, full of fresh and glowing memories, absolutely refused.

"It's too late, Marion," I said. "It can't be done like that."

"Then we can't very well go on living together," she said. "Can we?"

"Very well," I deliberated, "if you must have it so."

"Well, can we?"

"Can you stay in this house? I mean—if I go away?"

"I don't know. . . . I don't think I could."

"Then—what do you want?"

Slowly we worked our way from point to point, until at last the word "divorce" was before us.

"If we can't live together we ought to be free," said Marion.

"I don't know anything of divorce," I said—"if you mean that. I don't know how it is done. I shall have to ask

somebody—or look it up. . . . Perhaps, after all, it is the
thing to do. We may as well face it."

We began to talk ourselves into a realisation of what our
divergent futures might be. I came back on the evening
of that day with my questions answered by a solicitor.

"We can't, as a matter of fact," I said, "get divorced as
things are. Apparently, so far as the law goes you've got
to stand this sort of thing. It's silly—but that is the law.
However, it's easy to arrange a divorce. In addition to
adultery there must be desertion or cruelty. To establish
cruelty I should have to strike you, or something of that sort,
before witnesses. That's impossible—but it's simple to desert
you—legally. I have to go away from you ; that's all. I
can go on sending you money—and you bring a suit, what is
it ?—for Restitution of Conjugal Rights. The Court orders me
to return. I disobey. Then you can go on to divorce me.
You get a Decree Nisi, and once more the Court tries to make
me come back. If we don't make it up within six months and
if you don't behave scandalously—the Decree is made absolute.
That's the end of the fuss. That's how one gets unmarried.
It's easier, you see, to marry than unmarry."

"And then—how do I live ? What becomes of me ? "

"You'll have an income. They call it alimony. From a
third to a half of my present income—more if you like—I don't
mind—three hundred a year, say. You've got your old people
to keep and you'll need all that."

"And then—then you'll be free ? "

"Both of us."

"And all this life you've hated——"

I looked up at her wrung and bitter face. "I haven't
hated it," I lied, my voice near breaking with the pain of it
all. "Have you ? "

§ 9

The perplexing thing about life is the irresoluble complexity
of reality, of things and relations alike. Nothing is simple.
Every wrong done has a certain justice in it, and every good
deed has dregs of evil. As for us, young still, and still without
self-knowledge, we sounded a hundred discordant notes in
the harsh jangle of that shock. We were furiously angry with
each other, tender with each other, callously selfish, generously
self-sacrificing.

I remember Marion saying innumerable detached things
that didn't hang together one with another, that contradicted
one another, that were nevertheless all in their places profoundly true and sincere. I see them now as so many
vain experiments in her effort to apprehend the crumpled confusions of our complex moral landslip. Some I found irritating beyond measure. I answered her—sometimes quite
abominably.

"Of course," she would say again and again, "my life has been a failure."

"I've besieged you for three years," I would retort, "asking it not to be. You've done as you pleased. If I've turned away at last——"

Or again she would revive all the stresses before our marriage.

"How you must hate me! I made you wait. Well, now—I suppose you have your revenge."

"*Revenge!*" I echoed.

Then she would try over the aspects of our new separated lives.

"I ought to earn my own living," she would insist. "I want to be quite independent. I've always hated London. Perhaps I shall try a poultry farm and bees. You won't mind at first my being a burden. Afterwards——"

"We've settled all that," I said.

"I suppose you will hate me anyhow. . . ."

There were times when she seemed to regard our separation with absolute complacency, when she would plan all sorts of freedoms and characteristic interests.

"I shall go out a lot with Smithie," she said.

And once she said an ugly thing that I did indeed hate her for, that I cannot even now quite forgive her.

"Your aunt will rejoice at all this. She never cared for me. . . ."

Into my memory of these pains and stresses comes the figure of Smithie, full charged with emotion, so breathless in the presence of the horrid villain of the piece that she could make no articulate sounds. She had long tearful confidences with Marion, I know, sympathetic close clingings. There were moments when only absolute speechlessness prevented her giving me a stupendous "talking to"—I could see it in her eye. The wrong things she would have said! And I recall too, Mrs. Ramboat's slow awakening to something in the air, the growing expression of solicitude in her eye, only her well-trained fear of Marion keeping her from speech. . . .

And at last through all this welter, like a thing fated and altogether beyond our control, parting came to Marion and me.

I hardened my heart, or I could not have gone. For at the last it came to Marion that she was parting from me for ever. That overbore all other things, and turned our last hour to anguish. She forgot for a time the prospect of moving into a new house, she forgot the outrage on her proprietorship and pride. For the first time in her life she really showed strong emotions in regard to me, for the first time perhaps they really came to her. She began to weep slow reluctant tears. I came into her room, and found her asprawl on the bed weeping.

"I didn't know," she cried. "Oh! I didn't understand!

" I've been a fool.   All my life is a wreck !

" I shall be alone ! . . . *Mutney !* Mutney, don't leave me !   Oh ! Mutney ! I didn't understand."

I had to harden my heart indeed, for it seemed to me at moments in those last hours together that, too late, the longed-for thing had happened and Marion had come alive. A new-born hunger for me lit her eyes.

" Don't leave me ! " she said, " don't leave me ! "   She clung to me ; she kissed me with tear-salt lips. . . .

I was promised now and pledged, and I hardened my heart against this impossible dawn.   Yet it seems to me that it needed but a cry, but one word more to have united us again for all our lives.   Could we have united again ?   Would that passage have enlightened us for ever, or should we have fallen back in a week or so into the old estrangement, the old temperamental opposition ?

Of that there is now no telling.   Our own resolve carried us on our predestined way.   We behaved more and more like separating lovers, parting inexorably, but all the preparations we had set going worked on like a machine, and we made no attempt to stop them.   My trunks and boxes went to the station.   I packed my bag with Marion standing before me. We were like children who had hurt each other horribly in sheer stupidity, who didn't know now how to remedy it.   We belonged to each other immensely—immensely.   The cab came to the little iron gate.

" Good-bye ! " I said.

" Good-bye."

For a moment we embraced and kissed—incredibly without malice.   We heard our servant in the passage going to open the door.   For the last time we pressed ourselves to one another.   We were not lovers nor enemies, but two human souls in a frank community of pain.   I tore myself from her.

" Go away," I said to the servant, seeing that Marion had followed me down.

I felt her standing behind me as I spoke to the cabman.

I got into the cab, resolutely not looking back, and then as it started jumped up, craned out and looked at the door.

It was wide open, but she had disappeared. . . .

I wonder—I suppose she ran upstairs.

§ 10

So I parted from Marion at an extremity of perturbation and regret, and went, as I had promised and arranged, to Effie who was waiting for me in apartments near Orpington. I remember her upon the station platform, a bright, flitting figure looking along the train for me, and our walk over the fields in the twilight.   I had expected an immense sense of relief when at last the stresses of separation were over, but now I found I was beyond measure wretched and perplexed, full of the profoundest persuasion of irreparable error. The dusk and sombre Marion were so alike, her sorrow seemed to be all about me. I had to hold myself to my own plans, to remember that I must keep faith with Effie, with Effie who had made no terms, exacted no guarantees, but flung herself into my hands.

We went across the evening fields in silence, towards a sky of deepening gold and purple, and Effie was close beside me always, very close, glancing up ever and again at my face.

Certainly she knew I grieved for Marion, that ours was now no joyful reunion. But she showed no resentment and no jealousy. Extraordinarily she did not compete against Marion. Never once in all our time together did she say an adverse word of Marion. . . .

She set herself presently to dispel the shadow that brooded over me with the same instinctive skill that some women will show with the trouble of a child. She made herself my glad and pretty slave and handmaid ; she forced me at last to rejoice in her. Yet at the back of it all Marion remained, stupid and tearful and infinitely distressful, so that I was almost intolerably unhappy for her—for her and the dead body of my married love.

It is all, as I tell it now, unaccountable to me. I go back into these remote parts, these rarely visited uplands and lonely tarns of memory, and it seems to me still a strange country. I had thought I might be going to some sensuous paradise with Effie, but desire which fills the universe before its satisfaction, vanishes utterly—like the going of daylight—with achievement. All the facts and forms of life remain darkling and cold. It was an upland of melancholy questionings, a region from which I saw all the world at new angles and in new aspects ; I had outflanked passion and romance.

I had come into a condition of vast perplexities. For the first time in my life, at least so it seems to me now in this retrospect, I looked at my existence as a whole.

Since this was nothing, what was I doing ? What was I for ?

I was going to and fro about Tono-Bungay—the business I had taken up to secure Marion and which held me now in spite of our ultimate separation—and snatching odd week-ends and nights for Orpington, and all the while I struggled with these obstinate interrogations. I used to fall into musing in the trains. I became even a little inaccurate and forgetful about business things. I have the clearest memory of myself sitting thoughtful in the evening sunlight on a grassy hillside that looked towards Sevenoaks and commanded a wide sweep of country, and that I was thinking out my destiny. I could almost write my thoughts down now, I believe, as they came to me that afternoon. Effie, restless little Cockney that she was, rustled and struggled in a hedgerow below, gathering flowers, discovering flowers she had never seen before. I had, I remember, a letter from Marion in my pocket. I had even made some tentatives for return, for a reconciliation ; Heaven knows now how I had put it ! but her cold, ill-written letter repelled me. I perceived I could never face that old inconclusive dullness of life again, that stagnant disappointment. That, anyhow, wasn't possible. But what was possible ? I could see no way of honour or fine living before me at all.

" What am I to do with life ? " that was the question that besieged me.

I wondered if all the world was even as I, urged to this by one motive and to that by another, creatures of chance and impulse and unmeaning traditions. Had I indeed to abide by what I had said and done and chosen ? Was there nothing for me in honour but to provide for Effie, go back penitent to Marion and keep to my trade in rubbish—or find some fresh one—and so work out the residue of my days ? I didn't accept that for a moment. But what else was I to do ? I wondered if my case was the case of many men, whether in former ages men had been so guideless, so uncharted, so haphazard in their journey into life. In the Middle Ages, in the old Catholic days, one went to a priest, and he said with all the finality of natural law, this you are and this you must do. I wondered whether even in the Middle Ages I should have accepted that ruling without question. . . .

I remember very distinctly how Effie came and sat beside me on a little box that was before the casement window of our room.

" Gloomkins," said she.

I smiled and remained head on hand, looking out of the window forgetful of her.

" Did you love your wife so well ? " she whispered softly.

" Oh ! " I cried, recalled again ; " I don't know. I don't understand these things. Life is a thing that hurts, my dear ! It hurts without logic or reason. I've blundered ! I didn't understand. Anyhow—there is no need to go hurting you, is there ? "

And I turned about and drew her to me, and kissed her ear. . . .

" Yes, I had a very bad time—I still recall. I suffered, I suppose, from a sort of *ennui* of the imagination. I found myself without an object to hold my will together. I read restlessly and discursively. I tried Ewart and got no help from him. As I regard it all now in this retrospect, it seems to me as if in those days of disgust and abandoned aims I discovered myself for the first time. Before that I had seen only the world and things in it, had followed them self-forgetful of all but my impulse. Now I found myself *grouped,*

with a system of appetites and satisfactions, with much work
to do—and no desire, it seemed, left in me.

There were moments when I thought of suicide. At times
my life appeared before me in bleak, relentless light, a series
of ignorances, crude blunderings, degradation and cruelty.
I had what the old theologians call a "conviction of sin."
I sought salvation—not perhaps in the formulæ a Methodist
preacher would recognise—but salvation nevertheless.

Men find their salvation nowadays in many ways. Names
and forms don't, I think, matter very much, the real need is
something that we can hold and that holds one. I have
known a man find that determining factor in a dry-plate
factory, and another in writing a history of the Manor. So
long as it holds one, it does not matter. Many men and
women nowadays take up some concrete aspect of socialism
or social reform. But socialism for me has always been a
little bit too human, too set about with personalities and
foolishness. It isn't my line. I don't like things so human.
I don't think I'm blind to the fun, the surprises, the jolly
little coarsenesses and insufficiency of life, to the "humour
of it," as people say, and to adventure, but that isn't the root
of the matter with me. There's no humour in my blood. I'm
in earnest in warp and woof. I stumble and flounder, but
I know that over all these merry, immediate things, there are
other things that are great and serene, very high, beautiful
things—the reality. I haven't got it, but it's there nevertheless. I'm a spiritual guttersnipe in love with unimaginable
goddesses. I've never seen the goddesses nor ever shall—but
it takes all the fun out of the mud—and at times I fear it
takes all the kindliness too.

But I'm talking of things I can't expect the reader to understand, because I don't half understand them myself. There
is something links things for me, a sunset or so, a mood or
so, the high air, something there was in Marion's form and
colour, something I find and lose in Mantegna's pictures,
something in the lines of these boats I make. (You should
see X2, my last and best !)

I can't explain myself, I perceive. Perhaps it all comes
to this, that I am a hard and morally limited cad with a mind
beyond my merits. Naturally I resist that as a complete
solution. Anyhow, I had a sense of inexorable need, of
distress and insufficiency that was unendurable, and for a
time this aeronautical engineering allayed it. . . .

In the end of this particular crisis of which I tell so badly,
I idealised Science. I decided that in power and knowledge
lay the salvation of my life, the secret that would fill my
need ; that to these things I would give myself. I emerged
at last like a man who has been diving in darkness, clutching
at a new resolve for which he has groped desperately and long.

I came into the inner office suddenly one day—it must

have been just before the time of Marion's suit for restitution —and sat down before my uncle.

" Look here," I said, " I'm sick of this."

" Hal*lo* ! " he answered, and put some papers aside. " What's up, George ? "

" Things are wrong."

" As how ? "

" My life," I said, " it's a mess, an infinite mess."

" She's been a stupid girl, George," he said ; " I partly understand. But you're quit of her now, practically, and there's just as good fish in the sea——"

" Oh ! it's not that," I cried. " That's only the part that shows. I'm sick—— I'm sick of all this damned rascality."

" Eh ? Eh ? " said my uncle. " *What*—rascality ? "

" Oh, *you* know. I want some *stuff*, man. I want something to hold on to. I shall go amok if I don't get it. I'm a different sort of beast from you. You float in all this bunkum. *I* feel like a man floundering in a universe of soapsuds, up and down, east and west. I can't stand it. I must get my foot on something solid or—I don't know what."

I laughed at the consternation in his face.

" I mean it," I said. " I've been thinking it over. I've made up my mind. It's no good arguing. I shall go in for work—real work. No ! this isn't work ; it's only laborious cheating. But I've got an idea ! It's an old idea—I thought of years ago, but it came back to me. Look here ! Why should I fence about with you ? I believe the time has come for flying to be possible. Real flying ! "

" Flying ! "

" Up in the air. Aeronautics ! Machine heavier than air. It can be done. And I want to do it."

" Is there money in it, George ? "

" I don't know nor care ! But that's what I'm going to do."

I stuck to that, and it helped me through the worst time in my life. My uncle, after some half-hearted resistance and a talk with my aunt, behaved like the father of a spoilt son. He fixed up an arrangement that gave me capital to play with, released me from too constant a solicitude for the newer business developments—this was in what I may call the later Moggs period of our enterprises—and I went to work at once with grim intensity. . . .

But I will tell of my soaring and flying machines in the proper place. I've been leaving the story of my uncle alto- gether too long. I wanted merely to tell how it was I took to this work. I took to these experiments after I had sought something that Marion in some indefinable way had seemed to promise. I toiled and forgot myself for a time, and did many things. Science, too, has been something of an irresponsive mistress since, though I've served her better than I served

Marion.   But at the time Science, with her order, her
inhuman distance, her steely certainties, saved me from
despair.

Well, I have still to fly ; but incidentally I have invented
the lightest engines in the world. . . .

I am trying to tell of all the things that happened to me.
It's hard enough simply to get it put down in the remotest
degree right.   But this is a novel, not a treatise.   Don't
imagine that I'm coming presently to any sort of solution of
my difficulties.   Here among my drawings and hammerings
now, I still question unanswering problems.   All my life has
been at bottom, *seeking*, disbelieving always, dissatisfied
always with the thing seen and the thing believed, seeking
something in toil, in force, in danger, something whose name
and nature I do not clearly understand, something beautiful,
worshipful, enduring, mine profoundly and fundamentally,
and the utter redemption of myself ; I don't know—all I can
tell is that it is something I have ever failed to find.

§ 11

But before I finish this chapter and book altogether and
go on with the great adventure of my uncle's career, I may
perhaps tell what else remains of Marion and Effie, and then
set my private life behind me.

For a time Marion and I corresponded with some regularity,
writing friendly but rather uninforming letters about minor
business things.   The clumsy process of divorce completed
itself.   She left the house at Ealing and went into the country
with her aunt and parents, taking a small farm near Lewes
in Sussex.   She put up glass, she put in heat for her father,
happy man ! and spoke of figs and peaches.   The thing
seemed to promise well throughout a spring and summer, but
the Sussex winter after London was too much for the Ramboats.
They got very muddy and dull ; Mr. Ramboat killed a cow
by improper feeding, and that disheartened them all.   A
twelvemonth saw the enterprise in difficulties.   I had to help
her out of this, and then they returned to London and she
went into partnership with Smithie at Streatham, and ran
a business that was intimated on the firm's stationery as
" Robes."   The parents and aunt were stowed away in a
cottage somewhere.   After that the letters became infrequent.
But in one I remember a postscript that had a little stab of
our ancient intimacy : " Poor old Miggles is dead."

Nearly eight years slipped by.   I grew up.   I grew in
experience, in capacity, until I was fully a man, busy with
many new interests, living on a larger scale in a wider world
than I could have dreamt of in my Marion days.   Her letters
became rare and insignificant.   At last came a gap of silence
that made me curious.   For eighteen months or more I had

nothing from Marion save her quarterly receipts through the bank. Then I damned at Smithie, and wrote a card to Marion.

" Dear Marion," I said, " how goes it ? "

She astonished me tremendously by telling me she had married again—" a Mr. Wachorn, a leading agent in the paper-pattern trade." But she still wrote on the Ponderevo and Smith (Robes) notepaper, from the Ponderevo and Smith address.

And that, except for a little difference of opinion about the continuance of alimony which gave me some passages of anger, and the use of my name by the firm, which also annoyed me, is the end of Marion's history for me, and she vanishes out of this story. I do not know where she is nor what she is doing. I do not know whether she is alive or dead. It seems to me utterly grotesque that two people who have stood so close to one another as she and I should be so separated, but so it is between us.

Effie, too, I have parted from, though I still see her at times. Between us there was never any intention of marriage nor intimacy of soul. She had a sudden fierce hot-blooded passion for me, and I for her, but I was not her first lover nor her last. She was in another world from Marion. She had a queer delightful nature ; I've no memory of ever seeing her sullen or malicious. She was—indeed she was magnificently —eupeptic. That I think, was the central secret of her agreeableness, and moreover that she was infinitely kind-hearted. I helped her at last into an opening she coveted, and she amazed me by a sudden display of business capacity. She has now a typewriting bureau in Riffle's Inn, and she runs it with a brisk vigour and considerable success, albeit a certain plumpness has overtaken her. And she still loves her kind. She married a year or so ago a boy half her age—a wretch of a poet, a wretched poet and given to drugs, a thing with lank fair hair always getting into his blue eyes, and limp legs. She did it, she said, because he needed nursing. . . .

But enough of this disaster of my marriage and of my early love affairs ; I have told all that is needed for my picture to explain how I came to take up aeroplane experiments and engineering science ; let me get back to my essential story, to Tono-Bungay and my uncle's promotions and to the vision of the world these things have given me.

END OF BOOK II

Book Three
The Great Days
of Tono-Bungay

CHAPTER ONE

THE HARDINGHAM HOTEL, AND HOW WE BECAME BIG PEOPLE

§ 1

BUT now that I resume the main line of my story it may be well to describe the personal appearance of my uncle as I remember him during those magnificent years that followed his passage from trade to finance. The little man plumped up very considerably during the creation of the Tono-Bungay property, but with the increasing excitements that followed that first flotation came dyspepsia and a certain flabbiness and falling away. His abdomen—if the reader will pardon my taking his features in the order of their value— had at first a nice full roundness, but afterwards it lost tone, without however losing size. He always went as though he was proud of it and would make as much of it as possible. To the last his movements remained quick and sudden, his short firm legs, as he walked, seemed to twinkle rather than display the scissors-stride of common humanity, and he never seemed to have knees, but instead, a dispersed flexibility of limb. There was, I seem to remember, a secular intensification of his features, his nose developed character, became aggressive, stuck out at the world more and more ; the obliquity of his mouth, I think, increased. From the face that returns to my memory projects a long cigar that is sometimes cocked jauntily up from the higher corner, that sometimes droops from the lower ;—it was as eloquent as a dog's tail, and he removed it only for the more emphatic modes of speech. He assumed a broad black ribbon for his glasses, and wore them more and more askew as time went on. His hair seemed to stiffen with success, but towards the climax it thinned greatly over the crown and he brushed it hard back over his ears where, however, it stuck out fiercely. It always stuck out fiercely over his forehead, up and forward.

He adopted an urban style of dressing with the onset of Tono-Bungay and rarely abandoned it. He preferred silk hats with ample rich brims, often a trifle large for him by modern ideas, and he wore them at various angles to his axis ; his taste in trouserings was towards fairly emphatic stripes and his trouser cut was neat ; he liked his frock-coat long and full although that seemed to shorten him. He displayed a number of valuable rings, and I remember one upon his left little finger with a large red stone bearing Gnostic symbols. " Clever chaps, those Gnostics, George," he told me. " Means a lot. Lucky ! " He never had any but a black mohair watch-chain. In the country he affected grey and a large

grey cloth top-hat, except when motoring; then he would
have a brown deer-stalker cap and a fur suit of Esquimaux
cut with a sort of boot-end to the trousers. Of an evening he
would wear white waistcoats and plain gold studs. He hated
diamonds. " Flashy," he said they were. " Might as well
wear an income-tax receipt. All very well for Park Lane.
Unsold stock. Not my style. Sober financier, George."

So much for his visible presence. For a time it was very
familiar to the world, for at the crest of the boom he allowed
quite a number of photographs and at least one pencil sketch
to be published in the sixpenny papers. . . . His voice declined
during those years from his early tenor to a flat rich quality of
sound that my knowledge of music is inadequate to describe.
His Zzz-ing inrush of air became less frequent as he ripened,
but returned in moments of excitement. Throughout his
career, in spite of his increasing and at last astounding
opulence, his more intimate habits remained as simple as they
had been at Wimblehurst. He would never avail himself of
the services of a valet; at the very climax of his greatness his
trousers were folded by a housemaid and his shoulders brushed
as he left his house or hotel. He became wary about breakfast
as life advanced, and at one time talked much of Dr. Haig
and uric acid. But for other meals he remained reasonably
omnivorous. He was something of a gastronome, and would
eat anything he particularly liked in an audible manner, and
perspire upon his forehead. He was a studiously moderate
drinker—except when the spirit of some public banquet or
some great occasion caught him and bore him beyond his
wariness—then he would, as it were, drink inadvertently and
become flushed and talkative—about everything but his
business projects.

To make the portrait complete one wants to convey an
effect of sudden, quick bursts of movement like the jumps of
a Chinese-cracker to indicate that his pose, whatever it is,
has been preceded and will be followed by a rush. If I were
painting him, I should certainly give him for a background
that distressed, uneasy sky that was popular in the eighteenth
century, and at a convenient distance a throbbing motor-car,
very big and contemporary, a secretary hurrying with papers,
and an alert chauffeur.

Such was the figure that created and directed the great
property of Tono-Bungay, and from the successful reconstruction of that company passed on to a slow crescendo of
magnificent creations and promotions until the whole world
of investors marvelled. I have already, I think, mentioned
how, long before we offered Tono-Bungay to the public, we
took over the English agency of certain American specialities.
To this was presently added our exploitation of Moggs'
Domestic Soap, and so he took up the Domestic Convenience
Campaign that, coupled with his equatorial rotundity and a

certain resolute convexity in his bearing, won my uncle his
Napoleonic title.

§ 2

It illustrates the romantic element in modern commerce
that my uncle met young Moggs at a city dinner—I think
it was the Bottle-makers' Company—when both were some
way advanced beyond the initial sobriety of the occasion.
This was the grandson of the original Moggs, and a very
typical instance of an educated, cultivated, degenerate plutocrat. His people had taken him about in his youth like the
Ruskins took their John, and fostered a passion for history in
him, and the actual management of the Moggs' industry had
devolved upon a cousin and a junior partner. Mr. Moggs,
being of a studious and refined disposition, had just decided—
after a careful search for a congenial subject in which he would
not be constantly reminded of soap—to devote himself to the
History of the Thebaid when his cousin died suddenly and
precipitated responsibilities upon him. In the frankness of
conviviality, Moggs bewailed the uncongenial task thus thrust
into his hands, and my uncle offered to lighten his burden by
a partnership then and there. They even got to terms—
extremely muzzy terms, but terms nevertheless.

Each gentleman wrote the name and address of the other
on his cuff, and they separated in a mood of brotherly carelessness, and next morning neither seems to have thought
to rescue his shirt from the wash until it was too late. My
uncle made a painful struggle—it was one of my business
mornings—to recall name and particulars.

" He was an aquarium-faced, long, blond sort of chap,
George, with glasses and a genteel accent," he said.

I was puzzled. " Aquarium-faced ? "

" You know how they look at you. His stuff was soap,
I'm pretty nearly certain. And he had a name. And the
thing was the straightest Bit-of-All-Right you ever. I was
clear enough to spot that . . ."

We went out at last with knitted brows, and wandered up
into Finsbury seeking a good, well-stocked looking grocer.
We called first on a chemist for a pick-me-up for my uncle,
and then we found the shop we needed.

" I want," said my uncle, " half a pound of every sort of soap
you got. Yes, I want to take them now. . . . Wait a moment,
George. . . . Now whassort of soap d'you call *that* ? "

At the third repetition of that question the young man
said, " Moggs' Domestic."

" Right," said my uncle. " You needn't guess again.
Come along, George, let's go to a telephone and get on to
Moggs. Oh—the order ? Certainly. I confirm it. Send
it all—send it all to the Bishop of London ; he'll have some
good use for it—(First-rate man, George, he is—charities

and all that)—and put it down to me—here's a card—
Ponderevo—Tono-Bungay."

Then we went on to Moggs and found him in a camel-hair
dressing-jacket in a luxurious bed, drinking China tea, and
got the shape of everything but the figures fixed by lunch time.

Young Moggs enlarged my mind considerably ; he was a
sort of thing I hadn't met before ; he seemed quite clean and
well informed and he assured me he never read newspapers
nor used soap in any form at all.   " Delicate skin," he said.

" No objection to our advertising you wide and free ? "
said my uncle.

" I draw the line at railway stations," said Moggs, " south-
coast cliffs, theatre programmes, books by me and poetry
generally—scenery—oh !—and the *Mercure de France*."

" We'll get along," said my uncle.

" So long as you don't annoy me," said Moggs, lighting a
cigarette, " you can make me as rich as you like."

We certainly made him no poorer.   His was the first firm
that was advertised by a circumstantial history ; we even got
to illustrated magazine articles telling of the quaint past of
Moggs.   We concocted Moggsiana.   Trusting to our partner's
preoccupation with the uncommercial aspects of life, we gave
graceful histories of Moggs the First, Moggs the Second, Moggs
the Third, and Moggs the Fourth.   You must, unless you are
very young, remember some of them and our admirable block
of a Georgian shop window.   My uncle bought early nineteenth-century memoirs, soaked himself in the style, and
devised stories about old Moggs the First and the Duke of
Wellington, George the Third and the soap dealer (" almost
certainly old Moggs ").   Very soon we had added to the
original Moggs' Primrose several varieties of scented and
superfatted, a " special nursery—as used in the household of
the Duke of Kent and for the old Queen in Infancy," a plate
powder, " the Paragon," and a knife powder.   We roped
in a good little second-rate black-lead firm, and carried their
origins back into the mists of antiquity.   It was my uncle's
own unaided idea that we should associate that commodity
with the Black Prince.   He became industriously curious
about the past of black-lead.   I remember his button-holing
the president of the Pepys Society.

" I say, is there any black-lead in Pepys ?   You know—
black-lead—for grates !   *Or does he pass it over as a matter
of course ?* "

He became in those days the terror of eminent historians.
" Don't want your drum and trumpet history—no fear," he
used to say.   " Don't want to know who was who's mistress,
and why so-and-so devastated such a province ; that's bound
to be all lies and upsy-down anyhow.   Not my affair.
Nobody's affair now.   Chaps who did it didn't clearly know.
. . . What I want to know is, in the Middle Ages Did they Do

Anything for Housemaid's Knee ? What did they put in
their hot baths after jousting, and was the Black Prince—
you know the Black Prince—was he enamelled or painted, or
what ? I think myself, black-leaded—very likely—like pipe-
clay—but *did* they use blacking so early ? "

So it came about that in designing and writing those Moggs'
Soap Advertisements, that wrought a revolution in that department of literature, my uncle was brought to realise not
only the lost history, but also the enormous field for invention
and enterprise that lurked among the little articles, the dust-
pans and mincers, the mousetraps and carpet-sweepers that
fringe the shops of the oilman and domestic ironmonger. He
was recalled to one of the dreams of his youth, to his conception of the Ponderevo Patent Flat that had been in his mind
so early as the days before I went to serve him at Wimblehurst. "The Home, George," he said, "wants straightening
up. Silly muddle ! Things that get in the way. Got to
organise it."

For a time he displayed something like the zeal of a genuine
social reformer in relation to these matters.

"We've got to bring the Home Up to Date ? That's my
idee, George. We got to make a civilised d'mestic machine
out of these relics of barbarism. I'm going to hunt up inventors,
make a corner in d'mestic idees. Everything. Balls of string
that won't dissolve into a tangle, and gum that won't dry
into horn. See ? Then after conveniences—beauty. Beauty,
George ! All these new things ought to be made fit to look at,
it's your aunt's idee, that. Beautiful jam-pots ! Get one of
those new art chaps to design all the things they make ugly
now. Patent carpet-sweepers by these greenwood chaps,
housemaid's boxes it'll be a pleasure to fall over—rich coloured
house-flannels. Zzzz. Pails, f'rinstance. Hang 'em up on
the walls like warming-pans. All the polishes and things in
such tins—you'll want to cuddle 'em, George ! See the
notion ? 'Sted of all the silly, ugly things we got." . . .

We had some magnificent visions ; they so affected me that
when I passed ironmongers and oil-shops they seemed to me
as full of promise as trees in late winter, flushed with the effort
to burst into leaf and flower. . . . And really we did do much
towards that new brightness these shops display. They were
dingy things in the 'eighties compared to what our efforts have
made them now, grey quiet displays. . . .

Well, I don't intend to write down here the tortuous financial
history of Moggs Limited, which was our first development
of Moggs and Sons ; nor will I tell very much of how from
that we spread ourselves with a larger and larger conception
throughout the chandlery and minor ironmongery, how we
became agents for this little commodity, partners in that, got
a tentacle round the neck of a specialised manufacturer or so,
secured a pull upon this or that supply of raw material, and

so prepared the way for our second flotation, Domestic Utilities:
—" Do Ut," they rendered it in the city.   And then came the
reconstruction of Tono-Bungay, and then " Household
Services " and the Boom !

That sort of development is not to be told in detail in a
novel.   I have, indeed, told much of it elsewhere.   It is to
be found set out at length, painfully at length, in my uncle's
examination and mine in the bankruptcy proceedings, and in
my own various statements after his death.   Some people
know everything in that story, some know it all too well,
most do not want the details, it is the story of a man of imagination among figures, and unless you are prepared to collate
columns of pounds, shillings and pence, compare dates and
check additions, you will find it very unmeaning and perplexing.   And after all, you wouldn't find the early figures so
much wrong as *strained*.   In the matter of Moggs and Do Ut,
as in the first Tono-Bungay promotion and in its reconstruction,
we left the court by city standards without a stain on our characters.   The great amalgamation of Household Services was
my uncle's first really big-scale enterprise and his first display
of bolder methods ;   for this we bought back Do Ut, Moggs
(going strong with a seven per cent. dividend) and acquired
Skinnerton's polishes, the Riffleshaw properties and the
Runcorn's mincer and coffee-mill business.   To that Amalgamation I was really not a party ;   I left it to my uncle because
I was then beginning to get keen upon the soaring experiments I had taken on from the results then to hand of Lilienthal, Pilcher and the Wright brothers.   I was developing a
glider into a flyer.   I meant to apply power to this glider as
soon as I could work out one or two residual problems affecting
the longitudinal stability.   I knew that I had a sufficiently
light motor in my own modification of Bridger's light turbine,
but I knew, too, that until I had cured my aeroplane of a
tendency demanding constant alertness from me, a tendency
to jerk up its nose at unexpected moments and slide back upon
me, the application of an engine would be little short of suicide.

But that I will tell about later.   The point I was coming
to was that I did not realise until after the crash how recklessly
my uncle had kept his promise of paying a dividend of over
eight per cent. on the ordinary shares of that hugely over-
capitalised enterprise, Household Services.

I drifted out of business affairs into my research much more
than either I or my uncle had contemplated.   Finance was
much less to my taste than the organisation of the Tono-
Bungay factory.   In the new field of enterprise there was
a great deal of bluffing and gambling, of taking chances and
concealing material facts—and these are hateful things to the
scientific type of mind.   It wasn't fear I felt so much as an
uneasy inaccuracy.   I didn't realise dangers, I simply disliked
the sloppy, relaxing quality of this new sort of work.   I was

at last constantly making excuses not to come up to him in London. The latter part of his business career recedes therefore beyond the circle of my particular life. I lived more or less with him ; I talked, I advised, I helped him at times to fight his Sunday crowd at Crest Hill, but I did not follow nor guide him. From the Do Ut time onward he rushed up the financial world like a bubble in water and left me like some busy water-thing down below in the deeps.

Anyhow, he was an immense success. The public was, I think, particularly attracted by the homely familiarity of his field of work—you never lost sight of your investment, they felt, with the name on the house-flannel and shaving-strop—and its allegiance was secured by the Egyptian solidity of his apparent results. Tono-Bungay, after its reconstruction, paid thirteen, Moggs seven, Domestic Utilities had been a safe-looking nine ; here was Household Services with eight ; on such a showing he had merely to buy and sell Roeburn's Antiseptic fluid, Razor soaks and Bath crystals in three weeks to clear twenty thousand pounds. I do think that as a matter of fact Roeburn's was good value at the price at which he gave it to the public, at least until it was strained by ill-conceived advertisement. It was a period of expansion and confidence ; much money was seeking investment and " Industrials " were the fashion. Prices were rising all round. There remained little more for my uncle to do, therefore, in his climb to the high unstable crest of Financial Greatness but, as he said, to " grasp the cosmic oyster, George, while it gaped," which being translated meant for him to buy respectable businesses confidently and courageously at the vendor's estimate, add thirty or forty thousand to the price and sell them again. His sole difficulty indeed was the tactful management of the load of shares that each of these transactions left upon his hands. But I thought so little of these later things that I never fully appreciated the peculiar inconveniences of that until it was too late to help him.

§ 3

When I think of my uncle near the days of his Great Boom and in connection with the actualities of his enterprises, I think of him as I used to see him in the suite of rooms he occupied in the Hardingham Hotel, seated at a great old oak writing-table, smoking, drinking, and incoherently busy ; that was his typical financial aspect—our evenings, our mornings, our holidays, our motor-car expeditions, Lady Grove and Crest Hill belong to an altogether different set of memories.

These rooms in the Hardingham were a string of apartments along one handsome thick-carpeted corridor. All the doors upon the corridor were locked except the first ; and my uncle's bedroom, breakfast-room and private sanctum were the least accessible and served by an entrance from the adjacent passage, which he also used at times as a means of escape from importunate callers. The most external room was a general waiting-room and very business-like in quality ; it had one or two uneasy sofas, a number of chairs, a green baize table, and a collection of the very best Moggs and Tono posters ; and the plush carpets normal to the Hardingham had been replaced by a grey-green cork linoleum. Here I would always find a remarkable miscellany of people, presided over by a peculiarly faithful and ferocious-looking commissionaire, Ropper, who guarded the door that led a step nearer my uncle. Usually there would be a parson or so, one or two widows ; hairy, eye-glassy, middle-aged gentlemen, some of them looking singularly like Edward Ponderevos who hadn't come off, a variety of young and youngish men more or less attractively dressed, some with papers protruding from their pockets, others with their papers decently concealed. And wonderful incidental, frowsy people.

All these persons maintained a practically hopeless siege—sometimes for weeks together ; they had better have stayed at home. Next came a room full of people who had some sort of appointment, and here one would find smart-looking people, brilliantly dressed, nervous women hiding behind magazines, nonconformist divines, clergy in gaiters, real business men, these latter for the most part gentlemen in admirable morning dress who stood up and scrutinised my uncle's taste in water-colours manfully and sometimes by the hour together. Young men again were here of various social origins—young Americans, treasonable clerks from other concerns, university young men, keen-looking, most of them, resolute, reserved but on a sort of hair trigger, ready at any moment to be most voluble, most persuasive. This room had a window, too, looking out into the hotel courtyard with its fern-set fountains and mosaic pavement, and the young men would stand against this and sometimes even mutter. One day I heard one repeating in an urgent whisper as I passed, " But you don't quite see, Mr. Ponderevo, the full advantages, the *full* advantages——" I met his eye and he was embarrassed.

Then came a room with a couple of secretaries—no type-writers, because my uncle hated the clatter—and a casual person or two sitting about, projectors whose projects were being entertained. Here and in a further room nearer the private apartments, my uncle's correspondence underwent an exhaustive process of pruning and digestion before it reached him. Then the two little rooms in which my uncle talked ; my magic uncle who had *got* the investing public—to whom all things were possible.

As one came in one would find him squatting with his cigar up and an expression of dubious beatitude upon his

face, while some one urged him to grow still richer by this
or that.

"Thatju, George?" he used to say. "Come in. Here's
a thing. Tell him—Mister—over again. Have a drink,
George? No! Wise man! Liss'n."

I was always ready to listen. All sorts of financial marvels
came out of the Hardingham, more particularly during my
uncle's last great flurry, but they were nothing to the projects
that passed in. It was the little brown and gold room he
sat in usually. He had had it redecorated by Bordingly and
half a dozen Sussex pictures by Webster hung about it
Latterly he wore a velveteen jacket of a golden-brown colour
in this apartment that I think over-emphasised its æsthetic
intention, and he also added some gross Chinese bronzes. . . .

He was on the whole a very happy man throughout all
that wildly enterprising time. He made, and, as I shall tell
in its place, spent great sums of money. He was constantly
in violent motion, constantly stimulated mentally and physically and rarely tired. About him was an atmosphere of
immense deference ; much of his waking life was triumphal
and all his dreams. I doubt if he had any dissatisfaction
with himself at all until the crash bore him down. Things
must have gone very rapidly with him. . . . I think he must
have been very happy.

As I sit here writing about all these things, jerking down
notes and throwing them aside in my attempt to give some
literary form to the tale of our promotions, the marvel of it
all comes to me as if it came for the first time, the supreme
unreason of it. At the climax of his Boom, my uncle at the
most sparing estimate must have possessed in substance and
credit about two million pounds'-worth of property to set off
against his vague colossal liabilities, and from first to last he
must have had a controlling influence in the direction of nearly
thirty millions. This irrational muddle of a community in
which we live gave him that, paid him at that rate for sitting
in a room and scheming and telling it lies. For he created
nothing, he invented nothing, he economised nothing. I
cannot claim that a single one of the great businesses we
organised added any real value to human life at all. Several
like Tono-Bungay were unmitigated frauds by any honest
standard, the giving of nothing coated in advertisements
for money. And the things the Hardingham gave out, I
repeat, were nothing to the things that came in. I think
of the long procession of people who sat down before us
and propounded this and that. Now it was a device for
selling bread under a fancy name and so escaping the laws
as to weight—this was afterwards floated as the Decorticated
Health-Bread Company and bumped against the law—
now it was a new scheme for still more strident advertisement,
now it was a story of unsuspected deposits of minerals, now a

cheap and nasty substitute for this or that common necessity, now the treachery of a too well-informed employee, anxious to become our partner. It was all put to us tentatively, persuasively. Sometimes one had a large pink blusterous person trying to carry us off our feet by his pseudo-boyish frankness, now some dyspeptically yellow whisperer, now some earnest, specially dressed youth with an eyeglass and a buttonhole, now some homely-speaking, shrewd Manchester man or some Scotchman eager to be very clear and full. Many came in couples or trios, often in tow of an explanatory solicitor. Some were white and earnest, some flustered beyond measure at their opportunity. Some of them begged and prayed to be taken up. My uncle chose what he wanted and left the rest. He became very autocratic to these applicants. He felt he could make them, and they felt so too. He had but to say "No!" and they faded out of existence. . . . He had become a sort of vortex to which wealth flowed of its own accord. His possessions increased by heaps ; his shares, his leaseholds and mortgages and debentures.

Behind his first-line things he found it necessary at last, and sanctioned by all the precedents, to set up three general trading companies, the London and African Investment Company, the British Traders' Loan Company, and Business Organisations Limited. That was in the culminating time when I had least to do with affairs. I don't say that with any desire to exculpate myself, I admit I was a director of all three, and I will confess I was wilfully incurious in that capacity. Each of these companies ended its financial year solvent by selling great holdings of shares to one or other of its sisters, and paying a dividend out of the proceeds. I sat at the table and agreed. That was our method of equilibrium at the iridescent climax of the bubble. . . .

You perceive now, however, the nature of the services for which this fantastic community gave him unmanageable wealth and power and real respect. It was all a monstrous payment for courageous fiction, a gratuity in return for the one reality of human life—illusion. We gave them a feeling of hope and profit ; we sent a tidal wave of water and confidence into their stranded affairs. "We mint Faith, George," said my uncle one day. "That's what we do. And by Jove we got to keep minting ! We been making human confidence ever since I drove the first cork of Tono-Bungay."

"Coining" would have been a better word than minting ! And yet, you know, in a sense he was right. Civilisation is possible only through confidence, so that we can bank our money and go unarmed about the streets. The bank reserve or a policeman keeping order in a jostling multitude of people, are only slightly less impudent bluffs than my uncle's prospectuses. They couldn't for a moment "make good" if the quarter of what they guarantee was demanded

of them. The whole of this modern mercantile investing
civilisation is indeed such stuff as dreams are made of. A
mass of people swelters and toils, great railway systems
grow, cities arise to the skies and spread wide and far, mines
are opened, factories hum, foundries roar, ships plough the
seas, countries are settled ; about this busy striving world
the rich owners go, controlling all, enjoying all, confident and
creating the confidence that draws us all together into a reluctant, nearly unconscious brotherhood. I wonder and plan
my engines. The flags flutter, the crowds cheer, the legis-
latures meet. Yet it seems to me indeed at times that all this
present commercial civilisation is no more than my poor uncle's
career writ large, a swelling, thinning bubble of assurances ;
that its arithmetic is just as unsound, its dividends as ill-
advised, its ultimate aim as vague and forgotten ; that it all
drifts on perhaps to some tremendous parallel to his individual disaster. . . .

Well, so it was we Boomed, and for four years and a half
we lived a life of mingled substance and moonshine. Until
our particular unsoundness overtook us we went about in the
most magnificent of motor-cars upon tangible high-roads, made
ourselves conspicuous and stately in splendid houses, ate
sumptuously and had a perpetual stream of notes and money
trickling into our pockets ; hundreds of thousands of men and
women respected us, saluted us and gave us toil and honour ;
I asked, and my work sheds rose, my aeroplanes swooped out
of nothingness to scare the downland pewits ; my uncle waved
his hand and Lady Grove and all its associations of chivalry
and ancient peace were his ; waved again, and architects were
busy planning the great palace he never finished at Crest
Hill and an army of workmen gathered to do his bidding,
blue marble came from Canada, and timber from New Zealand ;
and beneath it all, you know, there was nothing but fictitious
values as evanescent as rainbow gold.

§ 4

I pass the Hardingham ever and again and glance aside
through the great archway at the fountain and the ferns,
and think of those receding days when I was so near the
centre of our eddy of greed and enterprise. I see again
my uncle's face white and intent, and hear him discourse,
hear him make consciously Napoleonic decisions, " grip " his
nettles, put his " finger on the spot," " bluff," say " snap."
He became particularly addicted to the last idiom. Towards
the end every conceivable act took the form of saying
" snap ! " . . .

The odd fish that came to us ! And among others came
Gordon-Nasmyth, that queer blend of romance and illegality
who was destined to drag me into the most irrelevant ad-

venture in my life, the Mordet Island affair; and leave me, as they say, with blood upon my hands. It is remarkable how little it troubles my conscience and how much it stirs my imagination, that particular memory of the life I took. The story of Mordet Island has been told in a government report and told all wrong; there are excellent reasons for leaving it wrong in places, but the liveliest appeals of discretion forbid my leaving it out altogether.

I've still the vividest memory of Gordon-Nasmyth's appearance in the inner sanctum, a lank, sunburnt person in tweeds with a yellow-brown, hatchet face and one faded blue eye—the other was a closed and sunken lid—and how he told us with a stiff affectation of ease his incredible story of this great heap of quap that lay abandoned or undiscovered on the beach behind Mordet's Island among white dead mangroves and the black ooze of brackish water.

"What's quap?" said my uncle on the fourth repetition of the word.

"They call it quap, or quab, or quabb," said Gordon-Nasmyth; "but our relations weren't friendly enough to get the accent right. . . . But there the stuff is for the taking. They don't know about it. Nobody knows about it. I got down to the damned place in a canoe alone. The boys wouldn't come. I pretended to be botanising." . . .

To begin with, Gordon-Nasmyth was inclined to be dramatic.

"Look here," he said when he first came in, shutting the door rather carefully behind him as he spoke, "do you two men—yes or no—want to put up six thousand—for a clear good chance of fifteen hundred per cent. on your money in a year?"

"We're always getting chances like that," said my uncle, cocking his cigar offensively, wiping his glasses and tilting his chair back. "We stick to a safe twenty."

Gordon-Nasmyth's quick temper showed in a slight stiffening of his attitude.

"Don't you believe him," said I, getting up before he could reply. "*You're* different, and I know your books. We're very glad you've come to us. Confound it, uncle! It's Gordon-Nasmyth! Sit down. What is it? Minerals?"

"Quap," said Gordon-Nasmyth, fixing his eye on me, "in heaps."

"In heaps," said my uncle softly, with his glasses very oblique.

"You're only fit for the grocery," said Gordon-Nasmyth scornfully, sitting down and helping himself to one of my uncle's cigars. "I'm sorry I came. But, still, now I'm here. . . . And first as to quap; quap, sir, is the most radio-active stuff in the world. That's quap! It's a festering mass of earths and heavy metals, polonium, radium, ythorium,

thorium, carium, and new things too.   There's a stuff called
Xk—provisionally.   There they are, mucked up together in a
sort of rotting sand.   What it is, how it got made, I don't
know.   It's like as if some young creator had been playing
about there.   There it lies in two heaps, one small, one great,
and the world for miles about it is blasted and scorched and
dead.   You can have it for the getting.   You've got to take
it—that's all ! " . . .

"That sounds all right," said I.   "Have you samples ? "

"Well—*should* I ?   You can have anything—up to two
ounces."

"Where is it ? " . . .

His blue eye smiled at me and scrutinised me.   He smoked
and was fragmentary for a time, fending off my questions ;
then his story began to piece itself together.   He conjured
up a vision of this strange forgotten kink in the world's littoral,
of the long meandering channels that spread and divaricate
and spend their burthen of mud and silt within the thunderbelt
of Atlantic surf, of the dense, tangled vegetation that creeps
into the shimmering water with root and sucker.   He gave
a sense of heat and a perpetual reek of vegetable decay, and
told how at last comes a break among these things, an arena
fringed with bone-white dead trees, a sight of the hard blue
sea-line byond the dazzling surf and a wide desolation of dirty
shingle and mud, bleached and scarred. . . . A little way
off among charred dead weeds stands the abandoned station—
abandoned because every man who stayed two months at that
station stayed to die, eaten up mysteriously like a leper—with
its dismantled sheds and its decaying pier of worm-rotten
and oblique piles and planks, still insecurely possible.   And in
the midst, two clumsy heaps shaped like the backs of hogs,
one small, one great, sticking out under a rib of rock that cuts
the space across—quap !

"There it is," said Gordon-Nasmyth, "worth three pounds
an ounce, if it's worth a penny ; two great heaps of it, rotten
stuff and soft, ready to shovel and wheel, and you may get
it by the ton ! "

"How did it get there ? "

"God knows ! . . . There it is—for the taking !   In a
country where you mustn't trade.   In a country where the
company waits for good, kind men to find its riches and then
take 'em away from 'em.   There you have it—derelict."

"Can't you do any sort of deal ? "

"They're too damned stupid.   You've got to go and
take it.   That's all."

"They might catch you."

"They might, of course.   But they're not great at catching."

We went into the particulars of that difficulty.   "They
wouldn't catch me, because I'd sink first.   Give me a yacht,"
said Gordon-Nasmyth ; "that's all I need."

" But if you get caught," said my uncle. . . .

I am inclined to think Gordon-Nasmyth imagined we would give him a cheque for six thousand pounds on the strength of his talk. It was very good talk, but we didn't do that. I stipulated for samples of his stuff for analysis, and he consented—reluctantly. I think, on the whole, he would rather I didn't examine samples. He made a motion pocketwards, that gave us an invincible persuasion that he had a sample upon him, and that at the last instant he decided not to produce it prematurely. There was evidently a curious strain of secretiveness in him. He didn't like to give us samples, and he wouldn't indicate within three hundred miles the position of this Mordet Island of his. He had it clear in his mind that he had a secret of immense value, and he had no idea at all of just how far he ought to go with business people. And so presently, to gain time for these hesitations of his, he began to talk of other things.

He talked very well. He talked of the Dutch East Indies and of the Congo, of Portuguese East Africa and Paraguay, of Malays and rich Chinese merchants, Dyaks and negroes and the spread of the Mohammedan world in Africa to-day. And all this time he was trying to judge if we were good enough to trust with his adventure. Our cosy inner office became a little place, and all our businesses cold and lifeless exploits beside his glimpses of strange minglings of men, of slayings unavenged and curious customs, of trade where no writs run, and the dark treacheries of eastern ports and uncharted channels.

We had neither of us gone abroad except for a few vulgar raids on Paris, our world was England, and the places of origin of half the raw material of the goods we sold had seemed to us as remote as fairyland or the forest of Arden. But Gordon-Nasmyth made it so real and intimate for us that afternoon—for me, at any rate—that it seemed like something seen and forgotten and now again remembered.

And in the end he produced his sample, a little lump of muddy clay speckled with brownish grains, in a glass bottle wrapped about with lead and flannel—red flannel it was, I remember—a hue which is, I know, popularly supposed to double all the mystical efficacies of flannel.

" Don't carry it about on you," said Gordon-Nasmyth. " It makes a sore."

I took the stuff to Thorold, and Thorold had the exquisite agony of discovering two new elements in what was then a confidential analysis. He has christened them and published since, but at the time Gordon-Nasmyth wouldn't hear for a moment of our publication of any facts at all; indeed, he flew into a violent passion and abused me mercilessly even for showing the stuff to Thorold. " I thought you were going to analyse it yourself," he said with the touching persuasion of the layman that a scientific man knows and practises all the sciences.

I made some commercial inquiries, and there seemed even then much truth in Gordon-Nasmyth's estimate of the value of the stuff. It was before the days of Capern's discovery of the value of canadium and his use of it in the Capern filament, but the cerium and thorium alone were worth the money he extracted for the gas-mantles then in vogue. There were, however, doubts. Indeed, there were numerous doubts. What were the limits of the gas-mantle trade ? How much thorium, not to speak of cerium, could they take at a maximum ? Suppose that quantity was high enough to justify our ship-load, came doubts in another quarter. Were the heaps up to sample ? Were they as big as he said ? Was Gordon Nasmyth—imaginative ? And if these values held, could we after all get the stuff. It wasn't ours. It was on forbidden ground. You see, there were doubts of every grade and class in the way of this adventure.

We went some way, nevertheless, in the discussion of his project, though I think we tried his patience. Then suddenly he vanished from London, and I saw no more of him for a year and a half.

My uncle said that was what he had expected, and when at last Gordon-Nasmyth reappeared and mentioned in an incidental way that he had been to Paraguay on private (and we guessed passionate) affairs, the business of the " quap " expedition had to be begun again at the beginning. My uncle was disposed to be altogether sceptical, but I wasn't so decided. I think I was drawn by its picturesque aspects. But we neither of us dreamt of touching it seriously until Capern's discovery. . . .

Nasmyth's story had laid hold of my imagination like one small, intense picture of tropical sunshine hung on a wall of grey business affairs. I kept it going during Gordon-Nasmyth's intermittent appearances in England. Every now and then he and I would meet and reinforce its effect. We would lunch in London, or he would come to see my gliders at Crest Hill, and make new projects for getting at those heaps again, now with me, now alone. At times they became a sort of fairy story with us, an imaginative exercise. And then came Capern's discovery of what he called the ideal filament, and with it an altogether less problematical quality about the business side of quap. For the ideal filament needed five per cent. of canadium, and canadium was known to the world only as a newly separated constitutent of a variety of the rare mineral rutile. But to Thorold it was better known as an element in a mysterious sample brought to him by me, and to me it was known as one of the elements in quap. I told my uncle, and we jumped on to the process at once. We found that Gordon-Nasmyth, still unaware of the altered value of the stuff, and still thinking of the experimental prices of radium and the rarity value of cerium, had got hold of a cousin named Pollack, made some extraordinary transaction about his life-insurance policy, and was buying a brig. We cut in, put down three thousand pounds and forthwith the life-insurance transaction and the Pollack side of this finance vanished into thin air, leaving Pollack, I regret to say, in the brig and in the secret—except so far as canadium and the filament went—as residuum. We discussed earnestly whether we should charter a steamer or go on with the brig, but we decided on the brig as a less conspicuous instrument for an enterprise that was after all, to put it plainly, stealing.

But that was one of our last enterprises before our great crisis, and I will tell of it in its place.

So it was quap came into our affairs, came in as a fairy-tale and became real. More and more real it grew until at last it was real, until at last I saw with my eyes the heaps my imagination had seen for so long and felt between my fingers again that half-gritty, half-soft texture of quap, like sanded moist-sugar mixed with clay in which there stirs something——

One must feel it to understand.

§ 5

All sorts of things came to the Hardingham and offered themselves to my uncle. Gordon-Nasmyth stands out only because he played a part at last in the crisis of our fortunes. So much came to us that it seemed to me at times as though the whole world of human affairs was ready to prostitute itself to our real and imaginary millions. As I look back, I am still dazzled and incredulous to think of the quality of our opportunities. We did the most extraordinary things; things that it seems absurd to me to leave to any casual man of wealth and enterprise who cares to do them. I had some amazing perceptions of just how modern thought and the supply of fact to the general mind may be controlled by money. Among other things that my uncle offered for, he tried very hard to buy the *British Medical Journal* and the *Lancet*, and run them on what he called modern lines, and when they resisted him he talked very vigorously for a time of organising a rival enterprise. That was a very magnificent idea indeed in its way; it would have given a tremendous advantage in the handling of innumerable specialities, and indeed I scarcely know how far it would not have put the medical profession in our grip. It still amazes me—I shall die amazed—that such a thing can be possible in the modern state. If my uncle failed to bring the thing off, some one else may succeed. But I doubt, even if he had got both those weeklies, whether his peculiar style would have suited them.

The change of purpose would have shown. He would have
found it difficult to keep up their dignity.

He certainly did not keep up the dignity of the *Sacred
Grove*, an important critical organ which he acquired one
day—by saying " snap "—for eight hundred pounds. He
got it " lock, stock, and barrel "—under one or other of which
three aspects the editor was included. Even at that price it
didn't pay. If you are a literary person you will remember
the bright new cover he gave that representative organ of
British intellectual culture, and how his sound business instincts jarred with the exalted pretensions of a vanishing age.
One old wrapper I discovered the other day runs :—

" THE SACRED GROVE."

*A Weekly Magazine of Art, Philosophy, Science and
Belles Lettres.*

HAVE YOU A NASTY TASTE IN YOUR MOUTH ?

IT IS LIVER.

YOU NEED ONE TWENTY-THREE PILL.

(JUST ONE.)

NOT A DRUG BUT A LIVE AMERICAN REMEDY.

CONTENTS.

A Hitherto Unpublished Letter from Walter
   Pater.
Charlotte Brontë's Maternal Great Aunt.
A New Catholic History of England.
The Genius of Shakespeare.
Correspondence :—The Mendelian Hypothesis ;
   The Split Infinitive ; " Commence," or
   " Begin " ; Claverhouse ; Socialism and the
   Individual ; The Dignity of Letters.
Folk-lore Gossip.
The Stage ; the Paradox of Acting.
Travel, Biography, Verse, Fiction, etc.

THE BEST PILL IN THE WORLD FOR AN IRREGULAR LIVER.

I suppose it is some lingering traces of the Bladesover
tradition in me that makes this combination of letters and

pills seem so incongruous, just as I suppose it is a lingering
trace of Plutarch and my ineradicable boyish imagination
that at bottom our State should be wise, sane and dignified,
that makes me think a country which leaves its medical
and literary criticism, or indeed any such vitally important
criticism, entirely to private enterprise and open to the
advances of any purchaser must be in a frankly hopeless
condition. These are ideal conceptions of mine. As a
matter of fact, nothing could be more entirely natural and
representative of the relations of learning, thought and the
economic situation in the world at the present time than this
cover of the *Sacred Grove*—the quiet conservatism of the one
element embedded in the aggressive brilliance of the other ;
the contrasted notes of bold physiological experiment and
extreme mental immobility.

§ 6

There comes back, too, among these Hardingham memories
an impression of a drizzling November day, and how we looked
out of the windows upon a procession of the London unemployed.

It was like looking down a well into some momentarily
revealed nether world. Some thousands of needy ineffectual
men had been raked together to trail their spiritless misery
through the West End with an appeal that was also in its
way a weak and unsubstantial threat : " It is Work we need,
not Charity."

There they were, half-phantom through the fog, a silent,
foot-dragging, interminable, grey procession. They carried
wet, dirty banners, they rattled boxes for pence ; these
men who had not said " snap " in the right place, the men
who had " snapped " too eagerly, the men who had never
said " snap," the men who had never had a chance of saying
" snap." A shambling, shameful stream they made, oozing
along the street, the gutter waste of competitive civilisation.
And we stood high out of it all, as high as if we looked godlike
from another world, standing in a room beautifully lit and
furnished, skilfully warmed, filled with costly things.

" There," thought I, " but for the grace of God, go George
and Edward Ponderevo."

But my uncle's thoughts ran in a different channel, and
he made that vision the text of a spirited but inconclusive
harangue upon Tariff Reform.

CHAPTER TWO

§ 1

So far my history of my aunt and uncle has dealt chiefly with his industrial and financial exploits. But side by side with that history of inflation from the infinitesimal to the immense is another development, the change year by year from the shabby impecuniosity of the Camden Town lodging to the lavish munificence of the Crest Hill marble staircase and my aunt's golden bed, the bed that was facsimiled from Fontainebleau. And the odd thing is that as I come to this nearer part of my story I find it much more difficult to tell than the clear little perspective memories of the earlier days. Impressions crowd upon one another and overlap one another ; I was presently to fall in love again, to be seized by a passion to which I still faintly respond, a passion that still clouds my mind. I came and went between Ealing and my aunt and uncle, and presently between Effie and clubland, and then between business and a life of research that became far more continuous, infinitely more consecutive and memorable than any of these other sets of experiences. I didn't witness a regular social progress therefore ; my aunt and uncle went up in the world so far as I was concerned as if they were displayed by an early cinematograph, with little jumps and flickers.

As I recall this side of our life, the figure of my round-eyed, button-nosed, pink-and-white Aunt Susan tends always to the central position. We drove the car and sustained the car, she sat in it with a magnificent variety of headgear poised upon her delicate neck, and—always with that faint ghost of a lisp no misspelling can render—commented on and illuminated the new aspects.

I've already sketched the little home behind the Wimblehurst chemist's shop, the lodging near the Cobden statue, and the apartments in Gower Street. Thence my aunt and uncle went into a flat in Redgauntlet Mansions. There they lived when I married. It was a compact flat, with very little for a woman to do in it. In those days my aunt, I think, used to find the time heavy upon her hands, and so she took to books and reading, and after a time even to going to lectures in the afternoon. I began to find unexpected books upon her table ; sociological books, travels, Shaw's plays.

" Hallo ! " I said, at the sight of some volume of the latter.

" I'm keeping a mind, George," she explained.

" Eh ? "

" Keeping a mind. Dogs I never cared for. It's been a toss-up between setting up a mind and setting up a soul. It's jolly lucky for Him and you it's a mind. I've joined the London Library, and I'm going in for the Royal Institution and every blessed lecture that comes along next winter. You'd better look out." . . .

And I remember her coming in late one evening with a note-book in her hand.

" Where ye been, Susan ? " said my uncle.

" Birkbeck—Physiology. I'm getting on." She sat down and took off her gloves. " You're just glass to me," she sighed, and then in a note of grave reproach : " You old *Package* ! I had no idea ! The Things you've kept from me ! " . . .

Presently they were setting up the house at Beckenham, and my aunt intermitted her intellectual activities. The house at Beckenham was something of an enterprise for them at that time, a reasonably large place by the standards of the early years of Tono-Bungay. It was a big, rather gaunt villa, with a conservatory and a shrubbery, a tennis-lawn, a quite considerable vegetable garden, and a small disused coach-house. I had some glimpses of the excitements of its inauguration, but not many because of the estrangement between my aunt and Marion.

My aunt went into that house with considerable zest, and my uncle distinguished himself by the thoroughness with which he did the repainting and replumbing. He had all the drains up and most of the garden with them, and stood administrative on heaps—administrating whisky to the workmen. I found him there one day, most Napoleonic, on a little Elba of dirt, in an atmosphere that defies print. He also, I remember, chose what he considered cheerful contrasts of colours for the painting of the woodwork. This exasperated my aunt extremely—she called him a " Pestilential old Splosher " with an unusual note of earnestness—and he also enraged her into novelties of abuse by giving each bedroom the name of some favourite hero—Clive, Napoleon, Cæsar, and so forth—and having it painted on the door in gilt letters on a black label. " Martin Luther " was kept for me. Only her respect for domestic discipline, she said, prevented her retaliating with " Old Pondo " on the housemaid's cupboard.

Also he went and ordered one of the completest sets of garden requisites I have ever seen—and had them all painted a hard, clear blue. My aunt got herself large tins of a kindlier hued enamel and had everything secretly recoated, and this done, she found great joy in the garden and became an ardent rose grower and herbaceous borderer, leaving her Mind, indeed, to damp evenings and the winter months. When I think of her at Beckenham, I always think first of her as dressed in that blue cotton stuff she affected, with her arms in huge gauntleted gardening gloves, a trowel in one hand and a small but no doubt hardy and promising seedling, limp and very young-looking and sheepish, in the other.

Beckenham, in the persons of a vicar, a doctor's wife, and a large proud lady called Hogberry, "called" on my uncle and aunt almost at once, so soon as the lawn was down again, and afterwards my aunt made friends with a quiet gentlewoman next door, à propos of an overhanging cherry tree and the need of repairing the party fence. So she resumed her place in society from which she had fallen with the disaster of Wimblehurst. She made a partially facetious study of the etiquette of her position, had cards engraved and retaliated calls. And then she received a card for one of Mrs. Hogberry's At Homes, gave an old garden party herself, participated in a bazaar and sale of work, and was really becoming quite cheerfully entangled in Beckenham society when she was suddenly taken up by the roots again by my uncle and transplanted to Chislehurst.

"Old Trek, George," she said compactly, "Onward and Up," when I found her superintending the loading of two big furniture vans. "Go up and say good-bye to 'Martin Luther,' and then I'll see what you can do to help me."

§ 2

I look into the jumbled stores of the middle distance of memory, and Beckenham seems to me a quite transitory phase. But really they were there several years; through nearly all my married life in fact, and far longer than the year and odd months we lived together at Wimblehurst. But the Wimblehurst time with them is fuller in my memory by far than the Beckenham period. There comes back to me with a quite considerable amount of detail the effect of that garden party of my aunt's and of a little social misbehaviour of which I was guilty on that occasion. It's like a scrap from another life. It's all set in what is for me a kind of cutaneous feeling, the feeling of rather ill-cut city clothes, frock-coat and grey trousers, and of a high collar and tie worn in sunshine among flowers. I have still a quite vivid memory of the little trapezoidal lawn, of the gathering and particularly of the hats and feathers of the gathering, of the parlour-maid and the blue tea-cups, and of the magnificent presence of Mrs. Hogberry and of her clear resonant voice. It was a voice that would have gone with a garden party on a larger scale; it went into adjacent premises; it included the gardener who was far up the vegetable patch and technically out of play. The only other men were my aunt's doctor, two of the clergy, amiable contrasted men, and Mrs. Hogberry's imperfectly grown-up son, a youth just bursting into collar. The rest were women, except for a young girl or so in a state of speechless good behaviour. Marion also was there.

Marion and I had arrived a little estranged, and I remember
her as a silent presence, a shadow across all that sunlit
emptiness of intercourse.   We had embittered each other with
one of those miserable disputes that seemed so unavoidable
between us.   She had, with the help of Smithie, dressed rather
elaborately for the occasion, and when she saw me prepared
to accompany her in, I think it was, a grey suit, she protested
that silk hat and frock-coat were imperative.   I was recalcitrant, she quoted an illustrated paper showing a garden party
with the King present, and finally I capitulated—but after my
evil habit, resentfully. . . .

Eh dear !   those old quarrels, how pitiful they were, how
trivial !   And how sorrowful they are to recall !   I think they
grow more sorrowful as I grow older, and all the small
passionate reasons for our mutual anger fade and fade out of
memory.

The impression that Beckenham company has left on my
mind is one of a modest unreality ;   they were all maintaining
a front of unspecified social pretension, and evading the display
of the economic facts of the case.   Most of the husbands were
" in business " off stage—it would have been outrageous to
ask what the business was—and the wives were giving their
energies to produce with the assistance of novels and the illustrated magazines, a moralised version of the afternoon life
of the aristocratic class.   They hadn't the intellectual or
moral enterprise of the upper-class woman, they had no
political interests, they had no views about anything, and
consequently they were, I remember, extremely difficult to
talk to.   They all sat about in the summer-house and in
garden-chairs, and were very hatty and ruffley and sunshadey.
Three ladies and the curate played croquet with a general
immense gravity broken by occasional loud cries of feigned
distress from the curate.   " Oh !   Whacking me about
again !   Augh ! "

The dominant social fact that afternoon was Mrs. Hogberry ;   she took up a central position commanding the croquet
and went on, as my aunt said to me in an incidental aside,
" like an old Roundabout."   She talked of the way in which
Beckenham society was getting mixed, and turned on to a
touching letter she had recently received from her former nurse
at Little Gossdean.   Followed a loud account of Little Gossdean and how much she and her eight sisters had been looked
up to there.   " My poor mother was quite a little Queen
there," she said.   " And such *nice* Common People !   People
say the country labourers are getting disrespectful nowadays.
It isn't so—not if they're properly treated.   Here, of course, in
Beckenham it's different.   I don't call the people we get here a
Poor—they're certainly not a proper Poor.   They're Masses.
I always tell Mr. Bugshoot they're Masses, and ought to be
treated as such." . .

Dim memories of Mrs. Mackridge floated through my mind as I listened to her. . . .

I was whirled on this roundabout for a bit, and then had the fortune to fall off into a *tête-à-tête* with a lady whom my aunt introduced as Mrs. Mumble—but then she introduced everybody to me as Mumble that afternoon, either by way of humour or necessity.

That must have been one of my earliest essays in the art of polite conversation, and I remember that I began by criticising the local railway service, and that at the third sentence or thereabouts Mrs. Mumble said in a distinctly bright and encouraging way that she feared I was a very " frivolous " person.

I wonder now what it was I said that was " frivolous."

I don't know what happened to end that conversation, or if it had an end. I remember talking to one of the clergy for a time rather awkwardly, and being given a sort of topographical history of Beckenham, which he assured me time after time, was " Quite an old place. *Quite* an old place." As though I had treated it as new and he meant to be very patient but very convincing. Then we hung up in a distinct pause, and my aunt rescued me. " George," she said in a confidential undertone, " keep the pot-a-boiling." And then audibly, " I say, will you both old trot about with tea a bit ? "

" Only too delighted to *trot* for you, Mrs. Ponderevo," said the clergyman, becoming fearfully expert and in his element ; " only too delighted."

I found we were near a rustic table, and that the housemaid was behind us in a suitable position to catch us on the rebound with the tea things.

" Trot ! " repeated the clergyman to me, much amused ; " excellent expression ! " and I just saved him from the tray as he turned about.

We handed tea for a while. . . .

" Give 'em cakes," said my aunt, flushed but well in hand. " Helps 'em to talk, George. Always talk best after a little nushment. Like throwing a bit of turf down an old geyser."

She surveyed the gathering with a predominant blue eye and helped herself to tea.

" They keep on going stiff," she said in an undertone. . . . " I've done my best."

" It's been a huge success," I said encouragingly.

" That boy has had his legs crossed in that position and hasn't spoken for ten minutes. Stiffer and stiffer. Brittle. He's beginning a dry cough—always a bad sign, George. . . . Walk 'em about, shall I ?—rub their noses with snow ? "

Happily she didn't. I got myself involved with the gentlewoman from next door, a pensive, languid-looking little woman with a low voice, and fell talking ; our topic, Cats and Dogs, and which it was we liked best.

"I always feel," said the pensive little woman, "that there's something about a dog—— A cat hasn't got it."

"Yes," I found myself admitting with great enthusiasm, "there *is* something. And yet again——"

"Oh! I know there's something about a cat too. But it isn't the same."

"Not quite the same," I admitted; "but still it's something."

"Ah! But such a different something!"

"More sinuous."

"Much more."

"Ever so much more." . . .

"It make all the difference, don't you think?"

"Yes," I said, "*all.*"

She glanced at me gravely and sighed a long, deep-felt "*Yes.*" A long pause.

The thing seemed to me to amount to a stalemate. Fear came into my heart and much perplexity.

"The -er, Roses," I said. I felt like a drowning man. "Those roses—don't you think they are—very beautiful flowers?"

"Aren't they!" she agreed gently. "There seems to be something in roses—something—I don't know how to express it."

"Something," I said helpfully.

"Yes," she said, "something. Isn't there?"

"So few people see it," I said; "more's the pity!"

She sighed and said again very softly, "*Yes.*" . . .

There was another long pause. I looked at her, and she was thinking dreamily. The drowning sensation returned, the fear and enfeeblement. I perceived by a sort of inspiration that her tea-cup was empty.

"Let me take your cup," I said abruptly, and, that secured, made for the table by the summer-house. I had no intention then of deserting my aunt. But close at hand the big French window of the drawing-room yawned inviting and suggestive. I can feel all that temptation now, and particularly the provocation of my collar. In an instant I was lost. I would—— Just for a moment!

I dashed in, put down the cup on the keys of the grand piano and fled upstairs, softly, swiftly, three steps at a time, to the sanctuary of my uncle's study, his snuggery. I arrived there breathless, convinced there was no return for me. I was very glad and ashamed of myself and desperate. By means of a penknife I contrived to break open his cabinet of cigars, drew a chair to the window, took off my coat, collar and tie, and remained smoking guiltily and rebelliously, and peeping through the blind at the assembly on the lawn until it was altogether gone. . . .

The clergymen, I thought, were wonderful.

§ 3

A few such pictures of those early days at Beckenham stand out, and then I find myself among the Chislehurst memories. The Chislehurst mansion had " grounds " rather than a mere garden, and there was a gardener's cottage and a little lodge at the gate. The ascendant movement was always far more in evidence there than at Beckenham. The velocity was increasing.

One night picks itself out as typical, as in its way marking an epoch. I was there, I think, about some advertisement stuff, on some sort of business anyhow, and my uncle and aunt had come back in a fly from a dinner at the Runcorns. (Even then he was nibbling at Runcorn with the idea of our great Amalgamation budding in his mind.) I got down there, I suppose, about eleven. I found the two of them sitting in the study, my aunt on a chair-arm with a whimsical pensiveness on her face, regarding my uncle, and he, much extended and very rotund, in the low arm-chair drawn up to the fender.

" Look here, George," said my uncle after my first greetings, " I just been saying : We aren't Oh Fay ! "

" Eh ? "

" Not Oh Fay ! Socially ! "

" Old *Fly*, he means, George—French ! "

" Oh ! Didn't think of French. One never knows where to have him. What's gone wrong to-night ? "

" I been thinking. It isn't any particular thing. I ate too much of that fishy stuff at first, like salt frog spawn, and was a bit confused by olives ; and—well, I didn't know which wine was which. Had to say *that* each time. It puts your talk all wrong. And she wasn't in evening dress, not like the others. We can't go on in that style, George—not a proper ad'."

" I'm not sure you were right," I said, " in having a fly."

" We got to do it all better," said my uncle, " we got to do it in Style. Smart business, smart men. She tries to pass it off as humorous "—my aunt pulled a grimace—" it isn't humorous ! See ! We're on the up-grade now, fair and square. We're going to be big. We aren't going to be laughed at as Poovenoos, see ! "

" Nobody laughed at you," said my aunt. " Old Bladder ! "

" Nobody isn't going to laugh at me," said my uncle, glancing at his contours and suddenly sitting up.

My aunt raised her eyebrows slightly, swung her foot, and said nothing.

" We aren't keeping pace with our own progress, George. We got to. We're bumping against new people, and they set up to be gentlefolks—etiquette dinners and all the rest of it. They give themselves airs and expect us to be fish-out-of-water. We aren't going to be. They think we've no Style. Well, we give them Style for our advertisements, and we're

going to give 'em Style all through. . . . You needn't be born
to it to dance well on the wires of the Bond Street tradesmen.
See ? "

I handed him the cigar-box.

" Runcorn hadn't cigars like these," he said, truncating one
lovingly. " We beat him at cigars. We'll beat him all round."

My aunt and I regarded him, full of apprehensions.

" I got idees," he said darkly to the cigar, deepening our
dread.

He pocketed his cigar-cutter and spoke again.

" We got to learn all the rotten little game first. See ?
F'rinstance, we got to get samples of all the blessed wines
there are—and learn 'em up. Stern, Smoor, Burgundy,
all of 'em ! She took Stern to-night—and when she tasted
it first—— You pulled a face, Susan, you did. I saw
you. It surprised you. You bunched your nose. We got
to get used to wine and not do that. We got to get used to
wearing evening dress—*you*, Susan, too."

" Always have had a tendency to stick out of my clothes,"
said my aunt. " However—— Who cares ? " She shrugged
her shoulders.

I had never seen my uncle so immensely serious.

" Got to get the hang of etiquette," he went on to the
fire. " Horses even. Practise everything. Dine every night
in evening dress. . . . Get a brougham or something. Learn
up golf and tennis and things. Country gentleman. Oh
Fay. It isn't only freedom from Goochery."

" Eh ? " I said.

" Oh !—Gawshery, if you like ! "

" French, George," said my aunt. " But *I'm* not old
Gooch. I made that face for fun."

" It isn't only freedom from Gawshery. We got to have
Style. See ! Style ! Just all right and one better. That's
what I call Style. We can do it, and we will."

He mumbled his cigar and smoked for a space, leaning
forward and looking into the fire.

" What is it," he asked, " after all ? What is it ? Tips
about eating ; tips about drinking. Clothes. How to hold
yourself, and not say jes' the few little things they know for
certain are wrong—jes' the shibboleth things." . . .

He was silent again, and the cigar crept up from the horizontal towards the zenith as the confidence of his mouth
increased.

" Learn the whole bag of tricks in six months," he said,
becoming more cheerful. " Eh, Susan ? Beat 'em out !
George, you in particular ought to get hold of it. Ought
to get into a good club, and all that."

" Always ready to learn," I said. " Ever since you gave
me the chance of Latin. So far we don't seem to have hit
upon any Latin-speaking stratum in the population."

" We've come to French," said my aunt, " anyhow."

" It's a very useful language," said my uncle. " Puts a point on things. Zzzz. As for accent, no Englishman has an accent. No Englishman pronounces French properly. Don't you tell *me*. It's a Bluff. It's all a Bluff. Life's a Bluff—practically. That's why it's so important, Susan, for us to attend to Style. Le Steel Say Lum. The Style it's the man. Whad you laughing at, Susan ? . . . George, you're not smoking. These cigars are good for the mind. . . . What do *you* think of it all ? We got to adapt ourselves. We have—so far. . . . Not going to be beat by these silly things."

§ 4

" What do you think of it, George ? " he insisted.

What I said I thought of it I don't now recall. Only I have very distinctly the impression of meeting for a moment my aunt's impenetrable eye. And anyhow he started in with his accustomed energy to rape the mysteries of the Costly Life, and become the calmest of its lords. On the whole I think he did it—thoroughly. I have crowded memories, a little difficult to disentangle, of his experimental stages, his experimental proceedings. It's hard at times to say which memory comes in front of which. I recall him as presenting on the whole a series of small surprises, as being again and again, unexpectedly, a little more self-confident, a little more polished, a little richer and finer, a little more aware of the positions and values of things and men. There was a time— it must have been very early—when I saw him deeply impressed by the splendours of the dining-room of the National Liberal Club. Heaven knows who our host was or what that particular little " feed " was about now !—all that sticks is the impression of our straggling entry, a string of six or seven guests, and my uncle looking about him at the numerous bright red-shaded tables, at the exotics in great Majolica jars, at the shining ceramic columns and pilasters, at the impressive portraits of Liberal statesmen and heroes, and all that contributes to the ensemble of that palatial spectacle. He was betrayed into a whisper to me, "This is all Right, George ! " he said. That artless comment seems almost incredible as I set it down ; there came a time so speedily when not even the clubs of New York could have overawed my uncle, and when he could walk through the bowing magnificence of the Royal Grand Hotel to his chosen table in that aggressively exquisite gallery upon the river, with all the easy calm of one of earth's legitimate kings.

The two of them learned the new game rapidly and well ; they experimented abroad, they experimented at home. At Chislehurst, with the aid of a new, very costly, but highly instructive cook, they tried over everything they heard of that roused their curiosity and had any reputation for difficulty, from asparagus to plover's eggs. They afterwards got a gardener who could wait at table—and he brought the soil home to one. Then there came a butler.

I remember my aunt's first dinner-gown very brightly, and how she stood before the fire in the drawing-room con fessing once unsuspected pretty arms with all the courage she possessed, and looking over her shoulder at herself in a mirror.

"A ham," she remarked reflectively, "must feel like this. Just a necklace." . . .

I attempted, I think, some commonplace compliment.

My uncle appeared at the door in a white waistcoat and with his hands in his trouser pockets ; he halted and surveyed her critically.

"Couldn't tell you from a duchess, Susan," he remarked. "I'd like to have you painted, standin' at the fire like that. Sargent ! You look—spirited, somehow. Lord !—I wish some of those damned tradesmen at Wimblehurst could see you." . . .

They did a lot of week-ending at hotels, and sometimes I went down with them. We seemed to fall into a vast drifting crowd of social learners. I don't know whether it is due simply to my changed circumstances, but it seems to me there have been immensely disproportionate developments of the hotel-frequenting and restaurant-using population during the last twenty years. It is not only, I think, that there are crowds of people who, like we were, are in the economically ascendant phase, but whole masses of the prosperous section of the population must be altering their habits, giving up high-tea for dinner and taking to evening dress, using the week-end hotels as a practice-ground for these new social arts. A swift and systematic conversion to gentility has been going on, I am convinced, throughout the whole commercial upper-middle class since I was twenty-one. Curiously mixed was the personal quality of the people one saw in these raids. There were conscientiously refined and low-voiced people reeking with proud bashfulness ; there were aggressively smart people using pet diminutives for each other loudly and seeking fresh occasions for brilliant rudeness ; there were awkward husbands and wives quarrelling furtively about their manners and ill at ease under the eye of the waiter—cheerfully amiable and often discrepant couples with a disposition to inconspicuous corners, and the jolly sort, affecting an unaffected ease ; plump happy ladies who laughed too loud, and gentlemen in evening dress who subsequently " got their pipes." And nobody, you knew, was anybody, however expensively they dressed and whatever rooms they took.

I look back now with a curious remoteness of spirit to those crowded dining-rooms with their dispersed tables and their inevitable red-shaded lights and the unsympathetic,

unskilful waiters, and the choice of " Thig or Glear, sir ? "
I've not dined in that way, in that sort of place, now for five
years—it must be quite five years, so specialised and narrow
is my life becoming.

My uncle's earlier motor-car phases work in with these
associations, and there stands out a little bright vignette
of the hall of the Magnificent, Bexhill-on-Sea, and people
dressed for dinner and sitting about amidst the scarlet furni-
ture-satin and white enamelled woodwork until the gong should
gather them ; and my aunt is there, very marvellously wrapped
about in a dust cloak and a cage-like veil, and there are hotel
porters and under-porters very alert, and an obsequious
manager, and the tall young lady in black from the office is
surprised into admiration, and in the middle of the picture is
my uncle making his first appearance in that Esquimaux
costume I have already mentioned, a short figure, compactly
immense, hugely goggled, wearing a sort of brown rubber
proboscis, and surmounted by a table-land of motoring cap.

§ 5

So it was we recognised our new needs as fresh invaders
of the upper levels of the social system, and set ourselves
quite consciously to the acquisition of Style and *Savoir
Faire.* We became part of what is nowadays quite an important element in the confusion of our world, that multitude
of economically ascendant people who are learning how to
spend money. It is made up of financial people, the owners of
the businesses that are eating up their competitors, inventors
of new sources of wealth such as ourselves ; it includes nearly
all America as one sees it on the European stage. It is a
various multitude having only this in common ; they are
all moving, and particularly their womenkind are moving,
from conditions in which means were insistently finite, things
were few and customs simple, towards a limitless expenditure
and the sphere of attraction of Bond Street, Fifth Avenue, and
Paris. Their general effect is one of progressive revelation,
of limitless rope.

They discover suddenly indulgences their moral code
never foresaw and has no provision for, elaborations, ornaments, possessions beyond their wildest dreams. With an
immense astonished zest they begin *shopping,* begin a systematic adaptation to a new life crowded and brilliant with
things shopped, with jewels, maids, butlers, coachmen,
electric broughams, hired town and country houses. They
plunge into it as one plunges into a career ; as a class, they
talk, think, and dream possessions. Their literature, their
Press, turns all on that ; immense illustrated weeklies of un-
surpassed magnificence guide them in domestic architecture,
in the art of owning a garden, in the achievement of the

sumptuous in motor-cars, in an elaborate sporting equipment, in the purchase and control of their estates, in travel
and stupendous hotels. Once they begin to move they go far
and fast. Acquisition becomes the substance of their lives.
They find a world organised to gratify that passion. In a
brief year or so they are connoisseurs. They join in the plunder
of the eighteenth century, buy rare old books, fine old pictures,
good old furniture. Their first crude conception of dazzling
suites of the newly perfect is replaced almost from the outset
by a jackdaw dream of accumulating costly discrepant old
things. . . .

I seem to remember my uncle taking to shopping quite
suddenly. In the Beckenham days and in the early Chislehurst days he was chiefly interested in getting money, and
except for his onslaught on the Beckenham house, bothered
very little about his personal surroundings and possessions.
I forget now when the change came and he began to spend.
Some accident must have revealed to him this new source of
power, or some subtle shifting occurred in the tissues of his
brain. He began to spend and " shop." So soon as he began
to shop, he began to shop violently. He began buying pictures,
and then, oddly enough, old clocks. For the Chislehurst
house he bought nearly a dozen grandfather clocks and three
copper warming-pans. After that he bought much furniture.
Then he plunged into art patronage, and began to commission
pictures and to make presents to churches and institutions.
His buying increased with a regular acceleration. Its development was a part of the mental changes that came to him in the
wild excitements of the last four years of his ascent. Towards
the climax he was a furious spender ; he shopped with large,
unexpected purchases, he shopped like a mind seeking expression, he shopped to astonish and dismay ; shopped
crescendo, shopped *fortissimo, con molto expressione* until the
magnificent smash of Crest Hill ended his shopping for ever.
Always it was he who shopped. My aunt did not shine as a
purchaser. It is a curious thing, due to I know not what fine
strain in her composition, that my aunt never set any great
store upon possessions. She plunged through that crowded
bazaar of Vanity Fair during those feverish years, spending
no doubt freely and largely, but spending with detachment
and a touch of humorous contempt for the things, even the
" old " things, that money can buy. It came to me suddenly
one afternoon just how detached she was, as I saw her going towards the Hardingham, sitting up as she always did rather stiffly
in her electric brougham, regarding the glittering world with interested and ironically innocent blue eyes from under the brim
of a hat that defied comment. " No one," I thought, " would
sit so apart if she hadn't dreams—and what are her dreams ? "
I'd never thought.

And I remember, too, an outburst of scornful description

after she had lunched with a party of women at the Imperial
Cosmic Club. She came round to my rooms on the chance
of finding me there, and I gave her tea. She professed herself
tired and cross, and flung herself into my chair. . . .

"George," she cried, "the Things women are ! Do *I* stink
of money ? "

"Lunching ? " I asked.

She nodded.

"Plutocratic ladies ? "

"Yes."

"Oriental type ? "

"Oh !   Like a burst hareem ! . . . Bragging of possessions.
. . . They feel you. They feel your clothes, George, to see if
they are good ! "

I soothed her as well as I could. "They *are* Good, aren't
they ? " I said.

"It's the old pawnshop in their blood," she said, drinking
tea ; and then in infinite disgust, "They run their hands
over your clothes—they paw you."

I had a moment of doubt whether perhaps she had not
been discovered in possession of unsuspected forgeries. I
don't know. After that my eyes were quickened, and I
began to see for myself women running their hands over other
women's furs. scrutinising their lace, even demanding to
handle jewellery, appraising, envying, testing. They have a
kind of etiquette. The woman who feels says, "What
beautiful sables ! "   "What lovely lace ! "   The woman felt
admits proudly : "It's Real, you know," or disavows pretension modestly and hastily, "It's not Good." In each
other's houses they peer at the pictures, handle the selvage of
hangings, look at the bottoms of china. . . .

I wonder if it *is* the old pawnshop in the blood.

I doubt if Lady Drew and the Olympians did that sort of
thing, but there I may be only clinging to another of my
former illusions about aristocracy and the State. Perhaps
always possessions have been Booty, and never anywhere
has there been such a thing as house and furnishings native
and natural to the women and men who made use of them. . . .

§ 6

For me, at least, it marked an epoch in my uncle's career
when I learnt one day that he had "shopped" Lady Grove.
I realised a fresh, wide, unpreluded step. He took me by
surprise with the sudden change of scale from such portable
possessions as jewels and motor-cars to a stretch of country-
side. The transaction was Napoleonic ; he was told of the
place ; he said "snap" ; there were no preliminary desirings
or searchings. Then he came home and said what he had
done. Even my aunt was for a day or so measurably

awe-stricken by this exploit in purchase, and we both went
down with him to see the house in a mood near consternation.
It struck us then as a very lordly place indeed. I remember
the three of us standing on the terrace that looked westward,
surveying the sky-reflecting windows of the house, and a feeling
of unwarrantable intrusion comes back to me.

Lady Grove, you know, is a very beautiful house indeed,
a still and gracious place, whose age-long seclusion was only
effectively broken with the toot of the coming of the motor-
car. An old Catholic family had died out in it, century by
century, and was now altogether dead. Portions of the fabric
are thirteenth century, and its last architectural revision was
Tudor ; within, it is for the most part dark and chilly, save
for two or three favoured rooms and its tall-windowed, oak-
galleried hall. Its terrace is its noblest feature, a very wide,
broad lawn it is, bordered by a low stone battlement, and there
is a great cedar in one corner under whose level branches one
looks out across the blue distances of the Weald—blue distances that are made extraordinarily Italian in quality by virtue
of the dark masses of that single tree. It is a high-hung
terrace ; southward one looks down upon the tops of way-
faring trees and spruces, and westward on a steep slope of
beechwood, through which the road comes. One turns back to
the still old house, and sees a grey and lichenous façade
with a finely arched entrance. It was warmed by the
afternoon light and touched with the colour of a few neglected
roses and a pyracanthus. It seemed to me that the most
modern owner conceivable in this serene fine place was some
bearded scholarly man in a black cassock, gentle-voiced
and white-handed, or some soft-robed, grey gentlewoman.
And there was my uncle holding his goggles in a sealskin
glove, wiping the glass with a pocket-handkerchief, and asking
my aunt if Lady Grove wasn't a " Bit of all Right."

My aunt made him no answer.

"The man who built this," I speculated, "wore armour
and carried a sword."

" There's some of it inside still," said my uncle.

We went inside. An old woman with very white hair was
in charge of the place, and cringed rather obviously to the new
master. She evidently found him a strange and frightful
apparition, and was dreadfully afraid of him. But if
the surviving present bowed down to us, the past did not.
We stood up to the dark long portraits of the extinguished
race—one was a Holbein—and looked them in their sidelong
eyes. They looked back at us. We all, I know, felt the enigmatical quality in them. Even my uncle was momentarily
embarrassed, I think, by that invincibly self-complacent expression. It was just as though, after all, he had *not* bought
them up and replaced them altogether, as though that, secretly,
they knew better and could smile at him. . . .

The spirit of the place was akin to Bladesover but touched with something older and remoter. That armour that stood about had once served in tilt-yards, if indeed it has not served in battle, and this family had sent its blood and treasure, time after time, upon the most romantic quest in history, to Palestine. Dreams, loyalties, place and honour, how utterly had it all evaporated, leaving at last the final expression of its spirit, these quaint painted smiles, these smiles of triumphant completion. It had evaporated, indeed, long before the ultimate Durgan had died, and in his old age he had cumbered the place with Early-Victorian cushions and carpets and tapestry tablecloths and invalid appliances of a type even more extinct it seemed to us than the Crusades. . . . Yes, it was different from Bladesover.

"Bit stuffy, George," said my uncle. "They hadn't much idee of ventilation when this was built."

One of the panelled rooms was half-filled with presses and a four-poster bed. "Might be the ghost room," said my uncle ; but it did not seem to me that so retiring a family as the Durgans, so old and completed and exhausted a family as the Durgans, was likely to haunt anybody. What living thing now had any concern with their honour and judgments and good and evil deeds ? Ghosts and witchcraft were a later innovation ; that fashion came from Scotland with the Stuarts. . . .

Afterwards, prying for epitaphs, we found a marble crusader with a broken nose, under a battered canopy of fretted stone, outside the restricted limits of the present Duffield church, and half-buried in nettles. "Ichabod," said my uncle. "Eh ? We shall be like that, Susan, some day. . . . I'm going to clean him up a bit and put a railing to keep off the children."

"Old saved at the eleventh hour," said my aunt, quoting one of the less successful advertisements of Tono-Bungay.

But I don't think my uncle heard her.

It was by our captured crusader that the vicar found us. He came round the corner at us briskly, a little out of breath. He had an air of having been running after us since the first toot of our horn had warned the village of our presence. He was an Oxford man, clean-shaven, with a cadaverous complexion and a guardedly respectful manner, a cultivated intonation, and a general air of accommodation to the new order of things. These Oxford men are the Greeks of our plutocratic empire. He was a Tory in spirit, and what one may call an adapted Tory by stress of circumstances, that is to say he was no longer a legitimist, he was prepared for the substitution of new lords for old. We were pill vendors, he knew, and no doubt horribly vulgar in soul ; but then it might have been some polygamous Indian rajah, a great strain on a good man's tact, or some Jew with an inherited expression of contempt. Anyhow, we were English and neither Dissenters nor Socialists, and he was cheerfully prepared to do what he could to make gentlemen of both of us. He might have preferred Americans for some reasons ; they are not so obviously taken from one part of the social system and dumped down in another, and they are more teachable ; but in this world we cannot always be choosers. So he was very bright and pleasant with us, showed us the church, gossiped inform- ingly about our neighbours on the country-side, Tux the banker, Lord Boom the magazine and newspaper proprietor, Lord Carnaby, that great sportsman, and old Lady Osprey. And finally he took us by way of a village lane—three children bobbed convulsively with eyes of terror for my uncle—through a meticulous garden to a big, slovenly Vicarage with faded Victorian furniture and a faded Victorian wife, who gave us tea and introduced us to a confusing family dispersed among a lot of disintegrating basket chairs upon the edge of a well- used tennis lawn.

These people interested me. They were a common type, no doubt, but they were new to me. There were two lank sons who had been playing singles at tennis, red-eared youths growing black moustaches, and dressed in conscientiously untidy tweeds and unbuttoned and ungirt Norfolk jackets. There were a number of ill-nourished-looking daughters, sensible and economical in their costume, the younger still with long, brown-stockinged legs, and the eldest present— there were, we discovered, one or two hidden away—displaying a large gold cross and other aggressive ecclesiastical symbols ; there were two or three fox-terriers, a retrieverish mongrel, and an old, bloody-eyed and very evil-smelling St. Bernard. There was a jackdaw. There was, moreover, an ambiguous silent lady that my aunt subsequently decided must be a very deaf paying guest. Two or three other people had concealed themselves at our coming and left unfinished teas behind them. Rugs and cushions lay among the chairs, and two of the latter were, I noted, covered with Union Jacks.

The vicar introduced us sketchily, and the faded Victorian wife regarded my aunt with a mixture of conventional scorn and abject respect, and talked to her in a languid persistent voice about people in the neighbourhood whom my aunt could not possibly know. My aunt received these personalia cheerfully, with her blue eyes flitting from point to point, and coming back again and again to the pinched faces of the daughters and the cross upon the eldest's breast. Encouraged by my aunt's manner the vicar's wife grew patronising and kindly, and made it evident that she could do much to bridge the social gulf between ourselves and the people of family about us.

I had just snatches of that conversation. " Mrs. Merridew brought him quite a lot of money. Her father, I believe,

had been in the Spanish wine trade—quite a lady, though.
And after that he fell off his horse and cracked his brain pan
and took to fishing and farming. I'm sure you'll like to know
them. He's *most* amusing. . . . The daughter had a disappointment and went to China as a missionary and got mixed
up in a massacre. . . .

" The most beautiful silks and things she brought back,
you'd hardly believe ! . . .

" Yes, they gave them to propitiate her. You see, they
didn't understand the difference, and they thought that as
they'd been massacring people, *they'd* be massacred. They
didn't understand the difference Christianity makes. . . .

" Seven bishops they've had in the family ! . . .

" Married a Papist and was quite lost to them. . . .

" He failed some dreadful examination and had to go into
the militia. . . .

" So she bit his leg as hard as ever she could and he let
go. . . .

" Had four of his ribs amputated. . . .

" Caught meningitis and was carried off in a week.

" Had to have a large piece of silver tube let into his throat,
and if he wants to talk he puts his finger on it. It makes him
so interesting, I think. You feel he's sincere, somehow. A
most charming man in every way.

" Preserved them both in spirits very luckily, and there
they are in his study, though of course he doesn't show them
to everybody."

The silent lady, unperturbed by these apparently exciting
topics, scrutinised my aunt's costume with a singular intensity,
and was visibly moved when she unbuttoned her dust cloak
and flung it wide. Meanwhile, we men conversed, one of the
more spirited daughters listened brightly, and the youths
lay on the grass at our feet. My uncle offered them cigars,
but they both declined—out of bashfulness, it seemed to me,
whereas the vicar, I think, accepted out of tact. When we
were not looking at them directly, these young men would
kick each other furtively.

Under the influence of my uncle's cigar, the vicar's mind had
soared beyond the limits of the district. " This Socialism,"
he said, " seems making great headway."

My uncle shook his head. " We're too individualistic in this
country for that sort of nonsense," he said. " Everybody's
business is nobody's business. That's where they go wrong."

" They have some intelligent people in their ranks, I am
told," said the vicar, " writers and so forth. Quite a distinguished playwright, my eldest daughter was telling me—I
forget his name. Milly dear ! Oh ! she's not here. Painters,
too, they have. This Socialism, it seems to me, is part of the
Unrest of the Age. . . . But, as you say, the spirit of the
people is against it. In the country at any rate. The people

down here are too sturdily independent in their small way—
and too sensible altogether." . . .

"It's a great thing for Duffield to have Lady Grove occupied
again," he was saying when my wandering attention came
back from some attractive casualty in his wife's discourse.
"People have always looked up to the house—and considering
all things, old Mr. Durgan really was extraordinarily good—
extraordinarily good.   You intend to give us a good deal of
your time here I hope."

"I mean to do my duty by the Parish," said my uncle.

"I'm sincerely glad to hear it—sincerely.   We've missed
—the house influence.   An English village isn't complete——
People get out of hand.   Life grows dull.   The young people
drift away to London."

He enjoyed his cigar gingerly for a moment.

"We shall look to you to liven things up," he said—poor
man !

My uncle cocked his cigar and removed it from his mouth.

"Whad you think the place wants ?" he asked.

He did not wait for an answer.   "I been thinking while
you been talking—things one might do.   Cricket—a good
English game—sports.   Build the chaps a pavilion perhaps.
Then every village ought to have a miniature rifle-range."

"Ye-ees," said the vicar.   "Provided, of course, there
isn't a constant popping." . . .

"Manage *that* all right," said my uncle.   "Thing'd be a
sort of long shed.   Paint it red.   British colour.   Then
there's a Union Jack for the church and the village school.
Paint the school red, too, p'raps.   Not enough colour about
now.   Too grey.   Then a maypole."

"How far our people would take up that sort of thing——"
began the vicar.

"I'm all for getting that good old English spirit back
again," said my uncle.   "Merrymakings.   Lads and lasses
dancing on the village green.   Harvest home.   Fairings.
Yule Log—all the rest of it."

"How would old Sally Glue do for a May Queen ?" asked
one of the sons in the slight pause that followed.

"Or Annie Glassbound ?" said the other, with the huge,
virile guffaw of a young man whose voice has only recently
broken.

"Sally Glue is eighty-five," explained the vicar, "and
Annie Glassbound is, well—a young lady of extremely generous
proportions.   And not quite right, you know.   Not quite
right—here."   He tapped his brow.

"Generous proportions !" said the eldest son, and the
guffaws were renewed.

"You see," said the vicar, "all the brisker girls go into
service in or near London.   The life of excitement attracts
them.   And no doubt the higher wages have something to do

with it. And the liberty to wear finery. And generally—
freedom from restraint. So that there might be a little difficulty, perhaps, to find a May Queen here just at present who
was really young and, er—pretty. . . . Of course I couldn't
think of any of my girls—or anything of that sort."

"We got to attract 'em back," said my uncle. "That's
what I feel about it. We got to Buck-Up the country. The
English country is a going concern still ; just as the Established Church—if you'll excuse me saying it, is a going concern.
Just as Oxford is—or Cambridge. Or any of those old, fine
old things. Only it wants fresh capital, fresh idees, and fresh
methods. Light   railways,   f'rinstance—scientific   use   of
drainage. Wire fencing—machinery—all that."

The vicar's face for one moment betrayed dismay. Perhaps
he was thinking of his country walks amidst the hawthorns
and honeysuckle.

"There's great things," said my uncle, "to be done on
Mod'un lines with Village Jam and Pickles—boiled in the
country."

It was the reverberation of this last sentence in my mind,
I think, that sharpened my sentimental sympathy as we
went through the straggling village street and across the trim
green on our way back to London. It seemed that afternoon
the most tranquil and idyllic collection of creeper-sheltered
homes you can imagine ; thatch still lingered on a whitewashed
cottage or two, pyracanthus, wallflowers, and daffodils
abounded, and an unsystematic orchard or so was white with
blossom above and gay with bulbs below. I noted a row of
straw beehives, beehive shaped, beehives of the type long since
condemned as inefficient by all progressive minds, and in the
doctor's acre of grass a flock of two whole sheep was grazing—
no doubt he'd taken them on account. Two men and one
old woman made gestures of abject vassalage, and my uncle
replied with a lordly gesture of his great motoring glove. . . .

"England's full of Bits like this," said my uncle, leaning
over the front seat and looking back with great satisfaction.
The black glare of his goggles rested for a time on the receding
turrets of Lady Grove just peeping over the trees.

"I shall have a flagstaff, I think," he considered. "Then
one could show when one is in residence. The villagers will
like to know." . . .

I reflected. "They will," I said. "They're used to liking
to know." . . .

My aunt had been unusually silent. Suddenly she spoke.
"He says Snap," she remarked ; "he buys that place. And
a nice old job of Housekeeping he gives me ! He sails through
the village swelling like an old Turkey. And who'll have
to scoot the butler ? Me ! Who's got to forget all she ever
knew and start again ? Me ! Who's got to trek from Chislehurst and be a great lady ? Me ! . . . You old Bother !

Just when I was settling down and beginning to feel at home."

My uncle turned his goggles to her. " Ah ! *this* time it
is home, Susan. . . . We got there."

§ 7

It seems to me now but a step from the buying of Lady
Grove to the beginning of Crest Hill, from the days when
the former was a stupendous achievement to the days when
it was too small and dark and inconvenient altogether for a
great financier's use. For me that was a period of increasing
detachment from our business and the great world of London.
I saw it more and more in broken glimpses, and sometimes
I was working in my little pavilion above Lady Grove for a
fortnight together ; even when I came up it was often solely
for a meeting of the aeronautical society or for one of the
learned societies or to consult literature or employ searchers
or some such special business. For my uncle it was a period
of stupendous inflation. Each time I met him I found him
more confident, more comprehensive, more consciously a
factor in great affairs. Soon he was no longer an associate of
merely business men, he was big enough for the attentions of
greater powers.

I grew used to discovering some item of personal news
about him in my evening paper or to the sight of a full-page
portrait of him in a sixpenny magazine. Usually the news
was of some munificent act, some romantic piece of buying
or giving, or some fresh rumour of reconstruction. He saved,
you will remember, the Parbury Reynolds for the country.
Or at times it would be an interview or my uncle's contribution
to some symposium on the " Secret of Success," or such-like
topic. Or wonderful tales of his power of work, of his wonderful organisation to get things done, of his instant decisions
and remarkable power of judging his fellow-men. They
repeated his great *mot* : " Eight-hour working-day—I want
eighty hours ! "

He became modestly but resolutely " public." They
cartooned him in *Vanity Fair*. One year my aunt, looking
indeed a very gracious, slender lady, faced the portrait of
the King in the great room at Burlington House, and the
next year saw a medallion of my uncle by Ewart, looking
out upon the world, proud and imperial but on the whole
a trifle too prominently convex, from the walls of the New
Gallery.

I shared only intermittently in his social experiences.
People knew of me, it is true, and many of them sought to
make through me a sort of flank attack upon him, and there
was a legend, owing, very unreasonably, partly to my growing
scientific reputation and partly to an element of reserve in my
manner, that I played a much larger share in planning his

operations than was actually the case. This led to one or
two very intimate private dinners, to my inclusion in one or
two house parties and various odd offers of introductions and
services that I didn't for the most part accept. Among other
people who sought me in this way was Archie Garvell, now a
smart, impecunious soldier of no particular distinction, who
would, I think, have been quite prepared to develop any
sporting instincts I possessed, and who was beautifully unaware of our former contact. He was always offering me
winners ; no doubt in a spirit of anticipatory exchange for
some really good thing in our more scientific and certain
method of getting something for nothing. . . .

In spite of my preoccupation with my experimental work,
I did, I find now that I come to ransack my impressions, see
a great deal of the great world during those eventful years ;
I had a near view of the machinery by which our astounding
Empire is run, rubbed shoulders and exchanged experiences
with bishops and statesmen, political women and women who
were not political, physicians and soldiers, artists and authors,
the directors of great journals, philanthropists and all sort of
eminent, significant people. I saw the statesmen without
their orders and the bishops with but a little purple silk left
over from their canonicals, inhaling not incense but cigar
smoke. I could look at them all the better because for the
most part they were not looking at me but at my uncle, and
calculating consciously or unconsciously how they might use
him and assimilate him to their system, the most unpre-
meditated, subtle, successful and aimless plutocracy that ever
encumbered the destinies of mankind. Not one of them,
so far as I could see, until disaster overtook him, resented his
lies, his almost naked dishonesty of method, the disorderly
disturbance of this trade and that, caused by his spasmodic
operations. I can see them now about him, see them polite,
watchful, various ; his stiff, compact little figure always a
centre of attention, his wiry hair, his brief nose, his under-lip,
electric with self-confidence. Wandering marginally through
distinguished gatherings, I would catch the whispers : " That's
Mr. Ponderevo ! "

" The little man ? "

" Yes, the little bounder with the glasses."

" They say he's made——" . . .

Or I would see him on some parterre of a platform beside
my aunt's hurraying hat, amidst titles and costumes, " holding
his end up," as he would say, subscribing heavily to obvious
charities, even at times making brief convulsive speeches in
some good cause before the most exalted audiences. " Mr.
Chairman, your Royal Highness, my Lord, Ladies and Gentlemen," he would begin amidst subsiding applause, and adjust
those obstinate glasses and thrust back the wings of his frock-
coat and rest his hands upon his hips and speak his fragment

with ever and again an incidental Zzzz. His hands would fret about him as he spoke, fiddle his glasses, feel in his waist-coat pockets; ever and again he would rise slowly to his toes as a sentence unwound jerkily like a clockwork snake, and drop back on his heels at the end. They were the very gestures of our first encounter when he had stood before the empty fireplace in his minute draped parlour and talked of my future to my mother.

In those measurelessly long hot afternoons in the little shop at Wimblehurst he had talked and dreamt of the Romance of Modern Commerce. Here surely was his romance come true.

§ 8

People say that my uncle lost his head at the crest of his fortunes, but if one may tell so much truth of a man one has in a manner loved, he never had very much head to lose. He was always imaginative, erratic, inconsistent, recklessly inexact, and his inundation of wealth merely gave him scope for these qualities. It is true indeed that towards the climax he became intensely irritable at times and impatient of contra-diction, but that I think was rather the gnawing uneasiness of sanity than any mental disturbance. But I find it hard either to judge him or convey the full development of him to the reader. I saw too much of him; my memory is choked with disarranged moods and aspects. Now he is distended with megalomania, now he is deflated, now he is quarrelsome, now impenetrably self-satisfied, but always he is sudden, jerky, fragmentary, energetic, and—in some subtle funda-mental way that I find difficult to define—absurd.

There stands out—because of the tranquil beauty of its setting, perhaps—a talk we had in the veranda of the little pavilion near my work-sheds behind Crest Hill in which my aeroplanes and navigable balloons were housed. It was one of many similar conversations, and I do not know why it in particular should survive its fellows. It happens so. He had come up to me after his coffee to consult me about a certain chalice which in a moment of splendour and under the importunity of a countess he had determined to give to a deserving church in the East End. I in a moment of even rasher generosity had suggested Ewart as a possible artist. Ewart had produced at once an admirable sketch for the sacred vessel surrounded by a sort of wreath of Millies with open arms and wings, and had drawn fifty pounds on the strength of it. After that came a series of vexatious delays. The chalice became less and less of a commercial-man's chalice, acquired more and more the elusive quality of the Holy Grail, and at last even the drawing receded.

My uncle grew restive. . . . " You see, George, they'll begin to want the blasted thing ! "

" What blasted thing ? "

" That chalice, damn it ! They're beginning to ask questions.
It isn't Business, George."

" It's art," I protested, " and religion."

" That's all very well. But it's not a good ad' for us,
George, to make a promise and not deliver the goods. . . .
I'll have to write off your friend Ewart as a bad debt, that's
what it comes to, and go to a decent firm." . . .

We sat outside on deck chairs in the veranda of the pavilion,
smoked, drank whisky, and the chalice disposed of, meditated.
His temporary annoyance passed. It was an altogether
splendid summer night, following a blazing, indolent day.
Full moonlight brought out dimly the lines of the receding
hills, one wave beyond another ; far beyond were the pin-
point lights of Leatherhead, and in the foreground the little
stage from which I used to start upon my gliders gleamed
like wet steel. The season must have been high June, for
down in the woods that hid the lights of the Lady Grove
windows, I remember the nightingales thrilled and gurgled. . . .

" We got here, George," said my uncle, ending a long
pause. " Didn't I say ? "

" Say !—when ? " I asked.

" In that hole in the To'nem Court Road, eh ? It's been
a Straight Square fight, and here we are ! "

I nodded.

" 'Member me telling you—Tono-Bungay ? . . . Well.
. . . I'd just that afternoon thought of it ! "

" I've fancied at times——" I admitted.

" It's a great world, George, nowadays, with a fair chance
for every one who lays hold of things. The career *ouvert*
to the Talons—eh ? Tono-Bungay. Think of it ! It's a
great world and a growing world, and I'm glad we're in it—
and getting a pull. We're getting big people, George. Things
come to us. Eh ? This Palestine thing." . . .

He meditated for a time and Zzzzed softly. Then he
became still.

His theme was taken up by a cricket in the grass until
he himself was ready to resume it. The cricket, too, seemed
to fancy that in some scheme of its own it had got there.
" Chirrrrrrup," it said ; " chirrrrrrup." . . .

Lord, what a place that was at Wimblehurst ! " he broke
out. " If ever I get a day off we'll motor there, George, and
run over that dog that sleeps in the High Street. Always
was a dog asleep there—always. Always. . . . I'd like to
see the old shop again. I dare say old Ruck still stands
between the sheep at his door, grinning with all his teeth, and
Marbel, silly beggar ! comes out with his white apron on
and a pencil stuck behind his ear, trying to look awake. . . .
Wonder if they know it's me ? I'd like 'em somehow to know
it's me."

"They'll have had the International Tea Company and all sorts of people cutting them up," I said. "And that dog's been on the pavement this six years—can't sleep even there, poor dear, because of the motor-horns and its shattered nerves."

"Movin' everywhere," said my uncle. "I expect you're right. . . . It's a big time we're in, George. It's a big Progressive On-coming Imperial Time. This Palestine business—the daring of it. . . . It's—it's a Process, George. And we got our hands on it. Here we sit—with our hands on it, George. Entrusted.

"It seems quiet to-night. But if we could see and hear." He waved his cigar towards Leatherhead and London.

"There they are, millions, George. Jes' think of what they've been up to to-day—those ten millions—each one doing his own particular job. You can't grasp it. It's like old Whitman says—what is it he says ? Well, anyway, it's like old Whitman. Fine chap, Whitman ! Fine old chap ! Queer, you can't quote him ! . . . And these millions aren't anything. There's the millions over seas, hundreds of millions, Chinee, M'rocco, Africa generally, 'Merica. . . . Well, here we are, with power, with leisure, picked out—because we've been energetic, because we've seized opportunities, because we've made things hum when other people have waited for them to hum. See ? Here we are—with our hands on it. Big people. Big growing people. In a sort of way—Forces."

He paused. "It's wonderful, George," he said.

"Anglo-Saxon energy," I said softly to the night.

"That's it, George—energy. It's put things in our grip—threads, wires, stretching out and out, George, from that little office of ours, out to West Africa, out to Egypt, out to Inja, out east, west, north and south. Running the world practically. Running it faster and faster. Creative. There's that Palestine canal affair. Marvellous idee ! Suppose we take that up, suppose we let ourselves in for it, us and the others, and run that water sluice from the Mediterranean into the Dead Sea Valley—think of the difference it will make ! All the desert blooming like a rose, Jericho lost for ever, all the Holy Places under water. . . . Very likely destroy Christianity." . . .

He mused for a space. "Cuttin' canals," murmured my uncle. "Making tunnels. . . . New countries. . . . New centres. . . . Zzzz. . . . Finance. . . . Not only Palestine.

"I wonder where we shall get before we done, George ? We got a lot of big things going. We got the investing public sound and sure. I don't see why in the end we shouldn't be very big. There's difficulties—but I'm equal to them. We're still a bit soft in our bones, but they'll harden all right. . . . I suppose, after all, I'm worth something like a million, George—cleared up and settled. If I got out of things now. It's a great time, George, a wonderful time ! " . . .

I glanced through the twilight at his convexity—and I must confess it struck me that on the whole he wasn't particularly good value.

"We got our hands on things, George—us big people. We got to hang together, George—run the show. Join up with the old order like that mill-wheel of Kipling's. (Finest thing he ever wrote, George ;—I jes' been reading it again. Made me buy Lady Grove.) Well, we got to run the country, George. It's ours. Make it a Scientific—Organised—Business—Enterprise. Put idees into it. 'Lectrify it. Run the Press. Run all sorts of developments. All sorts of developments. I been talking to Lord Bloom. I been talking to all sorts of people. Great things. Progress. The world on business lines. Only jes' beginning." . . .

He fell into a deep meditation.

He Zzzzed for a time and ceased.

"Yes," he said at last in the tone of a man who has at last emerged with ultimate solutions to the profoundest problems.

"What ? " I said, after a seemly pause.

My uncle hung fire for a moment, and it seemed to me the fate of nations trembled in the balance. Then he spoke as one who speaks from the very bottom of his heart—and I think it was the very bottom of his heart.

"I'd jes' like to drop into the Eastry Arms, jes' when all those beggars in the parlour are sittin' down to whist, Ruck and Marbel and all, and give 'em ten minutes of my mind, George. Straight from the shoulder. Jes' exactly what I think of them. It's a little thing, but I'd like to do it—jes' once before I die." . . .

He rested on that for some time—Zzzz-ing.

Then he broke out at a new place in a tone of detached criticism.

"There's Boom," he reflected.

"It's a wonderful system—this old British system, George. It's staid and stable, and yet it has a place for new men. We come up and take our places. It's almost expected. We take a hand. That's where our Democracy differs from America. Over there a man succeeds ; all he gets is money. Here there's a system—open to every one—practically. . . . Chaps like Boom—come from nowhere."

His voice ceased. I reflected upon the spirit of his words. Suddenly I kicked my feet in the air, rolled on my side and sat up suddenly on my deck chair with my legs down.

"You don't mean it ! " I said.

"Mean what, George ? "

"Subscription to the party funds. Reciprocal advantage. Have we got to that ? "

"Whad you driving at, George ? "

"You know. They'd never do it, man ! "

"Do what ?" he said feebly ; and, "Why shouldn't they ? "

"They'd not even go to a baronetcy. *No !* . . . And yet, of course, there's Boom ! And Collingshead—and Gorver. They've done beer, they've done snippets ! After all Tono-Bungay—it's not like a turf commission agent or anything like that ! . . . There have, of course, been some very gentlemanly commission agents. It isn't like a fool of a scientific man who can't make money ! "

My uncle grunted ; we'd differed on that issue before.

A malignant humour took possession of me. "What would they call you ? " I speculated. "The vicar would like Duffield. Too much like Duffer ! Difficult thing a title." I ran my mind over various possibilities. "Why not take a leaf from a socialist tract I came upon yesterday. Chap says we're all getting delocalised. Beautiful word—delocalised ! Why not be the first delocalised peer ? That gives you—Tono-Bungay ! There is a Bungay, you know. Lord Tono of Bungay—in bottles everywhere. Eh ? "

My uncle astonished me by losing his temper.

"Damn it, George, you don't seem to see I'm serious ! You're always sneering at Tono-Bungay ! As though it was some sort of swindle. It was perfec'ly legitimate trade, perfec'ly legitimate. Good value and a good article. . . . When I come up here and tell you plans and exchange idees—you sneer at me. You *do*. You don't see—it's a big thing. It's a big thing. You got to get used to new circumstances. You got to face what lies before us. You got to drop that tone." . . .

§ 9

My uncle was not altogether swallowed up in business and ambition. He kept in touch with modern thought. For example, he was, I know, greatly swayed by what he called " This Overman idee, Nietzsche—all that stuff."

He mingled those comforting suggestions of a potent and exceptional human being emancipated from the pettier limitations of integrity with the Napoleonic legend. It gave his imagination a considerable outlet. That Napoleonic legend ! The real mischief of Napoleon's immensely disastrous and accidental career began only when he was dead and the romantic type of mind was free to elaborate his character. I do believe that my uncle would have made a far less egregious smash if there had been no Napoleonic legend to misguide him. He was in many ways better and infinitely kinder than his career. But when in doubt between decent conduct and a base advantage, that cult came in more and more influentially ; " think of Napoleon ; think what the inflexibly-wilful Napoleon would have done with such scruples as yours " ; that was the rule, and the end was invariably a new step in dishonour.

My uncle was in an unsystematic way a collector of Napoleonic relics ; the bigger the book about his hero, the more readily he bought it ; he purchased letters and tinsel and weapons that bore however remotely upon the Man of Destiny, and he even secured in Geneva, though he never brought home, an old coach in which Buonaparte might have ridden ; he crowded the quiet walls of Lady Grove with engravings and figures of him, preferring, my aunt remarked, the more convex portraits with the white vest and those statuettes with the hands behind the back which throw forward the figure. The Durgans watched him through it all, sardonically.

And he would stand after breakfast at times in the light of the window at Lady Grove, a little apart, with two fingers of one hand stuck between his waistcoat-buttons and his chin sunken, thinking—the most preposterous little fat man in the world. It made my aunt feel, she said, " like an old Field-Marshal—knocks me into a cocked hat, George ! "

Perhaps this Napoleonic bias made him a little less frequent with his cigars than he would otherwise have been, but of that I cannot be sure, and it certainly caused my aunt a considerable amount of vexation after he had read *Napoleon and the Fair Sex*, because for a time that roused him to a sense of a side of life he had in his commercial preoccupations very largely forgotten. Suggestion plays so great a part in this field. My uncle took the next opportunity and had an " affair ! "

It was not a very impassioned affair, and the exact particulars never of course reached me. It is quite by chance I know anything of it at all. One evening I was surprised to come upon my uncle in a mixture of Bohemia and smart people at an At Home in the flat of Robbert, the R.A. who painted my aunt, and he was standing a little apart in a recess, talking or rather being talked to in undertones by a plump, blonde woman in pale blue, a Helen Scrymgeour who wrote novels and was organising a weekly magazine. I elbowed a large lady who was saying something about them, but I didn't need to hear the thing she said to perceive the relation-ship of the two. It hit me like a placard on a hoarding. I was amazed the whole gathering did not see it. Perhaps they did. She was wearing a remarkably fine diamond necklace, much too fine for journalists, and regarding him with that quality of questionable proprietorship, of leashed but straining intimacy, that seems inseparable from this sort of affair. It is so much more palpable than matrimony. If anything was wanted to complete my conviction it was my uncle's eyes when presently he became aware of mine, a certain embarrassment and a certain pride and defiance. And the next day he made an opportunity to praise the lady's intelligence to me concisely, lest I should miss the point of it all.

After that I heard some gossip—from a friend of the lady's. I was much too curious to do anything but listen. I had never in all my life imagined my uncle in an amorous attitude. It would appear that she called him her " God in the Car "—after the hero in a novel of Anthony Hope's. It was essential to the convention of their relations that he should go relentlessly whenever business called, and it was generally arranged that it did call. To him women were an incident, it was understood between them ; Ambition was the master-passion. A great world called him and the noble hunger for Power. I have never been able to discover just how honest Mrs. Scrymgeour was in all this, but it is quite possible the immense glamour of his financial largeness prevailed with her and that she did bring a really romantic feeling to their encounters. There must have been some extraordinary moments. . . .

I was a good deal exercised and distressed about my aunt when I realised what was afoot. I thought it would prove a terrible humiliation to her. I suspected her of keeping up a brave front with the loss of my uncle's affections fretting at her heart, but there I simply underestimated her. She didn't hear for some time, and when she did hear she was extremely angry and energetic. The sentimental situation didn't trouble her for a moment. She decided that my uncle " wanted smacking." She accentuated herself with an unexpected new hat, went and gave him an inconceivable talking-to at the Hardingham, and then came round to " blow-up " me for not telling her what was going on before. . . .

I tried to bring her to a proper sense of the accepted values in this affair, but my aunt's originality of outlook was never so invincible. " Men don't tell on one another in affairs of passion," I protested, and suchlike worldly excuses.

" Women ! " she said in high indignation, " and men ! It isn't women and men—it's him and me, George ! Why don't you talk sense ?

" Old passion's all very well, George, in its way, and I'm the last person to be jealous. But this is old nonsense. . . . I'm not going to let him show off what a silly old lobster he is to other women. . . . I'll mark every scrap of his underclothes with red letters, ' Ponderevo—Private '—every scrap. . . .

" Going about making love, indeed !—in abdominal belts ! —at his time of life ! "

I cannot imagine what passed between her and my uncle. But I have no doubt that for once her customary badinage was laid aside. How they talked then I do not know, for I who knew them so well had never heard that much of intimacy between them. At any rate it was a concerned and preoccupied " God in the Car " I had to deal with during the next few days, unusually Zzzz-y and given to slight impatient gestures that had nothing to do with the current conversation.

And it was evident that in all directions he was finding things unusually difficult to explain.

The intimate moments in this affair were hidden from me, but in the end my aunt triumphed. He did not so much throw as jerk over Mrs. Scrymgeour, and she did not so much make a novel of it as upset a huge pailful of attenuated and adulterated female soul upon this occasion. My aunt did not appear in that, even remotely. So that it is doubtful if the lady knew the real causes of her abandonment. The Napoleonic hero was practically unmarried, and he threw over his lady as Napoleon threw over Josephine, for a Great Alliance. . . .

It was a triumph for my aunt, but it had its price. For some time it was evident things were strained between them. He gave up the lady, but he resented having to do so, deeply. She had meant more to his imagination than one could have supposed. He wouldn't for a long time " come round." He became touchy and impatient and secretive towards my aunt, and she, I noted, after an amazing check or so, stopped that stream of kindly abuse that had flowed for so long and had been so great a refreshment in their lives. They were both the poorer for its cessation, both less happy. She devoted herself more and more to Lady Grove and the humours and complications of its management. The servants took to her —as they say—she godmothered three Susans during her rule, the coachman's, the gardener's, and the Up Hill game-keeper's. She got together a library of old household books that were in the vein of the place. She revived the still-room, and became a great artist in jellies and elder and cowslip wine.

§ 10

And while I neglected the development of my uncle's finances—and my own, in my scientific work and my absorbing conflict with the difficulties of flying—his schemes grew more and more expansive and hazardous, and his spending wilder and laxer. I believe that a haunting sense of the intensifying unsoundness of his position accounts largely for his increasing irritability and his increasing secretiveness with my aunt and myself during these crowning years. He dreaded, I think, having to explain, he feared our jests might pierce unwittingly to the truth. Even in the privacy of his mind he would not face the truth. He was accumulating unrealis-able securities in his safes until they hung a potential avalanche over the economic world. But his buying became a fever, and his restless desire to keep it up with himself that he was making a triumphant progress to limitless wealth gnawed deeper and deeper. A curious feature of this time with him was his buying over and over again of similar things. His ideas seemed to run in series. Within a twelvemonth he

bought five new motor-cars, each more swift and powerful
than its predecessor, and only the repeated prompt resignation
of his chief chauffeur at each moment of danger, prevented
his driving them himself. He used them more and more.
He developed a passion for locomotion for its own sake.

Then he began to chafe at Lady Grove, fretted by a chance
jest he had overheard at a dinner. " This house, George,"
he said. " It's a misfit. There's no elbow-room in it ; it's
choked with old memories. . . . And I can't stand all these
damned Durgans !

" That chap in the corner, George. No ! the other corner !
The man in a cherry-colour coat. He watches you ! He'd
look silly if I stuck a poker through his Gizzard ! "

" He'd look," I reflected, " much as he does now. As
though he was amused."

He replaced his glasses, which had fallen at his emotion,
and glared at his antagonists. " What are they ? What
are they all, the lot of 'em ? Dead as Mutton ! They just
stuck in the mud. They aidn't even rise to the Reformation.
The old out-of-date Reformation ! Move with the times !—
they moved against the times. Just a Family of Failure ;—
they never even tried ! . . .

" They're jes', George, exactly what I'm not. Exactly.
It isn't suitable. . . . All this living in the Past.

" And I want a bigger place, too, George. I want air and
sunlight and room to move about and more service. A house
where you can get a Move on things ! Zzzz. Why ! it's
like a discord—it jars—even to have the telephone. . . .
There's nothing, nothing except the terrace, that's worth a
Rap. It's all dark and old and dried up and full of old-
fashioned things—musty old idees—fitter for a silver-fish
than a modern man. . . . I don't know how I got here."

He broke out into a new grievance. " That damned
vicar," he complained, " thinks I ought to think myself lucky
to get this place ! Every time I meet him I can see him
think it. . . . One of these days, George, I'll show him what
a Mod'un house is like ! "

And he did.

I remember the day when he declared, as Americans say,
for Crest Hill. He had come up to see my new gas plant,
for I was then only just beginning to experiment with auxiliary
collapsible balloons, and all the time the shine of his glasses
was wandering away to the open down beyond. " Let's go
back to Lady Grove over the hill," he said. " Something
I want to show you. Something fine ! "

It was an empty sunlit place that summer evening, sky
and earth warm with sundown, and a pewit or so just accentu-
ating the pleasant stillness that ends a long clear day. A
beautiful peace, it was, to wreck for ever. And there was
my uncle, the modern man of power, in his grey top-hat and

his grey suit and his black-ribboned glasses, short, thin-legged, large-stomached, pointing and gesticulating, threatening this calm.

He began with a wave of his arm. "That's the place, George," he said. "See ? "

"Eh ! " I cried—for I had been thinking of remote things.

"I got it."

"Got what ? "

"For a house !—a Twentieth-Century house ! That's the place for it ! "

One of his characteristic phrases was begotten in him. "Four-square to the winds of heaven, George ! " he said. "Eh ? Four-square to the winds of heaven ! "

"You'll get the winds up here," I said.

"A mammoth house it ought to be, George—to suit these hills."

"Quite," I said.

"Great galleries and things—running out there and there— See ? I been thinking of it, George ! Looking out all this way—across the Weald. With its back to Lady Grove."

"And the morning sun in its eye."

"Like an eagle, George—like an eagle ! "

So he broached to me what speedily became the leading occupation of his culminating years, Crest Hill. But all the world has heard of that extravagant place which grew and changed its plans as it grew, and bubbled like a salted snail, and burgeoned and bulged and evermore grew. I know not what delirium of pinnacles and terraces and arcades and corridors glittered at last upon the uplands of his mind ; the place, for all that its expansion was terminated abruptly by our collapse, is wonderful enough as it stands—that empty instinctive building of a childless man. His chief architect was a young man named Westminster, whose work he had picked out in the architecture room of the Royal Academy on account of a certain grandiose courage in it, but with him he associated from time to time a number of fellow pro-fessionals, stonemasons, sanitary engineers, painters, sculptors, scribes, metal workers, wood carvers, furniture designers, ceramic specialists, landscape gardeners, and the man who designs the arrangement and ventilation of the various new houses in the London Zoological Gardens. In addition he had his own ideas. The thing occupied his mind at all times, but it held it completely from Friday night to Monday morn-ing. He would come down to Lady Grove on Friday night in a crowded motor-car that almost dripped architects. He didn't, however, confine himself to architects, every one was liable to an invitation to week-end and view Crest Hill, and many an eager promoter, unaware of how Napoleonically and completely my uncle had departmentalised his mind, tried to creep up to him by way of tiles and ventilators and new electric fittings. Always on Sunday mornings, unless the weather was vile, he would, so soon as breakfast and his secretaries were disposed of, visit the site with a considerable retinue, and alter and develop plans, making modifications, Zzzz-ing, giving immense new orders verbally—an unsatisfactory way, as Westminster and the contractors ultimately found.

There he stands in my memory, the symbol of this age for me, the man of luck and advertisement, the current master of the world. There he stands upon the great outward sweep of the terrace before the huge main entrance, a little figure, ridiculously disproportionate to that forty-foot arch, with the granite ball behind him—the astronomical ball, brass coopered, that represented the world, with a little adjustable tube of lenses on a gun-metal arm that focused the sun upon just that point of the earth on which it chanced to be shining vertically. There he stands, Napoleonically grouped with his retinue, men in tweeds and golfing-suits, a little solicitor, whose name I forget, in grey trousers and a black jacket, and Westminster in Jaeger underclothing, a floriferous tie, and a peculiar brown cloth of his own. The downland breeze flutters my uncle's coat-tails, disarranges his stiff hair, and insists on the evidence of undisciplined appetites in face and form, as he points out this or that feature in the prospect to his attentive collaborator.

Below are hundreds of feet of wheeling-planks, ditches, excavations, heaps of earth, piles of garden stone from the Wealden ridges. On either hand the walls of his irrelevant unmeaning palace rise. At one time he had working in that place—disturbing the economic balance of the whole countryside by their presence—upwards of three thousand men. . . .

So he poses for my picture amidst the raw beginnings that were never to be completed. He did the strangest things about that place, things more and more detached from any conception of financial scale, things more and more apart from sober humanity. He seemed to think himself at last released from any such limitations. He moved a quite considerable hill, and nearly sixty mature trees were moved with it to open his prospect eastward, moved it about two hundred feet to the south. At another time he caught a suggestion from some city restaurant and made a billiard-room roofed with plate-glass beneath the waters of his ornamental lake. He furnished one wing while the roof still awaited completion. He had a swimming-bath thirty feet square next to his bedroom upstairs, and to crown it all he commenced a great wall to hold all his dominions together, free from the invasion of common men. It was a ten-foot wall, glass surmounted, and had it been completed as he intended it, it would have had a total length of nearly eleven miles. Some of it towards the last was so dishonestly built that it collapsed within a year upon its foundations, but some miles of it still stand. I never think of it now but what I think of the hundreds of eager little investors who followed his "star," whose hopes and lives, whose wives' security and children's prospects are all mixed up beyond redemption with that flaking mortar. . . .

It is curious how many of these modern financiers of chance and bluff have ended their careers by building. It was not merely my uncle. Sooner or later they all seem to bring their luck to the test of realisation, try to make their fluid opulence coagulate out as bricks and mortar, bring moonshine into relations with a weekly wages-sheet. Then the whole fabric of confidence and imagination totters—and down they come. . . .

When I think of that despoiled hillside, that colossal litter of bricks and mortar and crude roads and paths, the scaffolding and sheds, the general quality of unforeseeing outrage upon the peace of nature, I am reminded of a chat I had with the vicar one bleak day after he had witnessed a glide. He talked to me of aeronautics as I stood in jersey and shorts beside my machine, fresh from alighting, and his cadaverous face failed to conceal a peculiar desolation that possessed him.

"Almost you convince me," he said, coming up to me, "against my will. . . . A marvellous invention! But it will take you a long time, sir, before you can emulate that perfect mechanism—the wing of a bird."

He looked at my sheds.

"You've changed the look of this valley, too," he said.

"Temporary defilements," I remarked, guessing what was in his mind.

"Of course. Things come and go. Things come and go. But—— H'm. I've just been up over the hill to look at Mr. Edward Ponderevo's new house. That—that is something more permanent. A magnificent place!—in many ways. Imposing. I've never somehow brought myself to go that way before. . . . Things are greatly advanced. . . . We find—the great number of strangers introduced into the villages about here by these operations, working-men chiefly, a little embarrassing—— It puts us out. They bring a new spirit into the place ; betting—ideas—all sorts of queer notions. Our publicans like it, of course. And they come and sleep in one's outhouses—and make the place a little unsafe at nights. The other morning I couldn't sleep—a slight dyspepsia—and I looked out of the window. I was amazed to see people going by on bicycles. A silent procession. I counted ninety-seven—in the dawn. All going up to the new road for Crest Hill. Remarkable I thought it. And so I've been up to see what they were doing."

"They would have been more than remarkable thirty years ago," I said.

"Yes, indeed. Things change. We think nothing of it now at all—comparatively. And that big house——"

He raised his eyebrows. " Really stupendous ! . . . Stupendous.

" All the hillside—the old turf—cut to ribbons ! "

His eye searched my face. " We've grown so accustomed to look up to Lady Grove," he said, and smiled in search of sympathy. " It shifts our centre of gravity."

" Things will readjust themselves," I lied.

He snatched at the phrase. "Of course," he said. "They'll readjust themselves—settle down again. Must. In the old way. It's bound to come right again—a comforting thought. Yes. After all, Lady Grove itself had to be built once upon a time—was—to begin with—artificial."

His eye returned to my aeroplane. He sought to dismiss his graver preoccupations. "I should think twice," he remarked, "before I trusted myself to that concern. . . . But I suppose one grows accustomed to the motion."

He bade me good-morning and went his way, bowed and thoughtful. . . .

He had kept the truth from his mind a long time, but that morning it had forced its way to him with an aspect that brooked no denial that this time it was not just changes that were coming in his world, but that all his world lay open and defenceless, conquered and surrendered, doomed so far as he could see, root and branch, scale and form alike, to change.

CHAPTER THREE

SOARING

§ 1

FOR nearly all the time that my uncle was incubating and hatching Crest Hill I was busy in a little transverse valley between that great beginning and Lady Grove with more and more costly and ambitious experiments in aerial navigation. This work was indeed the main substance of my life through all the great time of the Tono-Bungay symphony.

I have told already how I came to devote myself to this system of inquiries, how in a sort of disgust with the common adventure of life I took up the dropped ends of my college studies, taking them up again with a man's resolution instead of a boy's ambition. From the first I did well at this work. It was, I think, largely a case of special aptitude, of a peculiar irrelevant vein of faculty running through my mind. It is one of those things men seem to have by chance, that has little or nothing to do with their general merit, and which it is ridiculous to be either conceited or modest about. I did get through a very big mass of work in those years, working for a time with a concentrated fierceness that left little of such energy or capacity as I possess unused. I worked out a series of problems connected with the stability of bodies pitching in the air and the internal movements of the wind, and I also revolutionised one leading part at least of the theory of explosive engines. These things are to be found in the *Philosophical Transactions*, the *Mathematical Journal*, and less frequently in one or two other such publications, and they needn't detain us here. Indeed, I doubt if I could write about them here. One acquires a sort of shorthand for one's notes and mind in relation to such special work. I have never taught nor lectured, that is to say I have never had to express my thoughts about mechanical things in ordinary everyday language, and I doubt very much if I could do so now without extreme tedium. . . .

My work was to begin with very largely theoretical. I was able to attack such early necessities of verification as arose with quite little models, using a turntable to get the motion through the air, and cane, whalebone and silk as building material. But a time came when incalculable factors crept in, factors of human capacity and factors of insufficient experimental knowledge, when one must needs guess and try. Then I had to enlarge the scale of my operations, and soon I had enlarged them very greatly. I set to work almost concurrently on the balance and stability of gliders and upon the steering of inflated bags, the latter a particularly expensive branch of work. I was no doubt moved by something of the same spirit of lavish expenditure that was running away with my uncle in these developments. Presently my establishment above Lady Grove had grown to a painted wood châlet big enough to accommodate six men, in which I would sometimes live for three weeks together ; to a gasometer, to a motor-house, to three big corrugated-roofed sheds and lock-up houses, to a stage from which to start gliders, to a workshop and so forth. A rough road was made. We brought up gas from Cheaping and electricity from Woking, which place I found also afforded a friendly workshop for larger operations than I could manage. I had the luck also to find a man who seemed my heaven-sent second-in-command—Cothope his name was. He was a self-educated man ; he had formerly been a sapper and he was one of the best and handiest working engineers alive. Without him I do not think I could have achieved the half of what I have done. At times he has been not so much my assistant as my collaborator, and has followed my fortunes to this day. Other men came and went as I needed them.

I do not know how far it is possible to convey to any one who has not experienced it, the peculiar interest, the peculiar satisfaction that lies in a sustained research when one is not hampered by want of money. It is a different thing from any other sort of human effort. You are free from the exasperating conflict with your fellow-creatures altogether—at least so far as the essential work goes—that for me is its peculiar merit. Scientific truth is the remotest of mistresses, she hides in strange places, she is attained by tortuous and laborious roads, but *she is always there* ! Win to her and she will not fail you ; she is yours and mankind's for ever. She is reality, the one reality I have found in this strange disorder of existence. She will not sulk with you nor misunderstand you nor cheat you of your reward upon some petty doubt. You cannot change her by advertisement or clamour, nor stifle her in vulgarities. Things grow under your hands when you serve her, things that are permanent as nothing else is permanent in the whole life of man. That, I think, is the peculiar satisfaction of science and its enduring reward. . . .

The taking up of experimental work produced a great change in my personal habits. I have told how already once in my life at Wimblehurst I had a period of discipline and continuous effort, and how when I came to South Kensington I became demoralised by the immense effect of London, by its innumerable imperative demands upon my attention and curiosity. And I parted with much of my personal pride when I gave up science for the development of Tono-Bungay. But my poverty kept me abstinent and my youthful romanticism kept me chaste until my married life was well under way. Then in all directions I relaxed. I did a large amount of work, but I never troubled to think whether it was my maximum nor whether the moods and indolences that came to me at times were avoidable things. With the coming of plenty I ate abundantly and foolishly, drank freely and followed my impulses more and more carelessly. I felt no reason why I should do anything else. Never at any point did I use myself to the edge of my capacity. The emotional crisis of my divorce did not produce any immediate change in these matters of personal discipline. I found some difficulty at first in concentrating my mind upon scientific work, it was so much more exacting than business, but I got over that difficulty by smoking. I became an inordinate cigar smoker ; it gave me moods of profound depression, but I treated these usually by the homœopathic method—by lighting another cigar. I didn't realise at all how loose my moral and nervous fibre had become till I reached the practical side of my investigations and was face to face with the necessity of finding out just how it felt to use a glider and just what a man could do with one.

I got into this relaxed habit of living in spite of very real tendencies in my nature towards discipline. I've never been in love with self-indulgence. That philosophy of the loose lip and the lax paunch is one for which I've always

had an instinctive distrust. I like bare things, stripped
things, plain, austere and continent things, fine lines and
cold colours. But in these plethoric times when there is
too much coarse stuff for everybody and the struggle for
life takes the form of competitive advertisement and the
effort to fill your neighbour's eye, when there is no urgent
demand either for personal courage, sound nerves or stark
beauty, we find ourselves by accident. Always before these
times the bulk of the people did not over-eat themselves
because they couldn't whether they wanted to do so or not,
and all but a very few were kept " fit " by unavoidable exercise
and personal danger. Now, if only he pitch his standard
low enough and keep free from pride, almost any one can
achieve a sort of excess. You can go through contemporary
life fudging and evading, indulging and slacking, never really
hungry nor frightened nor passionately stirred, your highest
moment a mere sentimental orgasm, and your first real contact
with primary and elemental necessities, the sweat of your
death-bed. So I think it was with my uncle ; so, very nearly,
it was with me.

But the glider brought me up smartly. I had to find out
how these things went down the air, and the only way to find
out is to go down with one. And for a time I wouldn't face it.

There is something impersonal about a book, I suppose.
At any rate I find myself able to write down here just the
confession I've never been able to make to any one face to
face, the frightful trouble it was to me to bring myself to do
what I suppose every other coloured boy in the West Indies
could do without turning a hair, and that is to fling myself
off for my first soar down the wind. The first trial was
bound to be the worst, it was an experiment I made with life,
and the chance of death or injury was, I supposed, about
equal to the chance of success. I believed that with a dawn-
like lucidity. I had begun with a glider that I imagined was
on the lines of the Wright Brothers' aeroplane, but I could
not be sure. It might turn over. I might upset it. It
might burrow its nose at the end and smash itself and me.
The conditions of the flight necessitated alert attention ; it
wasn't a thing to be done by jumping off and shutting one's
eyes or getting angry or drunk to do it. One had to use
one's weight to balance. And when at last I did it it was
horrible—for ten seconds. For ten seconds or so, as I swept
down the air flattened on my infernal framework and with
the wind in my eyes, the rush of the ground beneath me filled
me with sick and helpless terror ; I felt as though some violent
oscillatory current was throbbing in brain and backbone,
and I groaned aloud. I set my teeth and groaned. It was
a groan wrung out of me in spite of myself. My sensations
of terror swooped to a climax.

And then, you know, they ended !

Suddenly my terror was over and done with. I was soaring through the air right way up, steadily, and no mischance had happened. I felt intensely alive and my nerves were strung like a bow. I shifted a limb, swerved and shouted between fear and triumph as I recovered from the swerve and heeled the other way and steadied myself.

I thought I was going to hit a rook that was flying athwart me—it was queer with what projectile silence that jumped upon me out of nothingness, and I yelled helplessly, " Get out of the way ! " The bird doubled itself up like a partly inverted V, flapped, went up to the right abruptly and vanished from my circle of interest. Then I saw the shadow of my aeroplane keeping a fixed distance before me and very steady, and the turf as it seemed streaming out behind it. The turf ! —it wasn't after all streaming so impossibly fast. . . .

When I came gliding down to the safe spread of level green I had chosen, I was as cool and ready as a city clerk who drops off an omnibus in motion, and I had learned much more than soaring. I tilted up her nose at the right moment, levelled again and grounded like a snowflake on a windless day. I lay flat for an instant, and then knelt up and got on my feet atremble but very satisfied with myself. Cothope was running down the hill to me. . . .

But from that day I went into training, and I kept myself in training for many months. I had delayed my experiments for very nearly six weeks on various excuses because of my dread of this first flight, because of the slackness of body and spirit that had come to me with the business life. The shame of that cowardice spurred me none the less because it was probably altogether my own secret. I felt that Cothope at any rate might suspect. Well—he shouldn't suspect again.

It is curious that I remember that shame and self-accusation and its consequences far more distinctly than I recall the weeks of vacillation before I soared. For a time I went altogether without alcohol, I stopped smoking altogether and ate very sparingly, and every day I did something that called a little upon my nerves and muscles. I soared as frequently as I could. I substituted a motor-bicycle for the London train and took my chances in the southward traffic, and I even tried what thrills were to be got upon a horse. But they put me on made horses, and I conceived a perhaps unworthy contempt for the certitudes of equestrian exercise in comparison with the adventures of mechanism. Also I walked along the high wall at the back of Lady Grove garden, and at last brought myself to stride the gap where the gate comes. If I didn't altogether get rid of a certain giddy instinct by such exercises, at least I trained my will until it didn't matter. And soon I no longer dreaded flight but was eager to go higher into the air, and I came to esteem soaring upon a glider that even over the deepest dip in the ground

had barely forty feet of fall beneath it, a mere mockery of
what flight might be. I began to dream of the keener freshness in the air high above the beechwoods, and it was rather
to satisfy that desire than as any legitimate development of
my proper work that presently I turned a part of my energies
and the bulk of my private income to the problem of the
navigable balloon.

§ 2

I had gone far beyond that initial stage ; I had had two
smashes and a broken rib which my aunt nursed with great
energy, and was getting some reputation in the aeronautic
world when suddenly, as though she had never really left it,
the Honourable Beatrice Normandy, dark-eyed, and with
the old disorderly wave of the hair from her brow, came back
into my life. She came riding down a grass path in the
thickets below Lady Grove, perched up on a huge black horse,
and the old Earl of Carnaby and Archie Garvell, her half-
brother, were with her. My uncle had been bothering me
about the Crest Hill hot-water pipes, and we were returning
by a path transverse to theirs and came out upon them suddenly. Old Carnaby was trespassing on our ground and so he
hailed us in a friendly fashion and pulled up to talk to us.

I didn't note Beatrice at all at first. I was interested in
Lord Carnaby, that remarkable vestige of his own brilliant
youth. I had heard of him but never seen him. For a man
of sixty-five who had sinned all the sins, so they said, and
laid waste the most magnificent political debut of any man
of his generation, he seemed to me to be looking remarkably
fit and fresh. He was a lean little man with grey-blue eyes
in his brown face, and his cracked voice was the worst thing
in his effect.

" Hope you don't mind us coming this way, Ponderevo,"
he cried ; and my uncle, who was sometimes a little too
general and generous with titles, answered, " Not at all,
my lord, not at all ! Glad you make use of it ! "

" You're building a great place over the hill," said Carnaby
" Thought I'd make a show for once," said my uncle
" It looks big because it's spread out for the sun."

" Air and sunlight," said the earl. " You can't have too
much of them. But before our time they used to build for
shelter and water and the high road." . . .

Then I discovered that the silent figure behind the earl
was Beatrice.

I'd forgotten her sufficiently to think for a moment that
she hadn't changed at all since she had watched me from
behind the skirts of Lady Drew. She was looking at me,
and her dainty brow under her broad-brimmed hat—she was
wearing a grey hat and loose unbuttoned coat—was knit
with perplexity, trying, I suppose, to remember where she

had seen me before. Her shaded eyes met mine with that mute question.

It seemed incredible to me she didn't remember.

"Well," said the earl, and touched his horse.

Garvell was patting the neck of his horse, which was inclined to fidget, and disregarding me. He nodded over his shoulder and followed. His movement seemed to release a train of memories in her. She glanced suddenly at him and then back at me with a flash of recognition that warmed instantly to a faint smile. She hesitated as if to speak to me, smiled broadly and understandingly and turned to follow the others. All three broke into a canter and she did not look back. I stood for a second or so at the crossing of the lanes, watching her recede, and then became aware that my uncle was already some paces off and talking over his shoulder in the belief that I was close behind.

I turned about and strode to overtake him.

My mind was full of Beatrice and this surprise. I remembered her simply as a Normandy. I'd clean forgotten that Garvell was the son and she the stepdaughter of our neighbour, Lady Osprey. Indeed, I'd probably forgotten at that time that we had Lady Osprey as a neighbour. There was no reason at all for remembering it. It was amazing to find her in this Surrey country-side, when I'd never thought of her as living anywhere in the world but at Bladesover Park, near forty miles and twenty years away. She was so alive—so unchanged! The same quick warm blood was in her cheeks. It seemed only yesterday that we had kissed among the bracken stem . . . .

"Eh ?" I said.

"I say he's good stuff," said my uncle. "You can say what you like against the aristocracy, George; Lord Carnaby's rattling good stuff. There's a sort of *Savoir Faire*, something —it's an old-fashioned phrase, George, but a good one—there's a Bong-Tong. . . . It's like the Oxford turf, George, you can't grow it in a year. I wonder how they do it ? It's living always on a Scale, George. It's being there from the beginning." . . .

"She might," I said to myself, "be a picture by Romney come alive ! "

"They tell all these stories about him," said my uncle, "but what do they all amount to ? "

"Gods ! " I said to myself ; "but why have I forgotten for so long ? Those queer little brows of hers—the touch of mischief in her eyes—the way she breaks into a smile ! "

"I don't blame him," said my uncle. "Mostly it's imagination. That and leisure, George. When I was a young man I was kept pretty busy. So were you. Even then——! "

What puzzled me more particularly was the queer trick of my memory that had never recalled anything vital of

Beatrice whatever when I met Garvell again, that had, indeed, recalled nothing except a boyish antagonism and our fight. Now when my senses were full of her, it seemed incredible that I could ever have forgotten. . . .

§ 3

" Oh, Crikey ! " said my aunt, reading a letter behind her coffee-machine. " *Here's* a young woman, George ! "

We were breakfasting together in the big window bay at Lady Grove that looks upon the iris beds ; my uncle was in London.

I sounded an interrogative note and decapitated an egg.

" Who's Beatrice Normandy ? " asked my aunt. " I've not heard of her before."

" She the young woman ? "

" Yes. Says she knows you. I'm no hand at old etiquette, George, but her line is a bit unusual. Practically she says she's going to make her mother——"

" Eh ? Step-mother, isn't it ? "

" You seem to know a lot about her. She says ' mother,'— Lady Osprey. They're to call on me, anyhow, next Wednesday week at four, and there's got to be you for tea."

" Eh ? "

" You—for tea."

" H'm. She had rather—force of character when I knew her before."

I became aware of my aunt's head sticking out obliquely from behind the coffee-machine and regarding me with wide blue curiosity. I met her gaze for a moment, flinched, coloured and laughed.

" I've known her longer than I've known you," I said, and explained at length.

My aunt kept her eye on me over and round the coffee-machine as I did so. She was greatly interested, and asked several elucidatory questions.

" Why didn't you tell me the day you saw her ? You've had her on your mind for a week," she said.

" It *is* odd I didn't tell you," I admitted.

" You thought I'd get a Down on her," said my aunt conclusively. " That's what you thought," and opened the rest of her letters.

The two ladies came in a pony-carriage with conspicuous punctuality, and I had the unusual experience of seeing my aunt entertaining callers. We had tea upon the terrace under the cedar, but old Lady Osprey being an embittered Protestant had never before seen the inside of the house, and we made a sort of tour of inspection that reminded me of my first visit to the place. In spite of my preoccupation with Beatrice, I stored a queer little memory of the contrast between the two other women ; my aunt, tall, slender and awkward, in a simple blue home-keeping dress, an omnivorous reader and a very authentic wit, and the lady of pedigree, short and plump, dressed with Victorian fussiness, living at the intellectual level of palmistry and genteel fiction, pink in the face and generally flustered by a sense of my aunt's social strangeness and disposed under the circumstances to behave rather like an imitation of the more queenly moments of her own cook. The one seemed made of whalebone, the other of dough. My aunt was nervous, partly through the intrinsic difficulty of handling the lady and partly because of her passionate desire to watch Beatrice and me, and her nervousness took a common form with her, a wider clumsiness of gesture and an exacerbation of her habitual oddity of phrase which did much to deepen the pink perplexity of the lady of title. For instance, I heard my aunt admit that one of the Stuart Durgan ladies did look a bit " balmy on the crumpet," she described the knights of the age of chivalry as "korvorting about on the off-chance of a dragon," she explained she was "always old mucking about the garden," and instead of offering me a Garibaldi biscuit, she asked me with that faint lisp of hers, to " have some squashed flies, George." I felt convinced Lady Osprey would describe her as " a most eccentric person " on the very first opportunity ;—" a *most* eccentric person." One could see her, as people say, " shaping " for that.

Beatrice was dressed very quietly in brown with a simple but courageous broad-brimmed hat, and an unexpected quality of being grown-up and responsible. She guided her step-mother through the first encounter, scrutinised my aunt and got us all well in movement through the house, and then she turned her attention to me with a quick and half-confident smile.

" We haven't met," she said, " since——"

" It was in the Warren."

" Of course," she said, " the Warren ! I remembered it all except just the name. . . . I was eight."

Her smiling eyes insisted on my memories being thorough. I looked up and met them squarely, a little at a loss for what I should say.

" I gave you away pretty completely," she said, meditating upon my face. " And afterwards I gave away Archie."

She turned her face away from the others, and her voice fell ever so little.

" They gave him a licking for telling lies ! " she said, as though that was a pleasant memory. " And when it was all over I went to our wigwam. You remember the wigwam ? "

" Out in the West Wood ? "

" Yes—and cried—for all the evil I had done you, I suppose . . . I've often thought of it since. . . ."

Lady Osprey stopped for us to overtake her. " My dear ! "

she said to Beatrice. "Such a beautiful gallery!" Then
she stared very hard at me, puzzled in the most naked fashion
to understand who I might be.

"People say the oak staircase is rather good," said my
aunt, and led the way.

Lady Osprey, with her skirts gathered for the ascent to
the gallery and her hand on the newel, turned and addressed
a look full of meaning—overflowing indeed with meanings—
at her charge. The chief meaning no doubt was caution about
myself, but much of it was just meaning at large. I chanced to
catch the response in a mirror and detected Beatrice with her
nose wrinkled into a swift and entirely diabolical grimace.
Lady Osprey became a deeper shade of pink and speechless
with indignation—it was evident she disavowed all further
responsibility, as she followed my aunt upstairs.

"It's dark, but there's a sort of dignity," said Beatrice
very distinctly, regarding the hall with serene tranquillity,
and allowing the unwilling feet on the stairs to widen their
distance from us. She stood a step up, so that she looked
down a little upon me and over me at the old hall.

She turned upon me abruptly when she thought her step-
mother was beyond ear-shot.

"But how did you get here?" she asked.

"Here?"

"All this." She indicated space and leisure by a wave
of the hand at hall and tall windows and sunlit terrace.
"Weren't you the housekeeper's son?"

"I've adventured. My uncle has become—a great
financier. He used to be a little chemist about twenty miles
from Bladesover. We're promoters now, amalgamators, big
people on the new model."

"I understand." She regarded me with interested eyes,
visibly thinking me out.

"And you recognised me?" I asked.

"After a second or so. I saw you recognised me. I
couldn't place you, but I knew I knew you. Then Archie
being there helped me to remember."

"I'm glad to meet again," I ventured. "I'd never forgotten you."

"One doesn't forget those childish things."

We regarded one another for a moment with a curiously
easy and confident satisfaction in coming together again.
I can't explain our ready zest in one another. The thing
was so. We pleased each other, we had no doubt in
our minds that we pleased each other. From the first we
were at our ease with one another. "So picturesque, so
very picturesque," came a voice from above, and then:
"Bee-atrice!"

"I've a hundred things I want to know about you," she said
with an easy intimacy, as we went up the winding steps. . . .

As the four of us sat at tea together under the cedar on the
terrace, she asked questions about my aeronautics. My aunt
helped with a word or so about my broken ribs. Lady Osprey
evidently regarded flying as a most undesirable and improper
topic—a blasphemous intrusion upon the angels. " It isn't
flying," I explained. " We don't fly yet."

" You never will," she said compactly. " You never
will."

" Well," I said, " we do what we can."

The little lady lifted a small gloved hand and indicated
a height of about four feet from the ground. " Thus far,"
she said, " thus far—*and no farther !* No ! "

She became emphatically pink. " *No,*" she said again
quite conclusively, and coughed shortly. " Thank you,"
she said to her ninth or tenth cake. Beatrice burst into
cheerful laughter with her eye on me. I was lying on the
turf, and this perhaps caused a slight confusion about the
primordial curse in Lady Osprey's mind.

" Upon his belly shall he go," she said with quiet distinct-
ness, " all the days of his life."

After which we talked no more of aeronautics.

Beatrice sat bunched together in a chair and regarded
me with exactly the same scrutiny, I thought, the same
adventurous aggression, that I had faced long ago at the tea-
table in my mother's room. She was amazingly like that
little Princess of my Bladesover memories, the wilful mis-
behaviours of her hair seemed the same—her voice ; things one
would have expected to be changed altogether. She formed
her plans in the same quick way, and acted with the same
irresponsible decision.

She stood up abruptly.

" What is there beyond the terrace ? " she said, and found
me promptly beside her.

I invented a view for her.

At the farther corner from the cedar she perched herself
up upon the parapet and achieved an air of comfort among
the lichenous stones. " Now tell me," she said, " all about
yourself. Tell me about yourself ; I know such duffers of
men ! They all do the same things. How did you get—
here ? All my men *were* here. They couldn't have got here
if they hadn't been here always. They wouldn't have thought
it right. You've climbed."

" If it's climbing," I said.

She went off at a tangent. " It's—I don't know if you'll
understand—interesting to meet you again. I've remembered you. I don't know why, but I have. I've used you as
a sort of lay figure—when I've told myself stories. But you've
always been rather stiff and difficult in my stories—in ready-
made clothes—a Labour Member or a Bradlaugh, or something
like that. You're not like that a bit. And yet you *are* ! "

She looked at me. "Was it much of a fight ? They make out it is. I don't know why ? "

" I was shot up here by an accident," I said. "There was no fight at all. Except to keep honest perhaps—and I made no great figure in that. I and my uncle mixed a medicine and it blew us up. No merit in that ! But you've been here all the time. Tell me what you have done first."

" One thing we didn't do." She meditated for a moment.

" What ? " said I.

" Produce a half-brother for Bladesover. So it went to the Phillbrick gang. And they let it ! And I and my step-mother—we let too. And live in a little house."

She nodded her head vaguely over her shoulder, and turned to me again. "Well, suppose it was an accident. Here you are ! Now you're here, what are you going to do ? You're young. Is it to be Parliament ? I heard some men the other day talking about you. Before I knew you were you. They said that was what you ought to do." . . .

She put me through my intentions with a close and vital curiosity. It was just as she had tried to imagine me a soldier and place me years ago. She made me feel more planless and incidental than ever. " You want to make a flying-machine," she pursued. "And when you fly ? What then ? Would it be for fighting ? " . . .

I told her something of my experimental work. She had never heard of the soaring aeroplane, and was excited by the thought, and keen to hear about it. She had thought all the work so far had been a mere projecting of impossible machines. For her Pilcher and Lilienthal had died in vain. She did not know such men had lived in the world.

" But that's dangerous ! " she said, with a note of discovery.

" Oh !—it's dangerous." . . .

" Bee-atrice ! " Lady Osprey called.

Beatrice dropped from the wall to her feet.

" Where do you do this soaring ? "

" Beyond the high Barrows. East of Crest Hill and the wood."

" Do you mind people coming to see ? "

" Whenever you please. Only let me know——"

" I'll take my chance some day. Some day soon." She looked at me thoughtfully, smiled, and our talk was at an end.

§ 4

All my later work in aeronautics is associated in my memory with the quality of Beatrice, with her incidental presence, with things she said and did and things I thought of that had reference to her.

In the spring of that year I had got to a flying-machine that lacked nothing but longitudinal stability. My model

flew like a bird for fifty or a hundred yards or so, and then
either dived and broke its nose or, what was commoner,
reared up, slid back and smashed its propeller. The rhythm
of the pitching puzzled me. I felt it must obey some laws
not yet quite clearly stated. I became, therefore, a student
of theory and literature for a time, I hit upon the string
of considerations that led me to what is called Ponderevo's
Principle and my F.R.S., and I worked this out in three long
papers. Meanwhile I made a lot of turntable and glider models
and started in upon an idea of combining gas-bags and gliders.
Balloon work was new to me. I had made one or two ascents
in the balloons of the Aero Club before I started my gasometer
and the balloon shed and gave Cothope a couple of months
with Sir Peter Rumchase. My uncle found part of the money
for these developments; he was growing interested and
competitive in this business because of Lord Boom's prize
and the amount of *réclame* involved, and it was at his request
that I named my first navigable balloon Lord Roberts Alpha.

Lord Roberts *a* very nearly terminated all my investigations. My idea both in this and its more successful and
famous younger brother, Lord Roberts *β*, was to utilise the idea
of a contractile balloon with a rigid flat base, a balloon shaped
rather like an inverted boat that should almost support the
apparatus but not quite. The gas-bag was of the chambered
sort used for these long forms, and not with an internal
balloonette. The trouble was to make the thing contractile.
This I sought to do by fixing a long, fine-meshed silk net over
it that was fastened to be rolled up on two longitudinal rods.
Practically I contracted my sausage gas-bag by netting it
down. The ends were too complex for me to describe here,
but I thought them out elaborately and they were very carefully
planned. Lord Roberts *a* was furnished with a single big screw
forward and there was a rudder aft. The engine was the first
one to be, so to speak, right in the plane of the gas-bag. I lay
immediately under the balloon on a sort of glider framework
far away from either engine or rudder, controlling them by wire-
pulls constructed on the principle of the well-known Bowden
brake of the cyclist.

But Lord Roberts *a* has been pretty exhaustively figured
and described in various aeronautical publications. The
unforeseen defect was the badness of the work in the silk
netting. It tore aft as soon as I began to contract the balloon
and the last two segments immediately bulged through the
hole, exactly as an inner tube will bulge through the ruptured
outer cover of a pneumatic tyre, and then the sharp edge of
the torn net cut the oiled-silk of the distended last segment
along a weak seam and burst it with a loud report.

Up to that point the whole thing had been going on extremely
well. As a navigable balloon and before I contracted it, the
Lord Roberts *a* was an unqualified success. It had run

out of the shed admirably at nine or ten miles an hour or
more, and although there was a gentle south-wester blowing,
it had gone up and turned and faced it as well as any craft
of the sort I have ever seen.

I lay in my customary glider position, horizontal and face
downward, and the invisibility of all the machinery gave an
extraordinary effect of independent levitation. Only by
looking up, as it were, and turning my head back could I
see the flat aeroplane bottom of the balloon and the rapid
successive passages, swish, swish, swish of the vans of the propeller. I made a wide circle over Lady Grove and Duffield
and out towards Effingham and came back quite successfully
to the starting-point.

Down below in the October sunlight were my sheds and
the little group that had been summoned to witness the
start, their faces craned upward and most of them scrutinising
my expression through field-glasses. I could see Carnaby
and Beatrice on horseback, and two girls I did not know
with them, Cothope and three or four workmen I employed,
my aunt and Mrs. Levinstein, who was staying with her, on
foot, and Dimmock, the veterinary surgeon, and one or two
others. My shadow moved a little to the north of them like
the shadow of a fish. At Lady Grove the servants were out
on the lawn, and the Duffield school playground swarmed with
children too indifferent to aeronautics to cease their playing.
But in the Crest Hill direction—the place looked extraordinarily squat and ugly from above—there were knots and strings
of staring workmen everywhere—not one of them working but
all agape. (But now I write of it, it occurs to me that perhaps
it was their dinner-hour ; it was certainly near twelve.)
I hung for a moment or so enjoying the soar, then turned
about to face a clear stretch of open down, let the engine
out to full speed and set my rollers at work rolling in the
net and so tightening the gas-bags. Instantly the pace
quickened with the diminished resistance. . . .

In that moment before the bang I think I must have been
really flying. Before the net ripped, just in the instant
when my balloon was at its systole, the whole apparatus was,
I am convinced, heavier than air. That, however, is a claim
that has been disputed, and in any case this sort of priority
is a very trivial thing.

Then came a sudden retardation, instantly followed by
an inexpressibly disconcerting tilt downward of the machine.
That I still recall with horror. I couldn't see what was
happening at all and I couldn't imagine. It was a mysterious,
inexplicable dive. The thing, it seemed, without rhyme or
reason was kicking up its heels in the air. The bang followed
immediately and I perceived I was falling rapidly.

I was too much taken by surprise to think of the proper
cause of the report. I don't even know what I made of it.

I was obsessed I suppose by that perpetual dread of the modern aeronaut, a flash between engine and balloon. Yet obviously I wasn't wrapped in flames. I ought to have realised instantly it wasn't that. I did at any rate, whatever other impressions there were, release the winding of the outer net and let the balloon expand again, and that no doubt did something to break my fall. I don't remember doing that. Indeed, all I do remember is the giddy effect upon the landscape of falling swiftly upon it down a flat spiral, the hurried rush of fields and trees and cottages on my left shoulder and the overhung feeling as if the whole apparatus was pressing down the top of my head. I didn't stop or attempt to stop the screw. That was going on swish, swish, swish all the time.

Cothope really knows more about the fall than I do. He describes the easterly start, the tilt, and the appearance and bursting of a sort of bladder aft. Then down I swooped, very swiftly but not nearly so steeply as I imagined I was doing. "Fifteen or twenty degrees," said Cothope, "to be exact." From him it was that I learnt that I let the nets loose again and so arrested my fall. He thinks I was more in control of myself than I remember. But I do not see why I should have forgotten so excellent a resolution. His impression is that I was really steering and trying to drop into the Farthing Down beeches. "You hit the trees," he said, "and the whole affair stood on its nose among them and then very slowly crumpled up. I saw you'd been jerked out as I thought and I didn't stay for more. I rushed for my bicycle."

As a matter of fact it was purely accidental that I came down in the woods. I am reasonably certain that I had no more control then than a thing in a parcel. I remember I felt a sort of wincing, "Now it comes!" as the trees rushed up to me. If I remember that I should remember steering. Then the propeller smashed, everything stopped with a jerk and I was falling into a mass of yellowing leaves, and Lord Roberts a, so it seemed to me, was going back into the sky.

I felt twigs and things hit me in the face, but I didn't feel injured at the time; I clutched at things that broke, tumbled through a froth of green and yellow into a shadowy world of great bark-covered arms, and there snatching wildly, got a grip on a fair round branch and hung.

I became intensely alert and clear-headed. I held by that branch for a moment and looked about me and caught at another and then found myself holding to a practicable fork. I swung forward to that and got a leg round it below its junction and so was able presently to clamber down, climbing very coolly and deliberately. I dropped ten feet or so from the lowest branch and fell on my feet. "That's all right," I said and stared up through the tree to see what I could of the deflated and crumpled remains that had once been Lord Roberts a festooned on the branches it had broken. " Gods ! " I said, " What a tumble ! "

I wiped something that trickled from my face and was shocked to see my hand covered with blood. I looked at myself and saw what seemed to me an astonishing quantity of blood running down my arm and shoulder. I perceived my mouth was full of blood. It's a queer moment when one realises one is hurt and perhaps badly hurt, and has still to discover just how far one is hurt. I explored my face carefully and found unfamiliar contours on the left side. The broken end of a branch had driven right through my cheek, damaging my cheek and teeth and gums, and left a splinter of itself stuck like an explorer's farthest-point flag in the upper maxillary. That and a sprained wrist were all my damage. But I bled as though I had been chopped to pieces, and it seemed to me that my face had been driven in. I can't describe just the horrible disgust I felt at that.

" This blood must be stopped, anyhow," I said, thick-headedly. " I wonder where there's a spider's web "—an odd twist for my mind to take. But it was the only treatment that occurred to me.

I must have conceived some idea of going home unaided, because I was thirty yards from the tree before I dropped.

Then a kind of black disc appeared in the middle of the world and rushed out to the edge of things and blotted them out. I don't remember falling down. I fainted from excite-ment, disgust at my injury and loss of blood, and lay there until Cothope found me.

He was the first to find me, scorching as he did over the downland turf, and making a wide course to get the Carnaby plantations at their narrowest. Then presently, while he was trying to apply the methodical teachings of the St. John's Ambulance classes to a rather abnormal case, Beatrice came galloping through the trees full-tilt with Lord Carnaby hard behind her, and she was hatless, muddy from a fall and white as death. " And cool as a cucumber, too," said Cothope, turning it over in his mind as he told me.

(" They never seem quite to have their heads, and never seem quite to lose 'em," said Cothope, generalising about the sex.)

Also he witnessed she acted with remarkable decision. The question was whether I should be taken to the house her step-mother occupied at Bedley Corner, the Carnaby dower-house, or down to Carnaby's place at Easting. Beatrice had no doubt in the matter, for she meant to nurse me. Carnaby didn't seem to want that to happen. " She *would* have it wasn't half so far," said Cothope. " She faced us out. . . .

" I hate to be faced out of my opinions, so I've taken a pedometer over it since. It's exactly forty-three yards farther.

"Lord Carnaby looked at her pretty straight," said Cothope, finishing the picture; "and then he gave in."

§ 5

But my story has made a jump from June to October, and during that time my relations with Beatrice and the country-side that was her setting had developed in many directions. She came and went, moving in an orbit for which I had no data, going to London and Paris, into Wales and Northampton, while her step-mother on some independent system of her own also vanished and recurred intermittently. At home they obeyed the rule of an inflexible old maid, Charlotte, and Beatrice exercised all the rights of proprietorship in Carnaby's extensive stables. Her interest in me was from the first undisguised. She found her way to my work-sheds and developed rapidly, in spite of the sincere discouragement of Cothope, into a keen amateur of aeronautics. She would come sometimes in the morning, sometimes in the afternoon, sometimes afoot with an Irish terrier, sometimes riding. She would come for three or four days every day, vanish for a fortnight or three weeks, return.

It was not long before I came to look for her. From the first I found her immensely interesting. To me she was a new feminine type altogether—I have made it plain, I think, how limited was my knowledge of women. But she made me not simply interested in her, but in myself. She became for me something that greatly changes a man's world. How shall I put it? She became an audience. Since I've emerged from the emotional developments of the affair I have thought it out in a hundred aspects, and it does seem to me that this way in which men and women make audiences for one another is a curiously influential force in their lives. For some it seems an audience is a vital necessity, they seek audiences as creatures seek food; others again, my uncle among them, can play to an imaginary audience. I, I think, have lived and can live without one. In my adolescence I was my own audience and my own court of honour. And to have an audience in one's mind is to play a part, to become self-conscious and dramatic. For many years I had been self-forgetful and scientific. I had lived for work and impersonal interests until I found scrutiny, applause and expectation in Beatrice's eyes. Then I began to live for the effect I imagined I made upon her, to make that very soon the principal value in my life. I played to her. I did things for the look of them. I began to dream more and more of beautiful situations and fine poses and groupings with her and for her.

I put these things down because they puzzle me. I think I was in love with Beatrice, as being in love is usually understood, but it was a different state altogether from my

passionate hunger for Marion, or my keen sensuous desire
for and pleasure in Effie. These were selfish sincere things,
fundamental and instinctive, as sincere as the leap of a tiger.
But until matters drew to a crisis with Beatrice, there was an
immense imaginative insurgence of a quite different quality.
I am setting down here very gravely, and perhaps absurdly,
what are no doubt elementary commonplaces for innumerable
people. This love that grew up between Beatrice and myself
was, I think—I put it quite tentatively and rather curiously
—romantic love. That unfortunate and truncated affair
of my uncle and the Scrymgeour lady was really of the same
stuff, if a little different in quality. I have to admit that.
The factor of audience was of primary importance in either case.

Its effect upon me was to make me in many respects adolescent again. It made me keener upon the point of honour,
and anxious and eager to do high and splendid things, and in
particular, brave things. So far it ennobled and upheld me.
But it did also push me towards vulgar and showy things.
At bottom it was disingenuous ; it gave my life the quality
of stage scenery, with one side to the audience, another side
that wasn't meant to show, and an economy of substance. It
certainly robbed my work of high patience and quality. I
cut down the toil of research in my eagerness and her eagerness for fine flourishes in the air, flights that would tell. I
shirked the longer road.

And it robbed me, too, of any fine perception of
absurdity. . . .

Yet that was not everything in our relationship. The
elemental thing was there also. It came in very suddenly.

It was one day in the summer, though I do not now recall
without reference to my experimental memoranda whether
it was in July or August. I was working with a new and more
bird-like aeroplane with wing curvatures studied from Lilienthal, Pilcher and Phillips, that I thought would give a different
rhythm for the pitching oscillations than anything I'd had
before. I was soaring my long course from the framework
on the old barrow by my sheds down to Tinker's Corner. It is
a clear stretch of downland, except for two or three thickets
of box and thorn to the right of my course ; one transverse
trough, in which there is bush and a small rabbit warren, comes
in from the east. I had started, and was very intent on the
peculiar long swoop with which my new arrangement flew.
Then, without any sort of notice, right ahead of me appeared
Beatrice riding towards Tinker's Corner to waylay and talk
to me. She looked round over her shoulder, saw me coming,
touched her horse to a gallop, and then the brute bolted right
into the path of my machine.

There was a queer moment of doubt whether we shouldn't
all smash together. I had to make up my mind very quickly
whether I would pitch-up and drop backward at once and

take my chance of falling undamaged, a poor chance it would
have been, in order to avoid any risk to her, or whether I
would lift against the wind and soar right over her. This
latter I did. She had already got her horse in hand when I
came up to·her. Her woman's body lay along his neck, and
she glanced up as I, with wings aspread, and every nerve in a
state of tension, swept over her.

Then I had landed, and was going back to where her horse
stood still and trembling.

We exchanged no greetings. She slid from her saddle
into my arms, and for one instant I held her. " Those great
wings," she said, and that was all.

She lay in my arms, and I thought for a moment she had
fainted.

" Very near a nasty accident," said Cothope, coming up
and regarding our grouping with disfavour. He took her
horse by the bridle. " Very dangerous thing coming across
us like that."

Beatrice disengaged herself from me, stood for a moment
trembling, and then sat down on the turf. " I'll just sit
down for a moment," she said.

" Oh ! " she said.

She covered her face with her hands while Cothope looked
at her with an expression between suspicion and impatience.

For some moments nobody moved. Then Cothope remarked that perhaps he'd better get her water.

As for me I was filled with a new, outrageous idea, begotten
I scarcely know how from this incident with its instant contacts and swift emotions, and that was that I must make
love to and possess Beatrice. I see no particular reason why
that thought should have come to me in that moment, but it
did. I do not believe that before then I had thought of our
relations in such terms at all. Suddenly, as I remember it,
the factor of passion came. She crouched there, and I stood
over her and neither of us said a word. But it was just as
though something had been shouted from the sky.

Cothope had gone twenty paces perhaps, when she un-
covered her face. " I shan't want any water," she said.
" Call him back."

§ 6

After that the spirit of our relations changed. The old
ease had gone. She came to me less frequently, and when
she came she would have some one with her, usually old
Carnaby, and he would do the bulk of the talking. All
through September she was away. When we were alone
together there was a curious constraint. We became clouds
of inexpressible feeling towards one another ; we could think
of nothing that was not too momentous for words.

Then came the smash of Lord Roberts *a*, and I found

myself with a bandaged face in a bedroom in the Bedley
Corner dower-house with Beatrice presiding over an inefficient
nurse, Lady Osprey very pink and shocked in the background,
and my aunt jealously intervening.

My injuries were much more showy than serious, and I
could have been taken to Lady Grove next day, but Beatrice
would not permit that, and kept me at Bedley Corner three
clear days. In the afternoon of the second day she became
extremely solicitous for the proper aeration of the nurse,
packed her off for an hour in a brisk rain, and sat by me alone.

I asked her to marry me.

On the whole I must admit it was not a situation that
lent itself to eloquence. I lay on my back and talked through
bandages and with some little difficulty, for my tongue and
mouth had swollen. But I was feverish and in pain, and the
emotional suspense I had been in so long with regard to her,
became now an unendurable impatience.

" Comfortable ? " she asked.

" Yes."

" Shall I read to you ? "

" No. I want to talk."

" You can't. I'd better talk to you."

" No," I said, " I want to talk to you."

She came and stood by my bedside and looked me in the
eyes. " I don't—I don't want you to talk to me," she said.
" I thought you couldn't talk."

" I get few chances—of you."

" You'd better not talk. Don't talk now. Let me chatter
instead. You ought not to talk."

" It isn't much," I said.

" I'd rather you didn't."

" I'm not going to be disfigured," I said. " Only a scar."

" Oh ! " she said, as if she had expected something quite
different. " Did you think you'd become a sort of gargoyle ? "

" L'Homme qui Rit !—I didn't know. But that's all
right. Jolly flowers those are ! "

" Michaelmas daisies," she said. " I'm glad you're not
disfigured. And those are perennial sunflowers. Do you
know no flowers at all ? When I saw you on the ground I
certainly thought you were dead. You ought to have been,
by all the rules of the game."

She said some other things, but I was thinking of my next
move.

" Are we social equals ? " I said abruptly.

She stared at me. " Queer question," she said.

" But are we ? "

" H'm. Difficult to say. But why do you ask ? Is the
daughter of a courtesy Baron who died—of general disre-
putableness, I believe—before his father—— ? I give it up.
Does it matter ? "

"No. My mind is confused. I want to know if you will marry me."

She whitened and said nothing. I suddenly felt I must plead with her. "Damn these bandages!" I said, breaking into ineffectual febrile rage.

She roused herself to her duties as nurse. "What are you doing? Why are you trying to sit up? Lie down! Don't touch your bandages. I told you not to talk."

She stood helpless for a moment, then took me firmly by the shoulders and pushed me back upon the pillow. She gripped the wrist of the hand I had raised to my face. "I told you not to talk," she whispered close to my face. "I asked you not to talk. Why couldn't you do as I asked you?"

"You've been avoiding me for a month," I said.

"I know. You might have known. Put your hand back —down by your side."

I obeyed. She sat on the edge of the bed. A flush had come to her cheeks, and her eyes were very bright. "I asked you," she repeated, "not to talk."

My eyes questioned her mutely.

She put her hand on my chest. Her eyes were tormented. "How can I answer you now?" she said. "How *can* I say anything now?"

"What do you mean?" I asked.

She made no answer.

"Do you mean it must be No?"

She nodded.

"But——" I said, and my whole soul was full of accusations.

"I know," she said. "I can't explain. I can't. But it has to be No! It can't be. It's utterly, finally, for ever impossible. . . . Keep your hands still!"

"But," I said, "when we met again——"

"I can't marry. I can't and won't."

She stood up. "Why did you talk?" she cried. "Couldn't you *see*?"

She seemed to have something it was impossible to say.

She came to the table beside my bed and pulled the Michaelmas daisies awry. "Why did you talk like that?" she said in a tone of infinite bitterness. "To begin like that——!"

"But what is it?" I said. "Is it some circumstance— my social position?"

"Oh *damn* your social position!" she cried.

She went and stood at the farther window staring out at the rain. For a long time we were absolutely still. The wind and rain came in little gusts upon the pane. She turned to me abruptly.

"You didn't ask me if I loved you," she said.

"Oh, if it's *that*!" said I.

" It's not that," she said.   " But if you want to know——"
She paused.

" I do," she said.

We stared at one another.

" I do—with all my heart, if you want to know."

" Then why the devil—— ? " I asked.

She made no answer.   She walked across the room to
the piano and began to play, rather noisily and rapidly, with
odd gusts of emphasis, the shepherd's pipe music from the
last act in *Tristan and Isolde*.   Presently she missed a note,
failed again, ran her finger heavily up the scale, struck the
piano passionately with her fist, making a feeble jar in the
treble, jumped up, and went out of the room. . . .

The nurse found me still wearing my helmet of bandages,
partially dressed and pottering round the room to find the
rest of my clothes.   I was in a state of exasperated hunger
for Beatrice and I was too inflamed and weakened to conceal
the state of my mind.   I was feebly angry because of the
irritation of dressing and particularly of the struggle to put
on my trousers without being able to see my legs.   I was
staggering about, and once I had fallen over a chair, and I had
upset the jar of Michaelmas daisies.

I must have been a detestable spectacle.   " I'll go back
to bed," said I, " if I may have a word with Miss Normandy.
I've got something to say to her.   That's why I'm dressing."

My point was conceded, but there were long delays.   Whethe
the household had my ultimatum or whether she told Beatrice
directly I do not know, and what Lady Osprey can have made
of it in the former case I can't imagine. . . .

At last Beatrice came and stood by my bedside.   " Well ? "
she said.

" All I want to say," I said with the querulous note of a
misunderstood child, " is that I can't take this as final.   I
want to see you and talk when I'm better—and write.   I
can't do anything now.   I can't argue."

I was overtaken with self-pity and began to snivel.

" I can't rest.   You see ?   I can't do anything."

She sat down beside me again and spoke softly.   " I promise
I will talk it all over with you again.   When you are well.
I promise I will meet you somewhere so that we can talk.
You can't talk now.   I asked you not to talk now.   All you
want to know you shall know. . . . Will that do ? "

" I'd like to know——"

She looked round to see the door was closed, stood up
and went to it.

Then she crouched beside me and began whispering very
softly and rapidly with her face close to me.

" Dear," she said, " I love you.   If it will make you happy
to marry me, I will marry you.   I was in a mood just now
—a stupid, inconsiderate mood.   Of course I will marry

you. You are my prince, my king. Women are such things
of mood—or I would have—behaved differently. We say
' No ' when we means ' Yes '—and fly into crises. So now,
Yes—yes—yes. I will. . . . I can't even kiss you. Give
me your hand to kiss that. Understand I am yours. Do you
understand ? I am yours just as if we had been married
fifty years. Your wife—Beatrice. Is that enough ? Now—
now will you rest ? "

" Yes," I said ; " but why—— ? "

" There are complications. There are difficulties. When
you are better you will be able to—understand them. But
now they don't matter. Only you know this must be secret—
for a time. Absolutely secret between us. Will you promise
that ? "

" Yes," I said, " I understand. I wish I could kiss you."

She laid her head down beside mine for a moment, and
then she kissed my hand.

" I don't care what difficulties there are," I said, and shut
my eyes.

§ 7

But I was only beginning to gauge the unaccountable
elements in Beatrice. For a week after my return to Lady
Grove I had no sign of her, and then she called with Lady
Osprey and brought a huge bunch of perennial sunflowers
and Michaelmas daisies, " just the old flowers there were
in your room," said my aunt with a relentless eye on me. I
didn't get any talk alone with Beatrice then, and she took
occasion to tell us she was going to London for some indefinite
number of weeks. I couldn't even pledge her to write to me,
and when she did it was a brief, enigmatical friendly letter
with not a word of the reality between us.

I wrote back a love letter—my first love letter—and she
made no reply for eight days. Then came a scrawl : " I
can't write letters. Wait till we can talk. Are you better ? "

I think the reader would be amused if he could see the papers
on my desk as I write all this, the mangled and disfigured
pages, the experimental arrangements of notes, the sheets of
suggestions balanced in constellations, the blottesque intellectual battlegrounds over which I have been fighting. I
find this account of my relations to Beatrice quite the most
difficult part of my story to write. I happen to be a very
objective-minded person, I forget my moods, and this was so
much an affair of moods. And even such moods and emotions
as I recall are very difficult to convey. To me it is about as
difficult as describing a taste or a scent.

Then the objective story is made up of little things that
are difficult to set in a proper order. And love is an hysterical
passion, now high, now low, now exalted, and now intensely

physical.   No one has ever yet dared to tell a love story completely, its alternations, its comings and goings, its debased
moments, its hate.   The love stories we tell, tell only the net
consequence, the ruling effect. . . .

How can I rescue from the past now the mystical quality
of Beatrice ; my intense longing for her ; the overwhelming,
irrational, formless desire ?   How can I explain how intimately
that worship mingled with a high impatient resolve to make her
mine, to take her by strength and courage, to do my loving
in a violent heroic manner ?   And then the doubts, the
puzzled arrest at the fact of her fluctuations, at her refusal
to marry me, at the fact that even when at last she returned to
Bedley Corner she seemed to evade me ?

That exasperated me and perplexed me beyond measure.
I felt that it was treachery.   I thought of every conceivable
explanation, and the most exalted and romantic confidence
in her did not simply alternate but mingled with the basest
misgivings.

And into the tangle of memories comes the figure of Carnaby,
coming out slowly from the background to a position of
significance, as an influence, as a predominant strand in the
nets that kept us apart, as a rival.   What were the forces that
pulled her away from me when it was so clearly manifest she
loved me ?   Did she think of marrying him ?   Had I invaded
some long-planned scheme ?   It was evident he did not like
me, that in some way I spoiled the world for him.   She returned
to Bedley Corner, and for some weeks she was flitting about me,
and never once could I have talk with her alone.   When she
came to my sheds Carnaby was always with her, jealously
observant.   (Why the devil couldn't she send him about his
business ?)   The days slipped by and my anger gathered.

All this mingles with the making of Lord Roberts β.   I
had resolved upon that one night as I lay awake at Bedley
Corner, I got it planned out before the bandages were off my
face.   I conceived this second navigable balloon in a grandiose
manner.   It was to be a second Lord Roberts a only more so ;
it was to be three times as big, large enough to carry three
men, and it was to be an altogether triumphant vindication
of my claims upon the air.   The framework was to be hollow
like a bird's bones, airtight, and the air pumped in or out
as the weight of fuel I carried changed.   I talked much and
boasted to Cothope—whom I suspected of scepticism about
this new type—of what it would do, and it progressed, slowly.
It progressed slowly because I was restless and uncertain.
At times I would go away to London to snatch some chance
of seeing Beatrice there, at times nothing but a day of gliding
and hard and dangerous exercise would satisfy me.   And now
in the newspapers, in conversation, in everything about me,
arose a new invader of my mental states.   Something was
happening to the great schemes of my uncle's affairs ; people

were beginning to doubt, to question.   It was the first quiver
of his tremendous insecurity, the first wobble of that gigantic
credit top he had kept spinning so long.

There were comings and goings, November and December
slipped by.   I had two unsatisfactory meetings with Beatrice,
meetings that had no privacy—in which we said things of the
sort that need atmosphere, baldly and furtively.   I wrote to
her several times and she wrote back notes that I would sometimes respond to altogether, sometimes condemn as insincere
evasions.   " You don't understand.   I can't just now explain.
Be patient with me.   Leave things a little while to me."   So
she wrote.

I would talk aloud to these notes and wrangle over them
in my workroom—while the plans of Lord Roberts β waited.

"You don't give me a chance!" I would say.   "Why
don't you let me know the secret ?   That's what I'm for—
to settle difficulties !—to tell difficulties to ! "

And at last I could hold out no longer against these accumulating pressures.

I took an arrogant, outrageous line that left her no loop-
holes ; I behaved as though we were living in a melodrama.

"You must come and talk to me," I wrote, " or I will come
and take you.   I want you—and the time runs away."

We met in a ride in the upper plantations.   It must have
been early in January, for there was snow on the ground
and on the branches of the trees.   We walked to and fro
for an hour or more, and from the first I pitched the key high
in romance and made understandings impossible.   It was our
worst time together.   I boasted like an actor, and she, I
know not why, was tired and spiritless.

Now I think over that talk in the light of all that has
happened since, I can imagine how she came to me full of a
human appeal I was too foolish to let her make.   I don't
know.   I confess I have never completely understood Beatrice.
I confess I am still perplexed at many things she said and did.
That afternoon, anyhow, I was impossible.   I posed and
scolded.   I was—I said it—for " taking the Universe by the
throat ! "

" If it was only that," she said, but though I heard I did
not heed her.

At last she gave way to me and talked no more.   Instead
she looked at me—as a thing beyond her controlling but none
the less interesting—much as she had looked at me from behind
the skirts of Lady Drew in the Warren when we were children
together.   Once even I thought she smiled faintly.

" What are the difficulties ? " I cried.   " There's no difficulty I will not overcome for you !   Do your people think
I'm no equal for you ?   Who says it ?   My dear, tell me to
win a title !   I'll do it in five years ! . . .

" Here am I just grown a man at the sight of you.   I

have wanted something to fight for. Let me fight for
you ! . . .

"I'm rich without intending it. Let me mean it, give me
an honourable excuse for it, and I'll put all this rotten old
warren of England at your feet ! "

I said such things as that. I write them down here in all their
resounding base pride. I said these empty and foolish things
and they are part of me. Why should I still cling to pride and
be ashamed. I shouted her down.

I passed from such megalomania to petty accusations.

"You think Carnaby is a better man than I ? " I said.

"No ! " she cried, stung to speech ; "No ! "

"You think we're unsubstantial. You've listened to all
these rumours Boom has started because we talked of a
newspaper of our own. When you are with me you know
I'm a man ; when you get away from me you think I'm a
cheat and a cad. . . . There's not a word of truth in the
things they say about us. I've been slack. I've left things.
But we have only to exert ourselves. You do not know how
wide and far we have spread our nets. Even now we have
a coup—an expedition—in hand. It will put us on a
footing." . . .

Her eyes asked mutely and asked in vain that I would
cease to boast of the very qualities she admired in me.

In the night I could not sleep for thinking of that talk
and the vulgar things I had said in it. I could not understand the drift my mind had taken. I was acutely disgusted.
And my unwonted doubts about myself spread from a merely
personal discontent to our financial position. It was all very
well to talk as I had done of wealth and power and peerages,
but what did I know nowadays of my uncle's position ?
Suppose in the midst of such boasting and confidence there
came some turn I did not suspect, some rottenness he had
concealed from me ! I resolved I had been playing with
aeronautics long enough, that next morning I would go to
him and have things clear between us.

I caught an early train and went up to the Hardingham.

I went up to the Hardingham through a dense London fog
to see how things really stood. Before I had talked to my
uncle for ten minutes I felt like a man who has just awakened
in a bleak inhospitable room out of a grandiose dream.

CHAPTER FOUR

HOW I STOLE THE HEAPS OF QUAP FROM MORDET ISLAND

§ I

"WE got to make a fight for it," said my uncle. "We got to face the music!"

I remember that even at the sight of him I had a sense of impending calamity. He sat under the electric light with the shadow of his hair making bars down his face. He looked shrunken and as though his skin had suddenly got loose and yellow. The decorations of the room seemed to have lost freshness, and outside—the blinds were up—there was not so much fog as a dun darkness. One saw the dingy outlines of the chimneys opposite quite distinctly, and then a sky of such a brown as only London can display.

"I saw a placard," I said; "'More Ponderevity.'"

"That's Boom," he said. "Boom and his damned news-papers. He's trying to fight me down. Ever since I offered to buy the *Daily Decorator* he's been at me. And he thinks consolidating Do Ut cut down the ads. He wants everything, damn him! He's got no sense of dealing. I'd like to bash his face!"

"Well," I said; "what's to be done?"

"Keep going," said my uncle.

"I'll smash Boom yet," he said with sudden savagery.

"Nothing else?" I asked.

"We got to keep going. There's a scare on. Did you notice the rooms? Half the people out there this morning are reporters. And if I talk they touch it up! . . . They didn't use to touch things up! Now they put in character touches—insulting you. Don't know what journalism's coming to. It's all Boom's doing."

He cursed Lord Boom with considerable imaginative vigour.

"Well," said I, "what can he do?"

"Shove us up against time, George; make money tight for us. We been handling a lot of money—and he tightens us up."

"We're sound?"

"Oh, we're sound, George. Trust me for that! But all the same—— There's such a lot of imagination in these things. . . . We're sound enough. That's not it."

He blew. "Damn Boom!" he said, and his eyes over his glasses met mine defiantly.

"We can't, I suppose, run close hauled for a bit—stop expenditure?"

" Where ? "

" Well—Crest Hill."

" What ! " he shouted. " Me stop Crest Hill for Boom ! "
He waved a fist as if to hit his ink-pot and controlled himself
with difficulty. He spoke at last in a reasonable voice. " If
I did," he said, " he'd kick up a fuss. It's no good even if I
wanted to. Everybody's watching the place. If I was
to stop building we'd be down in a week."

He had an idea. " I wish I could do something to start a
strike or something. No such luck. Treat those workmen
a sight too well. No, sink or swim, Crest Hill goes on until
we're under water."

I began to ask questions and irritated him instantly.

" Oh, dash these explanations, George ! " he cried ; " you
only make things look rottener than they are. It's your
way. It isn't a case of figures. We're all right—there's
only one thing we got to do."

" Yes ? "

" Show value, George. That's where this quap comes in ;
that's why I fell in so readily with what you brought to me
week before last. Here we are, we got our option on the
perfect filament, and all we want's canadium. Nobody
knows there's more canadium in the world than will go on the
edge of a sixpence except me and you. Nobody has an idee
the perfect filament's more than just a bit of theorising.
Fifty tons of quap and we'd turn that bit of theorising into
somethin'—— We'd make the lamp trade sit on its tail and
howl. We'd put Ediswan and all of 'em into a parcel with
our last year's trousers and a hat, and swap 'em off for a pot
of geraniums. See ? We'd do it through Business Organisations, and there you are ! See ? Capern's Patent Filament !
The Ideal and the Real ! George, we'll do it ! We'll bring it
off ! And then we'll give such a facer to Boom : he'll think
for fifty years. He's laying up for our London and African
meeting. Let him. He can turn the whole paper on to us.
He says the Business Organisations shares aren't worth fifty-
two—and we quote 'em at eighty-four. Well, here we are.
Gettin' ready for him—loading our gun."

His pose was triumphant.

" Yes," I said, " that's all right. But I can't help thinking
where should we be if we hadn't just by accident got Capern's
Perfect Filament. Because, you know, it was an accident—
my buying up that."

He crumpled up his nose into an expression of impatient
distaste at my unreasonableness.

" And after all, the meeting's in June, and you haven't
begun to get the quap ! After all, we've still got to load
our gun——"

" They start on Toosday."

" Have they got the brig ? "

"They've got a brig."

"Gordon-Nasymth !" I doubted.

"Safe as a bank," he said.   "More I see of that man the more I like him.   All I wish is we'd got a steamer instead of a sailing ship——"

"And," I went on, "you seem to overlook what used to weigh with us a bit.   This canadium side of the business and the Capern chance has rushed you off your legs.   After all—it's stealing, and in its way an international outrage. They've got two gunboats on the coast."

I jumped up and went and stared out at the fog.

"And, by Jove, it's about our only chance ! . . . I didn't dream."

I turned on him.   "I've been up in the air," I said. "Heaven knows where I haven't been.   And here's our only chance—and you give it to that adventurous lunatic to play in his own way—in a brig ! "

"Well, you had a voice——"

"I wish I'd been in this before.   We ought to have run out a steamer to Lagos or one of those West Coast places and done it from there.   Fancy a brig in the Channel at this time of year, if it blows south-west ! "

"I dessay you'd have shoved it, George.   Still—— You know, George. . . . I believe in him."

"Yes," I said.   "Yes, I believe in him too.   In a way. Still——"

He took up a telegram that was lying on his desk and opened it.   His face became a livid yellow.   He put the flimsy pink paper down with a slow reluctant movement and took off his glasses.

"George," he said, " the luck's against us."

"What ? "

He grimaced with his mouth in the queerest way at the telegram.

"That."

I took it up and read :—

"Motor smash compound fracture of the leg gordon naismith what price mordet now."

For a moment neither of us spoke.

"That's all right," I said at last.

"Eh ? " said my uncle.

"*I'm* going.   I'll get that quap or bust."

§ 2

I had a ridiculous persuasion that I was "saving the situation."

'I'm going," I said quite consciously and dramatically. I saw the whole affair—how shall I put it ?—in American colours.

I sat down beside him. " Give me all the data you've got," I said, " and I'll pull this thing off."

" But nobody knows exactly where——"

" Nasmyth does, and he'll tell me."

" He's been very close," said my uncle, and regarded me.

" He'll tell me all right now he's smashed."

He thought. " I believe he will."

" George," he said, " if you pull this thing off——! Once or twice before you've stepped in—with that sort of Woosh of yours——"

He left the sentence unfinished.

" Give me that note-book," I said, " and tell me all you know. Where's the ship ? Where's Pollack ? And where's that telegram from ? If that quap's to be got, I'll get it or bust. If you'll hold on here until I get back with it." . . .

And so it was I jumped into the wildest adventure of my life.

I requisitioned my uncle's best car forthwith. I went down that night to the place of dispatch named on Nasmyth's telegram, Bampton S.O., Oxon, routed him out with a little trouble from that centre, made things right with him and got his explicit directions ; and I was inspecting the *Maud Mary* with young Pollack, his cousin and aide, the following after-noon. She was rather a shock to me and not at all in my style, a beast of a brig inured to the potato trade, and she reeked from end to end with the faint subtle smell of raw potatoes so that it prevailed even over the temporary smell of new paint. She was a beast of a brig, all hold and dirty framework, and they had ballasted her with old iron and old rails and iron sleepers, and got a miscellaneous lot of spades and iron wheelbarrows against the loading of the quap. I thought her over with Pollack, one of those tall, blond young men who smoke pipes and don't help much, and then by myself, and as a result I did my best to sweep Gravesend clean of wheeling planks, and got in as much cord and small rope as I could for lashing. I had an idea we might need to run up a jetty. In addition to much ballast she held remotely hidden in a sort of inadvertent way a certain number of ambiguous cases which I didn't examine, but which I gathered were a provision against the need of a trade.

The captain was a most extraordinary creature, under the impression we were after copper ore ; he was a Roumanian Jew, with twitching excitable features, who had made his way to a certificate after some preliminary naval experiences in the Black Sea. The mate was an Essex man of impenetrable reserve. The crew was astoundingly ill-clad and destitute and dirty ; most of them youths, unwashed, out of colliers. One, the cook, was a mulatto ; and one, the best-built fellow of them all, was a Breton. There was some subterfuge about our position on board—I forget the particulars now—I was

called the supercargo and Pollack was the steward. This
added to the piratical flavour that insufficient funds and
Gordon-Nasmyth's original genius had already given the
enterprise.

Those two days of bustle at Gravesend, under dingy skies,
in narrow, dirty streets, was a new experience for me. It is
like nothing else in my life. I realised that I was a modern
and civilised man. I found the food filthy and the coffee
horrible; the whole town stank in my nostrils, the landlord
of the Good Intent on the quay had a stand-up quarrel with
us before I could get even a hot bath, and the bedroom I slept
in was infested by a quantity of exotic but voracious flat
parasites called locally " bugs," in the walls, in the woodwork,
everywhere. I fought them with insect powder, and found
them comatose in the morning. I was dipping down into the
dingy underworld of the contemporary state, and I liked it no
better than I did my first dip into it when I stayed with my
Uncle Nicodemus Frapp at the bakery at Chatham—where,
by the bye, we had to deal with cockroaches of a smaller,
darker variety, and also with bugs of sorts.

Let me confess that through all this time before we started
I was immensely self-conscious, and that Beatrice played the
part of audience in my imagination throughout. I was, as I
say, " saving the situation," and I was acutely aware of that.
The evening before we sailed, instead of revising our medicine-
chest as I had intended, I took the car and ran across country
to Lady Grove to tell my aunt of the journey I was
making, dress, and astonish Lady Osprey by an after-dinner
call.

The two ladies were at home and alone beside a big fire
that seemed wonderfully cheerful after the winter night. I
remember the effect of the little parlour in which they sat as
very bright and domestic. Lady Osprey in a costume of
mauve and lace sat on a chintz sofa and played an elaborately
spread-out patience by the light of a tall, shaded lamp;
Beatrice in a white dress that showed her throat, smoked a
cigarette in an arm-chair and read with a lamp at her elbow.
The room was white-panelled and chintz-curtained. About
those two bright centres of light were warm, dark shadows
in which a circular mirror shone like a pool of brown water.
I carried off my raid by behaving like a slave of etiquette.
There were moments when I think I really made Lady Osprey
believe that my call was an unavoidable necessity, that it
would have been negligent of me not to call just how and when
I did. But at the best those were transitory moments.

They received me with disciplined amazement. Lady
Osprey was interested in my face and scrutinised the scar.
Beatrice stood behind her solicitude. Our eyes met, and
in hers I could see startled interrogations.

" I'm going," I said, " to the west coast of Africa."

They asked questions, but it suited my mood to be vague.

" We've interests there. It is urgent I should go. I don't know when I may return."

After that I perceived Beatrice surveyed me steadily.

The conversation was rather difficult. I embarked upon lengthy thanks for their kindness to me after my accident. I tried to understand Lady Osprey's game of patience, but it didn't appear that Lady Osprey was anxious for me to understand her patience. I came to the verge of taking my leave.

" You needn't go yet," said Beatrice, abruptly.

She walked across to the piano, took a pile of music from the cabinet near, surveyed Lady Osprey's back, and with a gesture to me dropped it all deliberately on to the floor.

" Must talk," she said, kneeling close to me as I helped her to pick it up. " Turn my pages. At the piano."

" I can't read music."

" Turn my pages."

Presently we were at the piano, and Beatrice was playing with noisy inaccuracy. She glanced over her shoulder and Lady Osprey had resumed her patience. The old lady was very pink, and appeared to be absorbed in some attempt to cheat herself without our observing it.

" Isn't West Africa a vile climate ? "   " Are you going to live there ? "   " Why are you going ? "

Beatrice asked these questions in a low voice and gave me no chance to answer. Then taking a rhythm from the music before her, she said—

" At the back of the house is a garden—a door in the wall— on the lane. Understand ? "

I turned over two pages without any effect on her playing.

" When ? " I asked.

She dealt in chords. " I wish I *could* play this ! " she said. " Midnight."

She gave her attention to the music for a time.

" You may have to wait."

" I'll wait."

She brought her playing to an end by—as schoolboys say—" stashing it up."

" I can't play to-night," she said, standing up and meeting my eyes. " I wanted to give you a parting voluntary."

" Was that Wagner, Beatrice ? " asked Lady Osprey, looking up from her cards. " It sounded very confused." . . .

I took my leave. I had a curious twinge of conscience as I parted from Lady Osprey. Either a first intimation of middle-age or my inexperience in romantic affairs was to blame, but I felt a very distinct objection to the prospect of invading this good lady's premises from the garden door. I motored up to the pavilion, found Cothope reading in bed, told him for the first time of West Africa, spent an hour with him in settling all the outstanding details of Lord Roberts β, and left that in his hands to finish against my return. I sent the motor back to Lady Grove, and still wearing my fur coat—for the January night was damp and bitterly cold—walked back to Bedley Corner. I found the lane to the back of the dower-house without any difficulty, and was at the door in the wall with ten minutes to spare. I lit a cigar and fell to walking up and down. This queer flavour of intrigue, this nocturnal garden-door business, had taken me by surprise and changed my mental altitudes. I was startled out of my egotistical pose, and thinking intently of Beatrice, of that elfin quality in her that always pleased me, that always took me by surprise, that had made her for example so instantly conceive this meeting.

She came within a minute of midnight ; the door opened softly and she appeared, a short grey figure in a motor-coat of sheepskin, bare-headed to the cold drizzle. She flitted up to me, and her eyes were shadows in her dusky face.

"Why are you going to West Africa ?" she asked at once.

"Business crisis. I have to go."

"You're not going—— ? You're coming back ?"

"Three or four months," I said, "at most."

"Then, it's nothing to do with me ?"

"Nothing," I said. "Why should it have ?"

"Oh, that's all right. One never knows what people think or what people fancy." She took me by the arm. "Let's go for a walk," she said.

I looked about me at darkness and rain.

"That's all right," she laughed. "We can go along the lane and into the Old Woking Road. Do you mind ? Of course you don't. My head. It doesn't matter. One never meets anybody."

"How do you know ?"

"I've wandered like this before. . . . Of course! Did you think"—she nodded her head back at her home—"that's all ?"

"No, by Jove !" I cried ; "it's manifest it isn't."

She took my arm and turned me down the lane. "Night's my time," she said by my side. "There's a touch of the werewolf in my blood. One never knows in these old families. . . . I've wondered often. . . . Here we are, anyhow, alone in the world. Just darkness and cold and a sky of clouds and wet. And we—together. I like the wet on my face and hair, don't you ? When do you sail ?"

I told her to-morrow.

"Oh, well, there's no to-morrow now. You and I !" She stopped and confronted me.

"You don't say a word except to answer !"

"No," I said.

"Last time you did all the talking."

"Like a fool. Now——"

We looked at each other's two dim faces. " You're glad to be here ? "

" I'm glad—I'm beginning to be—it's more than glad."

She put her hands on my shoulders and drew me down to kiss her.

" Ah ! " she said, and for a moment or so we just clung to one another.

" That's all," she said, releasing herself. " What bundles of clothes we are to-night. I felt we should kiss some day again. Always. The last time was ages ago."

" Among the fern stalks."

" Among the bracken. You remember. And your lips were cold. Were mine ? The same lips—after so long— after so much ! . . . And now let's trudge through this blotted-out world together for a time. Yes, let me take your arm. Just trudge, see ? Hold tight to me because I know the way—and don't talk—don't talk. Unless you want to talk. . . . Let me tell you things ! You see, dear, the whole world *is* blotted out—it's dead and gone, and we're in this place. This dark wild place. . . . We're dead. Or all the world is dead. No ! We're dead. No one can see us. We're shadows. We've got out of our positions, out of our bodies—and together. That's the good thing of it— together. But that's why the world can't see us and why we hardly see the world. Sssh ! Is it all right ? "

" It's all right," I said.

We stumbled along for a time in a close silence. We passed a dim-lit, rain-veiled window.

" The silly world," she said, " the silly world ! It eats and sleeps. If the wet didn't patter so from the trees we'd hear it snoring. It's dreaming such stupid things—stupid judg-ments. It doesn't know we are passing, we two—free of it— clear of it. You and I ! "

We pressed against each other reassuringly.

" I'm glad we're dead," she whispered. " I'm glad we're dead. I was tired of it, dear. I was so tired of it, dear, and so entangled."

She stopped abruptly.

We splashed through a string of puddles. I began to remember things I had meant to say.

" Look here ! " I cried. " I want to help you beyond measure. You are entangled. What is the trouble ? I asked you to marry me. You said you would. But there's something."

My thoughts sounded clumsy as I said them.

" Is it something about my position ? . . . Or is it some-thing—perhaps—about some other man ? "

There was an immense assenting silence.

" You've puzzled me so. At first—I mean quite early— I thought you meant to make me marry you."

" I did."

" And then—— ? "

" To-night," she said after a long pause, " I can't explain. No! I can't explain. I love you ? But—explanations! To-night—— My dear, here we are in the world alone—and the world doesn't matter. Nothing matters. Here am I in the cold with you—and my bed away there deserted. I'd tell you—— I *will* tell you when things enable me to tell you, and soon enough they will. But to-night—— I won't. I won't."

She left my side and went in front of me.

She turned upon me. " Look here," she said, " I insist upon your being dead. Do you understand ? I'm not joking. To-night you and I are out of life. It's our time together. There may be other times, but this we won't spoil. We're —in Hades if you like. Where there's nothing to hide and nothing to tell. No bodies even. No bothers. We loved each other—down there—and were kept apart, but now it doesn't matter. It's over. . . . If you won't agree to that —I will go home."

" I wanted——" I began.

" I know. Oh! my dear, if you'd only understand I understand. If you'd only not care—and love me to-night."

" I do love you," I said.

" Then *love* me," she answered, " and leave all these things that bother you. Love me ! Here I am ! "

" But——"

" No ! " she said.

" Well, have your way."

So she carried her point, and we wandered into the night together and Beatrice talked to me of love. . . .

I'd never heard a woman before in all my life who could talk of love, who could lay bare and develop and touch with imagination all that mass of fine emotion every woman, it may be, hides. She had read of love, she had thought of love, a thousand sweet lyrics had sounded through her brain and left fine fragments in her memory ; she poured it out, all of it, shamelessly, skilfully, for me. I cannot give any sense of that talk, I cannot even tell how much of the delight of it was the magic of her voice, the glow of her near presence. And always we walked swathed warmly through a chilly air, along dim, interminable greasy roads—with never a soul abroad it seemed but us, never a beast in the fields.

" Why do people love each other ? " I said.

" Why not ? "

" But why do I love you ? Why is your voice better than any voice, your face sweeter than any face ? "

" And why do I love you ? " she asked ; " not only what is fine in you, but what isn't ? Why do I love your dullness, your arrogance ? For I do. To-night I love the very rain-drops on the fur of your coat ! " . . .

So we talked ; and at last very wet, still glowing but a little tired, we parted at the garden door. We had been wandering for two hours in our strange irrational community of happiness, and all the world about us, and particularly Lady Osprey and her household, had been asleep—and dreaming of anything rather than Beatrice in the night and rain.

She stood in the doorway a muffled figure with eyes that glowed.

" Come back," she whispered.   " I shall wait for you."

She hesitated.

She touched the lapel of my coat. " I love you *now*," she said, and lifted her face to mine.

I held her to me and was atremble from top to toe. " O God ! " I cried.   " And I must go ! "

She slipped from my arms and paused regarding me.   For an instant the world seemed full of fantastic possibilities.

" Yes, *Go !* " she said, and vanished and slammed the door upon me, leaving me alone like a man new fallen from fairy-land in the black darkness of the night.

§ 3

That expedition to Mordet Island stands apart from all the rest of my life, detached, a piece by itself with an atmosphere of its own.   It would, I suppose, make a book by itself —it has made a fairly voluminous official report—but so far as this novel of mine goes it is merely an episode, a contributory experience, and I mean to keep it at that.

Vile weather, an impatient fretting against unbearable slowness and delay, sea-sickness, general discomfort and humiliating self-revelation are the master values of these memories.

I was sick all through the journey out.   I don't know why.   It was the only time I was ever sea-sick, and I have seen some pretty bad weather since I became a boat-builder.   But that phantom smell of potatoes was peculiarly vile to me.   Coming back on the brig we were all ill, every one of us, so soon as we got to sea, poisoned I firmly believe by quap.   On the way out most of the others recovered in a few days, but the stuffiness below, the coarse food, the cramped dirty accommodation kept me, if not actually sea-sick, in a state of acute physical wretchedness the whole time.   The ship abounded in cockroaches and more intimate vermin.   I was cold all the time until after we passed Cape Verde, then I became steamily hot ; I had been too pre-occupied with Beatrice and my keen desire to get the *Maud Mary* under way at once, to consider a proper wardrobe for myself, and in particular I lacked a coat.   Heavens ! how I lacked that coat !   And, moreover, I was cooped up with

two of the worst bores in Christendom, Pollack and the
captain. Pollack, after conducting his illness in a style better
adapted to the capacity of an opera house than a small compartment, suddenly got insupportably well and breezy, and
produced a manly pipe in which he smoked a tobacco as
blond as himself, and divided his time almost equally between
smoking it and trying to clean it. "There's only three
things you *can* clean a pipe with," he used to remark with
a twist of paper in hand. "The best's a feather, the second's
a straw, and the third's a girl's hairpin. I never see such a
ship. You can't find any of 'em. Last time I came this
way I did find hairpins anyway, and found 'em on the floor
of the captain's cabin. Regular deposit. Eh ? . . . Feelin'
better ? "

At which I usually swore.

" Oh, you'll be all right soon. Don't mind my puffin' a
bit ? Eh ? "

He never tired of asking me to " have a hand at Nap.
Good game. Makes you forget it, and that's half the battle."

He would sit swaying with the rolling of the ship and suck
at his pipe of blond tobacco and look with an inexpressibly
sage but somnolent blue eye at the captain by the hour
together. "Captain's a Card," he would say over and over
again as the outcome of these meditations. "He'd like to
know what we're up to. He'd like to know—no end."

That did seem to be the captain's ruling idea. But he
also wanted to impress me with the notion that he was a
gentleman of good family and to air a number of views adverse
to the English, to English literature, to the English constitution, and the like. He had learned the sea in the
Roumanian navy, and English out of a book ; he would still
at times pronounce the e's at the end of " there " and " here " ;
he was a naturalised Englishman, and he drove me into a
reluctant and uncongenial patriotism by his everlasting
carping at things English. Pollack would set himself to
" draw him out." Heaven alone can tell how near I came
to murder.

Fifty-three days I had outward, cooped up with these
two and a shy and profoundly depressed mate who read the
Bible on Sundays and spent the rest of his leisure in lethargy,
three and fifty days of life cooped up in a perpetual smell,
in a persistent sick hunger that turned from the sight of food,
in darkness, cold and wet, in a lightly ballasted ship that
rolled and pitched and swayed. And all the time the sands
in the hour-glass of my uncle's fortunes were streaming out.
Misery ! Amidst it all I remember only one thing brightly,
one morning of sunshine in the Bay of Biscay and a vision
of frothing waves, sapphire green, a bird following our wake
and our masts rolling about the sky. Then wind and rain
closed in on us again.

You must not imagine they were ordinary days, days I
mean of an average length ; they were not so much days
as long damp slabs of time that stretched each one to the
horizon, and much of that length was night. One paraded
the staggering deck in a borrowed sou'-wester hour after
hour in the chilly, windy, splashing and spitting darkness,
or sat in the cabin, bored and ill, and looked at the faces of
those inseparable companions by the help of a lamp that
gave smell rather than light. Then one would see going up,
up, up, and then sinking down, down, down, Pollack, extinct
pipe in mouth, humorously observant, bringing his mind
slowly to the seventy-seventh decision that the captain was
a Card, while the words flowed from the latter in a nimble
incessant flood. " Dis England eet is not a country aristocratic, no ! Eet is a glorified bourgeoisie ! Eet is plutocratic. In England dere is no aristocracy since de Wars of
Roses. In the rest of Europe east of the Latins, yes ; in
England, no.
" Eet is all middle-class, youra England. Everything you
look at, middle-class. Respectable ! Everything good—eet
is, you say, shocking. Madame Grundy ! Eet is all limited
and computing and self-seeking. Dat is why your art is so
limited, youra fiction, your philosophia, why you are all so
inartistic. You want nothing but profit ! What will pay !
What would you ? " . . .
He had all those violent adjuncts to speech we Western
Europeans have abandoned, shruggings of the shoulders,
waving of the arms, thrusting out of the face, wonderful
grimaces and twiddlings of the hands under your nose until
you wanted to hit them away. Day after day it went on,
and I had to keep my anger to myself, to reserve myself for
the time ahead when it would be necessary to see the quap
was got aboard and stowed—knee deep in this man's astonishment. I knew he would make a thousand objections to all
we had before us. He talked like a drugged man. It ran
glibly over his tongue. And all the time one could see his
seamanship fretting him, he was gnawed by responsibility,
perpetually uneasy about the ship's position, perpetually
imagining dangers. If a sea hit us exceptionally hard he'd
be out of the cabin in an instant making an outcry of inquiries,
and he was pursued by a dread of the hold, of ballast shifting,
of insidious wicked leaks. As we drew near the African
coast his fear of rocks and shoals became infectious.
" I do not know dis coast," he used to say. " I cama
nera because Gordon-Nasmyth was coming too. Den he
does not come ! "
" Fortunes of war," I said, and tried to think in vain if
any motive but sheer haphazard could have guided Gordon-
Nasmyth in the choice of these two men. I think perhaps
Gordon-Nasmyth had the artistic temperament and wanted

contrasts, and also that the captain helped him to express his own malignant Anti-Britishism. He was indeed an exceptionally inefficient captain. On the whole I was glad I had come even at the eleventh hour to see to things.

(The captain, by the bye, did at last, out of sheer nervousness, get aground at the end of Mordet's Island, but we got off in an hour or so with a swell and a little hard work in the boat.)

I suspected the mate of his opinion of the captain long before he expressed it. He was, I say, a taciturn man, but one day speech broke through him. He had been sitting at the table with his arms folded on it, musing drearily, pipe in mouth, and the voice of the captain drifted down from above.

The mate lifted his heavy eyes to me and regarded me for a moment. Then he began to heave with the beginnings of speech. He disembarrassed himself of his pipe. I cowered with expectation. Speech was coming at last. Before he spoke he nodded reassuringly once or twice.

" E——"

He moved his head strangely and mysteriously, but a child might have known he spoke of the captain.

" E's a foreigner."

He regarded me doubtfully for a time, and at last decided for the sake of lucidity to clench the matter.

" That's what E is—a *Dago* ! "

He nodded like a man who gives a last tap to a nail, and I could see he considered his remark well and truly laid. His face, though still resolute, became as tranquil and uneventful as a huge hall after a public meeting has dispersed out of it, and finally he closed and locked it with his pipe.

" Roumanian Jew, isn't he ? " I said.

He nodded darkly and almost forbiddingly.

More would have been too much. The thing was said. But from that time forth I knew I could depend upon him and that he and I were friends. It happens I never did have to depend upon him, but that does not affect our relationship.

Forward the crew lived lives very much after the fashion of ours, more crowded, more cramped and dirty, wetter, steamier, more verminous. The coarse food they had was still not so coarse but that they did not think they were living " like fighting cocks." So far as I could make out they were all nearly destitute men, hardly any of them had a proper sea outfit, and what small possessions they had were a source of mutual distrust. And as we pitched and floundered southward they gambled and fought, were brutal to one another, argued and wrangled loudly, until we protested at the uproar. . . .

There's no romance about the sea in a small sailing ship as I saw it. The romance is in the mind of the landsman dreamer. These brigs and schooners and brigantines that still stand out from every little port are relics from an age of petty trade, as rotten and obsolescent as a Georgian house that has sunken into a slum. They are indeed just floating fragments of slum, much as icebergs are floating fragments of glacier. The civilised man who has learned to wash, who has developed a sense of physical honour, of cleanly temperate feeding, of time, can endure them no more. They pass, and the clanking coal-wasting steamers will follow them, giving place to cleaner, finer things. . . .

But so it was I made my voyage to Africa, and came at last into a world of steamy fogs and a hot smell of vegetable decay, and into sound and sight of surf and distant intermittent glimpses of the coast. I lived a strange concentrated life through all that time, such a life as a creature must do that has fallen in a well. All my former ways ceased, all my old vistas became memories.

The situation I was saving was very small and distant now ; I felt its urgency no more. Beatrice and Lady Grove, my uncle and the Hardingham, my soaring in the air and my habitual wide vision of swift effectual things, became as remote as if they were in some world I had left for ever. . . .

§ 4

All these African memories stand by themselves. It was for me an expedition into the realms of undisciplined nature out of the world that is ruled by men, my first bout with that hot side of our mother that gives you the jungle—that cold side that gives you the air-eddy I was beginning to know passing well. They are memories woven upon a fabric of sunshine and heat and a constant warm smell of decay. They end in rain—such rain as I had never seen before, a vehement, a frantic downpouring of water, but our first slow passage through the channels behind Mordet's Island was in incandescent sunshine.

There we go in my memory still, a blistered dirty ship with patched sails and a battered mermaid to present *Maud Mary*, sounding and taking thought between high banks of forest whose trees come out knee-deep at last in the water. There we go with a little breeze on our quarter, Mordet Island rounded and the quap it might be within a day of us.

Here and there strange blossoms woke the dank intensities of green with a trumpet call of colour. Things crept among the jungle and peeped and dashed back rustling into stillness. Always in the sluggishly drifting, opaque water were eddyings and stirrings ; little rushes of bubbles came chuckling up light-heartedly from this or that submerged conflict and tragedy ; now and again were crocodiles like a stranded fleet of logs basking in the sun. Still it was by day, a dreary

stillness broken only by insect sounds and the creaking and
flapping of our progress, by the calling of the soundings and
the captain's confused shouts ; but in the night as we lay
moored to a clump of trees the darkness brought a thousand
swampy things to life and out of the forest came screamings
and howlings, screamings and yells that made us glad to be
afloat. And once we saw between the tree stems long blazing
fires. We passed two or three villages landward and brown-
black women and children came and stared at us and gesticulated, and once a man came out in a boat from a creek and
hailed us in an unknown tongue ; and so at last we came to a
great open place, a broad lake rimmed with a desolation of
mud and bleached refuse and dead trees, free from crocodiles
or water birds or sight or sound of any living thing, and
saw far off, even as Nasmyth had described, the ruins of the
deserted station and hard by two little heaps of buff-hued
rubbish under a great rib of rock, the quap ! The forest
receded. The land to the right of us fell away and became
barren, and far off across a notch in its backbone was surf
and the sea.

We took the ship in towards those heaps and the ruined
jetty slowly and carefully. The captain came and talked.

" This is eet ? " he said.

" Yes," said I.

" Is eet for trade we have come ? "

This was ironical.

" No," said I. . . .

" Gordon-Nasmyth would haf told me long ago what it
ees for we haf come."

" I'll tell you now," I said. " We are going to lay in as
close as we can to those two heaps of stuff—you see them ?—
under the rock. Then we are going to chuck all our ballast
overboard and take those in. Then we're going home."

" May I presume to ask—is eet gold ? "

" No," I said uncivilly, " it isn't."

" Then what is it ? "

" It's stuff—of some commercial value."

" We can't do eet," he said.

" We can," I answered reassuringly.

" We can't," he said as confidently. " I don't mean what
you mean. You know so liddle—But—Dis is forbidden
country."

I turned on him suddenly angry and met bright excited
eyes. For a minute we scrutinised one another. Then I
said, " That's our risk. Trade is forbidden. But this isn't
trade. . . . This thing's got to be done."

His eyes glittered and he shook his head. . . .

The brig stood in slowly through the twilight towards this
strange scorched and blistered stretch of beach, and the
man at the wheel strained his ears to listen to the low-voiced

angry argument that began between myself and the captain, that was presently joined by Pollack. We moored at last within a hundred yards of our goal, and all through our dinner and far into the night we argued intermittently and fiercely with the captain about our right to load just what we pleased. " I will haf nothing to do with it," he persisted. " I wash my hands." It seemed that night as though we argued in vain. " If it is not trade," he said, " it is prospecting and mining. That is worse. Any one who knows anything—outside England—knows that is worse."

We argued and I lost my temper and swore at him. Pollack kept cooler and chewed his pipe watchfully with that blue eye of his upon the captain's gestures. Finally I went on deck to cool. The sky was overcast. I discovered all the men were in a knot forward, staring at the faint quivering luminosity that had spread over the heaps of quap, a phosphorescence such as one sees at times on rotting wood. And about the beach east and west there were patches and streaks of something like diluted moonshine. . . .

In the small hours I was still awake and turning over scheme after scheme in my mind whereby I might circumvent the captain's opposition. I meant to get that quap aboard if I had to kill some one to do it. Never in my life had I been so thwarted ! After this intolerable voyage ! There came a rap at my cabin door, and then it opened and I made out a bearded face. " Come in," I said, and a black voluble figure I could just see obscurely came in to talk in my private ear and fill my cabin with its whisperings and gestures. It was the captain. He too had been awake and thinking things over. He had come to explain—enormously. I lay there hating him and wondering if I and Pollack could lock him in his cabin and run the ship without him. " I do not want to spoil dis expedition," emerged from a cloud of protestations, and then I was able to disentangle " a commission —shush a small commission—for special risks ! " " Special risks " became frequent. I let him explain himself out. It appeared he was also demanding an apology for something I had said. No doubt I had insulted him generously. At last came definite offers. I broke my silence and bargained.

" Pollack ! " I cried and hammered the partition.

" What's up ? " asked Pollack.

I stated the case concisely.

There came a silence.

" He's a Card," said Pollack. " Let's give him his commission. I don't mind."

" Eh ? " I cried.

" I said he was a Card, that's all," said Pollack. " I'm coming."

He appeared in my doorway a faint white figure and joined our vehement whisperings. . . .

We had to buy the captain off ; we had to promise him
ten per cent. of our problematical profits. We were to give
him ten per cent. on what we sold the cargo for over and
above his legitimate pay, and I found in my out-bargained
and disordered state small consolation in the thought that I,
as the Gordon-Nasmyth expedition, was to sell the stuff to
myself as Business Organisations. And he further exasperated me by insisting on having our bargain in writing.
" In the form of a letter," he insisted.

" All right," I acquiesced, " in the form of a letter. Here
goes ! Get a light ! "

" And the apology," he said, folding up the letter.

" All right," I said ; " apology."

My hand shook with anger as I wrote, and afterwards I
could not sleep for hate of him. At last I got up. I suffered,
I found, from an unusual clumsiness. I struck my toe
against my cabin door, and cut myself as I shaved. I found
myself at last pacing the deck under the dawn in a mood of
extreme exasperation. The sun rose abruptly and splashed
light blindingly into my eyes and I swore at the sun. I
found myself imagining fresh obstacles with the men and
talking aloud in anticipatory rehearsal of the consequent
row.

The malaria of the quap was already in my blood.

§ 5

Sooner or later the ridiculous embargo that now lies upon
all the coast eastward of Mordet Island will be lifted and
the reality of the deposits of quap ascertained. I am sure
myself that we were merely taking the outcrop of a stratum
of nodulated deposits that dip steeply seaward. Those
heaps were merely the crumbled-out contents of two irregular
cavities in the rock, they are as natural as any talus or heap
of that kind, and the mud along the edge of the water for
miles is mixed with quap, and is radio-active and lifeless
and faintly phosphorescent at night. But the reader will
find the full particulars of my impression of all this in the
Geological Magazine for October, 1905, and to that I must
refer him. There, too, he will find my unconfirmed theories
of its nature. If I am right it is something far more significant from the scientific point of view than those incidental
constituents of various rare metals, pitchblende, rutile, and
the like, upon which the revolutionary discoveries of the
last decade are based. Those are just little molecular centres
of disintegration, of that mysterious decay and rotting of
those elements, elements once regarded as the most stable
things in nature. But there is something—the only word
that comes near it is *cancerous*—and that is not very near,
about the whole of quap, something that creeps and lives

as a disease lives by destroying ; an elemental stirring and disarrangement, incalculably maleficent and strange.

This is no imaginative comparison of mine. To my mind radio-activity is a real disease of matter. Moreover it is a contagious disease. It spreads. You bring those debased and crumbling atoms near others and those too presently catch the trick of swinging themselves out of coherent existence. It is in matter exactly what the decay of our old culture is in society, a loss of traditions and distinctions and assured reactions. When I think of these inexplicable dissolvent centres that have come into being in our globe— these quap heaps are surely by far the largest that have yet been found in the world ; the rest as yet mere specks in grains and crystals—I am haunted by a grotesque fancy of the ultimate eating away and dry-rotting and dispersal of all our world. So that while man still struggles and dreams his very substance will change and crumble from beneath him. I mention this here as a queer persistent fancy. Suppose, indeed, that is to be the end of our planet ; no splendid climax and finale, no towering accumulation of achievements but just—atomic decay ! I add that to the ideas of the suffocating comet, the dark body out of space, the burning out of the sun, the distorted orbit, as a new and far more possible end—as Science can see ends—to this strange by-play of matter that we call human life. I do not believe this can be the end ; no human soul can believe in such an end and go on living, but to it science points as a possible thing, science and reason alike. If single human beings—if one single rickety infant—can be born as it were by accident and die futile, why not the whole race ? These are questions I have never answered, that now I never attempt to answer, but the thought of quap and its mysteries brings them back to me.

I can witness that the beach and mud for two miles or more either way was a lifeless beach—lifeless as I could have imagined no tropical mud could ever be, and all the dead branches and leaves and rotting dead fish and so forth that drifted ashore became presently shrivelled and white. Sometimes crocodiles would come up out of the water and bask, and now and then water birds would explore the mud and rocky ribs that rose out of it, in a mood of transitory speculation. That was its utmost animation. And the air felt at once hot and austere, dry and blistering, and altogether different to the warm moist embrace that had met us at our first African landfall and to which we had grown accustomed.

I believe that the primary influence of the quap upon us was to increase the conductivity of our nerves, but that is a mere unjustifiable speculation on my part. At any rate it gave a sort of east-wind effect to life. We all became irritable, clumsy, languid and disposed to be impatient with our

languor. We moored the brig to the rocks with difficulty,
and got aground on mud, and decided to stick there and tow
off when we had done—the bottom was as greasy as butter.
Our efforts to fix up planks and sleepers in order to wheel
the quap aboard were as ill conceived as that sort of work
can be—and that sort of work can at times be very ill conceived. The captain had a superstitious fear of his hold ;
he became wildly gesticulatory and expository and incompetent at the bare thought of it. His shouts still echo in
my memory, becoming as each crisis approached less and
less like any known tongue.

But I cannot now write the history of those days of blundering and toil, of how Milton, one of the boys, fell from a plank
to the beach, thirty feet perhaps, with his barrow and broke
his arm and I believe a rib, of how I and Pollack set the
limb and nursed him through the fever that followed, of
how one man after another succumbed to a feverish malaria,
and how I—by virtue of my scientific reputation—was
obliged to play the part of doctor and dose them with quinine,
and then finding that worse than nothing, with rum and
small doses of Easton's Syrup, of which there chanced to be
a case of bottles aboard—Heaven and Gordon-Nasmyth
know why. For three long days we lay in misery and never
shipped a barrow-load. Then, when they resumed, the
men's hands broke out into sores. There were no gloves
available ; and I tried to get them, while they shovelled and
wheeled, to cover their hands with stockings or greased rags.
They would not do this on account of the heat and discomfort.
This attempt of mine did, however, direct their attention
to the quap as the source of their illness and precipitated
what in the end finished our lading, an informal strike.
" We've had enough of this," they said, and they meant
it. They came aft to say as much. They cowed the captain.

Through all these days the weather was variously vile,
first a furnace heat under a sky of a scowling intensity of
blue, then a hot fog that stuck in one's throat like wool and
turned the men on the planks into colourless figures of giants,
then a wild burst of thunderstorms, mad elemental uproar
and rain. Through it all, against illness, heat, confusion of
mind, one master impetus prevailed with me, to keep the
shipping going, to maintain one motif at least, whatever
else arose or ceased, the chuff of the spades, the squeaking
and shriek of the barrows, the pluppa, pluppa, pluppa, as
the men came trotting along the swinging high planks, and
then at last, the dollop, dollop as the stuff shot into the
hold. " Another barrow-load, thank God ! Another fifteen
hundred, or it may be two thousand pounds, for the saving
of Ponderevo ! . . . ! "

I found out many things about myself and humanity in
those weeks of effort behind Mordet Island. I understand

now the heart of the sweater, of the harsh employer, of the nigger-driver. I had brought these men into a danger they didn't understand, I was fiercely resolved to overcome their oppositions and bend and use them for my purpose, and I hated the men. But I hated all humanity during the time that the quap was near me. . . .

And my mind was pervaded, too, by a sense of urgency and by the fear that we should be discovered and our proceedings stopped. I wanted to get out to sea again—to be beating up northward with our plunder. I was afraid our masts showed to seaward and might betray us to some curious passer on the high sea. And one evening near the end I saw a canoe with three natives far off down the lake ; I got field-glasses from the captain and scrutinised them, and I could see them staring at us. One man might have been a half-breed and was dressed in white. They watched us for some time very quietly and then paddled off into some channel in the forest shadows.

And for three nights running, so that it took a painful grip upon my inflamed imagination, I dreamt of my uncle's face, only that it was ghastly white like a clown's, and the throat was cut from ear to ear—a long ochreous cut. " Too late," he said ; " too late ! . . ."

§ 6

A day or so after we had got to work upon the quap I found myself so sleepless and miserable that the ship became unendurable. Just before the rush of sunrise I borrowed Pollack's gun, walked down the planks, clambered over the quap heaps and prowled along the beach. I went perhaps a mile and a half that day and some distance beyond the ruins of the old station. I became interested in the desolation about me, and found when I returned that I was able to sleep for nearly an hour. It was delightful to have been alone for so long—no captain, no Pollack, no one. Accordingly I repeated this expedition the next morning and the next until it became a custom with me. There was little for me to do once the digging and wheeling was organised, and so these prowlings of mine grew longer and longer, and presently I began to take food with me.

I pushed these walks far beyond the area desolated by the quap. On the edges of that was first a zone of stunted vegetation, then a sort of swampy jungle that was difficult to penetrate, and then the beginnings of the forest, a scene of huge tree stems and tangled creeper ropes and roots mingled with oozy mud. Here I used to loaf in a state between botanising and reverie—always very anxious to know what was up above in the sunlight—and here it was I murdered a man.

It was the most unmeaning and purposeless murder imaginable. Even as I write down its well-remembered particulars there comes again the sense of its strangeness, its pointlessness, its incompatibility with any of the neat and definite theories people hold about life and the meaning of the world. I did this thing and I want to tell of my doing it, but why I did it and particularly why I should be held responsible for it I cannot explain.

That morning I had come upon a track in the forest, and it had occurred to me as a disagreeable idea that this was a human pathway. I didn't want to come upon any human beings. The less our expedition saw of the African population the better for its prospects. Thus far we had been singularly free from native pestering. So I turned back and was making my way over mud and roots and dead fronds and petals scattered from the green world above when abruptly I saw my victim.

I became aware of him perhaps forty feet off, standing quite still and regarding me.

He wasn't by any means a pretty figure. He was very black and naked except for a dirty loin-cloth, his legs were ill-shaped and his toes spread wide, and the upper edge of his cloth and a girdle of string cut his clumsy abdomen into folds. His forehead was low, his nose very flat, and his lower lip swollen and purplish red. His hair was short and fuzzy, and about his neck was a string and a little purse of skin. He carried a musket, and a powder flask was stuck in his girdle. It was a curious confrontation. There opposed to him stood I, a little soiled perhaps, but still a rather elaborately civilised human being born, bred and trained in a vague tradition. In my hand was an unaccustomed gun. And each of us was essentially a teeming vivid brain, tensely excited by the encounter, quite unaware of the other's mental content or what to do with him.

He stepped back a pace or so. Stumbled and turned to run.

"Stop," I cried ; "stop, you fool ! " and started to run after him shouting such things in English. But I was no match for him over the roots and mud.

I had a preposterous idea. "He mustn't get away and tell them ! "

And with that instantly I brought both feet together, raised my gun, aimed quite coolly, drew the trigger carefully and shot him neatly in the back.

I saw, and saw with a leap of pure exultation, the smash of my bullet between his shoulder blades. "Got him," said I, dropping my gun, and down he flopped and died without a groan. "By Jove," I cried with a note of surprise, " I've killed him." I looked about me and then went forward cautiously in a mood between curiosity and astonishment to look at this man whose soul I had flung so unceremoniously out of our common world. I went to him not as one goes to something one has made or done, but as one approaches something found.

He was frightfully smashed out in front ; he must have died in the instant. I stooped and raised him by his shoulder and realised that. I dropped him, and stood about and peered about me through the trees. " My word ! " I said. He was the second dead human being—apart I mean from surgical properties and mummies and common shows of that sort—that I had ever seen. I stood over him wondering, wondering beyond measure.

A practical idea came into that confusion. Had any one heard the gun ?

I reloaded.

After a time I felt securer, and gave my mind again to the dead I had killed. What must I do ?

It occurred to me that perhaps I ought to bury him. At any rate, I ought to hide him. I reflected coolly, and then put my gun within easy reach and dragged him by the arm towards a place where the mud seemed soft, and thrust him in. His powder-flask slipped from his loin-cloth, and I went back to get it. Then I pressed him down with the butt of my rifle.

Afterwards this all seemed to me most horrible, but at the time it was entirely a matter-of-fact transaction. I looked round for any other visible evidence of his fate, looked round as one does when one pack's one portmanteau in an hotel bedroom.

Then I got my bearings, and carefully returned towards the ship. I had the mood of grave concentration of a boy who has lapsed into poaching. And the business only began to assume proper proportions for me as I got near the ship, to seem any other kind of thing than the killing of a bird or rabbit.

In the night, however, it took on enormous and portentous forms. " By God ! " I cried suddenly, starting wide awake ; " but it was murder ! "

I lay after that outcry, staring at my memories. In some odd way these visions mixed up with my dream of my uncle in his despair. The black body which I saw now damaged and partly buried, but which, nevertheless, I no longer felt was dead but acutely alive and perceiving, I mixed up with the ochreous slash under my uncle's face. I tried to dismiss this horrible obsession from my mind, but it prevailed over all my efforts.

The next day was utterly black with my sense of that ugly creature's body. I am the least superstitious of men, but it drew me. It drew me back into those thickets to the very place where I had hidden him.

Some evil and detestable beast had been at him, and he lay disinterred.

Methodically I buried his swollen and mangled carcass again, and returned to the ship for another night of dreams. Next day for all the morning I resisted the impulse to go to him, and played Nap with Pollack with my secret gnawing at me, and in the evening started to go and was near benighted. I never told a soul of them of this thing I had done.

Next day I went early and he had gone, and there were human footmarks and ugly stains round the muddy hole from which he had been dragged.

I returned to the ship, disconcerted and perplexed. That day it was the men came aft, with blistered hands and faces, and sullen eyes. When they proclaimed, through Edwards, their spokesman, " We've had enough of this, and we mean it," I answered very readily, " So have I. Let's go."

§ 7

We were none too soon. People had been reconnoitring us, the telegraph had been at work, and we were not four hours at sea before we ran against the gunboat that had been sent down the coast to look for us and that would have caught us behind the island like a beast in a trap. It was a night of driving cloud that gave intermittent gleams of moonlight, the wind and sea were strong and we were rolling along through a drift of rain and mist. Suddenly the world was white with moonshine. The gunboat came out as a long dark shape wallowing on the water to the east. She sighted the *Maud Mary* at once, and fired some sort of pop-gun to arrest us.

The mate turned to me.

" Shall I tell the captain ? "

" The captain be damned ! " said I, and we let him sloop through two hours of chase till a rainstorm swallowed us up. Then we changed our course and sailed right across them, and by morning only her smoke was showing.

We were clear of Africa—and with the booty aboard. I did not see what stood between us and home.

For the first time since I had fallen sick in the Thames my spirits rose. I was sea-sick and physically disgusted of course, but I felt kindly in spite of my qualms. So far as I could calculate then the situation was saved. I saw myself triumphantly returning into the Thames, and nothing on earth to prevent old Capern's Perfect Filament going on the market in a fortnight. I had the monopoly of electric lamps beneath my feet.

I was released from the spell of that blood-stained black body all mixed up with grey-black mud. I was going back to baths and decent food and aeronautics and Beatrice. I was going back to Beatrice and my real life again—out of this well into which I had fallen. It would have needed something more than sea-sickness and quap fever to prevent my spirits rising.

I told the captain that I agreed with him that the British were the scum of Europe, the westward drift of all the people, a disgusting rabble, and I lost three pounds by attenuated retail to Pollack at ha-penny nap and euchre.

And then you know, as we got out into the Atlantic this side of Cape Verde, the ship began to go to pieces. I don't pretend for one moment to understand what happened. But I think Greiffenhagen's recent work on the effects of radium upon ligneous tissue does rather carry out my idea that emanations from quap have a rapid rotting effect upon woody fibre.

From the first there had been a different feel about the ship, and as the big winds and waves began to strain her she commenced leaking. Soon she was leaking—not at any particular point, but everywhere. She did not spring a leak, I mean, but water came in first of all near the decaying edges of her planks, and then through them.

I firmly believe the water came through the wood. First it began to ooze, then to trickle. It was like trying to carry moist sugar in a thin paper bag. Soon we were taking in water as though we had opened a door in her bottom.

Once it began, the thing went ahead beyond all fighting. For a day or so we did our best, and I can still remember in my limbs and back the pumping—the fatigue in my arms and the memory of a clear little dribble of water that jerked as one pumped, and of knocking off and the being awakened to go on again, and of fatigue piling up upon fatigue. At last we ceased to think of anything but pumping; one became a thing of torment enchanted, doomed to pump for ever. I still remember it as pure relief when at last Pollack came to me pipe in mouth.

"The captain says the damned thing's going down right now," he remarked, chewing his mouthpiece. "Eh ? "

"Good idea ! " I said. "One can't go on pumping for ever."

And without hurry or alacrity, sullenly and wearily we got into the boats and pulled away from the *Maud Mary* until we were clear of her, and then we stayed resting on our oars, motionless upon a glassy sea, waiting for her to sink. We were all silent, even the captain was silent until she went down. And then he spoke quite mildly in an undertone.

"Dat is the first ship I haf ever lost. . . . And it was not a fair game ! It wass not a cargo any man should take. No ! "

I stared at the slow eddies that circled above the departed *Maud Mary*, and the last chance of Business Organisations.

I felt weary beyond emotion. I thought of my heroics to Beatrice and my uncle, of my prompt " *I'll* go," and of all the ineffectual months I had spent after this headlong decision. I was moved to laughter at myself and fate.

But the captain and the men did not laugh. The men scowled at me and rubbed their sore and blistered hands, and set themselves to row. . . .

As all the world knows, we were picked up by the Union Castle liner *Portland Castle*.

The hairdresser aboard was a wonderful man, and he even improvised me a dress suit, and produced a clean shirt and warm underclothing. I had a hot bath, and dressed and dined and drank a bottle of Burgundy.

" Now," I said, " are there any newspapers ? I want to know what's been happening in the world."

My steward gave me what he had, but I landed at Plymouth still largely ignorant of the course of events. I shook off Pollack, and left the captain and mate in an hotel, and the men in a Sailor's Home until I could send to pay them off, and I made my way to the station.

The newspapers I bought, the placards I saw, all England indeed resounded to my uncle's bankruptcy.

END OF BOOK III

CHAPTER ONE

THE STICK OF THE ROCKET

§ 1

THAT evening I talked with my uncle in the Hardingham for the last time. The atmosphere of the place had altered quite shockingly. Instead of the crowd of importunate courtiers there were just half a dozen uninviting men, journalists waiting for an interview. Ropper the big commissionaire was still there, but now indeed he was defending my uncle from something more than time-wasting intrusions. I found the little man alone in the inner office pretending to work but really brooding. He was looking yellow and deflated.

"Lord !" he said at the sight of me. "You're lean, George. It makes that scar of yours show up."

We regarded each other gravely for a time.

"Quap," I said, "is at the bottom of the Atlantic. There's some bills—— We've got to pay the men." . . .

"Seen the papers ? "

"Read 'em all in the train."

"At bay," he said. "I been at bay for a week. . . . Yelping round me. . . . And me facing the music. I'm feelin' a bit tired."

He blew and wiped his glasses.

"My stomach isn't what it was," he explained. "One finds it—these times. How did it all happen, George ? Your Marconigram—it took me in the wind a bit."

I told him concisely. He nodded to the paragraphs of my narrative, and at the end he poured something from a medicine bottle into a sticky little wineglass and drank it. I became aware of the presence of drugs, of three or four small bottles before him among his disorder of papers, of a faint elusively familiar odour in the room.

"Yes," he said, wiping his lips and recorking the bottle. "You've done your best, George. The luck's been against us."

He reflected, bottle in hand. "Sometimes the luck goes with you and sometimes it doesn't. Sometimes it doesn't. And then where are you ? Grass in the oven ! Fight or no fight."

He asked a few questions and then his thoughts came back to his own urgent affairs. I tried to get some comprehensive account of the situation from him, but he would not give it.

"Oh, I wish I'd had you. I wish I'd had you, George. I've had a lot on my hands. You're clear-headed at times."

"What has happened ? "

"Oh ! Boom !—infernal things."

"Yes, but—how ? I'm just off the sea, remember."

" It'd worry me too much to tell you now.   It's tied up in a skein."

He muttered something to himself and mused darkly, and roused himself to say :

" Besides—you'd better keep out of it. It's getting tight. Get 'em talking. Go down to Crest Hill and fly. That's *your* affair."

For a time his manner set free queer anxieties in my brain again.   I will confess that that Mordet Island nightmare of mine returned, and as I looked at him his hand went out for the drug again.   " Stomach, George," he said.

" I been fightin' on that.   Every man fights on something— gives way somewhere,—head, heart, liver—something. Zzzz. Gives way somewhere. Napoleon did at last. All through the Waterloo campaign, his stomach—it wasn't a stomach ! Worse than mine, no end."

The mood of depression passed as the drug worked within him.   His eyes brightened.   He began to talk big.   He began to dress up the situation for my eyes, to recover what he had admitted to me.   He put it as a retreat from Russia. There were still the chances of Leipzig.

" It's a battle, George—a big fight.   We're fighting for millions.   I've still chances.   There's still a card or so.   I can't tell all my plans—like speaking on the stroke."

" You might," I began.

" I can't, George.   It's like asking to look at some embryo. You got to wait.   I know.   In a sort of way, I know.   But to tell it—— No ! You been away so long. And everything's got complicated."

My perception of disastrous entanglements deepened with the rise of his spirits.   It was evident that I could not help to tie him up in whatever net was weaving round his mind by forcing questions and explanations upon him.   My thoughts flew off at another angle.   " How's Aunt Susan ? " said I.

I had to repeat the question.   His busy whispering lips stopped for a moment, and he answered in the note of one who repeats a formula.

" She'd like to be in the battle with me.   She'd like to be here in London.   But there's corners I got to turn alone." His eye rested for a moment on the little bottle beside him. " And things have happened.

" You might go down now and talk to her," he said, in a directer voice.   " I shall be down to-morrow night, I think."

He looked up as though he hoped that would end our talk.

" For the week-end ? "

" For the week-end.   Thank God for week-ends, George ! "

§ 2

My return home to Lady Grove was a very different thing from what I had anticipated when I had got out to sea with

my load of quap and fancied the Perfect Filament was safe
within my grasp. As I walked through the evening light
along the Downs, the summer stillness seemed like the stillness
of something newly dead. There were no lurking workmen
any more, no cyclists on the high-road.

Cessation was manifest everywhere. There had been, I
learned from my aunt, a touching and quite voluntary demonstration when the Crest Hill work had come to an end and
the men had drawn their last pay ; they had cheered my
uncle and hooted the contractors and Lord Boom.

I cannot now recall the manner in which my aunt and I
greeted one another. I must have been very tired then,
but whatever impression was made has gone out of my
memory. But I recall very clearly how we sat at the little
round table near the big window that gave on the terrace,
and dined and talked. I remember her talking of my uncle.

She asked after him, and whether he seemed well. " I wish
I could help," she said. " But I've never helped him much,
never. His way of doing things was never mine. And since
—since— Since he began to get so rich, he's kept things
from me. In the old days—it was different. . . .

" There he is—I don't know what he's doing. He won't
have me near him. . . .

" More's kept from me than any one. The very servants
won't let me know. They try and stop the worst of the
papers—Boom's things—from coming upstairs. . . . I suppose
they've got him in a corner, George.

" Poor old Teddy ! Poor old Adam and Eve we are !
Ficial Receivers with flaming swords to drive us out of our
garden ! I'd hoped we'd never have another Trek. Well—
anyway, it won't be Crest Hill. . . . But it's hard on Teddy.
He must be in such a mess up there. Poor old chap. I
suppose we can't help him. I suppose we'd only worry him.
Have some more soup, George—while there is some ? . . ."

The next day was one of those days of strong perception
that stand out clear in one's memory when the common
course of days is blurred. I can recall now the awakening
in the large familiar room that was always kept for me, and
how I lay staring at its chintz-covered chairs, its spaced fine
furniture, its glimpse of the cedars without, and thought that
all this had to end.

I have never been greedy for money, I have never wanted
to be rich, but I felt now an immense sense of impending
deprivation. I read the newspapers after breakfast—I and
my aunt together—and then I walked up to see what Cothope
had done in the matter of Lord Roberts β. Never before had
I appreciated so acutely the ample brightness of the Lady
Grove gardens, the dignity and wide peace of all about me.
It was one of those warm mornings in late May that have
won all the glory of summer without losing the gay delicacy of

spring. The shrubbery was bright with laburnum and lilac,
the beds swarmed with daffodils and narcissi and with lilies
of the valley in the shade.

I went along the well-kept paths among the rhododendra
and through the private gate into the woods where the bluebells and common orchid were in profusion. Never before
had I tasted so completely the fine sense of privilege and
ownership. And all this has to end, I told myself, all this
has to end.

Neither my uncle nor I had made any provision for disaster,
all we had was in the game, and I had little doubt now of the
completeness of our ruin. For the first time in my life since
he had sent me that wonderful telegram of his I had to consider that common anxiety of mankind,—Employment. I
had to come off my magic carpet and walk once more in the
world.

And suddenly I found myself at the cross drives where I
had seen Beatrice for the first time after so many years. It
is strange, but so far as I can recollect I had not thought of
her once since I had landed at Plymouth. No doubt she had
filled the background of my mind, but I do not remember
one definite clear thought. I had been intent on my uncle
and the financial collapse.

It came like a blow in the face now, all that too has to end !

Suddenly I was filled with the thought of her and a great
longing for her. What would she do when she realised our
immense disaster ? What would she do ? How would she
take it ? It filled me with astonishment to realise how little
I could tell. . . .

Should I perhaps presently happen upon her ?

I went on through the plantations and out upon the Downs,
and thence I saw Cothope with a new glider of his own design
soaring down wind to my old familiar " grounding " place.
To judge by its long rhythm it was a very good glider. " Like
Cothope's cheek," thought I, " to go on with the research. I
wonder if he's keeping notes. . . . But all this will have to
stop."

He was sincerely glad to see me. " It's been a rum go,"
he said.

He had been there without wages for a month, a man
forgotten in the rush of events.

" I just stuck on and did what I could with the stuff. I got
a bit of money of my own—and I said to myself, ' well, here
you are with the gear and no one to look after you. You
won't get such a chance again, my boy, not in all your born
days. Why not make what you can with it ? ' "

" How's Lord Roberts β ? "

Cothope lifted his eyebrows. " I've had to refrain," he
said. " But he's looking very handsome."

" Gods ! " I said, " I'd like to get him up just once before

we smash. You read the papers ? You know we're going
to smash ? "

"Oh ! I read the papers. It's scandalous, sir, such work
as ours should depend on things like that. You and I ought
to be under the State, sir, if you'll excuse me——"

"Nothing to excuse," I said. "I've always been a Socialist
—of a sort—in theory. Let's go and have a look at him.
How is he ?   Deflated ? "

"Just about quarter full. That last oil glaze of yours
holds the gas something beautiful. He's not lost a cubic
metre a week. . . ."

Cothope returned to Socialism as we went towards the sheds.

"Glad to think you're a Socialist, sir," he said, "it's the
only civilised state. I been a Socialist some years—off the
Clarion. It's a rotten scramble, this world. It takes the
things we make and invent and it plays the silly fool with 'em.
We scientific people, we'll have to take things over and stop
all this financing and advertisement and that. It's too silly.
It's a noosance. Look at us ! "

Lord Roberts β even in his partially deflated condition
in his shed was a fine thing to stare up at. I stood side by
side with Cothope regarding him, and it was borne in upon me
more acutely than ever that all this had to end. I had a
feeling just like the feeling of a boy who wants to do wrong,
that I would use up the stuff while I had it before the creditors
descended. I had a queer fancy too, I remember, that if I
could get into the air it would advertise my return to Beatrice.

"We'll fill her," I said concisely.

"It's all ready," said Cothope, and added as an after-
thought, "unless they cut off the gas. . . ."

I worked and interested myself with Cothope all the morning
and for a time forgot my other troubles. But the thought
of Beatrice flooded me slowly and steadily. It became an
unintelligent sick longing to see her. I felt that I could not
wait for the filling of Lord Roberts β, that I must hunt her
up and see her soon. I got everything forward and lunched
with Cothope, and then with the feeblest excuses left him
in order to prowl down through the woods towards Bedley
Corner. I became a prey to wretched hesitations and diffi-
dence. Ought I to go near her now ? I asked myself,
reviewing all the social abasements of my early years. At
last about five I called at the dower house. I was greeted by
their Charlotte—with a forbidding eye and a cold astonishment.
Both Beatrice and Lady Osprey were out.

There came into my head some prowling dream of meeting
her. I went along the lane towards Woking, the lane down
which we had walked five months ago in the wind and rain.

I mooned for a time in our former footsteps, then swore
and turned back across the fields, and then conceived a distaste
for Cothope and went Downward. At last I found myself

looking down on the huge abandoned masses of the Crest
Hill house.

That gave my mind a twist into a new channel. My uncle
came uppermost again. What a strange melancholy emptiness of intention that stricken enterprise seemed in the even
evening sunlight, what vulgar magnificence and crudity and
utter absurdity ! It was as idiotic as the pyramids. I sat
down on the stile, staring at it as though I had never seen that
forest of scaffold poles, that waste of walls and bricks and
plaster and shaped stones, that wilderness of broken soil and
wheeling tracks and dumps before. It struck me suddenly
as the compactest image and sample of all that passes for
Progress, of all the advertisement-inflated spending, the aimless
building up and pulling down, the enterprise and promise of
my age. This was our fruit, this was what we had done, I
and my uncle, in the fashion of our time. We were its leaders
and exponents, we were the thing it most flourishingly produced. For this futility in its end, for an epoch of such
futility, the solemn scroll of history had unfolded. . . .

" Great God ! " I cried, " but is this Life ? "

For this the armies drilled, for this the Law was administered and the prisons did their duty, for this the millions
toiled and perished in suffering, in order that a few of us should
build palaces we never finished, make billiard-rooms under
ponds, run imbecile walls round irrational estates, scorch
about the world in motor-cars, devise flying-machines, play
golf and a dozen such foolish games of ball, crowd into chatter-
ing dinner parties, gamble and make our lives one vast dismal
spectacle of witless waste ! So it struck me then, and for a
time I could think of no other interpretation. This was Life !
It came to me like a revelation, a revelation at once incredible
and indisputable of the abysmal folly of our being.

§ 3

I was roused from such thoughts by the sound of footsteps
behind me.

I turned half hopeful—so foolish is a lover's imagination,
and stopped amazed. It was my uncle. His face was white—
white as I had seen it in my dream.

" Hullo ! " I said and stared. " Why aren't you in London ? "

" It's all up," he said. . . .

" Adjudicated ? "

" No ! " . . .

I stared at him for a moment and then got off the stile.

He stood swaying and then came forward with a weak
motion of his arms like a man who cannot see distinctly, and
caught at and leaned upon the stile. For a moment we were
absolutely still. He made a clumsy gesture towards the great
futility below and choked. I discovered that his face was

wet with tears, that his wet glasses blinded him. He put up
his little fat hand and clawed them off clumsily, felt ineffi-
ciently for his pocket-handkerchief and then to my horror,
as he clung to me, he began to weep aloud, this little old
world-worn swindler. It wasn't just sobbing or shedding
tears, it was crying as a child cries. It was—oh! terrible!

"It's cruel," he blubbered at last. "They asked me
questions. They *kep'* asking me questions, George. . . ."

He sought for utterance, and spluttered.

"The Bloody bullies!" he shouted. "The Blöööödy Bullies."

He ceased to weep. He became suddenly rapid and
explanatory.

"It's not a fair game, George. They tire you out. And
I'm not well. My stomach's all wrong. And I been and got
a cold. I always been li'ble to cold and this one's on my chest.
And then they tell you to speak up. They bait you—and
bait you, and bait you. It's torture. The strain of it. You
can't remember what you said. You're bound to contradict
yourself. It's like Russia, George. . . . It isn't fair play.
. . . Prominent man. I've been next at dinners with that
chap, Neal, I've told him stories—and he's bitter! Sets
out to ruin me. Don't ask a civil question—bellows."

He broke down again. "I been bellowed at, I been bullied,
I been treated like a dog. Dirty cads they are! Dirty cads!
I'd rather be a Three-Card Sharper than a barrister; I'd
rather sell cat's-meat in the streets.

"They sprung things on me this morning, things I didn't
expect. They rushed me! I'd got it all in my hands and
then I was jumped. By Neal! Neal I've given city tips
to! Neal! I've helped Neal. . . .

"I couldn't swallow a mouthful—not in the lunch hour.
I couldn't face it. It's true, George—I couldn't face it. I
said I'd get a bit of air and slipped out and down to the
Embankment, and there I took a boat to Richmond. Some
idee. I took a rowing boat when I got there and rowed about
on the river for a bit. A lot of chaps and girls there was on
the bank laughed at my shirt-sleeves and top hat. Dessay
they thought it was a pleasure trip. Fat lot of pleasure!
I rowed round for a bit and came in. Then I came on here.
Windsor way. And there they are in London doing what they
like with me. . . . I don't care!"

"But——" I said, looking down at him perplexed.

"It's abscondin'. They'll have a warrant."

"I don't understand," I said.

"It's all up, George—all up and over.

"And I thought I'd live in that place, George—and die a
lord! It's a great place, reely, an imperial place—if any one
has the sense to buy it and finish it. That terrace——"

I stood thinking him over.

"Look here!" I said. "What's that about a warrant?

Are you sure they'll get a warrant ? I'm sorry, uncle ; but what have you done ? "

" Haven't I tole you ? "

" Yes," but they won't do very much to you for that. They'll only bring you up for the rest of your examination."

He remained silent for a time. At last he spoke—speaking with difficulty.

" It's worse than that. I done something. . . . They're bound to get it out. Practically they *have* got it out."

" What ? "

" Writin' things down—— I done something."

For the first time in his life, I believe, he felt and looked ashamed. It filled me with remorse to see him suffer so.

" We've all done things," I said. " It's part of the game the world makes us play. If they want to arrest you—and you've got no cards in your hand——! They mustn't arrest you."

" No. That's partly why I went to Richmond. But I never thought——"

His little bloodshot eyes stared at Crest Hill.

" That chap Wittaker Wright," he said, " he had his stuff ready. I haven't. Now you got it, George. That's the sort of hole I'm in."

§ 4

That memory of my uncle at the gate is very clear and full. I am able to recall even the undertow of my thoughts while he was speaking. I remember my pity and affection for him in his misery growing and stirring within me, my realisation that at any risk I must help him. But then comes indistinctness again. I was beginning to act. I know I persuaded him to put himself in my hands, and began at once to plan and do. I think that when we act most we remember least, that just in the measure that the impulse of our impressions translates itself into schemes and movements, it ceases to record itself in memories. I know I resolved to get him away at once, and to use the Lord Roberts β in effecting that. It was clear he was soon to be a hunted man, and it seemed to me already unsafe for him to try the ordinary Continental routes in his flight. I had to evolve some scheme, and evolve it rapidly, how we might drop most inconspicuously into the world across the water. My resolve to have one flight at least in my airship fitted with this like hand to glove. It seemed to me we might be able to cross over the water in the night, set our airship adrift, and turn up as pedestrian tourists in Normandy or Brittany, and so get away. That, at any rate, was my ruling idea. I sent off Cothope with a dummy note to Woking because I did not want to implicate him, and took my uncle to the pavilion. I went down to my aunt, and made a clean breast of the situation. She became admirably competent. We went into his dressing-room, and

ruthlessly broke his locks.   I got a pair of brown boots, a tweed
suit and cap of his, and indeed a plausible walking outfit, and
a little game bag for his pedestrian gear ; and, in addition,
a big motoring overcoat and a supply of rugs to add to those
I had at the pavilion.   I also got a flask of brandy, and she
made sandwiches.   I don't remember any servants appearing,
and I forget where she got those sandwiches.   Meanwhile we
talked.   Afterwards I thought with what a sure confidence
we talked to each other.

" What's he done ? " she said.

" D'you mind knowing ? "

" No conscience left, thank God ! "

" I think—forgery ! "

There was just a little pause.   " Can you carry this
bundle ? " she asked.

I lifted it.

" No woman ever has respected the law—ever," she said.
" It's too silly. . . . The things it lets you do ! And then
pulls you up.   Like a mad nurse minding a child."

She carried some rugs for me through the shrubbery in the
darkling.

" They'll think we're going mooning," she said, jerking
her head at the household.   " I wonder what they make
of us—criminals. . . ."   An immense droning note came as
if in answer to that.   It startled us both for a moment.   " The
dears ! " she said.   " It's the gong for dinner ! . . . But I
wish I could help little Teddy, George.   It's awful to think of
him there with hot eyes, red and dry.   And I know—the sight
of me makes him feel sore.   Things I said, George.   If I
could have seen, I'd have let him have an omnibusful of
Scrymgeours.   I cut him up.   He'd never thought I meant
it before. . . . I'll help all I can, anyhow."

I turned at something in her voice, and got a moonlight
gleam of tears upon her face.

" Could *she* have helped ? " she asked abruptly.

" *She ?* "

" That woman."

" My God ! " I cried, " *helped !* Those—things don't
help ! . . . "

" Tell me again what I ought to do," she said after a silence.

I went over the plans I had made for communicating, and
the things I thought she might do.   I had given her the
address of a solicitor she might put some trust in.

" But you must act for yourself," I insisted.   " Roughly,"
I said, " it's a scramble.   You must get what you can for us,
and follow as you can."

She nodded.

She came right up to the pavilion, and hovered for a time
shyly, and then went away.

I found my uncle in my sitting-room in an arm-chair

with his feet upon the fender of the gas stove, which he had
lit, and now he was feebly drunken with my whisky, and very
weary in body and spirit, and inclined to be cowardly.

" I lef' my drops," he said.

He changed his clothes slowly and unwillingly. I had to
bully him, I had almost to shove him to the airship and tuck
him up upon its wicker flat. Single-handed I made but a
clumsy start ; we scraped along the roof of the shed and bent
a van of the propeller, and for a time I hung underneath
without his offering a hand to help me to clamber up. If it
hadn't been for a sort of anchoring trolley device of Cothope's,
a sort of slip anchor running on a rail, we should never have
got clear at all.

§ 5

The incidents of our flight in Lord Roberts β do not arrange
themselves in any consecutive order. To think of that
adventure is like dipping haphazard into an album of views.
One is reminded first of this and then of that. We were both
lying down on a horizontal plate of basketwork ; for Lord
Roberts β had none of the elegant accommodation of a balloon.
I lay forward, and my uncle behind me in such a position that
he could see hardly anything of our flight. We were pro-
tected from rolling over simply by netting between the steel
stays. It was impossible for us to stand up at all ; we had
either to lie or crawl on all fours over the basketwork. Amid-
ships were lockers made of Watson's Aulite material, and
between these it was that I had put my uncle wrapped in
rugs. I wore sealskin motoring boots and gloves, and a
motor fur coat over my tweeds, and I controlled the engine
by Bowden wires and levers forward.

The early part of that night's experience was made up of
warmth, of moonlit Surrey and Sussex landscape, and of a
rapid and successful flight, ascending and swooping, and then
ascending again southward. I could not watch the clouds
because the airship overhung me ; I could not see the stars
nor gauge the metereological happening, but it was fairly
clear to me that a wind, shifting between north and north-
east, was gathering strength, and after I had satisfied myself
by a series of entirely successful expansions and contractions
of the real air-worthiness of Lord Roberts β, I stopped the
engine to save my petrol, and let the monster drift, checking
its progress by the dim landscape below. My uncle lay quite
still behind me, saying little and staring in front of him, and
I was left to my own thoughts and sensations.

My thoughts, whatever they were, have long since faded
out of memory, and my sensations have merged into one
continuous memory of a country-side lying, as it seemed,
under snow, with square patches of dimness, white phantoms
of roads, rents and pools of velvety blackness, and lamp-

jewelled houses. I remember a train boring its way like a
hastening caterpillar of fire across the landscape, and how
distinctly I heard its clatter. Every town and street was
buttoned with street lamps. I came quite close to the South
Downs near Lewes, and all the lights were out in the houses,
and the people gone to bed. We left the land a little to the
east of Brighton, and by that time Brighton was well abed,
and the brightly lit seafront deserted. Then I let out the gas
chamber to its fullest extent and rose. I like to be high
above water.

I do not clearly know what happened in the night. I think
I must have dozed, and probably my uncle slept. 1 remember
that once or twice I heard him talking in an eager, muffled
voice to himself, or to an imaginary court. But there can be
no doubt the wind changed right round into the east, and that
we were carried far down the Channel without any suspicion
of the immense leeway we were making. I remember the kind
of stupid perplexity with which I saw the dawn breaking over
a grey waste of waters below, and realised that something
was wrong. I was so stupid that it was only after the sunrise
I really noticed the trend of the foam caps below, and perceived
we were in a severe easterly gale. Even then instead of head-
ing south-easterly, I set the engine going, headed south, and so
continued a course that must needs have either just hit Ushant,
or carry us over the Bay of Biscay. I thought I was east
of Cherbourg, when I was far to the west, and stopped my
engine in that belief, and then set it going again. I did actually
sight the coast of Brittany to the south-east in the late afternoon, and that it was woke me up to the gravity of our position.
I discovered it by accident in the south-east, when I was
looking for it in the south-west. I turned about east and
faced the wind for some time, and finding I had no chance in
its teeth, went high, where it seemed less violent, and tried
to make a course south-east. It was only then that I realised
what a gale I was in. I had been going westward, and perhaps
even in gusts north of west, at a pace of fifty or sixty miles
an hour.

Then I began what I suppose would be called a Fight
against the east wind. One calls it a Fight, but it was really
almost as unlike a fight as plain sewing. The wind tried
to drive me westwardly, and I tried to get as much as I could
eastwardly, with the wind beating and rocking us irregularly,
but by no means unbearably, for about twelve hours. My
hope lay in the wind abating, and our keeping in the air and
eastward of Finisterre until it did, and the chief danger
was the exhaustion of our petrol. It was a long and anxious
and almost meditative time ; we were fairly warm, and only
slowly getting hungry, and except that my uncle grumbled a
little and produced some philosophical reflections, and began
to fuss about having a temperature, we talked very little. I

was tired and sulky, and chiefly worried about the engine.   I
had to resist a tendency to crawl back and look at it.   I did
not care to risk contracting our gas chamber for fear of losing
gas.   Nothing was less like a fight.   I know that in popular
magazines, and so forth, all such occasions as this are depicted
in terms of hysteria.   Captains save their ships, engineers
complete their bridges, generals conduct their battles, in a state
of dancing excitement, foaming recondite technicalities at the
lips.   I suppose that sort of thing works up the reader, but
so far as it professes to represent reality, I am convinced it is
all childish nonsense.   Schoolboys of fifteen, girls of eighteen,
and literary men all their lives, may have these squealing fits,
but my own experience is that most exciting scenes are not
exciting, and most of the urgent moments in life are met by
steady-headed men.

Neither I nor my uncle spent the night in ejaculations, nor
in humorous allusions, nor any of these things.   We remained
lumpish.   My uncle stuck in his place and grumbled about
his stomach, and occasionally rambled off into expositions
of his financial position and denunciations of Neal—he
certainly struck out one or two good phrases for Neal—and I
crawled about at rare intervals in a vague sort of way and
grunted, and our basketwork creaked continually, and the
wind on our quarter made a sort of ruffled flapping in the wall
of the gas chamber.   For all our wraps we got frightfully cold
as the night wore on.

I must have dozed, and it was still dark when I realised with
a start that we were nearly due south of, and a long way from,
a regularly-flashing lighthouse, standing out before the glow
of some great town, and then that the thing that had awakened
me was the cessation of our engine, and that we were driving
back to the west.

Then, indeed, for a time I felt the grim thrill of life.   I
crawled forward to the cords of the release valves, made my
uncle crawl forward too, and let out the gas until we were
falling down through the air like a clumsy glider towards the
vague greyness that was land.

Something must have intervened here that I have forgotten.
I saw the lights of Bordeaux when it was quite dark, a nebulous
haze against black ; of that I am reasonably sure.   But
certainly our fall took place in the cold, uncertain light of
early dawn.   I am, at least, equally sure of that.   And
Mimizan, near where we dropped, is fifty miles from Bordeaux,
whose harbour lights I must have seen.

I remember coming down at last with a curious indifference,
and actually rousing myself to steer.   But the actual coming
to earth was exciting enough.   I remember our prolonged
dragging landfall, and the difficulty I had to get clear, and how
a gust of wind caught Lord Roberts β as my uncle stumbled
away from the ropes and litter, and dropped me heavily, and

threw me on to my knees. Then came the realisation that
the monster was almost consciously disentangling itself for
escape, and then the light leap of its rebound. The rope
slipped out of reach of my hand. I remember running knee-
deep in a salt pool in hopeless pursuit of the airship as it dragged
and rose seaward, and how only after it had escaped my uttermost effort to recapture it, did I realise that this was quite
the best thing that could have happened. It drove swiftly
over the sandy dunes, lifting and falling, and was hidden by a
clump of wind-bitten trees. Then it reappeared much further
off, and still receding. It soared for a time, and sank slowly,
and after that I saw it no more. I suppose it fell into the
sea and got wetted with salt water and heavy, and so became
deflated and sank.

It was never found, and there was never a report of any one
seeing it after it escaped from me.

§ 6

But if I find it hard to tell the story of our long flight through
the air overseas, at least that dawn in France stands cold and
clear and full. I see again almost as if I saw once more with
my bodily eyes the ridges of sand rising behind ridges of sand,
grey and cold and black-browed with an insufficient grass. I
feel again the clear, cold chill of dawn, and hear the distant
barking of a dog. I find myself asking again, " What shall we do
now ? " and trying to scheme with a brain tired beyond measure.

At first my uncle occupied my attention. He was shivering
a good deal, and it was all I could do to resist my desire to get
him into a comfortable bed at once. But I wanted to appear
plausibly in this part of the world. I felt it would not do to
turn up anywhere at dawn and rest, it would be altogether too
conspicuous ; we must rest until the day was well advanced,
and then appear as road-stained pedestrians seeking a meal.
I gave him most of what was left of the biscuits, emptied our
flasks, and advised him to sleep, but at first it was too cold,
albeit I wrapped the big fur rug around him.

I was struck now by the flushed weariness of his face, and the
look of age the grey stubble on his unshaved chin gave him.
He sat crumpled up, shivering and coughing, munching
reluctantly, but drinking eagerly, and whimpering a little, a
dreadfully pitiful figure to me. But we had to go through with
it, there was no way out for us.

Presently the sun rose over the pines, and the sand grew
rapidly warm. My uncle had done eating, and sat with his
wrists resting on his knees, the most hopeless-looking of lost
souls.

" I'm ill," he said, " I'm damnably ill ! I can feel it in my
skin ! "

Then—it was horrible to me—he cried, " I ought to be in

bed ; I ought to be in bed . . . instead of flying about," and suddenly he burst into tears.

I stood up. "Go to sleep, man!" I said, and took the rug from him, and spread it out and rolled him up in it.

"It's all very well," he protested ; "I'm not young enough——"

"Lift up your head," I interrupted, and put his knapsack under it.

"They'll catch us here, just as much as in an inn," he grumbled, and then lay still.

Presently, after a long time, I perceived he was asleep. His breath came with peculiar wheezings, and every now and again he would cough. I was very stiff and tired myself, and perhaps I dozed. I don't remember. I remember only sitting, as it seemed nigh interminably, beside him, too weary even to think in that sandy desolation.

No one came near us, no creature, not even a dog. I roused myself at last, feeling that it was vain to seek to seem other than abnormal ; and with an effort that was like lifting a sky of lead, we made our way through the wearisome sand to a farmhouse. There I feigned even a more insufficient French than I possess naturally, and let it appear that we were pedestrians from Biarritz who had lost our way along the shore and got benighted. This explained us pretty well, I thought, and we got most heartening coffee and a cart to a little roadside station. My uncle grew more and more manifestly ill with every stage of our journey. I got him to Bayonne, where he refused at first to eat, and was afterwards very sick, and then took him, shivering and collapsed, up a little branch line to a frontier place called Luzon Gare.

We found one homely inn with two small bedrooms, kept by a kindly Basque woman. I got him to bed, and that night shared his room, and after an hour or so of sleep he woke up in a raging fever and with a wandering mind, cursing Neal and repeating long inaccurate lists of figures. He was manifestly a case for a doctor, and in the morning we got one in. He was a young man from Montpelier, just beginning to practise, and very mysterious and technical and modern and unhelpful. He spoke of cold and exposure, and *la grippe* and pneumonia. He gave many explicit and difficult directions. . . . I perceived it devolved upon me to organise nursing and a sick-room. I installed a *religieuse* in the second bedroom of the inn, and took a room for myself in the inn of Port de Luzon, a quarter of a mile away.

§ 7

And now my story converges on what, in that queer corner of refuge out of the world, was destined to be my uncle's deathbed. There is a background of the Pyrenees, of blue hills and sunlit houses, of the old castle of Luzon and a noisy cascading river, and for a foreground the dim stuffy room whose windows both the *religieuse* and hostess conspired to shut, with its waxed floor, its four-poster bed, its character- istically French chairs and fireplace, its champagne bottles and dirty basins and used towels and packets of *Somatosé* on the table. And in the sickly air of the confined space behind the curtains of the bed lay my little uncle, with an effect of being enthroned and secluded, or sat up, or writhed and tossed in his last dealings with life. One went and drew back the edge of the curtains if one wanted to speak to him or look at him.

Usually he was propped up against pillows, because so he breathed more easily. He slept hardly at all.

I have a confused memory of vigils and mornings and afternoons spent by that bedside, and how the *religieuse* hovered about me, and how meek and good and inefficient she was, and how horribly black were her nails. Other figures come and go, and particularly the doctor, a young man plumply rococo, in bicycling dress, with fine waxen features, a little pointed beard, and the long black frizzy hair and huge tie of a minor poet. Bright and clear-cut and irrelevant are memories of the Basque hostess of my uncle's inn and of the family of Spanish people who entertained me and prepared the most amazingly elaborate meals for me, with soup and salad and chicken and remarkable sweets. They were all very kind and sympathetic people, systematically so. And con- stantly, without attracting attention, I was trying to get newspapers from home.

My uncle is central to all these impressions.

I have tried to make you picture him, time after time, as the young man of the Wimblehurst chemist's shop, as the shabby assistant in Tottenham Court Road, as the adventurer of the early days of Tono-Bungay, as the confident pre- posterous plutocrat. And now I have to tell of him strangely changed under the shadow of oncoming death, with his skin lax and yellow and glistening with sweat, his eyes large and glassy, his countenance unfamiliar through the growth of a beard, his nose pinched and thin. Never had he looked so small as now. And he talked to me in a whispering, strained voice of great issues, of why his life had been, and whither he was going. Poor little man ! that last phase is, as it were, disconnected from all the other phases. It was as if he crawled out from the ruins of his career, and looked about him before he died. For he had quite clear-minded states in the intervals of his delirium.

He knew he was almost certainly dying. In a way that took the burthen of his cares off his mind. There was no more Neal to face, no more flights or evasions, no punishments.

" It has been a great career, George," he said, " but I shall be glad to rest. Glad to rest ! . . . Glad to rest."

His mind ran rather upon his career, and usually, I am glad
to recall, with a note of satisfaction and approval. In his
delirious phases he would most often exaggerate this self-
satisfaction, and talk of his splendours. He would pluck at
the sheet and stare before him, and whisper half-audible
fragments of sentences.

"What is this great place, these cloud-capped towers,
these airy pinnacles ? . . . Ilion. Sky-y-pointing. . . . Ilion
House, the residence of one of our great merchant princes. . . .
Terrace above terrace. Reaching to the Heavens. . . .
Kingdoms Cæsar never knew. . . . A great poet, George.
Zzzz. Kingdoms Cæsar never knew. . . . Under entirely
new management.

"Greatness. . . . Millions. . . . Universities. . . . He
stands on the terrace—on the upper terrace—directing—
directing—by the globe—directing —the trade. . . ."

It was hard at times to tell when his sane talk ceased and
his delirium began. The secret springs of his life, the vain
imaginations, were revealed, I sometimes think that all the
life of man sprawls abed, careless and unkempt, until it must
needs clothe and wash itself and come forth seemly in act and
speech for the encounter with one's fellow-men. I suspect
that all things unspoken in our souls partake somewhat of the
laxity of delirium and dementia. Certainly from those slimy
tormented lips above the bristling grey beard came nothing
but dreams and disconnected fancies. . . .

Sometimes he raved about Neal, threatened Neal. " What
has he got invested ? " he said. " Does he think he can
escape me ? . . . If I followed him up. . . . Ruin. Ruin.
. . . One would think *I* had taken his money."

And sometimes he reverted to our airship flight. " It's too
long, George, too long and too cold. I'm too old a man—too
old—for this sort of thing. . . . You know you're not saving
—you're killing me."

Towards the end it became evident our identity was discovered. I found the press, and especially Boom's section
of it, had made a sort of hue and cry for us, sent special commissioners to hunt for us, and though none of these emissaries
reached us until my uncle was dead, one felt the forewash of
that storm of energy. The thing got into the popular French
press. People became curious in their manner towards us,
and a number of fresh faces appeared about the weak little
struggle that went on in the closeness behind the curtains of
the bed. The young doctor insisted on consultations, and a
motor-car came up from Biarritz, and suddenly odd people
with questioning eyes began to poke in with inquiries and help.
Though nothing was said, I could feel that we were no longer
regarded as simple middle-class tourists ; about me, as I went,
I perceived almost as though it trailed visibly, the prestige
of Finance and a criminal notoriety. Local personages of a

plump and prosperous quality appeared in the inn making inquiries, the Luzon priest became helpful, people watched our window, and stared at me as I went to and fro ; and then we had a raid from a little English clergyman and his amiable, capable wife in severely Anglican black, who swooped down upon us like virtuous but resolute vultures from the adjacent village of Saint Jean de Pollack.

The clergyman was one of those odd types that oscillate between remote country towns in England and the conduct of English church services on mutual terms in enterprising hotels abroad, a tremulous, obstinate little being with sporadic hairs upon his face, spectacles, a red button nose, and aged black raiment. He was evidently enormously impressed by my uncle's monetary greatness, and by his own inkling of our identity, and he shone and brimmed over with tact and fussy helpfulness. He was eager to share the watching of the bedside with me, he proffered services with both hands, and as I was now getting into touch with affairs in London again, and trying to disentangle the gigantic details of the smash from the papers I had succeeded in getting from Biarritz, I accepted his offers pretty generously, and began the studies in modern finance that lay before me. I had got so out of touch with the old traditions of religion, that I overlooked the manifest possibility of his attacking my poor sinking vestiges of an uncle with theological solicitudes. My attention was called to that, however, very speedily by a polite but urgent quarrel between himself and the Basque landlady as to the necessity of her hanging a cheap crucifix in the shadow over the bed, where it might catch my uncle's eye, where, indeed, I found it had caught his eye.

"Good Lord ! " I cried ; " is *that* still going on ! "

That night the little clergyman watched, and in the small hours he raised a false alarm that my uncle was dying, and made an extraordinary fuss. He raised the house. I shall never forget that scene, I think, which began with a tapping at my bedroom door just after I had fallen asleep, and his voice—

" If you want to see your uncle before he goes, you must come now."

The stuffy little room was crowded when I reached it, and lit by three flickering candles. I felt I was back in the eighteenth century. There lay my poor uncle amidst indescribably tumbled bedclothes, weary of life beyond measure, weary and rambling, and the little clergyman trying to hold his hand and his attention, and repeating over and over again—

" Mr. Ponderevo, Mr. Ponderevo, it is all right. It is all right. Only believe ! ' Believe on Me, and ye shall be saved ' ! "

Close at hand was the doctor with one of those cruel and idiotic injection needles modern science puts in the hands of these half-educated young men, keeping my uncle flickeringly alive for no reason whatever. The *religieuse* hovered sleepily in the background with an overdue and neglected dose. In addition, the landlady had not only got up herself, but roused an aged crone of a mother and a partially imbecile husband, and there was also a fattish, stolid man in grey alpaca, with an air of importance—who he was and how he got there, I don't know. I rather fancy the doctor explained him to me in French I did not understand. And they were all there, wearily nocturnal, hastily and carelessly dressed, intent upon the life that flickered and sank, making a public and curious show of its going, queer shapes of human beings lit by three uncertain candles, and every soul of them keenly and avidly resolved to be in at the death. The doctor stood, the others were all sitting on chairs the landlady had brought in and arranged for them.

And my uncle spoiled the climax, and did not die.

I replaced the little clergyman on the chair by the bedside, and he hovered about the room.

" I think," he whispered to me mysteriously, as he gave place to me, " I believe—it is well with him."

I heard him trying to render the stock phrases of Low Church piety into French for the benefit of the stolid man in grey alpaca. Then he knocked a glass off the table, and scrabbled for the fragments. From the first I doubted the theory of an immediate death. I consulted the doctor in urgent whispers. I turned round to get champagne, and nearly fell over the clergyman's legs. He was on his knees at the additional chair the Basque landlady had got on my arrival, and he was praying aloud, " Oh, Heavenly Father, have mercy on this thy Child. . . ." I hustled him up and out of the way, and in another minute he was down at another chair praying again, and barring the path of the *religieuse* who had found me the corkscrew. Something put into my head that tremendous blasphemy of Carlyle's about " the last mew of a drowning kitten." He found a third chair vacant presently ; it was as if he was playing a game.

" Good Heavens," said I, " we must clear these people out," and with a certain urgency I did.

I had a temporary lapse of memory, and forgot all my French. I drove them out mainly by gesture, and opened the window to the universal horror. I intimated the death scene was postponed, and, as a matter of fact, my uncle did not die until the next night.

I did not let the little clergyman come near him again, and I was watchful for any sign that his mind had been troubled. But he made none. He talked once about "that parson chap."

" Didn't bother you ? " I asked.

" Wanted something," he said.

I kept silence, listening keenly to his mutterings. I understood him to say, " they wanted too much." His face puckered like a child's going to cry. "You can't *get* a safe six per cent.," he said. I had for a moment a wild suspicion that those urgent talks had not been altogether spiritual, but that, I think, was a quite unworthy and unjust suspicion. The little clergyman was as simple and honest as the day. My uncle was simply generalising about his class.

But it may have been these talks that set loose some long dormant string of ideas in my uncle's brain, ideas the things of this world had long suppressed and hidden altogether. Near the end he suddenly became clear-minded and lucid, albeit very weak, and his voice was little, but clear.

"George," he said.

"I'm here," I said, "close beside you."

"George. You have always been responsible for the science. George. You know better than I do. Is—— Is it proved?"

"What proved?"

"Either way?"

"I don't understand."

"Death ends all. After so much—— Such splendid beginnings. Somewhere. Something."

I stared at him amazed. His sunken eyes were very grave.

"What do you expect?" I said in wonder.

He would not answer. "Aspirations," he whispered.

He fell into a broken monologue, regardless of me. "Trailing clouds of glory," he said, and "first-rate poet, first-rate. . . . George was always hard. Always."

For a long time there was silence.

Then he made a gesture that he wished to speak.

"Seems to me, George——"

I bent my head down, and he tried to lift his hand to my shoulder. I raised him a little on his pillows, and listened.

"It seems to me, George, always—there must be something in me—that won't die."

He looked at me as though the decision rested with me.

"I think," he said; "—something."

Then, for a moment, his mind wandered. "Just a little link," he whispered almost pleadingly, and lay quite still, but presently he was uneasy again.

"Some other world——"

"Perhaps," I said. "Who knows?"

"Some other world."

"Not the same scope for enterprise," I said. "No."

He became silent. I sat leaning down to him, and following out my own thoughts, and presently the *religieuse* resumed her periodic conflict with the window fastening. For a time he struggled for breath. . . . It seemed such nonsense that he should have to suffer so—poor silly little man!

"George," he whispered, and his weak little hand came out. "*Perhaps*——"

He said no more, but I perceived from the expression of his
eyes that he thought the question had been put.

" Yes, I think so," I said stoutly.

" Aren't you sure ? "

" Oh—practically sure," said I, and I think he tried to
squeeze my hand. And there I sat, holding his hand tight,
and trying to think what seeds of immortality could be found
in all his being, what sort of ghost there was in *him* to wander
out into the bleak immensities. Queer fancies came to me.
. . . He lay still for a long time, save for a brief struggle or so
for breath, and ever and again I wiped his mouth and lips.

I fell into a pit of thought. I did not remark at first the
change that was creeping over his face. He lay back on his
pillow, made a faint zzzing sound that ceased, and presently
and quite quietly he died—greatly comforted by my assurance. I do not know when he died. His hand relaxed
insensibly. Suddenly, with a start, with a shock, I found
that his mouth had fallen open, and that he was dead. . . .

§ 8

It was dark night when I left his deathbed and went back
to my own inn down the straggling street of Luzon.

That return to my inn sticks in my memory also as a thing
apart, as an experience apart. Within was a subdued bustle
of women, a flitting of lights, and the doing of petty offices
to that queer exhausted thing that had once been my active
and urgent little uncle. For me those offices were irksome
and impertinent. I slammed the door, and went out into the
warm, foggy drizzle of the village street lit by blurred specks of
light in great voids of darkness, and never a soul abroad.
That warm veil of fog produced an effect of vast seclusion.
The very houses by the roadside peered through it as if from
another world. The stillness of the night was marked by an
occasional remote baying of dogs ; all these people kept dogs
because of the near neighbourhood of the frontier.

Death !

It was one of those rare seasons of relief, when for a brief
time one walks a little outside of and beside life. I felt as I
sometimes feel after the end of a play. I saw the whole
business of my uncle's life as something familiar and completed. It was done, like a play one leaves, like a book one
closes. I thought of the push and the promotions, the noise
of London, the crowded, various company of people through
which our lives had gone, the public meetings, the excitements, the dinners and disputations, and suddenly it appeared
to me that none of these things existed. It came to me like a
discovery that none of these things existed. Before and after
I have thought and called life a phantasmagoria, but never
have I felt its truth as I did that night. . . . We had parted ;

we two who had kept company so long had parted. But there was, I knew, no end to him or me. He had died a dream death, and ended a dream, his pain dream was over. It seemed to me almost as though I had died too. What did it matter, since it was unreality, all of it, the pain and desire, the beginning and the end ? There was no reality except this solitary road, this quite solitary road, along which one went rather puzzled, rather tired. . . .

Part of the fog became a big mastiff that came towards me and stopped and slunk round me growling, barked gruffly and shortly and presently became fog again.

My mind swayed back to the ancient beliefs and fears of our race. My doubts and disbeliefs slipped from me like a loosely-fitting garment. I wondered quite simply what dogs bayed about the path of that other walker in the darkness, what shapes, what lights, it might be, loomed about him as he went his way from our last encounter on earth—along the paths that are real, and the way that endures for ever ?

§ 9

Last belated figure in that grouping round my uncle's death-bed is my aunt. When it was beyond all hope that my uncle could live I threw aside whatever concealment remained to us and telegraphed directly to her. But she came too late to see him living. She saw him calm and still, strangely unlike his habitual garrulous animation, an unfamiliar inflexibility.

" It isn't like him," she whispered, awed by this alien dignity.

I remember her chiefly as she talked and wept upon the bridge below the old castle. We had got rid of some amateurish reporters from Biarritz, and had walked together in the hot morning sunshine down through Port Luzon. There, for a time, we stood leaning on the parapet of the bridge and surveying the distant peaks, the rich blue masses of the Pyrenees. For a long time we said nothing, and then she began talking.

" Life's a rum Go, George ! " she began. " Who would have thought, when I used to darn your stockings at old Wimblehurst, that this would be the end of the story ? It seems far away now—that little shop, his and my first home. The glow of the bottles, the big coloured bottles ! Before he stuck those old retorts there. Do you remember how the light shone on the mahogany drawers ? The little gilt letters ! *Ol Amjig*, and *S'nap !* I can remember it all—bright and shining—like a Dutch picture. Real ! And yesterday. And here we are in a dream. You a man—and me an old woman, George. And poor little Teddy, who used to rush about and talk—making that noise he did—Oh ! "

She choked, and the tears flowed unrestrained. She wept, and I was glad to see her weeping. . . .

She stood leaning over the bridge, her tear-wet hand-kerchief gripped in her clenched hand.

" Just an hour in the old shop again—and him talking. Before things got done. Before they got hold of him. And fooled him.

" Men oughtn't to be so tempted with business and things. . . .

" They didn't hurt him, George ? " she asked suddenly.

For a moment I was puzzled.

" Here, I mean," she said.

" No," I lied stoutly, suppressing the memory of that foolish injection needle I had caught the young doctor using.

" I wonder, George, if they'll let him talk in Heaven ? . . ."

She faced me. " Oh ! George, dear, my heart aches, and I don't know what I say and do. Give me your arm to lean on—it's good to have you, dear, and lean upon you. . . . Yes, I know you care for me. That's why I'm talking. We've always loved one another, and never said anything about it, and you understand, and I understand. But my heart's torn to pieces by this, torn to rags, and things drop out I've kept in it. It's true he wasn't a husband much for me at the last. But he was my child, George, he was my child and all my children, my silly child, and life has knocked him about for me, and I've never had a say in the matter ; never a say ; it's puffed him up and smashed him—like an old bag—under my eyes. I was clever enough to see it, and not clever enough to prevent it, and all I could do was to jeer. I've had to make what I could of it. Like most people. Like most of us. . . . But it wasn't fair, George. It wasn't fair. Life and Death—great serious things—why couldn't they leave him alone, and his lies and ways ? If we could see the light-ness of it——

" Why couldn't they leave him alone ? " she repeated in a whisper as we went towards the inn.

CHAPTER TWO

LOVE AMONG THE WRECKAGE

§ 1

WHEN I came back I found that my share in the escape and death of my uncle had made me for a time a notorious and even popular character. For two weeks I was kept in London " facing the music," as he would have said, and making things easy for my aunt, and I still marvel at the consideration with which the world treated me. For now it was open and manifest that I and my uncle were no

more than specimens of a modern species of brigand, wasting
the savings of the public out of the sheer wantonness of enterprise. I think that, in a way, his death produced a reaction
in my favour, and my flight, of which some particulars now
appeared, stuck in the popular imagination. It seemed a
more daring and difficult feat than it was, and I couldn't very
well write to the papers to sustain my private estimate.
There can be little doubt that men infinitely prefer the appearance of dash and enterprise to simple honesty. No one
believed I was not an arch plotter in his financing. Yet they
favoured me. I even got permission from the trustee to
occupy my châlet for a fortnight while I cleared up the mass
of papers, calculations, notes of work, drawings and the like,
that I left in disorder when I started on that impulsive raid
upon the Mordet quap heaps. I was there alone. I got work
for Cothope with the Ilchesters, for whom I now build these
destroyers. They wanted him at once, and he was short of
money, so I let him go, and managed very philosophically by
myself.

But I found it hard to fix my attention on aeronautics.
I had been away from the work for a full half-year and more,
a half-year crowded with intense disconcerting things. For a
time my brain refused these fine problems of balance and
adjustment altogether ; it wanted to think about my uncle's
dropping jaw, my aunt's reluctant tears, about dead negroes
and pestilential swamps, about the evident realities of cruelty
and pain, about life and death. Moreover, it was weary with
the frightful pile of figures and documents at the Hardingham,
a task to which this raid to Lady Grove was simply an interlude. And there was Beatrice.

On the second morning, as I sat out upon the verandah
recalling memories and striving in vain to attend to some too
succinct pencil notes of Cothope's, Beatrice rode up suddenly
from behind the pavilion, and pulled rein and became still ;
Beatrice a little flushed from riding and sitting on a big black
horse.

I did not instantly rise. I stared at her. " *You !* " I said.
She looked at me steadily. " Me," she said.
I did not trouble about any civilities. I stood up and asked
pointblank a question that came into my head.
" Whose horse is that ? " I said.
She looked me in the eyes. " Carnaby's," she answered.
" How did you get here—this way ? "
" The wall's down."
" Down ? Already ? "
" A great bit of it between the plantations."
" And you rode through, and got here by chance ? "
" I saw you yesterday. And I rode over to see you."
I had now come close to her, and stood looking up into her face.
" I'm a mere vestige," I said.

She made no answer, but remained regarding me steadfastly with a curious air of proprietorship.

"You know I'm the living survivor now of the great smash. I'm rolling and dropping down through all the scaffolding of the social system. . . . It's all a chance whether I roll out free at the bottom, or go down a crack into the darkness out of sight for a year or two."

"The sun," she remarked irrelevantly, "has burned you. . . . I'm getting down."

She swung herself down into my arms, and stood beside me face to face.

"Where's Cothope ?" she asked.

"Gone."

Her eyes flitted to the pavilion and back to me. We stood close together, extraordinarily intimate, and extraordinarily apart.

"I've never seen this cottage of yours," she said, "and I want to."

She flung the bridle of her horse round the verandah post, and I helped her tie it.

"Did you get what you went for to Africa ?" she asked.

"No," I said, "I lost my ship."

"And that lost everything ?"

"Everything."

She walked before me into the living-room of the châlet, and I saw that she gripped her riding-whip very tightly in her hand. She looked about her for a moment, and then at me.

"It's comfortable," she remarked.

Our eyes met in a conversation very different from the one upon our lips. A sombre glow surrounded us, drew us together ; an unwonted shyness kept us apart. She roused herself, after an instant's pause, to examine my furniture.

"You have chintz curtains. I thought men were too feckless to have curtains without a woman— But, of course, your aunt did that ! And a couch and a brass fender, and— is that a pianola ? That is your desk. I thought men's desks were always untidy, and covered with dust and tobacco ash."

She flitted to my colour prints and my little case of books. Then she went to the pianola. I watched her intently.

"Does this thing play ?" she said.

"What ?" I asked.

"Does this thing play ?"

I roused myself from my preoccupation.

"Like a musical gorilla with fingers all of one length. And a sort of soul. . . . It's all the world of music to me."

"What do you play ?"

"Beethoven, when I want to clear up my head while I'm working. He is—how one would always like to work. Sometimes Chopin and those others, but Beethoven. Beethoven mainly. Yes."

Silence again between us. She spoke with an effort.

"Play me something." She turned from me and explored the rack of music rolls, became interested and took a piece, the first part of the Kreutzer Sonata, hesitated. "No," she said, "that!"

She gave me Brahm's Second Concerto, Op. 58, and curled up on the sofa watching me as I set myself slowly to play. . . .

"I say," she said when I had done, "that's fine. I didn't know those things could play like that. I'm all astir. . . ."

She came and stood over me, looking at me. "I'm going to have a concert," she said abruptly, and laughed uneasily and hovered at the pigeon-holes. "Now—now what shall I have?" She chose more of Brahms. Then we came to the Kreutzer Sonata. It is queer how Tolstoy has loaded that with suggestions, debauched it, made it a scandalous and intimate symbol. When I had played the first part of that, she came up to the pianola and hesitated over me. I sat stiffly—waiting.

Suddenly she seized my downcast head and kissed my hair. She caught at my face between her hands and kissed my lips. I put my arms about her and we kissed together. I sprang to my feet and clasped her.

"Beatrice," I said. "Beatrice!"

"My dear," she whispered, nearly breathless, with her arms about me. "Oh! my dear!"

§ 2

Love, like everything else in this immense process of social disorganisation in which we live, is a thing adrift, a fruitless thing broken away from its connections. I tell of this love affair here because of its irrelevance, because it is so remarkable that it should mean nothing, and be nothing except itself. It glows in my memory like some bright casual flower starting up amidst the *débris* of a catastrophe. For nearly a fortnight we two met and made love together. Once more this mighty passion, that our aimless civilisation has fettered and maimed and sterilised and debased, gripped me and filled me with passionate delights and solemn joys—that were all, you know, futile and purposeless. Once more I had the persuasion "This matters. Nothing else matters so much as this." We were both infinitely grave in such happiness as we had. I do not remember any laughter at all between us.

Twelve days it lasted from that encounter in my châlet until our parting.

Except at the end, they were days of supreme summer, and there was a waxing moon. We met recklessly day by day. We were so intent upon each other at first, so intent upon expressing ourselves to each other, and getting at each other, that we troubled very little about the appearance of our relationship. We met almost openly. . . . We talked of ten thousand things, and of ourselves. We loved. We made love. There is no prose of mine that can tell of hours transfigured. The facts are nothing. Everything we touched, the meanest things, became glorious. How can I render bare tenderness and delight and mutual possession ?

I sit here at my desk thinking of untellable things.

I have come to know so much of love that I know now what love might be. We loved, scarred and stained ; we parted—basely and inevitably, but at least I met love.

I remember as we sat in a Canadian canoe, in a reedy, bush-masked shallow we had discovered opening out of that pine-shaded Woking canal, how she fell talking of the things that happened to her before she met me again. . . .

She told me things, and they so joined and welded together other things that lay disconnected in my memory, that it seemed to me I had always known what she told me. And yet indeed I had not known nor suspected it, save perhaps for a luminous, transitory suspicion ever and again.

She made me see how life had shaped her. She told me of her girlhood after I had known her. " We were poor and pretending and managing. We hacked about on visits and things. I ought to have married. The chances I had weren't particularly good chances. I didn't like 'em."

She paused. " Then Carnaby came along."

I remained quite still. She spoke now with downcast eyes, and one finger just touching the water.

" One gets bored, bored beyond redemption. One goes about to these huge expensive houses. I suppose—the scale's immense. One makes one's self useful to the other women, and agreeable to the men. One has to dress. . . . One has food and exercise and leisure. It's the leisure, and the space, and the blank opportunity it seems a sin not to fill. Carnaby isn't like the other men. He's bigger. . . . They go about making love. Everybody's making love. I did. . . . And I don't do things by halves."

She stopped.

" You knew ? " she asked, looking up, quite steadily.

I nodded.

" Since when ? "

" Those last days. . . . It hasn't seemed to matter really. I was a little surprised——"

She looked at me quietly. " Cothope knew," she said. " By instinct. I could feel it."

" I suppose," I began, " once, this would have mattered immensely. Now——"

" Nothing matters," she said, completing me. " I felt I had to tell you. I wanted you to understand why I didn't marry you—with both hands. I have loved you "—she paused—" have loved you ever since the day I kissed you in the bracken. Only—I forgot."

And suddenly she dropped her face upon her hands, and sobbed passionately—

"I forgot—I forgot," she cried, and became still. . . .

I dabbed my paddle in the water. "Look here!" I said; "forget again! Here am I—a ruined man. Marry me."

She shook her head without looking up.

We were still for a long time. "Marry me," I whispered.

She looked up, twined back a wisp of hair, and answered dispassionately—

"I wish I could. Anyhow, we have had this time. It has been a fine time—has it been—for you also? I haven't grudged you all I had to give. It's a poor gift—except for what it means and might have been. But we are near the end of it now."

"Why?" I asked. "Marry me! Why should we two——"

"You think," she said, "I could take courage and come to you and be your everyday wife—while you work and are poor?"

"Why not?" said I.

She looked at me gravely, with extended finger. "Do you really think that?—of me? Haven't you seen me—all?"

I hesitated.

"Never once have I really meant marrying you," she insisted. "Never once. I fell in love with you from the first. But when you seemed a successful man, I told myself I wouldn't. I was love-sick for you, and you were so stupid, I came near it then. But I knew I wasn't good enough. What could I have been to you? A woman with bad habits and bad associations, a woman smirched. And what could I do for you or be to you? If I wasn't good enough to be a rich man's wife I'm certainly not good enough to be a poor one's. Forgive me for talking sense to you now, but I wanted to tell you this somewhen——"

She stopped at my gesture. I sat up, and the canoe rocked with my movement.

"I don't care," I said. "I want to marry you and make you my wife!"

"No," she said, "don't spoil things. That is impossible!"

"Impossible!"

"Think! I can't do my own hair! Do you mean you will get me a maid?"

"Good God!" I cried, disconcerted beyond measure, "won't you learn to do your own hair for me? Do you mean to say you can love a man——"

She flung out her hands at me. "Don't spoil it," she cried. "I have given you all I have, I have given you all I can. If I could do it, if I was good enough to do it, I would. But I am a woman spoiled and ruined, dear, and you are a ruined man. When we are making love we are lovers—but think of the gulf between us in habits and ways of thought, in will and training, when we are not making love. Think of it—and don't think of it ! Don't think of it yet. We have snatched some hours. We still may have some hours ! "

She suddenly knelt forward toward me, with a glowing darkness in her eyes. "Who cares if it upsets ? " she cried. " If you say another word I will kiss you. And go to the bottom clutching you. I'm not afraid of that. I'm not a bit afraid of that. I'll die with you. Choose a death, and I'll die with you—readily. Do listen to me ! I love you. I shall always love you. It's because I love you that I won't go down to become a dirty familiar thing with you amidst the grime. I've given all I can. I've had all I can. . . . Tell me," and she crept nearer, " have I been like the dusk to you, like the warm dusk ? Is there magic still ? Listen to the ripple of water from your paddle. Look at the warm evening light in the sky. Who cares if the canoe upsets ? Come nearer to me. Oh, my love ! come near ! So."

She drew me to her and our lips met.

§ 3

I asked her to marry me once again.

It was our last morning together, and we had met very early, about sunrise, knowing that we were to part. No sun shone that day. The sky was overcast, the morning chilly, and lit by a clear, cold spiritless light. A heavy dampness in the air verged close on rain. When I think of that morning, it has always the quality of greying ashes wet with rain.

Beatrice too had changed. The spring had gone out of her movement ; it came to me, for the first time, that some day she might grow old. She had become one flesh with the rest of common humanity ; the softness had gone from her voice and manner, the dusky magic of her presence had gone. I saw these things with perfect clearness, and they made me sorry for them and for her. But they altered my love not a whit, abated it nothing. And when we had talked awkwardly for half a dozen sentences, I came dully to my point.

" And now," I cried, " will you marry me ? "

" No," she said, " I shall keep to my life here."

I asked her to marry me in a year's time. She shook her head.

" This world is a soft world," I said, " in spite of my present disasters. I know now how to do things. If I had you to work for—in a year I could be a prosperous man——"

" No," she said, " I will put it brutally, I shall go back to Carnaby."

" But——! " I did not feel angry. I had no sort of jealousy, no wounded pride, no sense of injury. I had only a sense of grey desolation, of hopeless cross-purposes.

" Look here," she said.   " I have been awake all night and
every night.   I have been thinking of this—every moment
when we have not been together.   I'm not answering you on
an impulse.   I love you.   I love you.   I'll say that over
ten thousand times.   But here we are——"

" The rest of life together," I said.

" It wouldn't be together.   Now we are together.   Now
we have been together.   We are full of memories.   I do not
feel I can ever forget a single one."

" Nor I."

" And I want to close it and leave it at that.   You see,
dear, what else is there to do ? "

She turned her white face to me.   " All I know of love, all
I have ever dreamed or learned of love I have packed into
these days for you.   You think we might live together and go
on loving.   No !   For you I will have no vain repetitions.
You have had the best and all of me.   Would you have us,
after this, meet again in London or Paris or somewhere, scuffle
to some wretched dressmaker's, meet in a *cabinet particulier ?* "

" No," I said.   " I want you to marry me.   I want you
to play the game of life with me as an honest woman should.
Come and live with me.   Be my wife and squaw.   Bear me
children."

I looked at her white, drawn face, and it seemed to me I
might carry her yet.   I spluttered for words.

" My God !   Beatrice ! " I cried ;   " but this is cowardice
and folly !   Are *you* afraid of life ?   You of all people !   What
does it matter what has been or what we were ?   Here we are
with the world before us !   Start clean and new with me.
We'll fight it through !   I'm not such a simple lover that I'll
not tell you plainly when you go wrong, and fight our difference out with you.   It's the one thing I want, the one thing I
need—to have you, and more of you and more !   This love-
making—it's love-making.   It's just a part of us, an incident——"

She shook her head and stopped me abruptly.   "It's all,"
she said.

" All ! " I protested.

" I'm wiser than you.   Wiser beyond words."   She turned
her eyes to me and they shone with tears.

" I wouldn't have you say anything—but what you're
saying," she said.   " But it's nonsense, dear.   You know it's
nonsense as you say it."

I tried to keep up the heroic note, but she would not listen
to it.

" It's no good," she cried almost petulantly.   " This little
world has made—made us what we are.   Don't you see—
don't you see what I am ?   I can make love.   I can make
love and be loved, prettily.   Dear, don't blame me !   I have
given you all I have.   If I had anything more——   I have

gone through it all over and over again—thought it out. This morning my head aches, my eyes ache. The light has gone out of me and I am a sick and tired woman. But I'm talking wisdom—bitter wisdom. I couldn't be any sort of helper to you, any sort of wife, any sort of mother. I'm spoiled. I'm spoiled by this rich idle way of living, until every habit is wrong, every taste wrong. The world is wrong. People can be ruined by wealth just as much as by poverty. Do you think I wouldn't face life with you if I could, if I wasn't absolutely certain I should be down and dragging in the first half-mile of the journey ? Here I am—damned ! Damned ! But I won't damn you. You know what I am ! You know. You are too clear and simple not to know the truth. You try to romance and hector, but you know the truth. I am a little cad—sold and done. I'm—— My dear, you think I've been misbehaving, but all these days I've been on my best behaviour. . . . You don't understand, because you're a man. A woman, when she's spoiled, is *spoiled*. She's dirty in grain. She's done."

She walked on weeping.

" You're a fool to want me," she said. " You're a fool to want me—for my sake just as much as yours. We've done all we can. It's just romancing——"

She dashed the tears from her eyes and turned upon me. " Don't you understand ? " she challenged. " Don't you know ? "

We faced one another in silence for a moment.

" Yes," I said, " I know."

For a long time we spoke never a word, but talked on together, slowly and sorrowfully, reluctant to turn about towards our parting. When at last we did, she broke silence again.

" I've had you," she said.

" Heaven and hell," I said, " can't alter that."

" I've wanted——" she went on. " I've talked to you in the nights and made up speeches. Now when I want to make them I'm tongue-tied. But to me it's just as if the moments we have had lasted for ever. Moods and states come and go. To-day my light is out. . . ."

To this day I cannot determine whether she said or whether I imagined she said " chloral." Perhaps a half-conscious diagnosis flashed it on my brain. Perhaps I am the victim of some perverse imaginative freak of memory, some hinted possibility that scratched and seared. There the word stands in my memory, as if it were written in fire.

We came to the door of Lady Osprey's garden at last, and it was beginning to drizzle.

She held out her hands and I took them.

" Yours," she said, in a weary unimpassioned voice ; " all that I had—such as it was. Will you forget ? "

" Never," I answered.

" Never a touch or a word of it ? "

" No."

" You will," she said.

We looked at one another in silence, and her face was full of
fatigue and misery.

What could I do ?   What was there to do ?

" I wish——" I said, and stopped.

" Good-bye."

§ 4

That should have been the last I saw of her, but, indeed, I
was destined to see her once again. Two days after I was
at Lady Grove, I forget altogether upon what errand, and as I
walked back to the station believing her to be gone away, she
came upon me, and she was riding with Carnaby, just as I had
seen them first. The encounter jumped upon us unprepared.
She rode by, her eyes dark in her white face, and scarcely
noticed me. She winced and grew stiff at the sight of me and
bowed her head. But Carnaby, because he thought I was a
broken and discomfited man, saluted me with an easy friendliness, and shouted some genial commonplace to me.

They passed out of sight and left me by the roadside. . . .

And then indeed I tasted the ultimate bitterness of life.
For the first time I felt utter futility, and was wrung by
emotion that begot no action, by shame and pity beyond
words. I had parted from her dully and I had seen my uncle
break and die with dry eyes and a steady mind, but this chance
sight of my lost Beatrice brought me to tears. My face was
wrung, and tears came pouring down my cheeks. All the
magic she had for me had changed to wild sorrow. " Oh
God ! " I cried, " this is too much," and turned my face after
her and made appealing gestures to the beech trees and cursed
at fate. I wanted to do preposterous things, to pursue her,
to save her, to turn life back so that she might begin again.
I wonder what would have happened had I overtaken them
in pursuit, breathless with running, uttering incoherent words,
weeping, expostulatory ?   I came near to doing that.

There was nothing in earth or heaven to respect my curses
or weeping.   In the midst of it a man who had been trimming
the opposite hedge appeared and stared at me.

Abruptly, ridiculously, I dissembled before him and went
on and caught my train. . . .

But the pain I felt then I have felt a hundred times ; it is
with me as I write. It haunts this book, I see ; that is what
haunts this book, from end to end. . . .

CHAPTER THREE

NIGHT AND THE OPEN SEA

§ 1

I HAVE tried throughout all this story to tell things as they
happened to me. In the beginning—the sheets are still
here on the table, grimy and dogs-eared and old-looking—
I said I wanted to tell *myself* and the world in which I found
myself, and I have done my best. But whether I have succeeded I cannot imagine. All this writing is grey now and
dead and trite and unmeaning to me ; some of it I know by
heart. I am the last person to judge it.

As I turn over the big pile of manuscript before me, certain
things become clearer to me, and particularly the immense
inconsequence of my experiences. It is, I see now that I have
it all before me, a story of activity and urgency and sterility.
I have called it *Tono-Bungay*, but I had far better have called
it *Waste*. I have told of childless Marion, of my childless
aunt, of Beatrice wasted and wasteful and futile. What
hope is there for a people whose women become fruitless ?
I think of all the energy I have given to vain things. I think
of my industrious scheming with my uncle, of Crest Hill's
vast cessation, of his resonant strenuous career. Ten thousand
men have envied him, and wished to live as he lived. It is
all one spectacle of forces running to waste, of people who
use and do not replace, the story of a country hectic with a
wasting aimless fever of trade and money-making and pleasure-
seeking. And now I build destroyers !

Other people may see this country in other terms ; this is
how I have seen it. In some early chapter in this heap I
compared all our present colour and abundance to October
foliage before the frosts nip down the leaves. That I still
feel was a good image. Perhaps I see wrongly. It may be I
see decay all about me because I am, in a sense, decay. To
others it may be a scene of achievement and construction
radiant with hope. I too have a sort of hope, but it is a
remote hope, a hope that finds no promise in this Empire
or in any of the great things of our time. How they will look
in history I do not know, how time and chance will prove
them I cannot guess ; that is how they have mirrored themselves on one contemporary mind.

§ 2

Concurrently with writing the last chapter of this book
I have been much engaged by the affairs of a new destroyer
we have completed. It has been an oddly complementary

alternation of occupations. Three weeks or so ago this novel had to be put aside in order that I might give all my time day and night to the fitting and finishing of the engines. Last Thursday X2, for so we call her, was done, and I took her down the Thames, and went out nearly to Texel for a trial of speed.

It is curious how at times one's impressions will all fuse and run together into a sort of unity and become continuous with things that have hitherto been utterly alien and remote. That rush down the river became mysteriously connected with this book. As I passed down the Thames I seemed in a new and parallel manner to be passing all England in review. I saw it then as I had wanted my readers to see it. The thought came to me slowly as I picked my way through the Pool; it stood out clear as I went dreaming into the night out upon the wide North Sea. . . .

It wasn't so much thinking at the time as a sort of photographic thought that came and grew clear. X2 went ripping through the dirty oily water as scissors rip through canvas, and the front of my mind was all intent with getting her through under the bridges and in and out among the steamboats and barges and rowing-boats and piers. I lived with my hands and eyes hard ahead. I thought nothing then of any appearances but obstacles, but for all that the back of my mind took the photographic memory of it complete and vivid. . . .

"This," it came to me, "is England. This is what I wanted to give in my book. This!"

We started in the late afternoon. We throbbed out of our yard above Hammersmith Bridge, fussed about for a moment, and headed down stream. We came at an easy rush down Craven Reach, past Fulham and Hurlingham, past the long stretches of muddy meadow and muddy suburb to Battersea and Chelsea, round the cape of tidy frontage that is Grosvenor Road and under Vauxhall Bridge, and Westminster opened before us. We cleared a string of coal barges, and there on the left in the October sunshine stood the Parliament houses and the flag was flying and Parliament was sitting. . . .

I saw it at the time unseeingly; afterwards it came into my mind as the centre of the whole broad panoramic effect of that afternoon. The stiff square lace of Victorian Gothic with its Dutch clock of a tower came upon me suddenly and stared and whirled past in a slow half pirouette and became still, I know, behind me as if watching me recede. "Aren't you going to respect me, then?" it seemed to say.

Not I! There in that great pile of Victorian architecture the landlords and the lawyers, the bishops, the railway men and the magnates of commerce go to and fro—in their incurable tradition of commercialised Bladesovery, of meretricious gentry and nobility sold for riches. I have been near enough

to know. The Irish and the Labour men run about among
their feet, making a fuss, effecting little ; they've got no
better plans that I can see. Respect it indeed ! There's
a certain paraphernalia of dignity, but whom does it deceive ?
The King comes down in a gilt coach to open the show and
wears long robes and a crown ; and there's a display of stout
and slender legs in white stockings and stout and slender legs
in black stockings and artful old gentlemen in ermine. I was
reminded of one congested afternoon I had spent with my
aunt amidst a cluster of agitated women's hats in the Royal
Gallery of the House of Lords and how I saw the King going to
open Parliament, and the Duke of Devonshire looking like a
gorgeous pedlar and terribly bored with the cap of maintenance on a tray before him hung by slings from his shoulders.
A wonderful spectacle ! . . .

It is quaint, no doubt, this England—it is even dignified
in places—and full of mellow associations. That does not
alter the quality of the realities these robes conceal. The
realities are greedy trade, base profit-seeking, bold advertisement—and kingship and chivalry, spite of this wearing of
treasured robes, are as dead among it all as that crusader my
uncle championed against the nettles outside the Duffield
church. . . .

I have thought much of that bright afternoon's panorama.

To run down the Thames so is to run one's hand over the
pages in the book of England from end to end. One begins
in Craven Reach and it is as if one were in the heart of old
England. Behind us are Kew and Hampton Court with their
memories of Kings and Cardinals, and one runs at first between
Fulham's episcopal garden parties and Hurlingham's playground for the sporting instinct of our race. The whole effect
is English. There is space, there are old trees and all the best
qualities of the home-land in that upper reach. Putney too,
looks Anglican on a dwindling scale. And then for a stretch
the newer developments slop over, one misses Bladesover and
there come first squalid stretches of mean homes right and
left and then the dingy industrialism of the south side, and
on the north bank the polite long front of nice houses, artistic,
literary, administrative people's residences, that stretches
from Cheyne Walk nearly to Westminster and hides a wilderness of slums. What a long slow crescendo that is, mile after
mile, with the houses crowding closelier, the multiplying
succession of church towers, the architectural moments, the
successive bridges, until you come out into the second movement of the piece with Lambeth's old palace under your
quarter and the houses of Parliament on your bow ! Westminster Bridge is ahead of you then and through it you flash,
and in a moment the round-faced clock tower cranes up to peer
at you again and New Scotland Yard squares at you, a fat
beef-eater of a policeman disguised miraculously as a Bastille.

For a stretch you have the essential London ; you have Charing Cross railway station, heart of the world, and the Embankment on the north side with its new hotels overshadowing its Georgian and Victorian architecture, and mud and great warehouses and factories, chimneys, shot towers, advertisements on the south. The northward skyline grows more intricate and pleasing, and more and more does one thank God for Wren. Somerset House is as picturesque as the civil war, one is reminded again of the original England, one feels in the fretted sky the quality of Restoration lace.

And then comes Astor's strong box and the lawyers' Inns. . . .

(I had a passing memory of myself there, how once I had trudged along the Embankment westward, weighing my uncle's offer of three hundred pounds a year. . . .)

Through that central essential London reach I drove, and X2 bored her nose under the foam regardless of it all like a black hound going through reeds—on what trail even I who made her cannot tell.

And in this reach too, one first meets the seagulls and is reminded of the sea. Blackfriars one takes—just under these two bridges and just between them is the finest bridge moment in the world—and behold, soaring up, hanging in the sky over a rude tumult of warehouses, over a jostling competition of traders, irrelevantly beautiful and altogether remote, Saint Paul's ! " Of course ! " one says, " Saint Paul's ! " It is the very figure of whatever fineness the old Anglican culture achieved, detached, a more dignified and chastened Saint Peter's, colder, greyer but still ornate, it has never been overthrown, never disavowed, only the tall warehouses and all the roar of traffic have forgotten it, every one has forgotten it ; the steamships, the barges, go heedlessly by regardless of it, intricacies of telephone wires and poles cut blackly into its thin mysteries and presently, when in a moment the traffic permits you and you look round for it, it has dissolved like a cloud into the grey-blues of the London sky.

And then the traditional and ostensible England falls from you altogether. The third movement begins, the last great movement in the London symphony, in which the trim scheme of the old order is altogether dwarfed and swallowed up. Comes London Bridge, and the great warehouses tower up about you waving stupendous cranes, the gulls circle and scream in your ears, large ships lie among their lighters, and one is in the port of the world. Again and again in this book I have written of England as a feudal scheme overtaken by fatty degeneration and stupendous accidents of hypertrophy. For the last time I must strike that note as the memory of the dear neat little sunlit ancient Tower of London lying away in a gap among the warehouses comes back to me, that little accumulation of buildings so provincially pleasant and digni-

fied, overshadowed by the vulgarest, most typical exploit of
modern England, the sham Gothic casings to the ironwork of
the Tower Bridge. That Tower Bridge is the very balance
and confirmation of Westminster's dull pinnacles and tower.
That sham Gothic bridge ; in the very gates of our mother of
change, the Sea !

But after that one is in a world of accident and nature.
For the third part of the panorama of London is beyond all
law, order, and precedence, it is the seaport and the sea.   One
goes down the widening reaches through a monstrous variety
of shipping, great steamers, great sailing-ships, trailing the
flags of all the world, a monstrous confusion of lighters,
witches' conferences of brown-sailed barges, wallowing tugs,
a tumultuous crowding and jostling of cranes and spars,
and wharves and stores, and assertive inscriptions.   Huge
vistas of dock open right and left of one, and here and there
beyond and amidst it all are church towers, little patches of
indescribably old-fashioned and worn-out houses, riverside
pubs and the like, vestiges of townships that were long since
torn to fragments and submerged in these new growths.   And
amidst it all no plan appears, no intention, no comprehensive
desire.   That is the very key of it all.   Each day one feels
that the pressure of commerce and traffic grew, grew insensibly
monstrous, and first this man made a wharf and that erected
a crane, and then this company set to work and then that,
and so they jostled together to make this unassimilable
enormity of traffic.   Through it we dodged and drove, eager
for the high seas.

I remember how I laughed aloud at the glimpse of the name
of a London County Council steamboat that ran across me.
Caxton it was called, and another was *Pepys* and another was
Shakespeare.   They seemed so wildly out of place, splashing
about in that confusion.   One wanted to take them out and
wipe them and put them back in some English gentleman's
library.   Everything was alive about them, flashing, splashing,
and passing, ships moving, tugs panting, hawsers taut, barges
going down with men toiling at the sweeps, the water all a-
swirl with the wash of shipping scaling into millions of little
wavelets, curling and frothing under the whip of the unceasing
wind.   Past it all we drove.   And at Greenwich to the south,
you know, there stands a fine stone frontage where all the
victories are recorded in a Painted Hall, and beside it is the
" Ship " where once upon a time those gentlemen of Westminster used to have an annual dinner—before the port of
London got too much for them altogether.   The old façade
of the Hospital was just warming to the sunset as we went
by, and after that, right and left, the river opened, the sense of
the sea increased and prevailed reach after reach from North-
fleet to the Nore.

And out you come at last with the sun behind you into the

eastern sea.   You speed up and tear the oily water louder and
faster, sirroo, sirroo—swish—sirroo, and the hills of Kent—
over which I once fled from the Christian teachings of Nicodemus Frapp—fall away on the right hand and Essex on the
left.   They fall away and vanish into blue haze ; and the tall
slow ships behind the tugs, scarce moving ships and wallowing sturdy tugs, are all wrought of wet gold as one goes frothing
by.   They stand out bound on strange missions of life and
death, to the killing of men in unfamiliar lands.   And now
behind us is blue mystery and the phantom flash of unseen
lights, and presently even these are gone, and I and my
destroyer tear out to the unknown across a great grey space.
We tear into the great spaces of the future and the turbines
fall to talking in unfamiliar tongues.   Out to the open we go,
to windy freedom and trackless ways.   Light after light goes
down.   England and the Kingdom, Britain and the Empire,
the old prides and the old devotions, glide abeam, astern, sink
down upon the horizon, pass—pass.   The river passes—London
passes, England passes. . . .

§ 3

This is the note I have tried to emphasise, the note that
sounds clear in my mind when I think of anything beyond the
purely personal aspects of my story.
It is a note of crumbling and confusion, of change and
seemingly aimless swelling, of a bubbling up and medley of
futile loves and sorrows.   But through the confusion sounds
another note.   Through the confusion something drives,
something that is at once human achievement and the most
inhuman of all existing things.   Something comes out of
it. . . .   How can I express the values of a thing at once so
essential and so immaterial ?   It is something that calls upon
such men as I with an irresistible appeal.
I have figured it in my last section by the symbol of my
destroyer, stark and swift, irrelevant to most human interests.
Sometimes I call this reality Science, sometimes I call it
Truth.   But it is something we draw by pain and effort out of
the heart of life, that we disentangle and make clear.   Other
men serve it, I know, in art, in literature, in social invention,
and see it in a thousand different figures, under a hundred
names.   I see it always as austerity, as beauty.   This thing
we make clear is the heart of life.   It is the one enduring
thing.   Men and nations, epochs and civilisations pass, each
making its contribution.   I do not know what it is, this something, except that it is supreme.   It is a something, a quality,
an element, one may find now in colours, now in forms, now
in sounds, now in thoughts.   It emerges from life with each
year one lives and feels, and generation by generation and age

by age, but the how and why of it are all beyond the compass of my mind. . . .

Yet the full sense of it was with me all that night as I drove, lonely above the rush and murmur of my engines, out upon the weltering circle of the sea. . . .

Far out to the north-east there came the flicker of a squadron of warships waving white swords of light about the sky. I kept them hull-down, and presently they were mere summer lightning over the watery edge of the globe. . . . I fell into thought that was nearly formless, into doubts and dreams that have no words, and it seemed good to me to drive ahead and on and on through the windy starlight, over the long black waves.

§ 4

It was morning and day before I returned with the four sick and starving journalists who had got permission to come with me, up the shining river, and past the old grey Tower. . . .

I recall the back views of those journalists very distinctly, going with a certain damp weariness of movement along a side street away from the river. They were good men and bore me no malice, and they served me up to the public in turgid degenerate Kiplingese, as a modest button on the complacent stomach of the Empire. Though as a matter of fact, X2 isn't intended for the Empire, or indeed for the hands of any European power. We offered it to our own people first, but they would have nothing to do with me, and I have long since ceased to trouble much about such questions. I have come to see myself from the outside, my country from the outside—without illusions. We make and pass.

We are all things that make and pass, striving upon a hidden mission, out to the open sea.

END OF BOOK IV

A MODERN UTOPIA

A NOTE TO THE READER

THIS book is in all probability the last of a series of writings, of which—disregarding certain earlier disconnected essays—my *Anticipations* was the beginning. Originally I intended *Anticipations* to be my sole digression from my art or trade (or what you will) of an imaginative writer. I wrote that book in order to clear up the muddle in my own mind about innumerable social and political questions, questions I could not keep out of my work, which it distressed me to touch upon in a stupid haphazard way, and which no one, so far as I knew, had handled in a manner to satisfy my needs. But *Anticipations* did not achieve its end. I have a slow constructive hesitating sort of mind, and when I emerged from that undertaking I found I had still most of my questions to state and solve. In *Mankind in the Making*, therefore, I tried to review the social organisation in a different way, to consider it as an educational process instead of dealing with it as a thing with a future history, and if I made this second book even less satisfactory from a literary standpoint than the former (and this is my opinion), I blundered, I think, more edifyingly—at least from the point of view of my own instruction. I ventured upon several themes with a greater frankness than I had used in *Anticipations*, and came out of that second effort guilty of much rash writing, but with a considerable development of formed opinion. In many matters I had shaped out at last a certain personal certitude, upon which I feel I shall go for the rest of my days. In this present book I have tried to settle accounts with a number of issues left over or opened up by its two predecessors, to correct them in some particulars, and to give the general picture of a *Utopia* that has grown up in my mind during the course of these speculations as a state of affairs at once possible and more desirable than the world in which I live. But this book has brought me back to imaginative writing again. In its two predecessors the treatment of social organisation had been purely objective ; here my intention has been a little wider and deeper, in that I have tried to present not simply an ideal, but an ideal in reaction with two personalities. Moreover, since this may be the last book of the kind I shall ever publish, I have written into it as well as I can the heretical metaphysical scepticism upon which all my thinking rests, and I have inserted certain sections reflecting upon the established methods of sociological and economic science. . . .

The last four words will not attract the butterfly reader, I know. I have done my best to make the whole of this book as lucid and entertaining as its matter permits, because I want it read by as many people as possible, but I do not promise anything but rage and confusion to him who proposes to glance through my pages just to see if I agree with him, or to begin in the middle, or to read without a constantly alert attention. If you are not already a little interested and open-minded with regard to social and political questions, and a little exercised in self-examination, you will find neither interest nor pleasure here. If your mind is " made up " upon such issues your time will be wasted on these pages. And even if you are a willing reader you may require a little patience for the peculiar method I have this time adopted.

That method assumes an air of haphazard, but it is not so careless as it seems. I believe it to be—even now that I am through with the book—the best way to a sort of lucid vagueness which has always been my intention in this matter. I tried over several beginnings of a Utopian book before I adopted this. I rejected from the outset the form of the argumentative essay, the form which appeals most readily to what is called the " serious " reader, the reader who is often no more than the solemnly impatient parasite of great questions. He likes everything in hard, heavy lines, black and white, yes and no, because he does not understand how much there is that cannot be presented at all in that way ; wherever there is any effect of obliquity, of incommensurables, wherever there is any levity or humour or difficulty of multiplex presentation, he refuses attention. Mentally he seems to be built up upon an invincible assumption that the Spirit of Creation cannot count beyond two, he deals only in alternatives. Such readers I have resolved not to attempt to please here. Even if I presented all my tri-clinic crystals as systems of cubes——! Indeed I felt it would not be worth doing. But having rejected the " serious " essay as a form, I was still greatly exercised, I spent some vacillating months, over the scheme of this book. I tried first a recognised method of viewing questions from divergent points that has always attracted me and which I have never succeeded in using, the discussion novel, after the fashion of Peacock's (and Mr. Mallock's) development of the ancient dialogue ; but this encumbered me with unnecessary characters and the inevitable complications of intrigue among them, and I abandoned it. After that I tried to cast the thing into a shape resembling a little the double personality of Boswell's Johnson, a sort of interplay between monologue and commentator ; but that too, although it got nearer to the quality I sought, finally failed. Then I hesitated over what one might call " hard narrative." It will be evident to the experienced reader that by omitting certain speculative and metaphysical elements and by elaborating incident this book might have been reduced to a straightforward story. But I did not want to omit as much on this occasion. I do not see why I should always pander to the vulgar appetite for stark stories. And in short, I made it this. I explain all this in order to make it clear to the reader that, however queer this book appears at the first examination, it is the outcome of trial and deliberation, it is intended to be as it is. I am aiming throughout at a sort of shot-silk texture between philosophical discussion on the one hand and imaginative narrative on the other.

H. G. WELLS.

CONTENTS

Chapter   Page

		Page
	A NOTE TO THE READER	309
	THE OWNER OF THE VOICE	313
I.	TOPOGRAPHICAL	315
II.	CONCERNING FREEDOMS	327
III.	UTOPIAN ECONOMICS	346
IV.	THE VOICE OF NATURE	367
V.	FAILURE IN A MODERN UTOPIA	378
VI.	WOMEN IN A MODERN UTOPIA	397
VII.	A FEW UTOPIAN IMPRESSIONS	416
VIII.	MY UTOPIAN SELF	432
IX.	THE SAMURAI	437
X.	RACE IN UTOPIA	466
XI.	THE BUBBLE BURSTS	482
	APPENDIX. SCEPTICISM OF THE INSTRUMENT	494

THE OWNER OF THE VOICE

*T*HERE *are works, and this is one of them, that are best begun with a portrait of the author. And here, indeed, because of a very natural misunderstanding this is the only course to take. Throughout these papers sounds a note, a distinctive and personal note, a note that tends at times towards stridency ; and all that is not, as these words are, in Italics, is in one voice. Now, this Voice, and this is the peculiarity of the matter, is not to be taken as the Voice of the ostensible author who fathers these pages. You have to clear your mind of any preconceptions in that respect. The Owner of the Voice you must figure to yourself as a whitish plump man, a little under the middle size and age, with such blue eyes as many Irishmen have, and agile in his movements and with a slight tonsorial baldness—a penny might cover it—of the crown. His front is convex. He droops at times like most of us, but for the greater part he bears himself as valiantly as a sparrow. Occasionally his hand flies out with a fluttering gesture of illustration. And his voice (which is our medium henceforth) is an unattractive tenor that becomes at times aggressive. Him you must imagine as sitting at a table reading a manuscript about Utopias, a manuscript he holds in two hands that are just a little fat at the wrist. The curtain rises upon him so. But afterwards, if the devices of this declining art of literature prevail, you will go with him through curious and interesting experiences. Yet, ever and again, you will find him back at that little table, the manuscript in his hand, and the expansion of his ratiocinations about Utopia conscientiously resumed. The entertainment before you is neither the set drama of the work of fiction you are accustomed to read, nor the set lecturing of the essay you are accustomed to evade, but a hybrid of these two. If you figure this owner of the Voice as sitting, a little nervously, a little modestly, on a stage, with table, glass of water and all complete, and myself as the intrusive chairman insisting with a bland ruthlessness upon his " few words " of introduction before he recedes into the wings, and if furthermore you figure a sheet behind our friend on which moving pictures intermittently appear, and if finally you suppose his subject to be the story of the adventure of his soul among Utopian inquiries, you will be prepared for some at least of the difficulties of this unworthy but unusual work.*

But over against this writer here presented, there is also another earthly person in the book, who gathers himself together into a distinct personality only after a preliminary complication with the reader. This person is spoken of as the botanist, and he is a leaner, rather taller, graver and much less garrulous man. His face is weakly handsome and done in tones of grey, he is fairish and grey-eyed, and you would suspect him of dyspepsia. It is a justifiable suspicion. Men of this type, the chairman remarks with a sudden intrusion of exposition, are romantic with a shadow of meanness, they seek at once to conceal and shape their sensuous cravings beneath egregious sentimentalities, they get into mighty tangles and troubles with women, and he has had his troubles. You will hear of them, for that is the quality of his type. He gets no personal expression in this book, the Voice is always that other's, but you gather much of the matter and something of the manner of his interpolations from the asides and the tenour of the Voice.

So much by way of portraiture is necessary to present the explorers of the Modern Utopia, which will unfold itself as a background to these two inquiring figures. The image of a cinematograph entertainment is the one to grasp. There will be an effect of these two people going to and fro in front of the circle of a rather defective lantern, which sometimes jams and sometimes gets out of focus, but which does occasionally succeed in displaying on a screen a momentary moving picture of Utopian conditions. Occasionally the picture goes out altogether, the Voice argues and argues, and the footlights return, and then you find yourself listening again to the rather too plump little man at his table laboriously enunciating propositions, upon whom the curtain rises now.

CHAPTER ONE

§ 1

THE Utopia of a modern dreamer must needs differ in one fundamental aspect from the Nowheres and Utopias men planned before Darwin quickened the thought of the world. Those were all perfect and static States, a balance of happiness won for ever against the forces of unrest and disorder that inhere in things. One beheld a healthy and simple generation enjoying the fruits of the earth in an atmosphere of virtue and happiness, to be followed by other virtuous, happy, and entirely similar generations, until the Gods grew weary. Change and development were dammed back by invincible dams for ever. But the Modern Utopia must be not static but kinetic, must shape not as a permanent state but as a hopeful stage, leading to a long ascent of stages. Nowadays we do not resist and overcome the great stream of things, but rather float upon it. We build now not citadels, but ships of state. For one ordered arrangement of citizens rejoicing in an equality of happiness safe and assured to them and their children for ever, we have to plan " a flexible common compromise, in which a perpetually novel succession of individualities may converge most effectually upon a comprehensive onward development." That is the first, most generalised difference between a Utopia based upon modern conceptions and all the Utopias that were written in the former time.

Our business here is to be Utopian, to make vivid and creditable if we can, first this facet and then that, of an imaginary whole and happy world. Our deliberate intention is to be not, indeed, impossible, but most distinctly impracticable, by every scale that reaches only between to-day and to-morrow. We are to turn our backs for a space upon the insistent examination of the thing that is, and face towards the freer air, the ampler spaces of the thing that perhaps might be, to the projection of a State or city " worth while," to designing upon the sheet of our imaginations the picture of a life conceivably possible, and yet better worth living than our own. That is our present enterprise. We are going to lay down certain necessary starting propositions, and then we shall proceed to explore the sort of world these propositions give us. . . .

It is no doubt an optimistic enterprise. But it is good for awhile to be free from the carping note that must needs be audible when we discuss our present imperfections, to release ourselves from practical difficulties and the tangle of ways and means. It is good to stop by the track for a space, put

aside the knapsack, wipe the brows, and talk a little of the
upper slopes of the mountain we think we are climbing, would
but the trees let us see it.

There is to be no inquiry here of policy and method. This
is to be a holiday from politics and movements and methods.
But for all that, we must needs define certain limitations.
Were we free to have our untrammelled desire, I suppose we
should follow Morris to his Nowhere, we should change the
nature of man and the nature of things together ; we should
make the whole race wise, tolerant, noble, perfect—wave our
hands to a splendid anarchy, every man doing as it pleases
him, and none pleased to do evil, in a world as good in its
essential nature, as ripe and sunny, as the world before the
Fall. But that golden age, that perfect world, comes out
into the possibilities of space and time. In space and time
the pervading Will to Live sustains for evermore a perpetuity
of aggressions. Our proposal here is upon a more practical
plane at least than that. We are to restrict ourselves first to
the limitations of human possibility as we know them in the
men and women of this world to-day, and then to all the inhumanity, all the insubordination of nature. We are to shape
our state in a world of uncertain seasons, sudden catastrophes,
antagonistic diseases, and inimical beasts and vermin, out of
men and women with like passions, like uncertainties of mood
and desire to our own. And, moreover, we are going to accept
this world of conflict, to adopt no attitude of renunciation towards it, to face it in no ascetic spirit, but in the mood of the
Western peoples, whose purpose is to survive and overcome.
So much we adopt in common with those who deal not in
Utopias, but in the world of Here and Now.

Certain liberties, however, following the best Utopian
precedents, we may take with existing fact. We assume that
the tone of public thought may be entirely different from what
it is in the present world. We permit ourselves a free hand
with the mental conflict of life, within the possibilities of the
human mind as we know it. We permit ourselves also a free
hand with all the apparatus of existence that man has, so to
speak, made for himself, with houses, roads, clothing, canals,
machinery, with laws, boundaries, conventions and traditions,
with schools, with literature and religious organization,
with creeds and customs, with everything, in fact, that it lies
within man's power to alter. That, indeed, is the cardinal
assumption of all Utopian speculations old and new ; the
Republic and Laws of Plato, and More's Utopia, Howells'
implicit Altruria, and Bellamy's future Boston, Comte's great
Western Republic, Hertzka's Freeland, Cabet's Icaria, and
Campanella's City of the Sun, are built, just as we shall build,
upon that, upon the hypothesis of the complete emancipation
of a community of men from tradition, from habits, from legal
bonds, and that subtler servitude possessions entail. And

much of the essential value of all such speculations lies in this assumption of emancipation, lies in that regard towards human freedom, in the undying interest of the human power of self-escape, the power to resist the causation of the past, and to evade, initiate, endeavour, and overcome.

§ 2

There are very definite artistic limitations also.

There must always be a certain effect of hardness and thinness about Utopian speculations. Their common fault is to be comprehensively jejune. That which is the blood and warmth and reality of life is largely absent ; there are no individualities, but only generalised people. In almost every Utopia—except, perhaps, Morris's *News from Nowhere*—one sees handsome but characterless buildings, symmetrical and perfect cultivations, and a multitude of people, healthy, happy, beautifully dressed, but without any personal distinction whatever. Too often the prospect resembles the key to one of those large pictures of coronations, royal weddings, parliaments, conferences, and gatherings so popular in Victorian times, in which, instead of a face, each figure bears a neat oval with its index number legibly inscribed. This burthens us with an incurable effect of unreality, and I do not see how it is altogether to be escaped. It is a disadvantage that has to be accepted. Whatever institution has existed or exists, however irrational, however preposterous, has, by virtue of its contact with individualities, an effect of realness and rightness no untried thing may share. It has ripened, it has been christened with blood, it has been stained and mellowed by handling, it has been rounded and dented to the softened contours that we associate with life ; it has been salted, maybe, in a brine of tears. But the thing that is merely proposed, the thing that is merely suggested, however rational, however necessary, seems strange and inhuman in its clear, hard, uncompromising lines, its unqualified angles and surfaces.

There is no help for it, there it is ! The Master suffers with the last and least of his successors. For all the humanity he wins to, through his dramatic device of dialogue, I doubt if any one has ever been warmed to desire himself a citizen in the Republic of Plato ; I doubt if any one could stand a month of the relentless publicity of virtue planned by More. . . . No one wants to live in any community of intercourse really, save for the sake of the individualities he would meet there. The fertilising conflict of individualities is the ultimate meaning of the personal life, and all our Utopias no more than schemes for bettering that interplay. At least, that is how life shapes itself more and more to modern perceptions. Until you bring in individualities, nothing comes into being, and a Universe ceases when you shiver the mirror of the least of individual minds.

T.-B.—M.U.   L

§ 3

No less than a planet will serve the purpose of a modern
Utopia. Time was when a mountain valley or an island
seemed to promise sufficient isolation for a polity to maintain
itself intact from outward force ; the Republic of Plato stood
armed ready for defensive war, and the New Atlantis and the
Utopia of More in theory, like China and Japan through many
centuries of effectual practice, held themselves isolated from
intruders. Such late instances as Butler's satirical *Erewhon*,
and Mr. Stead's queendom of inverted sexual conditions
in Central Africa, found the Tibetan method of slaughtering
the inquiring visitor a simple, sufficient rule. But the whole
trend of modern thought is against the permanence of any
such enclosures. We are acutely aware nowadays that, however subtly contrived a State may be, outside your boundary
lines the epidemic, the breeding barbarian or the economic
power, will gather its strength to overcome you. The swift
march of invention is all for the invader. Now, perhaps you
might still guard a rocky coast or a narrow pass ; but what of
that near to-morrow when the flying machine soars overhead,
free to descend at this point or that ? A state powerful
enough to keep isolated under modern conditions would be
powerful enough to rule the world, would be, indeed, if not
actively ruling, yet passively acquiescent in all other human
organisations, and so responsible for them altogether. World-
state, therefore, it must be.

That leaves no room for a modern Utopia in Central Africa,
or in South America, or round about the pole, those last
refuges of ideality. The floating isle of *La Cité Morellyste*
no longer avails. We need a planet. Lord Erskine, the
author of a Utopia (" Armata ") that might have been inspired by Mr. Hewins, was the first of all Utopists to perceive
this—he joined his twin planets pole to pole by a sort of
umbilical cord. But the modern imagination, obsessed by
physics, must travel further than that.

Out beyond Sirius, far in the deeps of space, beyond the
flight of a cannon-ball flying for a billion years, beyond the
range of unaided vision, blazes the star that is *our* Utopia's
sun. To those who know where to look, with a good opera-
glass aiding good eyes, it and three fellows that seem in a
cluster with it—though they are incredible billions of miles
nearer—make just the faintest speck of light. About it go
planets, even as our planets, but weaving a different fate,
and in its place among them is Utopia, with its sister mate, the
Moon. It is a planet like our planet, the same continents,
the same islands, the same oceans and seas, another Fuji-
Yama is beautiful there dominating another Yokohama—and
another Matterhorn overlooks the icy disorder of another
Theodule. It is so like our planet that a terrestrial botanist

might find his every species there, even to the meanest pond-weed or the remotest Alpine blossom. . . .

Only when he had gathered that last and turned about to find his inn again, perhaps he would not find his inn !

Suppose now that two of us were actually to turn about in just that fashion. Two, I think, for to face a strange planet, even though it be a wholly civilised one, without some other familiar backing, dashes the courage overmuch. Suppose that we were indeed so translated even as we stood. You figure us upon some high pass in the Alps, and though I—being one easily made giddy by stooping—am no botanist myself, if my companion were to have a specimen tin under his arm—so long as it is not painted that abominable popular Swiss apple green—I would make it no occasion for quarrel ! We have tramped and botanised and come to a rest, and, sitting among rocks, we have eaten our lunch and finished our bottle of Yvorne, and fallen into a talk of Utopias, and said such things as I have been saying. I could figure it myself upon that little neck of the Lucendro Pass, upon the shoulder of the Piz Lucendro, for there once I lunched and talked very pleasantly, and we are looking down upon the Val Bedretto, and Villa and Fontana and Airolo try to hide from us under the mountain side—three-quarters of a mile they are vertically below. (*Lantern.*) With that absurd nearness of effect one gets in the Alps, we see the little train a dozen miles away, running down the Biaschina to Italy, and the Lukmanier Pass beyond Piora left of us, and the San Giacomo right, mere foot-paths under our feet. . . .

And behold ! in the twinkling of an eye we are in that other world !

We should scarcely note the change. Not a cloud would have gone from the sky. It might be the remote town below would take a different air, and my companion the botanist, with his educated observation, might almost see as much, and the train, perhaps, would be gone out of the picture, and the embanked straightness of the Ticino in the Ambri-Piotta meadows—that might be altered, but that would be all the visible change. Yet I have an idea that in some obscure manner we should come to feel at once a difference in things.

The botanist's glance would, under a subtle attraction, float back to Airolo. " It's queer," he would say quite idly, " but I never noticed that building there to the right before."

" Which building ? "

" That to the right—with a queer sort of thing——"

" I see now. Yes. Yes, it's certainly an odd-looking affair. . . . And big, you know ! Handsome ! I wondered——"

That would interrupt our Utopian speculations. We should both discover that the little towns below had changed —but how, we should not have marked them well enough to know. It would be indefinable, a change in the quality of their grouping, a change in the quality of their remote, small shapes.

I should flick a few crumbs from my knee, perhaps. "It's odd," I should say, for the tenth or eleventh time, with a motion to rise, and we should get up and stretch ourselves, and, still a little puzzled, turn our faces towards the path that clambers down over the tumbled rocks and runs round by the still clear lake and down towards the Hospice of St. Gothard—if perchance we could still find that path.

Long before we got to that, before even we got to the great high road, we should have hints from the stone cabin in the nape of the pass—it would be gone or wonderfully changed—from the very goats upon the rocks, from the little hut by the rough bridge of stone, that a mighty difference had come to the world of men.

And presently, amazed and amazing, we should happen on a man—no Swiss—dressed in unfamiliar clothing and speaking an unfamiliar speech. . . .

§ 4

Before nightfall we should be drenched in wonders, but still we should have wonder left for the thing my companion, with his scientific training, would no doubt be the first to see. He would glance up, with that proprietary eye of the man who knows his constellations down to the little Greek letters. I imagine his exclamation. He would at first doubt his eyes. I should inquire the cause of his consternation, and it would be hard to explain. He would ask me with a certain singularity of manner for "Orion," and I should not find him ; for the Great Bear, and it would have vanished. "Where ? " I should ask, and "where ? " seeking among that scattered starriness, and slowly I should acquire the wonder that possessed him.

Then, for the first time, perhaps, we should realise from this unfamiliar heaven that not the world had changed, but ourselves—that we had come into the uttermost deeps of space.

§ 5

We need suppose no linguistic impediments to intercourse. The whole world will surely have a common language, that is quite elementarily Utopian, and since we are free of the trammels of convincing story-telling, we may suppose that language to be sufficiently our own to understand. Indeed should we be in Utopia at all, if we could not talk to every one ? That accursed bar of language, that hostile inscription in the foreigner's eyes, "deaf and dumb to you, sir, and so—your enemy," is the very first of the defects and complications one has fled the earth to escape.

But what sort of language would we have the world speak, if we were told the miracle of Babel was presently to be reversed ?

If I may take a daring image, a mediæval liberty, I would suppose that in this lonely place the Spirit of Creation spoke to us on this matter. " You are wise men," that Spirit might say—and I, being a suspicious, touchy, over-earnest man for all my predisposition to plumpness, would instantly scent the irony (while my companion, I fancy, might even plume himself), "and to beget your wisdom is chiefly why the world was made. You are so good as to propose an acceleration of that tedious multitudinous evolution upon which I am engaged. I gather, a universal tongue would serve you there. While I sit here among these mountains—I have been filing away at them for this last aeon or so, just to attract your hotels, you know—will you be so kind——? A few hints——? "

Then the Spirit of Creation might transiently smile, a smile that would be like the passing of a cloud. All the mountain wilderness about us would be radiantly lit. (You know those swift moments, when warmth and brightness drift by, in lonely and desolate places.)

Yet, after all, why should two men be smiled into apathy by the Infinite ? Here we are, with our knobby little heads, our eyes and hands and feet and stout hearts, and if not us or ours, still the endless multitudes about us and in our loins are to come at last to the World State and a greater fellowship and the universal tongue. Let us to the extent of our ability, if not answer that question, at any rate try to think ourselves within sight of the best thing possible. That, after all, is our purpose, to imagine our best and strive for it, and it is a worse folly and a worse sin than presumption, to abandon striving because the best of all our bests looks mean amidst the suns.

Now you as a botanist would, I suppose, incline to something, as they say, " *scientific.*" You wince under that most offensive epithet—and I am able to give you my intelligent sympathy—though " pseudo-scientific " and " quasi-scientific " are worse by far for the skin. You would begin to talk of scientific languages, of Esperanto, La Langue Bleue, New Latin, Volapuk, and Lord Lytton, of the philosophical language of Archbishop Whateley, Lady Welby's work upon Significs and the like. You would tell me of the remarkable precisions, the encyclopædic quality of chemical terminology, and at the word terminology I should insinuate a comment on that eminent American biologist, Professor Mark Baldwin, who has carried the language biological to such heights of expressive clearness as to be triumphantly and invincibly unreadable. (Which foreshadows the line of my defence.)

You make your ideal clear, a scientific language you demand, without ambiguity, as precise as mathematical formulæ, and with every term in relations of exact logical consistency with every other. It will be a language with all the inflexions of verbs and nouns regular and all its constructions inevitable, each word clearly distinguishable from every other word in sound as well as spelling.

That, at any rate, is the sort of thing one hears demanded, and if only because the demand rests upon implications that reach far beyond the region of language, it is worth considering here. It implies, indeed, almost everything that we are endeavouring to repudiate in this particular work. It implies that the whole intellectual basis of mankind is established, that the rules of logic, the systems of counting and measurement, the general categories and schemes of resemblance and difference, are established for the human mind for ever—blank Comte-ism, in fact, of the blankest description. But, indeed, the science of logic and the whole framework of philosophical thought men have kept since the days of Plato and Aristotle, has no more essential permanence as a final expression of the human mind, than the Scottish Longer Catechism. Amidst the welter of modern thought, a philosophy long lost to men rises again into being, like some blind and almost formless embryo, that must presently develop sight, and form, and power, a philosophy in which this assumption is denied.[1]

All through this Utopian excursion, I must warn you, you shall feel the thrust and disturbance of that insurgent movement. In the reiterated use of " Unique," you will, as it were, get the gleam of its integument ; in the insistence upon individuality, and the individual difference as the significance of life, you will feel the texture of its shaping body. Nothing endures, nothing is precise and certain (except the mind of a pedant), perfection is the mere repudiation of that ineluctable marginal inexactitude which is the mysterious inmost quality of Being. Being, indeed !—there is no being, but a universal becoming of individualities, and Plato turned his back on truth when he turned towards his museum of specific ideals. Heraclitus, that lost and misinterpreted giant, may perhaps be coming to his own. . . .

There is no abiding thing in what we know. We change from weaker to stronger lights, and each more powerful light pierces our hitherto opaque foundations and reveals fresh and different opacities below. We can never foretell which of our seemingly assured fundamentals the next change will not affect. What folly, then, to dream of mapping out our minds in however general terms, of providing for the endless mysteries of the future a terminology and an idiom ! We follow the vein, we mine and accumulate our treasure, but who can tell which way the vein may trend ? Language is the nourishment of the thought of man, that serves only as it undergoes

[1] The serious reader may refer at leisure to Sidgwick's *Use of Words in Reasoning* (particularly), and to Bosanquet's *Essentials of Logic, Bradley's Principles of Logic,* and Sigwart's *Logik* ; the lighter minded may read and mark the temper of Professor Case in the *British Encyclopædia*, article " Logic " (vol. xxx.). I have appended to this book a rude sketch of a philosophy upon the new lines, originally read by me to the Oxford Phil. Soc. in 1903.

metabolism, and becomes thought and lives, and in its very living passes away. You scientific people, with your fancy of a terrible exactitude in language, of indestructible foundations built, as that Wordsworthian doggerel on the title-page of *Nature* says, " for aye," are marvellously without imagination !

The language of Utopia will no doubt be one and indivisible ; all mankind will, in the measure of their individual differences in quality, be brought into the same phase, into a common resonance of thought, but the language they will speak will still be a living tongue, an animated system of imperfections, which every individual man will infinitesimally modify. Through the universal freedom of exchange and movement, the developing change in its general spirit will be a worldwide change ; that is the quality of its universality. I fancy it will be a coalesced language, a synthesis of many. Such a language as English is a coalesced language ; it is a coalescence of Anglo-Saxon and Norman French and Scholar's Latin, welded into one speech more ample and more powerful and beautiful than either. The Utopian tongue might well present a more spacious coalescence, and hold in the frame of such an uninflected or slightly inflected idiom as English already presents, a profuse vocabulary into which have been cast a dozen once separate tongues, superposed and then welded together through bilingual and trilingual compromises.[1] In the past ingenious men have speculated on the inquiry, " Which language will survive ? " The question was badly put. I think now that this wedding and survival of several in a common offspring is a far more probable thing.

§ 6

This talk of languages, however, is a digression. We were on our way along the faint path that runs round the rim of the Lake of Lucendro, and we were just upon the point of coming upon our first Utopian man. He was, I said, no Swiss. Yet he would have been a Swiss on mother Earth, and here he would have the same face, with some difference, maybe, in the expression ; the same physique, though a little better developed perhaps—the same complexion. He would have different habits, different traditions, different knowledge, different ideas, different clothing, and different appliances, but, except for all that, he would be the same man. We very distinctly provided at the outset that the modern Utopia must have people inherently the same as those in the world.

There is more, perhaps, in that than appears at the first suggestion.

That proposition gives one characteristic difference between a modern Utopia and almost all its predecessors. It is to be a world Utopia, we have agreed, no less ; and so we must

[1] *Vide* an excellent article, " La Langue Française en l'an 2003," par Leon Bollack, in *La Revue*, 15 Juillet, 1903.

needs face the fact that we are to have differences of race.
Even the lower class of Plato's Republic was not specifically
of different race. But this is a Utopia as wide as Christian
charity, and white and black, brown, red and yellow, all tints
of skin, all types of body and character, will be there. How
we are to adjust their differences is a master question, and
the matter is not even to be opened in this chapter. It will
need a whole chapter even to glance at its issues. But here
we underline that stipulation ; every race of this planet earth
is to be found in the strictest parallelism there, in numbers
the same—only, as I say, with an entirely different set of
traditions, ideals, ideas, and purposes, and so moving under
those different skies to an altogether different destiny.

There follows a curious development of this to anyone
clearly impressed by the uniqueness and the unique significance of individualities. Races are no hard and fast things,
no crowd of identically similar persons, but massed sub-races,
and tribes and families, each after its kind unique, and these
again are clusterings of still smaller uniques and so down to
each several person. So that our first convention works out
to this, that not only is every earthly mountain, river, plant,
and beast in that parallel planet beyond Sirius also, but every
man, woman, and child alive has a Utopian parallel. From
now onward, of course, the fates of these two planets will
diverge, men will die here whom wisdom will save there, and
perhaps conversely here we shall save men ; children will be
born to them and not to us, to us and not to them, but this,
this moment of reading, is the starting moment, and for the first
and last occasion the populations of our planets are abreast.

We must in these days make some such supposition. The
alternative is a Utopia of dolls in the likeness of angels—
imaginary laws to fit incredible people, an unattractive
undertaking.

For example, we must assume there is a man such as I might
have been, better informed, better disciplined, better employed, thinner and more active—and I wonder what he is
doing !—and you, Sir or Madam, are in duplicate also, and all
the men and women that you know and I. I doubt if we shall
meet our doubles, or if it would be pleasant for us to do so ;
but as we come down from these lonely mountains to the roads
and houses and living places of the Utopian world-state, we
shall certainly find, here and there, faces that will remind us
singularly of those who have lived under our eyes.

There are some you never wish to meet again, you say,
and some, I gather, you do. " And One—— ! "

It is strange, but this figure of the botanist will not keep
in place. It sprang up between us, dear reader, as a passing
illustrative invention. I do not know what put him into my
head, and for the moment, it fell in with my humour for a
space to foist the man's personality upon you as yours and call

you scientific—that most abusive word. But here he is, indisputably, with me in Utopia, and lapsing from our high speculative theme into halting but intimate confidences. He declares he has not come to Utopia to meet again with his sorrows.

What sorrows?

I protest, even warmly, that neither he nor his sorrows were in my intention.

He is a man, I should think, of thirty-nine, a man whose life has been neither tragedy nor a joyous adventure, a man with one of those faces that have gained interest rather than force or nobility from their commerce with life. He is something refined, with some knowledge, perhaps, of the minor pains and all the civil self-controls; he has read more than he has suffered, and suffered rather than done. He regards me with his blue-grey eye, from which all interest in this Utopia has faded.

"It is a trouble," he says, "that has come into my life only for a month or so—at least acutely again. I thought it was all over. There was some one——"

It is an amazing story to hear upon a mountain crest in Utopia, this Hampstead affair, this story of a Frognal heart. "Frognal," he says, is the place where they met, and it summons to my memory the word on a board at the corner of a flint-dressed new road, an estate development road, with a vista of villas up a hill. He had known her before he got his professorship, and neither her "people" nor his—he speaks that detestable middle-class dialect in which aunts and things with money and the right of intervention are called "people!"—approved of the affair. "She was, I think, rather easily swayed," he says. "But that's not fair to her, perhaps. She thought too much of others. If they seemed distressed, or if they seemed to think a course right——" . . .

Have I come to Utopia to hear this sort of thing?

§ 7

It is necessary to turn the botanist's thoughts into a worthier channel. It is necessary to override these modest regrets, this intrusive, petty love story. Does he realise this is indeed Utopia? Turn your mind, I insist, to this Utopia of mine, and leave these earthly troubles to their proper planet. Do you realise just where the propositions necessary to a modern Utopia are taking us? Every one on earth will have to be here;—themselves, but with a difference. Somewhere here in this world is, for example, Mr. Chamberlain, and the King is here (no doubt *incognito*), and all the Royal Academy, and Sandow, and Mr. Arnold White.

But these famous names do not appeal to him.

My mind goes from this prominent and typical personage to that, and for a time I forget my companion. I am distracted by the curious side issues this general proposition trails after it. There will be so-and-so, and so-and-so. The name and figure of Mr. Roosevelt jerks into focus, and obliterates an attempt to acclimatise the Emperor of the Germans. What, for instance, will Utopia do with Mr. Roosevelt ? There drifts across my inner vision the image of a strenuous struggle with Utopian constables, the voice that has thrilled terrestrial millions in eloquent protest. The writ of arrest, drifting loose in the conflict, comes to my feet ; I impale the scrap of paper, and read—but can it be ?—" attempted disorganisation ? . . . incitements to disarrange ? . . . the balance of population ? "

The trend of my logic for once has led us into a facetious alley. One might indeed keep in this key, and write an agreeable little Utopia, that like the holy families of the mediæval artists (or Michael Angelo's " Last Judgment ") should compliment one's friends in various degrees. Or one might embark upon a speculative treatment of the entire *Almanach de Gotha*, something on the lines of Epistemon's vision of the damned great, when

" Xerxes was a crier of mustard.
Romulus was a salter and a patcher of patterns. . . ."

That incomparable catalogue ! That incomparable catalogue ! Inspired by the Muse of Parody, we might go on to the pages of *Who's Who*, and even, with an eye to the obdurate republic, to *Who's Who in America*, and make the most delightful and extensive arrangements. Now where shall we put this most excellent man ? And this ? . . .

But, indeed, it is doubtful if we shall meet any of these doubles during our Utopian journey, or know them when we meet them. I doubt if any one will be making the best of both these worlds. The great men in this still unexplored Utopia may be but village Hampdens in our own, and earthly goatherds and obscure illiterates sit here in the seats of the mighty.

That again opens agreeable vistas left of us and right.

But my botanist obtrudes his personality again. His thoughts have travelled by a different route.

" I know," he says, "that she will be happier here, and that they will value her better than she has been valued upon earth."

His interruption serves to turn me back from my momentary contemplation of those popular effigies inflated by old newspapers and windy report, the earthly great. He sets me thinking of more personal and intimate applications, of the human beings one knows with a certain approximation to real knowledge, of the actual common substance of life. He turns me to the thought of rivalries and tendernesses, of differences and disappointments. I am suddenly brought painfully against the things that might have been. What if instead of that Utopia of vacant ovals we meet relinquished

loves here, and opportunities lost and faces as they might have
looked to us ?

I turn to my botanist almost reprovingly.   " You know, she
won't be quite the same lady here that you knew in Frognal,"
I say, and wrest myself from a subject that is no longer agreeable by rising to my feet.

" And besides," I say, standing above him, " the chances
against our meeting here are a million to one. . . . And we
loiter !   This is not the business we have come upon, but a
mere incidental kink in our larger plan.   The fact remains,
these people we have come to see are people with like in-
firmities to our own—and only the conditions are changed.
Let us pursue the tenour of our inquiry."

With that I lead the way round the edge of the Lake of
Lucendro towards our Utopian world.

(You figure him doing it.)

Down the mountain we shall go and down the passes,
and as the valleys open the world will open, Utopia, where
men and women are happy and laws are wise, and where all
that is tangled and confused in human affairs has been un-
ravelled and made right.

CHAPTER TWO

CONCERNING FREEDOMS

§ I

NOW what sort of question would first occur to two
men descending upon the planet of a Modern Utopia ?
Probably grave solicitude about their personal freedom.   Towards the Stranger, as I have already remarked,
the Utopias of the past displayed their least amiable aspect.
Would this new sort of Utopian State, spread to the dimensions
of a world, be any less forbidding ?

We should take comfort in the thought that universal
Toleration is certainly a modern idea, and it is upon modern
ideas that this World State rests.   But even suppose we are
tolerated and admitted to this unavoidable citizenship, there
will still remain a wide range of possibility. . . . I think we
should try to work the problem out from an inquiry into first
principles, and that we should follow the trend of our time and
kind by taking up the question as one of " Man *versus* the State,"
and discussing the compromise of Liberty.

The idea of individual liberty is one that has grown in
importance and grows with every development of modern
thought.   To the classical Utopists freedom was relatively
trivial.   Clearly they considered virtue and happiness as

entirely separable from liberty, and as being altogether more important things. But the modern view, with its deepening insistence upon individuality and upon the significance of its uniqueness, steadily intensifies the value of freedom, until at last we begin to see liberty as the very substance of life, that indeed it is life, and that only the dead things, the choiceless things, live in absolute obedience to law. To have free play for one's individuality is, in the modern view, the subjective triumph of existence, as survival in creative work and offspring is its objective triumph. But for all men, since man is a social creature, the play of will must fall short of absolute freedom. Perfect human liberty is possible only to a despot who is absolutely and universally obeyed. Then to will would be to command and achieve, and within the limits of natural law we could at any moment do exactly as it pleased us to do. All other liberty is a compromise between our own freedom of will and the wills of those with whom we come in contact. In an organised state each one of us has a more or less elaborate code of what he may do to others and to himself, and what others may do to him. He limits others by his rights, and is limited by the rights of others, and by considerations affecting the welfare of the community as a whole.

Individual liberty in a community is not, as mathematicians would say, always of the same sign. To ignore this is the essential fallacy of the cult called Individualism. But in truth, a general prohibition in a state may increase the sum of liberty, and a general permission may diminish it. It does not follow, as these people would have us believe, that a man is more free where there is least law and more restricted where there is most law. A socialism or a communism is not necessarily a slavery, and there is no freedom under Anarchy. Consider how much liberty we gain by the loss of the common liberty to kill. Thereby one may go to and fro in all the ordered parts of the earth, unencumbered by arms or armour, free of the fear of playful poison, whimsical barbers, or hotel trap-doors. Indeed, it means freedom from a thousand fears and precautions. Suppose there existed even the limited freedom to kill in vendetta, and think what would happen in our suburbs. Consider the inconvenience of two households in a modern suburb estranged and provided with modern weapons of precision, the inconvenience not only to each other, but to the neutral pedestrian, the practical loss of freedoms all about them. The butcher, if he came at all, would have to come round in an armoured cart. . . .

It follows, therefore, in a modern Utopia, which finds the final hope of the world in the evolving interplay of unique individualities, that the State will have effectually chipped away just all those spendthrift liberties that waste liberty, and not one liberty more, and so have attained the maximum general freedom.

There are two distinct and contrasting methods of limiting liberty ; the first is Prohibition, " thou shalt not," and the second Command, " thou shalt." There is, however, a sort of prohibition that takes the form of a conditional command, and this one needs to bear in mind. It says if you do so-and-so, you must also do so-and-so ; if, for example, you go to sea with men you employ, you must go in a seaworthy vessel. But the pure command is unconditional ; it says, whatever you have done or are doing or want to do, you are to do this, as when the social system, working through the base necessities of base parents and bad laws, sends a child of thirteen into a factory. Prohibition takes one definite thing from the indefinite liberty of a man, but it still leaves him an unbounded choice of actions. He remains free, and you have merely taken a bucketful from the sea of his freedom. But compulsion destroys freedom altogether. In this Utopia of ours there may be many prohibitions, but no indirect compulsions— if one may so contrive it—and few or no commands. As far as I see it now, in this present discussion, I think, indeed, there should be no positive compulsions at all in Utopia, at any rate for the adult Utopian—unless they fall upon him as penalties incurred.

§ 2

What prohibitions should we be under, we two Uitlanders in this Utopian world ? We should certainly not be free to kill, assault, or threaten any one we met, and in that we earth-trained men would not be likely to offend. And until we knew more exactly the Utopian idea of property we should be very chary of touching anything that might conceivably be appropriated. If it was not the property of individuals it might be the property of the State. But beyond that we might have our doubts. Are we right in wearing the strange costumes we do, in choosing the path that pleases us athwart this rock and turf, in coming striding with unfumigated rücksacks and snow-wet hobnails into what is conceivably an extremely neat and orderly world ? We have passed our first Utopian now, with an answered vague gesture, and have noted, with secret satisfaction, there is no access of dismay ; we have rounded a bend, and down the valley in the distance we get a glimpse of what appears to be a singularly well-kept road. . . .

I submit that to the modern minded man it can be no sort of Utopia worth desiring that does not give the utmost freedom of going to and fro. Free movement is to many people one of the greatest of life's privileges—to go wherever the spirit moves them, to wander and see—and though they have every comfort, every security, every virtuous discipline, they will still be unhappy if that is denied them. Short of damage to things cherished and made, the Utopians will surely have this right, so we may expect no unclimbable walls and fences, nor the discovery of any laws we may transgress in coming down these mountain places.

And yet, just as civil liberty itself is a compromise defended by prohibitions, so this particular sort of liberty must also have its qualifications. Carried to the absolute pitch the right of free movement ceases to be distinguishable from the right of free intrusion. We have already, in a comment on More's *Utopia*, hinted at an agreement with Aristotle's argument against communism, that it flings people into an intolerable continuity of contact. Schopenhauer carried out Aristotle in the vein of his own bitterness and with the truest of images when he likened human society to hedgehogs clustering for warmth, and unhappy when either too closely packed or too widely separated. Empedocles found no significance in life whatever except as an unsteady play of love and hate, of attraction and repulsion, of assimilation and the assertion of difference. So long as we ignore difference, so long as we ignore individuality, and that I hold has been the common sin of all Utopias hitherto, we can make absolute statements, prescribe communisms or individualisms, and all sorts of hard theoretic arrangements. But in the world of reality, which— to modernise Heraclitus and Empedocles—is nothing more nor less than the world of individuality, there are no absolute rights and wrongs, there are no qualitative questions at all, but only quantitative adjustments. Equally strong in the normal civilised man is the desire for freedom of movement and the desire for a certain privacy, for a corner definitely his, and we have to consider where the line of reconciliation comes.

The desire for absolute personal privacy is perhaps never a very strong or persistent craving. In the great majority of human beings, the gregarious instinct is sufficiently powerful to render any but the most temporary isolations not simply disagreeable, but painful. The savage has all the privacy he needs within the compass of his skull ; like dogs and timid women, he prefers ill-treatment to desertion, and it is only a scarce and complex modern type that finds comfort and refreshment in quite lonely places and quite solitary occupations. Yet such there are, men who can neither sleep well nor think well, nor attain to a full perception of beautiful objects, who do not savour the best of existence until they are securely alone, and for the sake of these even it would be reasonable to draw some limits to the general right of free movement. But their particular need is only a special and exceptional aspect of an almost universal claim to privacy among modern people, not so much for the sake of isolation as for congenial companionship. We want to go apart from the great crowd, not so much to be alone as to be with those who appeal to us particularly and to whom we particularly appeal ; we want to form households and societies with them, to give our individualities play in intercourse with them, and in the appointments and furnishings of that intercourse. We want gardens and enclosures and exclusive freedoms for our like and our choice, just as spacious as we can get them—and it is only the multitudinous uncongenial, anxious also for similar developments in some opposite direction, that checks this expansive movement of personal selection and necessitates a compromise on privacy.

Glancing back from our Utopian mountain side down which this discourse marches, to the confusions of old earth, we may remark that the need and desire for privacies there is exceptionally great at the present time, and it was less in the past, that in the future it may be less again, and that under the Utopian conditions to which we shall come when presently we strike yonder road, it may be reduced to quite manageable dimensions. But this is to be effected not by the suppression of individualities to some common pattern,[1] but by the broadening of public charity and the general amelioration of mind and manners. It is not by assimilation, that is to say, but by understanding that the modern Utopia achieves itself. The ideal community of man's past was one with a common belief, with common customs and common ceremonies, common manners and common formulæ ; men of the same society dressed in the same fashion, each according to his defined and understood grade, behaved in the same fashion, loved, worshipped, and died in the same fashion. They did or felt little that did not find a sympathetic publicity. The natural disposition of all peoples, white, black, or brown, a natural disposition that education seeks to destroy, is to insist upon uniformity, to make publicity extremely unsympathetic to even the most harmless departures from the code. To be dressed " odd," to behave "oddly," to eat in a different manner or of different food, to commit, indeed, any breach of the established convention is to give offence and to incur hostility among unsophisticated men. But the disposition of the more original and enterprising minds at all times has been to make such innovations.

This is particularly in evidence in this present age. The almost cataclysmal development of new machinery, the discovery of new materials, and the appearance of new social possibilities through the organised pursuit of material science, has given enormous and unprecedented facilities to the spirit of innovation. The old local order has been broken up or is now being broken up all over the earth, and everywhere societies deliquesce, everywhere men are afloat amidst the wreckage of their flooded conventions, and still tremendously unaware of the thing that has happened. The old local orthodoxies of behaviour, of precedence, the old accepted amusements and employments, the old ritual of conduct in

[1] More's *Utopia*. " Whoso will may go in, for there is nothing within the houses that is private or anie man's owne."

the important small things of the daily life and the old ritual of thought in the things that make discussion, are smashed up and scattered and mixed discordantly together, one use with another, and no world-wide culture of toleration, no courteous admission of differences, no wider understanding has yet replaced them. And so publicity in the modern earth has become confusedly unsympathetic for every one. Classes are intolerable to classes and sets to sets, contact provokes aggressions, comparisons, persecutions and discomforts, and the subtler people are excessively tormented by a sense of observation, unsympathetic always and often hostile. To live without some sort of segregation from the general mass is impossible in exact proportion to one's individual distinction.

Of course things will be very different in Utopia. Utopia will be saturated with consideration. To us, clad as we are in mountain-soiled tweeds and with no money but British bank-notes, negotiable only at a practically infinite distance, this must needs be a reassuring induction. And Utopian manners will not only be tolerant, but almost universally tolerable. Endless things will be understood perfectly and universally that on earth are understood only by a scattered few; baseness of bearing, grossness of manner, will be the distinctive mark of no section of the community whatever. The coarser reasons for privacy, therefore, will not exist here. And that savage sort of shyness, too, that makes so many half-educated people on earth recluse and defensive, that too the Utopians will have escaped by their more liberal breeding. In the cultivated State we are assuming it will be ever so much easier for people to eat in public, rest and amuse themselves in public, and even work in public. Our present need for privacy in many things marks, indeed, a phase of transition from an ease in public in the past due to homogeneity, to an ease in public in the future due to intelligence and good breeding, and in Utopia that transition will be complete. We must bear that in mind throughout the consideration of this question.

Yet, after this allowance has been made, there still remains a considerable claim for privacy in Utopia. The room, or apartments, or home, or mansion, whatever it may be a man or woman maintains, must be private, and under his or her complete dominion ; it seems harsh and intrusive to forbid a central garden plot or peristyle, such as one sees in Pompeii, within the house walls, and it is almost as difficult to deny a little private territory beyond the house. Yet if we concede that, it is clear that without some further provision we concede the possibility that the poorer townsman (if there are to be rich and poor in the world) will be forced to walk through endless miles of high fenced villa gardens before he may expand in his little scrap of reserved open country. Such is already the poor Londoner's miserable fate. . . . Our Utopia will

have, of course, faultless roads and beautifully arranged
inter-urban communications, swift trains or motor services
or what not, to diffuse its population, and without some
anticipatory provisions, the prospect of the residential areas
becoming a vast area of defensively walled villa Edens is all
too possible.

This is a quantitive question, be it remembered, and not
to be dismissed by any statement of principle. Our Utopians
will meet it, I presume, by detailed regulations, very probably
varying locally with local conditions. Privacy beyond the
house might be made a privilege to be paid for in proportion
to the area occupied, and the tax on these licences of privacy
might increase as the square of the area affected. A maximum
fraction of private enclosure for each urban and suburban
square mile could be fixed. A distinction could be drawn
between an absolutely private garden and a garden private
and closed only for a day or a couple of days a week, and at
other times open to the well-behaved public. Who, in a
really civilised community, would grudge that measure of
invasion ? Walls could be taxed by height and length, and
the enclosure of really natural beauties, of rapids, cascades,
gorges, viewpoints, and so forth made impossible. So a
reasonable compromise between the vital and conflicting
claims of the freedom of movement and the freedom of
seclusion might be attained. . . .

And as we argue thus we draw nearer and nearer to the
road that goes up and over the Gotthard crest and down the
Val Tremola towards Italy.

What sort of road would that be ?

§ 3

Freedom of movement in a Utopia planned under modern
conditions must involve something more than unrestricted
pedestrian wanderings, and the very proposition of a world-
state speaking one common tongue carries with it the idea of a
world population travelled and travelling to an extent quite
beyond anything our native earth has seen. It is now our
terrestrial experience that whenever economic and political
developments set a class free to travel, that class at once
begins to travel ; in England, for example, above the five or
six hundred pounds a year level, it is hard to find any one
who is not habitually migratory, who has not been frequently,
as people say, " abroad." In the Modern Utopia travel must
be in the common texture of life. To go into fresh climates
and fresh scenery, to meet a different complexion of humanity
and a different type of home and food and apparatus, to mark
unfamiliar trees and plants and flowers and beasts, to climb
mountains, to see the snowy night of the North and the blaze
of the tropical midday, to follow great rivers, to taste loneliness
in desert places, to traverse the gloom of tropical forests and

to cross the high seas, will be an essential part of the reward and adventure of life, even for the commonest people. . . . This is a bright and pleasant particular in which a modern Utopia must differ again, and differ diametrically, from its predecessors.

We may conclude from what has been done in places upon our earth that the whole Utopian world will be open and accessible, and as safe for the wayfarer as France or England is to-day. The peace of the world will be established for ever, and everywhere, except in remote and desolate places, there will be convenient inns, at least as convenient and trustworthy as those of Switzerland to-day ; the touring clubs and hotel associations that have tariffed that country and France so effectually will have had their fine Utopian equivalents, and the whole world will be habituated to the coming and going of strangers. The greater part of the world will be as secure and cheaply and easily accessible to every one as is Zermatt or Lucerne to a Western European of the middle-class at the present time.

On this account alone no places will be so congested as these two are now on earth. With freedom to go everywhere, with easy access everywhere, with no dread of difficulties about language, coinage, custom, or law, why should every one continue to go to just a few special places ? Such congestions are merely the measure of the general inaccessibility and insecurity and costliness of contemporary life, an awkward transitory phase in the first beginnings of the travel age of mankind.

No doubt the Utopian will travel in many ways. It is unlikely there will be any smoke-disgorging steam railway trains in Utopia, they are already doomed on earth, already threatened with that obsolescence that will endear them to the Ruskins of to-morrow, but a thin spider's web of inconspicuous special routes will cover the land of the world, pierce the mountain masses and tunnel under the seas. These may be double railways or monorails or what not—we are no engineers to judge between such devices—but by means of them the Utopian will travel about the earth from one chief point to another at a speed of two or three hundred miles or more an hour. That will abolish the greater distances. . . . One figures these main communications as something after the manner of corridor trains, smooth-running and roomy, open from end to end, with cars in which one may sit and read cars in which one may take refreshment, cars into which the news of the day comes printing itself from the wires beside the track ; cars in which one may have privacy and sleep if one is so disposed, bath-room cars, library cars ; a train as comfortable as a good club. There will be no distinctions of class in such a train, because in a civilised world there would be no offence between one kind of man and another, and for the good of the whole world such travelling will be as cheap as it can be, and well within the reach of any but the almost criminally poor.

Such great tramways as this will be used when the Utopians wish to travel fast and far ; thereby you will glide all over the land surface of the planet ; and feeding them and distributing from them, innumerable minor systems, clean little electric tramways I picture them, will spread out over the land in finer reticulations, growing close and dense in the urban regions and thinning as the population thins. And running beside these lighter railways, and spreading beyond their range, will be the smooth minor high roads such as this one we now approach, upon which independent vehicles, motor-cars, cycles, and what not will go. I doubt if we shall see any horses upon this fine, smooth, clean road ; I doubt if there will be many horses on the high roads of Utopia, and, indeed, if they will use draught horses at all upon that planet. Why should they ? Where the world gives turf or sand, or along special tracts, the horse will perhaps be ridden for exercise and pleasure, but that will be all the use for him ; and as for the other beasts of burthen, on the remoter mountain tracts the mule will no doubt still be a picturesque survival, in the desert men will still find a use for the camel, and the elephant may linger to play a part in the pageant of the East. But the burthen of the minor traffic, if not the whole of it, will certainly be mechanical. This is what we shall see even while the road is still remote, swift and shapely motor-cars going past, cyclists, and in these agreeable mountain regions there will also be pedestrians upon their way. Cycle tracks will abound in Utopia, sometimes following beside the great high roads, but oftener taking their own more agreeable line amidst woods and crops and pastures ; and there will be a rich variety of footpaths and minor ways. There will be many footpaths in Utopia. There will be pleasant ways over the scented needles of the mountain pinewoods, primrose-strewn tracks amidst the budding thickets of the lower country, paths running beside rushing streams, paths across the wide spaces of the corn land, and, above all, paths through the flowery garden spaces amidst which the houses in the towns will stand. And everywhere about the world, on road and path, by sea and land, the happy holiday Utopians will go.

The population of Utopia will be a migratory population beyond any earthly precedent, not simply a travelling population, but migratory. The old Utopias were all localised, as localised as a parish councillor ; but it is manifest that nowadays even quite ordinary people live over areas that would have made a kingdom in those former days, would have filled the Athenian of the *Laws* with incredulous astonishment. Except for the habits of the very rich during the Roman Empire, there was never the slightest precedent for this modern detachment from place. It is nothing to us that we go eighty or ninety miles from home to place of business, or take an hour's spin of fifty miles to our week-end golf ; every summer it has become a fixed custom to travel wide and far. Only the clumsiness of communications limit us now, and every facilitation of locomotion widens not only our potential, but our habitual range. Not only this, but we change our habitations with a growing frequency and facility ; to Sir Thomas More we should seem a breed of nomads. That old fixity was of necessity and not of choice, it was a mere phase in the development of civilisation, a trick of rooting man learnt for a time from his new-found friends, the corn and the vine and the hearth ; the untamed spirit of the young has turned for ever to wandering and the sea. The soul of man has never yet in any land been willingly adscript to the glebe. Even Mr. Belloc, who preaches the happiness of a peasant proprietary, is so much wiser than his thoughts that he sails about the seas in a little yacht or goes afoot from Belgium to Rome. We are winning our freedom again once more, a freedom renewed and enlarged, and there is now neither necessity nor advantage in a permanent life servitude to this place or that. Men may settle down in our Modern Utopia for love and the family at last, but first and most abundantly they will see the world.

And with this loosening of the fetters of locality from the feet of men, necessarily there will be all sorts of fresh distributions of the factors of life. On our own poor haphazard earth, wherever men work, wherever there are things to be grown, minerals to be won, power to be used, there, regardless of all the joys and decencies of life, the households needs must cluster. But in Utopia there will be wide stretches of cheerless or unhealthy or toilsome or dangerous land with never a household ; there will be regions of mining and smelting, black with the smoke of furnaces and gashed and desolated by mines, with a sort of weird inhospitable grandeur of industrial desolation, and the men will come thither and work for a spell and return to civilisation again, washing and changing their attire in the swift gliding train. And by way of compensation there will be beautiful regions of the earth specially set apart and favoured for children ; in them the presence of children will remit taxation, while in other less wholesome places the presence of children will be taxed ; the lower passes and fore hills of these very Alps, for example, will be populous with homes, serving the vast arable levels of Upper Italy.

So we shall see, as we come down by our little lake in the lap of Lucendro, and even before we reach the road, the first scattered chalets and households in which these migrant people live, the upper summer homes. With the coming of summer, as the snows on the high Alps recede, a tide of households and schools, teachers and doctors, and all such attendant services will flow up the mountain masses, and ebb again when the September snows return. It is essential to the modern ideal of life that the period of education and growth should be prolonged to as late a period as possible and puberty correspondingly retarded, and by wise regulation the statesmen of Utopia will constantly adjust and readjust regulations and taxation to diminish the proportion of children reared in hot and stimulating conditions. These high mountains will, in the bright sweet summer, be populous with youth. Even up towards this high place where the snow is scarce gone until July, these households will extend, and below, the whole long valley of Urseren will be a scattered summer town.

One figures one of the more urban highways, one of those along which the light railways of the second order run, such as that in the valley of Urseren, into which we should presently come. I figure it as one would see it at night, a band a hundred yards perhaps in width, the footpath on either side shaded with high trees and lit softly with orange glowlights ; while down the centre the tramway of the road will go, with sometimes a nocturnal tram-car gliding, lit and gay but almost noiselessly, past. Lantern-lit cyclists will flit along the track like fireflies, and ever and again some humming motor-car will hurry by, to or from the Rhoneland or the Rhineland or Switzerland or Italy. Away on either side the lights of the little country homes up the mountain slopes will glow.

I figure it at night, because so it is we should see it first.

We should come out from our mountain valley into the minor road that runs down the lonely rock wilderness of the San Gotthard Pass, we should descend that nine miles of winding route, and so arrive towards twilight among the clustering homes and upland unenclosed gardens of Realp and Hospenthal and Andermatt. Between Realp and Andermatt, and down the Schoellenen gorge, the greater road would run. By the time we reached it, we should be in the way of understanding our adventure a little better. We should know already, when we saw those two familiar clusters of chalets and hotels replaced by a great dispersed multitude of houses—we should see their window lights, but little else— that we were the victims of some strange transition in space or time, and we should come down by dimly-seen buildings into the part that would answer to Hospenthal, wondering and perhaps a little afraid. We should come out into this great main roadway—this roadway like an urban avenue— and look up it and down, hesitating whether to go along the valley Furka-ward, or down by Andermatt through the gorge that leads to Göschenen. . . .

People would pass us in the twilight, and then more people ; we should see they walked well and wore a graceful, unfamiliar dress, but more we should not distinguish.

" Good-night ! " they would say to us in clear, fine voices.
Their dim faces would turn with a passing scrutiny towards us.

We should answer out of our perplexity : " Good-night ! "
—for by the conventions established in the beginning of this
book, we are given the freedom of their tongue.

§ 4

Were this a story, I should tell at length how much we
were helped by the good fortune of picking up a Utopian
coin of gold, how at last we adventured into the Utopian inn
and found it all marvellously easy. You see us the shyest
and most watchful of guests ; but of the food they put before
us and the furnishings of the house, and all our entertainment,
it will be better to speak later. We are in a migratory world,
we know, one greatly accustomed to foreigners ; our mountain
clothes are not strange enough to attract acute attention,
though ill-made and shabby, no doubt, by Utopian standards ;
we are dealt with as we might best wish to be dealt with,
that is to say as rather untidy, inconspicuous men. We look
about us and watch for hints and examples, and, indeed, get
through with the thing. And after our queer, yet not unpleasant, dinner, in which we remark no meat figures, we go
out of the house for a breath of air and for quiet counsel one
with another, and there it is we discover those strange constellations overhead. It comes to us then, clear and full, that
our imagination has realised itself ; we dismiss quite finally a
Rip-Van-Winkle fancy we have entertained, all the unfamili-
arities of our descent from the mountain pass gather together
into one fullness of conviction, and we know, we know, we are
in Utopia.

We wander under the trees by the main road, watching
the dim passers-by as though they were the phantoms of a
dream. We say little to one another. We turn aside into a
little pathway and come to a bridge over the turbulent Reuss,
hurrying down towards the Devil's Bridge in the gorge below.
Far away over the Furka ridge a pallid glow preludes the
rising of the moon.

Two lovers pass us whispering, and we follow them with our
eyes. This Utopia has certainly preserved the fundamental
freedom, to love. And then a sweet-voiced bell from somewhere high up towards Oberalp chimes two-and-twenty times.

I break the silence. " That might mean ten o'clock," I say.

My companion leans upon the bridge and looks down into
the dim river below. I become aware of the keen edge of the
moon like a needle of incandescent silver creeping over the
crest, and suddenly the river is alive with flashes.

He speaks, and astonishes me with the hidden course his
thoughts have taken.

" We two were boy and girl lovers like that," he says, and
jerks a head at the receding Utopians. " I loved her first

and I do not think I have ever thought of loving any one but her."

It is a curiously human thing, and, upon my honour, not one I had designed, that when at last I stand in the twilight in the midst of a Utopian township, when my whole being should be taken up with speculative wonder, this man should be standing by my side, and lugging my attention persistently towards himself, towards his limited futile self. This thing perpetually happens to me, this intrusion of something small and irrelevant and alive, upon my great impressions. The time I first saw the Matterhorn, that Queen among the Alpine summits, I was distracted beyond appreciation by the tale of a man who could not eat sardines—always sardines did this with him and that ; and my first wanderings along the brown streets of Pompeii, an experience I had anticipated with a strange intensity, was shot with the most stupidly intelligent discourse on vehicular tariffs in the chief capitals of Europe that it is possible to imagine. And now this man, on my first night in Utopia, talks and talks and talks of his poor little love affair.

It shapes itself as the most trite and feeble of tragedies, one of those stories of effortless submission to chance and custom in which Mr. Hardy or George Gissing might have found a theme. I do but half listen at first—watching the black figures in the moonlit roadway pacing to and fro. Yet— I cannot trace how he conveys the subtle conviction to my mind—the woman he loves is beautiful.

They were boy and girl together, and afterwards they met again as fellow students in a world of comfortable discretions. He seems to have taken the decorums of life with a confiding good faith, to have been shy and innocent in a suppressed sort of way, and of a mental type not made for worldly suc- cesses ; but he must have dreamt about her and loved her well enough. How she felt for him I could never gather ; it seemed to be all of that fleshless friendliness into which we train our girls. Then abruptly happened stresses. The man who became her husband appeared, with a very evident passion. He was a year or so older than either of them, and he had the habit and quality of achieving his ends ; he was already successful, and with the promise of wealth, and I, at least, perceived, from my botanist's phrasing, that his desire was for her beauty.

As my botanist talked I seemed to see the whole little drama, rather clearer than his words gave it me, the actors all absurdly in Hampstead middle-class raiment, meetings of a Sunday after church (the men in silk hats, frock coats, and tightly-rolled umbrellas), rare excursions into evening dress, the decorously vulgar fiction read in their homes, its ambling sentimentalities of thought, the amiably worldly mothers, the respectable fathers, the aunts, the " people "—his " people " and her " people "—the piano music and the song, and in this

setting our friend, " quite clever " at botany and " going in "
for it " as a profession," and the girl, gratuitously beautiful ;
so I figured the arranged and orderly environment into which
this claw of an elemental force had thrust itself to grip.

The stranger who had come in got what he wanted ; the
girl considered that she thought she had never loved the
botanist, had had only friendship for him—though little she
knew of the meaning of those fine words—they parted a little
incoherently and in tears, and it had not occurred to the
young man to imagine she was not going off to conventional
life in some other of the endless Frognals he imagined as the
cellular tissue of the world.

But she wasn't.

He had kept her photograph and her memory sweet, and if
ever he had strayed from the severest constancy, it seemed
only in the end to strengthen with the stuff of experience, to
enhance by comparative disappointment his imagination of
what she might have meant to him. . . . Then eight years
afterwards they met again.

By the time he gets to this part of his story we have, at my
initiative, left the bridge and are walking towards the Utopian
guest house. The Utopian guest house ! His voice rises and
falls, and sometimes he holds my arm. My attention comes
and goes. "Good-night," two sweet-voiced Utopians cry to us
in their universal tongue, and I answer them " Good-night."

" You see," he persists, " I saw her only a week ago. It
was in Lucerne, while I was waiting for you to come on from
England. I talked to her three or four times altogether.
And her face—the change in her ! I can't get it out of my
head—night or day. The miserable waste of her. . . ."

Before us, through the tall pine stems, shine the lights of
our Utopian inn.

He talks vainly of ill-usage. The husband is vain, boastful,
dishonest to the very confines of the law, and a drunkard.
There are scenes and insults——"

" She told you ? "

" Not much, but some one else did. He brings other
women almost into her presence to spite her."

" And it's going on ? " I interrupt.

" Yes. *Now*."

" Need it go on ? "

" What do you mean ? "

" Lady in trouble," I say. " Knight at hand. Why not
stop this dismal grizzling and carry her off ? " (*You figure
the heroic sweep of the arm that belongs to the Voice.*) I positively forget for the moment that we are in Utopia at all.

" You mean ? "

" Take her away from him ! What's all this emotion of
yours worth if it isn't equal to that ! "

Positively he seems aghast at me.

" Do you mean elope with her ? "

" It seems a most suitable case."

For a space he is silent, and we go on through the trees. A Utopian tram-car passes and I see his face, poor bitted wretch! looking pinched and scared in its trailing glow of light.

" That's all very well in a novel," he says. " But how could I go back to my laboratory, mixed classes with young ladies, you know, after a thing like that ? How could we live and where could we live ? We might have a house in London, but who would call upon us ? . . . Besides, you don't know her. She is not the sort of woman. . . . Don't think I'm timid or conventional. Don't think I don't feel. . . . Feel! *You* don't know what it is to feel in a case of this sort. . . ."

He halts and then flies out viciously : " Ugh ! There are times when I could strangle him with my hands."

Which is nonsense.

He flings out his lean botanising hands in an impotent gesture.

" My dear Man ! " I say, and say no more.

For a moment I forget we are in Utopia altogether.

§ 5

Let us come back to Utopia. We were speaking of travel.

Besides roadways and railways and tramways, for those who go to and fro in the earth the Modern Utopians will have very many other ways of travelling. There will be rivers, for example, with a vast variety of boats ; canals with diverse sorts of haulage ; there will be lakes and lagoons; and when one comes at last to the borders of the land, the pleasure craft will be there, coming and going, and the swift great passenger vessels, very big and steady, doing thirty knots an hour or more, will trace long wakes as they go dwindling out athwart the restless vastness of the sea.

They will be just beginning to fly in Utopia. We owe much to M. Santos Dumont ; the world is immeasurably more disposed to believe this wonder is coming, and coming nearly, than it was five years ago. But unless we are to suppose Utopian scientific knowledge far in advance of ours— and though that supposition was not proscribed in our initial undertaking, it would be inconvenient for us and not quite in the vein of the rest of our premises—they, too, will only be in the same experimental stage as ourselves. In Utopia, however, they will conduct research by the army corps while we conduct it—we don't conduct it ! We let it happen. Fools make researches and wise men exploit them—that is our earthly way of dealing with the question, and we thank Heaven for an assumed abundance of financially impotent and sufficiently ingenious fools.

fallen from some wayfarer's pocket. (This, in our first hour or so before we reach the inn in the Urseren Thal.) You figure us upon the high Gotthard road, heads together over the little disk that contrives to tell us so much of this strange world.

It is, I imagine, of gold, and it will be a convenient accident if it is sufficient to make us solvent for a day or so, until we are a little more informed of the economic system into which we have come. It is, moreover, of a fair round size, and the inscription declares it one Lion, equal to "twaindy" bronze Crosses. Unless the ratio of metals is very different here, this latter must be a token coin, and therefore legal tender for but a small amount. (That would be pain and pleasure to Mr. Wordsworth Donisthorpe if he were to chance to join us, for once he planned a Utopian coinage,[1] and the words Lion and Cross are his. But a token coinage and "legal tender" he cannot abide. They make him argue.) And being in Utopia, that unfamiliar "twaindy" suggests at once we have come upon that most Utopian of all things, a duodecimal system of counting.

My author's privilege of details serves me here. This Lion is distinctly a beautiful coin, admirably made, with its value in fine, clear letters circling the obverse side, and a head thereon—of Newton, as I live! One detects American influence here. Each year, as we shall find, each denomination of coins celebrates a centenary. The reverse shows the universal goddess of the Utopian coinage—Peace, as a beautiful woman, reading with a child out of a great book, and behind them are stars, and an hour-glass, halfway run. Very human these Utopians, after all, and not by any means above the obvious in their symbolism !

So for the first time we learn definitely of the World State, and we get our first clear hint, too, that there is an end to Kings. But our coin raises other issues also. It would seem that this Utopia has no simple community of goods, that there is, at any rate, a restriction upon what one may take, a need for evidences of equivalent value, a limitation to human credit.

It dates—so much of this present Utopia of ours dates. Those former Utopists were bitterly against gold. You will recall the undignified use Sir Thomas More would have us put it to, and how there was no money at all in the Republic of Plato, and in that later community for which he wrote his Laws an iron coinage of austere appearance and doubtful efficacy. . . . It may be these great gentlemen were a little hasty with a complicated difficulty, and not a little unjust to a highly respectable element.

Gold is abused and made into vessels of dishonour, and abolished from ideal society as though it were the cause instead of the instrument of human baseness ; but, indeed, there is nothing bad in gold. Making gold into vessels of

[1] *A System of Measures*, by Wordsworth Donisthorpe.

the mystery of balancing justice against the good of the future, amidst these violent and elusive passions. Where falls the balance of freedoms here ? I pass for a time from Utopianising altogether, to ask the question that, after all, Schopenhauer failed completely to answer, why sometimes in the case of hurtful, pointless, and destructive things we want so vehemently. . . .

I come back from this unavailing glance into the deeps to the general question of freedoms in this new relation. I find myself far adrift from the case of the Frognal botanist, and asking how far a modern Utopia will deal with personal morals.

As Plato demonstrated long ago, the principles of the relation of State control to personal morals may be best discussed in the case of intoxication, the most isolated and least complicated of all this group of problems. But Plato's treatment of this issue as a question of who may or may not have the use of wine, though suitable enough in considering a small State in which everybody was the effectual inspector of everybody, is entirely beside the mark under modern conditions, in which we are to have an extraordinarily higher standard of individual privacy and an amplitude and quantity of migration inconceivable to the Academic imagination. We may accept this principle and put this particular freedom (of the use of wine) among the distinctive privileges of maturity, and still find all that a modern would think of as the Drink Question untouched.

That question in Utopia will differ perhaps in the proportion of its factors, but in no other respect, from what it is upon earth. The same desirable ends will be sought, the maintenance of public order and decency, the reduction of inducements to form this bad and wasteful habit to their lowest possible minimum, and the complete protection of the immature. But the modern Utopians, having systematised their sociology, will have given some attention to the psychology of minor officials, a matter altogether too much neglected by the social reformer on earth. They will not put into the hands of a common policeman powers direct and indirect that would be dangerous to the public in the hands of a judge. And they will have avoided the immeasurable error of making their control of the drink traffic a source of public revenue. Privacies they will not invade, but they will certainly restrict the public consumption of intoxicants to specified licensed places and the sale of them to unmistakable adults, and they will make the temptation of the young a grave offence. In so migratory a population as the Modern Utopian, the licensing of inns and bars would be under the same control as the railways and high roads. Inns exist for the stranger and not for the locality, and we shall meet with nothing there to correspond with our terrestrial absurdity of Local Option.

The Utopians will certainly control this trade, and as certainly punish personal excesses. Public drunkenness (as distinguished from the mere elation that follows a generous but controlled use of wine) will be an offence against public decency, and will be dealt with in some very drastic manner. It will, of course, be an aggravation of, and not an excuse for, crime.

But I doubt whether the State will go beyond that. Whether an adult shall use wine or beer or spirits, or not, seems to me entirely a matter for his doctor and his own private conscience. I doubt if we explorers shall meet any drunken men, and I doubt not we shall meet many who have never availed themselves of their adult freedom in this respect. The conditions of physical happiness will be better understood in Utopia, it will be worth while to be well there, and the intelligent citizen will watch himself closely. Half and more of the drunkenness of earth is an attempt to lighten dull days and hopelessly sordid and disagreeable lives, and in Utopia they do not suffer these things. Assuredly Utopia will be temperate, not only drinking, but eating with the soundest discretion. Yet I do not think wine and good ale will be altogether wanting there, nor good, mellow whisky, nor, upon occasion, the engaging various liqueur. I do not think so. My botanist, who abstains altogether, is of another opinion. We differ here and leave the question to the earnest reader. I have the utmost respect for all Teetotalers, Prohibitionists, and Haters and Persecutors of Innkeepers, their energy of reform awakens responsive notes in me, and to their species I look for a large part of the urgent repair of our earth ; yet for all that——

There is Burgundy, for example, a bottle of soft and kindly Burgundy, taken to make a sunshine on one's lunch when four strenuous hours of toil have left one on the further side of appetite. Or ale, a foaming tankard of ale, ten miles of sturdy tramping in the sleet and slush as a prelude, and then good bread and good butter and a ripe hollow Stilton and celery and ale——ale with a certain quantitative freedom. Or, again, where is the sin in a glass of tawny port three or four times, or it may be five, a year, when the walnuts come round in their season ? If you drink no port, then what are walnuts for ? Such things I hold for the reward of vast intervals of abstinence ; they justify your wide, immaculate margin, which is else a mere unmeaning blankness on the page of palate God has given you ! I write of these things as a fleshly man, confessedly and knowingly fleshly, and more than usually aware of my liability to err ; I know myself for a gross creature more given to sedentary world-mending than to brisk activities, and not one-tenth as active as the dullest newspaper boy in London. Yet still I have my uses, uses that vanish in monotony, and still I must ask why should we bury the talent of these bright sensations altogether? Under no circumstances can I think of my Utopians maintaining their fine order of life on ginger ale and lemonade and the ale that is Kops'. Those terrible Temperance Drinks, solutions of qualified sugar mixed with vast volumes of gas, as, for example, soda, seltzer, lemonade, and *fire-extincteurs* hand grenades—*minerals*, they call such stuff in England—fill a man with wind and self-righteousness. Indeed they do! Coffee destroys brain and kidney, a fact now universally recognised and advertised throughout America; and tea, except for a kind of green tea best used with discretion in punch, tans the entrails and turns honest stomachs into leather bags. Rather would I be Metchnikoffed [1] at once and have a clean, good stomach of German silver. No! If we are to have no ale in Utopia, give me the one clean temperance drink that is worthy to set beside wine, and that is simple water. Best it is when not quite pure and with a trace of organic matter, for then it tastes and sparkles. . . .

My botanist would still argue.

Thank Heaven this is my book, and that the ultimate decision rests with me. It is open to him to write his own Utopia and arrange that everybody shall do nothing except by the consent of the savants of the Republic, either in his eating, drinking, dressing or lodging, even as Cabet proposed. It is open to him to try a *News from Nowhere* Utopia with the wine left out. I have my short way with him here quite effectually. I turn in the entrance of our inn to the civil but by no means obsequious landlord, and with a careful ambiguity of manner—for the thing may be considered an outrage, and I try to make it possible the idea is a jest—put my test demand. . . .

"You see, my dear Teetotaler?—he sets before me tray and glass and . . ." Here follows the necessary experiment and a deep sigh. . . . "Yes, a bottle of quite *excellent* light beer! So there are also cakes and ale in Utopia! Let us in this saner and more beautiful world drink perdition to all earthly excesses. Let us drink more particularly to the coming of the day when men beyond there will learn to distinguish between qualitative and quantitative questions, to temper good intentions with good intelligence, and righteousness with wisdom. One of the darkest evils of our world is surely the unteachable wildness of the Good."

§ 7

So presently to bed and to sleep, but not at once to sleep. At first my brain, like a dog in unfamiliar quarters, must turn itself round for a time or so before it lies down. This strange mystery of a world of which I have seen so little as yet—a mountain slope, a twilit road, a traffic of ambiguous vehicles

[1] See *The Nature of Man*, by Professor Elie Metchnikoff.

and dim shapes, the window lights of many homes—fills me with curiosities. Figures and incidents come and go, the people we have passed, our landlord, quietly attentive and yet, I feel, with the keenest curiosity peeping from his eyes, the unfamiliar forms of the house parts and furnishings, the unfamiliar courses of the meal. Outside this little bedroom is a world, a whole unimagined world. A thousand million things lie outside in the darkness beyond this lit inn of ours, unthought-of possibilities, overlooked considerations, surprises, riddles, incommensurables, a whole monstrous intricate universe of consequences that I have to do my best to unravel. I attempt impossible recapitulations and mingle the weird quality of dream stuff with my thoughts.

Athwart all this tumult of my memory goes this queer figure of my unanticipated companion, so obsessed by himself and his own egotistical love that this sudden change to another world seems only a change of scene for his gnawing, uninvigorating passion. It occurs to me that she also must have an equivalent in Utopia, and then that idea and all ideas grow thin and vague, and are dissolved at last in the rising tide of sleep. . . .

CHAPTER THREE

UTOPIAN ECONOMICS

§ 1

THESE modern Utopians with the universally diffused good manners, the universal education, the fine freedoms we shall ascribe to them, their world unity, world language, world-wide travellings, world-wide freedom of sale and purchase, will remain mere dreamstuff, incredible even by twilight, until we have shown that at that level the community will still sustain itself. At any rate, the common liberty of the Utopians will not embrace the common liberty to be unserviceable, the most perfect economy of organisation still leaves the fact untouched that all order and security in a State rests on the certainty of getting work done ? How will the work of this planet be done ? What will be the economics of a modern Utopia ?

Now in the first place, a state so vast and complex as this world Utopia, and with so migratory a people, will need some handy symbol to check the distribution of services and commodities. Almost certainly they will need to have money. They will have money, and it is not inconceivable that, for all his sorrowful thoughts, our botanist, with his trained observation, his habit of looking at little things upon the ground, would be the one to see and pick up the coin that has

In Utopia, a great multitude of selected men, chosen volunteers, will be collaborating upon this new step in man's struggle with the elements. Bacon's visionary House of Saloman [1] will be a thing realised, and it will be humming with this business. Every university in the world will be urgently working for priority in this aspect of the problem or that. Reports of experiments, as full and as prompt as the telegraphic reports of cricket in our more sportive atmosphere, will go about the world All this will be passing, as it were, behind the act drop of our first experience, behind this first picture of the urbanised Urseren valley. The literature of the subject will be growing and developing with the easy swiftness of an eagle's swoop as we come down the hillside; unseen in that twilight, unthought of by us until this moment, a thousand men at a thousand glowing desks, a busy specialist press, will be perpetually sifting, criticising, condensing, and clearing the ground for further speculation. Those who are concerned with the problems of public locomotion will be following these aeronautic investigations with a keen and enterprising interest, and so will the physiologist and the sociologist. That Utopian research will, I say, go like an eagle's swoop in comparison with the blind-man's fumbling of our terrestrial way. Even before our own brief Utopian journey is out, we may get a glimpse of the swift ripening of all this activity that will be in progress at our coming. To-morrow, perhaps, or in a day or so, some silent, distant thing will come gliding into view over the mountains, will turn and soar and pass again beyond our astonished sight. . . .

§ 6

But my friend and his great trouble turn my mind from these questions of locomotion and the freedoms that cluster about them. In spite of myself I find myself framing his case. He is a lover, the most conventional of Anglican lovers, with a heart that has had its training, I should think, in the clean but limited schoolroom of Mrs. Henry Wood. . . .

In Utopia I think they will fly with stronger pinions, it will not be in the superficialities of life merely that movement will be wide and free, they will mount higher and swoop more steeply than he in his cage can believe. What will their range be, their prohibitions ? what jars to our preconceptions will he and I receive here ?

My mind flows with the free, thin flow that it has at the end of an eventful day, and as we walk along in silence towards our inn I rove from issue to issue, I find myself ranging amidst the fundamental things of the individual life and all the per-plexity of desires and passions. I turn my questionings to the most difficult of all sets of compromises, those mitigations of spontaneous freedom that constitute the marriage laws,

[1] In The New Atlantis.

dishonour and banishing it from the State is punishing the
hatchet for the murderer's crime. Money, did you but use it
right, is a good thing in life, a necessary thing in civilised
human life, as complicated, indeed, for its purposes, but as
natural a growth as the bones in a man's wrist, and I do not
see how one can imagine anything at all worthy of being called
a civilisation without it. It is the water of the body social,
it distributes and receives, and renders growth and assimilation and movement and recovery possible. It is the reconciliation of human interdependence with liberty. What
other device will give a man so great a freedom with so strong
an inducement to effort ? The economic history of the world,
where it is not the history of the theory of property, is very
largely the record of the abuse, not so much of money as of
credit devices to supplement money, to amplify the scope of
this most precious invention ; and no device of labour credits[1]
or free demand of commodities from a central store[2] or the
like has ever been suggested that does not give ten thousand
times more scope for that inherent moral dross in man that
must be reckoned with in any sane Utopia we may design and
plan. . . . Heaven knows where progress may not end, but
at any rate this developing State, into which we two men have
fallen, this Twentieth Century Utopia, has still not passed
beyond money and the use of coins.

§ 2

Now if this Utopian world is to be in some degree parallel to
contemporary thought, it must have been concerned, it may
be still concerned, with many unsettled problems of currency,
and with the problems that centre about a standard of value.
Gold is perhaps of all material substances the best adapted to
the monetary purpose, but even at that best it falls far short of
an imaginable ideal. It undergoes spasmodic and irregular
cheapening through new discoveries of gold, and at any time
it may undergo very extensive and sudden and disastrous
depreciation through the discovery of some way of trans-
muting less valuable elements. The liability to such deprecia-
tions introduces an undesirable speculative element into the
relations of debtor and creditor. When, on the one hand,
there is for a time a check in the increase of the available
stores of gold, or an increase in the energy applied to social
purposes, or a checking of the public security that would
impede the free exchange of credit and necessitate a more
frequent production of gold in evidence, then there comes an
undue appreciation of money as against the general commodities of life, and an automatic improverishment of the
citizens in general as against the creditor class. The common
people are mortgaged into the bondage of debt. And on the

[1] Edward Bellamy's *Looking Backward,* ch. ix.
[2] More's *Utopia* and Cabet's *Icaria.*

other hand an unexpected spate of gold production, the discovery of a single nugget as big as St. Paul's, let us say—a quite possible thing—would result in a sort of jail delivery of debtors and a financial earthquake.

It has been suggested by an ingenious thinker that it is possible to use as a standard of monetary value no substance whatever, but instead, force, and that value might be measured in units of energy. An excellent development this, in theory, at any rate, of the general idea of the modern State as kinetic and not static ; it throws the old idea of the social order and the new into the sharpest antithesis. The old order is presented as a system of institutions and classes ruled by men of substance ; the new, of enterprises and interests led by men of power.

Now I glance at this matter in the most incidental manner, as a man may skim through a specialist's exposition in a popular magazine. You must figure me, therefore, finding from a casual periodical paper in our inn, with a certain surprise at not having anticipated as much, the Utopian self of that same ingenious person quite conspicuously a leader of thought, and engaged in organising the discussion of the currency changes Utopia has under consideration. The article, as it presents itself to me, contains a complete and lucid, though occasionally rather technical, explanation of his newest proposals. They have been published, it seems, for general criticism, and one gathers that in the modern Utopia the administration presents the most elaborately detailed schemes of any proposed alteration in law or custom, some time before any measure is taken to carry it into effect, and the possibilities of every detail are acutely criticised, flaws anticipated, side issues raised, and the whole minutely tested and fined down by a planetful of critics, before the actual process of legislation begins.

The explanation of these proposals involves an anticipatory glance at the local administration of a Modern Utopia. To any one who has watched the development of technical science during the last decade or so, there will be no shock in the idea that a general consolidation of a great number of common public services over areas of considerable size is now not only practicable, but very desirable. In a little while heating and lighting and the supply of power for domestic and industrial purposes and for urban and inter-urban communications will all be managed electrically from common generating stations. And the trend of political and social speculation points decidedly to the conclusion that so soon as it passes out of the experimental stage, the supply of electrical energy, just like drainage and the supply of water, will fall to the local authority. Moreover, the local authority will be the universal landowner. Upon that point so extreme an individualist as Herbert Spencer was in agreement with the Socialist. In Utopia

T.-B.—M.U.   M

we conclude that, whatever other types of property may exist, all natural sources of force, and indeed all strictly natural products, coal, water power, and the like, are inalienably vested in the local authorities (which, in order to secure the maximum of convenience and administrative efficiency, will probably control areas as large sometimes as half England) they will generate electricity by water power, by combustion, by wind or tide or whatever other natural force is available, and this electricity will be devoted, some of it to the authority's lighting and other public works, some of it, as a subsidy, to the World-State authority which controls the high roads, the great railways, the inns and other apparatus of world communication, and the rest will pass on to private individuals or to distributing companies at a uniform fixed rate for private lighting and heating, for machinery and industrial applications of all sorts. Such an arrangement of affairs will necessarily involve a vast amount of book-keeping between the various authorities, the World-State government and the customers, and this book-keeping will naturally be done most conveniently in units of physical energy.

It is not incredible that the assessment of the various local administrations for the central world government would be already calculated upon the estimated total of energy, periodically available in each locality, and booked and spoken of in these physical units. Accounts between central and local governments could be kept in these terms. Moreover, one may imagine Utopian local authorities making contracts in which payment would be no longer in coinage upon the gold basis, but in notes good for so many thousand or millions of units of energy at one or other of the generating stations.

Now the problems of economic theory will have undergone an enormous clarification if, instead of measuring in fluctuating money values, the same scale of energy units can be extended to their discussion, if, in fact, the idea of trading could be entirely eliminated. In my Utopia, at any rate, this has been done, the production and distribution of common commodities have been expressed as a problem in the conversion of energy, and the scheme that Utopia was now discussing was the application of this idea of energy as the standard of value to the entire Utopian coinage. Every one of those giant local authorities was to be free to issue energy notes against the security of its surplus of saleable available energy, and to make all its contracts for payment in those notes up to a certain maximum defined by the amount of energy produced and disposed of in that locality in the previous year. This power of issue was to be renewed just as rapidly as the notes came in for redemption. In a world without boundaries, with a population largely migratory and emancipated from locality, the price of the energy notes of these various local bodies would constantly tend to be uniform, because employment would constantly shift into the areas where energy was cheap. Accordingly, the price of so many millions of units of energy at any particular moment in coins of the gold currency would be approximately the same throughout the world. It was proposed to select some particular day when the economic atmosphere was distinctly equable, and to declare a fixed ratio between the gold coinage and the energy notes ; each gold Lion and each Lion of credit representing exactly the number of energy units it could buy on that day. The old gold coinage was at once to cease to be legal tender beyond certain defined limits, except to the central government, which would not re-issue it as it came in. It was, in fact, to become a temporary token coinage, a token coinage of full value for the day of conversion at any rate, if not afterwards, under the new standard of energy, and to be replaceable by an ordinary token coinage as time went on. The old computation by Lions and the values of the small change of daily life were therefore to suffer no disturbance whatever.

The economists of Utopia, as I apprehended them, had a different method and a very different system of theories from those I have read on earth, and this makes my exposition considerably more difficult. This article upon which I base my account floated before me in an unfamiliar, perplexing, and dream-like phraseology. Yet I brought away an impression that here was a rightness that earthly economists have failed to grasp. Few earthly economists have been able to disentangle themselves from patriotisms and politics, and their obsession has always been international trade. Here in Utopia the World State cuts that away from beneath their feet ; there are no imports but meteorites, and no exports at all. Trading is the earthly economists' initial notion, and they start from perplexing and insoluble riddles about exchange value, insoluble because all trading finally involves individual preferences which are incalculable and unique. Nowhere do they seem to be handling really defined standards, every economic dissertation and discussion reminds one more strongly than the last of the game of croquet Alice played in Wonderland, when the mallets were flamingoes and the balls were hedgehogs and crawled away, and the hoops were soldiers and kept getting up and walking about. But economics in Utopia must be, it seems to me, not a theory of trading based on bad psychology. but physics applied to problems in the theory of sociology. The general problem of Utopian economics is to state the conditions of the most efficient application of the steadily increasing quantities of material energy the progress of science makes available for human service, to the general needs of mankind. Human labour and existing material are dealt with in relation to that. Trading and relative wealth are merely episodical in such a scheme. The trend of the article I read, as I understood it, was that a

monetary system based upon a relatively small amount
gold, upon which the business of the whole world had hither
been done, fluctuated unreasonably and supplied no re
criterion of well-being, that the nominal values of things an
enterprises had no clear and simple relation to the real physic
prosperity of the community, that the nominal wealth of
community in millions of pounds or dollars or Lions, measure
nothing but the quantity of hope in the air, and in increas
of confidence meant an inflation of credit and a pessimist
phase a collapse of this hallucination of possessions. The ne
standards, this advocate reasoned, were to alter all that, an
it seemed to me they would.

I have tried to indicate the drift of these remarkable pre
posals, but about them clustered an elaborate mass of kee
and temperate discussion. Into the details of that discussic
I will not enter now, nor am I sure I am qualified to rende
the multitudinous aspect of this complicated question at a
precisely. I read the whole thing in the course of an hour o
two of rest after lunch—it was either the second or third da
of my stay in Utopia—and we were sitting in a little inn a
the end of the Lake of Uri. We had loitered there, and I ha
fallen reading because of a shower of rain. . . . But certain
as I read it the proposition struck me as a singularly simple an
attractive one, and its exposition opened out to me for th
first time clearly, in a comprehensive outline, the general co
ception of the economic nature of the Utopian State.

§ 3

The difference between the social and economic scienc
as they exist in our world [1] and in this Utopia deserv
perhaps a word or so more. I write with the utmost diffidenc
because upon earth economic science has been raised to a ve
high level of tortuous abstraction by the industry of its pr
fessors, and I can claim neither a patient student's intima
with their productions nor—what is more serious—anythi
but the most generalised knowledge of what their Utopi
equivalents have achieved. The vital nature of econom
issues to a Utopia necessitates, however, some attempt
interpretation between the two.

In Utopia there is no distinct and separate science
economics. Many problems that we should regard as econom
come within the scope of Utopian psychology. My Utopia
make two divisions of the science of psychology, first, t
general psychology of individuals, a sort of mental physiolo
separated by no definite line from physiology proper, a
secondly, the psychology of relationship between individua
This second is an exhaustive study of the reaction of peop

[1] But see Gidding's *Principles of Sociology*, a modern and richly suggestive Americ
work, imperfectly appreciated by the British student. See also Walter Bageho
Economic Studies.

upon each other and of all possible relationships. It is a science of human aggregations, of all possible family groupings, of neighbours and neighbourhood, of companies, associations, unions, secret and public societies, religious groupings, of common ends and intercourse, and of the methods of intercourse and collective decision that hold human groups together, and finally of government and the State. The elucidation of economic relationships, depending as it does on the nature of the hypothesis of human aggregation actually in operation at any time, is considered to be subordinate and subsequent to this general science of Sociology. Political economy and economics, in our world now, consist of a hopeless muddle of social assumptions and preposterous psychology, and a few geographical and physical generalisations. Its ingredients will be classified out and widely separated in Utopian thought. On the one hand there will be the study of physical economies, ending in the descriptive treatment of society as an organisation for the conversion of all the available energy in nature to the material ends of mankind—a physical sociology which will be already at such a stage of practical development as to be giving the world this token coinage representing energy— and on the other there will be the study of economic problems as problems in the division of labour, having regard to a social organisation whose main ends are reproduction and education in an atmosphere of personal freedom. Each of these inquiries, working unencumbered by the other, will be continually contributing fresh valid conclusions for the use of the practical administrator.

In no region of intellectual activity will our hypothesis of freedom from tradition be of more value in devising a Utopia from here. From its beginning the earthly study of economics has been infertile and unhelpful, because of the mass of unanalysed and scarcely suspected assumptions upon which it rested. The facts were ignored that trade is a by-product and not an essential factor in social life, that property is a plastic and fluctuating convention, that value is capable of impersonal treatment only in the case of the most generalised requirements. Wealth was measured by the standards of exchange. Society was regarded as a practically unlimited number of avaricious adult units incapable of any other subordinate groupings than business partnerships, and the sources of competition were assumed to be inexhaustible. Upon such quicksands rose an edifice that aped the securities of material science, developed a technical jargon and professed the discovery of " laws." Our liberation from these false presumptions through the rhetoric of Carlyle and Ruskin and the activities of the Socialists, is more apparent than real. The old edifice oppresses us still, repaired and altered by indifferent builders, underpinned in places, and with a slight change of name. " Political Economy " has been painted out, and

instead we read " Economics—under entirely new management." Modern Economics differs mainly from old Political
Economy in having produced no Adam Smith. The old
" Political Economy " made certain generalisations, and they
were mostly wrong ; new Economics evades generalisations,
and seems to lack the intellectual power to make them. The
science hangs like a gathering fog in a valley, a fog which
begins nowhere and goes nowhere, an incidental, unmeaning
inconvenience to passers-by. Its most typical exponents
display a disposition to disavow generalisations altogether,
to claim consideration as " experts," and to make immediate
political application of that conceded claim. Now Newton,
Darwin, Dalton, Davy, Joule, and Adam Smith did not affect
this " expert " hankey-pankey, becoming enough in a hairdresser or a fashionable physician, but indecent in a philosopher
or a man of science. In this state of impotent expertness,
however, or in some equally unsound state, economics must
struggle on—a science that is no science, a floundering lore
wallowing in a mud of statistics—until either the study of the
material organisation of production on the one hand as a
development of physics and geography, or the study of social
aggregation on the other, renders enduring foundations possible.

§ 4

The older Utopias were all relatively small states ; Plato's
Republic, for example, was to be smaller than the average
English borough, and no distinction was made between the
Family, the Local Government, and the State. Plato and
Campanella—for all that the latter was a Christian priest—
carried communism to its final point and prescribed even a
community of husbands and wives, an idea that was brought
at last to the test of effectual experiment in the Oneida Community of New York State (1848–1879). This latter body did
not long survive its founder, at least as a veritable communism,
by reason of the insurgent individualism of its vigorous sons.
More, too, denied privacy and ruled an absolute community
of goods, at any rate, and so, coming to the Victorian Utopias,
did Cabet. But Cabet's communism was one of the " free
store " type, and the goods were yours only after you had
requisitioned them. That seems the case in the " Nowhere "
of Morris also. Compared with the older writers Bellamy and
Morris have a vivid sense of individual separation, and their
departure, from the old homogeneity is sufficiently marked
to justify a doubt whether there will be any more thoroughly
communistic Utopias for ever.

A Utopia such as this present one, written in the opening
of the Twentieth Century, and after the most exhaustive
discussion—nearly a century long—between Communistic
and Socialistic ideas on the one hand, and Individualism on the
other, emerges upon a sort of effectual conclusion to those

controversies. The two parties have so chipped and amended each other's initial propositions that, indeed, except for the labels still flutteringly adhesive to the implicated men, it is hard to choose between them. Each side established a good many propositions, and we profit by them all. We of the succeeding generation can see quite clearly that for the most part the heat and zeal of these discussions arose in the confusion of a quantitative for a qualitative question. To the onlooker, both Individualism and Socialism are, in the absolute, absurdities ; the one would make men the slaves of the violent or rich, the other the slaves of the State official, and the way of sanity runs, perhaps even sinuously, down the intervening valley. Happily the dead past buries its dead, and it is not our function now to adjudicate the preponderance of victory. In the very days when our political and economic order is becoming steadily more Socialistic, our ideals of intercourse turn more and more to a fuller recognition of the claims of individuality. The State is to be progressive, it is no longer to be static, and this alters the general condition of the Utopian problem profoundly ; we have to provide not only for food and clothing, for order and health, but for initiative. The factor that leads the World State on from one phase of development to the next is the interplay of individualities ; to speak teleologically, the world exists for the sake of and through initiative, and individuality is the method of initiative. Each man and woman, to the extent that his or her individuality is marked, breaks the law of precedent, transgresses the general formula, and makes a new experiment for the direction of the life force. It is impossible, therefore, for the State, which represents all and is preoccupied by the average to make effectual experiments and intelligent innovations, and so supply the essential substance of life. As against the individual the state represents the species, in the case of the Utopian World State it absolutely represents the species. The individual emerges from the species, makes his experiment, and either fails, dies, and comes to an end, or succeeds and impresses himself in offspring, in consequences and results, intellectual, material and moral, upon the world.

Biologically the species is the accumulation of the experiments of all its successful individuals since the beginning, and the World State of the Modern Utopist will, in its economic aspect, be a compendium of established economic experience, about which individual enterprise will be continually experimenting, either to fail and pass, or to succeed and at last become incorporated with the undying organism of the World State. This organism is the universal rule, the common restriction, the rising level platform on which individualities stand.

The World State in this ideal presents itself as the sole landowner of the earth, with the great local governments I have adumbrated, the local municipalities, holding, as it were, feudally under it as landlords. The State or these subordinates holds all the sources of energy, and either directly or through its tenants, farmers and agents, develops these sources, and renders the energy available for the work of life. It or its tenants will produce food, and so human energy, and the exploitation of coal and electric power, and the powers of wind and wave and water will be within its right. It will pour out this energy by assignment and lease and acquiescence and what not upon its individual citizens. It will maintain order, maintain roads, maintain a cheap and efficient administration of justice, maintain cheap and rapid locomotion and be the common carrier of the planet, convey and distribute labour, control, let, or administer all natural productions, pay for and secure healthy births and a healthy and vigorous new generation, maintain the public health, coin money and sustain standards of measurement, subsidise research, and reward such commercially unprofitable undertakings as benefit the community as a whole ; subsidise when needful chairs of criticism and authors and publications, and collect and distribute information. The energy developed and the employment afforded by the State will descend like water that the sun has sucked out of the sea to fall upon a mountain range, and back to the sea again it will come at last, debouching in ground rent and royalty and licence fees, in the fees of travellers and profits upon carrying and coinage and the like, in death duty, transfer tax, legacy and forfeiture, returning to the sea. Between the clouds and the sea it will run, as a river system runs, down through a great region of individual enterprise and interplay, whose freedom it will sustain. In that intermediate region between the kindred heights and deeps those beginnings and promises will arise that are the essential significance, the essential substance, of life. From our human point of view the mountains and sea are for the habitable lands that lie between. So likewise the State is for Individualities. The State is for Individuals, the law is for freedoms, the world is for experiment, experience, and change : these are the fundamental beliefs upon which a modern Utopia must go.

§ 5

Within this scheme, which makes the State the source of all energy, and the final legatee, what will be the nature of the property a man may own ? Under modern conditions— indeed, under any conditions—a man without some negotiable property is a man without freedom, and the extent of his property is very largely the measure of his freedom. Without any property, without even shelter or food, a man has no choice but to set about getting these things ; he is in servitude to his needs until he has secured property to satisfy them. But with a certain small property a man is free to do many things, to take a fortnight's holiday when he chooses, for example, and to try this new departure from his work or that ; with so much more, he may take a year of freedom and go to the ends of the earth ; with so much more, he may obtain elaborate apparatus and try curious novelties, build himself houses and make gardens, establish businesses and make experiments at large. Very speedily, under terrestrial conditions, the property of a man may reach such proportions that his freedom oppresses the freedom of others. Here, again, is a quantitative question, an adjustment of conflicting freedoms, a quantitative question that too many people insist on making a qualitative one.

The object sought in the code of property laws that one would find in operation in Utopia would be the same object that pervades the whole Utopian organisation, namely, a universal maximum of individual freedom. Whatever far-reaching movements the State or great rich men or private corporations may make, the starvation by any complication of employment, the unwilling deportation, the destruction of alternatives to servile submissions, must not ensue. Beyond such qualifications, the object of Modern Utopian statesmanship will be to secure to a man the freedom given by all his legitimate property, that is to say, by all the values his toil or skill or foresight and courage have brought into being. Whatever he has justly made he has a right to keep, that is obvious enough ; but he will also have a right to sell and exchange, and so this question of what may be property takes really the form of what may a man buy in Utopia ?

A modern Utopian most assuredly must have a practically unqualified property in all those things that become, as it were, by possession, extensions and expressions of his personality ; his clothing, his jewels, the tools of his employment, his books, the objects of art he may have bought or made, his personal weapons (if Utopia have need of such things), insignia, and so forth. All such things that he has bought with his money or acquired—provided he is not a professional or habitual dealer in such property—will be inalienably his, his to give or lend or keep, free even from taxation. So intimate is this sort of property that I have no doubt Utopia will give a man posthumous rights over it—will permit him to assign it to a successor with at the utmost the payment of a small redemption. A horse, perhaps, in certain districts, or a bicycle, or any such mechanical conveyance personally used, the Utopians might find it well to rank with these possessions. No doubt, too, a house and privacy owned and occupied by a man, and even a man's own household furniture, might be held to stand as high or almost as high in the property scale, might be taxed as lightly and transferred under only a slightly heavier redemption, provided he had not let these things on hire, or otherwise alienated them from his intimate self. A thoroughgoing, Democratic Socialist will no doubt be inclined at first to object that if the Utopians make these things a specially free sort of property in this way, men would spend much more upon them than they would otherwise do, but indeed that will be an excellent thing. We are too much affected by the needy atmosphere of our own mismanaged world. In Utopia no one will have to hunger because some love to make and have made and own and cherish beautiful things. To give this much property to individuals will tend to make clothing, ornamentation, implements, books, and all the arts finer and more beautiful, because by buying such things a man will secure something inalienable—save in the case of bankruptcy—for himself and for those who belong to him. Moreover, a man may in his lifetime set aside sums to ensure special advantages of education and care for the immature children of himself and others, and in this manner also exercise a posthumous right.[1]

For all other property, the Utopians will have a scantier respect ; even money unspent by a man, and debts to him that bear no interest, will at his death stand upon a lower level than these things. What he did not choose to gather and assimilate to himself, or assign for the special education of his children, the State will share in the lion's proportion with heir and legatee.

This applies, for example, to the property that a man creates and acquires in business enterprises, which are presumably undertaken for gain, and as a means of living rather than for themselves. All new machinery, all new methods, all uncertain and variable and non-universal undertakings, are no business for the State ; they commence always as experiments of unascertained value, and next after the invention of money, there is no invention has so facilitated freedom and progress as the invention of the limited liability company to do this work of trial and adventure. The abuses, the necessary reforms of company law on earth are no concern of ours here and now, suffice it that in a Modern Utopia such laws must be supposed to be as perfect as mortal laws can possibly be made. *Caveat vendor* will be a sound qualification of *Caveat emptor* in the beautifully codified Utopian law. Whether the Utopian company will be allowed to prefer this class of share to that or to issue debentures, whether indeed usury, that is to say lending money at fixed rates of interest, will be permitted at all in Utopia, one may venture to doubt. But whatever the nature of the shares a man may hold, they will all be sold at his death, and whatever he has not clearly assigned for special educational purposes will—with possibly

[1] But a Statute of Mortmain will set a distinct time limit to the continuance of such benefactions. A periodic revision of endowments is a necessary feature in any modern Utopia.

some fractional concession to near survivors—lapse to the
State. The "safe investment," that permanent, undying
claim upon the community, is just one of those things Utopia
will discourage ; which indeed the developing security of
civilisation quite automatically discourages through the fall
in the rate of interest. As we shall see at a later stage, the
State will insure the children of every citizen, and those legitimately dependent upon him, against the inconvenience of his
death ; it will carry out all reasonable additional dispositions
he may have made for them in the same event, and it will
insure him against old age and infirmity ; and the object of
Utopian economics will be to give a man every inducement to
spend his surplus money in intensifying the quality of his
surroundings, either by economic adventures and experiments, which may yield either losses or large profits, or in increasing the beauty, the pleasure, the abundance and promise
of life.

Besides strictly personal possessions and shares in business
adventures, Utopia will no doubt permit associations of its
citizens to have a property in various sorts of contracts and
concessions, in leases of agricultural and other land, for
example ; in houses they may have built, factories and
machinery they may have made, and the like. And if a citizen
prefer to adventure into business single-handed, he will have
all the freedoms of enterprise enjoyed by a company ; in
business affairs he will be a company of one, and his single
share will be dealt with at his death like any other shares. . . .
So much for the second kind of property. And these two kinds
of property will probably exhaust the sorts of property a
Utopian may possess.

The trend of modern thought is entirely against private
property in land or natural objects or products, and in Utopia
these things will be the inalienable property of the World
State. Subject to the rights of free locomotion, land will be
leased out to companies or individuals, but—in view of the
unknown necessities of the future—never for a longer period
than, let us say, fifty years.

The property of a parent in his children, and of a husband
in his wife, seems to be undergoing a steadily increasing
qualification in the world of to-day, but the discussion of the
Utopian state of affairs in regard to such property may be
better reserved until marriage becomes our topic. Suffice it
here to remark, that the increasing control of a child's welfare
and upbringing by the community, and the growing disposition to limit and tax inheritance are complementary aspects
of the general tendency to regard the welfare and free intra-
play of future generations no longer as the concern of parents
and altruistic individuals, but as the predominant issue of
statesmanship, and the duty and moral meaning of the world
community as a whole.

§ 6

From the conception of mechanical force as coming in from Nature to the service of man, a conception the Utopian proposal of a coinage based on energy units would emphasise, arise profound contrasts between the modern and the classical Utopias. Except for a meagre use of water power for milling, and the wind for sailing—so meagre in the latter case that the classical world never contrived to do without the galley slave— and a certain restricted help from oxen in ploughing, and from horses in locomotion, all the energy that sustained the old-fashioned State was aerived from the muscular exertion of toiling men. They ran their world by hand. Continual bodily labour was a condition of social existence. It is only with the coming of coal burning, of abundant iron and steel, and of scientific knowledge that this condition has been changed. To-day, I suppose, if it were possible to indicate, in units of energy, the grand total of work upon which the social fabric of the United States or England rests, it would be found that a vastly preponderating moiety is derived from non-human sources, from coal and liquid fuel, and explosives and wind and water. There is every indication of a steady increase in this proportion of mechanical energy, in this emancipation of men from the necessity of physical labour. There appears no limit to the invasion of life by the machine.

Now it is only in the last three hundred years that any human being seems to have anticipated this. It stimulates the imagination to remark how entirely it was overlooked as a modifying cause in human development.[1] Plato clearly had no ideas about machines at all as a force affecting social organisation. There was nothing in his world to suggest them to him. I suppose there arose no invention, no new mechanical appliance or method of the slightest social importance through all his length of years. He never thought of a State that did not rely for its force upon human muscle, just as he never thought of a State that was not primarily organised for warfare hand to hand. Political and moral inventions he saw enough of and to spare, and in that direction he still stimulates the imagination. But in regard to all material possibilities he deadens rather than stimulates.[2] An infinitude of nonsense about the Greek mind would never have been written if the distinctive intellectual and artistic quality of Plato's time, its extraordinarily clear definition of certain material conditions as absolutely permanent, coupled with its politico-social instability, had been borne in mind. The food of the Greek imagination was the very antithesis of our own nourishment. We are educated by our circumstances to think no revolution

[1] It is interesting to note how little even Bacon seems to see of this in his *New Atlantis*.
[2] The lost Utopia of Hippodamus provided rewards for inventors, but unless Aristotle misunderstood him, and it is certainly the fate of all Utopias to be more or less misread, the inventions contemplated were political devices.

in appliances and economic organisation incredible, our minds play freely about possibilities that would have struck the men of the Academy as outrageous extravagance, and it is in regard to politico-social expedients that our imaginations fail. Sparta, for all the evidence of history, is scarcely more credible to us than a motor-car throbbing in the agora would have been to Socrates.

By sheer inadvertence, therefore, Plato commenced the tradition of Utopias without machinery, a tradition we find Morris still loyally following, except for certain mechanical barges and such-like toys, in his *News from Nowhere*. There are some foreshadowings of mechanical possibilities in the *New Atlantis*, but it is only in the nineteenth century that Utopias appeared in which the fact is clearly recognised that the social fabric rests no longer upon human labour. It was, I believe, Cabet [1] who first in a Utopian work insisted upon the escape of man from irksome labours through the use of machinery. He is the great primitive of modern Utopias, and Bellamy is his American equivalent. Hitherto, either slave labour (Phaleas),[2] or at least class distinctions involving unavoidable labour in the lower class, have been assumed— as Plato does, and as Bacon in the *New Atlantis* probably intended to do (More gave his Utopians bondsmen *sans phrase* for their most disagreeable toil) ; or there is—as in Morris and the outright Return-to-Nature Utopians—a bold make-believe that all toil may be made a joy, and with that a levelling down of all society to an equal participation in labour. But indeed this is against all the observed behaviour of mankind. It needed the Olympian unworldliness of an irresponsible rich man of the shareholding type, a Ruskin or a Morris playing at life, to imagine as much. Road-making under Mr. Ruskin's auspices was a joy at Oxford no doubt, and a distinction, and it still remains a distinction ; it proved the least contagious of practices. And Hawthorne did not find bodily toil anything more than the curse the Bible says it is, at Brook Farm.[3]

If toil is a blessing, never was blessing so effectually disguised, and the very people who tell us that, hesitate to suggest more than a beautiful ease in the endless day of Heaven. A certain amount of bodily or mental exercise, a considerable amount of doing things under the direction of one's free imagination is quite another matter. Artistic production, for example, when it is at its best, when a man is freely obeying himself, and not troubling to please others, is really not toil at all. It is quite a different thing digging potatoes, as boys say, "for a lark," and digging them because otherwise you will starve, digging them day after day as a dull, unavoidable

[1] Cabet, *Voyage en Icarie*, 1848.
[2] Aristotle's *Politics*, bk. ii., ch. viii.
[3] *The Blythedale Experiment*, and see also his *Notebook*.

imperative. The essence of toil is that imperative, and the
fact that the attention *must* cramp itself to the work in hand—
that it excludes freedom, and not that it involves fatigue.
So long as anything but a quasi-savage life depended upon
toil, so long was it hopeless to expect mankind to do anything
but struggle to confer just as much of this blessing as possible
upon one another. But now that the new conditions physical
science is bringing about, not only dispense with man as a
source of energy but supply the hope that all routine work
may be made automatic, it is becoming conceivable that presently there may be no need for any one to toil habitually at
all ; that a labouring class—that is to say, a class of workers
without personal initiative—will become unnecessary to the
world of men.

The plain message physical science has for the world at
large is this, that were our political and social and moral
devices only as well contrived to their ends as a linotype
machine, an antiseptic operating plant, or an electric tram-
car, there need now at the present moment be no appreciable
toil in the world, and only the smallest fraction of the pain,
the fear, and the anxiety that now makes human life so doubtful in its value. There is more than enough for every one
alive. Science stands, a too competent servant, behind her
wrangling underbred masters, holding out resources, devices,
and remedies they are too stupid to use.[1] And on its material
side a modern Utopia must needs present these gifts as taken,
and show a world that is really abolishing the need of labour,
abolishing the last base reason for any one's servitude or
inferiority.

§ 7

The effectual abolition of a labouring and servile class
will make itself felt in every detail of the inn that will shelter
us, of the bedrooms we shall occupy. You conceive my
awakening to all these things on the morning after our arrival.
I shall lie for a minute or so with my nose peeping over the
coverlet, agreeably and gently coming awake, and with some
vague nightmare of sitting at a common table with an unavoidable dustman in green and gold called Boffin,[2] fading out of
my mind. Then I should start up. You figure my apprehension, startled inspection of my chamber. " Where am
I ? " that classic phrase, recurs. Then I perceive quite clearly
that I am in bed in Utopia.

Utopia ! The word is enough to bring any one out of bed
to the nearest window, but thence I see no more than the great
mountain mass behind the inn, a very terrestrial looking mountain mass. I return to the contrivances about me, and make

---

[1] See that most suggestive little book, *Twentieth Century Inventions,* by Mr. George
Sutherland.
[2] *Vide* William Morris's *News from Nowhere.*

my examination as I dress, pausing garment in hand to hover
over first this thing of interest and then that.

The room is, of course, very clear and clean and simple ;
not by any means cheaply equipped, but designed to economise
the labour of redding and repair just as much as is possible.
It is beautifully proportioned and rather lower than most
rooms I know on earth. There is no fireplace, and I am perplexed by that until I find a thermometer beside six switches
on the wall. Above this switch-board is a brief instruction :
one switch warms the floor, which is not carpeted, but covered
by a substance like soft oilcloth ; one warms the mattress
(which is of metal with resistance coils threaded to and fro in
it); and the others warm the wall in various degrees, each
directing current through a separate system of resistances.
The casement does not open, but above, flush with the ceiling,
a noiseless rapid fan pumps air out of the room. The air
enters by a Tobin shaft. There is a recess dressing-room,
equipped with a bath and all that is necessary to one's toilet,
and the water, one remarks, is warmed, if one desires it warm,
by passing it through an electrically heated spiral of tubing.
A cake of soap drops out of a store machine on the turn of a
handle, and when you have done with it, you drop that and
your soiled towels and so forth, which also are given you by
machines, into a little box, through the bottom of which they
drop at once, and sail down a smooth shaft. A little notice
tells you the price of your room, and you gather the price is
doubled if you do not leave the toilet as you found it. Beside
the bed, and to be lit at night by a handy switch over the
pillow, is a little clock, its face flush with the wall. The room
has no corners to gather dirt, wall meets floor with a gentle
curve, and the apartment could be swept out effectually by a
few strokes of a mechanical sweeper. The door frames and
window frames are of metal, rounded and impervious to
draught. You are politely requested to turn a handle at the
foot of your bed before leaving the room, and forthwith the
frame turns up into a vertical position, and the bedclothes
hang airing. You stand at the doorway and realise that there
remains not a minute's work for any one to do. Memories
of the fœtid disorder of many an earthly bedroom after a
night's use float across your mind.

And you must not imagine this dustless, spotless, sweet
apartment as anything but beautiful. Its appearance is a
little unfamiliar of course, but all the muddle of dust-collect-
ing hangings and witless ornament that cover the earthly
bedroom, the valances, the curtains to check the draught from
the ill-fitting wood windows, the worthless irrelevant pictures,
usually a little askew, the dusty carpets, and all the paraphernalia about the dirty, black-leaded fireplace are gone. But
the faintly tinted walls are framed with just one clear coloured
line, as finely placed as the member of a Greek capital ; the

door handles and the lines of the panels of the door, the two chairs, the framework of the bed, the writing table, have all that final simplicity, that exquisite finish of contour that is begotten of sustained artistic effort. The graciously shaped windows each frame a picture—since they are draughtless the window seats are no mere mockeries as are the window seats of earth—and on the sill, the sole thing to need attention in the room, is one little bowl of blue Alpine flowers.

The same exquisite simplicity meets one downstairs.

Our landlord sits down at table with us for a moment, and seeing we do not understand the electrically heated coffee-pot before us, shows us what to do. Coffee and milk we have, in the Continental fashion, and some excellent rolls and butter.

He is a swarthy little man, our landlord, and overnight we saw him preoccupied with other guests. But we have risen either late or early by Utopian standards, we know not which, and this morning he has us to himself. His bearing is kindly and inoffensive, but he cannot conceal the curiosity that possesses him. His eye meets ours with a mute inquiry, and then as we fall to, we catch him scrutinising our cuffs, our garments, our boots, our faces, our table manners. He asks nothing at first, but says a word or so about our night's comfort and the day's weather, phrases that have an air of being customary. Then comes a silence that is interrogative.

" Excellent coffee," I say to fill the gap.

" And excellent rolls," says my botanist.

Our landlord indicates his sense of our approval.

A momentary diversion is caused by the entry of an elfin-tressed little girl, who stares at us half impudently, half shyly, with bright black eyes, hesitates at the botanist's clumsy smile and nod, and then goes and stands by her father and surveys us steadfastly.

" You have come far ? " ventures our landlord, patting his daughter's shoulder.

I glance at the botanist. " Yes," I say, " we have."

I expand. " We have come so far that this country of yours seems very strange indeed to us."

" The mountains ? "

" Not only the mountains."

" You came up out of the Ticino valley ? "

" No—not that way."

" By the Oberalp ? "

" No."

" The Furka ? "

" No."

" Not up from the lake ? "

" No."

He looks puzzled.

" We came," I say, " from another world."

He seems trying to understand. Then a thought strikes

him, and he sends away his little girl with a needless message to her mother.

" Ah ! " he says. " Another world—eh ? Meaning—— ? "

" Another world—far in the deeps of space."

Then at the expression of his face one realises that a Modern Utopia will probably keep its more intelligent citizens for better work than inn-tending. He is evidently inaccessible to the idea we think of putting before him. He stares at us a moment, and then remarks, " There's the book to sign."

We find ourselves confronted with a book, a little after the fashion of the familiar hotel visitors' book of earth. He places this before us, and beside it puts pen and ink and a slab, upon which ink has been freshly smeared.

"Thumbmarks," says my scientific friend hastily in English.

" You show me how to do it," I say as quickly.

He signs first, and I look over his shoulder.

He is displaying more readiness than I should have expected. The book is ruled in broad transverse lines, and has a space for a name, for a number, and a thumbmark. He puts his thumb upon the slab and makes the thumbmark first with the utmost deliberation. Meanwhile he studies the other two entries. The " numbers " of the previous guests above are complex muddles of letters and figures. He writes his name, then with a calm assurance writes down his number, A.M.a.1607.2.$a\beta\oplus$ I am wrung with momentary admiration. I follow his example, and fabricate an equally imposing signature. We think ourselves very clever. The landlord proffers finger bowls for our thumbs, and his eye goes, just a little curiously, to our entries.

I decide it is advisable to pay and go before any conversation about our formulæ arises.

As we emerge into the corridor, and the morning sunlight of the Utopian world, I see the landlord bending over the book.

" Come on," I say. " The most tiresome thing in the world is explanations, and I perceive that if we do not get along, they will fall upon us now."

I glance back to discover the landlord and a gracefully robed woman standing outside the pretty simplicity of the Utopian inn, watching us doubtfully as we recede.

"Come on," I insist.

§ 8

We should go towards the Schoellenen gorge, and as we went, our fresh morning senses would gather together a thousand factors for our impression of this more civilised world. A Modern Utopia will have done with yapping about nationality, and so the ugly fortifications, the barracks and military defilements of the earthly vale of Urseren will be wanting. Instead there will be a great multitude of gracious little houses clustering in college-like groups, no doubt about their common kitchens and halls, down and about the valley slopes. And there will be many more trees, and a great variety of trees—all the world will have been ransacked for winter conifers. Despite the height of the valley there will be a double avenue along the road. This high road with its tramway would turn with us to descend the gorge, and we should hesitate upon the adventure of boarding the train. But now we should have the memory of our landlord's curious eye upon us, and we should decide at last to defer the risk of explanations such an enterprise might precipitate.

We should go by the great road for a time, and note something of the difference between Utopian and terrestrial engineering.

The tramway, the train road, the culverts, and bridges, the Urnerloch tunnel, into which the road plunges, will all be beautiful things.

There is nothing in machinery, there is nothing in embankments and railways and iron bridges and engineering devices to oblige them to be ugly. Ugliness is the measure of imperfection ; a thing of human making is for the most part ugly in proportion to the poverty of its constructive thought, to the failure of its producer fully to grasp the purpose of its being. Everything to which men continue to give thought and attention, which they make and remake in the same direction, and with a continuing desire to do as well as they can, grows beautiful inevitably. Things made by mankind under modern conditions are ugly, primarily because our social organisation is ugly, because we live in an atmosphere of snatch and uncertainty, and do everything in an underbred strenuous manner. This is the misfortune of machinery, and not its fault. Art, like some beautiful plant, lives on its atmosphere, and when the atmosphere is good, it will grow everywhere, and when it is bad nowhere. If we smashed and buried every machine, every furnace, every factory in the world, and without any further change set ourselves to home industries, hand labour, spade husbandry, sheep-folding and pig-minding, we should still do things in the same haste, and achieve nothing but dirtiness, inconvenience, bad air, and another gaunt and gawky reflection of our intellectual and moral disorder. We should mend nothing.

But in Utopia a man who designs a tram road will be a cultivated man, an artist craftsman ; he will strive, as a good writer, or a painter strives, to achieve the simplicity of perfection. He will make his girders and rails and parts as gracious as that first engineer, Nature, has made the stems of her plants and the joints and gestures of her animals. To esteem him a sort of anti-artist, to count every man who makes things with his unaided thumbs an artist, and every man who uses machinery as a brute, is merely a passing phase of human stupidity. This tram road beside us will be a triumph of design. The idea will be so unfamiliar to us that for a time it will not occur to us that it is a system of beautiful objects at all. We shall admire its ingenious adaptation to the need of a district that is buried half the year in snow, the hard bed below, curved and guttered to do its own clearing, the great arched sleeper masses, raising the rails a good two yards above the ground, the easy, simple standards and insulators. Then it will creep in upon our minds, " But, by Jove ! *This is designed !* "

Indeed the whole thing will be designed.

Later on, perhaps, we may find students in an art school working in competition to design an electric tram, students who know something of modern metallurgy, and something of electrical engineering, and we shall find people as keenly critical of a signal box or an iron bridge as they are on earth of—— ! Heavens ! what *are* they critical about on earth ?

The quality and condition of a dress tie !

We should make some unpatriotic comparisons with our own planet, no doubt.

CHAPTER FOUR

THE VOICE OF NATURE

§ I

PRESENTLY we recognise the fellow of the earthly Devil's Bridge, still intact as a footway, spanning the gorge, and old memories turn us off the road down the steep ruin of an ancient mule track towards it. It is our first reminder that Utopia too must have a history. We cross it and find the Reuss, for all that it has already lit and warmed and ventilated and cleaned several thousands of houses in the dale above, and for all that it drives those easy trams in the gallery overhead, is yet capable of as fine a cascade as ever it flung on earth. So we come to a rocky path, wild as one could wish, and descend, discoursing how good and fair an ordered world may be, but with a certain unformulated qualification in our minds about those thumbmarks we have left behind.

" Do you recall the Zermatt valley ? " says my friend, " and how on earth it reeks and stinks with smoke ? "

" People make that an argument for obstructing change, instead of helping it forward ! "

And here perforce an episode intrudes. We are invaded by a talkative person.

He overtakes us and begins talking forthwith in a fluty,

but not unamiable, tenor. He is a great talker, this man, and a fairly respectable gesticulator, and to him it is we make our first ineffectual tentatives at explaining who indeed we are ; but his flow of talk washes that all away again. He has a face of that rubicund, knobby type I have heard an indignant mineralogist speak of as botryoidal, and about it waves a quantity of disorderly blond hair. He is dressed in leather doublet and knee breeches, and he wears over these a streaming woollen cloak of faded crimson that give him a fine dramatic outline as he comes down towards us over the rocks. His feet, which are large and handsome, but bright pink with the keen morning air, are bare, except for sandals of leather. (It was the only time that we saw any one in Utopia with bare feet.) He salutes us with a scroll-like waving of his stick, and falls in with our slower paces.

"Climbers, I presume ? " he says, " and you scorn these trams of theirs ? I like you. So do I ! Why a man should consent to be dealt with as a bale of goods holding an indistinctive ticket—when God gave him legs and a face—passes my understanding."

As he speaks, his staff indicates the great mechanical road that runs across the gorge and high overhead through a gallery in the rock, follows it along until it turns the corner, picks it up as a viaduct far below, traces it until it plunges into an arcade through a jutting crag, and there dismisses it with a spiral whirl. " *No !* " he says.

He seems sent by Providence, for just now we had been discussing how we should broach our remarkable situation to these Utopians before our money is spent.

Our eyes meet, and I gather from the botanist that I am to open our case.

I do my best.

"You came from the other side of space ! " says the man in the crimson cloak, interrupting me. " Precisely ! I like that—it's exactly my note ! So do I ! And you find this world strange ! Exactly my case ! We are brothers ! We shall be in sympathy. I am amazed, I have been amazed as long as I can remember, and I shall die, most certainly, in a state of incredulous amazement, at this remarkable world. Eh ? . . . You found yourselves suddenly upon a mountain top ! Fortunate men ! " He chuckled. " For my part I found myself in the still stranger position of infant to two parents of the most intractable dispositions ! "

"The fact remains," I protest.

"A position, I can assure you, demanding Tact of an altogether superhuman quality ! "

We desist for a space from the attempt to explain our remarkable selves, and for the rest of the time this picturesque and exceptional Utopian takes the talk entirely under his control. . . .

§ 2

An agreeable person, though a little distracting, he was, and he talked, we recall, of many things. He impressed us, we found afterwards, as a *poseur* beyond question, a conscious Ishmaelite in the world of wit, and in some subtly inexplicable way as a most consummate ass. He talked first of the excellent and commodious trams that came from over the passes, and ran down the long valley towards middle Switzerland, and of all the growth of pleasant homes and châlets amidst the heights that made the opening gorge so different from its earthly parallel, with a fine disrespect. " But they are beautiful," I protested. " They are graciously proportioned, they are placed in well-chosen positions ; they give no offence to the eye."

" What do we know of the beauty they replace ? They are a mere rash. Why should we men play the part of bacteria upon the face of our Mother ? "

" All life is that ! "

" No ! not natural life, not the plants and the gentle creatures that live their wild shy lives in forest and jungle. That is a part of her. That is the natural bloom of her complexion. But these houses and tramways and things, all made from ore and stuff torn from her veins—— ! You can't better my image of the rash. It's a morbid breaking out ! I'd give it all for one—what is it ?—free and natural chamois."

" You live at times in a house ? " I asked.

He ignored my question. For him, untroubled Nature was the best, he said, and, with a glance at his feet, the most beautiful. He professed himself a Nazarite, and shook back his Teutonic poet's shock of hair. So he came to himself, and for the rest of our walk he kept to himself as the thread of his discourse, and went over himself from top to toe, and strung thereon all topics under the sun by way of illustrating his splendours. But especially his foil was the relative folly, the unnaturalness and want of logic in his fellow-men. He held strong views about the extreme simplicity of everything, only that men, in their muddle-headedness, had confounded it all. " Hence, for example, these trams ! They are always running up and down as though they were looking for the lost simplicity of nature. ' We dropped it here ! ' " He earned a living, we gathered, " some considerable way above the minimum wage," which threw a chance light on the labour problem—by perforating records for automatic musical machines —no doubt of the Pianotist and Pianola kind—and he spent all the leisure he could gain in going to and fro in the earth lecturing on " The Need of a Return to Nature," and on " Simple Foods and Simple Ways." He did it for the love of it. It was very clear to us he had an inordinate impulse to lecture, and esteemed us fair game. He had been lecturing

on these topics in Italy, and he was now going back through the
mountains to lecture in Saxony, lecturing on the way, to
perforate a lot more records, lecturing the while, and so start
out lecturing again. He was undisguisedly glad to have us
to lecture to by the way.

He called out attention to his costume at an early stage.
It was the embodiment of his ideal of Nature-clothing, and
it had been made especially for him at very great cost.
" Simply because naturalness has fled the earth, and has to
be sought now, and washed out from your crushed complexities
like gold."

" I should have thought," said I, " that any clothing whatever was something of a slight upon the natural man."

" Not at all," said he, " not at all ! You forget his natural
vanity ! "

He was particularly severe on our artificial hoofs, as he called
our boots, and our hats or hair destructors. " Man is the real
King of Beasts and should wear a mane. The lion only wears
it by consent and in captivity." He tossed his head.

Subsequently while we lunched and he waited for the specific
natural dishes he ordered—they taxed the culinary resources
of the inn to the utmost—he broached a comprehensive
generalisation. " The animal kingdom and the vegetable
kingdom are easily distinguished, and for the life of me I see
no reason for confusing them. It is, I hold, a sin against
Nature. I keep them distinct in my mind and I keep them
distinct in my person. No animal substance inside, no vegetable without ;—what could be simpler or more logical ?
Nothing upon me but leather and all-wool garments, within,
cereals, fruit, nuts, herbs, and the like. Classification—order
—man's function. He is here to observe and accentuate
Nature's simplicity. These people "—he swept an arm that
tried not too personally to include us—" are filled and covered
with confusion."

He ate great quantities of grapes and finished with a
cigarette. He demanded and drank a great horn of unfermented grape juice, and it seemed to suit him well.

We three sat about the board—it was in an agreeable little
arbour on a hill hard by the place where Wassen stands on
earth, and it looked down the valley to the Uri Rothstock,
and ever and again we sought to turn his undeniable gift of
exposition to the elucidation of our own difficulties.

But we seemed to get little, his style was so elusive. Afterwards, indeed, we found much information and many per-
suasions had soaked into us, but at the time it seemed to us he
told us nothing. He indicated things by dots and dashes,
instead of by good hard assertive lines. He would not pause
to see how little we knew. Sometimes his wit rose so high
that he would lose sight of it himself, and then he would pause,
purse his lips as if he whistled, and then till the bird came

back to the lure, fill his void mouth with grapes. He talked of the relations of the sexes, and love—a passion he held in great contempt as being in its essence complex and disingenuous —and afterwards we found we had learnt much of what the marriage laws of Utopia allow and forbid.

"A simple natural freedom," he said, waving a grape in an illustrative manner, and so we gathered the Modern Utopia did not at any rate go to that. He spoke, too, of the regulation of unions, of people who were not allowed to have children, of complicated rules and interventions. "Man," he said, "had ceased to be a natural product!"

We tried to check him with questions at this most illuminating point, but he drove on like a torrent, and carried his topic out of sight. The world, he held, was overmanaged, and that was the root of all evil. He talked of the overmanagement of the world, and among other things of the laws that would not let a poor simple idiot, a "natural," go at large. And so we had our first glimpse of what Utopia did with the feeble and insane. "We make all these distinctions between man and man, we exalt this and favour that, and degrade and seclude that ; we make birth artificial, life artificial, death artificial."

"You say *We*," said I, with the first glimmering of a new idea, "but *you* don't participate?"

"Not I! I'm not one of your *samurai*, your voluntary noblemen who have taken the world in hand. I might be, of course, but I'm not."

"*Samurai!*" I repeated, "voluntary noblemen!" and for the moment could not frame a question.

He whirled on to an attack on science, that stirred the botanist to controversy. He denounced with great bitterness all specialists whatever, and particularly doctors and engineers.

"Voluntary noblemen!" he said, "voluntary Gods I fancy they think themselves," and I was left behind for a space in the perplexed examination of this parenthesis, while he and the botanist—who is sedulous to keep his digestion up to date with all the newest devices—argued about the good of medicine men.

"The natural human constitution," said the blond-haired man, "is perfectly simple, with one simple condition—you must leave it to Nature. But if you mix up things so distinctly and essentially separated as the animal and vegetable kingdoms, for example, and ram *that* in for it to digest, what can you expect?

"Ill health! There isn't such a thing—in the course of Nature. But you shelter from Nature in houses, you protect yourselves by clothes that are useful instead of being ornamental, you wash—with such abstersive chemicals as soap, for example—and above all you consult doctors." He approved himself with a chuckle. "Have you ever found any one seriously ill without doctors and medicine about? Never!

You say a lot of people would die without shelter and medical attendance ! No doubt—but a natural death. A natural death is better than an artificial life, surely ? That's—to be frank with you—the very citadel of my position."

That led him, and rather promptly, before the botanist could rally to reply, to a great tirade against the laws that forbade " sleeping out." He denounced them with great vigour, and alleged that for his own part he broke that law whenever he could, found some corner of moss, shaded from an excess of dew, and there sat up to sleep. He slept, he said, always in a sitting position, with his head on his wrists, and his wrists on his knees—the simple natural position for sleep in man. . . . He said it would be far better if all the world slept out, and all the houses were pulled down.

You will understand, perhaps, the subdued irritation I felt, as I sat and listened to the botanist entangling himself in the logical net of this wild nonsense. It impressed me as being irrelevant. When one comes to a Utopia one expects a Cicerone, one expects a person as precise and insistent and instructive as an American advertisement—the advertisement of one of those land agents, for example, who print their own engaging photographs to instil confidence and begin, " You want to buy real estate." One expects to find all Utopians absolutely convinced of the perfection of their Utopia, and incapable of receiving a hint against its order. And here was this purveyor of absurdities !

And yet now that I come to think it over, is not this too one of the necessary differences between a Modern Utopia and those finite compact settlements of the older school of dreamers ? It is not to be a unanimous world any more, it is to have all and more of the mental contrariety we find in the world of the real ; it is no longer to be perfectly explicable, it is just our own vast mysterious welter, with some of the blackest shadows gone, with a clearer illumination, and a more conscious and intelligent will. Irrelevance is not irrelevant to such a scheme, and our blond-haired friend is exactly just where he ought to be here.

Still——

§ 3

I ceased to listen to the argumentation of my botanist with this apostle of Nature. The botanist, in his scientific way, was, I believe, defending the learned professions. (He thinks and argues like drawing on squared paper.) It struck me as transiently remarkable that a man who could not be induced to forget himself and his personal troubles on coming into a whole new world, who could waste our first evening in Utopia upon a paltry egotistical love story, should presently become quite heated and impersonal in the discussion of scientific professionalism. He was—absorbed. I can't attempt to explain these vivid spots and blind spots in the imaginations of sane men ; there they are !

" You say," said the botanist, with a prevalent index finger, and the resolute deliberation of a big siege gun being lugged into action over rough ground by a number of in-experienced men, " you prefer a natural death to an artificial life. But what is your *definition* (stress) of artificial ? . . ."

And after lunch too ! I ceased to listen, flicked the end of my cigarette ash over the green trellis of the arbour, stretched my legs with a fine restfulness, leant back, and gave my mind to the fields and houses that lay adown the valley.

What I saw interwove with fragmentary things our garrulous friend had said, and with the trend of my own speculations. . . .

The high road, with its tramways and its avenues on either side, ran in a bold curve, and with one great loop of descent, down the opposite side of the valley, and below crossed again on a beautiful viaduct, and dipped into an arcade in the side of the Bristenstock. Our inn stood out boldly, high above the level this took. The houses clustered in their collegiate groups over by the high road, and near the subordinate way that ran almost vertically below us and past us and up towards the valley of the Meien Reuss. There were one or two Utopians cutting and packing the flowery mountain grass in the care-fully levelled and irrigated meadows by means of swift, light machines that ran on things like feet and seemed to devour the herbage, and there were many children and a woman or so, going to and fro among the houses near at hand. I guessed a central building towards the high road must be the school from which these children were coming. I noted the health and cleanliness of these young heirs of Utopia as they passed below.

The pervading quality of the whole scene was a sane order, the deliberate solution of problems, a progressive intention steadily achieving itself, and the aspect that particularly occupied me was the incongruity of this with our blond-haired friend.

On the one hand here was a state of affairs that implied a power of will, an organising and controlling force, the co-operation of a great number of vigorous people to establish and sustain its progress, and on the other this creature of pose and vanity, with his restless wit, his perpetual giggle at his own cleverness, his manifest incapacity for comprehensive co-operation.

Now, had I come upon a hopeless incompatibility ? Was this the *reductio ad absurdum* of my vision, and must it even as I sat there fade, dissolve, and vanish before my eyes ?

There was no denying our blond friend. If this Utopia is indeed to parallel our earth, man for man—and I see no other reasonable choice to that—there must be this sort of person and kindred sorts of persons in great abundance. The desire and gift to see life whole is not the lot of the great majority of men, the service of truth is the privilege of the elect, and these clever fools who choke the avenues of the world of thought, who stick at no inconsistency, who oppose, obstruct, confuse, will find only the freer scope amidst Utopian freedoms.

(They argued on, these two, as I worried my brains with riddles. It was like a fight between a cock sparrow and a tortoise ; they both went on in their own way, regardless of each other's proceedings. The encounter had an air of being extremely lively, and the moments of contact were few. " But you mistake my point," the blond man was saying, disordering his hair—which had become unruffled in the preoccupation of dispute—with a hasty movement of his hand, " you don't appreciate the position I take up.")

" Ugh ! " said I privately, and lighted another cigarette and went away into my own thoughts with that.

The position he takes up ! That's the way of your intellectual fool, the Universe over. He takes up a position, and he's going to be the most brilliant, delightful, engaging and invincible of gay delicious creatures defending that position you can possibly imagine. And even when the case is not so bad as that, there still remains the quality. We "take up our positions," silly little contentious creatures that we are, we will not see the right in one another, we will not patiently state and restate, and honestly accommodate and plan, and so we remain at sixes and sevens. We've all a touch of Gladstone in us, and try to the last moment to deny we have made a turn. And so our poor broken-springed world jolts athwart its trackless destiny. Try to win into line with some fellow weakling, and see the little host of suspicions, aggressions, misrepresentations, your approach will stir—like summer flies on a high road—the way he will try to score a point and claim you as a convert to what he has always said, his fear lest the point should be scored to you.

It is not only such gross and palpable cases as our blond and tenoring friend. I could find the thing negligible were it only that. But when one sees the same thread woven into men who are leaders, men who sway vast multitudes, who are indeed great and powerful men ; when one sees how unfair they can be, how unteachable, the great blind areas in their eyes also, their want of generosity, then one's doubts gather like mists across this Utopian valley, its vistas pale, its people become unsubstantial phantoms, all its orders and its happiness dim and recede. . . .

If we are to have any Utopia at all, we must have a clear common purpose, and a great and steadfast movement of will to override all these incurably egotistical dissentients. Something is needed wide and deep enough to float the worst of egotisms away. The world is not to be made right by acclamation and in a day, and then for ever more trusted to run alone. It is manifest this Utopia could not come about

by chance and anarchy, but by co-ordinated effort and a
community of design, and to tell of just land laws and wise
government, a wisely balanced economic system, and wise
social arrangements without telling how it was brought about,
and how it is sustained against the vanity and self-indulgence,
the moody fluctuations and uncertain imaginations, the heat
and aptitude for partisanship that lurk, even when they do
not flourish, in the texture of every man alive, is to build a
palace without either door or staircase.

I had not this in mind when I began.

Somewhere in the Modern Utopia there must be adequate
men, men the very antithesis of our friend, capable of self-
devotion, of intentional courage, of honest thought, and steady
endeavour. There must be a literature to embody their
common idea, of which this Modern Utopia is merely the
material form ; there must be some organisation, however
slight, to keep them in touch one with the other.

Who will these men be ? Will they be a caste ? a race ?
an organisation in the nature of a Church ? . . . And there
came into my mind the words of our acquaintance, that he
was not one of these " voluntary noblemen."

At first that phrase struck me as being merely queer, and
then I began to realise certain possibilities that were wrapped
up in it.

The animus of our chance friend, at any rate, went to
suggest that here was his antithesis. Evidently what he is
not, will be the class to contain what is needed here. Evidently.

§ 4

I was recalled from my meditations by the hand of the
blond-haired man upon my arm.

I looked up to discover the botanist had gone into the inn.

The blond-haired man was for a moment almost stripped of
pose.

" I say," he said. " Weren't you listening to me ? "

" No," I said bluntly.

His surprise was manifest. But by an effort he recalled
what he had meant to say.

" Your friend," he said, " has been telling me, in spite of
my sustained interruptions, a most incredible story."

I wondered how the botanist managed to get it in. " About
that woman ? " I said.

" About a man and a woman who hate each other and can't
get away from each other."

" I know," I said.

" It sounds absurd."

" It is."

" Why can't they get away ? What is there to keep them
together ? It's ridiculous. I——"

" Quite."

"' He *would* tell it to me."

"' It's his way."

"' He interrupted me. And there's no point in it. Is he——" he hesitated, " mad ? "

" There's a whole world of people mad with him," I answered after a pause.

The perplexed expression of the blond-haired man intensified. It is vain to deny that he enlarged the scope of his inquiry, visibly if not verbally. " Dear me ! " he said, and took up something he had nearly forgotten. " And you found yourselves suddenly on a mountain side ? . . . I thought you were joking."

I turned round upon him with a sudden access of earnestness. At least I meant my manner to be earnest, but to him it may have seemed wild.

" You," I said, " are an original sort of man. Do not be alarmed. Perhaps you will understand. . . . We were not joking."

" But, my dear fellow ! "

" I mean it ! We come from an inferior world ! Like this, but out of order."

" No world could be more out of order——"

" You play at that and have your fun. But there's no limit to the extent to which a world of men may get out of gear. In our world——"

He nodded, but his eye had ceased to be friendly.

" Men die of starvation ; people die by the hundred thousand needlessly and painfully ; men and women are lashed together to make hell for each other ; children are born—abominably, and reared in cruelty and folly ; there is a thing called war, a horror of blood and vileness. The whole thing seems to me at times a cruel and wasteful wilderness of muddle. You in this decent world have no means of understanding——"

" No ? " he said, and would have begun, but I went on too quickly.

" No ! When I see you dandering through this excellent and hopeful world, objecting, obstructing, and breaking the law, displaying your wit on science and order, on the men who toil so ingloriously to swell and use the knowledge that is salvation, this salvation for which *our* poor world cries to heaven——"

" You don't mean to say," he said, " that you really come from some other world where things are different and worse ? "

" I do."

" And you want to talk to me about it instead of listening to me ? "

" Yes."

" Oh, nonsense ! " he said abruptly. " You can't do it—really. I can assure you this present world touches the nadir of imbecility. You and your friend, with his love for the

lady who's so mysteriously tied—you're romancing ! People
could not possibly do such things. It's—if you'll excuse
me—ridiculous. *He* began—he would begin. A most tiresome story—simply bore me down. We'd been talking very
agreeably before that, or rather *I* had, about the absurdity of
marriage laws, the interference with a free and natural life,
and so on, and suddenly he burst like a dam. No ! " He
paused. " It's really impossible. You behave perfectly
well for a time, and then you begin to interrupt. . . . And
such a childish story, too ! "

He spun round upon his chair, got up, glanced at me over
his shoulder, and walked out of the arbour. He stepped aside
hastily to avoid too close an approach to the returning botanist.
" Impossible," I heard him say. He was evidently deeply
aggrieved by us. I saw him presently a little way off in the
garden, talking to the landlord of our inn, and looking towards
us as he talked—they both looked towards us—and after that,
without the ceremony of a farewell, he disappeared, and
we saw him no more. We waited for him a little while, and
then I expounded the situation to the botanist. . . .

" We are going to have a very considerable amount of
trouble explaining ourselves," I said in conclusion. " We
are here by an act of the imagination, and that is just one
of those metaphysical operations that are so difficult to make
credible. We are, by the standard of bearing and clothing I
remark about us, unattractive in dress and deportment. We
have nothing to produce to explain our presence here, no bit
of a flying machine or a space travelling sphere or any of the
apparatus customary on these occasions. We have no means
beyond a dwindling amount of small change out of a gold
coin, upon which I suppose in ethics and the law some native
Utopian had a better claim. We may already have got ourselves into trouble with the authorities with that confounded
number of yours ! "

" You did one too ! "

" All the more bother, perhaps, when the thing is brought
home to us. There's no need for recriminations. The thing
of moment is that we find ourselves in the position—not to
put too fine a point upon it—of tramps in this admirable
world. The question of all others of importance to us at
present is what do they do with their tramps ? Because
sooner or later, and the balance of probability seems to incline
to sooner, whatever they do with their tramps that they will
do with us."

" Unless we can get some work."

" Exactly—unless we can get some work."

" Get work ! "

The botanist leant forward on his arms and looked out of
the arbour with an expression of despondent discovery.
" I say," he remarked ; " this is a strange world—quite strange

and new. I'm only beginning to realise just what it means for us. The mountains there are the same, the old Bristenstock and all the rest of it ; but these houses, you know, and that roadway, and the costumes, and that machine that is licking up the grass there—only. . . ."

He sought expression. "Who knows what will come in sight round the bend of the valley there ? Who knows what may happen to us anywhere ? We don't know who rules over us even . . . we don't know that ! "

" No," I echoed, " we don't know *that*."

CHAPTER FIVE

FAILURE IN A MODERN UTOPIA

§ 1

THE old Utopias—save for the breeding schemes of Plato and Campanella—ignored that reproductive competition among individualities which is the substance of life, and dealt essentially with its incidentals. The endless variety of men, their endless gradation of quality, over which the hand of selection plays, and to which we owe the unmanageable complication of real life, is tacitly set aside. The real world is a vast disorder of accidents and incalculable forces in which men survive or fail. A Modern Utopia, unlike its predecessors, dare not pretend to change the last condition ; it may order and humanise the conflict, but men must still survive or fail.

Most Utopias present themselves as going concerns, as happiness in being ; they make it an essential condition that a happy land can have no history, and all the citizens one is permitted to see are well looking and upright and mentally and morally in tune. But we are under the dominion of a logic that obliges us to take over the actual population of the world with only such moral and mental and physical improvements as lie within their inherent possibilities, and it is our business to ask what Utopia will do with its congenital invalids, its idiots and madmen, its drunkards and men of vicious mind, its cruel and furtive souls, its stupid people, too stupid to be of use to the community, its lumpish, unteachable and unimaginative people ? And what will it do with the man who is " poor " all round, the rather spiritless, rather incompetent low-grade man who on earth sits in the den of the sweater, tramps the streets under the banner of the unemployed, or trembles—in another man's cast-off clothing, and with an infinity of hat-touching—on the verge of rural employment ?

These people will have to be in the descendant phase, the species must be engaged in eliminating them ; there is no escape from that, and conversely the people of exceptional quality must be ascendant. The better sort of people, so far as they can be distinguished, must have the fullest freedom of public service, and the fullest opportunity of parentage. And it must be open to every man to approve himself worthy of ascendancy.

The way of Nature in this process is to kill the weaker and the sillier, to crush them, to starve them, to overwhelm them, using the stronger and more cunning as her weapon. But man is the unnatural animal, the rebel child of Nature, and more and more does he turn himself against the harsh and fitful hand that reared him. He sees with a growing resentment the multitude of suffering ineffectual lives over which his species tramples in its ascent. In the Modern Utopia he will have set himself to change the ancient law. No longer will it be that failures must suffer and perish lest their breed increase, but the breed of failure must not increase, lest they suffer and perish, and the race with them.

Now we need not argue here to prove that the resources of the world and the energy of mankind, were they organised sanely, are amply sufficient to supply every material need of every living human being. And if it can be so contrived that every human being shall live in a state of reasonable physical and mental comfort, without the reproduction of inferior types, there is no reason whatever why that should not be secured. But there must be a competition in life of some sort to determine who are to be pushed to the edge, and who are to prevail and multiply. Whatever we do, man will remain a competitive creature, and though moral and intellectual training may vary and enlarge his conception of success and fortify him with refinements and consolations, no Utopia will ever save him completely from the emotional drama of struggle, from exultations and humiliations, from pride and prostration and shame. He lives in success and failure just as inevitably as he lives in space and time.

But we may do much to make the margin of failure endurable. On earth, for all the extravagance of charity, the struggle for the mass of men at the bottom resolves itself into a struggle, and often a very foul and ugly struggle, for food, shelter, and clothing. Deaths outright from exposure and starvation are now perhaps uncommon, but for the multitude there are only miserable houses, uncomfortable clothes, and bad and insufficient food ; fractional starvation and exposure, that is to say. A Utopia planned upon modern lines will certainly have put an end to that. It will insist upon every citizen being properly housed, well nourished, and in good health, reasonably clean and clothed healthily, and upon that insistence its labour laws will be founded. In a phrasing that will be familiar to every one interested in social reform, it will maintain a standard of life. Any house, unless it be a public monument, that does not come up to its rising standard of healthiness and convenience, the Utopian State will incontinently pull down, and pile the material and charge the owner for the labour ; any house unduly crowded or dirty, it must in some effectual manner, directly or indirectly, confiscate and clear and clean. And any citizen indecently dressed, or ragged and dirty, or publicly unhealthy, or sleeping abroad homeless, or in any way neglected or derelict, must come under its care. It will find him work if he can and will work, it will take him to it, it will register him and lend him the money wherewith to lead a comely life until work can be found or made for him, and it will give him credit and shelter him and strengthen him if he is ill. In default of private enterprises it will provide inns for him and food, and it will—by itself acting as the reserve employer—maintain a minimum wage which will cover the cost of a decent life. The State will stand at the back of the economic struggle as the reserve employer of labour. This most excellent idea does, as a matter of fact, underlie the British institution of the workhouse, but it is jumbled up with the relief of old age and infirmity, it is administered parochially and on the supposition that all population is static and localised whereas every year it becomes more migratory ; it is administered without any regard to the rising standards of comfort and self-respect in a progressive civilisation, and it is administered grudgingly. The thing that is done is done as unwilling charity by administrators who are often, in the rural districts at least, competing for low-priced labour, and who regard want of employment as a crime. But if it were possible for any citizen in need of money to resort to a place of public employment as a right, and there work for a week or month without degradation upon certain minimum terms, it seems fairly certain that no one would work, except as the victim of some quite exceptional and temporary accident, for less.

The work publicly provided would have to be toilsome, but not cruel or incapacitating. A choice of occupations would need to be afforded, occupations adapted to different types of training and capacity, with some residual employment of a purely laborious and mechanical sort for those who were incapable of doing the things that required intelligence. Necessarily this employment by the State would be a relief of economic pressure, but it would not be considered a charity done to the individual, but a public service. It need not pay, any more than the police need pay, but it could probably be done at a small margin of loss. There is a number of durable things bound finally to be useful that could be made and stored whenever the tide of more highly paid employment ebbed and labour sank to its minimum, bricks, iron from inferior ores, shaped and preserved timber, pins, nails, plain fabrics of cotton and linen, paper, sheet glass, artificial fuel,

and so on ; new roads could be made and public buildings
reconstructed, inconveniences of all sorts removed, until
under the stimulus of accumulating material, accumulating
investments or other circumstances, the tide of private enterprise flowed again.

The State would provide these things for its citizen as
though it was his right to require them ; he would receive as
a shareholder in the common enterprise and not with any
insult of charity.   But on the other hand it will require that
the citizen who renders the minimum of service for these
concessions shall not become a parent until he is established
in work at a rate above the minimum, and free of any debt
he may have incurred.   The State will never press for its debt,
nor put a limit to its accumulation so long as a man or woman
remains childless ; it will not even grudge them temporary
spells of good fortune when they may lift their earnings above
the minimum wage.   It will pension the age of every one
who cares to take a pension, and it will maintain special guest
homes for the very old to which they may come as paying
guests, spending their pensions there.   By such obvious
devices it will achieve the maximum elimination of its feeble
and spiritless folk in every generation with the minimum of
suffering and public disorder.

§ 2

But the mildly incompetent, the spiritless and dull, the
poorer sort who are ill, do not exhaust our Utopian problem.
There remains idiots and lunatics, there remain perverse
and incompetent persons, there are people of weak character
who become drunkards, drug takers, and the like.   Then
there are persons tainted with certain foul and transmissible
diseases.   All these people spoil the world for others.   They
may become parents, and with most of them there is manifestly
nothing to be done but to seclude them from the great body
of the population.   You must resort to a kind of social surgery.
You cannot have social freedom in your public ways, your
children cannot speak to whom they will, your girls and gentle
women cannot go abroad while some sorts of people go free.
And there are violent people, and those who will not respect the
property of others, thieves and cheats, they, too, so soon
as their nature is confirmed, must pass out of the free life of
our ordered world.   So soon as there can be no doubt of the
disease or baseness of the individual, so soon as the insanity
or other disease is assured, or the crime repeated a third time,
or the drunkenness or misdemeanour past its seventh occasion
(let us say), so soon must he or she pass out of the common
ways of men.

The dreadfulness of all such proposals as this lies in the
possibility of their execution falling into the hands of hard, dull,
and cruel administrators.   But in the case of a Utopia one

T.-B.—M.U.   N assumes the best possible government, a government as merciful and deliberate as it is powerful and decisive. You must not too hastily imagine these things being done—as they would be done on earth at present—by a number of zealous half-educated people in a state of panic at a quite imaginary " Rapid Multiplication of the Unfit."

No doubt for first offenders, and for all offenders under five-and-twenty, the Modern Utopia will attempt cautionary and remedial treatment. There will be disciplinary schools and colleges for the young, fair and happy places, but with less confidence and more restraint than the schools and colleges of the ordinary world. In remote and solitary regions these enclosures will lie, they will be fenced in and forbidden to the common run of men, and there, remote from all temptation, the defective citizen will be schooled. There will be no masking of the lesson ; " which do you value most, the wide world of humanity, or this evil trend in you ? " From that discipline at last the prisoners will return.

But the others ; what would a saner world do with them ?

Our world is still vindictive, but the all-reaching State of Utopia will have the strength that begets mercy. Quietly the outcast will go from among his fellow-men. There will be no drumming of him out of the ranks, no tearing off of epaulettes, no smiting in the face. The thing must be just public enough to obviate secret tyrannies, and that is all.

There would be no killing, no lethal chambers. No doubt Utopia will kill all deformed and monstrous and evilly diseased births, but for the rest, the State will hold itself accountable for their being. There is no justice in Nature perhaps, but the idea of justice must be sacred in any good society. Lives that statesmanship has permitted, errors it has not foreseen and educated against, must not be punished by death. If the State does not keep faith, no one will keep faith. Crime and bad lives are the measure of a State's failure, all crime in the end is the crime of the community. Even for murder Utopia will not, I think, kill.

I doubt even if there will be jails. No men are quite wise enough, good enough and cheap enough to staff jails as a jail ought to be staffed. Perhaps islands will be chosen, islands lying apart from the highways of the sea, and to these the State will send its exiles, most of them thanking Heaven, no doubt, to be quit of a world of prigs. The State will, of course, secure itself against any children from those people, that is the primary object in their seclusion, and perhaps it may even be necessary to make these island prisons a system of island monasteries and island nunneries. Upon that I am not competent to speak, but if I may believe the literature of the subject—unhappily a not very well criticised literature—it is not necessary to enforce this separation.[1]

[1] See, for example, Dr. W. A. Chapple's *The Fertility of the Unfit*.

About such islands patrol boats will go, there will be no
freedoms of boat-building, and it may be necessary to have
armed guards at the creeks and quays. Beyond that the
State will give these segregated failures just as full a liberty
as they can have. If it interferes any further it will be simply
to police the islands against the organisation of serious cruelty,
to maintain the freedom of any of the detained who wish it to
transfer themselves to other islands, and so to keep a check
upon tyranny. The insane, of course, will demand care and
control, but there is no reason why the islands of the hopeless
drunkard, for example, should not each have a virtual
autonomy, have at the most a Resident and a guard. I
believe that a community of drunkards might be capable of
organising even its own bad habit to the pitch of tolerable
existence. I do not see why such an island should not build
and order for itself and manufacture and trade. "Your
ways are not our ways," the World State will say ; "but
here is freedom and a company of kindred souls. Elect your
jolly rulers, brew if you will, and distil ; here are vine cuttings
and barley fields ; do as it pleases you to do. We will take
care of the knives, but for the rest—deal yourselves with
God ! "

And you see the big convict steamship standing in to the
Island of Incurable Cheats. The crew are respectfully at
their quarters, ready to lend a hand overboard, but wide
awake, and the captain is hospitably on the bridge to bid his
guests good-bye and keep an eye on the movables. The new
citizens for this particular Alsatia, each no doubt with his
personal belongings securely packed and at hand, crowd the
deck and study the nearing coast. Bright, keen faces would be
there, and we, were we by any chance to find ourselves beside
the captain, might recognise the double of this great earthly
magnate or that, Petticoat Lane and Park Lane cheek by
jowl. The landing part of the jetty is clear of people, only a
government man or so stands there to receive the boat and
prevent a rush, but beyond the gates a number of engagingly
smart-looking individuals loiter speculatively. One figures a
remarkable building labelled Custom House, an interesting
fiscal revival this population has made, and beyond, crowding
up the hill, the painted walls of a number of comfortable inns
clamour loudly. One or two inhabitants in reduced circumstances would act as hotel touts, there are several hotel omnibuses and a Bureau de Change, certainly a Bureau de Change.
And a small house with a large board, aimed point-blank
seaward, declares itself a Gratis Information Office, and next
to it rises the graceful dome of a small Casino. Beyond, great
hoardings proclaim the advantages of many island specialities,
a hustling commerce, and the opening of a Public Lottery.
There is a large cheap-looking barrack, the school of Commercial Science for gentlemen of inadequate training. . . .

Altogether a very go-ahead looking little port it would be, and though this disembarkation would have none of the flow of hilarious good fellowship that would throw a halo of genial noise about the Islands of Drink, it is doubtful if the new arrivals would feel anything very tragic in the moment. Here at last was scope for adventure after their hearts.

This sounds more fantastic than it is. But what else is there to do, unless you kill ? You must seclude, but why should you torment ? All modern prisons are places of torture by restraint, and the habitual criminal plays the part of a damaged mouse at the mercy of the cat of our law. He has his little painful run, and back he comes again to a state more horrible even than destitution. There are no Alsatias left in the world. For my own part I can think of no crime, unless it is reckless begetting or the wilful transmission of contagious disease, for which the bleak terrors, the solitudes and ignominies of the modern prison do not seem outrageously cruel. If you want to go so far as that then kill. Why, once you are rid of them, should you pester criminals to respect an uncongenial standard of conduct ? Into such islands of exile as this a modern Utopia will have to purge itself. There is no alternative that I can contrive.

§ 3

Will a Utopian be free to be idle ?

Work has to be done, every day humanity is sustained by its collective effort, and without a constant recurrence of effort in the single man as in the race as a whole, there is neither health nor happiness. The permanent idleness of a human being is not only burthensome to the world, but his own secure misery. But unprofitable occupation is also intended by idleness, and it may be considered whether that freedom also will be open to the Utopian. Conceivably it will, like privacy, locomotion, and almost all the freedoms of life, and on the same terms—if he possess the money to pay for it.

The last condition may produce a shock in minds accustomed to the proposition that money is the root of all evil, and to the idea that Utopia necessarily implies something rather oaken and hand-made and primitive in all these relations. Of course, money is not the root of any evil in the world ; the root of all evil in the world, and the root of all good too, is the Will to Live, and money becomes harmful only when by bad laws and bad economic organisation it is more easily attained by bad men than good. It is as reasonable to say food is the root of all disease, because so many people suffer from excessive and unwise eating. The sane economic ideal is to make the possession of money the clear indication of public serviceableness, and the more nearly that ideal is attained, the smaller is the justification of poverty and the less the hardship of being poor. In barbaric and disorderly countries it is almost honourable to be indigent and unquestionably virtuous to give to a beggar, and even in the more or less civilised societies of earth, so many children come into life hopelessly handicapped, that austerity to the poor is regarded as the meanest of mean virtues. But in Utopia every one will have had an education and a certain minimum of nutrition and training ; every one will be insured against ill-health and accidents ; there will be the most efficient organisation for balancing the pressure of employment and the presence of disengaged labour, and so to be moneyless will be clear evidence of unworthiness. In Utopia, no one will dream of giving to a casual beggar, and no one will dream of begging.

There will need to be, in the place of the British casual wards, simple but comfortable inns with a low tariff—controlled to a certain extent no doubt, and even in some cases maintained, by the State. This tariff will have such a definite relation to the minimum permissible wage, that a man who has incurred no liabilities through marriage or the like relationship, will be able to live in comfort and decency upon that minimum wage, pay his small insurance premium against disease, death, disablement, or ripening years, and have a margin for clothing and other personal expenses. But he will get neither shelter nor food, except at the price of his freedom, unless he can produce money.

But suppose a man without money in a district where employment is not to be found for him ; suppose the amount of employment to have diminished in the district with such suddenness as to have stranded him there. Or suppose he has quarrelled with the only possible employer, or that he does not like his particular work. Then no doubt the Utopian State, which wants every one to be just as happy as the future welfare of the race permits, will come to his assistance. One imagines him resorting to a neat and business-like post office, and stating his case to a civil and intelligent official. In any sane State the economic conditions of every quarter of the earth will be watched as constantly as its meteorological phases, and a daily map of the country within a radius of three or four hundred miles showing all the places where labour is needed will hang upon the post office wall. To this his attention will be directed. The man out of work will decide to try his luck in this place or that, and the public servant, the official, will make a note of his name, verify his identity— the freedom of Utopia will not be incompatible with the universal registration of thumb-marks—and issue passes for travel and coupons for any necessary inn accommodation on his way to the chosen destination. There he will seek a new employer.

Such a free change of locality once or twice a year from a

region of restricted employment to a region of labour shortage will be among the general privileges of the Utopian citizen.

But suppose that in no district in the world is there work within the capacity of this particular man ?

Before we suppose that, we must take into consideration the general assumption one is permitted to make in all Utopian speculations. All Utopians will be reasonably well educated upon Utopian lines ; there will be no illiterates unless they are unteachable imbeciles, no rule-of-thumb toilers as inadaptable as trained beasts. The Utopian worker will be as versatile as any well-educated man is on earth to-day, and no Trade Union will impose a limit to his activities. The world will be his Union. If the work he does best and likes best is not to be found, there is still the work he likes second best. Lacking his proper employment, he will turn to some kindred trade.

But even with that adaptability, it may be that sometimes he will not find work. Such a disproportion between the work to be done and the people to do it may arise as to present a surplus of labour everywhere. This disproportion may be due to two causes : to an increase of population without a corresponding increase of enterprises, or to a diminution of employment throughout the world due to the completion of great enterprises, to economies achieved, or to the operation of new and more efficient labour-saving appliances. Through either cause, a World State may find itself doing well except for an excess of citizens of mediocre and lower quality.

But the first cause may be anticipated by wise marriage laws. . . . The full discussion of these laws will come later, but here one may insist that Utopia will control the increase of its population. Without the determination and ability to limit that increase as well as to stimulate it whenever it is necessary, no Utopia is possible. That was clearly demonstrated by Malthus for all time.

The second cause is not so easily anticipated, but then, though its immediate result in glutting the labour market is similar, its final consequences are entirely different from those of the first. The whole trend of a scientific mechanical civilisation is continually to replace labour by machinery and to increase it in its effectiveness by organisation, and so quite independently of any increase in population labour must either fall in value until it can compete against and check the cheapening process, or if that is prevented, as it will be in Utopia, by a minimum wage, come out of employment. There is no apparent limit to this process. But a surplus of efficient labour at the minimum wage is exactly the condition that should stimulate new enterprises, and that in a State saturated with science and prolific in invention will stimulate new enterprises. An increasing surplus of available labour without an absolute increase of population, an increasing surplus of labour due to increasing economy and not to pro-

liferation, and which, therefore, does not press on and disarrange the food supply, is surely the ideal condition for a
progressive civilisation. I am inclined to think that, since
labour will be regarded as a delocalised and fluid force, it will
be the World State and not the big municipalities ruling the
force areas that will be the reserve employer of labour. Very
probably it will be convenient for the State to hand over the
surplus labour for municipal purposes, but that is another
question. All over the world the labour exchanges will be
reporting the fluctuating pressure of economic demand and
transferring workers from this region of excess to that of
scarcity ; and whenever the excess is universal, the World
State—failing an adequate development of private enterprise—will either reduce the working day and so absorb the
excess, or set on foot some permanent special works of its own,
paying the minimum wage and allowing them to progress just
as slowly or just as rapidly as the ebb and flow of labour
dictated. But with sane marriage and birth laws there is no
reason to suppose such calls upon the resources and initiative
of the world more than temporary and exceptional occasions.

§ 4

The existence of our blond bare-footed friend was evidence
enough that in a modern Utopia a man will be free to be
just as idle or uselessly busy as it pleases him, after he has
earned the minimum wage. He must do that, of course, to
pay for his keep, to pay his assurance tax against ill health or
old age, and any charge or debt paternity may have brought
upon him. The World State of the modern Utopist is no state
of moral compulsions. If, for example, under the restricted
Utopian scheme of inheritance, a man inherited sufficient
money to release him from the need to toil, he would be free
to go where he pleased and do what he liked. A certain
proportion of men at ease is good for the world ; work as a
moral obligation is the morality of slaves, and so long as no
one is overworked there is no need to worry because some
few are underworked. Utopia does not exist as a solace for
envy. From leisure, in a good moral and intellectual atmosphere, come experiments, come philosophy and the new
departures.

In any modern Utopia there must be many leisurely people.
We are all too obsessed in the real world by the strenuous
ideal, by the idea that the vehement incessant fool is the only
righteous man. Nothing done in a hurry, nothing done under
strain, is really well done. A State where all are working hard,
where none go to and fro, easily and freely, loses touch with
the purpose of freedom.

But inherited independence will be the rarest and least
permanent of Utopian facts ; for the most part that wider
freedom will have to be earned, and the inducements to men

and women to raise their personal value far above the minimum wage will be very great indeed. Thereby will come privacies, more space in which to live, liberty to go everywhere and do no end of things, the power and freedom to initiate interesting enterprises and assist and co-operate with interesting people, and indeed all the best things of life. The modern Utopia will give a universal security indeed, and exercise the minimum of compulsions to toil, but it will offer some acutely desirable prizes. The aim of all these devices, the minimum wage, the standard of life, provision for all the feeble and unemployed and so forth, is not to rob life of incentives but to change their nature, to make life not less energetic, but less panic-stricken and violent and base, to shift the incidence of the struggle for existence from our lower to our higher emotions, so to anticipate and neutralise the motives of the cowardly and bestial, that the ambitious and energetic imagination which is man's finest quality may become the incentive and determining factor in survival.

§ 5

After we have paid for our lunch in the little inn that corresponds to Wassen, the botanist and I would no doubt spend the rest of the forenoon in the discussion of various aspects and possibilities of Utopian labour laws. We should examine our remaining change, copper coins of an appearance ornamental rather than reassuring, and we should decide that after what we had gathered from the man with the blond hair, it would, on the whole, be advisable to come to the point with the labour question forthwith. At last we should draw the deep breath of resolution and arise and ask for the Public Office. We should know by this time that the labour bureau sheltered with the post office and other public services in one building.

The public office of Utopia would of course contain a few surprises for two men from terrestrial England. You imagine us entering, the botanist lagging a little behind me, and my first attempts to be off-hand and commonplace in a demand for work.

The office is in charge of a quick-eyed little woman of six-and-thirty perhaps, and she regards us with a certain keenness of scrutiny.

" Where are your papers ? " she asks.

I think for a moment of the documents in my pocket, my passport chequered with visas and addressed in my commendation and in the name of her late Majesty by *We, Robert Arthur Talbot Gascoigne Cecil, Marquess of Salisbury, Earl of Salisbury, Viscount Cranborne, Baron Cecil*, and so forth, to all whom it may concern, my *Carte d'Identité* (useful on minor occasions) of the Touring Club de France, my green ticket to the Reading Room of the British Museum, and my

Letter d'Indication from the London and County Bank. A foolish humour prompts me to unfold all these, hand them to her and take the consequences, but I resist.

"Lost," I say briefly.

"Both lost ? " she asks, looking at my friend.

"Both," I answer.

"How ? "

I astonish myself by the readiness of my answer.

"I fell down a snow slope and they came out of my pocket."

"And exactly the same thing happened to both of you ? "

"No.   He'd given me his to put with my own."   She raised her eyebrows.   "His pocket is defective," I add, a little hastily.

Her manners are too Utopian for her to follow that up. She seems to reflect on procedure.

"What are your numbers ? " she asks abruptly.

A vision of that confounded visitors' book at the inn above comes into my mind.   "Let me *see*," I say, and pat my forehead and reflect, refraining from the official eye before me. "Let me *see*."

"What is yours ? " she asks the botanist.

"A. B.," he says slowly, "little *a*, nine four seven, I *think*——"

"Don't you know ? "

"Not exactly," says the botanist, very agreeably.   "No."

"Do you mean to say neither of you know your own numbers ? " says the little postmistress, with a rising note.

"Yes," I say, with an engaging smile and trying to keep up a good social tone.   "It's queer, isn't it ?   We've both forgotten."

"You're joking," she suggests.

"Well," I temporise.

"I suppose you've got your thumbs ? "

"The fact is——" I say and hesitate.   "We've got our thumbs, of course."

"Then I shall have to send a thumb-print down to the office and get your number from that.   But are you sure you haven't your papers or numbers ?   It's very queer."

We admit rather sheepishly that it's queer, and question one another silently.

She turns thoughtfully for the thumb-marking slab, and as she does so, a man enters the office.   At the sight of him she asks with a note of relief, "What am I to do, sir, here ? "

He looks from her to us gravely, and his eye lights to curiosity at our dress.   "What is the matter, madam ? " he asks, in a courteous voice.

She explains.

So far the impression we have had of our Utopia is one of a quite unearthly sanity, of good management and comprehensive design in every material thing, and it has seemed to us a little incongruous that all the Utopians we have talked to, our host of last night, the postmistress and our garrulous tramp, have been of the most commonplace type. But suddenly there looks out from this man's pose and regard a different quality, a quality altogether nearer that of the beautiful tramway and of the gracious order of the mountain houses. Here is a well-built man of perhaps five-and-thirty, with the easy movement that comes with perfect physical condition, his face is clean shaven and shows the firm mouth of a disciplined man, and his grey eyes are clear and steady. His legs are clad in some woven stuff deep-red in colour, and over this he wears a white shirt fitting pretty closely, and with a woven purple hem. His general effect reminds me somehow of the Knights Templars. On his head is a cap of thin leather and still thinner steel, and with the vestiges of ear-guards—rather like an attenuated version of the caps that were worn by Cromwell's Ironsides.

He looks at us, and we interpolate a word or so as she explains, and feel a good deal of embarrassment at the foolish position we have made for ourselves. I determine to cut my way out of this entanglement before it complicates itself further

" The fact is——" I say.

" Yes ? " he says, with a faint smile.

" We've perhaps been disingenuous. Our position is so entirely exceptional, so difficult to explain——"

" What have you been doing ? "

" No," I say, with decision ; " it can't be explained like that."

He looks down at his feet. " Go on," he says.

I try to give the thing a quiet, matter-of-fact air. " You see," I say, in the tone one adopts for really lucid explanations, " we come from another world. Consequently, whatever thumb-mark registration or numbering you have in this planet doesn't apply to us, and we don't know our numbers because we haven't got any. We are really, you know, explorers, strangers——"

" But what world do you mean ? "

" It's a different planet—a long way away. Practically at an infinite distance."

He looks up in my face with the patient expression of a man who listens to nonsense.

" I know it sounds impossible," I say, " but here is the simple fact—we *appear* in your world. We appeared suddenly upon the neck of Lucendro—the Passo Lucendro—yesterday afternoon, and I defy you to discover the faintest trace of us before that time. Down we marched into the San Gotthard road and here we are ! That's our fact. And as for papers——! Where in your world have you seen papers like this ? "

I produce my pocket-book, extract my passport, and present it to him.

His expression has changed. He takes the document and examines it, turns it over, looks at me, and smiles that faint smile of his again.

"Have some more," I say, and proffer the card of the T C.F.

I follow up that blow with my green British Museum ticket as tattered as a flag in a knight's chapel.

"You'll get found out," he says, with my documents in his hand. "You've got your thumbs. You'll be measured. They'll refer to the central registers, and there you'll be ! "

"That's just it," I say. " we shan't be."

He reflects. "It's a queer sort of joke for you two men to play," he decides, handing me back my documents.

"It's no joke at all," I say, replacing them in my pocket-book.

The postmistress intervenes. "What would you advise me to do ? "

"No money ? " he asks.

"No."

He makes some suggestions. "Frankly," he says, "I think you have escaped from some island. How you got so far as here I can't imagine, or what you think you'll do. . . . But anyhow, there's the stuff for your thumbs."

He points to the thumb-marking apparatus and turns to attend to his own business.

Presently we emerge from the office in a state between discomfiture and amusement, each with a tramway ticket for Lucerne in his hand and with sufficient money to pay our expenses until the morrow. We are to go to Lucerne because there there is a demand for comparatively unskilled labour in carving wood, which seems to us a sort of work within our range and a sort that will not compel our separation.

§ 6

The old Utopias are sessile organisations ; the new must square itself to the needs of a migratory population, to an endless coming and going, to a people as fluid and tidal as the sea. It does not enter into the scheme of earthly statesman-ship, but indeed all local establishments, all definitions of place, are even now melting under our eyes. Presently all the world will be awash with anonymous stranger men.

Now the simple laws of custom, the homely methods of identification that served in the little communities of the past when every one knew every one, fail in the face of this lique-faction. If the modern Utopia is indeed to be a world of responsible citizens, it must have devised some scheme by which every person in the world can be promptly and certainly recognised, and by which any one missing can be traced and found.

This is by no means an impossible demand. The total

population of the world is, on the most generous estimate, not more than 1,500,000,000, and the effectual indexing of this number of people, the record of their movement hither and thither, the entry of various material facts, such as marriage, parentage, criminal convictions and the like, the entry of the new-born and the elimination of the dead, colossal task though it would be, is still not so great as to be immeasurably beyond comparison with the work of the post offices in the world of to-day, or the cataloguing of such libraries as that of the British Museum, or such collections as that of the insects in Cromwell Road. Such an index could be housed quite comfortably on one side of Northumberland Avenue, for example. It is only a reasonable tribute to the distinctive lucidity of the French mind to suppose the central index housed in a vast series of buildings at or near Paris. The index would be classified primarily by some unchanging physical characteristic, such as we are told the thumb-mark and finger-mark afford, and to these would be added any other physical traits that were of material value. The classification of thumb-marks and of inalterable physical characteristics goes on steadily, and there is every reason for assuming it possible that each human being could be given a distinct formula, a number or " scientific name," under which he or she could be docketed.[1] About the buildings in which this great main index would be gathered, would be a system of other indices with cross references to the main one, arranged under names, under professional qualifications, under diseases, crimes and the like.

These index cards might conceivably be transparent and so contrived as to give a photographic copy promptly whenever it was needed, and they could have an attachment into which would slip a ticket bearing the name of the locality in which the individual was last reported. A little army of attendants would be at work upon this index day and night. From sub-stations constantly engaged in checking back thumb-marks and numbers, an incessant stream of information would come, of births, of deaths, of arrivals at inns, of applications to post offices for letters, of tickets taken for long journeys, of criminal convictions, marriages, applications for public doles and the like. A filter of offices would sort the stream, and all day and all night for ever a swarm of clerks would go to and fro correcting this central register, and photographing copies of its entries for transmission to the subordinate local stations, in response to their inquiries. So the inventory of the State would watch its every man and the wide world write its history as the fabric of its destiny flowed on. At last, when the citizen died, would come the last entry of all,

[1] It is quite possible that the actual thumbmark may play only a small part in the work of identification, but it is an obvious convenience to our thread of story to assume that it is the one sufficient feature.

his age and the cause of his death and the date and place of his cremation, and his card would be taken out and passed on to the universal pedigree, to a place of greater quiet, to the ever-growing galleries of the records of the dead.

Such a record is inevitable if a Modern Utopia is to be achieved.

Yet at this, too, our blond-haired friend would no doubt rebel. One of the many things to which some will make claim as a right, is that of going unrecognised and secret whither one will. But that, so far as one's fellow wayfarers were concerned, would still be possible. Only the State would share the secret of one's little concealment. To the eighteenth-century Liberal, to the old-fashioned nineteenth-century Liberal, that is to say to all professed Liberals, brought up to be against the Government on principle, this organised clairvoyance will be the most hateful of dreams. Perhaps, too, the Individualist would see it in that light. But these are only the mental habits acquired in an evil time. The old Liberalism assumed bad government, the more powerful the government the worse it was, just as it assumed the natural righteousness of the free individual. Darkness and secrecy were, indeed, the natural refuges of liberty when every government had in it the near possibility of tyranny, and the English-man or American looked at the papers of a Russian or a German as one might look at the chains of a slave. You imagine that father of the old Liberalism, Rousseau, slinking off from his offspring at the door of the Foundling Hospital, and you can understand what a crime against natural virtue this quiet eye of the State would have seemed to him. But suppose we do not assume that government is necessarily bad, and the individual necessarily good—and the hypothesis upon which we are working practically abolishes either alterna-tive—then we alter the case altogether. The government of a modern Utopia will be no perfection of intentions ignorantly ruling the world. . . .[1]

Such is the eye of the State that is now slowly beginning to apprehend our existence as two queer and inexplicable parties disturbing the fine order of its field of vision, the eye that will presently be focusing itself upon us with a growing astonishment and interrogation. "Who in the name of Galton and Bertillon," one fancies Utopia exclaiming, "are *you* ?"

[1] In the typical modern State of our own world, with its population of many millions and its extreme facility of movement, undistinguished men who adopt an alias can make themselves untraceable with the utmost ease. The temptation of the opportunities thus offered has developed a new type of criminality, the Deeming or Crossman type, base men who subsist and feed their heavy imaginations in the wooing, betrayal, ill-treatment, and sometimes even the murder of undistinguished women. This is a large, a growing, and, what is gravest, a prolific class, fostered by the practical anonymity of the common man. It is only the murderers who attract much public attention, but the supply of low-class prostitutes is also largely due to these free adventures of the base. It is one of the by-products of State Liberalism, and at present it is very probably drawing ahead in the race against the development of police organisation.

I perceive I shall cut a queer figure in that focus. I shall affect a certain spurious ease of carriage no doubt. "The fact is, I shall begin. . . ."

§ 7

And now see how an initial hypothesis may pursue and overtake its maker. Our thumb-marks have been taken, they have travelled by pneumatic tube to the central office of the municipality hard by Lucerne, and have gone on thence to the headquarters of the index at Paris. There, after a rough preliminary classification, I imagined them photographed on glass, and flung by means of a lantern in colossal images upon a screen, all finely squared, and the careful experts marking and measuring their several convolutions. And then off goes a brisk clerk to the long galleries of the index building.

I have told them they will find no sign of us, but you see him going from gallery to gallery, from bay to bay, from drawer to drawer, and from card to card. "Here he is ! " he mutters to himself, and he whips out a card and reads. "But that is impossible ! " he says. . . .

You figure us returning after a day or so of such Utopian experiences as I must presently describe, to the central office in Lucerne, even as we have been told to do.

I make my way to the desk of the man who has dealt with us before. "Well ? " I say, cheerfully, "have you heard ! "

His expression dashes me a little. "We've heard," he says, and adds, "it's very peculiar."

"I told you you wouldn't find out about us," I say triumphantly.

"But we have," he says ; "but that makes your freak none the less remarkable."

"You've heard ! You know who we are ! Well—tell us ! We had an idea, but we're beginning to doubt."

"You," says the official, addressing the botanist, "are——!"

And he breathes his name. Then he turns to me and gives me mine.

For a moment I am dumbfounded. Then I think of the entries we made at the inn in the Urserenthal, and then in a flash I have the truth. I rap the desk smartly with my finger-tips and shake my index-finger in my friend's face.

"By Jove ! " I say in English. "They've got our doubles ! "

The botanist snaps his fingers. "Of course ! I didn't think of that."

"Do you mind," I say to this official, "telling us some more about ourselves ? "

"I can't think why you keep it up," he remarks, and then almost wearily tells me the facts about my Utopian self. They are a little difficult to understand. He says I am one of the *samurai*, which sounds Japanese, "but you will be degraded," he says, with a gesture almost of despair. He describes my position in this world in phrases that convey very little.

"The queer thing," he remarks, "is that you were in Norway only three days ago."

"I am there still. At least—— I'm sorry to be so much trouble to you, but do you mind following up that last clue and inquiring if the person to whom the thumb-mark really belongs isn't in Norway still ? "

The idea needs explanation. He says something incomprehensible about a pilgrimage. "Sooner or later," I say, "you will have to believe there are two of us with the same thumb-mark. I won't trouble you with any apparent nonsense about other planets and so forth again. Here I am. If I was in Norway a few days ago, you ought to be able to trace my journey hither. And my friend ? "

"He was in India." The official is beginning to look perplexed.

"It seems to me," I say, "that the difficulties in this case are only just beginning. How did I get from Norway hither ? Does my friend look like hopping from India to the Saint Gotthard at one hop ? The situation is a little more difficult than that——"

"But here ! " says the official, and waves what are no doubt photographic copies of the index cards.

"But we are not those individuals ! "

"You *are* those individuals."

"You will see," I say.

He dabs his finger argumentatively upon the thumb-marks. "I see now," he says.

"There is a mistake," I maintain, "an unprecedented mistake. There's the difficulty. If you inquire you will find it begin to unravel. What reason is there for us to remain casual workmen here, when you allege we are men of position in the world, if there isn't something wrong ? We shall stick to this wood-carving work you have found us here, and meanwhile I think you ought to inquire again. That's how the thing shapes to me."

"Your case will certainly have to be considered further," he says, with the faintest of threatening notes in his tone. "But at the same time "—hand out to those copies from the index again—" there you are, you know ! "

§ 8

When my botanist and I have talked over and exhausted every possibility of our immediate position, we should turn, I think, to more general questions.

I should tell him the thing that was becoming more and more apparent in my own mind. Here, I should say, is a world, obviously on the face of it well organised. Compared with our world, it is like a well-oiled engine beside a scrap-heap. It has even got this confounded visual organ swivelling about in the most alert and lively fashion. But that's by the way. . . . You have only to look at all these houses below. (We should be sitting on a seat on the Gütsch and looking down on the Lucerne of Utopia, a Lucerne that would, I insist, quite arbitrarily, still keep the Wasserthurm and the Kapell-brucke.) You have only to mark the beauty, the simple cleanliness and balance of this world, you have only to see the free carriage, the unaffected graciousness of even the common people, to understand how fine and complete the arrangements of this world must be. How are they made so ? We of the twentieth century are not going to accept the sweetish, faintly nasty slopes of Rousseauism that so gratified our great-great-grandparents in the eighteenth. We know that order and justice do not come by Nature—" if only the police-man would go away." These things mean intention, will, carried to a scale that our poor vacillating, hot and cold earth has never known. What I am really seeing more and more clearly is the will beneath this visible Utopia. Convenient houses, admirable engineering that is no offence amidst natural beauties, beautiful bodies, and a universally gracious carriage, these are only the outward and visible signs of an inward and spiritual grace. Such an order means discipline. It means triumph over the petty egotisms and vanities that keep men on our earth apart ; it means devotion and a nobler hope ; it cannot exist without a gigantic process of inquiry, trial, forethought and patience in an atmosphere of mutual trust and concession. Such a world as this Utopia is not made by the chance occasional co-operations of self-indulgent men, by autocratic rulers or by the bawling wisdom of the demo-cratic leader. And an unrestricted competition for gain, an enlightened selfishness, that too fails us. . . .

I have compared the system of indexing humanity we have come upon to an eye, an eye so sensitive and alert that two strangers cannot appear anywhere upon the planet without discovery. Now an eye does not see without a brain, an eye does not run round and look without a will and purpose. A Utopia that deals only with appliances and arrangements is a dream of superficialities ; the essential problem here, the body within these garments, is a moral and an intellectual problem. Behind all this material order, these perfected communica-tions, perfected public services and economic organisations, there must be men and women willing these things. There must be a considerable number and a succession of these men and women of will. No single person, no transitory group of people, could order and sustain this vast complexity. They must have a collective if not a common width of aim, and that involves a spoken or written literature, a living litera-ture to sustain the harmony of their general activity. In some

way they must have put the more immediate objects of desire
into a secondary place, and that means renunciation. They
must be effectual in action and persistent in will, and that
means discipline. But in the modern world in which progress
advances without limits, it will be evident that whatever
common creed or formula they have must be of the simplest
sort ; that whatever organisation they have must be as
mobile and flexible as a thing alive. All this follows inevitably from the general propositions of our Utopian dream.
When we made those, we bound ourselves helplessly to come
to this. . . .

The botanist would nod an abstracted assent.

I should cease to talk. I should direct my mind to the
confused mass of memories three days in Utopia will have
given us. Besides the personalities with whom we have come
into actual contact, our various hosts, our foreman and work-
fellows, the blond man, the public officials, and so on, there
will be a great multitude of other impressions. There will be
many bright snapshots of little children, for example, of girls
and women and men, seen in shops and offices and streets, on
quays, at windows and by the wayside, people riding hither
and thither and walking to and fro. A very human crowd it
has seemed to me. But among them were there any who might
be thought of as having a wider interest than the others, who
seemed in any way detached from the rest by a purpose that
passed beyond the seen ?

Then suddenly I recall that clean-shaven man who talked
with us for a little while in the public office at Wassen, the
man who reminded me of my boyish conception of a Knight
Templar, and with him come momentary impressions of other
lithe and serious-looking people dressed after the same manner,
words and phrases we have read in such scraps of Utopian
reading as have come our way, and expressions that fell from
the loose mouth of the man with the blond hair. . . .

CHAPTER SIX

WOMEN IN A MODERN UTOPIA

§ 1

BUT though I have come to a point where the problem
of a Utopia has resolved itself very simply into the
problem of government and direction, I find I have
not brought the botanist with me. Frankly he cannot think
so steadily onward as I can. I feel to think, he thinks to feel.
It is I and my kind that have the wider range, because we can
be impersonal as well as personal. We can escape ourselves.
In general terms, at least, I understand him, but he does not

understand me in any way at all. He thinks me an incomprehensive brute because his obsession is merely one of my incidental interests, and wherever my reasoning ceases to be explicit and full, the slightest ellipsis, the most transitory digression, he evades me and is back at himself again. He may have a personal liking for me, though I doubt it, but also he hates me pretty distinctly, because of this bias he cannot understand. My philosophical insistence that things shall be reasonable and hang together, that what can be explained shall be explained, and that what can be done by calculation and certain methods shall not be left to chance, he loathes. He just wants adventurously to feel. He wants to feel the sunset, and he thinks that on the whole he would feel it better if he had not been taught the sun was about ninety-two million miles away. He wants to feel free and strong, and he would rather feel so than be so. He does not want to accomplish great things, but to have dazzling things occur to him. He does not know that there are feelings also up in the clear air of the philosophic mountains, in the long ascents of effort and design. He does not know that thought itself is only a finer sort of feeling than his—good hock to the mixed gin, porter, and treacle of his emotions, a perception of similitudes and oppositions that carries even thrills. And naturally he broods on the source of all his most copious feelings and emotions, women, and particularly upon the woman who has most made him feel. He forces me also to that.

Our position is unfortunate for me. Our return to the Utopian equivalent of Lucerne revives in him all the melancholy distresses that so preoccupied him when first we were transferred to this better planet. One day, while we are still waiting there for the public office to decide about us, he broaches the matter. It is early evening, and we are walking beside the lake after our simple dinner. "About here," he says, " the quays would run and all those big hotels would be along here, looking out on the lake. It's so strange to have seen them so recently, and now not to see them at all. . . . Where have they gone ? "

" Vanished by hypothesis."

" What ? "

" Oh ! They're there still. It's we that have come hither."

" Of course. I forgot. But still—— You know, there was an avenue of little trees along this quay with seats, and she was sitting looking out upon the lake. . . . I hadn't seen her for ten years."

He looks about him still a little perplexed. "Now we are here," he says, "it seems as though that meeting and the talk we had must have been a dream."

He falls musing.

Presently he says : " I knew her at once. I saw her in profile. But, you know, I didn't speak to her directly. I

walked past her seat and on for a little way, trying to control
myself. . . . Then I turned back and sat down beside her,
very quietly. She looked up at me. Everything came back—
everything. For a moment or so I felt I was going to cry. . . .

That seems to give him a sort of satisfaction even in the
reminiscence.

" We talked for a time just like casual acquaintances—
about the view and the weather, and things like that."

He muses again.

" In Utopia everything would have been different," I say.

" I suppose it would."

He goes on before I can say anything more.

" Then, you know, there was a pause. I had a sort of
intuition that the moment was coming. So I think had she.
You may scoff, of course, at these intuitions——"

I don't as a matter of fact. Instead, I swear secretly.
Always this sort of man keeps up the pretence of highly distinguished and remarkable mental processes, whereas—have
not I, in my own composition, the whole diapason of emotional
fool ? Is not the suppression of these notes my perpetual
effort, my undying despair ? And then, am I to be accused of
poverty ?

But to his story.

" She said, quite abruptly, ' I am not happy,' and I told
her, ' I knew that the instant I saw you.' Then, you know,
she began to talk to me very quietly, very frankly, about
everything. It was only afterwards I began to feel just what
it meant, her talking to me like that."

I cannot listen to this !

" Don't you understand," I cry, " that we are in Utopia.
She may be bound unhappily upon earth and you may be
bound, but not here. Here I think it will be different. Here
the laws that control all these things will be humane and just.
So that all you said and did, over there, does not signify here—
does not signify here ! "

He looks up for a moment at my face, and then carelessly
at my wonderful new world.

" Yes," he says, without interest, with something of the
tone of an abstracted elder speaking to a child, " I dare say
it will be all very fine here." And he lapses, thwarted from his
confidences, into musing.

There is something almost dignified in this withdrawal into
himself. For a moment I entertain an illusion that really I
am unworthy to hear the impalpable inconclusiveness of what
he said to her and of what she said to him.

I am snubbed. I am also amazed to find myself snubbed.
I become breathless with indignation. We walk along side
by side, but now profoundly estranged.

I regard the façade of the Utopian public offices of Lucerne
—I had meant to call his attention to some of the architec-

tural features of these—with a changed eye, with all the spirit
gone out of my vision. I wish I had never brought this intro-
spective carcass, this mental ingrate, with me.

I incline to fatalistic submission. I suppose I had no
power to leave him behind. . . . I wonder and I wonder.
The old Utopists never had to encumber themselves with this
sort of man.

§ 2

How would things be " different " in the Modern Utopia ?
After all it is time we faced the riddle of the problems of
marriage and motherhood. . . .

The Modern Utopia is not only to be a sound and happy
World State, but it is to be one progressing from good to
better. But as Malthus [1] demonstrated for all time, a State
whose population continues to increase in obedience to un-
checked instinct, can progress only from bad to worse. From
the view of human comfort and happiness, the increase of
population that occurs at each advance in human security is
the greatest evil of life. The way of Nature is for every
species to increase nearly to its possible maximum of numbers,
and then to improve through the pressure of that maximum
against its limiting conditions by the crushing and killing of
all the feebler individuals. The way of Nature has also been
the way of humanity so far, and except when a temporary
alleviation is obtained through an expansion of the general
stock of sustenance by invention or discovery, the amount of
starvation and of the physical misery of privation in the world,
must vary almost exactly with the excess of the actual birth-
rate over that required to sustain population at a number
compatible with a universal contentment. Neither has
Nature evolved, nor has man so far put into operation, any
device by which paying this price of progress, this misery of a
multitude of starved and unsuccessful lives can be evaded.
A mere indiscriminating restriction of the birth-rate—an end
practically attained in the homely, old-fashioned civilisation
of China by female infanticide, involves not only the cessation
of distresses but stagnation, and the minor good of a sort of
comfort and social stability is won at too great a sacrifice.
Progress depends essentially on competitive selection, and
that we may not escape.

But it is a conceivable and possible thing that this margin
of futile struggling, pain and discomfort and death might be
reduced to nearly nothing without checking physical and
mental evolution, with indeed an acceleration of physical and
mental evolution, by preventing the birth of those who would
in the unrestricted interplay of natural forces be born to suffer
and fail. The method of Nature " red in tooth and claw "
is to degrade, thwart, torture, and kill the weakest and least

Essay on the Principles of Population.

adapted members of every species in existence in each generation, and so keep the specific average rising ; the ideal of a
scientific civilisation is to prevent those weaklings being born.
There is no other way of evading Nature's punishment of
sorrow. The struggle for life among the beasts and uncivilised
men means misery and death for the inferior individuals,
misery and death in order that they may not increase and
multiply ; in the civilised State it is now clearly possible to
make the conditions of life tolerable for every living creature,
provided the inferiors can be prevented from increasing and
multiplying. But this latter condition must be respected.
Instead of competing to escape death and wretchedness, we
may compete to give birth, and we may heap every sort of
consolation prize upon the losers in that competition. The
modern State tends to qualify inheritance, to insist upon education and nurture for children, to come in more and more in
the interests of the future between father and child. It is
taking over the responsibility of the general welfare of the
children more and more, and as it does so, its right to decide
which children it will shelter becomes more and more reasonable.

How far will such conditions be prescribed ? how far can
they be prescribed in a Modern Utopia ?

Let us set aside at once all nonsense of the sort one hears
in certain quarters about the human stud farm.[1] State
breeding of the population was a reasonable proposal for
Plato to make, in view of the biological knowledge of his time
and the purely tentative nature of his metaphysics ; but from
any one in the days after Darwin, it is preposterous. Yet we
have it given to us as the most brilliant of modern discoveries
by a certain school of sociological writers, who seem totally
unable to grasp the modification of meaning " species " and
" individual " have undergone in the last fifty years. They
do not seem capable of the suspicion that the boundaries of
species have vanished, and that individuality now carries with
it the quality of the unique ! To them individuals are still
defective copies of a Platonic ideal of the species, and the
purpose of breeding no more than an approximation to that
perfection. Individuality is indeed a negligible difference
to them, an impertinence, and the whole flow of modern
biological ideas has washed over them in vain.

But to the modern thinker individuality is the significant
fact of life, and the idea of the State, which is necessarily
concerned with the average and general, selecting individualities in order to pair them and improve the race, an absurdity. It is like fixing a crane on the plain in order to raise
the hill-tops. In the initiative of the individual above the
average, lies the reality of the future, which the State, presenting the average, may subserve but cannot control. And
the natural centre of the emotional life, the cardinal will,

[1] See *Mankind in the Making*, ch. ii.

the supreme and significant expression of individuality, should lie in the selection of a partner for procreation.

But compulsory pairing is one thing, and the maintenance of general limiting conditions is another, and one well within the scope of State activity. The State is justified in saying, before you may add children to the community for the community to educate and in part to support, you must be above a certain minimum of personal efficiency, and this you must show by holding a position of solvency and independence in the world ; you must be above a certain age, and a certain minimum of physical development, and free of any transmissible disease. You must not be a criminal unless you have expiated your offence. Failing these simple qualifications, if you and some person conspire and add to the population of the State, we will, for the sake of humanity, take over the innocent victim of your passions, but we shall insist that you are under a debt to the State of a peculiarly urgent sort, and one you will certainly pay, even if it is necessary to use restraint to get the payment out of you ; it is a debt that has in the last resort your liberty as a security, and, moreover, if this thing happens a second time, or if it is disease or imbecility you have multiplied, we will take an absolutely effectual guarantee that neither you nor your partner offend again in this matter.

" Harsh ! " you say, and " Poor Humanity ! "

You have the gentler alternative to study in your terrestrial slums and asylums.

It may be urged that to permit conspicuously inferior people to have one or two children in this way would be to fail to attain the desired end, but, indeed, this is not so. A suitably qualified permission, as every statesman knows, may produce the social effects without producing the irksome pressure of an absolute prohibition. Amidst bright and comfortable circumstances, and with an easy and practicable alternative, people will exercise foresight and self-restraint to escape even the possibilities of hardship and discomfort ; and free life in Utopia is to be well worth this trouble even for inferior people. The growing comfort, self-respect, and intelligence of the English is shown, for example, in the fall in the proportion of illegitimate births from 2·2 per 1000 in 1846–50 to 1·2 per 1000 in 1890–1900, and this without any positive preventive laws whatever. This most desirable result is pretty certainly not the consequence of any great exaltation of our moral tone, but simply of a rising standard of comfort and a livelier sense of consequences and responsibilities. If so marked a change is possible in response to such progress as England has achieved in the past fifty years, if discreet restraint can be so effectual as this, it seems reasonable to suppose that in the ampler knowledge and the cleaner, franker atmosphere of our Utopian planet the birth of a child to diseased or inferior parents, and contrary to the sanctions of the State, will be the rarest of disasters.

And the death of a child, too, that most tragic event, Utopia will rarely know. Children are not born to die in childhood. But in our world, at present, through the defects of our medical science and nursing methods, through defects in our organisation, through poverty and carelessness, and through the birth of children that never ought to have been born, one out of every five children born dies within five years. It may be the reader has witnessed this most distressful of all human tragedies. It is sheer waste of suffering. There is no reason why ninety-nine out of every hundred children born should not live to a ripe age. Accordingly, in any Modern Utopia, it must be insisted they will.

§ 3

All former Utopias have, by modern standards, erred on the side of over regulation in these matters. The amount of State interference with the marriage and birth of the citizens of a modern Utopia will be much less than in any terrestrial State. Here, just as in relation to property and enterprise, the law will regulate only in order to secure the utmost freedom and initiative.

Up to the beginning of this chapter, our Utopian speculations, like many Acts of Parliament, have ignored the difference of sex. " He " indeed is to be read as " He and She " in all that goes before. But we may now come to the sexual aspects of the modern ideal of a constitution of society in which, for all purposes of the individual, women are to be as free as men. This will certainly be realised in the Modern Utopia, if it can be realised at all—not only for woman's sake, but for man's.

But women may be free in theory and not in practice, and as long as they suffer from their economic inferiority, from the inability to produce as much value as a man for the same amount of work—and there can be no doubt of this inferiority—so long will their legal and technical equality be a mockery. It is a fact that almost every point in which a woman differs from a man is an economic disadvantage to her, her incapacity for great stresses of exertion, her frequent liability to slight illnesses, her weaker initiative, her inferior invention and resourcefulness, her relative incapacity for organisation and combination, and the possibilities of emotional complications whenever she is in economic dependence on men. So long as women are compared economically with men and boys they will be inferior in precisely the measure in which they differ from men. All that constitutes this difference they are supposed not to trade upon except in one way, and that is by winning or luring a man to marry, selling themselves in an almost irrevocable bargain, and then following and sharing his fortunes for " better or worse."

But—do not let the proposition in its first crudity alarm you—suppose the Modern Utopia equalises things between the sexes in the only possible way, by insisting that motherhood is a service to the State and a legitimate claim to a living ; and that, since the State is to exercise the right of forbidding or sanctioning motherhood, a woman who is, or is becoming, a mother, is as much entitled to wages above the minimum wage, to support, to freedom, and to respect and dignity as a policeman, a solicitor-general, a king, a bishop in the State Church, a Government professor, or any one else the State sustains.   Suppose the State secures to every woman who is, under legitimate sanctions, becoming or likely to become a mother, that is to say who is duly married, a certain wage from her husband to secure her against the need of toil and anxiety, suppose it pays her a certain gratuity upon the birth of a child, and continues to pay at regular intervals sums sufficient to keep her and her child in independent freedom, so long as the child keeps up to the minimum standard of health and physical and mental development.   Suppose it pays more upon the child when it rises markedly above certain minimum qualifications, physical or mental, and, in fact, does its best to make thoroughly efficient motherhood a profession worth following.   And suppose in correlation with this it forbids the industrial employment of married women and of mothers who have children needing care, unless they are in a position to employ qualified efficient substitutes to take care of their offspring. What differences from terrestrial conditions will ensue ?

This extent of intervention will at least abolish two or three salient hardships and evils of the civilised life.   It will abolish the hardship of the majority of widows, who on earth are poor and encumbered exactly in proportion as they have discharged the chief distinctive duty of a woman, and miserable, just in proportion as their standard of life and of education is high.   It will abolish the hardship of those who do not now marry on account of poverty, or who do not dare to have children.   The fear that often turns a woman from a beautiful to a mercenary marriage will vanish from life.   In Utopia a career of wholesome motherhood would be, under such conditions as I have suggested, the normal and remunerative calling for a woman, and a capable woman who has borne, bred, and begun the education of eight or nine well-built, intelligent, and successful sons and daughters would be an extremely prosperous woman, quite irrespective of the economic fortunes of the man she has married.   She would need to be an exceptional woman, and she would need to have chosen a man at least a little above the average as her partner in life. But his death, or misbehaviour, or misfortunes would not ruin her.

Now such an arrangement is merely the completed induction from the starting propositions that make some measure of education free and compulsory for every child in the State. If you prevent people making profit out of their children—and every civilised State—even that compendium of old-fashioned Individualism, the United States of America—is now disposed to admit the necessity of that prohibition—and if you provide for the aged instead of leaving them to their children's sense of duty, the practical inducements to parentage, except among very wealthy people, are greatly reduced. The sentimental factor in the case rarely leads to more than a solitary child or at most two to a marriage, and with a high and rising standard of comfort and circumspection it is unlikely that the birth-rate will ever rise very greatly again. The Utopians will hold that if you keep the children from profitable employment for the sake of the future, then, if you want any but the exceptionally rich, secure, pious, unselfish, or reckless to bear children freely, you must be prepared to throw the cost of their maintenance upon the general community.

In short, Utopia will hold that sound childbearing and rearing is a service done, not to a particular man, but to the whole community, and all its legal arrangements for motherhood will be based on that conception.

§ 4

And after these preliminaries we must proceed to ask, first, what will be the Utopian marriage law, and then what sort of customs and opinions are likely to be superadded to that law ?

The trend of our reasoning has brought us to the conclusion that the Utopian State will feel justified in intervening between men and women on two accounts, first on account of paternity, and secondly on account of the clash of freedoms that may otherwise arise. The Utopian State will effectually interfere with and prescribe conditions for all sorts of contract, and for this sort of contract in particular it will be in agreement with almost every earthly State, in defining in the completest fashion what things a man or woman may be bound to do, and what they cannot be bound to do. From the point of view of a statesman, marriage is the union of a man and woman in a manner so intimate as to involve the probability of offspring, and it is of primary importance to the State, first in order to secure good births, and secondly good home conditions, that these unions should not be free, nor promiscuous, nor practically universal throughout the adult population.

Prolific marriage must be a profitable privilege. It must occur only under certain obvious conditions, the contracting parties must be in health and condition, free from specific transmissible taints, above a certain minimum age, and sufficiently intelligent and energetic to have acquired a minimum education. The man at least must be in receipt of a net income above the minimum wage, after any outstanding charges against him have been paid. All this much it is surely reasonable to insist upon before the State becomes responsible for the prospective children. The age at which men and women may contract to marry is difficult to determine. But if we are, as far as possible, to put women on an equality with men, if we are to insist upon a universally educated population, and if we are seeking to reduce the infantile death-rate to zero, it must be much higher than it is in any terrestrial State. The woman should be at least one-and-twenty ; the man twenty-six or twenty-seven.

One imagines the parties to a projected marriage first obtaining licences which will testify that these conditions are satisfied. From the point of view of the theoretical Utopian State, these licences are the feature of primary importance. Then, no doubt, that universal register at Paris would come into play. As a matter of justice, there must be no deception between the two people, and the State will ensure that in certain broad essentials this is so. They would have to communicate their joint intention to a public office after their personal licences were granted, and each would be supplied with a copy of the index card of the projected mate, on which would be recorded his or her age, previous marriages, legally important diseases, offspring, domiciles, public appointments, criminal convictions, registered assignments of property, and so forth. Possibly it might be advisable to have a little ceremony for each party, for each in the absence of the other, in which this record could be read over in the presence of witnesses, together with some prescribed form of address of counsel in the matter. There would then be a reasonable interval for consideration and withdrawal on the part of either spouse. In the event of the two people persisting in their resolution, they would after this minimum interval signify as much to the local official and the necessary entry would be made in the registers. These formalities would be quite independent of any religious ceremonial the contracting parties might choose, for with religious belief and procedure the modern State has no concern.

So much for the preliminary conditions of matrimony. For those men and women who chose to ignore these conditions and to achieve any sort of union they liked, the State would have no concern, unless offspring were born illegitimately. In that case, as we have already suggested, it would be only reasonable to make the parents chargeable with every duty, with maintenance, education, and so forth, that in the normal course of things would fall to the State. It would be necessary to impose a life-assurance payment upon these parents, and to exact effectual guarantees against every possible evasion of the responsibility they had incurred. But the further control of private morality, beyond the protection of the immature from corruption and evil example, will be no concern of the State's. When a child comes in, the future of the species comes in ; and the State comes in as the guardian of interests wider than the individual's ; but the adult's private life is the entirely private life into which the State may not intrude.

Now what will be the nature of the Utopian contract of matrimony ?

From the first of the two points of view named above, that of parentage, it is obvious that one unavoidable condition will be the chastity of the wife. Her infidelity being demonstrated, must at once terminate the marriage, and release both her husband and the State from any liability for the support of her illegitimate offspring. That, at any rate, is beyond controversy ; a marriage contract that does not involve that, is a triumph of metaphysics over common sense. It will be obvious that under Utopian conditions it is the State that will suffer injury by a wife's misconduct, and that a husband who condones anything of the sort will participate in her offence. A woman, therefore, who is divorced on this account will be divorced as a public offender, and not in the key of a personal quarrel ; not as one who has inflicted a private and personal wrong. This, too, lies within the primary implications of marriage.

Beyond that, what conditions should a marriage contract in Utopia involve ?

A reciprocal restraint on the part of the husband is clearly of no importance whatever, so far as the first end of matrimony goes, the protection of the community from inferior births. It is no wrong to the State. But it does carry with it a variable amount of emotional offence to the wife ; it may wound her pride and cause her violent perturbations of jealousy ; it may lead to her neglect, her solitude and unhappiness, and it may even work to her physical injury. There should be an implication that it is not to occur. She has bound herself to the man for the good of the State, and clearly it is reasonable that she should look to the State for relief if it does occur. The extent of the offence given her is the exact measure of her injury ; if she does not mind nobody minds, and if her self-respect does not suffer nothing whatever is lost to the world ; and so it should rest with her to establish his misconduct, and, if she thinks fit, to terminate the marriage.

A failure on either side to perform the elementary duties of companionship, desertion, for example, should obviously give the other mate the right to relief, and clearly the development of any disqualifying habit, drunkenness, or drug-taking, or the like, or any serious crime or acts of violence, should give grounds for a final release. Moreover, the modern Utopian State intervenes between the sexes only because of the coming generation, and for it to sustain restrictions upon conduct in a continually fruitless marriage is obviously to lapse into purely moral intervention. It seems reasonable, therefore, to set a term to a marriage that remains childless, to let it expire at the end of three or four or five unfruitful years, but with no restriction upon the right of the husband and wife to marry each other again.

These are the fairly easy primaries of this question. We now come to the more difficult issues of the matter. The first of these is the question of the economic relationships of husband and wife, having regard to the fact that even in Utopia women, at least until they become mothers, are likely to be on the average poorer than men. The second is the question of the duration of a marriage. But the two interlock, and are, perhaps, best treated together in one common section. And they both ramify in the most complicated manner into the consideration of the general morale of the community.

§ 5

This question of marriage is the most complicated and difficult in the whole range of Utopian problems. But it is happily not the most urgent necessity that it should be absolutely solved. The urgent and necessary problem is the ruler. With rulers rightly contrived and a provisional defective marriage law a Utopia may be conceived as existing and studying to perfect itself, but without rulers a Utopia is impossible though the theory of its matrimony be complete. And the difficulty in this question is not simply the difficulty of a complicated chess problem, for example, in which the whole tangle of considerations does at least lie in one plane, but a series of problems upon different levels and containing incommensurable factors.

It is very easy to repeat our initial propositions, to recall that we are on another planet, and that all the customs and traditions of the earth are set aside, but the faintest realisation of that demands a feat of psychological insight. We have all grown up into an invincible mould of suggestion about sexual things ; we regard this with approval, that with horror, and this again with contempt, very largely because the thing has always been put to us in this light or that. The more emancipated we think ourselves the more subtle are our bonds. The disentanglement of what is inherent in these feelings from what is acquired is an extraordinary complex undertaking. Probably all men and women have a more or less powerful disposition to jealousy, but what exactly they will be jealous about and what exactly they will suffer seems part of the superposed factor. Probably all men and women are capable of ideal emotions and wishes beyond merely physical desires, but the shape these take are almost entirely a reaction to external images. And you really cannot strip the external off ; you cannot get your stark natural man, jealous, but not jealous about anything in particular, imaginative without any imaginings, proud at large. Emotional dispositions can no

more exist without form than a man without air. Only a
very observant man who had lived all over the planet Earth,
in all sorts of social strata, and with every race and tongue,
and who was endowed with great imaginative insight, could
hope to understand the possibilities and the limitations of
human plasticity in this matter, and say what any men and
any women could be induced to do willingly, and just exactly
what no man and no woman could stand, provided one had
the training of them.   Though very young men will tell you
readily enough.   The proceedings of other races and other
ages do not seem to carry conviction ; what our ancestors did,
or what the Greeks or Egyptians did, though it is the direct
physical cause of the modern young man or the modern young
lady, is apt to impress these remarkable consequences merely
as an arrangement of quaint, comical, or repulsive proceedings.

But there emerges to the modern inquirer certain ideals
and desiderata that at least go some way towards completing
and expanding the crude primaries of a Utopian marriage law
set out in § 4.

The sound birth being assured, does there exist any valid
reason for the persistence of the Utopian marriage union ?

There are two lines of reasoning that go to establish a
longer duration for marriage.   The first of these rests upon
the general necessity for a home and for individual attention
in the case of children.   Children are the results of a choice
between individuals ; they grow well, as a rule, only in relation to sympathetic and kindred individualities, and no wholesale character-ignoring method of dealing with them has ever
had a shadow of the success of the individualised home.
Neither Plato nor Socrates, who repudiated the home, seems
ever to have had to do with anything younger than a young
man.   Procreation is only the beginning of parentage, and
even where the mother is not the direct nurse and teacher of
her child, even where she delegates these duties, her super-
vision is, in the common case, essential to its welfare.   Moreover, though the Utopian State will pay the mother, and the
mother only, for the being and welfare of her legitimate
children, there will be a clear advantage in fostering the natural
disposition of the father to associate his child's welfare with
his individual egotism, and to dispense some of his energies
and earnings in supplementing the common provision of the
State.   It is an absurd disregard of a natural economy to
leave the innate philoprogenitiveness of either sex unculti-
vated.   Unless the parents continue in close relationship, if
each is passing through a series of marriages, the dangers of a
conflict of rights, and of the frittering away of emotions,
become very grave.   The family will lose homogeneity, and its
individuals will have for the mother varied and perhaps incompatible emotional associations.   The balance of social
advantage is certainly on the side of much more permanent

unions, on the side of an arrangement that, subject to ample provisions for a formal divorce without disgrace in cases of incompatibility, would bind, or at least enforce ideals that would tend to bind, a man and woman together for the whole term of her maternal activity, until, that is, the last born of her children was no longer in need of her help.

The second system of considerations arises out of the artificiality of woman's position. It is a less conclusive series than the first, and it opens a number of interesting side vistas.

A great deal of nonsense is talked about the natural equality or inferiority of women to men. But it is only the same quality that can be measured by degrees and ranged in ascending and descending series, and the things that are essentially feminine are different qualitatively from and incommensurable with the distinctly masculine things. The relationship is in the region of ideals and conventions, and a State is perfectly free to determine that men and women shall come to intercourse on a footing of conventional equality, or with either the man or woman treated as the predominating individual. Aristotle's criticism of Plato in this matter, his insistence upon the natural inferiority of slaves and women, is just the sort of confusion between inherent and imposed qualities that was his most characteristic weakness. The spirit of the European people, of almost all the peoples now in the ascendant, is towards a convention of equality ; the spirit of the Mahometan world is towards the intensification of a convention that the man alone is a citizen and that the woman is very largely his property. There can be no doubt that the latter of these two convenient fictions is the more primitive way of regarding this relationship. It is quite unfruitful to argue between these ideals as if there were a demonstrable conclusion, the adoption of either is an arbitrary act, and we shall simply follow our age and time if we display a certain bias for the former.

If one looks closely into the various practical expansions of these ideas, we find their inherent falsity works itself out in a very natural way so soon as reality is touched. Those who insist upon equality work in effect for assimilation, for a similar treatment of the sexes. Plato's women of the governing class, for example, were to strip for gymnastics like men, to bear arms and go to war, and follow most of the masculine occupations of their class. They were to have the same education and to be assimilated to men at every doubtful point. The Aristotelian attitude, on the other hand, insists upon specialisation. The men are to rule and fight and toil ; the women are to support motherhood in a state of natural inferiority. The trend of evolutionary forces through long centuries of human development has been on the whole in this second direction, has been towards differentiation.[1] An adult white woman differs far more from a white man than a negress

[1] See Havelock Ellis's *Man and Woman*.

or pigmy woman from her equivalent male. The education, the mental disposition, of a white or Asiatic woman, reeks of sex ; her modesty, her decorum is not to ignore sex but to refine and put a point to it ; her costume is clamorous with the distinctive elements of her form. The white woman in the materially prosperous nations is more of a sexual specialist than her sister of the poor and austere peoples, of the prosperous classes more so than the peasant woman. The contemporary woman of fashion who sets the tone of occidental intercourse is a stimulant rather than a companion for a man. Too commonly she is an unwholesome stimulant turning a man from wisdom to appearance, from beauty to beautiful pleasures, from form to colour, from persistent aims to belief and stirring triumphs. Arrayed in what she calls distinctly " dress," scented, adorned, displayed, she achieves by artifice a sexual differentiation profounder than that of any other vertebrated animal. She outshines the peacock's excess above his mate, one must probe among the domestic secrets of the insects and crustacea to find her living parallel. And it is a question by no means easy and yet of the utmost importance, to determine how far the wide and widening differences between the human sexes is inherent and inevitable, and how far it is an accident of social development that may be converted and reduced under a different social regimen. Are we going to recognise and accentuate this difference and to arrange our Utopian organisation to play upon it, are we to have two primary classes of human being, harmonising indeed and reacting, but following essentially different lives, or are we going to minimise this difference in every possible way ?

The former alternative leads either to a romantic organisation of society in which men will live and fight and die for wonderful, beautiful, exaggerated creatures, or it leads to the hareem. It would probably lead through one phase to the other. Women would be enigmas and mysteries and maternal dignitaries that one would approach in a state of emotional excitement and seclude piously when serious work was in hand. A girl would blossom from the totally negligible to the mystically desirable at adolescence, and boys would be removed from their mother's educational influence at as early an age as possible. Whenever men and women met together, the men would be in a state of inflamed competition towards one another, and the women likewise, and the intercourse of ideas would be in suspense. Under the latter alternative the sexual relation would be subordinated to friendship and companionship ; boys and girls would be co-educated—very largely under maternal direction, and women, disarmed of their distinctive barbaric adornments, the feathers, beads, lace, and trimmings that enhance their clamorous claim to a directly personal attention would mingle, according to their quality, in the counsels and intellectual development of men.

Such women would be fit to educate boys even up to adolescence. It is obvious that a marriage law embodying a
decision between these two sets of ideas would be very different
according to the alternative adopted. In the former case a
man would be expected to earn and maintain in an adequate
manner the dear delight that had favoured him. He would
tell her beautiful lies about her wonderful moral effect upon
him, and keep her sedulously from all responsibility and knowledge. And, since there is an undeniably greater imaginative
appeal to men in the first bloom of a woman's youth, she
would have a distinct claim upon his energies for the rest of her
life. In the latter case a man would no more pay for and
support his wife than she would do so for him. They would
be two friends, differing in kind no doubt but differing reciprocally, who had linked themselves in a matrimonial
relationship. Our Utopian marriage, so far as we have
discussed it, is indeterminate between these alternatives.

We have laid it down as a general principle that the private
morals of an adult citizen are no concern for the State. But
that involves a decision to disregard certain types of bargain.
A sanely contrived State will refuse to sustain bargains wherein
there is no plausibly fair exchange, and if private morality is
really to be outside the scope of the State then the affections
and endearments most certainly must not be regarded as
negotiable commodities. The State, therefore, will absolutely
ignore the distribution of these favours unless children, or at
least the possibility of children, is involved. It follows that it
will refuse to recognise any debts or transfers of property that
are based on such considerations. It will be only consistent,
therefore, to refuse recognition in the marriage contract to any
financial obligation between husband and wife, or any settlements qualifying that contract, except when they are in the
nature of accessory provision for the prospective children.[2]
So far the Utopian State will throw its weight upon the side
of those who advocate the independence of women and their
conventional equality with men.

But to any further definition of the marriage relation the
World State of Utopia will not commit itself. The wide range
of relationships that are left possible, within and without the
marriage code, are entirely a matter for the individual choice
and imagination. Whether a man treat his wife in private as
a goddess to be propitiated, as a " mystery " to be adored, as
an agreeable auxiliary, as a particularly intimate friend, or as
the wholesome mother of his children, is entirely a matter for
their private intercourse : whether he keep her in Oriental
idleness or active co-operation, or leave her to live her independent life, rests with the couple alone, and all the possible

[1] Unqualified gifts for love by solvent people will, of course, be quite possible and
permissible, unsalaried services and the like, provided the standard of life is maintained
and the joint income of the couple between whom the services hold does not sink below
twice the minimum wage.

friendship and intimacies outside marriage also lie quite
beyond the organisation of the modern State. Religious
teaching and literature may affect these ; customs may arise ;
certain types of relationship may involve social isolation ;
the justice of the statesman is blind to such things. It may
be urged that according to Atkinson's illuminating analysis [1]
the control of love-making was the very origin of the human
community. In Utopia, nevertheless, love-making is no
concern of the State's beyond the province that the protection
of children covers. [2] Change of function is one of the ruling
facts in life, the sac that was in our remotest ancestors a
swimming bladder is now a lung, and the State which was once,
perhaps, no more than the jealous and tyrannous will of the
strongest male in the herd, the instrument of justice and
equality. The State intervenes now only where there is want
of harmony between individuals—individuals who exist or
who may presently come into existence.

§ 6

It must be reiterated that our reasoning still leaves
Utopian marriage an institution with wide possibilities of
variation. We have tried to give effect to the ideal of a
virtual equality, an equality of spirit between men and
women, and in doing so we have overridden the accepted
opinion of the great majority of mankind. Probably the first
writer to do as much was Plato. His argument in support of
this innovation upon natural human feeling was thin enough—
a mere analogy to illustrate the spirit of his propositions ; it
was his creative instinct that determined him. In the atmosphere of such speculations as this, Plato looms very large
indeed, and in view of what we owe to him, it seems reasonable
that we should hesitate before dismissing as a thing prohibited
and evil, a type of marriage that he made almost the central
feature in the organisation of the ruling class, at least, of his
ideal State. He was persuaded that the narrow monogamic
family is apt to become illiberal and anti-social, to withdraw the
imagination and energies of the citizen from the services of
the community as a whole, and the Roman Catholic Church has
so far endorsed and substantiated his opinion as to forbid
family relations to its priests and significant servants. He
conceived of a poetic devotion to the public idea, a devotion
of which the mind of Aristotle, as his criticisms of Plato show,
was incapable, as a substitute for the warm and tender but

[1] See Lang and Atkinson's *Social Origins and Primal Law.*
[2] It cannot be made too clear that though the control of morality is outside the law
the State must maintain a general decorum, a systematic suppression of powerful and
moving examples, and of incitations and temptations of the young and inexperienced,
and to that extent it will, of course, in a sense, exercise a control over morals. But
this will be only part of a wider law to safeguard the tender mind. For example, lying
advertisements, and the like, when they lean towards adolescent interests, will encounter
a specially disagreeable disposition in the law, over and above the treatment of their
general dishonesty.

T.-B.—M.U.   O illiberal emotions of the home. But while the Church made the alternative to family ties celibacy [1] and participation in an organisation, Plato was far more in accordance with modern ideas in perceiving the disadvantage that would result from precluding the nobler types of character from offspring. He sought a way to achieve progeny, therefore, without the narrow concentration of the sympathies about the home, and he found it in a multiple marriage in which every member of the governing class was considered to be married to all the others. But the detailed operation of this system he put tentatively and very obscurely. His suggestions have the experimental inconsistency of an inquiring man. He left many things altogether open, and it is unfair to him to adopt Aristotle's forensic method and deal with his discussion as though it was a fully-worked-out project. It is clear that Plato intended every member of his governing class to be so " changed at birth " as to leave paternity untraceable ; mothers were not to know their children, nor children their parents, but there is nothing to forbid the supposition that he intended these people to select and adhere to congenial mates within the great family. Aristotle's assertion that the Platonic republic left no scope for the virtue of continence shows that he had jumped to just the same conclusions a contemporary London errand boy, hovering a little shamefacedly over Jowett in a public library, might be expected to reach.

Aristotle obscures Plato's intention, it may be accidentally, by speaking of his marriage institution as a community of wives. When reading Plato he could not or would not escape reading in his own conception of the natural ascendency of men, his idea of property in women and children. But as Plato intended women to be conventionally equal to men, this phrase belies him altogether ; community of husbands and wives would be truer to his proposal. Aristotle condemns Plato as roundly as any commercial room would condemn him to-day, and in much the same spirit ; he asserts rather than proves that such a grouping is against the nature of man. He wanted to have women property just as he wanted to have slaves property, he did not care to ask why, and it distressed his conception of convenience extremely to imagine any other arrangement. It is no doubt true that the natural instinct of either sex is exclusive of participators in intimacy during a period of intimacy, but it was probably Aristotle who gave Plato an offensive interpretation in this matter. No one would freely submit to such a condition of affairs as multiple marriage carried out, in the spirit of the Aristotelian interpretation, to an obscene completeness, but that is all the more reason why the modern Utopia should not refuse a grouped marriage to three or more freely consenting persons. There is no sense

[1] The warm imagination of Campanella, that quaint Calabrian monastic, fired by Plato, reversed this aspect of the Church.

in prohibiting institutions which no sane people could ever want to abuse. It is claimed—though the full facts are difficult to ascertain—that a group marriage of over two hundred persons was successfully organised by John Humphrey Noyes at Oneida Creek.[1] It is fairly certain in the latter case that there was no " promiscuity," and that the members mated for variable periods, and often for life, within the group. The documents are reasonably clear upon that point. This Oneida community was, in fact, a league of two hundred persons to regard their children as " common." Choice and preference were not abolished in the community, though in some cases they were set aside—just as they are by many parents under our present conditions. There seems to have been a premature attempt at " stirpiculture," at what Mr. Francis Galton now calls " Eugenics," in the mating of the members, and there was also a limitation of offspring. Beyond these points the inner secrets of the community do not appear to be very profound ; its atmosphere was almost commonplace, it was made up of very ordinary people. There is no doubt that it had a career of exceptional success throughout the whole lifetime of its founder, and it broke down with the advent of a new generation, with the onset of theological differences, and the loss of its guiding intelligence. The Anglo-Saxon spirit, it has been said by one of the ablest children of the experiment, is too individualistic for communism. It is possible to regard the temporary success of this complex family as a strange accident, as the wonderful exploit of what was certainly a very exceptional man. Its final disintegration into frankly monogamic couples—it is still a prosperous business association—may be taken as an experimental verification of Aristotle's common-sense psychology, and was probably merely the public acknowledgment of conditions already practically established.

Out of respect for Plato we cannot ignore this possibility of multiple marriage altogether in our Utopian theorising, but even if we leave this possibility open we are still bound to regard it as a thing so likely to be rare as not to come at all under our direct observation during our Utopian journeyings. But in one sense, of course, in the sense that the State guarantees care and support for all properly born children, our entire Utopia is to be regarded as a comprehensive marriage group.[1]

It must be remembered that a modern Utopia must differ from the Utopias of any preceding age in being world-wide ; it is not, therefore, to be the development of any special race or type of culture, as Plato's developed an Athenian-Spartan

[1] See John H. Noyes's *History of American Socialisms* and his writings generally. The bare facts of this and the other American experiments are given, together with more recent matter, by Morris Hillquirt, in *The History of Socialism in the United States*.
[1] The Thelma of Rabelais, with its principle of " Fay ce que vouldras " within the limits of the order, is probably intended to suggest a Platonic complex marriage after the fashion of our interpretation.

blend, or More, Tudor England. The modern Utopia is to be, before all things, synthetic. Politically and socially, as linguistically, we must suppose it a synthesis ; politically it will be a synthesis at once widely different forms of government ; socially and morally, a synthesis of a great variety of domestic traditions and ethical habits. Into the modern Utopia there must have entered the mental tendencies and origins that give our own world the polygamy of the Zulus and of Utah, the polyandry of Tibet, the latitudes of experiment permitted in the United States, and the divorceless wedlock of Comte. The tendency of all synthetic processes in matters of law and custom is to reduce and simplify the compulsory canon, to admit alternatives and freedoms ; what were laws before become traditions of feeling and style, and in no matter will this be more apparent than in questions affecting the relations of the sexes.

CHAPTER SEVEN

A FEW UTOPIAN IMPRESSIONS

§ 1

BUT now we are in a better position to describe the houses and ways of the Utopian townships about the Lake of Lucerne, and to glance a little more nearly at the people who pass. You figure us as curiously settled down in Utopia, as working for a low wage at wood-carving, until the authorities at the central registry in Paris can solve the perplexing problem we have set them. We stay in an inn looking out upon the lake, and go to and fro for our five hours' work a day, with a curious effect of having been born Utopians. The rest of our time is our own.

Our inn is one of those inns and lodging houses which have a minimum tariff, inns which are partly regulated, and, in the default of private enterprise, maintained and controlled by the World State throughout the entire world. It is one of several such establishments in Lucerne. It possesses many hundreds of practically self-cleaning little bedrooms, equipped very much after the fashion of the rooms we occupied in the similar but much smaller inn at Hospenthal, differing only a little in the decoration. There is the same dressing-room recess with its bath, the same graceful proportion in the succinct simplicity of its furniture. This particular inn is a quadrangle after the fashion of an Oxford college ; it is perhaps forty feet high, and with about five stories of bedrooms above its lower apartments ; the windows of the rooms look either outward or inward to the quadrangle, and the doors give upon artificially-lit passages with staircases passing up and down. These passages are carpeted with a sort of cork carpet, but are otherwise bare. The lower story is occupied by the equivalent of a London club, kitchens and other offices, dining-room, writing-room, smoking and assembly-rooms, a barber's shop, and a library. A colonnade with seats runs about the quadrangle, and in the middle is a grass-plot. In the centre of this a bronze figure, a sleeping child, reposes above a little basin and fountain, in which water lilies are growing. The place has been designed by an architect happily free from the hampering traditions of Greek temple building, and of Roman and Italian palaces ; it is simple, unaffected, gracious. The material is some artificial stone with the dull surface and something of the tint of yellow ivory ; the colour is a little irregular, and a partial confession of girders and pillars breaks this front of tender colour with lines and mouldings of greenish grey, that blend with the tones of the leaden gutters and rain pipes from the light red roof. At one point only does any explicit effort towards artistic effect appear, and that is in the great arched gateway opposite my window. Two or three abundant yellow roses climb over the face of the building, and when I look out of my window in the early morning—for the usual Utopian working day com-mences within an hour of sunrise—I see Pilatus above this outlook, rosy in the morning sky.

This quadrangle type of building is the prevalent element in Utopian Lucerne, and one may go from end to end of the town along corridors and covered colonnades without emerging by a gateway into the open roads at all. Small shops are found in these colonnades, but the larger stores are usually housed in buildings specially adapted to their needs. The majority of the residential edifices are far finer and more substantial than our own modest shelter, though we gather from such chance glimpses as we get of their arrangements that the labour-saving ideal runs through every grade of this servant-less world ; and what we should consider a complete house in earthly England is hardly known here.

The autonomy of the household has been reduced far below terrestrial conditions by hotels and clubs, and all sorts of co-operative expedients. People who do not live in hotels seem usually to live in clubs. The fairly prosperous Utopian belongs, in most cases, to one or two residential clubs of con-genial men and women. These clubs usually possess, in addition to furnished bedrooms, more or less elaborate suites of apartments, and if a man prefers it one of these latter can be taken and furnished according to his personal taste. A pleasant boudoir, a private library and study, a private garden plot, are among the commonest of such luxuries. Devices to secure roof gardens, loggias, verandahs, and such-like open-air privacies to the more sumptuous of these apartments, give interest and variety to Utopian architecture. There are sometimes little cooking corners in these flats—as one would call them on earth—but the ordinary Utopian would no more think of a special private kitchen for his dinners than he would think of a private flour mill or dairy farm. Business, private work, and professional practice go on sometimes in the house apartments, but often in special offices in the great warren of the business quarter. A common garden, an infant school, play rooms, and a playing garden for children, are universal features of the club quadrangles.

Two or three main roads, with their tramways, their cyclists' paths, and swift traffic paths, will converge on the urban centre, where the public offices will stand in a group close to the two or three theatres and the larger shops, and hither, too, in the case of Lucerne, the head of the swift railway to Paris and England and Scotland, and to the Rhineland and Germany will run. And as one walks out from the town centre one will come to that mingling of homesteads and open country which will be the common condition of all the more habitable parts of the globe.

Here and there, no doubt, will stand quite solitary homesteads, homesteads that will nevertheless be lit and warmed by cables from the central force station, that will share the common water supply, will have their perfected telephonic connection with the rest of the world, with doctor, shop, and so forth, and may even have a pneumatic tube for books and small parcels to the nearest post office. But the solitary homestead, as a permanent residence, will be something of a luxury—the resort of rather wealthy garden lovers ; and most people with a bias for retirement will probably get as much residential solitude as they care for in the hire of a holiday châlet in a forest, by remote lagoons or high up the mountain side.

The solitary house may indeed prove to be very rare indeed in Utopia. The same forces, the same facilitation of communications that will diffuse the towns will tend to little concentrations of the agricultural population over the countryside. The field workers will probably take their food with them to their work during the day, and for the convenience of an interesting dinner and of civilised intercourse after the working day is over, they will most probably live in a college quadrangle with a common room and club. I doubt if there will be any agricultural labourers drawing wages in Utopia. I am inclined to imagine farming done by tenant associations, by little democratic unlimited liability companies working under elected managers, and paying not a fixed rent but a share of the produce to the State. Such companies could reconstruct annually to weed out indolent members.[1] A minimum standard of efficiency in farming would be insured

[1] Schemes for the co-operative association of producers will be found in Dr. Hertzka's *Freeland.*

by fixing a minimum beneath which the rent must not fall, and perhaps by inspection. The general laws respecting the standard of life would, of course, apply to such associations. This type of co-operation presents itself to me as socially the best arrangement of productive agriculture and horticulture, but such enterprises as stock breeding, seed farming, and the stocking of loan and agricultural implements are probably, and agricultural research and experiment certainly, best handled directly by large companies or the municipality of the State.

But I should do little to investigate this question ; these are presented as quite incidental impressions. You must suppose that for the most part our walks and observations keep us within the more urban quarters of Lucerne. From a number of beautifully printed placards at the streets corners, adorned with caricatures of considerable pungency, we discover an odd little election is in progress. This is the selection, upon strictly democratic lines, with a suffrage that includes every permanent resident in the Lucerne ward over the age of fifteen, of the ugliest local building. The old little urban and local governing bodies, we find, have long since been superseded by great provincial municipalities for all the more serious administrative purposes, but they still survive to discharge a number of curious minor functions, and not the least among these is this sort of æsthetic ostracism. Every year every minor local governing body pulls down a building selected by local plebiscite, and the greater Government pays a slight compensation to the owner, and resumes possession of the land it occupies. The idea would strike us at first as simply whimsical, but in practice it appears to work as a cheap and practical device for the æsthetic education of builders, engineers, business men, opulent persons, and the general body of the public. But when we come to consider its application to our own world we should perceive it was the most Utopian thing we had so far encountered.

§ 2

The factory that employs us is something very different from the ordinary earthly model. Our business is to finish making little wooden toys—bears, cattle men, and the like—for children. The things are made in the rough by machinery, and then finished by hand, because the work of unskilful but interested men—and it really is an extremely amusing employment—is found to give a personality and interest to these objects no machine can ever attain.

We carvers—who are the riff-raff of Utopia—work in a long shed together, nominally by time ; we must keep at the job for the length of the spell, but we are expected to finish a certain number of toys for each spell of work. The rules of the game as between employer and employed in this particular

industry hang on the wall behind us ; they are drawn up by a
conference of the Common Council of Wages Workers with
the employers, a common council which has resulted in Utopia
from a synthesis of the old Trades Unions, and which has
become a constitutional power ; but any man who has skill
or humour is presently making his own bargain with our
employer more or less above that datum line.

Our employer is a quiet blue-eyed man with a humorous
smile. He dresses wholly in an indigo blue, that later we
come to consider a sort of voluntary uniform for Utopian
artists. As he walks about the workshop, stopping to laugh
at this production or praise that, one is reminded inevitably
of an art school. Every now and then he carves a little himself
or makes a sketch or departs to the machinery to order some
change in the rough shapes it is turning out. Our work is by
no means confined to animals. After a time I am told to
specialise in a comical little Roman-nosed pony ; but several
of the better paid carvers work up caricature images of eminent
Utopians. Over these our employer is most disposed to
meditate, and from them he darts off most frequently to
improve the type.

It is high summer, and our shed lies open at either end.
On one hand is a steep mountain side down which there
comes, now bridging a chasm, now a mere straight groove
across a meadow, now hidden among green branches, the
water-slide that brings our trees from the purple forest overhead. Above us, but nearly hidden, hums the machine
shed, but we see a corner of the tank into which, with a mighty
splash, the pine trees are delivered. Every now and then,
bringing with him a gust of resinous smell, a white-clad
machinist will come in with a basketful of crude, unwrought
little images, and will turn them out upon the table from which
we carvers select them.

(Whenever I think of Utopia that faint and fluctuating
smell of resin returns to me, and whenever I smell resin,
comes the memory of the open end of the shed looking out
upon the lake, the blue-green lake, the boats mirrored in the
water, and far and high beyond floats the atmospheric fairy-
land of the mountains of Glarus, twenty miles away.)

The cessation of the second and last spell of work comes
about midday, and then we walk home, through this beautiful
intricacy of a town to our cheap hotel beside the lake.

We should go our way with a curious contentment, for all
that we were earning scarcely more than the minimum wage.
We should have, of course, our uneasiness about the final
decisions of that universal eye which has turned upon us,
we should have those ridiculous sham numbers on our con-
sciences ; but that general restlessness, that brooding stress
that pursues the weekly worker on earth, that aching anxiety
that drives him so often to stupid betting, stupid drinking,

and violent and mean offences will have vanished out of
mortal experience.

§ 3

I should find myself contrasting my position with my
preconceptions about a Utopian visit. I had always imagined
myself as standing outside the general machinery of the
State—in the distinguished visitors' gallery, as it were—and
getting the new world in a series of comprehensive perspective
views. But this Utopia, for all the sweeping floats of generalisation I do my best to maintain, is swallowing me up. I find
myself going between my work and the room in which I sleep
and the place in which I dine, very much as I went to and fro
in that real world into which I fell five-and-forty years ago.
I find about me mountains and horizons that limit my view,
institutions that vanish also without an explanation, beyond
the limit of sight, and a great complexity of things I do not
understand and about which, to tell the truth, I do not formulate acute curiosities. People, very unrepresentative people,
people just as casual as people in the real world, come into
personal relations with us, and little threads of private and
immediate interest spin themselves rapidly into a thickening
grey veil across the general view. I lose the comprehensive
interrogation of my first arrival ; I find myself interested in
the grain of the wood I work, in birds among the tree branches,
in little irrelevant things, and it is only now and then that I get
fairly back to the mood that takes all Utopia for its picture.

We spend our first surplus of Utopian money in the re-
organisation of our wardrobes upon more Utopian lines ; we
develop acquaintance with several of our fellow-workers, and
of those who share our table at the inn. We pass insensibly
into acquaintanceships and the beginnings of friendships.
The World Utopia, I say, seems for a time to be swallowing me
up. At the thought of detail it looms too big for me. The
question of government, of its sustaining ideas, of race, and
the wider future, hang like the arch of the sky over these daily
incidents, very great indeed, but very remote. These people
about me are everyday people, people not so very far from the
minimum wage accustomed much as the everyday people of
earth are accustomed to take their world as they find it. Such
inquiries as I attempt are pretty obviously a bore to them,
pass outside their range as completely as Utopian speculation
on earth outranges a stevedore or a member of Parliament
or a working plumber. Even the little things of daily life
interest them in a different way. So I get on with my facts
and reasoning rather slowly. I find myself looking among the
pleasant multitudes of the streets for types that promise
congenial conversation.

My sense of loneliness is increased during this interlude
by the better social success of the botanist. I find him

presently falling into conversation with two women who are
accustomed to sit at a table near our own. They wear the
loose, coloured robes of soft material that are the usual wear
of common adult Utopian women ; they are both dark and
sallow, and they affect amber and crimson in their garments.
Their faces strike me as a little unintelligent, and there is a
faint touch of middle-aged coquetry in their bearing that I
do not like. Yet on earth we should consider them women of
exceptional refinement. But the botanist evidently sees in
this direction scope for the feelings that have wilted a little
under my inattention, and he begins that petty intercourse of
a word, of a slight civility, of vague inquiries and comparisons
that leads at last to associations and confidences. Such
superficial confidences, that is to say, as he finds satisfactory.

This throws me back upon my private observations.

The general effect of a Utopian population is vigour. Every
one one meets seems to be not only in good health but in
training ; one rarely meets fat people, bald people, or bent or
grey. People who would be obese or bent and obviously
aged on earth are here, in good repair, and as a consequence
the whole effect of a crowd is livelier and more invigorating
than on earth. The dress is varied and graceful ; that of the
women reminds one most of the Italian fifteenth century ;
they have an abundance of soft and beautifully-coloured stuffs,
and the clothes, even of the poorest, fit admirably. Their
hair is very simply but very carefully and beautifully dressed,
and, except in very sunny weather, they do not wear hats or
bonnets. There is little difference in deportment between one
class and another ; they all are graceful and bear themselves
with quiet dignity, and among a group of them a European
woman of fashion in her lace and feathers, her hat and metal
ornaments, her mixed accumulations of " trimmings," would
look like a barbarian tricked out with the miscellaneous
plunder of a museum. Boys and girls wear much the same
sort of costume—brown leather shoes, then a sort of combination of hose and close-fitting trousers that reaches from toe to
waist, and over this a beltless jacket fitting very well, or a
belted tunic. Many slender women wear the same sort of
costume. We should see them in it very often in such a place
as Lucerne, as they returned from expeditions in the mountains,
The older men would wear long robes very frequently, but the
greater proportion of the men would go in variations of much
the same costume as the children. There would certainly be
hooded cloaks and umbrellas for rainy weather, high boots for
mud and snow, and cloaks and coats and furry robes for the
winter. There would be no doubt a freer use of colour than
terrestrial Europe sees in these days, but the costume of the
women at least would be soberer and more practical, and (in
harmony with our discussion in the previous chapter) less
differentiated from the men's.

But these, of course, are generalisations. These are the
mere translation of the social facts we have hypotheticated
into the language of costume. There will be a great variety of
costume and no compulsions. The doubles of people who
are naturally foppish on earth will be foppish in Utopia, and
people who have no natural taste on earth will have inartistic
equivalents. Every one will not be quiet in tone, or har-
monious, or beautiful. Occasionally, as I go through the
streets to my work, I shall turn round to glance again at some
robe shot with gold embroidery, some slashing of the sleeves,
some eccentricity of cut, or some discord or untidiness. But
these will be but transient flashes in a general flow of har-
monious graciousness ; dress will have scarcely any of that
effect of disorderly conflict, of self-assertion qualified by the
fear of ridicule, that it has in the crudely competitive civilisations of earth.

I shall have the seeker's attitude of mind during those few
days at Lucerne. I shall become a student of faces. I shall
be, as it were, looking for some one. I shall see heavy faces,
dull faces, faces with an uncongenial animation, alien faces,
and among these some with an immediate quality of appeal.
I should see desirable men approaching me, and I should think ;
" Now if I were to speak to you ? " Many of these latter I
should note wore the same clothing as the man who spoke to
us at Wassen ; I should begin to think of it as a sort of
uniform. . . .

Then I should see grave-faced girls, girls of that budding
age when their bearing becomes delusively wise, and the old
deception of my youth will recur to me ; " Could you and I
but talk together ? " I should think. Women will pass me
lightly, women with open and inviting faces, but they will
not attract me, and there will come beautiful women, women
with that touch of claustral preoccupation which forbids the
thought of any near approach. They are private and secret,
and I may not enter, I know, into their thoughts. . . .

I go as often as I can to the seat by the end of old Kapel-
brucke, and watch the people passing over.

I shall find a quality of dissatisfaction throughout all these
days. I shall come to see this period more and more distinctly as a pause, as a waiting interlude, and the idea of an
encounter with my double, which came at first as if it were a
witticism, as something verbal and surprising, begins to take
substance. The idea grows in my mind that after all this is
the " some one " I am seeking, this Utopian self of mine. I
had at first an idea of a grotesque encounter, as of something
happening in a looking-glass, but presently it dawns on me
that my Utopian self must be a very different person from me.
His training will be different, his mental content different.
But between us there will be a strange link of essential identity,
a sympathy, and understanding. I find the thing rising

suddenly to a preponderance in my mind. I find the interest of details dwindling to the vanishing point. That I have come to Utopia is the lesser thing now ; the greater is that I have come to meet myself.

I spend hours trying to imagine the encounter, inventing little dialogues. I go alone to the Bureau to find if any news has come to hand from the Great Index in Paris, but I am told to wait another twenty-four hours. I cease absolutely to be interested in anything else, except so far as it leads towards intercourse with this being who is to be at once so strangely alien and so totally mine.

§ 4

Wrapped up in these preoccupations as I am, it will certainly be the botanist who will notice the comparative absence of animals about us.

He will put it in the form of a temperate objection to the Utopian planet.

He is a professed lover of dogs and there are none. We have seen no horses and only one or two mules on the day of our arrival, and there seems not a cat in the world. I bring my mind round to his suggestion. " This follows," I say.

It is only reluctantly that I allow myself to be drawn from my secret musings into a discussion of Utopian pets.

I try to explain that a phase in the world's development is inevitable when a systematic world-wide attempt will be made to destroy for ever a great number of contagious and infectious diseases, and that this will involve, for a time at any rate, a stringent suppression of the free movement of familiar animals. Utopian houses, streets and drains will be planned and built to make rats, mice, and such-like house parasites impossible ; the race of cats and dogs—providing, as it does, living fastnesses to which such diseases as plague, influenza, catarrhs and the like, can retreat to sally forth again—must pass for a time out of freedom, and the filth made by horses and the other brutes of the highway vanish from the face of the earth. These things make an old story to me, and perhaps explicitness suffers through my brevity.

My botanist fails altogether to grasp what the disappearance of dieases means. His mind has no imaginative organ of that compass. As I talk his mind rests on one fixed image. This presents what the botanist would probably call a " dear old doggie "—which the botanist would make believe did not possess any sensible odour—and it has faithful brown eyes and understands everything you say. The botanist would make believe it understood him mystically, and I figure his long white hand—which seems to me, in my more jaundiced moments, to exist entirely for picking things and holding a lens—patting its head, while the brute looked things unspeakable. . . .

The botanist shakes his head after my explanation and says quietly, "I do not like your Utopia, if there are to be no dogs."

Perhaps that makes me a little malicious. Indeed, I do not hate dogs, but I care ten thousand times more for a man than for all the brutes on the earth, and I can see, what the botanist I think cannot, that a life spent in the delightful atmosphere of many pet animals may have too dear a price. . . .

I find myself back again at the comparison of the botanist and myself. There is a profound difference in our imaginations, and I wonder whether it is the consequence of innate character or of training, and whether he is really the human type or I. I am not altogether without imagination, but what imagination I have has the most insistent disposition to square itself with every fact in the universe. It hypothesises very boldly, but on the other hand it will not gravely make believe. Now the botanist's imagination is always busy with the most impossible make-believe. That is the way with all children I know. But it seems to me one ought to pass out of it. It isn't as though the world was an untidy nursery ; it is a place of splendours indescribable for all who will lift its veils. It may be he is essentially different from me, but I am much more inclined to think he is simply more childish. Always it is make-believe. He believes that horses are beautiful creatures, for example, dogs are beautiful creatures, that some women are inexpressibly lovely, and he makes believe that this is always so. Never a word of criticism of horse or dog or woman ! Never a word of criticism of his impeccable friends ! Then there is his botany. He makes believe that all the vegetable kingdom is mystically perfect and exemplary, that all flowers smell deliciously and are exquisitely beautiful, that *Drosera* does not hurt flies very much, and that onions do not smell. Most of the universe does not interest this nature lover at all. But I know, and I am querulously incapable of understanding why every one else does not know, that a horse is beautiful in one way and quite ugly in another, that everything has this shot-silk quality, and is all the finer for that. When people talk of a horse as an ugly animal I think of its beautiful moments, but when I hear a flow of indiscriminate praise of its beauty I think of such an aspect as one gets for example from a dog-cart, the fiddle-shaped back, and that distressing blade of the neck, the narrow clumsy place between the ears, and the ugly glimpse of cheek. There is, indeed, no beauty whatever save that transitory thing that comes and comes again ; all beauty is really the beauty of expression, is really kinetic and momentary. That is true even of those triumphs of static endeavour achieved by Greece. The Greek temple, for example, is a barn with a face that at a certain angle of vision and in a certain light has a great calm beauty.

But where are we drifting ? All such things, I hold, are cases of more and less, and of the right moment and the right aspect, even the things I most esteem.   There is no perfection, there is no enduring treasure.   This pet dog's beautiful affection, I say, or this other sensuous or imaginative delight, is no doubt good, but it can be put aside if it is incompatible with some other and wider good.   You cannot focus all good things together.

All right action and all wise action is surely sound judgment and courageous abandonment in the matter of such incompatibilities.   If I cannot imagine thoughts and feelings in a dog's brain that cannot possibly be there, at least I can imagine things in the future of men that might be there had we the will to demand them. . . .

"I don't like this Utopia," the botanist repeats.   "You don't understand about dogs.   To me they're human beings— and more !   There used to be such a jolly old dog at my aunt's at Frognal when I was a boy——"

But I do not heed his anecdote.   Something—something of the nature of conscience—has suddenly jerked back the memory of that beer I drank at Hospenthal, and puts an accusing finger on the memory.

I never have had a pet animal, I confess, though I have been fairly popular with kittens.   But with regard to a certain petting of myself—— ?

Perhaps I was premature about that beer.   I have had no pet animals, but I perceive if the Modern Utopia is going to demand the sacrifice of the love of animals, which is, in its way, a very fine thing indeed, so much the more readily may it demand the sacrifice of many other indulgencies, some of which are not even fine in the lowest degree.

It is curious this haunting insistence upon sacrifice and discipline !

It is slowly becoming my dominant thought that the sort of people whose will this Utopia embodies must be people a little heedless of small pleasures.   You cannot focus all good things at the same time.   That is my chief discovery in these meditations at Lucerne.   Much of the rest of this Utopia I had in a sort of way anticipated, but not this.   I wonder if I shall see my Utopian self for long and be able to talk to him freely. . . .

We lie in the petal-strewn grass under some Judas trees beside the lake shore, as I meander among these thoughts, and each of us, disregardful of his companion, follows his own associations.

"Very remarkable," I say, discovering that the botanist has come to an end with his story of that Frognal dog.

"You'd wonder how he knew," he says.

"You would."

I nibble a green blade.

"Do you realise quite," I ask, "that within a week we shall face our Utopian selves and measure something of what we might have been ? "

The botanist's face clouds. He rolls over, sits up abruptly and puts his lean hands about his knees.

"I don't like to think about it," he says. "What is the good of reckoning . . . might have beens ? "

§ 5

It is pleasant to think of one's puzzling the organised wisdom of so superior a planet as this Utopia, this moral monster State my Frankenstein of reasoning has made, and to that pitch we have come. When we are next in the presence of our Lucerne official, he has the bearing of a man who faces a mystification beyond his powers, an incredible disarrangement of the order of Nature. Here, for the first time in the records of Utopian science, are two cases—not simply one but two, and these in each other's company !—of duplicated thumb-marks. This, coupled with a cock-and-bull story of an instantaneous transfer from some planet unknown to Utopian astronomy. That he and all his world exists only upon a hypothesis that would explain every one of these difficulties absolutely, is scarcely likely to occur to his obviously un-philosophic mind.

The official eye is more eloquent than the official lips and asks almost urgently, "What in this immeasurable universe have you managed to do to your thumbs ? And why ? " But he is only a very inferior sort of official indeed, a mere clerk of the post, and he has all the guarded reserve of your thoroughly unoriginal man. "You are not the two persons I ascertained you were," he says, with the note of one resigned to communion with unreason ; "because you "—he indicates me—"are evidently at your residence in London. I smile. "That gentleman "—he points a pen at the botanist in a manner that is intended to dismiss my smile once for all—"will be in London next week. He will be returning next Friday from a special mission to investigate the fungoid parasites that have been attacking the cinchona trees in Ceylon."

The botanist blesses his heart.

"Consequently "—the official sighs at the burthen of such nonsense, "you will have to go and consult with—the people you ought to be."

I betray a faint amusement.

"You will have to end by believing in our planet," I say.

He waggles a negation with his head. He would intimate his position is too responsible a one for jesting, and both of us in our several ways enjoy the pleasure we poor humans have in meeting with intellectual inferiority. "The Standing Committee of Identification," he says, with an eye on a

memorandum, " has remitted your case to the Research Professor of Anthropology in the University of London, and they
want you to go there, if you will, and talk to him."

" What else can we do ? " says the botanist.

" There's no positive compulsion," he remarks, " but your
work here will probably cease.   Here——" he pushed the neat
slips of paper towards us—" are your tickets for London, and a
small but sufficient supply of money,"—he indicates two piles
of coins and paper on either hand of him—" for a day or so
there."   He proceeds in the same dry manner to inform us we
are invited to call at our earliest convenience upon our doubles,
and upon the Professor, who is to investigate our case.

" And then ? "

He pulls down the corners of his mouth in a wry deprecatory
smile, eyes us obliquely under a crumpled brow, shrugs his
shoulders, and shows us the palms of his hands.

On earth, where there is nationality, this would have been
a Frenchman—the inferior sort of Frenchman—the sort
whose only happiness is in the routine security of Government
employment.

§ 6

London will be the first Utopian city centre we shall see.

We shall find ourselves there with not a little amazement.
It will be our first experience of the swift long distance travel
of Utopia, and I have an idea—I know not why—that we
should make the journey by night.   Perhaps I think so
because the ideal of long-distance travel is surely a restful
translation less suitable for the active hours.

We shall dine and gossip and drink coffee at the pretty
little tables under the lantern-lit trees, we shall visit the
theatre, and decide to sup in the train, and so come at last to
the station.   There we shall find pleasant rooms with seats
and books—luggage all neatly elsewhere—and doors that we
shall imagine give upon a platform.   Our cloaks and hats and
such-like outdoor impedimenta will be taken in the hall and
neatly labelled for London, we shall exchange our shoes for
slippers there, and we shall sit down like men in a club.   An
officious little bell will presently call our attention to a label
" London " on the doorway, and an excellent phonograph will
enforce that notice with infinite civility.   The doors will open,
and we shall walk through into an equally comfortable gallery.

" Where is the train for London ? " we shall ask a uniformed
fellow Utopian.

" This is the train for London," he will say.

There will be a shutting of doors, and the botanist and I,
crying not to feel too childish, will walk exploring through
the capacious train.

The resemblance to a club will strike us both.   " A *good*
club," the botanist will correct me.

When one travels beyond a certain speed, there is nothing but fatigue in looking out of a window, and this corridor train, twice the width of its poor terrestrial brother, will have no need of that distraction. The simple device of abandoning any but a few windows, and those set high, gives the wall space of the long corridors to books ; the middle part of the train is indeed a comfortable library with abundant arm-chairs and couches, each with its green-shaded light, and soft carpets upon the sound-proof floor. Farther on will be a news-room, with a noiseless but busy tape, at one corner, printing off messages from the wires by the wayside, and farther still, rooms for gossip and smoking, a billiard room, and the dining car. Behind we shall come to bedrooms, bathrooms, the hairdresser, and so forth.

" When shall we start ? " I ask presently, as we return, rather like bashful yokels, to the library, and the old gentleman reading the *Arabian Nights* in the arm-chair in the corner glances up at me with a sudden curiosity.

The botanist touches my arm and nods towards a pretty little lead-paned window, through which we see a village sleeping under cloudy moonlight go flashing by. Then a skylit lake, and then a string of swaying lights, gone with the leap of a camera shutter.

Two hundred miles an hour !

We resort to a dignified Chinese steward and secure our berths. It is perhaps terrestrial of us that we do not think of reading the Utopian literature that lines the middle part of the train. I find a bed of the simple Utopian pattern, and lie for a time thinking—quite tranquilly—of this marvellous adventure.

I wonder why it is that to lie securely in bed, with the light out, seems ever the same place, wherever in space one may chance to be ? And asleep, there is no space for us at all. I become drowsy and incoherent and metaphysical. . . .

The faint and fluctuating drone of the wheels below the car, re-echoed by the flying track, is more perceptible now, but it is not unpleasantly loud, merely a faint tinting of the quiet. . . .

No sea crossing breaks our journey ; there is nothing to prevent a Channel tunnel in that other planet ; and I wake in London.

The train has been in London some time when I awake, for these marvellous Utopians have discovered that it is not necessary to bundle out passengers from a train in the small hours, simply because they have arrived. A Utopian train is just a peculiar kind of hotel corridor that flies about the earth while one sleeps.

§ 7

How will a great city of Utopia strike us ?

To answer that question well one must needs be artist and engineer, and I am neither. Moreover, one must employ words and phrases that do not exist, for this world still does not dream of the things that may be done with thought and steel, when the engineer is sufficiently educated to be an artist, and the artistic intelligence has been quickened to the accomplishment of an engineer. How can one write of these things for a generation which rather admires that inconvenient and gawky muddle of ironwork and Flemish architecture, the London Tower Bridge. When before this, temerarious anticipators have written of the mighty buildings that might some day be, the illustrator has blended with the poor ineffectual splutter of the author's words, his powerful suggestion that it amounted simply to something bulbous, florid and fluent in the vein of the onion, and *L'Art Nouveau.* But here, it may be, the illustrator will not intervene.

Art has scarcely begun in the world.

There have been a few forerunners and that is all. Leonardo Michael Angelo ; how they would have exulted in the liberties of steel ! There are no more pathetic documents in the archives of art than Leonardo's memoranda. In these, one sees him again and again reaching out as it were, with empty desirous hands, towards the unborn possibilities of the engineer. And Dürer, too, was a Modern, with the same turn towards creative invention. In our times these men would have wanted to make viaducts to bridge wild and inaccessible places, to cut and straddle great railways athwart the mountain masses of the world. You can see, time after time, in Dürer's work, as you can see in the imaginary architectural landscape of the Pompeian walls, the dream of structures, lighter and bolder than stone or brick can yield. . . . These Utopian town buildings will be the realisation of such dreams.

Here will be one of the great meeting-places of mankind. Here—I speak of Utopian London—will be the traditional centre of one of the great races in the commonalty of the World State—and here will be its social and intellectual exchange. There will be a mighty University here, with thousands of professors and tens of thousands of advanced students, and here great journals of thought and speculation, mature and splendid books of philosophy and science, and a glorious fabric of literature will be woven and shaped, and with a teeming leisureliness, put forth. Here will be stupendous libraries, and a mighty organisation of museums. About these centres will cluster a great swarm of people, and close at hand will be another centre, for I who am an Englishman must needs stipulate that Westminster shall still be a seat of world Empire, one of several seats, if you will—where the ruling council of the world assembles. Then the arts will cluster round this city, as gold gathers about wisdom, and here Englishmen will weave into wonderful prose and beautiful rhythms and subtly atmospheric forms, the intricate, austere and courageous imagination of our race.

One will come into this place as one comes into a noble mansion. They will have flung great arches and domes of glass above the wider spaces of the town, the slender beauty of the perfect metal-work far overhead will be softened to a fairy-like unsubstantiality by the mild London air. It will be the London air we know, clear of filth and all impurity, the same air that gives our October days their unspeakable clarity, and makes every London twilight mysteriously beautiful. We shall go along avenues of architecture that will be emancipated from the last memories of the squat temple boxes of the Greek, the buxom curvatures of Rome ; the Goth in us will have taken to steel and countless new materials as kindly as once he took to stone. The gay and swiftly moving platforms of the public ways will go past on either hand, carrying sporadic groups of people, and very speedily we shall find ourselves in a sort of central space, rich with palms and flowering bushes and statuary. We shall look along an avenue of trees, down a wide gorge between the cliffs of crowded hotels, the hotels that are still glowing with internal lights, to where the shining morning river streams dawnlit out to sea.

Great multitudes of people will pass softly to and fro in this central space, beautiful girls and youths going to the University classes that are held in the stately palaces about us, grave and capable men and women going to their businesses, children meandering along to their schools, holiday makers, lovers, setting out upon a hundred quests ; and here we shall ask for the two we more particularly seek. A graceful little telephone kiosk will put us within reach of them, and with a queer sense of unreality I shall find myself talking to my Utopian twin. He has heard of me, he wants to see me and he gives me clear directions how to come to him.

I wonder if my own voice sounds like that.

" Yes," I say, " then I will come as soon as we have been to our hotel."

We indulge in no eloquence upon this remarkable occasion. Yet I feel an unusual emotional stir. I tremble greatly, and the telephonic mouthpiece rattles as I replace it.

And thence the botanist and I walk on to the apartments that have been set aside for us, and into which the poor little rolls of the property that has accumulated about us in Utopia, our earthly raiment, and a change of linen and the like, have already been delivered. As we go I find I have little to say to my companion, until presently I am struck by a transitory wonder that he should have so little to say to me.

" I can still hardly realise," I say, " that I am going to see myself—as I might have been."

" No," he says, and relapses at once into his own pre-occupation.

For a moment my wonder as to what he should be thinking about brings me near to a double self-forgetfulness.

I realise we are at the entrance of our hotel before I can formulate any further remark.

" This is the place," I say.

CHAPTER EIGHT

MY UTOPIAN SELF

§ 1

IT falls to few of us to interview our better selves. My Utopian self is, of course, my better self—according to my best endeavours—and I must confess myself fully alive to the difficulties of the situation. When I came to this Utopia I had no thought of any such intimate self-examination.

The whole fabric of that other universe sways for a moment as I come into his room, into his clear and ordered work-room. I am trembling. A figure rather taller than myself stands against the light.

He comes towards me, and I, as I advance to meet him, stumble against a chair. Then, still without a word, we are clasping hands.

I stand now so that the light falls upon him, and I can see his face better. He is a little taller than I, younger looking and sounder looking ; he has missed an illness or so, and there is no scar over his eye. His training has been subtly finer than mine ; he has made himself a better face than mine. . . . These things I might have counted upon. I can fancy he winces with a twinge of sympathetic understanding at my manifest inferiority. Indeed, I come, trailing clouds of earthly confusion and weakness ; I bear upon me all the defects of my world. He wears, I see, that white tunic with the purple band that I have already begun to consider the proper Utopian clothing for grave men, and his face is clean shaven. We forget to speak at first in the intensity of our mutual inspection. When at last I do gain my voice it is to say something quite different from the fine, significant openings of my premeditated dialogues.

" You have a pleasant room," I remark, and look about a little, disconcerted because there is no fireplace for me to put my back against, or hearth-rug to stand upon. He pushed me a chair, into which I plump, and we hang over an immensity of conversational possibilities.

" I say," I plunge, " what do you think of me ? You don't think I'm an impostor ? "

" Not now that I have seen you. No."

" Am I so like you ? "

" Like me and your story—exactly."

" You haven't any doubt left ? " I ask.

" Not in the least since I saw you enter. You come from the world beyond Sirius, twin to this. Eh ? "

" And you don't want to know how I got here ? "

" I've ceased even to wonder how *I* got here," he says, with a laugh that echoes mine.

He leans back in his chair, and I in mine, and the absurd parody of our attitude strikes us both.

" Well ? " we say, simultaneously, and laugh together.

I will confess this meeting is more difficult even than I anticipated.

§ 2

Our conversation at that first encounter would do very little to develop the Modern Utopia in my mind. Inevitably, it would be personal and emotional. He would tell me how he stood in his world, and I how I stood in mine. I should have to tell him things, I should have to explain things——

No, the conversation would contribute nothing to a modern Utopia.

And so I leave it out.

§ 3

But I should go back to my botanist in a state of emotional relaxation. At first I should not heed the fact that he, too, had been in some manner stirred. " I have seen him," I should say, needlessly, and seem to be on the verge of telling the untellable. Then I should fade off into : " It's the strangest thing."

He would interrupt me with his own preoccupation. " You know," he would say, " I've seen some one."

I should pause and look at him.

" She is in this world," he says.

" Who is in this world ? "

" Mary ! "

I have not heard her name before, but I understand, of course, at once.

" I saw her," he explains.

" Saw her ? "

" I'm certain it was her. Certain. She was far away across those gardens near here—and before I had recovered from my amazement she had gone ! But it was Mary."

He takes my arm. " You know I did not understand this," he says. " I did not really understand that when you said Utopia, you meant I was to meet her—in happiness."

" I didn't."

" It works out at that."

" You haven't met her yet."

" I shall. It makes everything different. To tell you the truth I've rather hated this Utopia of yours at times. You mustn't mind my saying it, but there's something of the Gradgrind——"

Probably I should swear at that.

" What ? " he says.

" Nothing."

" But you spoke ? "

" I was purring. I'm a Gradgrind—it's quite right—anything you can say about Herbert Spencer, vivisectors, materialistic Science or Atheists, applies without correction to me. Begbie away ! But now you think better of a modern Utopia ? Was the lady looking well ? "

" It was her real self. Yes. Not the broken woman I met—in the real world."

" And as though she was pining for you."

He looks puzzled.

" Look there ! " I say.

He looks.

We are standing high above the ground in the loggia into which our apartments open, and I point across the soft haze of the public gardens to a tall white mass of University buildings that rises with a free and fearless gesture, to lift saluting pinnacles against the clear evening sky. " Don't you think that rather more beautiful than—say—our National Gallery ? "

He looks at it critically. " There's a lot of metal in it," he objects. " What ? "

I purred. " But, anyhow, whatever you can't see is that, you can, I suppose, see that it is different from anything in your world—it lacks the kindly humanity of a red-brick Queen Anne villa residence, with its gables and bulges and bow windows, and its stained glass fanlight, and so forth. It lacks the self-complacent unreasonableness of Board of Works classicism. There's something in its proportions—as though some one with brains had taken a lot of care to get it quite right, some one who not only knew what metal can do, but what a University ought to be, somebody who had found the Gothic spirit enchanted, petrified, in a cathedral, and had set it free."

" But what has this," he asks, " to do with her ? "

" Very much," I say. " This is not the same world. If she is here, she will be younger in spirit and wiser. She will be in many ways more refined——"

" No one——" he begins, with a note of indignation.

" No, no ! She couldn't be. I was wrong there. But she will be different. Grant that at any rate. When you go forward to speak to her, she may not remember—very many things *you* may remember. Things that happened at Frognal —dear romantic walks through the Sunday summer evenings, practically you two alone, you in your adolescent silk hat and your nice gentlemanly gloves. . . . Perhaps that did not happen here ! And she may have other memories—of things

—that down there haven't happened.   You noted her costume.
She wasn't by any chance one of the *samurai* ? "

He answers, with a note of satisfaction, " No !   She wore
a womanly dress of greyish green."

" Probably under the Lesser Rule."

" I don't know what you mean by the Lesser Rule.   She
wasn't one of the *samurai*."

" And, after all, you know—I keep on reminding you,
and you keep on losing touch with the fact, that this world
contains your double."

He pales, and his countenance is disturbed.   Thank Heaven,
I've touched him at last !

" This world contains your double.   But, conceivably,
everything may be different here.   The whole romantic story
may have run a different course.   It was as it was in our
world, by the accidents of custom and proximity.   Adolescence
is a defenceless plastic period.   You are a man to form great
affections—noble, great affections.   You might have met any
one almost at that season and formed the same attachment."

For a time he is perplexed and troubled by this suggestion.

" No," he says, a little doubtfully.   " No.   It was herself. . . ."   Then, emphatically, " *No !* "

§ 4

For a time we say no more, and I fall musing about my
strange encounter with my Utopian double.   I think of the
confessions I have just made to him, the strange admissions
both to him and myself.   I have stirred up the stagnations
of my own emotional life, the pride that has slumbered, the
hopes and disappointments that have not troubled me for
years.   There are things that happened to me in my adolescence
that no discipline of reason will ever bring to a just proportion
for me, the first humiliations I was made to suffer, the waste
of all the fine irrecoverable loyalties and passions of my youth.
The dull base caste of my little personal tragi-comedy—I have
ostensibly forgiven, I have for the most part forgotten—and
yet when I recall them I hate each actor still.   Whenever it
comes into my mind—I do my best to prevent it—there it is,
and these detestable people blot out the stars for me.

I have told all that story to my double, and he has listened
with understanding eyes.   But for a little while those squalid
memories will not sink back into the deeps.   We lean, side
by side, over our balcony, lost in such egotistical absorptions,
quite heedless of the great palace of noble dreams to which our
first enterprise has brought us.

§ 5

I can understand the botanist this afternoon ; for once we
are in the same key.   My own mental temper has gone for
the day, and I know what it means to be untempered.   Here

is a world and a glorious world, and it is for me to take hold of it, to have to do with it, here and now, and behold ! I can only think that I am burnt and scarred, and there rankles that wretched piece of business, the mean unimaginative triumph of my antagonist——

I wonder how many men have any real freedom of mind, are, in truth, unhampered by such associations, to whom all that is great and noble in life does not, at times at least, if not always, seem secondary to obscure rivalries and considerations, to the petty hates that are like germs in the blood, to the lust for self-assertion, to dwarfish pride, to affections they gave in pledge even before they were men.

The botanist beside me dreams, I know, of vindications for that woman.

All this world before us, and its order and liberty, are no more than a painted scene before which he is to meet Her at last freed from " that scoundrel."

He expects " that scoundrel " really to be present and, as it were, writhing under their feet. . . .

I wonder if that man *was* a scoundrel. He has gone wrong on earth, no doubt, has failed and degenerated, but what was it sent him wrong ? Was his failure inherent, or did some net of cross purposes tangle about his feet ? Suppose he is not a failure in Utopia ! . . .

I wonder that this has never entered the botanist's head.

He, with his vaguer mind, can overlook—spite of my ruthless reminders—all that would mar his vague anticipations. That, too, if I suggested it, he would overcome and disregard. He has the most amazing power of resistance to uncongenial ideas ; amazing that is, to me. He hates the idea of meeting his double, and, consequently, so soon as I cease to speak of that, with scarcely an effort of his will it fades again from his mind.

Down below in the gardens two children pursue one another, and one, near caught, screams aloud and rouses me from my reverie.

I follow their little butterfly antics until they vanish beyond a thicket of flowering rhododendra, and then my eyes go back to the great façade of the University buildings.

But I am in no mood to criticise architecture.

Why should a modern Utopia insist upon slipping out of the hands of its creator and becoming the background of a personal drama—of such a silly little drama ?

The botanist will not see Utopia in any other way. He tests it entirely by its reaction upon the individual persons and things he knows ; he dislikes it because he suspects it of wanting to lethal chamber his aunt's " dear old doggie," and now he is reconciled to it because a certain " Mary " looks much younger and better here than she did on earth. And here am I, near fallen into the same way of dealing !

We agree to purge this State and all the people in it of traditions, associations, bias, laws, and artificial entanglements, and begin anew ; but we have no power to liberate ourselves. Our past, even its accidents, its accidents above all, and ourselves, are one.

CHAPTER NINE

THE SAMURAI

§ 1

NEITHER my Utopian double nor I love emotion sufficiently to cultivate it, and my feelings are in a state of seemly subordination when we meet again. He is now in possession of some clear, general ideas about my own world, and I can broach almost at once the thoughts that have been growing and accumulating since my arrival in this planet of my dreams. We find our interest in a humanised state-craft makes us, in spite of our vast difference in training and habits, curiously akin.

I put it to him that I came to Utopia with but very vague ideas of the method of government, biased, perhaps, a little in favour of certain electoral devices, but for the rest indeterminate, and that I have come to perceive more and more clearly that the large intricacy of Utopian organisation demands more powerful and efficient method of control than electoral methods can give. I have come to distinguish among the varied costumes and the innumerable types of personality Utopia presents, certain men and women of a distinctive costume and bearing, and I know now that these people constitute an order, the *samurai*, the " voluntary nobility," which is essential in the scheme of the Utopian State. I know that this order is open to every physically and mentally healthy adult in the Utopian State who will observe its prescribed austere rule of living, that much of the responsible work of the State is reserved for it, and I am inclined now at the first onset of realisation to regard it as far more significant than it really is in the Utopian scheme, as being, indeed, in itself and completely the Utopian scheme. My predominant curiosity concerns the organisation of this order. As it has developed in my mind, it has reminded me more and more closely of that strange class of guardians which constitutes the essential substance of Plato's *Republic*, and it is with an implicit reference to Plato's profound intuitions that I and my double discuss this question.

To clarify our comparison he tells me something of the history of Utopia, and incidentally it becomes necessary to make a correction in the assumptions upon which I have based

my enterprise. We are assuming a world identical in every
respect with the real planet Earth, except for the profoundest
differences in the mental content of life. This implies a
different literature, a different philosophy, and a different
history, and so soon as I come to talk to him I find that though
it remains unavoidable that we should assume the correspondence of the two populations, man for man—unless we
would face unthinkable complications—we must assume also
that a great succession of persons of extraordinary character
and mental gifts, who on earth died in childhood or at birth,
or who never learnt to read, or who lived and died amidst
savage or brutalising surroundings that gave their gifts no
scope, did in Utopia encounter happier chances, and take up
the development and application of social theory—from
the time of the first Utopists in a steady onward progress,
down to the present hour.[1] The differences of conditions,
therefore, had widened with each successive year. Jesus
Christ had been born into a liberal and progressive Roman
Empire that spread from the Arctic Ocean to the Bight of
Benin, and was to know no Decline and Fall, and Mahomet,
instead of embodying the dense prejudices of Arab ignorance,
opened his eyes upon an intellectual horizon already nearly
as wide as the world.

And through this empire the flow of thought, the flow of
intention, poured always more abundantly. There were
wars, but they were conclusive wars that established new and
more permanent relations, that swept aside obstructions, and
abolished centres of decay ; there were prejudices tempered
to an ordered criticism, and hatreds that merged at last in
tolerant reactions. It was several hundred years ago that the
great organisation of the *samurai* came into its present form.
And it was this organisation's widely sustained activities that
had shaped and established the World State in Utopia.

This organisation of the *samurai* was a quite deliberate
invention. It arose in the course of social and political
troubles and complications, analogous to those of our own
time on earth, and was, indeed, the last of a number of political
and religious experiments dating back to the first dawn of
philosophical state-craft in Greece. That hasty despair of
specialisation for government that gave our poor world
individualism, democratic liberalism, and anarchism, and
that curious disregard of the fund of enthusiasm and self-
sacrifice in men, which is the fundamental weakness of worldly
economics, do not appear in the history of Utopian thought.
All that history is pervaded with the recognition of the fact
that self-seeking is no more the whole of human life than the
satisfaction of hunger ; that it is an essential of a man's

[1] One might assume as an alternative to this that amidst the four-fifths of the Greek
literature now lost to the world, there perished, neglected, some book of elementary
significance, some earlier *Novum Organum*, that in Utopia survived to achieve the
profoundest consequences.

existence no doubt, and that under stress of evil circumstances it may as entirely obsess him as would the food hunt during famine, but that life may pass beyond to an illimitable world of emotions and effort. Every sane person consists of possibilities beyond the unavoidable needs, is capable of disinterested feeling, even if it amounts only to enthusiasm for a sport or an industrial employment well done, for an art, or for a locality or class. In our world now, as in the Utopian past, this impersonal energy of a man goes out into religious emotion and work, into patriotic effort, into artistic enthusiasms, into games and amateur employments, and an enormous proportion of the whole world's fund of effort wastes itself in religious and political misunderstandings and conflicts, and in unsatisfying amusements and unproductive occupations. In a modern Utopia there will, indeed, be no perfection ; in Utopia there must also be friction, conflicts, and waste, but the waste will be enormously less than in our world. And the co-ordination of activities this relatively smaller waste will measure, will be the achieved end for which the order of the *samurai* was first devised.

Inevitably such an order must have first arisen among a clash of social forces and political systems as a revolutionary organisation. It must have set before itself the attainment of some such Utopian ideal as this modern Utopia does, in the key of mortal imperfection, realise. At first it may have directed itself to research and discussion, to the elaboration of its ideal, to the discussion of a plan of campaign, but at some stage it must have assumed a more militant organisation, and have prevailed against and assimilated the pre-existing political organisations, and to all intents and purposes have become this present synthesised World State. Traces of that militancy would, therefore, pervade it still, and a campaigning quality— no longer against specific disorders, but against universal human weaknesses, and the inanimate forces that trouble man—still remain as its essential quality.

" Something of this kind," I should tell my double, " had arisen in our thought "—I jerk my head back to indicate an infinitely distant planet—" just before I came upon these explorations. The idea had reached me, for example, of something to be called a New Republic, which was to be in fact an organisation for revolution something after the fashion of your *samurai*, as I understand them—only most of the organisation and the rule of life still remained to be invented. All sorts of people were thinking of something in that way about the time of my coming. The idea, as it reached me, was pretty crude in several respects. It ignored the high possibility of a synthesis of languages in the future ; it came from a literary man, who wrote only English, and, as I read him—he was a little vague in his proposals—it was to be a purely English-speaking movement. And his ideas were coloured too much by the peculiar opportunism of his time ; he seemed to have more than half an eye for a prince or a millionaire of genius ; he seemed looking here and there for support and the structural elements of a party. Still, the idea of a comprehensive movement of disillusioned and illuminated men behind the shams and patriotisms, the spites and personalities of the ostensible world, was there."

I added some particulars.

"Our movement had something of that spirit in the beginning," said my Utopian double. "But while your men seem to be thinking disconnectedly, and upon a very narrow and fragmentary basis of accumulated conclusions, ours had a fairly comprehensive science of human association, and a very careful analysis of the failures of preceding beginnings to draw upon. After all, your world must be as full as ours was of the wreckage and decay of previous attempts ; churches, aristocracies, orders, cults. . . ."

"Only at present we seem to have lost heart altogether and now there are no new religions, no new orders, no new cults—no beginnings any more."

"But that's only a resting phase, perhaps. You were saying——"

"Oh !—let that distressful planet alone for a time ! Tell me how you manage in Utopia."

§ 2

The social theorists of Utopia, my double explained, did not base their schemes upon the classification of men into labour and capital, the landed interest, the liquor trade, and the like. They esteemed these as accidental categories, indefinitely amenable to statesmanship, and they looked for some practical and real classification upon which to base organisation.[1] But, on the other hand, the assumption that men are unclassifiable, because practically homogeneous, which underlies modern democratic methods and all the fallacies of our equal justice, is even more alien to the Utopian mind. Throughout Utopia there is, of course, no other than provisional classifications, since every being is regarded as finally unique, but for political and social purposes things have long rested upon a classification of temperaments, which attends mainly to differences in the range and quality and character of the individual imagination.

This Utopian classification was a rough one, but it served its purpose to determine the broad lines of political organisation ; it was so far unscientific that many individuals fall between or within two or even three of its classes. But that

[1] In that they seem to have profited by a more searching criticism of early social and political speculations than our earth has yet undertaken. The social speculations of the Greeks, for example, had just the same primary defect as the economic speculations of the eighteenth century—they began with the assumption that the general conditions of the prevalent state of affairs were permanent.

was met by giving the correlated organisation a compensatory looseness of play. Four main classes of mind were distinguished, called, respectively, the Poietic, the Kinetic, the Dull, and the Base. The former two are supposed to constitute the living tissue of the State ; the latter are the fulcra and resistances, the bone and cover of its body. They are not hereditary classes, nor is there any attempt to develop any class by special breeding, simply because the intricate interplay of heredity is untraceable and incalculable. They are classes to which people drift of their own accord. Education is uniform until differentiation becomes unmistakable, and each man (and woman) must establish his position with regard to the lines of this abstract classification by his own quality, choice, and development. . . .

The Poietic or creative class of mental individuality embraces a wide range of types, but they agree in possessing imaginations that range beyond the known and accepted, and that involve the desire to bring the discoveries made in such excursions, into knowledge and recognition. The scope and direction of the imaginative excursion may vary very greatly. It may be the invention of something new or the discovery of something hitherto unperceived. When the invention or discovery is primarily beauty then we have the artistic type of Poietic mind ; when it is not so, we have the true scientific man. The range of discovery may be narrowed as it is in the art of Whistler or the science of a cytologist, or it may embrace a wide extent of relevance, until at last both artist or scientific inquirer merge in the universal reference of the true philosopher. To the accumulated activities of the Poietic type, reacted upon by circumstances, are due almost all the forms assumed by human thought and feeling. All religious ideas, all ideas of what is good or beautiful, entered life through the Poietic inspirations of man. Except for processes of decay, the forms of the human future must come also through men of this same type, and it is a primary essential to our modern idea of an abundant secular progress that these activities should be unhampered and stimulated.

The Kinetic class consists of types, various, of course, and merging insensibly along the boundary into the less representative constituents of the Poietic group, but distinguished by a more restricted range of imagination. Their imaginations do not range beyond the known, experienced, and accepted, though within these limits they may imagine as vividly or more vividly than members of the former group. They are often very clever and capable people, but they do not do, and they do not desire to do, new things. The more vigorous individuals of this class are the most teachable people in the world, and they are generally more moral and more trustworthy than the Poietic types. They live—while the Poietics are always something of experimentalists with life. The characteristics of either of these two classes may be associated with a good or bad physique, with excessive or defective energy, with exceptional keenness of the senses in some determinate direction or such-like "bent," and the Kinetic type, just as the Poietic type, may display an imagination of restricted or of the most universal range. But a fairly energetic Kinetic is probably the nearest thing to that ideal our earthly anthropologists have in mind when they speak of the "Normal" human being. The very definition of the Poietic class involves a certain abnormality.

The Utopians distinguished two extremes of this Kinetic class according to the quality of their imaginative preferences. the Dan and Beersheba, as it were, of this division. At one end is the mainly intellectual, unoriginal type, which, with energy of personality, makes an admirable judge or administrator and without it an uninventive, laborious, common mathematician, or common scholar, or common scientific man ; while at the other end is the mainly emotional, unoriginal man, the type to which—at a low level of personal energy—my botanist inclines. The second type includes, amidst its energetic forms, great actors, and popular politicians and preachers. Between these extremes is a long and wide region of varieties, into which one would put most of the people who form the reputable workmen, the men of substance, the trustworthy men and women, the pillars of society on earth.

Below these two classes in the Utopian scheme of things, and merging insensibly into them, come the Dull. The Dull are persons of altogether inadequate imagination, the people who never seem to learn thoroughly, or hear distinctly, or think clearly. (I believe if every one is to be carefully educated they would be considerably in the minority in the world, but it is quite possible that will not be the reader's opinion. It is clearly a matter of an arbitrary line.) They are the stupid people, the incompetent people, the formal, imitative people, the people who, in any properly organised State, should, as a class, gravitate towards and below the minimum wage that qualifies for marriage. The laws of heredity are far too mysterious for such offspring as they do produce to be excluded from a fair chance in the world, but for themselves, they count neither for work nor direction in the State.

Finally, with a bold disregard of the logician's classificatory rules, these Utopian statesmen who devised the World State, hewed out in theory a class of the Base. The Base may, indeed, be either poietic, kinetic, or dull, though most commonly they are the last, and their definition concerns not so much the quality of their imagination as a certain bias in it, that to a statesman makes it a matter for special attention. The Base have a narrower and more persistent egoistic reference than the common run of humanity ; they may boast, but they have no frankness ; they have relatively great powers of concealment, and they are capable of, and sometimes have an aptitude and inclination towards, cruelty. In the queer phrasing of earthly psychology with its clumsy avoidance of analysis, they have no " moral sense." They count as an antagonism to the State organisation.

Obviously, this is the rudest of classifications, and no Utopian has ever supposed it to be a classification for individual application, a classification so precise that one can say, this man is " poietic," and that man is " base." In actual experience these qualities mingle and vary in every possible way. It is not a classification for Truth, but a classification to an end. Taking humanity as a multitude, of unique individuals in mass, one may, for practical purposes, deal with it far more conveniently by disregarding its uniqueness and its mixed cases altogether, and supposing it to be an assembly of poietic, kinetic, dull, and base people. In many respects it behaves as if it were that. The State, dealing as it does only with non-individualised affairs, is not only justified in disregarding, but is bound to disregard, a man's special distinction, and to provide for him on the strength of his prevalent aspect as being on the whole poietic, kinetic, or what not. In a world of hasty judgments and carping criticism, it cannot be repeated too often that the fundamental ideas of a modern Utopia imply everywhere and in everything, margins and elasticities, a certain universal compensatory looseness of play.

§ 3

Now these Utopian statesmen who founded the World State put the problem of social organisation in the following fashion :—To contrive a revolutionary movement that shall absorb all existing governments and fuse them with itself, and that must be rapidly progressive and adaptable, and yet coherent, persistent, powerful, and efficient.

The problem of combining progress with political stability had never been accomplished in Utopia before that time, any more than it has been accomplished on earth. Just as on earth, Utopian history was a succession of powers rising and falling in an alternation of efficient conservative with unstable liberal States. Just as on earth, so in Utopia, the kinetic type of men had displayed a more or less unintentional antagonism to the poietic. The general life-history of a State had been the same on either planet. First, through poietic activities, the idea of a community has developed, and the State has shaped itself ; poietic men have arisen first in this department of national life, and then that, and have given place to kinetic men of a high type—for it seems to be in their nature that poietic men should be mutually repulsive, and not succeed and develop one another consecutively—and a period of expansion and vigour has set in. The general poietic activity has declined with the development of an efficient and settled social and political organisation ; the statesman has given way to the politician who has incorporated the wisdom of the statesman with his own energy, the original genius in arts, letters, science, and every department of activity to the cultivated and scholarly man. The kinetic man of wide range, who has assimilated his poietic predecessor, succeeds with far more readiness than his poietic contemporary in almost every human activity. The latter is by his very nature undisciplined and experimental, and is positively hampered by precedents and good order. With this substitution of the efficient for the creative type, the State ceases to grow, first in this department of activity, and then in that, and so long as its conditions remain the same it remains orderly and efficient. But it has lost its power of initiative and change ; its power of adaptation is gone, and with that secular change of conditions which is the law of life, stresses must arise within and without, and bring at last either through revolution or through defeat the release of fresh poietic power. The process, of course, is not in its entirety simple ; it may be masked by the fact that one department of activity may be in its poietic stage, while another is in a phase of realisation. In the United States of America, for example, during the nineteenth century, there was great poietic activity in industrial organisation, and none whatever in political philosophy ; but a careful analysis of the history of any period will show the rhythm almost invariably present, and the initial problem before the Utopian philosopher, therefore, was whether this was an inevitable alternation, whether human progress was necessarily a series of developments, collapses, and fresh beginnings, after an interval of disorder, unrest, and often great unhappiness, or whether it was possible to maintain a secure, happy, and progressive State beside an unbroken flow of poietic activity.

Clearly they decided upon the second alternative. If, indeed, I am listening to my Utopian self, then they not only decided the problem could be solved, but they solved it.

He tells me how they solved it.

A modern Utopia differs from all the older Utopias in its recognition of the need of poietic activities—one sees this new consideration creeping into thought for the first time in the phrasing of Comte's insistence that " spiritual " must precede political reconstruction, and in his admission of the necessity of recurrent books and poems about Utopias—and at first this recognition appears to admit only an added complication to a problem already unmanageably complex. Comte's separation of the activities of a State into the spiritual and material does, to a certain extent, anticipate this opposition of poietic and kinetic, but the intimate texture of his mind was dull and hard, the conception slipped from him again, and his suppression of literary activities, and his imposition of a rule of life upon the poietic types, who are least able to sustain it, mark how deeply he went under. To a large extent he followed the older Utopists in assuming that the philosophical and constructive problem could be done once for all, and he worked the results out simply under an organised kinetic government. But what seems to be merely an addition to the difficulty may in the end turn out to be a simplification, just as the introduction of a fresh term to an intricate irreducible mathematical expression will at times bring it to unity.

Now philosophers after my Utopian pattern, who find the ultimate significance in life in individuality, novelty, and the undefined, would not only regard the poietic element as the most important in human society, but would perceive quite clearly the impossibility of its organisation. This, indeed, is simply the application to the moral and intellectual fabric of the principles already applied in discussing the State control of reproduction (in Chapter Six, § 2). But just as in the case of births it was possible for the State to frame limiting conditions within which individuality plays more freely than in the void, so the founders of this modern Utopia believed it possible to define conditions under which every individual born with poietic gifts should be enabled and encouraged to give them a full development, in art, philosophy, invention, or discovery. Certain general conditions presented themselves as obviously reasonable :—to give every citizen as good an education as he or she could acquire, for example ; to so frame it that the directed educational process would never at any period occupy the whole available time of the learner, but would provide throughout a marginal free leisure with opportunities for developing idiosyncrasies, and to ensure by the expedient of a minimum wage for a specified amount of work, that leisure and opportunity did not cease throughout life.

But, in addition to thus making poietic activities universally possible, the founders of this modern Utopia sought to supply incentives, which was an altogether more difficult research, a problem in its nature irresolvably complex, and admitting of no systematic solution. But my double told me of a great variety of devices by which poetic men and women were given honour and enlarged freedoms, so soon as they produced an earnest of their quality, and he explained to me how great an ambition they might entertain.

There were great systems of laboratories attached to every municipal force station at which research could be conducted under the most favourable conditions, and every mine, and, indeed, almost every great industrial establishment, was saddled under its lease with similar obligations. So much for poietic ability and research in physical science. The World State tried the claims of every living contributor to any materially valuable invention, and paid or charged a royalty on its use that went partly to him personally, and partly to the research institution that had produced him. In the matter of literature and the philosophical and sociological sciences, every higher educational establishment carried its studentships, its fellowships, its occasional lectureships, and to produce a poem, a novel, a speculative work of force or merit, was to become the object of a generous competition between rival Universities. In Utopia, any author has the option either of publishing his works through the public bookseller as a private speculation, or, if he is of sufficient merit, of accepting a University endowment and conceding his copyright to the University press. All sorts of grants in the hands of committees of the most varied constitution, supplemented these academic resources, and ensured that no possible contributor to the wide flow of the Utopian mind slipped into neglect. Apart from those who engaged mainly in teaching and administration, my double told me that the world-wide House of Saloman [1] thus created sustained over a million men. For all the rarity of large fortunes, therefore, no original man with the desire and capacity for material or mental experiments went long without resources and the stimulus of attention, criticism, and rivalry.

" And finally," said my double, " our Rules ensure a considerable understanding of the importance of poietic activities in the majority of the *samurai*, in whose hands as a class all the real power of the world resides."

" Ah ! " said I, " and now we come to the thing that interests me most. For it is quite clear, in my mind, that these *samurai* form the real body of the State. All this time that I have spent going to and fro in this planet, it has been growing upon me that this order of men and women, wearing such a uniform as you wear, and with faces strengthened by discipline and touched with devotion, is the Utopian reality ; but that for them, the whole fabric of these fair appearances would crumble and tarnish, shrink and shrivel, until at last, back I should be amidst the grime and disorders of the life of earth. Tell me about these *samurai*, who remind me of Plato's guardians, who look like Knights Templars, who bear a name that recalls the swordsmen of Japan . . . and whose uniform you yourself are wearing. What are they ? Are they an hereditary caste, a specially educated order, an elected class ? For, certainly, this world turns upon them as a door upon its hinges."

§ 4

" I follow the Common Rule, as many men do," said my double, answering my allusion to his uniform almost apologetically. " But my own work is, in its nature, poietic ; there is much dissatisfaction with our isolation of criminals upon islands, and I am analysing the psychology of prison officials and criminals in general with a view to some better

[1] *The New Atlantis.*

scheme. I am supposed to be ingenious with expedients in this direction. Typically, the *samurai* are engaged in administrative work. Practically the whole of the responsible rule of the world is in their hands ; all our head teachers and disciplinary heads of colleges, our judges, barristers, employers of labour beyond a certain limit, practising medical men, legislators, must be *samurai*, and all the executive committees, and so forth, that play so large a part in our affairs are drawn by lot exclusively from them. The order is not hereditary—we know just enough of biology and the uncertainties of inheritance to know how silly that would be—and it does not require an early consecration or novitiate or ceremonies and initiations of that sort. The *samurai* are, in fact, volunteers. Any intelligent adult in a reasonably healthy and efficient state may, at any age after five-and-twenty, become one of the *samurai*, and take a hand in the universal control."

" Provided he follows the Rule."

" Precisely—provided he follows the Rule."

" I have heard the phrase, ' voluntary nobility.' "

" That was the idea of our Founders. They made a noble and privileged order—open to the whole world. No one could complain of an unjust exclusion, for the only thing that could exclude from the order was unwillingness or inability to follow the Rule."

" But the Rule might easily have been made exclusive of special lineages and races."

" That wasn't their intention. The Rule was planned to exclude the dull, to be unattractive to the base, and to direct and co-ordinate all sound citizens of good intent."

" And it has succeeded ? "

" As well as anything finite can. Life is still imperfect, still a thick felt of dissatisfactions and perplexing problems, but most certainly the quality of all its problems has been raised, and there has been no war, no grinding poverty, not half the disease, and an enormous increase of the order, beauty, and resources of life since the *samurai*, who began as a private aggressive cult, won their way to the rule of the world."

" I would like to have that history," I said. " I expect there was fighting ? " He nodded. " But first—tell me about the Rule."

" The Rule aims to exclude the dull and base altogether, to discipline the impulses and emotions, to develop a moral habit and sustain a man in periods of stress, fatigue, and temptation, to produce the maximum co-operation of all men of good intent, and, in fact, to keep all the *samurai* in a state of moral and bodily health and efficiency. It does as much of this as well as it can, but, of course, like all general propositions, it does not do it in any case with absolute precision. On the whole, it is so good that most men who, like myself, are doing poietic work, and who would be just as well off without obedience, find a satisfaction in adhesion. At first, in the militant days, it was a trifle hard and uncompromising ; it had rather too strong an appeal to the moral prig and harshly righteous man, but it has undergone, and still undergoes, revision and expansion, and every year it becomes a little better adapted to the need of a general rule of life that all men may try to follow. We have now a whole literature, with many very fine things in it, written about the Rule."

He glanced at a little book on his desk, took it up as if to show it me, then put it down again.

" The Rule consists of three parts ; there is the list of things that qualify, the list of things that must not be done, and the list of things that must be done. Qualification exacts a little exertion, as evidence of good faith, and it is designed to weed out the duller dull and many of the base. Our schooling period ends now about fourteen, and a small number of boys and girls— about three per cent.—are set aside then as unteachable, as, in fact, nearly idiotic ; the rest go on to a college or upper school."

" All your population ? "

" With that exception."

" Free ? "

" Of course. And they pass out of college at eighteen. There are several different college courses, but one or other must be followed and a satisfactory examination passed at the end—perhaps ten per cent. fail—and the Rule requires that the candidate for the *samurai* must have passed."

" But a very good man is sometimes an idle schoolboy."

" We admit that. And so any one who has failed to pass the college leaving examination may at any time in later life sit for it again and again and again. Certain carefully specified things excuse it altogether."

" That makes it fair. But aren't there people who cannot pass examinations ? "

" People of nervous instability——"

" But they may be people of great though irregular poietic gifts."

" Exactly. That is quite possible. But we don't want that sort of people among our *samurai*. Passing an examination is a proof of a certain steadiness of purpose, a certain self-control and submission——"

" Of a certain ' ordinariness.' "

" Exactly what is wanted."

" Of course, those others can follow other careers."

" Yes. That's what we want them to do. And, besides these two educational qualifications, there are two others of a similar kind of more debatable value. One is practically not in operation now. Our Founders put it that a candidate for the *samurai* must possess what they called a Technique, and, as it operated in the beginning, he had to hold the qualification for a doctor, for a lawyer, for a military officer

or an engineer, or teacher, or have painted acceptable pictures,
or written a book, or something of the sort. He had, in fact,
as people say, to ' be something,' or to have ' done something.'
It was a regulation of vague intention even in the beginning,
and it became catholic to the pitch of absurdity. To play a
violin skilfully has been accepted as sufficient for this qualification. There may have been a reason in the past for this provision ; in those days there were many daughters of prosperous
parents—and even some sons—who did nothing whatever but
idle uninterestingly in the world, and the organisation might
have suffered by their invasion, but that reason has gone
now, and the requirement remains a merely ceremonial requirement. But, on the other hand, another has developed.
Our Founders made a collection of several volumes, which
they called, collectively, the Book of the Samurai, a compila-
tion of articles and extracts, poems and prose pieces, which
were supposed to embody the idea of the order. It was to
play the part for the *samurai* that the Bible did for the ancient
Hebrews. To tell you the truth, the stuff was of very unequal merit ; there was a lot of very second-rate rhetoric,
and some nearly namby-pamby verse. There was also
included some very obscure verse and prose that had the trick
of seeming wise. But for all such defects, much of the Book,
from the very beginning, was splendid and inspiring matter.
From that time to this, the Book of the Samurai has been
under revision, much has been added, much rejected, and some
deliberately rewritten. Now, there is hardly anything in it
that is not beautiful and perfect in form. The whole range
of noble emotions finds expression there, and all the guiding
ideas of our Modern State. We have recently admitted some
terse criticism of its contents by a man named Henley."

" Old Henley ! "

" A man who died a little time ago."

" I knew that man on earth. And he was in Utopia, too !
He was a great red-faced man, with fiery hair, a noisy, in-
tolerant maker of enemies, with a tender heart—and he was
one of the *samurai* ? "

" He defied the Rules."

" He was a great man with wine. He wrote like wine ; in our
world he wrote wine ; red wine with the light shining through."

" He was on the Committee that revised our Canon. For
the revising and bracing of our Canon is work for poietic
as well as kinetic men. You knew him in your world ? "

" I wish I had. But I have seen him. On earth he wrote
a thing . . . it would run—

> " Out of the night that covers me,
>   Black as the pit from pole to pole,
> I thank whatever Gods may be,
>   For my unconquerable soul. . . ."

" We have that here. All good earthly things are in Utopia also. We put that in the Canon almost as soon as he died," said my double.

§ 5

" We have now a double Canon, a very fine First Canon, and a Second Canon of work by living men and work of inferior quality, and a satisfactory knowledge of both of these is the fourth intellectual qualification for the *samurai*."

" It must keep a sort of uniformity in your tone of thought."

" The Canon pervades our whole world. As a matter of fact, very much of it is read and learnt in the schools. . . . Next to the intellectual qualification comes the physical, the man must be in sound health, free from certain foul, avoidable, and demoralising diseases, and in good training. We reject men who are fat, or thin and flabby, or whose nerves are shaky —we refer them back to training. And finally the man or woman must be fully adult."

" Twenty-one ? But you said twenty-five ! "

" The age has varied. At first it was twenty-five or over ; then the minimum became twenty-five for men and twenty-one for women. Now there is a feeling that it ought to be raised. We don't want to take advantage of mere boy and girl emotions—men of my way of thinking, at any rate, don't— we want to get our *samurai* with experiences, with a settled mature conviction. Our hygiene and regimen are rapidly pushing back old age and death, and keeping men hale and hearty to eighty and more. There's no need to hurry the young. Let them have a chance of wine, love, and song ; let them feel the bite of full-bodied desire, and know what devils they have to reckon with."

" But there is a certain fine sort of youth that knows the desirability of the better things at nineteen."

" They may keep the Rule at any time—without its privi-leges. But a man who breaks the Rule after his adult ad-hesion at five-and-twenty is no more in the *samurai* for ever. Before that age he is free to break it and repent."

" And now, what is forbidden ? "

" We forbid a good deal. Many small pleasures do no great harm, but we think it well to forbid them, none the less, so that we can weed out the self-indulgent. We think that a constant resistance to little seductions is good for a man's quality. At any rate, its show that a man is prepared to pay something for his honour and privileges. We prescribe a regimen of food, forbid tobacco, wine, or any alcoholic drink, all narcotic drugs——"

" Meat ? "

" In all the round world of Utopia there is no meat. There used to be. But now we cannot stand the thought of slaughter-houses. And, in a population that is all educated, and at about the same level of physical refinement, it is practically impossible to find any one who will hew a dead ox or pig. We never settled the hygienic question of meat-eating at all. This other aspect decided us. I can still remember, as a boy, the rejoicings over the closing of the last slaughter-house."

" You eat fish."

" It isn't a matter of logic. In our barbaric past horrible flayed carcasses of brutes dripping blood were hung for sale in the public streets." He shrugged his shoulders.

" They do that still in London—in *my* world," I said.

He looked again at my laxer, coarser face, and did not say whatever thought had passed across his mind.

" Originally the *samurai* were forbidden usury, that is to say the lending of money at fixed rates of interest. They are still under that interdiction, but since our commercial code practically prevents usury altogether, and our law will not recognise contracts for interest upon private acccommodation loans to unprosperous borrowers, it is now scarcely necessary. The idea of a man growing richer by mere inaction and at the expense of an impoverishing debtor, is profoundly distasteful to Utopian ideas, and our State insists pretty effectually now upon the participation of the lender in the borrower's risks. This, however, is only one part of a series of limitations of the same character. It is felt that to buy simply in order to sell again brings out many unsocial human qualities ; it makes a man seek to enhance profits and falsify values, and so the *samurai* are forbidden to buy to sell on their own account or for any employer save the State, unless some process of manufacture changes the nature of the commodity (a mere change in bulk or packing does not suffice), and they are forbidden salesmanship and all its arts. Consequently they cannot be hotel-keepers, or hotel proprietors, or hotel shareholders, and a doctor—all practising doctors must be *samurai*— cannot sell drugs except as a public servant of the municipality or the State."

" That, of course, runs counter to all our current terrestrial ideas," I said. " We are obsessed by the power of money. These rules will work out as a vow of moderate poverty, and if your *samurai* are an order of poor men——"

" They need not be. *Samurai* who have invented, organised, and developed new industries, have become rich men, and many men who have grown rich by brilliant and original trading have subsequently become *samurai*."

" But these are exceptional cases. The bulk of your moneymaking business must be confined to men who are not *samurai*. You must have a class of rich, powerful outsiders——"

" *Have* we ? "

" I don't see the evidences of them."

" As a matter of fact, we have such people ! There are rich traders, men who have made discoveries in the economy of distribution, or who have called attention by intelligent, truthful advertisement to the possibilities of neglected commodities, for example."

" But aren't they a power ? "

" Why should they be ? "

" Wealth *is* power."

I had to explain that phrase.

He protested. " Wealth," he said, " is no sort of power at all unless you make it one. If it is so in your world it is so by inadvertency. Wealth is a State-made thing, a convention, the most artificial of powers. You can, by subtle statesmanship, contrive what it shall buy and what it shall not. In your world it would seem you have made leisure, movement, any sort of freedom, life itself, *purchasable*. The more fools you ! A poor working man with you is a man in discomfort and fear. No wonder your rich have power. But here a reasonable leisure, a decent life, is to be had by every man on easier terms than by selling himself to the rich. And rich as men are here, there is no private fortune in the whole world that is more than a little thing beside the wealth of the State. The *samurai* control the State and the wealth of the State, and by their vows they may not avail themselves of any of the coarser pleasures wealth can still buy. Where, then, is the power of your wealthy man ? "

" But, then—where is the incentive—— ? "

" Oh ! a man gets things for himself with wealth—no end of things. But little or no power over his fellows—unless they are exceptionally weak or self-indulgent persons."

I reflected. " What else may not the *samurai* do ? "

" Acting, singing, or reciting are forbidden them, though they may lecture authoritatively or debate. But professional mimicry is not only held to be undignified in a man or woman, but to weaken and corrupt the soul ; the mind becomes foolishly dependent on applause, over-skilful in producing tawdry and momentary illusions of excellence ; it is our experience that actors and actresses as a class are loud, ignoble, and insincere. If they have not such flamboyant qualities then they are tepid and ineffectual players. Nor may the *samurai* do personal services, except in the matter of medicine or surgery ; they may not be barbers, for example, nor inn waiters, nor boot cleaners. But, nowadays, we have scarcely any barbers or boot cleaners ; men do these things for themselves. Nor may a man under the Rule be any man's servant, pledged to do whatever he is told. He may neither be a servant nor keep one ; he must shave and dress and serve himself, carry his own food from the helper's place to the table, redd his sleeping room, and leave it clean. . . ."

" That is all easy enough in a world as ordered as yours. I suppose no *samurai* may bet ? "

" Absolutely not. He may insure his life and his old age for the better equipment of his children, or for certain other

specified ends, but that is all his dealings with chance. And he
is also forbidden to play games in public or to watch them being
played. Certain dangerous and hardy sports and exercises
are prescribed for him, but not competitive sports between
man and man or side and side. That lesson was learnt long
ago before the coming of the *samurai*. Gentlemen of honour,
according to the old standards, rode horses, raced chariots,
fought, and played competitive games of skill, and the dull,
cowardly and base came in thousands to admire, and howl, and
bet. The gentlemen of honour degenerated fast enough into a
sort of athletic prostitute, with all the defects, all the vanity,
trickery, and self-assertion of the common actor, and with even
less intelligence. Our Founders made no peace with this
organisation of public sports. They did not spend their lives
to secure for all men and women on the earth freedom, health,
and leisure, in order that they might waste lives in such folly."

"We have those abuses," I said, "but some of our earthly
games have a fine side. There is a game called cricket. It is
a fine, generous game."

"Our boys play that, and men too. But it is thought
rather puerile to give very much time to it ; men should have
graver interests. It was undignified and unpleasant for the
samurai to play conspicuously ill, and impossible for them to
play so constantly as to keep hand and eye in training against
the man who was fool enough and cheap enough to become an
expert. Cricket, tennis, fives, billiards—— You will find
clubs and a class of men to play all these things in Utopia, but
not the *samurai*. And they must play their games as games,
not as displays ; the price of a privacy for playing cricket, so
that they could charge for admission, would be overwhelmingly
high. . . . Negroes are often very clever at cricket. For a
time, most of the *samurai* had their sword-play, but few do
those exercises now, and until about fifty years ago they went
out for military training, a fortnight in every year, marching
long distances, sleeping in the open, carrying provisions, and
sham fighting over unfamiliar ground dotted with disappearing
targets. There was a curious inability in our world to realise
that war was really over for good and all."

"And now," I said, "haven't we got very nearly to the end
of your prohibitions ? You have forbidden alcohol, drugs,
smoking, betting, and usury, games, trade, servants. But
isn't there a vow of Chastity ? "

"That is the Rule for your earthly orders ? "

"Yes—except, if I remember rightly, for Plato's Guardians."

"There is a Rule of Chastity here—but not of Celibacy. We
know quite clearly that civilisation is an artificial arrangement,
and that all the physical and emotional instincts of man are too
strong, and his natural instinct of restraint too weak, for him
to live easily in the civilised State. Civilisation has developed
far more rapidly than man has modified. Under the unnatural

perfection of security, liberty, and abundance our civilisation has attained, the normal untrained human being is disposed to excess in almost every direction ; he tends to eat too much and too elaborately, to drink too much, to become lazy faster than his work can be reduced, to waste his interest upon displays, and to make love too much and too elaborately. He gets out of training, and concentrates upon egoistic or erotic broodings. The past history of our race is very largely a history of social collapses due to demoralisation by indulgences following security and abundance. In the time of our Founders the signs of a world-wide epoch of prosperity and relaxation were plentiful. Both sexes drifted towards sexual excesses, the men towards sentimental extravagances, imbecile devotions, and the complication and refinement of physical indulgences ; the women towards those expansions and differentiations of feeling that find expression in music and costly and distinguished dress. Both sexes became unstable and promiscuous. The whole world seemed disposed to do exactly the same thing with its sexual interest as it had done with its appetite for food and drink—make the most of it."

He paused.

" Satiety came to help you," I said.

" Destruction may come before satiety. Our Founders organised motives from all sorts of sources, but I think the chief force to give men self-control is Pride. Pride may not be the noblest thing in the soul, but it is the best King there, for all that. They looked to it to keep a man clean and sound and sane. In this matter, as in all matters of natural desire, they held no appetite must be glutted, no appetite must have artificial whets, and also and equally that no appetite should be starved. A man must come from the table satisfied, but not replete. And, in the matter of love, a straight and clean desire for a clean and straight fellow-creature was our Founders' ideal. They enjoined marriage between equals as the *samurai's* duty to the race, and they framed directions of the precisest sort to prevent that uxorious inseparableness, that connubiality which will reduce a couple of people to something jointly less than either. That Canon is too long to tell you now. A man under the Rule who loves a woman who does not follow it, must either leave the *samurai* to marry her, or induce her to accept what is called the Woman's Rule, which, while it excepts her from the severer qualifications and disciplines, brings her regimen of life into a working harmony with his."

" Suppose she breaks the Rule afterwards ? "

" He must leave either her or the order."

" There is matter for a novel or so in that."

" There has been matter for hundreds."

" Is the Woman's Rule a sumptuary law as well as a regimen ? I mean—may she dress as she pleases ? "

" Not a bit of it," said my double. " Every woman who

could command money used it, we found, to make underbred aggressions on other women. As men emerged to civilisation, women seemed going back to savagery—to paint and feathers. But the *samurai*, both men and women, and the women under the Lesser Rule also, all have a particular dress. No difference is made between women under either the Great or the Lesser Rule. You have seen the men's dress—always like this I wear. The women may wear the same, either with the hair cut short or plaited behind them, or they may have a high-waisted dress of very fine, soft woollen material, with their hair coiled up behind."

"I have seen it," I said. Indeed, nearly all the women had seemed to be wearing variants of that simple formula. "It seems to me a very beautiful dress. The other—I'm not used to. But I like it on girls and slender woman."

I had a thought, and added, "Don't they sometimes, well—take a good deal of care, dressing their hair ? "

My double laughed in my eyes. "They do," he said.

"And the Rule ? "

"The Rule is never fussy," said my double, still smiling.

"We don't want women to cease to be beautiful, and consciously beautiful, if you like," he added. "The more real beauty of form and face we have, the finer our world. But costly sexualised trappings——"

"I should have thought," I said, "a class of women who traded on their sex would have arisen, women, I mean, who found an interest and an advantage in emphasising their individual womanly beauty. There is no law to prevent it. Surely they would tend to counteract the severity of costume the Rule dictates."

"There are such women. But for all that the Rule sets the key of everyday dress. If a woman is possessed by the passion for gorgeous raiment she usually satisfies it in her own private circle, or with rare occasional onslaughts upon the public eye. Her everyday mood and the disposition of most people is against being conspicuous abroad. And I should say there are little liberties under the Lesser Rule ; a discreet use of fine needlework and embroidery, a wider choice of materials."

"You have no changing fashions ? "

"None. For all that, are not our dresses as beautiful as yours ? "

"Our women's dresses are not beautiful at all," I said, forced for a time towards the mysterious philosophy of dress. "Beauty ? That isn't their concern."

"Then what are they after ? "

"My dear man ! What is all my world after ? "

§ 6

I should come to our third talk with a great curiosity to hear of the last portion of the Rule, of the things that the *samurai* are obliged to do.

There would be many precise directions regarding his health, and rules that would aim at once at health and that constant exercise of will that makes life good. Save in specified exceptional circumstances, the *samurai* must bathe in cold water, and the men must shave every day; they have the precisest directions in such matters; the body must be in health, the skin and muscles and nerves in perfect tone, or the *samurai* must go to the doctors of the order, and give implicit obedience to the regimen prescribed. They must sleep alone at least four nights in five; and they must eat with and talk to any one in their fellowship who cares for their conversation for an hour, at least, at the nearest clubhouse of the *samurai* once on three chosen days in every week. Moreover, they must read aloud from the Book of the Samurai for at least ten minutes every day. Every month they must buy and read faithfully through at least one book that has been published during the past five years, and the only intervention with private choice in that matter is the prescription of a certain minimum of length for the monthly book or books. But the full Rule in these minor compulsory matters is voluminous and detailed, and it abounds with alternatives. Its aim is rather to keep before the *samurai* by a number of sample duties, as it were, the need of, and some of the chief methods towards health of body and mind, rather than to provide a comprehensive rule, and to ensure the maintenance of a community of feeling and interests among the *samurai* through habit, intercourse, and a living contemporary literature. These minor obligations do not earmark more than an hour in the day. Yet they serve to break down isolations of sympathy, all sorts of physical and intellectual sluggishness and the development of unsocial preoccupations of many sorts.

Women *samurai* who are married, my double told me, must bear children—if they are to remain married as well as in the order—before the second period for terminating a childless marriage is exhausted. I failed to ask for the precise figures from my double at the time, but I think it is beyond doubt that it is from *samurai* mothers of the Greater or Lesser Rule that a very large proportion of the future population of Utopia will be derived. There is one liberty accorded to women *samurai* which is refused to men, and that is to marry outside the Rule, and women married to men not under the Rule are also free to become *samurai*. Here, too, it will be manifest there is scope for novels and the drama of life. In practice, it seems that it is only men of great poietic distinction outside the Rule, or great commercial leaders, who have wives under it. The tendency of such unions is either to bring the husband under the Rule, or take the wife out of it. There can be no doubt that these marriage limitations tend to make the *samurai* something of an hereditary class. Their children, as a rule, become *samurai*. But it is not an exclusive caste; subject to the most reasonable qualifications, any one who sees fit can enter it at any time, and so, unlike all other privileged castes the world has seen, it increases relatively to the total population, and may indeed at last assimilate almost the whole population of the earth.

§ 7

So much my double told me readily.

But now he came to the heart of all his explanations, to the will and motives at the centre that made men and women ready to undergo discipline, to renounce the richness and elaboration of the sensuous life, to master emotions and control impulses, to keep in the key of effort while they had abundance about them to rouse and satisfy all desires, and his exposition was more difficult.

He tried to make his religion clear to me.

The leading principle of the Utopian religion is the repudiation of the doctrine of original sin ; the Utopians hold that man, on the whole, is good. That is their cardinal belief. Man has pride and conscience, they hold, that you may refine by training as you refine his eye and ear ; he has remorse and sorrow in his being, coming on the heels of all inconsequent enjoyments. How can one think of him as bad ? He is religious ; religion is as natural to him as lust and anger, less intense, indeed, but coming with a wide-sweeping inevitableness as peace comes after all tumults and noises. And in Utopia they understand this, or, at least, the *samurai* do, clearly. They accept Religion as they accept Thirst, as something inseparably in the mysterious rhythms of life. And just as thirst and pride and all desires may be perverted in an age of abundant opportunities, and men may be degraded and wasted by intemperance in drinking, by display, or by ambition, so, too, the nobler complex of desires that constitutes religion may be turned to evil by the dull, the base, and the careless. Slovenly indulgence in religious inclinations, a failure to think hard and discriminate as fairly as possible in religious matters, is just as alien to the men under the Rule as it would be to drink deeply because they were thirsty, eat until glutted, evade a bath because the day was chilly, or make love to any bright-eyed girl who chanced to look pretty in the dusk. Utopia, which is to have every type of character that one finds on earth, will have its temples and its priests, just as it will have its actresses and wine, but the *samurai*, will be forbidden the religion of dramatically lit altars, organ music, and incense, as distinctly as they are forbidden the love of painted women, or the consolations of brandy. And to all the things that are less than religion and that seek to comprehend it, to cosmogonies and philosophies, to creeds and formulæ, to catechisms and easy explanations, the attitude of the *samurai*, the note of the Book of Samurai, will be distrust. These things, the *samurai* will say, are part of the indulgences that should come before a man submits himself to the Rule they are like the early gratifications of young men, experiences to establish renunciation. The *samurai* will have emerged above these things.

The theology of the Utopian rulers will be saturated with that same philosophy of uniqueness, that repudiation of anything beyond similarities and practical parallelisms, that saturates all their institutions. They will have analysed exhaustively those fallacies and assumptions that arise between the One and the Many, that have troubled philosophy since philosophy began. Just as they will have escaped that delusive unification of every species under its specific definition that has dominated earthly reasoning, so they will have escaped the delusive simplification of God that vitiates all terrestrial theology. They will hold God to be complex and of an endless variety of aspects, to be expressed by no universal formula nor approved in any uniform manner. Just as the language of Utopia will be a synthesis, even so will its God be. The aspect of God is different in the measure of every man's individuality, and the intimate thing of religion must, therefore, exist in human solitude, between man and God alone. Religion in its quintessence is a relation between God and man ; it is perversion to make it a relation between man and man, and a man may no more reach God through a priest than love his wife through a priest. But just as a man in love may refine the interpretation of his feelings and borrow expression from the poems and music of poietic men, so an individual man may at his discretion read books of devotion and hear music that is in harmony with his inchoate feelings. Many of the *samurai*, therefore, will set themselves private regimens that will help their secret religious life, will pray habitually, and read books of devotion, but with these things the Rule of the order will have nothing to do.

Clearly the God of the *samurai* is a transcendental and mystical God. So far as the *samurai* have a purpose in common in maintaining the State, and the order and progress of the world, so far, by their discipline and denial, by their public work and effort, they worship God together. But the fount of motive lies in the individual life, it lies in silent and deliberate reflections, and at this, the most striking of all the rules of the *samurai* aims. For seven consecutive days in the year, at least, each man or woman under the Rule must go right out of all the life of man into some wild and solitary place, must speak to no man or woman, and have no sort of intercourse with mankind. They must go bookless and weaponless, without pen or paper, or money. Provisions must be taken for the period of the journey, a rug or sleeping sack—for they must sleep under the open sky—but no means of making a fire. They may study maps beforehand to guide them, showing any difficulties and dangers in the journey, but they may not carry such helps. They must not go by beaten ways or wherever there are inhabited houses, but into the bare, quiet places of the globe—the regions set apart for them.

This discipline, my double said, was invented to secure a certain stoutness of heart and body in the members of the order, which otherwise might have lain open to too many timorous, merely abstemious, men and women. Many things had been suggested, swordplay and tests that verged on torture, climbing in giddy places and the like, before this was chosen. Partly, it is to ensure good training and sturdiness of body and mind, but partly, also, it is to draw their minds for a space from the insistent details of life, from the intricate arguments and the fretting effort to work, from personal quarrels and personal affections, and the things of the heated room. Out they must go, clean out of the world.

Certain great areas are set apart for these yearly pilgrimages beyond the securities of the State. There are thousands of square miles of sandy desert in Africa and Asia set apart ; much of the Arctic and Antarctic circles ; vast areas of mountain land and frozen marsh ; secluded reserves of forest, and innumerable unfrequented lines upon the sea. Some are dangerous and laborious routes ; some merely desolate ; and there are even some sea journeys that one may take in the halcyon days as one drifts through a dream. · Upon the seas one must go in a little undecked sailing boat, that may be rowed in a calm ; all the other journeys one must do afoot, none aiding. There are, about all these desert regions and along most coasts, little offices at which the *samurai* says good-bye to the world of men, and at which they arrive after their minimum time of silence is overpast. For the intervening days they must be alone with Nature, necessity, and their own thoughts.

" It is good ? " I said.

" It is good," my double answered. " We civilised men go back to the stark Mother that so many of us would have forgotten were it not for this Rule. And one thinks. . . . Only two weeks ago I did my journey for the year. I went with my gear by sea to Tromso, and then inland to a starting-place, and took my ice-axe and rücksack, and said good-bye to the world. I crossed over four glaciers ; I climbed three high mountain passes, and slept on moss in desolate valleys. I saw no human being for seven days. Then I came down through pine woods to the head of a road that runs to the Baltic shore. Altogether it was thirteen days before I reported myself again, and had speech with fellow creatures."

" And the women do this ? "

" The women who are truly *samurai*—yes. Equally with the men. Unless the coming of children intervenes."

I asked him how it had seemed to him, and what he thought about during the journey.

" There is always a sense of effort for me," he said, " when I leave the world at the outset of the journey. I turn back again and again, and look at the little office as I go up my mountain side. The first day and night I'm a little disposed to shirk the job—every year it's the same—a little disposed, for example, to sling my pack from my back, and sit down, and go through its contents, and make sure I've got all my equipment."

" There's no chance of any one overtaking you ? "

" Two men mustn't start from the same office on the same route within six hours of each other. If they come within sight of each other, they must shun an encounter, and make no sign—unless life is in danger. All that is arranged beforehand."

" It would be, of course. Go on telling me of your journey."

" I dread the night. I dread discomfort and bad weather. I only begin to brace up after the second day."

" Don't you worry about losing your way ? "

" No. There are cairns and skyline signs. If it wasn't for that, of course, we should be worrying with maps the whole time. But I'm only sure of being a man after the second night, and sure of my power to go through."

" And then ? "

" Then one begins to get into it. The first two days one is apt to have the events of one's journey, little incidents of travel, and thoughts of one's work and affairs, rising and fading and coming again, but then the perspectives begin. I don't sleep much at nights on these journeys; I lie awake and stare at the stars. About dawn, perhaps, and in the morning sunshine, I sleep ! The nights this last time were very short, never more than twilight, and I saw the glow of the sun always, just over the edge of the world. But I had chosen the days of the new moon, so that I could have a glimpse of the stars. . . . Years ago, I went from the Nile across the Libyan Desert east, and then the stars the stars in the later days of that journey—brought me near weeping. . . . You begin to feel alone on the third day, when you find yourself out on some shiny snowfield, and nothing of mankind visible in the whole world save one landmark, one remote thin red triangle of iron, perhaps, in the saddle of the ridge against the sky. All this busy world that has done so much and so marvellously, and is still so little—you see it little as it is—and far off. All day long you go and the night comes, and it might be another planet. Then, in the quiet, waking hours, one thinks of one's self and the great external things, of space and eternity, and what one means by God."

He mused.

" You think of death ? "

" Not of my own. But when I go among snows and desolations—and usually I take my pilgrimage in mountains or the north—I think very much of the Night of this World—the time when our sun will be red and dull, and air and water will lie frozen together in a common snowfield where now the forests of the tropics are steaming. . . . I think very much of that, and whether it is indeed God's purpose that our kind should end, and the cities we have built, the books we have written, all that we have given substance and a form, should lie dead beneath the snows."

" You don't believe that ? "

" No. But if it is not so——. I went threading my way among gorges and precipices, with my poor brain dreaming of what the alternative should be, with my imagination straining and failing. Yet, in those high airs and in such solitude, a kind of exaltation comes to men. . . . I remember that one night I sat up and told the rascal stars very earnestly how they should not escape us in the end. "

He glanced at me for a moment as though he doubted I should understand.

" One becomes a personification up there," he said. " One becomes the ambassador of mankind to the outer world.

" There is time to think over a lot of things. One puts one's self and one's ambition in a new pair of scales. . . .

" Then there are hours when one is just exploring the wilderness like a child. Sometimes perhaps one gets a glimpse from some precipice edge of the plains far away, and houses and roadways, and remembers there is still a busy world of men. And at last one turns one's feet down some slope, some gorge that leads back. You come down, perhaps, into a pine forest, and hear that queer clatter reindeer make—and then, it may be, see a herdsman very far away, watching you. You wear your pilgrim's badge, and he makes no sign of seeing you. . . .

" You know, after these solitudes, I feel just the same queer disinclination to go back to the world of men that I feel when I have to leave it. I think of dusty roads and hot valleys, and being looked at by many people. I think of the trouble of working with colleagues and opponents. This last journey I outstayed my time, camping in the pine woods for six days. Then my thoughts came round to my proper work again. I got keen to go on with it, and so I came back into the world. You come back physically clean—as though you had had your arteries and veins washed out. And your brain has been cleaned, too. . . . I shall stick to the mountains now until I am old, and then I shall sail a boat in Polynesia. That is what so many old men do. Only last year one of the great leaders of the *samurai*—a white-haired man, who followed the Rule in spite of his one hundred and eleven years—was found dead in his boat far away from any land, far to the south, lying like a child asleep. . . ."

" That's better than a tumbled bed," said I, " and some boy of a doctor jabbing you with injections, and distressful people hovering about you."

" Yes," said my double ; " in Utopia we who are *samurai* die better than that. . . . Is that how your great men die ? "

It came to me suddenly as very strange that, even as we sat and talked, across deserted seas, on burning sands, through the still aisles of forests, and in all the high and lonely places of the world, beyond the margin where the ways and houses go, solitary men and women sailed alone or marched alone, or clambered—quiet, resolute exiles ; they stood alone amidst wildernesses of ice, on the precipitous banks of roaring torrents, in monstrous caverns, or steering a tossing boat in the little circle of the horizon amidst the tumbled, incessant sea, all in their several ways communing with the emptiness, the enig-matic spaces and silences, the winds and torrents and soulless forces that lie about the lit and ordered life of men.

I saw more clearly now something I had seen dimly already, in the bearing and the faces of this Utopian chivalry, a faint persistent tinge of detachment from the immediate heats and hurries, the little graces and delights, the tensions and stimula-tions of the daily world. It pleased me strangely to think of this steadfast yearly pilgrimage of solitude, and how near men might come then to the high distances of God.

§ 8

After that I remember we fell talking of the discipline of the Rule, of the Courts that try breaches of it, and interpret doubt-ful cases—for, though a man may resign with due notice and be free after a certain time to rejoin again, one deliberate breach may exclude a man for ever—of the system of law that has grown up about such trials, and of the triennial council that revises and alters the Rule. From that we passed to the dis-cussion of the general constitution of this World State. Practi-cally all political power vests in the *samurai*. Not only are they the only administrators, lawyers, practising doctors, and public officials of almost all kinds, but they are the only voters. Yet, by a curious exception, the supreme legislative assembly must have one-tenth, and may have one-half of its members outside the order, because, it is alleged, there is a sort of wisdom that comes of sin and laxness, which is necessary to the perfect ruling of life. My double quoted me a verse from the Canon on this matter that my unfortunate verbal memory did not retain, but it was in the nature of a prayer to save the world from " unfermented men." It would seem that Aris-totle's idea of a rotation of rulers, an idea that crops up again in Harrington's *Oceana*, that first Utopia of " the sovereign people " (a Utopia that, through Danton's readings in English, played a disastrous part in the French Revolution), gets a little respect in Utopia. The tendency is to give a practically permanent tenure to good men. Every ruler and official, it is true, is put on his trial every three years before a jury drawn by lot, according to the range of his activities, either from the *samurai* of his municipal area or from the general catalogue of the *samurai*, but the business of this jury is merely to decide whether to continue him in office or order a new election. In the majority of cases the verdict is continuation. Even if it is not so the official may still appear as a candidate before the second and separate jury which fills the vacant post. . . .

My double mentioned a few scattered details of the electoral methods, but as at that time I believed we were to have a number of further conversations, I did not exhaust my curiosities upon this subject. Indeed, I was more than a little preoccupied and inattentive. The religion of the *samurai* was after my heart, and it had taken hold of me very strongly. . . . But presently I fell questioning him upon the complications that arise in the Modern Utopia through the differences between the races of men, and found my attention returning. But the matter of that discussion I shall put apart into a separate chapter. In the end we came back to the particulars of this great Rule of Life that any man desiring of joining the *samurai* must follow.

I remember how, after our third bout of talking, I walked back through the streets of Utopian London to rejoin the botanist at our hotel.

My double lived in an apartment in a great building—I should judge about where, in our London, the Tate Gallery squats, and, as the day was fine, and I had no reason for hurry, I went not by the covered mechanical way, but on foot along the broad, tree-set terraces that follow the river on either side.

It was afternoon, and the mellow Thames Valley sunlight, warm and gentle, lit a clean and gracious world. There were many people abroad, going to and fro, unhurrying, but not aimless, and I watched them so attentively that were you to ask me for the most elementary details of the buildings and terraces that lay back on either bank, or of the pinnacles and towers and parapets that laced the sky, I could not tell you them. But of the people I could tell a great deal.

No Utopians wear black, and for all the frequency of the *samurai* uniform along the London ways the general effect is of a gaily-coloured population. You never see any one noticeably ragged or dirty ; the police, who answer questions and keep order (and are quite distinct from the organisation for the pursuit of criminals) see to that ; and shabby people are very infrequent. People who want to save money for other purposes, or who do not want much bother with their clothing, seem to wear costumes of rough woven cloth, dyed an unobtrusive brown or green, over fine woollen underclothing, and so achieve a decent comfort in its simplest form. Others outside the Rule of the *samurai* range the spectrum for colour, and have every variety of texture ; the colours attained by the Utopian dyers seem to me to be fuller and purer than the common range of stuffs on earth ; and the subtle folding of the woollen materials witness that Utopian Bradford is no whit behind her earthly sister. White is extraordinarily frequent ; white woollen tunics and robes into which are woven bands of brilliant colour, abound. Often these ape the cut and purple edge that distinguishes the *samurai*. In Utopian London the air is as clear and less dusty than it is among high mountains ; the roads are made of unbroken surfaces, and not of friable earth ; all heating is done by electricity, and no coal ever enters the town ; there are no horses or dogs, and so there is not a suspicion of smoke and scarcely a particle of any sort of dirt to render white impossible.

The radiated influence of the uniform of the *samurai* has been to keep costume simple, and this, perhaps, emphasises the general effect of vigorous health, of shapely bodies. Every one is well grown and well nourished ; every one seems in good condition ; every one walks well, and has that clearness of eye that comes with cleanness of blood. In London I am apt to consider myself of a passable size and carriage ; here I feel small and mean-looking. The faint suspicions of spinal curvatures, skew feet, unequal legs, and ill-grown bones, that haunt one in a London crowd, the plain intimations—in yellow faces, puffy faces, spotted and irregular complexions, in nervous movements and coughs and colds—of bad habits and an incompetent or disregarded medical profession, do not appear here. I notice few old people, but there seems to be a greater proportion of men and women at or near the prime of life.

I hang upon that. I have seen one two fat people here— they are all the more noticeable because they are rare. But wrinkled age ? Have I yet in Utopia set eyes on a bald head ?

The Utopians have brought a sounder physiological science than ours to bear upon regimen. People know better what to do and what to avoid, how to foresee and forestall coming trouble, and how to evade and suppress the subtle poisons that blunt the edge of sensation. They have put off the years of decay. They keep their teeth, they keep their digestions, they ward off gout and rheumatism, neuralgia and influenza, and all those cognate decays that bend and wrinkle men and women in the middle years of existence. They have extended the level years far into the seventies, and age, when it comes, comes swiftly and easily. The feverish hurry of our earth, the decay that begins before growth has ceased, is replaced by a ripe prolonged maturity. This modern Utopia is an adult world. The flushed romance, the predominant eroticisms, the adventurous uncertainty of a world in which youth prevails, gives place here to a grave deliberation, to a fuller and more powerful emotion, to a broader handling of life.

Yet youth is here.

Amidst the men whose faces have been made fine by thought and steadfast living, among the serene-eyed women, comes youth, gaily-coloured, buoyantly healthy, with challenging eyes, with fresh and eager face. . . .

For every one in Utopia who is sane enough to benefit, study and training last until twenty ; then comes the travel year, and many are still students until twenty-four or twenty-five. Most are still, in a sense, students throughout life, but it is thought that, unless responsible action is begun in some form in the early twenties, will undergo a partial atrophy. But the full swing of adult life is hardly attained until thirty is reached. Men marry before the middle thirties, and the women rather earlier, few are mothers before five-and-twenty. The majority of those who become *samurai* do so between twenty-seven and thirty-five. And, between seventeen and thirty, the Utopians have their dealings with love, and the play and excitement of love is a chief interest in life. Much freedom of act is allowed them so that their wills may grow freely. For the most part they end mated, and love gives place to some special and more enduring interest, though, indeed, there is love between older men and fresh girls, and between youths and maturer women. It is in these most graceful and beautiful years of life that such freedoms of dress as the atmosphere of Utopia permits are to be seen, and the crude bright will and imagination of youth peeps out in ornament and colour.

Figures come into my sight and possess me for a moment and pass, and give place to others ; there comes a dusky little Jewess, red-lipped and amber-clad, with a deep crimson flower—I know not whether real or sham—in the dull black of her hair. She passes me with an unconscious disdain ; and then I am looking at a brightly-smiling, blue-eyed girl, tall, ruddy, and freckled warmly, clad like a stage Rosalind, and talking gaily to a fair young man, a novice under the Rule. A red-haired mother under the Lesser Rule goes by, green-gowned, with dark green straps crossing between her breasts, and her two shock-headed children, bare-legged and lightly shod, tug at her hands on either side. Then a grave man in a long, fur-trimmed robe, a merchant, maybe, debates some serious matter with a white-tunicked clerk. And the clerk's face—— ? I turn to mark the straight, blue-black hair. The man must be Chinese. . . .

Then come two short-bearded men in careless indigo-blue raiment, both of them convulsed with laughter—men outside the Rule, who practise, perhaps, some art—and then one of the *samurai*, in cheerful altercation with a blue-robed girl of eight. " But you *could* have come back yesterday, Dadda," she persists. He is deeply sunburnt, and suddenly there passes before my mind the picture of a snowy mountain waste at nightfall and a solitary small figure under the stars. . . .

When I come back to the present thing again, my eye is caught at once by a young negro, carrying books in his hand, a prosperous-looking, self-respecting young negro, in a trimly-cut coat of purple-blue and silver.

I am reminded of what my double said to me of race.

CHAPTER TEN

RACE IN UTOPIA

§ 1

ABOVE the sphere of the elemental cravings and necessities, the soul of man is in a perpetual vacillation between two conflicting impulses : the desire to assert his individual differences, the desire for distinction, and his terror of isolation. He wants to stand out, but not too far out, and, on the contrary, he wants to merge himself with a group, with some larger body, but not altogether. Through all the things of life runs this tortuous compromise, men follow the fashions but resent ready-made uniforms on every plane of their being. The disposition to form aggregations and to imagine aggregations is part of the incurable nature of man ; it is one of the great natural forces the statesman must utilise, and against which he must construct effectual defences. The study of the aggregations and of the ideals of aggregations about which men's sympathies will twine, and upon which they will base a large proportion of their conduct and personal policy, is the legitimate definition of sociology.

Now the sort of aggregation to which men and women will refer themselves is determined partly by the strength and idiosyncrasy of the individual imagination, and partly by the reek of ideas that chances to be in the air at the time. Men and women may vary greatly both in their innate and their acquired disposition towards this sort of larger body or that, to which their social reference can be made. The " natural " social reference of a man is probably to some rather vaguely conceived tribe, as the " natural " social reference of a dog is to a pack. But just as the social reference of a dog may be educated until the reference to a pack is completely replaced by a reference to an owner, so on his higher plane of educability the social reference of the civilised man undergoes the most remarkable transformations. But the power and scope of his imagination and the need he has of response sets limits to this process. A highly intellectualised mature mind may refer for its data very consistently to ideas of a higher being so remote and indefinable as God, so comprehensive as humanity, so far-reaching as the purpose in things. I write " may," but I doubt if this exaltation of reference is ever permanently sustained. Comte, in his *Positive Polity*, exposes his soul with great freedom, and the curious may trace how, while he professes and quite honestly intends to refer himself always to his " Greater Being " Humanity, he narrows constantly to his projected " Western Republic " of civilised men, and quite frequently to the minute indefinite body of Positivist subscribers. And the history of the Christian Church, with its development of orders and cults, sects and dissents, the history of fashionable society with its cliques and sets, and every political history with its cabals and inner cabinets, witness to the struggle that goes on in the minds of men to adjust themselves to a body larger indeed than themselves, but which still does not strain and escape their imaginative grasp.

The statesman, both for himself and others, must recognise this inadequacy of grasp, and the necessity for real and imaginary aggregations to sustain men in their practical service of the order of the world. He must be a sociologist ; he must study the whole science of aggregations in relation to that World State to which his reason and his maturest thought direct him. He must lend himself to the development of aggregatory ideas that favour the civilising process, and he must do his best to promote the disintegration of aggregations and the effacement of aggregatory ideas, that keep men narrow and unreasonably prejudiced one against another.

He will, of course, know that few men are even rudely consistent in such matters, that the same man in different moods and on different occasions, is capable of referring himself in perfect good faith, not only to different, but to contradictory larger beings, and that the more important thing about an aggregatory idea from the State maker's point of view is not so much what it explicitly involves as what it implicitly repudiates. The natural man does not feel he is aggregating at all, unless he aggregates *against* something. He refers himself to the tribe ; he is loyal to the tribe, and quite inseparably he fears or dislikes those others outside the tribe. The tribe is always at least defensively hostile and usually actively hostile to humanity beyond the aggregation. The Anti-idea, it would seem, is inseparable from the aggregatory idea ; it is a necessity of the human mind. When we think of the class A as desirable, we think of Not-A as undesirable. The two things are as inevitably connected as the tendons of our hands, so that when we flatten down our little fingers on our palms, the fourth digit, whether we want it or not, comes down half-way. All real working gods, one may remark, all gods that are worshipped emotionally, are tribal gods, and every attempt to universalise the idea of God trails dualism and the devil after it as a moral necessity.

When we inquire, as well as the unformed condition of terrestrial sociology permits, into the aggregatory ideas that seem to satisfy men, we find a remarkable complex, a disorderly complex, in the minds of nearly all our civilised contemporaries.

For example, all sorts of aggregatory ideas come and go across the chameleon surfaces of my botanist's mind. He has a strong feeling for systematic botanists as against plant physiologists, whom he regards as lewd and evil scoundrels in this relation, but he has a strong feeling for all botanists, and, indeed, all biologists, as against physicists, and those who profess the exact sciences, all of whom he regards as dull, mechanical, ugly-minded scoundrels in this relation ; but he has a strong feeling for all who profess what is called Science as against psychologists, sociologists, philosophers, and literary men, whom he regards as wild, foolish, immoral scoundrels in this relation ; but he has a strong feeling for all educated men as against the working man, whom he regards as a cheating, lying, loafing, drunken, thievish, dirty scoundrel in this relation ; but so soon as the working man is comprehended together with those others, as Englishmen—which includes, in this case, I may remark, the Scottish and Welsh—he holds them superior to all other sorts of European, whom he regards, etc. . . .

Now one perceives in all these aggregatory ideas and re-arrangements of the sympathies one of the chief vices of human thought, due to its obsession by classificatory suggestions.[1] The necessity for marking our classes has brought with it a bias for false and excessive contrast, and we never invent a term but we are at once cramming it with implications beyond its legitimate content. There is no feat of irrelevance that people will not perform quite easily in this way ; there is no class, however accidental, to which they will not at once ascribe deeply distinctive qualities. The seventh sons of seventh sons have remarkable powers of insight ; people with a certain sort of ear commit crimes of violence ; people with red hair have souls of fire ; all democratic socialists are trustworthy persons ; all people born in Ireland have vivid imaginations and all Englishmen are clods ; all Hindoos are cowardly liars ; all curly-haired people are good-natured ; all hunchbacks are energetic and wicked, and all Frenchmen eat frogs. Such stupid generalisations have been believed with the utmost readiness, and acted upon by great numbers of sane, respectable people. And when the class is one's own class, when it expresses one of the aggregations to which one refers one's own activities, then the disposition to divide all qualities between this class and its converse, and to cram one's own class with every desirable distinction, becomes overwhelming.

It is part of the training of the philosopher to regard all such generalisations with suspicion ; it is part of the training of the Utopist and statesman, and all good statesmen are Utopists, to mingle something very like animosity with that suspicion. For crude classifications and false generalisations are the curse of all organised human life.

---

[1] See Chapter One, § 5, and the Appendix.

§ 2

Disregarding classes, cliques, sets, castes, and the like minor aggregations, concerned for the most part with details and minor aspects of life, one finds among the civilised peoples of the world certain broad types of aggregatory idea. There are, firstly, the national ideas, ideas which, in their perfection, require a uniformity of physical and mental type, a common idiom, a common religion, a distinctive style of costume, decoration, and thought, and a compact organisation acting with complete external unity. Like the Gothic cathedral, the national idea is never found complete with all its parts ; but one has in Russia, with her insistence on political and religious orthodoxy, something approaching it pretty closely, and again in the inland and typical provinces of China, where even a strange pattern of hat arouses hostility. We had it in vigorous struggle to exist in England under the earlier Georges in the minds of those who supported the Established Church. The idea of the fundamental nature of nationality is so ingrained in thought, with all the usual exaggeration of implication, that no one laughs at talk about Swedish painting or American literature. And I will confess and point out that my own detachment from these delusions is so imperfect and discontinuous that in another passage I have committed myself to a short assertion of the exceptionally noble quality of the English imagination.[1] I am constantly gratified by flattering untruths about English superiority which I should reject indignantly were the application bluntly personal, and I am ever ready to believe the scenery of England, the poetry of England, even the decoration and music of England, in some mystic and impregnable way, the best. This habit of intensifying all class definitions, and particularly those in which one has a personal interest, is in the very constitution of man's mind. It is part of the defect of that instrument. We may watch against it and prevent it doing any great injustices, or leading us into follies, but to eradicate it is an altogether different matter. There it is, to be reckoned with, like the coccyx, the pineal eye, and the vermiform appendix. And a too consistent attack on it may lead simply to its inversion, to a vindictively pro-foreigner attitude that is equally unwise.

The second sort of aggregatory ideas, running very often across the boundaries of national ideas and in conflict with them, are religious ideas. In Western Europe true national ideas only emerged to their present hectic vigour after the shock of the Reformation had liberated men from the great tradition of a Latin-speaking Christendom, a tradition the Roman Catholic Church has sustained as its modification of the old Latin-speaking Imperialism in the rule of the *pontifex maximus*. There was, and there remains to this day, a pro-

[1] Chapter Seven, § 6.

found disregard of local dialect and race in the Roman Catholic tradition, which has made that Church a persistently disintegrating influence in national life. Equally spacious and equally regardless of tongues and peoples is the great Arabic-speaking religion of Mahomet. Both Christendom and Islam are indeed on their secular sides imperfect realisations of a Utopian World State. But the secular side was the weaker side of these cults ; they produced no sufficiently great statesmen to realise their spiritual forces, and it is not in Rome under pontifical rule, nor in Munster under the Anabaptists, but rather in Thomas à Kempis and Saint Augustin's City of God that we must seek for the Utopias of Christianity.

In the last hundred years a novel development of material forces, and especially of means of communication, has done very much to break up the isolations in which nationality perfected its prejudices and so to render possible the extension and consolidation of such a world-wide culture as mediæval Christendom and Islam foreshadowed. The first onset of these expansive developments has been marked in the world of mind by an expansion of political ideals—Comte's *Western Republic* (1848) was the first Utopia that involved the synthesis of numerous States—by the development of " Imperialisms " in the place of national policies, and by the search for a basis for wider political unions in racial traditions and linguistic affinities. Anglo-Saxonism, Pan-Germanism, and the like are such synthetic ideas. Until the 'eighties, the general tendency of progressive thought was at one with the older Christian tradition which ignored " race," and the aim of the expansive liberalism movement, so far as it had a clear aim, was to Europeanise the world, to extend the franchise to negroes, put Polynesians into trousers, and train the teeming myriads of India to appreciate the exquisite lilt of *The Lady of the Lake*. There is always some absurdity mixed with human greatness, and we must not let the fact that the middle Victorians counted Scott, the suffrage, and pantaloons among the supreme blessings of life, conceal from us the very real nobility of their dream of England's mission to the world. . . .

We of this generation have seen a flood of reaction against such universalism. The great intellectual developments that centre upon the work of Darwin have exacerbated the realisation that life is a conflict between superior and inferior types, it has underlined the idea that specific survival rates are of primary significance in the world's development, and a swarm of inferior intelligences has applied to human problems elaborated and exaggerated versions of these generalisations. These social and political followers of Darwin have fallen into an obvious confusion between race and nationality, and into the natural trap of patriotic conceit. The dissent of the Indian and Colonial governing class to the first crude applications of liberal propositions in India has found a voice of unparalleled

penetration in Mr. Kipling, whose want of intellectual deliberation is only equalled by his poietic power. The search for a
basis for a new political synthesis in adaptable sympathies
based on linguistic affinities, was greatly influenced by Max
Müller's unaccountable assumption that language indicated
kindred, and led straight to wildly speculative ethnology, to
the discovery that there was a Keltic race, a Teutonic race,
an Indo-European race, and so forth. A book that has had
enormous influence in this matter, because of its use in teaching,
is J. R. Green's *Short History of the English People*, with its
grotesque insistence upon Anglo-Saxonism. And just now
the world is in a sort of delirium about race and the racial
struggle. The Briton forgetting his Defoe,[1] the Jew forgetting
the very word proselyte, the German forgetting his anthro-
pometric variations, and the Italian forgetting everything, are
obsessed by the singular purity of their blood, and the danger
of contamination the mere continuance of other races involves.
True to the law that all human aggregation involves the
development of a spirit of opposition to whatever is external
to the aggregation, extraordinary intensifications of racial
definition are going on ; the vileness, the inhumanity, the
incompatibility of alien races is being steadily exaggerated.
The natural tendency of every human being towards a stupid
conceit in himself and his kind, a stupid depreciation of all
unlikeness, is traded upon by this bastard science. With the
weakening of national references, and with the pause before
reconstruction in religious belief, these new arbitrary and
unsubstantial race prejudices become daily more formidable.
They are shaping policies and modifying laws, and they will
certainly be responsible for a large proportion of the wars,
hardships, and cruelties the immediate future holds in store for
our earth.

No generalisations about race are too extravagant for the
inflamed credulity of the present time. No attempt is ever
made to distinguish differences in inherent quality—the true
racial differences—from artificial differences due to culture.
No lesson seems ever to be drawn from history of the fluctuating incidence of the civilising process first upon this race and
then upon that. The politically ascendant peoples of the
present phase are understood to be the superior races, including
such types as the Sussex farm labourer, the Bowery tough,
the London hooligan, and the Paris apache ; the races not at
present prospering politically, such as the Egyptians, the
Greeks, the Spanish, the Moors, the Chinese, the Hindoos, the
Peruvians, and all uncivilised people are represented as the
inferior races, unfit to associate with the former on terms of
equality, unfit to intermarry with them on any terms, unfit
for any decisive voice in human affairs. In the popular
imagination of Western Europe, the Chinese are becoming

[1] *The True-born Englishman.*

bright gamboge in colour, and unspeakably abominable in
every respect ; the people who are black—the people who have
fuzzy hair and flattish noses, and no calves to speak of—are no
longer held to be within the pale of humanity. These superstitions work out along the obvious lines of the popular logic.
The depopulation of the Congo Free State by the Belgians,
the horrible massacre of Chinese by European soldiery during
the Pekin expedition, are condoned as a painful but necessary
part of the civilising process of the world. The world-wide
repudiation of slavery in the nineteenth century was done
against a vast sullen force of ignorant pride, which, reinvigorated
by the new delusions, swings back again to power.

    " Science " is supposed to lend its sanction to race mania,
but it is only " science " as it is understood by very illiterate
people that does anything of the sort—" scientists' " science,
in fact. What science has to tell about " The Races of Man "
will be found compactly set forth by Doctor J. Deinker, in the
book published under that title.[1] From that book one may
learn the beginnings of race charity. Save for a few isolated
pools of savage humanity, there is probably no pure race in
the whole world. The great continental populations are all
complex mixtures of numerous and fluctuating types. Even
the Jews present every kind of skull that is supposed to be
racially distinctive, a vast range of complexion—from blackness
in Goa, to extreme fairness in Holland—and a vast mental and
physical diversity. Were the Jews to discontinue all inter-
marriage with "other races" henceforth for ever, it would
depend upon quite unknown laws of fecundity, prepotency,
and variability, what their final type would be, or, indeed,
whether any particular type would ever prevail over diversity.
And, without going beyond the natives of the British Isles,
one can discover an enormous range of types, tall and short,
straight-haired and curly, fair and dark, supremely intelligent
and unteachably stupid, straightforward, disingenuous, and
what not. The natural tendency is to forget all this range
directly "race " comes under discussion, to take either an
average or some quite arbitrary ideal as the type, and think
only of that. The more difficult thing to do, but the thing
that must be done, if we are to get just results in this discussion,
is to do one's best to bear the range in mind.

    Let us admit that the average Chinaman is probably different
in complexion, and, indeed, in all his physical and psychical
proportions, from the average Englishman. Does that render
their association upon terms of equality in a World State
impossible ? What the average Chinaman or Englishman
may be, is of no importance whatever to our plan of a World
State. It is not averages that exist, but individuals. The
average Chinaman will never meet the average Englishman

---

[1] See also an excellent paper in the *American Journal of Sociology* for March, 1904,
" The Psychology of Race Prejudice," by W. I. Thomas.

anywhere ; only individual Chinamen will meet individual Englishmen. Now among Chinamen will be found a range of variety as extensive as among Englishmen, and there is no single trait presented by all Chinamen and no Englishman, or *vice versa*. Even the oblique eye is not universal in China, and there are probably many Chinamen who might have been " changed at birth," taken away and educated into quite passable Englishmen. Even after we have separated out and allowed for the differences in carriage, physique, moral pre-possessions, and so forth, due to their entirely divergent cultures, there remains, no doubt, a very great difference between the average Chinaman and the average Englishman ; but would that amount to a wider difference than is to be found between extreme types of Englishmen ?

For my own part I do not think that it would. But it is evident that any precise answer can be made only when anthropology has adopted much more exact and exhaustive methods of inquiry, and a far more precise analysis than its present resources permit.

Be it remembered how doubtful and tainted is the bulk of our evidence in these matters. These are extraordinarily subtle inquiries, from which few men succeed in disentangling the threads of their personal associations—the curiously interwoven strands of self-love and self-interest that affect their inquiries. One might almost say that instinct fights against such investigations, as it does undoubtedly against many necessary medical researches. But while a long special training, a high tradition and the possibility of reward and distinction, enable the medical student to face many tasks that are at once undignified and physically repulsive, the people from whom we get our anthropological information are rarely men of more than average intelligence, and of no mental training at all. And the problems are far more elusive. It surely needs at least the gifts and training of a first-class novelist, combined with a sedulous patience that probably cannot be hoped for in combination with these, to gauge the all-round differences between man and man. Even where there are no barriers of language and colour, understanding may be nearly impossible. How few educated people seem to understand the servant class in England, or the working men ! Except for Mr. Bart Kennedy's *A Man Adrift*, I know of scarcely any book that shows a really sympathetic and living understanding of the navvy, the longshore sailor man, the rough chap of our own race. Caricatures, luridly tragic or gaily comic, in which the misconceptions of the author blend with the preconceptions of the reader and achieve success, are, of course, common enough. And then consider the sort of people who pronounce judgments on the moral and intellectual capacity of the negro, the Malay, or the Chinaman. You have missionaries, native schoolmasters, employers of coolies, traders, simple downright men, who scarcely suspect the existence of any sources of error in their verdicts, who are incapable of understanding the difference between what is innate and what is acquired, much less of distinguishing them in their interplay. Now and then one seems to have a glimpse of something really living—in Mary Kingsley's buoyant work, for instance—and even that may be no more than my illusion.

For my own part I am disposed to discount all adverse judgments and all statements of insurmountable differences between race and race. I talk upon racial qualities to all men who have had opportunities of close observation, and I find that their insistence upon these differences is usually in inverse proportion to their intelligence. It may be the chance of my encounters, but that is my clear impression. Common sailors will generalise in the profoundest way about Irishmen, and Scotchmen, and Yankees, and Nova Scotians, and " Dutchies," until one might think one talked of different species of animal, but the educated explorer flings clear of all these delusions. To him men present themselves individualised, and if they classify it is by some skin-deep accident of tint, some trick of the tongue, or habit of gesture, or such-like superficiality. And after all there exists to-day available one kind at least of unbiased anthropological evidence. There are photographs. Let the reader turn over the pages of some such copiously illustrated work as *The Living Races of Mankind*,[1] and look into the eyes of one alien face after another. Are they not very like the people one knows ? For the most part, one finds it hard to believe that, with a common language and common social traditions, one would not get on very well with these people. Here or there is a brutish or evil face, but you can find as brutish and evil in the Strand on any afternoon. There are differences no doubt, but fundamental incompatibilities—*no !* And very many of them send out a ray of special resemblance and remind one more strongly of this friend or that, than they do of their own kind. One notes with surprise that one's good friend and neighbour X and an anonymous naked Gold Coast negro belong to one type, as distinguished from one's dear friend Y and a beaming individual from Somaliland, who as certainly belong to another.

In one matter the careless and prejudiced nature of accepted racial generalisations is particularly marked. A great and increasing number of people are persuaded that " half-breeds " are peculiarly evil creatures—as hunchbacks and bastards were supposed to be in the middle ages. The full legend of the wickedness of the half-breed is best to be learnt from a drunken mean white from Virginia or the Cape. The half-breed, one hears, combines all the vices of either parent, he is wretchedly poor in health and spirit, but vindictive, powerful,

[1] *The Living Races of Mankind*, by H. N. Hutchinson, J. W. Gregory, and R. Lydekker. (Hutchinson).

and dangerous to an extreme degree, his morals—the mean white has high and exacting standards —are indescribable even in whispers in a saloon, and so on, and so on. There is really not an atom of evidence an unprejudiced mind would accept to sustain any belief of the sort. There is nothing to show that the children of racial admixture are, as a class, inherently either better or worse in any respect than either parent. There is an equally baseless theory that they are better, a theory displayed to a fine degree of foolishness in the article on Shakespeare in the *Encyclopædia Britannica*. Both theories belong to the vast edifice of sham science that smothers the realities of modern knowledge. It may be that most "half-breeds" are failures in life, but that proves nothing. They are, in an enormous number of cases, illegitimate and outcast from the normal education of either race ; they are brought up in homes that are the battle-grounds of conflicting cultures ; they labour under a heavy premium of disadvantage. There is, of course, a passing suggestion of Darwin's to account for atavism that might go to support the theory of the vileness of half-breeds, if it had ever been proved. But, then, it never has been proved. There is no proof in the matter at all.

§ 3

Suppose, now, there is such a thing as an all-round inferior race. Is that any reason why we should propose to preserve it for ever in a condition of tutelage ? Whether there is a race so inferior I do not know, but certainly there is no race so superior as to be trusted with human charges. The true answer to Aristotle's plea for slavery, that there are "natural slaves," lies in that fact that there are no "natural " masters. Power is no more to be committed to men without discipline and restriction than alcohol. The true objection to slavery is not that it is unjust to the inferior but that it corrupts the superior. There is only one sane and logical thing to be done with a really inferior race, and that is to exterminate it.

Now there are various ways of exterminating a race, and most of them are cruel. You may end it with fire and sword after the old Hebrew fashion ; you may enslave it and work it to death, as the Spaniards did the Caribs ; you may set it boundaries and then poison it slowly with deleterious com- modities, as the Americans do with most of their Indians ; you may incite it to wear clothing to which it is not accustomed, and to live under new and strange conditions that will expose it to infectious diseases to which you yourselves are immune, as the missionaries do the Polynesians ; you may resort to honest simple murder, as we English did with the Tasmanians ; or you can maintain such conditions as conduce to " race suicide," as the British administration does in Fiji. Suppose, then, for a moment, that there is an all-round inferior race ; a Modern Utopia is under the hard logic of life, and it would have to exterminate such a race as quickly as it could. On the whole, the Fijian device seems the least cruel. But Utopia would do that without any clumsiness of race distinction, in exactly the same manner, and by the same machinery, as it exterminates all its own defective and inferior strains ; that is to say, as we have already discussed in Chapter Five, § 1, by its marriage laws, and by the laws of the minimum wage. That extinction need never be discriminatory. If any of the race did, after all, prove to be fit to survive they would survive—they would be picked out with a sure and automatic justice from the over-ready condemnation of all their kind.

Is there, however, an all-round inferior race in the world ? Even the Australian black-fellow is, perhaps, not quite so entirely eligible for extinction as a good, wholesome, horse-racing, sheep-farming Australian white may think. These queer little races, the black fellows, the Pigmies, the Bushmen, may have their little gifts, a greater keenness, a greater fineness of this sense or that, a quaintness of the imagination or what not, that may serve as their little unique addition to the totality of our Utopian civilisation. We are supposing that every individual alive on earth is alive in Utopia, and so all the surviving " black-fellows " are there. Every one of them in Utopia has had what none have had on earth, a fair education and fair treatment, justice, and opportunity. Suppose that the common idea is right about the general inferiority of these people, then it would follow that in Utopia most of them are childless, and working at or about the minimum wage, and some will have passed out of all possibility of offspring under the hand of the offended law ; but still—cannot we imagine some few of these little people—whom you must suppose neither naked nor clothed in the European style, but robed in the Utopian fashion—may have found some delicate art to practise, some peculiar sort of carving, for example, that justifies God in creating them ? Utopia has sound sanitary laws, sound social laws, sound economic laws ; what harm are these people going to do ?

Some may be even prosperous and admired, may have married women of their own or some other race, and so may be transmitting that distinctive thin thread of excellence, to take its due place in the great synthesis of the future.

And, indeed, coming along that terrace in Utopia, I see a little figure, a little bright-eyed, bearded man, inky black, frizzy haired, and clad in a white tunic and black hose, and with a mantle of lemon yellow wrapped about his shoulders. He walks, as most Utopians walk, as though he had reason to be proud of something, as though he had no reason to be afraid of anything in the world. He carries a portfolio in his hand. It is that, I suppose, as much as his hair, that recalls the *Quartier Latin* to my mind.

§ 4

I had already discussed the question of race with the botanist at Lucerne.

"But you would not like," he cried in horror, "your daughter to marry a Chinaman or a negro ? "

"Of course," said I, "when you say Chinaman, you think of a creature with a pigtail, long nails, and insanitary habits, and when you say negro you think of a filthy-headed, black creature in an old hat. You do this because your imagination is too feeble to disentangle the inherent qualities of a thing from its habitual associations."

"Insult isn't argument," said the botanist.

"Neither is unsound implication. You make a question of race into a question of unequal cultures. You would not like your daughter to marry the sort of negro who steals hens, but then you would also not like your daughter to marry a pure English hunchback with a squint, or a drunken cab tout of Norman blood. As a matter of fact, very few well-bred English girls do commit that sort of indiscretion. But you don't think it necessary to generalise against men of your own race because they are drunken cab touts, and why should you generalise against negroes ? Because the proportion of undesirables is higher among negroes, that does not justify a sweeping condemnation. You may have to condemn most, but why *all* ? There may be—neither of us knows enough to deny—negroes who are handsome, capable, courageous."

"Ugh ! " said the botanist.

"How detestable you must find Othello ! "

It is my Utopia, and for a moment I could almost find it in my heart to spite the botanist by creating a modern Desdemona and her lover sooty black to the lips, there before our eyes. But I am not so sure of my case as that, and for the moment there shall come nothing more than a swart-faced, dusky Burmese woman in the dress of the Greater Rule, with her tall Englishman (as he might be on earth) at her side. That, however, is a digression from my conversation with the botanist.

"And the Chinaman ? " said the botanist.

"I think we shall have all the buff and yellow peoples intermingling pretty freely."

"Chinamen and white women, for example."

"Yes," I said, "you've got to swallow that, anyhow ; you *shall* swallow that."

He finds the idea too revolting for comment.

I try to make the thing seem easier for him. "Do try," I said, "to grasp a Modern Utopian's conditions. The Chinaman will speak the same language as his wife—whatever her race may be—he will wear costume of the common civilised fashion, he will have much the same education as his European rival, read the same literature, bow to the same traditions. And you must remember a wife in Utopia is singularly not subject to her husband. . . ."

The botanist proclaims his invincible conclusion : " Every one would cut her ! "

" This is Utopia," I said, and then sought once more to tranquillise his mind. "No doubt among the vulgar, coarse-minded people outside the Rule there may be something of the sort. Every earthly moral blockhead, a little educated, perhaps, is to be found in Utopia. You will, no doubt, find the ' cut ' and the ' boycott,' and all those nice little devices by which dull people get a keen edge on life, in their place here, and their place here is somewhere——"

I turned a thumb earthward. " There ! "

The botanist did not answer for a little while. Then he said, with some temper and great emphasis : " Well, I'm jolly glad anyhow that I'm not to be a permanent resident in this Utopia, *if our daughters are to be married to Hottentots by regulation.* I'm jolly glad."

He turned his back on me.

Now did I say anything of the sort ? . . .

I had to bring him, I suppose ; there's no getting away from him in this life. But, as I have already observed, the happy ancients went to their Utopias without this sort of company.

§ 5

What gives the botanist so great an advantage in all his Anti-Utopian utterances is his unconsciousness of his own limitations. He thinks in little pieces that lie about loose, and nothing has any necessary link with anything else in his mind. So that I cannot retort upon him by asking him, if he objects to this synthesis of all nations, tongues, and peoples in a World State, what alternative ideal he proposes.

People of this sort do not even feel the need of alternatives. Beyond the scope of a few personal projects, meeting Her again, and things like that, they do not feel that there is a future. They are unencumbered by any baggage of convictions whatever, in relation to that. That, at least, is the only way in which I can explain our friend's high intellectual mobility. Attempts to correlate statesmanship, which they regard with interest as a dramatic interplay of personalities, with any secular movement of humanity, they class with the differential calculus and Darwinism, as things far too difficult to be anything but finally and subtly wrong.

So the argument must pass into a direct address to the reader.

If you are not prepared to regard a world-wide synthesis of all cultures and polities and races into one World State as the desirable end upon which all civilising efforts converge, what do you regard as the desirable end ? Synthesis, one may remark in passing, does not necessarily mean fusion, nor does it mean uniformity.

The alternatives fall roughly under three headings. The first is to assume there is a best race, to define as well as one can that best race, and to regard all other races as material for extermination. This has a fine, modern, biological air ("Survival of the Fittest"). If you are one of those queer German professors who write insanity about Welt-Politik, you assume the best race is the "Teutonic"; Cecil Rhodes affected that triumph of creative imagination, the "Anglo-Saxon race"; my friend, Moses Cohen, thinks there is much to be said for the Jew. On its premises, this is a perfectly sound and reasonable policy, and it opens out a brilliant prospect for the scientific inventor for what one might call Welt-Apparat in the future, for national harrowing and reaping machines, and race-destroying fumigations. The great plain of China ("Yellow Peril") lends itself particularly to some striking wholesale undertaking; it might, for example, be flooded for a few days, and then disinfected with volcanic chlorine. Whether, when all the inferior races have been stamped out, the superior race would not proceed at once, or after a brief millennial period of social harmony, to divide itself into sub-classes, and begin the business over again at a higher level, is an interesting residual question into which we need not now penetrate.

That complete development of a scientific Welt-Politik is not, however, very widely advocated at present, no doubt from a want of confidence in the public imagination. We have, however, a very audible and influential school, the Modern Imperialist school, which distinguishes its own race—there is a German, a British, and an Anglo-Saxon section in the school, and a wider teaching which embraces the whole "white race" in one remarkable tolerance—as the superior race, as one, indeed, superior enough to own slaves, collectively, if not individually; and the exponents of this doctrine look with a resolute, truculent, but slightly indistinct eye to a future in which all the rest of the world will be in subjection to these elect. The ideals of this type are set forth pretty clearly in Mr. Kidd's *Control of the Tropics*. The whole world is to be administered by the "white" Powers—Mr. Kidd did not anticipate Japan—who will see to it that their subjects do not "prevent the utilisation of the immense natural resources which they have in charge." Those other races are to be regarded as children, recalcitrant children at times, and without any of the tender emotions of paternity. It is a little doubtful whether the races lacking "in the elementary qualities of social efficiency" are expected to acquire them under the chastening hands of those races which, through "strength and energy of character, humanity, probity, and integrity, and a single-minded devotion to conceptions of duty," are developing " the resources of the richest regions of the earth " over their heads, or whether this is the ultimate ideal.

Next comes the rather incoherent alternative that one associates in England with official Liberalism.

Liberalism in England is not quite the same thing as Liberalism in the rest of the world ; it is woven of two strands. There is Whiggism, the powerful tradition of seventeenth-century Protestant and republican England, with its great debt to republican Rome, its strong constructive and disciplinary bias, its broad and originally very living and intelligent outlook ; and interwoven with this there is the sentimental and logical Liberalism that sprang from the stresses of the eighteenth century, that finds its early scarce differentiated expression in Harrington's *Oceana*, and after fresh draughts of the tradition of Brutus and Cato and some elegant trifling with noble savages, budded in *La Cité Morellyste*, flowered in the emotional democratic naturalism of Rousseau, and bore abundant fruit in the French Revolution. These are two very distinct strands. Directly they were freed in America from the grip of conflict with British Toryism, they came apart as the Republican and Democratic parties respectively. Their continued union in Great Britain is a political accident. Because of this mixture, the whole career of English-speaking Liberalism, though it has gone to one unbroken strain of eloquence, has never produced a clear statement of policy in relation to other peoples politically less fortunate. It has developed no definite ideas at all about the future of mankind. The Whig disposition, which once had some play in India, was certainly to attempt to anglicise the "native," to assimilate his culture, and then to assimilate his political status with that of his temporary ruler. But interwoven with this anglicising tendency, which was also, by the bye, a Christianising tendency, was a strong disposition, derived from the Rousseau strand, to leave other peoples alone, to facilitate even the separation and autonomy of detached portions of our own peoples, to disintegrate finally into perfect, because lawless, individuals. The official exposition of British " Liberalism " to-day still wriggles unstably because of these conflicting constituents, but on the whole the Whig strand now seems the weaker. The contemporary Liberal politician offers cogent criticism upon the brutality and conceit of modern imperialisms, but that seems to be the limit of his service. Taking what they do not say and do not propose as an indication of Liberal intentions, it would seem that the ideal of the British Liberals and of the American Democrats is to favour the existence of just as many petty, loosely allied, or quite independent nationalities as possible, just as many languages as possible, to deprecate armies and all controls, and to trust to the innate goodness of disorder and the powers of an ardent sentimentality to keep the world clean and sweet. The Liberals will not face the plain consequence that such a state of affairs is hopelessly unstable, that it involves the maximum risk of war with the minimum of permanent benefit and public order. They will not reflect that the stars in their courses rule inexorably against it. It is a vague, impossible ideal, with a rude sort of unworldly moral beauty, like the gospel of the Doukhobors. Besides that charm it has this most seductive quality to an official British Liberal, that it does not exact intellectual activity nor indeed activity of any sort whatever. It is, by virtue of that alone, a far less mischievous doctrine than the crude and violent Imperialism of the popular Press.

Neither of these two schools of policy, neither the international *laisser faire* of the Liberals, nor " hustle to the top " Imperialism, promise any reality of permanent progress for the world of men. They are the resort, the moral reference, of those who will not think frankly and exhaustively over the whole field of this question. Do that, insist upon solutions of more than accidental applicability, and you emerge with one or other of two contrasted solutions, as the consciousness of kind or the consciousness of individuality prevails in your mind. In the former case you will adopt aggressive Imperialism, but you will carry it out to its " thorough " degree of extermination. You will seek to develop the culture and power of your kind of men and women to the utmost in order to shoulder all other kinds from the earth. If on the other hand you appreciate the unique, you will aim at such a synthesis as this Utopia displays, a synthesis far more credible and possible than any other Welt-Politik. In spite of all the pageant of modern war, synthesis is in the trend of the world. To aid and develop it, could be made the open and secure policy of any great modern empire now. Modern war, modern international hostility is, I believe, possible only through the stupid illiteracy of the mass of men and the conceit and intellectual indolence of rulers and those who feed the public mind. Were the will of the mass of men lit and conscious, I am firmly convinced it would now burn steadily for synthesis and peace.

It would be so easy to bring about a world peace within a few decades, was there but the will for it among men ! The great empires that exist need but a little speech and frankness one with another. Within, the riddles of social order are already half solved in books and thoughts, there are the common people and the subject peoples to be educated and drilled, to be led to a common speech and a common literature, to be assimilated and made citizens ; without, there is the possibility of treaties. Why, for example, should Britain and France, or either and the United States, or Sweden and Norway, or Holland, or Denmark, or Italy, fight any more for ever ? And if there is no reason, how foolish and dangerous it is still to sustain linguistic differences and custom houses, and all sorts of foolish and irritating distinctions between their various citizens ! Why should not all these peoples agree to teach some common language, French, for example, in their common schools, or to teach each other's languages reciprocally ? Why should they not aim at a common literature, and bring their various common laws, their marriage laws, and so on, into uniformity ? Why should they not work for a uniform minimum of labour conditions through all their communities ? Why, then, should they not—except in the interests of a few rascal plutocrats—trade freely and exchange their citizenship freely throughout their common boundaries ? No doubt there are difficulties to be found, but they are quite finite difficulties. What is there to prevent a parallel movement of all the civilised Powers in the world towards a common ideal and assimilation ?

Stupidity—nothing but stupidity, a stupid brute jealousy, aimless and unjustifiable.

The coarser conceptions of aggregation are at hand, the hostile, jealous patriotisms, the blare of trumpets and the pride of fools ; they serve the daily need though they lead towards disaster. The real and the immediate has us in its grip, the accidental personal thing. The little effort of thought, the brief sustained effort of will, is too much for the contemporary mind. Such treaties, such sympathetic international movements, are but dream stuff yet on earth, though Utopia has realised them long since and already passed them by.

CHAPTER ELEVEN

THE BUBBLE BURSTS

§ 1

As I walk back along the river terrace to the hotel where the botanist awaits me, and observe the Utopians I encounter, I have no thought that my tenure of Utopia becomes every moment more precarious. There float in my mind vague anticipations of more talks with my double and still more, of a steady elaboration of detail, of interesting journeys of exploration. I forget that a Utopia is a thing of the imagination that becomes more fragile with every added circumstance, that, like a soap-bubble, it is most brilliantly and variously coloured at the very instant of its dissolution. This Utopia is nearly done. All the broad lines of its social organisation are completed now, the discussion of all its general difficulties and problems. Utopian individuals pass me by, fine buildings tower on either hand ; it does not occur to me that I may look too closely. To find the people assuming the concrete and individual, is not, as I fondly imagine, the last triumph of realisation, but the swimming moment of opacity before the film gives way. To come to individual emotional cases, is to return to the earth.

I find the botanist sitting at a table in the hotel courtyard.

" Well ? " I say, standing before him.

" I've been in the gardens on the river terrace," he answers, " hoping I might see her again."

" Nothing better to do ? "

" Nothing in the world."

" You'll have your double back from India to-morrow. Then you'll have conversation."

" I don't want it," he replies compactly.

I shrug my shoulders, and he adds, " At least with him."

I let myself down into a seat beside him.

For a time I sit restfully enjoying his companionable silence, and thinking fragmentarily of those *samurai* and their Rules. I entertain something of the satisfaction of a man who has finished building a bridge ; I feel that I have joined together things that I had never joined before. My Utopia seems real to me, very real, I can believe in it, until the metal chair-back gives to my shoulder blades, and Utopian sparrows twitter and hop before my feet. I have a pleasant moment of unhesitating self-satisfaction ; I feel a shameless exultation to be there. For a moment I forget the consideration the botanist demands ; the mere pleasure of completeness, of holding and controlling all the threads possesses me.

" You *will* persist in believing," I say, with an aggressive expository note, " that if you meet this lady she will be a person with the memories and sentiments of her double on earth. You think she will understand and pity, and perhaps love you. Nothing of the sort is the case." I repeat with confident rudeness, " Nothing of the sort is the case. Things are different altogether here ; you can hardly tell even now how different are——"

I discover he is not listening to me.

" What is the matter ? " I ask abruptly.

He makes no answer, but his expression startles me.

" What is the matter ? " and then I follow his eyes.

A woman and a man are coming through the great archway —and instantly I guess what has happened. She it is arrests my attention first—long ago I knew she was a sweetly beautiful woman. She is fair, with frank blue eyes, that look with a sort of tender receptivity into her companion's face. For a moment or so they remain, greyish figures in the cool shadow, against the sunlit greenery of the gardens beyond.

" It is Mary," the botanist whispers with white lips, but he stares at the form of the man. His face whitens, it becomes so transfigured with emotion that for a moment it does not look weak. Then I see that his thin hand is clenched.

I realise how little I understand his emotions.

A sudden fear of what he will do takes hold of me. He sits white and tense as the two come into the clearer light of the courtyard. The man, I see, is one of the *samurai*, a dark, strong-faced man, a man I have never seen before, and she is wearing the robe that shows her a follower of the Lesser Rule.

Some glimmering of the botanist's feelings strikes through to my slow sympathies. Of course—a strange man! I put out a restraining hand towards his arm. " I told you," I say, " that very probably, most probably, she would have met some other. I tried to prepare you."

" Nonsense," he whispers, without looking at me. " It isn't that. It's—that scoundrel——"

He has an impulse to rise. " That scoundrel," he repeats.

" He isn't a scoundrel," I say. " How do you know ? Keep still ! Why are you standing up ? "

He and I stand up quickly, I as soon as he. But now the full meaning of the group has reached me. I grip his arm. " Be sensible," I say, speaking very quickly, and with my back to the approaching couple. " He's not a scoundrel here. This world is different from that. It's caught his pride some-how and made a man of him. Whatever troubled them there——"

He turns a face of white wrath on me, of accusation, and for the moment of unexpected force. " This is *your* doing," he says. " You have done this to mock me. He—of all men ! " For a moment speech fails him, then ; " You—you have done this to mock me."

I try to explain very quickly. My tone is almost pro-pitiatory.

" I never thought of it until now. But he's—— How did I know he was the sort of man a disciplined world has a use for ? "

He makes no answer, but he looks at me with eyes that are positively baleful, and in the instant I read his mute but mulish resolve that Utopia must end.

" Don't let that old quarrel poison all this," I say almost entreatingly. " It happened all differently here—everything is different here. Your double will be back to-morrow. Wait for him. Perhaps then you will understand——"

He shakes his head, and then bursts out with, " What do I want with a double ? Double ! What do I care if things have been different here ? This——"

He thrusts me weakly back with his long, white hand. " My God ! " he says almost forcibly, " what nonsense all this is ! All these dreams ! All Utopias ! There she is—— ! Oh, but I have dreamt of her ! And now——"

A sob catches him. I am really frightened by this time. I still try to keep between him and these Utopians, and to hide his gestures from them.

" It's different here," I persist. " It's different here. The

emotion you feel has no place in it. It's a scar from the earth
—the sore scar of your past——"

"And what are we all but scars? What is life but a
scarring? It's *you*—you who don't understand ! Of course
we are covered with scars, we live to be scarred, we are scars !
We are the scars of the past ! These *dreams*, these childish
dreams—— ! "

He does not need to finish his sentence, he waves an unteachable destructive arm.

My Utopia rocks about me.

For a moment the vision of that great courtyard hangs real.
There the Utopians live real about me, going to and fro, and
the great archway blazes with sunlight from the green gardens
by the riverside. The man who is one of the *samurai*, and his
lady, whom the botanist loved on earth, pass out of sight
behind the marble flower-set Triton that spouts coolness in
the middle of the place. For a moment I see two working
men in green tunics sitting on a marble seat in the shadow of
the colonnade, and a sweet little silver-haired old lady, clad
all in violet, and carrying a book, comes towards us, and lifts
a curious eye at the botanist's gestures. And then——

"Scars of the past ! Scars of the past ! These fanciful,
useless dreams ! "

§ 2

There is no jerk, no sound, no hint of material shock. We
are in London, and clothed in the fashion of the town. The
sullen roar of London fills our ears. . . .

I see that I am standing beside an iron seat of poor design
in that grey and gawky waste of asphalt—Trafalgar Square,
and the botanist, with perplexity in his face, stares from me to
a poor, shrivelled, dirt-lined old woman—my God ! what a
neglected thing she is !—who proffers a box of matches. . . .

He buys almost mechanically, and turns back to me.

"I was saying," he says, "the past rules us absolutely.
These dreams——"

His sentence does not complete itself. He looks nervous and
irritated.

"You have a trick at times," he says instead, "of making
your suggestions so vivid——"

He takes a plunge. "If you don't mind," he says in a sort
of quavering ultimatum, "we won't discuss that aspect of the
question—the lady, I mean—further."

He pauses, and there still hangs a faint perplexity
between us.

"But——" I begin.

For a moment we stand there, and my dream of Utopia runs
off me like water from an oiled slab. Of course—we lunched at
our club. We came back from Switzerland by no dream train
but by the ordinary Bâle express. We have been talking of

that Lucerne woman he harps upon, and I have made some novel comment on his story. I have touched certain possibilities.

" You can't conceivably understand," he says.

" The fact remains," he goes on, taking up the thread of his argument again with an air of having defined our field, " we *are* the scars of the past. That's a thing one can discuss—without personalities."

" No," I say rather stupidly, " no."

" You are always talking as though you could kick the past to pieces ; as though one could get right out from oneself and begin afresh. It is your weakness—if you don't mind my being frank—it makes you seem harsh and dogmatic. Life has gone easily for you ; you have never been badly tried. You have been lucky—you do not understand the other way about. You are—hard."

I answer nothing.

He pants for breath. I perceive that in our discussion of his case I must have gone too far, and that he has rebelled. Clearly I must have said something wounding about that ineffectual love story of his.

" You don't allow for my position," he says, and it occurs to me to say, " I'm obliged to look at the thing from my own point of view. . . ."

One or other of us makes a move. What a lot of filthy, torn paper is scattered about the world ! We walk slowly side by side towards the dirt-littered basin of the fountain, and stand regarding two grimy tramps who sit and argue on a farther seat. One holds a horrible old boot in his hand, and gesticulates with it, while his other hand caresses his rag-wrapped foot. " Wot does Cham'lain *si* ? " his words drift to us. " W'y, 'e says, wot's the good of 'nvesting your kepital where these 'ere Americans may dump it flat any time they like. . . ."

(Were there not two men in green sitting on a marble seat ?)

§ 3

We walk on, our talk suspended, past a ruthlessly clumsy hoarding, towards where men and women and children are struggling about a string of omnibuses. A newsvendor at the corner spreads a newspaper placard upon the wood pavement, pins the corners down with stones, and we glimpse something about :

MASSACRE IN ODESSA

DISCOVERY OF HUMAN REMAINS AT CHERTSEY

SHOCKING LYNCHING OUTRAGE IN NEW YORK STATE

GERMAN INTRIGUES GET A SET-BACK

THE BIRTHDAY HONOURS—FULL LIST

Dear old familiar world !

An angry parent in conversation with a sympathetic friend
jostles against us. " I'll knock his blooming young 'ed orf
if 'e cheeks me again. It's these 'ere brasted Board
Schools——"

An omnibus passes, bearing on a board beneath an in-
correctly drawn Union Jack an exhortation to the true patriot
to " Buy Bumper's British-Boiled Jam." . . .

I am stunned beyond the possibility of discussion for a
space. In this very place it must have been that the high
terrace ran with the gardens below it, along which I came from
my double to our hotel. I am going back, but now through
reality, along the path I passed so happily in my dream. And
the people I saw then are the people I am looking at now—with
a difference.

The botanist walks beside me, white and nervously jerky in
his movements, his ultimatum delivered.

We start to cross the road. An open carriage drives by,
and we see a jaded, red-haired woman, smeared with paint,
dressed in furs, and petulantly discontented. Her face is
familiar to me, her face with a difference.

Why do I think of her as dressed in green ?

Of course !—she it was I saw leading her children by the hand !

Comes a crash to our left, and a running of people to see a
cab-horse down on the slippery, slanting pavement outside
St. Martin's Church.

We go on up the street.

A heavy-eyed young Jewess, a draggled prostitute—no
crimson flower for her hair, poor girl !—regards us with a
momentary speculation, and we get a whiff of foul language
from two newsboys on the kerb.

" We can't go on talking," the botanist begins, and ducks
aside just in time to save his eyes from the ferrule of a stupidly
held umbrella. He is going to treat our little tiff about that
lady as closed. He has the air of picking up our conversation
again at some earlier point.

He steps into the gutter, walks round outside a negro hawker,
just escapes the wheel of a hansom, and comes to my side again.

" We can't go on talking of your Utopia," he says, " in a
noise and crowd like this."

We are separated by a portly man going in the opposite
direction, and join again. " We can't go on talking of
Utopia," he repeats, " in London. . . . Up in the mountains
—and holiday-time—it was all right. We let ourselves go ! "

" I've been living in Utopia," I answer, tacitly adopting his
tacit proposal to drop the lady out of the question.

" At times," he says, with a queer laugh, " you've almost
made me live there, too."

He reflects. " It doesn't do, you know. *No !* And I don't
know whether, after all, I want——"

We are separated again by half a dozen lifted flagstones, a burning brazier, and two engineers concerned with some underground business or other—in the busiest hour of the day's traffic.

" Why shouldn't it do ? " I ask.

" It spoils the world of everyday to let your mind run on impossible perfections."

" I wish," I shout against the traffic, " I could *smash* the world of everyday."

My note becomes quarrelsome. " You may accept *this* as the world of reality, *you* may consent to be one scar in an ill-dressed compound wound, but so—not I ! This is a dream, too—this world. *Your* dream, and you bring me back to it—out of Utopia——"

The crossing of Bow Street gives me pause again.

The face of a girl who is passing westward, a student girl, rather carelessly dressed, her books in a carrying-strap, comes across my field of vision. The westward sun of London glows upon her face. She has eyes that dream, surely no sensuous nor personal dream.

After all, after all, dispersed, hidden, disorganised, undiscovered, unsuspected even by themselves, the *samurai* of Utopia are in this world, the motives that are developed and organised there stir dumbly here and stifle in ten thousand futile hearts. . . .

I overtake the botanist, who got ahead at the crossing by the advantage of a dust-cart.

" You think this is real because you can't wake out of it," I say. " It's all a dream, and there are people—I'm just one of the first of a multitude—between sleeping and waking—who will presently be rubbing it out of their eyes."

A pinched and dirty little girl, with sores upon her face stretches out a bunch of wilting violets, in a pitifully thin little fist, and interrupts my speech. " Bunch o' vi'lets—on'y a penny."

" No ! " I says curtly, hardening my heart.

A ragged and filthy nursing mother, with her last addition to our Imperial People on her arm, comes out of a drinkshop, and stands a little unsteadily, and wipes mouth and nose comprehensively with the back of a red chapped hand. . . .

§ 4

" Isn't *that* reality ? " says the botanist, almost triumphantly, and leaves me aghast at his triumph.

" *That !* " I say belatedly. " It's a thing in a nightmare ! "

He shakes his head and smiles—exasperatingly.

I perceive quite abruptly that the botanist and I have reached the limits of our intercourse.

" The world dreams things like that," I say, " because it suffers from an indigestion of such people as you."

His low-toned self-complacency, like the faded banner of an obstinate fort, still flies unconquered. And you know, he's not even a happy man with it all !

For ten seconds or more I am furiously seeking in my mind for a word, for a term of abuse, for one compendious verbal missile that shall smash this man for ever. It has to express total inadequacy of imagination and will, spiritual anæmia, dull respectability, gross sentimentality, a cultivated pettiness of heart. . . .

That word will not come. But no other word will do. Indeed the word does not exist. There is nothing with sufficient vituperative concentration for this moral and intellectual stupidity of educated people. . . .

" Er——" he begins.

No ! I can't endure him.

With a passionate rapidity of movement, I leave his side, dart between a carriage and a van, duck under the head of a cab-horse, and board a bus going westward somewhere—but anyhow, going in exactly the reverse direction to the botanist. I clamber up the steps and thread my swaying way to the seat immediately behind the driver.

" There ! " I say, as I whack myself down on the seat and pant.

When I look round the botanist is out of sight.

§ 5

But I am back in the world for all that, and my Utopia is done.

It is good discipline for the Utopist to visit this world occasionally.

But from the front seat on the top of an omnibus on a sunny September afternoon, the Strand, and Charing Cross corner, and Whitehall, and the great multitude of people, the great uproar of vehicles, streaming in all directions, is apt to look a world altogether too formidable. It has a glare, it has a tumult and vigour that shouts one down. It shouts one down, if shouting is to carry it. What good was it to trot along the pavement through this noise and tumult of life, pleading Utopia to that botanist ? What good would it be to recommend Utopia in this driver's preoccupied ear ?

There are moments in the life of every philosopher and dreamer when he feels himself the flimsiest of absurdities, when the Thing in Being has its way with him, its triumphant way, when it asks in a roar, unanswerably, with a fine solid use of the current vernacular, " What Good is all this—Rot about Utopias ? "

One inspects the Thing in Being with something of the diffident speculation of primitive man, peering from behind a tree at an angry elephant.

(There is an omen in that image. On how many occasions

must that ancestor of ours have had just the Utopist's feeling of ambitious unreality, have decided that on the whole it was wiser to go very quietly home again, and leave the big beast alone ? But, in the end, men rode upon the elephant's head, and guided him this way or that. . . . The Thing in Being that roars so tremendously about Charing Cross corner seems a bigger antagonist than an elephant, but then we have better weapons than chipped flint blades. . . .)

After all, in a very little time everything that impresses me so mightily this September afternoon will have changed or passed away for ever, everything. These omnibuses, these great, stalwart, crowded many-coloured things that jostle one another, and make so handsome a clatter-clamour, will all have gone ; they and their horses and drivers and organisation ; you will come here and you will not find them. Something else will be here, some different sort of vehicle, that is now perhaps the mere germ of an idea in some engineer student's brain. And this road and pavement will have changed, and these impressive great buildings ; other buildings will be here, buildings that are as yet more impalpable than this page you read, more formless and flimsy by far than anything that is reasoned here. Little plans sketched on paper, strokes of a pen or of a brush, will be the first materialisations of what will at last obliterate every detail and atom of these re-echoing actualities that overwhelm us now. And the clothing and gestures of these innumerable people, the character of their faces and bearing, these, too, will be recast in the spirit of what are now obscure and impalpable beginnings.

The new things will be indeed of the substance of the things that is, but differing just in the measure of the will and imagination that goes to make them. They will be strong and fair as the will is sturdy and organised and the imagination comprehensive and bold ; they will be ugly and smeared with wretchedness as the will is fluctuating and the imagination timid and mean.

Indeed Will is stronger than Fact, it can mould and overcome Fact. But this world has still to discover its will, it is a world that slumbers inertly, and all this roar and pulsation of life is no more than its heavy breathing. . . . My mind runs on to the thought of an awakening.

As my omnibus goes lumbering up Cockspur Street, through the clatter rattle of the cabs and carriages, there comes another fancy in my mind. . . . Could one but realise an apocalyptic image and suppose an angel, such as was given to each of the seven churches of Asia, given for a space to the service of the Greater Rule. I see him as a towering figure of flame and colour, standing between earth and sky, with a trumpet in his hands, over there above the Haymarket, against the October glow ; and when he sounds, all the *samurai*, all who are *samurai* in Utopia, will know themselves and one another. . . .

(Whup! says a motor brougham, and a policeman stays the traffic with his hand.)

All of us who partake of the *samurai* would know ourselves and one another!

For a moment I have a vision of this resurrection of the living, of a vague, magnificent answer, of countless myriads at attention, of all that is fine in humanity at attention, round the compass of the earth.

Then that philosophy of individual uniqueness resumes its sway over my thoughts, and my dream of a world's awakening fades.

I had forgotten. . . .

Things do not happen like that. God is not simple, God is not theatrical, the summons comes to each man in its due time for him, with an infinite subtlety of variety. . . .

If that is so, what of my Utopia?

This infinite world must needs be flattened to get it on one retina. The picture of a solid thing, although it is flattened and simplified, is not necessarily a lie. Surely, surely, in the end, by degrees, and steps, something of this sort, some such understanding, as this Utopia must come. First here, then there, single men and then groups of men will fall into line— not indeed with my poor faulty hesitating suggestions—but with a great and comprehensive plan wrought out by many minds and in many tongues. It is just because my plan is faulty, because it mis-states so much, and omits so much, that they do not now fall in. It will not be like *my* dream, the world that is coming. My dream is just my own poor dream, the thing sufficient for me. We fail in comprehension, we fail so variously and abundantly. We see as much as it is service-able for us to see, and we see no further. But the fresh un-daunted generations come to take on our work beyond our utmost effort, beyond the range of our ideas. They will learn with certainty things that to us are guesses and riddles. . . .

There will be many Utopias. Each generation will have its new version of Utopia, a little more certain and complete and real, with its problems lying closer and closer to the problems of the Thing in Being. Until at last from dreams Utopias will have come to be working drawings, and the whole world will be shaping the final World State, the fair and great and fruitful World State, that will only not be a Utopia because it will be this world. So surely it must be——

The policeman drops his hand. "Come up," says the bus driver, and the horses strain; "Clitter, clatter, cluck, clak," the line of hurrying hansoms overtakes the omnibus going west. A dexterous lad on a bicycle with a bale of newspapers on his back dodges nimbly across the head of the column and vanishes up a side street.

The omnibus sways forward. Rapt and prophetic, his plump

hands clasped round the handle of his umbrella, his billycock hat a trifle askew, this irascible little man of the Voice, this impatient dreamer, this scolding Optimist, who has argued so rudely and dogmatically about economics and philosophy and decoration, and indeed about everything under the sun, who has been so hard on the botanist and fashionable women, and so reluctant in the matter of beer, is carried onward, dreaming dreams, dreams that with all the inevitable ironies of difference, may be realities when you and I are dreams.

He passes, and for a little space we are left with his egoisms and idiosyncrasies more or less in suspense.

But why was he intruded ? you ask. Why could not a modern Utopia be discussed without this impersonation—impersonally ? It has confused the book, you say, made the argument hard to follow, and thrown a quality of insincerity over the whole. Are we but mocking at Utopias, you demand, using all these noble and generalised hopes as the backcloth against which two bickering personalities jar and squabble ? Do I mean we are never to view the promised land again except through a foreground of fellow-travellers ? There is a common notion that the reading of a Utopia should end with a swelling heart and clear resolves, with lists of names, formation of committees, and even the commencement of subscriptions. But this Utopia began upon a philosophy of fragmentation, and ends, confusedly, amidst a gross tumult of immediate realities, in dust and doubt, with, at the best, one individual's aspiration. Utopias were once in good faith, projects for a fresh creation of the world and of a most unworldly completeness ; this so-called Modern Utopia is a mere story of personal adventures among Utopian philosophies.

Indeed, that came about without the writer's intention. So it was the summoned vision came. For I see about me a great multitude of little souls and groups of souls as darkened, as derivative as my own ; with the passage of years I understand more and more clearly the quality of the motives that urge me and urge them to do whatever we do. . . . Yet that is not all I see, and I am not altogether bounded by my littleness. Ever and again, contrasting with this immediate vision, come glimpses of a comprehensive scheme, in which these personalities float, the scheme of a synthetic wider being, the great State, mankind, in which we all move and go, like blood corpuscles, like nerve cells, it may be at times like brain cells, in the body of a man. But the two visions are not seen consistently together, at least by me, and I do not surely know that they exist consistently together. The motives needed for those wider issues come not into the interplay of my vanities and wishes. That greater scheme lies about the men and women I know, as I have tried to make the vistas and spaces, the mountains, cities, laws, and order of Utopia lie about my talking couple, too great for their sustained comprehension. When one focuses upon these two that wide landscape becomes indistinct and distant, and when one regards that then the real persons one knows grow vague and

THE BUBBLE BURSTS

unreal. Nevertheless, I cannot separate these two aspects of human life, each commenting on the other. In that incongruity between great and individual inheres the incompatibility I could not resolve, and which, therefore, I have had to present in this conflicting form. At times that great scheme does seem to me to enter certain men's lives as a passion, as a real and living motive; there are those who know it almost as if it was a thing of desire; even for me, upon occasion, the little lures of the immediate life are seen small and vain, and the soul goes out to that mighty Being, to apprehend it and serve it and possess. But this is an illumination that passes as it comes, a rare transitory lucidity, leaving the soul's desire suddenly turned to presumption and hypocrisy upon the lips. One grasps at the Universe and attains—Bathos. The hungers, the jealousies, the prejudices and habits have us again, and we are forced back to think that it is so, and not otherwise, that we are meant to serve the mysteries; that in these blinkers it is we are driven to an end we cannot understand. And then, for measured moments in the night watches, or as one walks alone, or while one sits in thought and speech with a friend, the wider aspirations glow again with a sincere emotion, with the colours of attainable desire. . . .

That is my all about Utopia, and about the desire and need for Utopia, and how that planet lies to this planet that bears the daily lives of men.

APPENDIX

SCEPTICISM OF THE INSTRUMENT

A PORTION OF A PAPER READ TO THE OXFORD PHILOSOPHICAL SOCIETY, NOVEMBER 8, 1903, AND REPRINTED, WITH SOME REVISION, FROM THE VERSION GIVEN IN *Mind*, vol. xiii. (N.S.), No. 51.

(See also Chapter One, § 6, and Chapter Ten, §§ 1 and 2.)

IT seems to me that I may most propitiously attempt to interest you this evening by describing very briefly the particular metaphysical and philosophical system in which I do my thinking, and more particularly by setting out for your consideration one or two points in which I seem to myself to differ most widely from current accepted philosophy.

You must be prepared for things that will strike you as crude, for a certain difference of accent and dialect that you may not like, and you must be prepared, too, to hear what may strike you as the clumsy statement of my ignorant re-discovery of things already beautifully thought out and said. But in the end you may incline to forgive me some of this first offence. . . . It is quite unavoidable that, in setting out these intellectual foundations of mine, I should lapse for a moment or so towards autobiography.

A convergence of circumstances led to my having my knowledge of concrete things quite extensively developed before I came to philosophical examination at all. I have heard some one say that a savage or an animal is mentally a purely objective being, and in that respect I was like a savage or an animal until I was well over twenty. I was extremely unaware of the subjective or introverted element in my being. I was a Positivist without knowing it. My early education was a feeble one ; it was one in which my private observation, inquiry and experiment were far more important factors than any instruction, or rather perhaps the instruction I received was less even than what I learnt for myself, and it terminated at thirteen. I had come into pretty intimate contact with the harder realities of life, with hunger in various forms, and many base and disagreeable necessities, before I was fifteen. About that age, following the indication of certain theological and speculative curiosities, I began to learn something of what I will call deliberately and justly, Elementary Science—stuff I got out of *Cassell's Popular Educator* and cheap text-books— and then, through accidents and ambitions that do not matter in the least to us now, I came to three years of illuminating and good scientific work. The central fact of those three years was Huxley's course in Comparative Anatomy at the school in Exhibition Road. About that as a nucleus I arranged a spacious digest of facts. At the end of that time I had acquired what I still think to be a fairly clear and complete and ordered view of the ostensibly real universe. Let me try to give you the chief things I had. I had man definitely placed in the great scheme of space and time. I knew him incurably for what he was, finite and not final, a being of compromises and adaptations. I had traced his lungs, for example, from a swimming bladder, step by step, with scalpel and probe, through a dozen types or more, I had seen the ancestral cæcum shrink to that disease nest, the appendix of to-day, I had watched the gill slit patched slowly to the purposes of the ear and the reptile jaw suspension utilised to eke out the needs of a sense organ taken from its native and natural water. I had worked out the development of those extraordinarily unsatisfactory and untrustworthy instruments, man's teeth, from the skin scutes of the shark to their present function as a basis for gold stoppings, and followed the slow unfolding of the complex and painful process of gestation through which man comes into the world. I had followed all these things and many kindred things by dissection and in embryology—I had checked the whole theory of development again in a year's course of palæontology, and I had taken the dimensions of the whole process, by the scale of the stars, in a course of astronomical physics. And all that amount of objective elucidation came before I had reached the beginnings of any philosophical or metaphysical inquiry, any inquiry as to why I believed, how I believed, what I believed, or what the fundamental stuff of things was.

Now following hard upon this interlude with knowledge, came a time when I had to give myself to teaching, and it became advisable to acquire one of those Teaching Diplomas that are so widely and so foolishly despised, and that enterprise set me to a superficial, but suggestive study of educational method, of educational theory, of logic, of psychology, and so at last, when the little affair with the diploma was settled, to philosophy. Now to come to logic over the bracing uplands of comparative anatomy is to come to logic with a lot of very natural preconceptions blown clean out of one's mind. It is, I submit, a way of taking logic in the flank. When you have realised to the marrow that all the physical organs of man and all his physical structure are what they are through a series of adaptations and approximations, and that they are kept up to a level of practical efficiency only by the elimination of death, and that this is true also of his brain and of his instincts, and of many of his mental predispositions, you are not going to take his thinking apparatus unquestioningly as being in any way mysteriously different and better. And I had read only a little logic before I became aware of implications that I could not agree with, and assumptions that seemed to me to be altogether at variance with the general scheme of objective fact established in my mind.

I came to an examination of logical processes and of language with the expectation that they would share the profoundly provisional character, the character of irregular limitation and adaptation that pervades the whole physical and animal being of man. And I found the thing I had expected. And, as a consequence, I found a sort of intellectual hardihood about the assumptions of logic, that at first confused me and then roused all the latent scepticism in my mind.

My first quarrel with the accepted logic I developed long ago in a little paper that was printed in the *Fortnightly Review* in July 1891. It was called the " Rediscovery of the Unique," and re-reading it I perceive not only how bad and even annoying it was in manner—a thing I have long known—but also how remarkably bad it was in expression. I have good reason for doubting whether my powers of expression in these uses have very perceptibly improved, but at any rate I am doing my best now with that previous failure before me.

That unfortunate paper, among other oversights I can no longer regard as trivial, disregarded quite completely the fact that a whole literature upon the antagonism of the one and the many, of the specific ideal and the individual reality, was already in existence. It defined no relations to other thought or thinkers. I understand now, what I did not understand then, why it was totally ignored. But the idea underlying that paper I cling to to-day. I consider it an idea that will ultimately be regarded as one of primary importance to human thought, and I will try to present the substance of that early paper again now very briefly, as the best opening of my general case. My opening scepticism is essentially a doubt of *the objective reality of classification*. I have no hesitation in saying that is the first and primary proposition of my philosophy.

I have it in my mind that classification is a necessary condition of the working of the mental implement, but that it is a departure from the objective truth of things, that classification is very serviceable for the practical purposes of life, but a very doubtful preliminary to those fine penetrations the philosophical purpose, in its more arrogant moods, demands. All the peculiarities of my way of thinking derive from that.

A mind nourished upon anatomical study is, of course, permeated with the suggestion of the vagueness and instability of biological species. A biological species is quite obviously a great number of unique individuals which is separable from other biological species only by the fact that an enormous number of other linking individuals are inaccessible in time—are in other words dead and gone—and each new individual in that species does, in the distinction of its own individuality, break away in however infinitesimal degree from the previous average properties of the species. There is no property of any species, even the properties that constitute the specific definition, that is not a matter of more or less. If, for example, a species be distinguished by a single large red spot on the back, you will find if you go over a great number of specimens that red spot shrinking here to nothing, expanding there to a more general redness, weakening to pink, deepening to russet and brown, shading into crimson, and so on, and so on.   And this is true not only of biological species.   It is true of the mineral specimens constituting a mineral species, and I remember as a constant refrain in the lectures of Prof. Judd upon rock classification, the words " they pass into one another by insensible gradations."   That is true, I hold, of all things.

You will think perhaps of atoms of the elements as instances of identically similar things, but these are things not of experience but of theory, and there is not a phenomenon in chemistry that is not equally well explained on the supposition that it is merely the immense quantities of atoms necessarily taken in any experiment that mask by the operation of the law of averages the fact that each atom also has its unique quality, its special individual difference.   This idea of uniqueness in all individuals is not only true of the classifications of material science ; it is true, and still more evidently true, of the species of common thought, it is true of common terms.   Take the word *chair*.   When one says chair, one thinks vaguely of an average chair.   But collect individual instances, think of arm-chairs and reading chairs, and dining-room chairs and kitchen chairs, chairs that pass into benches, chairs that cross the boundary and become settees, dentists' chairs, thrones, opera stalls, seats of all sorts, those miraculous fungoid growths that cumber the floor of the Arts and Crafts Exhibition, and you will perceive what a lax bundle in fact is this simple straight-forward term.   In co-operation with an intelligent joiner I would undertake to defeat any definition of chair or chairish-ness that you gave me.   Chairs, just as much as individual organisms, just as much as mineral and rock specimens, are unique things—if you know them well enough you will find an individual difference even in a set of machine-made chairs— and it is only because we do not possess minds of unlimited capacity, because our brain has only a limited number of pigeon-holes for our correspondence with an unlimited universe of objective uniques, that we have to delude ourselves into the belief that there is a chairishness in this species common to and distinctive of all chairs.

Let me repeat ; this is of the very smallest importance in all the practical affairs of life, or, indeed, in relation to any-thing but philosophy and wide generalisations.   But in philosophy it matters profoundly.   If I order two new-laid eggs for breakfast, up come two unhatched but still unique avian individuals, and the chances are they serve my rude physiological purpose.   I can afford to ignore the hens' eggs of the past that were not quite so nearly this sort of thing, and the hens' eggs of the future that will accumulate modification age by age ; I can venture to ignore the rare chance of an abnormality in chemical composition and of any startling aberration in my physiological reaction ; I can, with a confidence that is practically perfect, say with unqualified simplicity " two eggs," but not if my concern is not my morning's breakfast but the utmost possible truth.

Now let me go on to point out whither this idea of uniqueness tends. I submit to you that syllogism is based on classification, that all hard logical reasoning tends to imply and is apt to imply a confidence in the objective reality of classification. Consequently in denying that I deny the absolute validity of logic. Classification and number, which in truth ignore the fine differences of objective realities, have in the past of human thought been imposed upon things. Let me for clearness' sake take a liberty here—commit, as you may perhaps think, an unpardonable insolence. Hindoo thought and Greek thought alike impress me as being overmuch obsessed by an objective treatment of certain necessary preliminary conditions of human thought—number and definition and class and abstract form. But these things, number, definition, class and abstract form, I hold, are merely unavoidable conditions of mental activity—regrettable conditions rather than essential facts. *The forceps of our minds are clumsy forceps, and crush the truth a little in taking hold of it.*

It was about this difficulty that the mind of Plato played a little inconclusively all his life. For the most part he tended to regard the *idea* as the something behind reality, whereas it seems to me that idea is the more proximate and less perfect thing, the thing by which the mind, by ignoring individual differences, attempts to comprehend an otherwise unmanageable number of unique realities.

Let me give you a rough figure of what I am trying to convey in this first attack upon the philosophical validity of general terms. You have seen the results of those various methods of black and white reproduction that involve the use of a rectangular net. You know the sort of process picture I mean—it used to be employed very frequently in reproducing photographs. At a little distance you really seem to have a faithful reproduction of the original picture, but when you peer closely you find not the unique form and masses of the original, but a multitude of little rectangles, uniform in shape and size. The more earnestly you go into the thing, the closer you look, the more the picture is lost in reticulations. I submit the world of reasoned inquiry has a very similar relation to the world I call objectively real. For the rough purposes of every day the network picture will do, but the finer your purpose the less it will serve, and for an ideally fine purpose, for absolute and general knowledge that will be as true for a man at a distance with a telescope as for a man with a microscope it will not serve at all.

It is true you can make your net of logical interpretation finer and finer, you can fine your classification more and more —up to a certain limit. But essentially you are working in limits, and as you come closer, as you look at finer and subtler things, as you leave the practical purpose for which the method exists, the element of error increases. Every species is vague, every term goes cloudy at its edges, and so in my way of thinking, relentless logic is only another phrase for a stupidity —for a sort of intellectual pigheadedness. If you push a philosophical or metaphysical inquiry through a series of valid syllogisms—never committing any generally recognised fallacy—you nevertheless leave a certain rubbing and marginal loss of objective truth, and you get deflections that are difficult to trace, at each phase in the process. Every species waggles about in its definition, every tool is a little loose in its handle, every scale has its individual error. So long as you are reasoning for practical purposes about the finite things of experience, you can every now and then check your process, and correct your adjustments. But not when you make what are called philosophical and theological inquiries, when you turn your implement towards the final absolute truth of things. Doing that is like firing at an inaccessible, unmarkable and indestructible target at an unknown distance, with a defective rifle and variable cartridges. Even if by chance you hit, you cannot know that you hit, and so it will matter nothing at all.

This assertion of the necessary untrustworthiness of all reasoning processes arising out of the fallacy of classification in what is quite conceivably a universe of uniques, forms only one introductory aspect of my general scepticism of the Instrument of Thought.

I have now to tell you of another aspect of this scepticism of the instrument which concerns negative terms.

Classes in logic are not only represented by circles with a hard firm outline, whereas they have no such definite limits, but also there is a constant disposition to think of negative terms as if they represented positive classes. With words just as with numbers and abstract forms there are definite phases of human development. There is, you know, with regard to number, the phase when man can barely count at all, or counts in perfect good faith and sanity upon his fingers. Then there is the phase when he is struggling with the development of number, when he begins to elaborate all sorts of ideas about numbers, until at last he develops complex superstitions about perfect numbers and imperfect numbers, about threes and sevens and the like. The same is the case with abstracted forms, and even to-day we are scarcely more than heads out of the vast subtle muddle of thinking about spheres and ideally perfect forms and so on, that was the price of this little necessary step to clear thinking. You know better than I do how large a part numerical and geometrical magic, numerical and geometrical philosophy has played in the history of the mind. And the whole apparatus of language and mental communication is beset with like dangers. The language of the savage is, I suppose, purely positive ; the thing has a name, the name has a thing. This indeed is the tradition of language, and to-day even, we, when we hear a name, are predisposed— and sometimes it is a very vicious disposition—to imagine forthwith something answering to the name. *We are disposed, as an incurable mental vice, to accumulate intension in terms.* If I say to you Wodget or Crump, you find yourself passing over the fact that these are nothings, these are, so to speak, mere blankety blanks, and trying to think what sort of thing a Wodget or a Crump may be. And where this disposition has come in, in its most alluring guise, is in the case of negative terms. Our instrument of knowledge persists in handling even such openly negative terms as the Absolute, the Infinite, as though they were real existences, and when the negative element is ever so little disguised, as it is in such a word as Omniscience, then the illusion of positive reality may be complete.

Please remember that I am trying to tell you my philosophy, and not arguing about yours. Let me try to express how in my mind this matter of negative terms has shaped itself. I think of something which I may perhaps best describe as being off the stage or out of court, or as the Void without Implications, or as Nothingness or as Outer Darkness. This is a sort of hypothetical Beyond to the visible world of human thought, and thither I think all negative terms reach at last, and merge and become nothing. Whatever positive class you make, whatever boundary you draw, straight away from that boundary begins the corresponding negative class and passes into the illimitable horizon of nothingness. You talk of pink things, you ignore, if you are a trained logician, the more elusive shades of pink, and draw your line. Beyond is the not pink, known and knowable, and still in the not pink region one comes to the Outer Darkness. Not blue, not happy, not iron, all the *not* classes meet in that Outer Darkness. That same Outer Darkness and nothingness is infinite space, and infinite time, and any being of infinite qualities, and all that region I rule out of court in my philosophy altogether. I will neither affirm nor deny if I can help it about any *not* things. I will not deal with not things at all, except by accident and inadvertence. If I use the word " infinite " I use it as one often uses " countless," " the countless hosts of the enemy "—or " immeasurable "—" immeasurable cliffs "—that is to say as the limit of measurement rather than as the limit of imaginary measurability, as a convenient equivalent to as many times this cloth yard as you can, and as many again and so on and so on. Now a great number of apparently positive terms are, or have become, practically negative terms and are under the same ban with me. A considerable number of terms that have played a great part in the world of thought, seem to me to be invalidated by this same defect, to have no content or an undefined content or an unjustifiable content. For example, that word Omniscient, as implying infinite knowledge, impresses me as being a word with a delusive air of being solid and full, when it is really hollow with no content whatever. I am persuaded that knowing is the relation of a conscious being to something not itself, that the thing known is defined as a system of parts and aspects and relationships, that knowledge is comprehension, and so that only finite things can know or be known. When you talk of a being of infinite extension and infinite duration, omniscient and omnipotent and Perfect, you seem to me to be talking in negatives of nothing whatever. When you speak of the Absolute you speak to me of nothing. If, however, you talk of a great yet finite and thinkable being, a being not myself, extending beyond my imagination in time and space, knowing all that I can think of as known and capable of doing all that I can think of as done, you come into the sphere of my mental operations, and into the scheme of my philosophy. . . .

These then are my first two charges against our Instrument of Knowledge, firstly, that it can work only by disregarding individuality and treating uniques as identically similar objects in this respect or that, so as to group them under one term, and that once it has done so it tends automatically to intensify the significance of that term, and secondly, that it can only deal freely with negative terms by treating them as though they were positive. But I have a further objection to the Instrument of Human Thought, that is not correlated to these former objections and that is also rather more difficult to convey.

Essentially this idea is to present a sort of stratification in human ideas. I have it very much in mind that various terms in our reasoning lie, as it were, at different levels and in different planes, and that we accomplish a large amount of error and confusion by reasoning terms together that do not lie or nearly lie in the same plane.

Let me endeavour to make myself a little less obscure by a most flagrant instance from physical things. Suppose some one began to talk seriously of a man seeing an atom through a microscope, or better perhaps of cutting one in half with a knife. There are a number of non-analytical people who would be quite prepared to believe that an atom could be visible to the eye or cut in this manner. But any one at all conversant with physical conceptions would almost as soon think of killing the square root of 2 with a rook rifle as of cutting an atom in half with a knife. Our conception of an atom is reached through a process of hypothesis and analysis, and in the world of atoms there are no knives and no men to cut.

If you have thought with a strong consistent mental movement, then when you have thought of your atom under the knife blade, your knife blade has itself become a cloud of swinging grouped atoms, and your microscope lens a little universe of oscillatory and vibratory molecules. If you think of the universe, thinking at the level of atoms, there is neither knife to cut, scale to weigh, nor eye to see. The universe *at that plane to which the mind of the molecular physicist descends* has none of the shapes or forms of our common life whatever. This hand with which I write is in the universe of molecular physics a cloud of warring atoms and molecules, combining and recombining, colliding, rotating, flying hither and thither in the universal atmosphere of ether.

You see, I hope, what I mean when I say that the universe of molecular physics is at a different level from the universe of common experience ;—what we call stable and solid is in that world a freely moving system of interlacing centres of force, what we call colour and sound is there no more than this length of vibration or that. We have reached to a conception of that universe of molecular physics by a great enterprise of organised analysis, and our universe of daily experiences stands in relation to that elemental world as if it were a synthesis of those elemental things.

I would suggest to you that this is only a very extreme instance of the general state of affairs, that there may be finer and subtler differences of level between one term and another, and that terms may very well be thought of as lying obliquely and as being twisted through different levels.

It will perhaps give a clearer idea of what I am seeking to convey if I suggest a concrete image for the whole world of a man's thought and knowledge. Imagine a large clear jelly, in which at all angles and in all states of simplicity or contortion his ideas are imbedded. They are all valid and possible ideas as they lie, none in reality incompatible with any. If you imagine the direction of up or down in this clear jelly being as it were the direction in which one moves by analysis or by synthesis, if you go down for example from matter to atoms and centres of force and up to men and states and countries—if you will imagine the ideas lying in that manner—you will get the beginning of my intention. But our Instrument, our process of thinking, like a drawing before the discovery of perspective, appears to have difficulties with the third dimension, appears capable only of dealing with or reasoning about ideas by projecting them upon the same plane. It will be obvious that a great multitude of things may very well exist together in a solid jelly, which would be overlapping and incompatible and mutually destructive, when projected together upon one plane. Through the bias in our Instrument to do this, through reasoning between terms not in the same plane, an enormous amount of confusion, perplexity, and mental deadlocking occurs.

The old theological deadlock between predestination and free-will serves admirably as an example of the sort of deadlock I mean. Take life at the level of common sensation and common experience, and there is no more indisputable fact than man's freedom of will, unless it is his complete moral responsibility. But make only the least penetrating of analyses and you perceive a world of inevitable consequences, a rigid succession of cause and effect. Insist upon a flat agreement between the two, and there you are ! The Instrument fails.

It is upon these three objections, and upon an extreme suspicion of abstract terms which arises materially out of my first and second objections, that I chiefly rest my case for a profound scepticism of the remoter possibilities of the Instrument of Thought. It is a thing no more perfect than the human eye or the human ear, though like those other instruments it may have undefined possibilities of evolution towards increased range, and increased power.

So much for my main contention. But before I conclude I may—since I am here—say a little more in the autobiographical vein, and with a view to your discussion to show how I reconcile this fundamental scepticism with the very positive beliefs about world-wide issues I possess, and the very definite distinction I make between right and wrong.

I reconcile these things by simply pointing out to you that if there is any validity in my image of that three dimensional jelly in which our ideas are suspended, such a reconciliation as you demand in logic, such a projection of the things as in accordance upon one plane, is totally unnecessary and impossible.

This insistence upon the element of uniqueness in being, this subordination of the class to the individual difference, not only destroys the universal claim of philosophy, but the universal claim of ethical imperatives, the universal claim of any religious teaching. If you press me back upon my fundamental position I must confess I put faith and standards and rules of conduct upon exactly the same level as I put my belief of what is right in art, and what I consider right practice in art. I have arrived at a certain sort of self-knowledge, and there are, I find, very distinct imperatives for me, but I am quite prepared to admit there is no proving them imperative on any one else. One's political proceedings, one's moral acts are, I hold, just as much self-expression as one's poetry or painting or music. But since life has for its primordial elements assimilation and aggression, I try not only to obey my imperatives, but to put them persuasively and convincingly into other minds, to bring about *my* good and to resist and overcome *my* evil as though they were the universal Good and the universal Evil in which unthinking men believe. And it is obviously in no way contradictory to this philosophy, for me, if I find others responding sympathetically to any notes of mine, or if I find myself responding sympathetically to notes sounding about me, to give that common resemblance between myself and others a name, to refer these others and myself in common to this thing as if it were externalised and spanned us all.

Scepticism of the Instrument is, for example, not incompatible with religious association and with organisation upon the basis of a common faith. It is possible to regard God as a Being synthetic in relation to men and societies, just as the idea of a universe of atoms and molecules and inorganic relationships is analytical in relation to human life.

The repudiation of demonstration in any but immediate and verifiable cases that this Scepticism of the Instrument amounts to, the abandonment of any universal validity for moral and religious propositions, brings ethical, social, and religious teaching into the province of poetry, and does something to correct the estrangement between knowledge and beauty that is a feature of so much mental existence at this time. All these things are self-expression. Such an opinion sets a new and greater value on that penetrating and illuminating quality of mind we call insight, insight which when it faces towards the contradictions that arise out of the imperfections of the mental instrument is called humour. In these innate, unteachable qualities I hold—in humour and the sense of beauty —lies such hope of intellectual salvation from the original sin of our intellectual instrument as we may entertain in this uncertain and fluctuating world of unique appearances. . . .

So frankly I spread my little equipment of fundamental assumptions before you, heartily glad of the opportunity you have given me of taking them out, of looking at them with the particularity the presence of hearers ensures, and of hearing the impression they make upon you. Of course, such a sketch must have an inevitable crudity of effect. The time I had for it—I mean the time I was able to give in preparation—was altogether too limited for any exhaustive finish of presentation ; but I think on the whole I have got the main lines of this sketch map of my mental basis true. Whether I have made myself comprehensible is a different question altogether. It is for you rather than me to say how this sketch map of mine lies with regard to your own more systematic cartography. . . .

Here followed certain comments upon *Personal Idealism,* and Mr. F. C. S. Schiller's *Humanism,* of no particular value.